Sea-Cursed

THIRTY TERRIFYING TALES OF THE DEEP

Sea-Cursed

THIRTY TERRIFYING TALES OF THE DEEP

Edited by

T. Liam McDonald,
Stefan Dziemianowicz,
and Martin H. Greenberg

BARNES
&NOBLE
BOOKS
NEW YORK

Acknowledgments

Grateful acknowledgment is made to the following for permission to reprint their copyrighted material:

"The Ship of Silent Men" by Philip M. Fisher—Copyright 1920 by Frank A. Munsey Publications. Reprinted by permission of Argosy Communications, Inc.

"The Temple" by H. P. Lovecraft—Copyright 1925 by the Popular Fiction Publishing Company for WEIRD TALES. Reprinted by the agents for the author's Estate, the Scott Meredith Literary Agency, Inc., 845 Third Avenue, New York, NY 10022.

"Bells of Oceana" by Arthur J. Burks—Copyright 1927 by the Popular Fiction Publishing Company for WEIRD TALES. Reprinted by permission of Forrest J. Ackerman, 2495 Glendower Ave., Hollywood, CA 90027.

"Second Night Out" by Frank Belknap Long—Copyright 1933 by the Popular Fiction Publishing Company for WEIRD TALES. Reprinted by permission of The Pimlico Agency, Inc.

"The Black Kiss" by Robert Bloch and Henry Kuttner—Copyright 1936 by the Popular Fiction Publishing Company for WEIRD TALES. Reprinted by permission of The Pimlico Agency, Inc.

"The Sea Thing" by A. E. van Vogt—Copyright 1940 by Street and Smith Publications, Inc. Reprinted by permission of Forrest J. Ackerman, 2495 Glendower Avenue, Hollywood, CA 90027.

"Sea Curse" by Robert E. Howard—Copyright 1929 by the Popular Fiction Publishing Company for WEIRD TALES. Reprinted by permission of Glenn Lord.

"A Vintage from Atlantis" by Clark Ashton Smith—Copyright 1933 by the Popular Fiction Publishing Company for WEIRD TALES. Reprinted by permission of the Scott Meredith Literary Agency, Inc., 845 Third Avenue, New York, NY 10022.

"Derelict" by Hugh B. Cave—Copyright 1937 by Hugh B. Cave. Reprinted by permission of the author.

"Sea Tiger" by Henry S. Whitehead—Copyright 1932 by Clayton Publications, Inc. Reprinted by permission of the Scott Meredith Literary Agency, Inc., 845 Third Avenue, New York, NY 10022.

"The Women" by Ray Bradbury—Copyright 1948; renewed © 1976 by Ray Bradbury. Reprinted by permission of Don Congdon Associates, Inc.

"The Doors of His Face, the Lamps of His Mouth" by Roger Zelazny—Copyright © 1965 by Mercury Press, Inc. First appeared in THE MAGAZINE OF FANTASY AND SCIENCE FICTION. Reprinted by permission of the author.

"The Wine-Dark Sea" by Robert Aickman—Copyright © 1966 by Robert Aickman. Reprinted by permission of The Pimlico Agency, Inc.

"The Ferries" by Ramsey Campbell—Copyright © 1982 by Ramsey Campbell. Reprinted by permission of the author.

"The Night *Sea Maid* Went Down" by Brian Lumley—Copyright © 1972 by Brian Lumley. Reprinted by permission of the author.

"Down by the Sea near the Great Big Rock" by Joe R. Lansdale—Copyright © 1984 by Joe R. Lansdale. Reprinted by permission of the author.

"Message Found in a Bottle II" by Nancy Holder—Copyright © 1990 by Nancy Holder. Reprinted by permission of Dell Publishing Inc.

"A Sailor's Pay" by Jack Cady—Copyright © 1991 by Jack Cady. Reprinted by permission of the author.

"Deep Sleep" by Matthew J. Costello—Copyright © 1992 by Matthew J. Costello. Reprinted by permission of the author.

"Scape-Goats" by Clive Barker—Copyright © 1984 by Clive Barker. Reprinted by permission of Little Brown, Ltd., London.

"Between the Windows of the Sea" by Jack Dann—Copyright © 1986 by Jack Dann. Reprinted by permission of the author.

"Dip in the Pool" by Roald Dahl—Copyright 1952, renewed © 1980 by Roald Dahl. Reprinted by permission of Alfred A. Knopf, Inc.

"The Night Ocean" by Robert H. Barlow—Copyright 1936 by Robert H. Barlow. Reprinted by permission of the Scott Meredith Literary Agency, Inc., 845 Third Avenue, New York, NY 10022.

"Spawn of the Sea" by Donald Wandrei—Copyright 1933 by the Popular Fiction Publishing Company for WEIRD TALES. Reprinted by permission of Lindquist and Vennum, Attorneys at Law.

Contents

Introduction

There is, one knows not what sweet mystery about this sea, whose great awful stirrings seem to speak of some hidden soul beneath . . . for here, millions of mixed shades and shadows, drowned dreams, somnambulisms, reveries; all that we call living souls, lie dreaming, dreaming, still; tossing like slumberers in their bed, but made so by their restlessness.

—Herman Melville, *Moby-Dick*

The sea never changes and its works, for all the talk of men, are wrapped in mystery.

—Joseph Conrad, *Typhoon*

ALL LIFE COMES from the sea, and mankind is not the least of its offspring. Yet this filial relationship is a troubled one that has given rise to myths and legends in many cultures. The biblical tale of Jonah, spat out on shore by the whale who swallowed him, is an archetype of the sea's rejection of humanity. Over the centuries, many writers have examined the sea's fundamental antipathy to human life in countless stories that depict the ocean as mankind's most formidable opponent. *Sea-Cursed: Thirty Terrifying Tales of the Deep* brings together stories from the last two centuries that depict the sea as an object of awe and mystery—one that threatens the very life it makes possible.

Much of the lore surrounding the sea comes from the golden age of exploration, when ships disappeared with alarming frequency and the sea claimed those foolish enough to think they could anticipate its actions, tame it, and bend it to their wills. Recognition of the sea as an incomprehensible force of nature persisted into the nineteenth century, where it gave rise to stories such as "A Descent into the Maelstrom," Edgar Allan Poe's attempt to describe a natural event so beyond human ken that it seems almost supernatural in its intensity. More than 150 years after Poe's story, we are still woefully ignorant of the true measure and nature of the sea. As Nancy Holder reminds us in her contemporary dramatic monologue, "Message Found in a Bottle II *or* An Invitation from Your Captain" (the title of which pays tribute to Poe's other sea horror story, "Ms. Found in a Bottle"), fear of drowning remains an instinctive dread more terrifying than the many "unnatural" forms of death we have become familiar with in the late twentieth century.

It is hardly surprising that the lives of those who made their living from the sea became rich source material for stories that take a dark view of deep waters. The constant threat of death, combined with the time spent in isolated, close quarters and long periods of separation from loved ones, made the sailor's life particularly hard. Intervals of hard work punctuated by stretches of excruciating monotony characterized months or even years of nautical service, during which men were as much at the mercy of the shipowners and officers as the sea. Reflecting on his own seafaring years, William Hope Hodgson, one of the greatest writers of sea fiction, wrote "I am not at sea because I object to bad treatment, poor food, poor wages and worse prospects. I am not at sea because very early on I discovered that it is a comfortless, weariful, and thankless life—a compact of hardness and sordidness such as shore people can scarcely conceive. I am not at sea because I dislike being a pawn with the sea for board and the shipowners for players." It is impossible not to sense the frustration Hodgson speaks of in Joseph Conrad's "The Brute," where a killer ship comes to symbolize the callous indifference of a business to its employees, or Philip M. Fisher's "The Ship of Silent Men," in which the ghost ship, whose undead crew somnambulistically repeats its tedious chores for all eternity, can be read as a Marxist allegory for the dehumanization of the working class.

No doubt, it was the harsh circumstances of the seaman's life that gave rise to fanciful tales of half-human creatures who inhabit the ocean depths. The preponderance of legends centered around enchantresses whose sole purpose is to bewitch sailors is easy to explain in a profession that denied men female companionship for long stretches of time. The mixture of beauty and horror these beings represent permeates the legend of the siren, as treated by Edward Lucas White in "The Song of the Sirens," the mermaid in Henry S. Whitehead's "Sea-Tiger," and the sea witch in Robert Bloch and Henry Kuttner's "The Black Kiss." Even when not dealing explicitly with creatures of myth, as in Ray Bradbury's "The Women" and Jack Dann's "Between the Windows of the Sea," writers invariably describe the mutually attractive and repulsive qualities of the sea in terms of sexual allure.

Of course, not all stories of the sailor's life are so bleak. In "The Derelict," Hugh Cave writes of the unnaturally strong emotional bonds that can develop between those who have shared the rigors of a life at sea. Even the inevitable retributions that await the characters in Jack Cady's "Sailor's Pay," Robert E. Howard's "Sea Curse," and Ramsey Campbell's "The Ferries," a take on the legend of the Flying Dutchman, suggest that a purer, if more relentless, code of honor than is found on land governs men at sea. Small wonder, then, that the protagonist of Roald Dahl's "A Dip in the Pool" discovers too late that the sea is merciless to those who would use it as a means to dishonest ends.

For many writers, the sheer vastness of the sea makes it the perfect remote setting in which horrors thrive. Indeed, several deep-sea horror stories simply transfer traditional themes of supernatural horror to maritime settings. Sir Arthur Conan Doyle's "The Captain of the *Pole-Star*" is the story of a haunting in which the encroaching ice floes of the arctic sea mirror the protagonist's pursuit by the specter of his own guilt. F. Marion Crawford's "The Upper Berth," Frank Belknap Long's "Second Night Out," and Arthur J. Burks' "The Bells of Oceana" all turn the ocean liner into a floating haunted house, while Matthew J. Costello's "Deep Sleep" uses the sea to give a twist to a tale involving one of horror fiction's most familiar monsters.

In contrast, the sea monster story acknowledges that the sea is a true *terra incognita* capable of breeding monsters that rival those of supernatural origin. The template for all such stories is *Moby-Dick*, in which Herman Melville applied his imagination to a factual account of the deliberate sinking of the *Essex* by an enraged sperm whale, and created a monster whose immense dimensions mocked all sense of human scale and proportion. Similarly, Donald Wandrei's "Spawn of the Sea," Brian Lumley's "The Night *Sea-Maid* Went Down," and Roger Zelazny's science fiction classic "The Doors of His Face, The Lamps of His Mouth," summon monsters whose immensity reflects the incomprehensible vastness of their environment. Even the scaled-down monsters of A. E. van Vogt's "The Sea Thing" and Joe R. Lansdale's "Down by the Sea near the Great Big Rock" show the limits of human understanding of the natural world through their ability to manipulate the vulnerabilities of their victims.

A similar element of scale is employed in stories that try to capture the awesome timelessness of the sea. In "A Vintage from Atlantis," Clark Ashton Smith conjures a remote human past that overwhelms the present. H. P. Lovecraft performs a similar feat in "The Temple," creating a civilization beneath the sea that predates the human race and mocks its impermanence. The terrifying realization of how insignificant human endeavor is in the face of such expansive vistas of time is the driving force of Clive Barker's "Scape-Goats," in which contemporary voyagers become caught up in a cycle of sacrifice to prehistoric sea gods, and Robert Aickman's "The Wine-Dark Sea," which evokes an inconceivably ancient time on earth when rock lived.

At the heart of all these stories is a single common theme: the sea is the alien in our midst. It is not bound by the same rules that govern human civilization and it resists all efforts to impose order upon it. As Robert H. Barlow implies through the series of bizarre images that make up his tale "The Night Ocean," there is no discernible pattern of cause and effect in what the sea takes from or yields to us. Rather, as the unfortunate sailors of William Hope Hodgson's "The Boats of the *Glen Carrig*" discover, the sea hides an abundance of marvels that defy human logic. Published in 1907, Hodgson's novel is remarkable not only for imagining a realm where horrors are everyday occurrences, but for suggesting that those horrors represent the mere surface of a world that can only be glimpsed safely and sanely through the veil of fiction.

And so we leave you with the ghost pirates and sea curses, with monsters, witches, devils, and cutthroats. Worst of all we leave you on the open sea, alone, with no sails and no compass, with only the endless waters stretching in all directions and the fathomless ocean beneath. In your hands is a map brown with age, and on it are vast uncharted spaces where the mapmaker has inked words of caution that afford you no protection: *Here there be monsters.*

—T. Liam McDonald and Stefan Dziemianowicz
1994

A Descent into the Maelstrom

Edgar Allan Poe

WE HAD NOW REACHED the summit of the loftiest crag. For some minutes the old man seemed too much exhausted to speak.
"Not long ago," said he at length, "and I could have guided you on this route as well as the youngest of my sons; but, about three years past, there happened to me an event such as never happened before to mortal man—or at least such as no man ever survived to tell of —and the six hours of deadly terror which I then endured have broken me up body and soul. You suppose me a *very* old man—but I am not. It took less than a single day to change these hairs from a jetty black to white, to weaken my limbs, and to unstring my nerves, so that I tremble at the least exertion, and am frightened at a shadow. Do you know I can scarcely look over this little cliff without getting giddy?"

The "little cliff", upon whose edge he had so carelessly thrown himself down to rest that the weightier portion of his body hung over it, while he was only kept from falling by the tenure of his elbow on its extreme and slippery edge—this "little cliff" arose, a sheer unobstructed precipice of black shining rock, some fifteen or sixteen hundred feet from the world of crags beneath us. Nothing would have tempted me to within half a dozen yards of its brink. In truth so deeply was I excited by the perilous position of my companion, that I fell at full length upon the ground, clung to the shrubs around me, and dared not even glance upward at the sky—while I struggled in vain to divest myself of the idea that the very foundations of the mountain were in danger from the fury of the winds. It was long before I could reason myself into sufficient courage to sit up and look out into the distance.

"You must get over these fancies," said the guide, "for I have brought you here that you might have the best possible view of the scene of that event I mentioned—and to tell you the whole story with the spot just under your eye."

"We are now," he continued, in that particularizing manner which distinguished him—"we are now close upon the Norwegian coast—in the sixty-eighth degree of latitude—in the great province of Nordland—and in the dreary district of Lofoden. The mountain upon whose top we sit is Helseggen, the Cloudy. Now raise yourself up a little higher—hold on to the grass if you feel giddy—so—and look out beyond the belt of vapor beneath us, into the sea."

I looked dizzily, and beheld a wide expanse of ocean, whose waters wore so inky a hue as to bring at once to my mind the Nubian geographer's account of the *Mare Tenebrarum*. A panorama more deplorably desolate no human imagination can conceive. To the right and left, as far as the eye could reach, there lay outstretched, like ramparts of the world, lines of horridly black and beetling cliff, whose character of gloom was but the more forcibly illustrated by the surf which reared high up against it its white and ghastly crest, howling and shrieking for ever. Just opposite the promontory upon whose apex we were placed, and at a distance of some five or six miles out at sea, there was visible a small, bleak-looking island; or, more properly, its position was discernible through the wilderness of surge in which it was enveloped. About two miles nearer the land, arose another of smaller size, hideously craggy and barren, and encompassed at various intervals by a cluster of dark rocks.

The appearance of the ocean, in the space between the more distant island and the shore, had something very unusual about it. Although, at the time, so strong a gale was blowing landward that a brig in the remote offing lay to under a double-reefed trysail, and constantly plunged her whole hull out of sight, still there was here nothing like a regular swell, but only a short, quick, angry cross dashing of water in every direction—as well in the teeth of the wind as otherwise. Of foam there was little except in the immediate vicinity of the rocks.

"The island in the distance," resumed the old man, "is called by the Norwegians Vurrgh. The one midway is Moskoe. That a mile to the northward is Ambaaren. Yonder are Iflesen, Hoeyholm, Kieldholm, Suarven, and Buckholm. Farther off—between Moskoe and Vurrgh—are Otterholm, Flimen, Sandflesen, and Skarholm. These are the true names of the places—but why it has been thought necessary to name them at all, is more than either you or I can understand. Do you hear any thing? Do you see any change in the water?"

We had now been about ten minutes upon the top of Helseggen, to which we had ascended from the interior of Lofoden, so that we had caught no glimpse of the sea until it had burst upon us from the summit. As the old man spoke, I became aware of a loud and gradually increasing sound, like the moaning of a vast herd of buffaloes upon an American prairie; and at the same moment I perceived that what seamen term the *chopping* character of the ocean beneath us, was rapidly changing into a current which set to the eastward. Even while I gazed, this current acquired a monstrous velocity. Each moment added to its speed—to its headlong impetuosity. In five minutes the whole sea, as far as Vurrgh, was lashed into ungovernable fury; but it was between Moskoe and the coast that the main uproar held its sway. Here the vast bed of the waters, seamed and scarred into a thousand conflicting channels, burst suddenly into phrensied convulsion—heaving, boiling, hissing—gyrating in gigantic and innumerable vortices, and all whirling and plunging on to the eastward with a rapidity which water never elsewhere assumes except in precipitous descents.

In a few minutes more, there came over the scene another radical alteration. The general surface grew somewhat more smooth, and the whirlpools, one by one, disappeared, while prodigious streaks of foam became apparent where none had been seen before. These streaks, at length, spreading out to a great distance, and entering into combination, took unto themselves the gyratory motion of the subsided vortices, and seemed to form the germ of another more vast. Suddenly—very suddenly—this assumed a distinct and definite existence, in a circle of more than half a mile in diameter. The edge of the whirl was represented by a broad belt of gleaming spray; but no particle of this slipped into the mouth of the terrific funnel, whose interior, as far as the eye could fathom it, was a smooth, shining, and jet-black wall of water, inclined to the horizon at an angle of some forty-five degrees, speeding dizzily round and round with a swaying and sweltering motion, and sending forth to the winds an appalling voice, half shriek, half roar, such as not even the mighty cataract of Niagara ever lifts up in its agony to Heaven.

The mountain trembled to its very base, and the rock rocked. I threw myself upon my face, and clung to the scant herbage in an excess of nervous agitation.

"This," said I at length, to the old man—"this *can* be nothing else than the great whirlpool of the Maelström."

"So it is sometimes termed," said he. "We Norwegians call it the Moskoe-ström, from the island of Moskoe in the midway."

The ordinary accounts of this vortex had by no means prepared me for what I saw. That of Jonas Ramus, which is perhaps the most circumstantial of any, cannot impart the faintest conception either of the magnificence, or of the horror of the scene—or of the wild bewildering sense of *the novel* which confounds the beholder. I am not sure from what point of view the writer in question surveyed it, nor at what time; but it could neither have been from the summit of Helseggen, nor during a storm. There are some passages of his description, nevertheless, which may be quoted for their details, although their effect is exceedingly feeble in conveying an impression of the spectacle.

"Between Lofoden and Moskoe," he says, "the depth of the water is between thirty-six and forty fathoms; but on the other side, toward Ver (Vurrgh) this depth decreases so as not to afford a convenient passage for a vessel, without the risk of splitting on the rocks, which happens even in the calmest weather. When it is flood, the stream runs up the country between Lofoden and Moskoe with a boisterous rapidity; but the roar of its impetuous ebb to the sea is scarce equalled by the loudest and most dreadful cataracts; the noise being heard several leagues off, and the vortices or pits are of such an extent and depth, that if a ship comes within its attraction, it is inevitably absorbed and carried down to the bottom, and there beat to pieces against the rocks; and when the water relaxes, the fragments thereof are thrown up again. But these intervals of tranquillity are only at the turn of the ebb and flood, and in calm weather, and last but a quarter of an hour, its violence gradually returning. When the stream is most boisterous, and its fury heightened by a storm, it is dangerous to come within a Norway mile of it. Boats, yachts, and ships have been carried away by not guarding against it before they were within its reach. It likewise happens frequently, that whales come too near the stream, and are overpowered by its violence; and then it is impossible to describe their howlings and bellowings in their fruitless struggles to disengage themselves. A bear once, attempting to swim from Lofoden to Moskoe, was caught by the stream and borne down, while he roared terribly, so as to be heard on shore. Large stocks of firs and pine trees, after being absorbed by the current, rise again broken and torn to such a degree as if bristles grew upon them. This plainly shows the bottom to consist of craggy rocks, among which they are whirled to and fro. This stream is regulated by the flux and reflux of the sea—it being constantly high and low water every six hours. In the year 1645, early in the morning of Sexagesima Sunday, it raged with such noise and impetuosity that the very stones of the houses on the coast fell to the ground."

In regard to the depth of the water, I could not see how this could have been ascertained at all in the immediate vicinity of the vortex. The "forty fathoms" must have reference only to portions of the channel close upon the shore either of Moskoe or Lofoden. The depth in the centre of the Moskoe-ström must be immeasurably greater; and no better proof of this fact is necessary than can be obtained from even the side-long glance into the abyss of the whirl which may be had from the highest crag of Helseggen. Looking down from this pinnacle upon the howling Phlegethon below, I could not help smiling at the simplicity with which the honest Jonas Ramus records, as a matter difficult of belief, the anecdotes of the whales and the bears; for it appeared to me, in fact, a self-evident thing, that the largest ships of the line in existence, coming within the influence of that deadly attraction, could resist it as little as a feather the hurricane, and must disappear bodily and at once.

The attempts to account for the phenomenon—some of which, I remember, seemed to me sufficiently plausible in perusal—now wore a very different and unsatisfactory aspect. The idea generally received is that this, as well as three smaller vortices among the Feroe islands, "have no other cause than the collision of waves rising and falling, at flux and reflux, against a ridge of rocks and shelves, which confines the water so that it precipitates itself like a cataract; and thus the higher the flood rises, the deeper must the fall be, and the natural result of all is a whirlpool or vortex, the prodigious suction of which is sufficiently known by lesser experiments."—These are the words of the Encyclopædia Britannica. Kircher and others imagine that in the centre of the channel of the Maelström is an abyss penetrating the globe, and issuing in some very remote part—the Gulf of Bothnia being somewhat decidedly named in one instance. This opinion, idle in itself, was the one to which, as I gazed, my imagination most readily assented; and, mentioning it to the guide, I was rather surprised to hear him say that, although it was the view almost universally entertained of the subject by the Norwegians, it nevertheless was not his own. As to the former notion he confessed his inability to comprehend it; and here I agreed with him—for, however conclusive on paper, it becomes altogether unintelligible, and even absurd, amid the thunder of the abyss.

"You have had a good look at the whirl now," said the old man, "and if you will creep round this crag, so as to get in its lee, and deaden the roar of the water, I will tell you a story that will convince you I ought to know something of the Moskoe-ström."

I placed myself as desired, and he proceeded.

"Myself and my two brothers once owned a schooner-rigged smack of about seventy tons burthen, with which we were in the habit of fishing among the islands beyond Moskoe, nearly to Vurrgh. In all violent eddies at sea there is good fishing, at proper opportunities, if one has only the courage to attempt it; but among the whole of the Lofoden coastmen, we three were the only ones who made a regular business of going out to the islands, as I tell you. The usual grounds are a great way lower down to the southward. There fish can be got at all hours, without much risk, and therefore these places are preferred. The choice spots over here among the rocks, however, not only yield the finest variety, but in far greater abundance; so that we often got in a single day, what the more timid of the craft could not scrape together in a week. In fact, we made it a matter of desperate speculation—the risk of life standing instead of labor, and courage answering for capital.

"We kept the smack in a cove about five miles higher up the coast than this; and it was our practice, in fine weather, to take advantage of the fifteen minutes' slack to push across the main channel of the Moskoeström, far above the pool, and then drop down upon anchorage somewhere near Otterholm, or Sandflesen, when the eddies are not so violent as elsewhere. Here we used to remain until nearly time for slack-water again, when we weighed and made for home. We never set out upon this expedition without a steady side wind for going and coming—one that we felt sure would not fail us before our return—and we seldom made a miscalculation upon this point. Twice, during six years, we were forced to stay all night at anchor on account of a dead calm, which is a rare thing indeed just about here; and once we had to remain on the grounds nearly a week, starving to death, owing to a gale which blew up shortly after our arrival, and made the channel too boisterous to be thought of. Upon this occasion we should have been driven out to sea in spite of everything, (for the whirlpools threw us round and round so violently, that, at length, we fouled our anchor and dragged it) if it had not been that we drifted into one of the innumerable cross currents—here today and gone tomorrow—which drove us under the lee of Flimen, where, by good luck, we brought up.

"I could not tell you the twentieth part of the difficulties we encountered 'on the ground'—it is a bad spot to be in, even in good weather—but we made shift always to run the gauntlet of the Moskoe-ström itself without accident; although at times my heart has been in my mouth when we happened to be a minute or so behind or before the slack. The wind sometimes was not as strong as we thought it at starting, and then we made rather less way than we could wish, while the current rendered the smack unmanageable. My eldest brother had a son eighteen years old, and I had two stout boys of my own. These would have been of great assistance at such times, in using the sweeps, as well as afterward in fishing—but, somehow, although we ran the risk ourselves, we had not the heart to let the young ones get into the danger—for, after all said and done, it *was* a horrible danger, and that is the truth.

"It is now within a few days of three years since what I am going to tell you occurred. It was on the tenth of July, 18—, a day which the people of this part of the world will never forget—for it was one in which blew the most terrible hurricane that ever came out of the heavens. And yet all the morning, and indeed until late in the afternoon, there was a gentle and steady breeze from the south-west, while the sun shone brightly, so that the oldest seaman among us could not have foreseen what was to follow.

"The three of us—my two brothers and myself—had crossed over to the islands about two o'clock P.M., and soon nearly loaded the smack with fine fish, which, we all remarked, were more plenty that day than we had ever known them. It was just seven, *by my watch,* when we weighed and started for home, so as to make the worst of the Ström at slack water, which we knew would be at eight.

"We set out with a fresh wind on our starboard quarter, and for some time spanked along at a great rate, never dreaming of danger, for indeed we saw not the slightest reason to apprehend it. All at once we were taken aback by a breeze from over Helseggen. This was most unusual—something that had never happened to us before—and I began to feel a little uneasy, without exactly knowing why. We put the boat on the wind, but could make no headway at all for the eddies, and I was upon the point of proposing to return to the anchorage, when, looking astern, we saw the whole horizon covered with a singular copper-colored cloud that rose with the most amazing velocity.

"In the meantime the breeze that had headed us off fell away, and we were dead becalmed, drifting about in every direction. This state of things, however, did not last long enough to give us time to think about it. In less than a minute the storm was upon us—in less than two the sky was entirely overcast—and what with this and the driving spray, it became suddenly so dark that we could not see each other in the smack.

"Such a hurricane as then blew it is folly to attempt describing. The oldest seaman in Norway never experienced any thing like it. We had let our sails go by the run before it cleverly took us; but, at the first puff, both our masts went by the board as if they had been sawed off—the mainmast taking with it my youngest brother, who had lashed himself to it for safety.

"Our boat was the lightest feather of a thing that ever sat upon water. It had a complete flush deck, with only a small hatch near the bow, and this hatch it had always been our custom to batten down when about to cross the Ström, by way of precaution against the chopping seas. But for this circumstance we should have foundered at once—for we lay entirely buried for some moments. How my elder brother escaped destruction I cannot say, for I never had an opportunity of ascertaining. For my part, as soon as I had let the foresail run, I threw myself flat on deck, with my feet against the narrow gunwale of the bow, and with my hands grasping a ring-bolt near the foot of the foremast. It was mere instinct that prompted me to do this—which was undoubtedly the very best thing I could have done—for I was too much flurried to think.

"For some moments we were completely deluged, as I say, and all this time I held my breath, and clung to the bolt. When I could stand it no longer I raised myself upon my knees, still keeping hold with my hands, and thus got my head clear. Presently our little boat gave herself a shake, just as a dog does in coming out of the water, and thus rid herself, in some measure, of the seas. I was now trying to get the better of the stupor that had come over me, and to collect my senses so as to see what was to be done, when I felt somebody grasp my arm. It was my elder brother, and my heart leaped for joy, for I had made sure that he was overboard—but the next moment all this joy was turned into horror—for he put his mouth close to my ear, and screamed out the word '*Moskoe-ström!*'

"No one ever will know what my feelings were at that moment. I shook from head to foot as if I had had the most violent fit of the ague. I knew what he meant by that one word well enough—I knew what he wished to make me understand. With the wind that now drove us on, we were bound for the whirl of the Ström, and nothing could save us!

"You perceive that in crossing the Ström *channel,* we always went a long way up above the whirl, even in the calmest weather, and then had to wait and watch carefully for the slack—but now we were driving right upon the pool itself, and in such a hurricane as this! 'To be sure,' I thought, 'we shall get there just about the slack—there is some little hope in that'—but in the next moment I cursed myself for being so great a fool as to dream of hope at all. I knew very well that we were doomed, had we been ten times a ninety-gun ship.

"By this time the first fury of the tempest had spent itself, or perhaps we did not feel it so much, as we scudded before it, but at all events the seas, which at first had been kept down by the wind, and lay flat and frothing, now got up into absolute mountains. A singular change, too, had come over the heavens. Around in every direction it was still as black as pitch, but nearly overhead there burst out, all at once, a circular rift of clear sky—as clear as I ever saw—and of a deep bright blue—and through it there blazed forth the full moon with a lustre that I never before knew her to wear. She lit up every thing about us with the greatest distinctness —but, oh God, what a scene it was to light up!

"I now made one or two attempts to speak to my brother—but in some manner which I could not understand, the din had so increased that I could not make him hear a single word, although I screamed at the top of my voice in his ear. Presently he shook his head, looking as pale as death, and held up one of his fingers, as if to say '*listen!*'

"At first I could not make out what he meant—but soon a hideous thought flashed upon me. I dragged my watch from its fob. It was not going. I glanced at its face by the moonlight, and then burst into tears as I flung it far away into the ocean. *It had run down at seven o'clock! We were behind the time of the slack, and the whirl of the Ström was in full fury!*

"When a boat is well built, properly trimmed, and not deep laden, the waves in a strong gale, when she is going large, seem always to slip from beneath her—which appears very strange to a landsman—and this is what is called *riding*, in sea phrase.

"Well, so far we had ridden the swells very cleverly; but presently a gigantic sea happened to take us right under the counter, and bore us with it as it rose—up—up—as if into the sky. I would not have believed that any wave could rise so high. And then down we came with a sweep, a slide, and a plunge, that made me feel sick and dizzy, as if I was falling from some lofty mountain-top in a dream. But while we were up I had thrown a quick glance around—and that one glance was all sufficient. I saw our exact position in an instant. The Moskoe-ström whirlpool was about a quarter of a mile dead ahead—but no more like the every-day Moskoe-ström, than the whirl as you now see it, is like a mill-race. If I had not known where we were, and what we had to expect, I should not have recognized the place at all. As it was, I involuntarily closed my eyes in horror. The lids clenched themselves together as if in a spasm.

"It could not have been more than two minutes afterwards until we suddenly felt the waves subside, and were enveloped in foam. The boat made a sharp half turn to larboard, and then shot off in its new direction like a thunderbolt. At the same moment the roaring noise of the water was completely drowned in a kind of shrill shriek—such a sound as you might imagine given out by the water-pipes of many thousand steam-vessels, letting off their steam all together. We were now in the belt of surf that always surrounds the whirl; and I thought, of course, that another moment would plunge us into the abyss—down which we could only see indistinctly on account of the amazing velocity with which we were borne along. The boat did not seem to sink into the water at all, but to skim like an air-bubble upon the surface of the surge. Her starboard side was next the whirl, and on the larboard arose the world of ocean we had left. It stood like a huge writhing wall between us and the horizon.

"It may appear strange, but now, when we were in the very jaws of the gulf, I felt more composed than when we were only approaching it. Having made up my mind to hope no more, I got rid of a great deal of that terror which unmanned me at first. I suppose it was despair that strung my nerves.

"It may look like boasting—but what I tell you is truth—I began to reflect how magnificent a thing it was to die in such a manner, and how foolish it was in me to think of so paltry a consideration as my own individual life, in view of so wonderful a manifestation of God's power. I do believe that I blushed with shame when this idea crossed my mind. After a little while I became possessed with the keenest curiosity about the whirl itself. I positively felt a *wish* to explore its depths, even at the sacrifice I was going to make; and my principal grief was that I should never be able to tell my old companions on shore about the mysteries I should see. These, no doubt, were singular fancies to occupy a man's mind in such extremity—and I have often thought since, that the revolutions of the boat around the pool might have rendered me a little light-headed.

"There was another circumstance which tended to restore my self-possession; and this was the cessation of the wind, which could not reach us in our present situation—for, as you saw yourself, the belt of surf is considerably lower than the general bed of the ocean, and this latter now towered above us, a high, black, mountainous ridge. If you have never been at sea in a heavy gale, you can form no idea of the confusion of mind occasioned by the wind and spray together. They blind, deafen, and strangle you, and take away all power of action or reflection. But we were now, in a great measure, rid of these annoyances—just as death-condemned felons in prison are allowed petty indulgences, forbidden them while their doom is yet uncertain.

"How often we made the circuit of the belt it is impossible to say. We careered round and round for perhaps an hour, flying rather than floating, getting gradually more and more into the middle of the surge, and then nearer and nearer to its horrible inner edge. All this time I had never let go of the ring-bolt. My brother was at the stern, holding on to a large empty water-cask which had been securely lashed under the coop of the counter, and was the only thing on deck that had not been swept overboard when the gale first took us. As we approached the brink of the pit he let go his hold upon this, and made for the ring, from which, in the agony of his terror, he endeavored to force my hands, as it was not large enough to afford us both a secure grasp. I never felt deeper grief than when I saw him attempt this act—although I knew he was a madman when he did it —a raving maniac through sheer fright. I did not care, however, to contest the point with him. I thought it could make no difference whether either of us held on at all; so I let him have the bolt, and went astern to the cask. This there was no great difficulty in doing; for the smack flew round steadily enough, and upon an even keel—only swaying to and fro, with the immense sweeps and swelters of the whirl. Scarcely had I secured myself in my new position, when we gave a wild lurch to starboard, and rushed headlong into the abyss. I muttered a hurried prayer to God, and thought all was over.

"As I felt the sickening sweep of the descent, I had instinctively tightened my hold upon the barrel, and closed my eyes. For some seconds I

dared not open them—while I expected instant destruction, and wondered that I was not already in my death-struggles with the water. But
moment after moment elapsed. I still lived. The sense of falling had
ceased; and the motion of the vessel seemed much as it had been before
while in the belt of foam, with the exception that she now lay more along.
I took courage and looked once again upon the scene.

"Never shall I forget the sensations of awe, horror, and admiration
with which I gazed about me. The boat appeared to be hanging, as if by
magic, midway down, upon the interior surface of a funnel vast in circum-
ference, prodigious in depth, and whose perfectly smooth sides might
have been mistaken for ebony, but for the bewildering rapidity with
which they spun around, and for the gleaming and ghastly radiance they
shot forth, as the rays of the full moon, from that circular rift amid the
clouds which I have already described, streamed in a flood of golden glory
along the black walls, and far away down into the inmost recesses of the
abyss.

"At first I was too much confused to observe anything accurately. The
general burst of terrific grandeur was all that I beheld. When I recovered
myself a little, however, my gaze fell instinctively downward. In this direction I was able to obtain an unobstructed view, from the manner in which
the smack hung on the inclined surface of the pool. She was quite upon an
even keel—that is to say, her deck lay in a plane parallel with that of the
water—but this latter sloped at an angle of more than forty-five degrees,
so that we seemed to be lying upon our beam-ends. I could not help
observing, nevertheless, that I had scarcely more difficulty in maintaining
my hold and footing in this situation, than if we had been upon a dead
level; and this, I suppose, was owing to the speed at which we revolved.

"The rays of the moon seemed to search the very bottom of the profound gulf; but still I could make out nothing distinctly, on account of a
thick mist in which everything there was enveloped, and over which there
hung a magnificent rainbow, like that narrow and tottering bridge which
Mussulmen say is the only pathway between Time and Eternity. This
mist, or spray, was no doubt occasioned by the clashing of the great walls
of the funnel, as they all met together at the bottom—but the yell that
went up to the Heavens from out of that mist, I dare not attempt to
describe.

"Our first slide into the abyss itself, from the belt of foam above, had
carried us to a great distance down the slope; but our farther descent was
by no means proportionate. Round and round we swept—not with any
uniform movement—but in dizzying swings and jerks, that sent us sometimes only a few hundred feet—sometimes nearly the complete circuit of

the whirl. Our progress downward, at each revolution, was slow, but very perceptible.

"Looking about me upon the wide waste of liquid ebony on which we were thus borne, I perceived that our boat was not the only object in the embrace of the whirl. Both above and below us were visible fragments of vessels, large masses of building timber and trunks of trees, with many smaller articles, such as pieces of house furniture, broken boxes, barrels and staves. I have already described the unnatural curiosity which had taken the place of my original terrors. It appeared to grow upon me as I drew nearer and nearer to my dreadful doom. I now began to watch, with a strange interest, the numerous things that floated in our company. I *must* have been delirious—for I even sought *amusement* in speculating upon the relative velocities of their several descents toward the foam below. 'This fir tree,' I found myself at one time saying, 'will certainly be the next thing that takes the awful plunge and disappears,'—and then I was disappointed to find that the wreck of a Dutch merchant ship overtook it and went down before. At length, after making several guesses of this nature, and being deceived in all—this fact—the fact of my invariable miscalculation, set me upon a train of reflection that made my limbs again tremble, and my heart beat heavily once more.

"It was not a new terror that thus affected me, but the dawn of a more exciting *hope*. This hope arose partly from memory, and partly from present observation. I called to mind the great variety of buoyant matter that strewed the coast of Lofoden, having been absorbed and then thrown forth by the Moskoe-ström. By far the greater number of the articles were shattered in the most extraordinary way—so chafed and roughened as to have the appearance of being stuck full of splinters—but then I distinctly recollected that there were *some* of them which were not disfigured at all. Now I could not account for this difference except by supposing that the roughened fragments were the only ones which had been *completely absorbed*—that the others had entered the whirl at so late a period of the tide, or, from some reason, had descended so slowly after entering, that they did not reach the bottom before the turn of the flood came, or of the ebb, as the case might be. I conceived it possible, in either instance, that they might thus be whirled up again to the level of the ocean, without undergoing the fate of those which had been drawn in more early or absorbed more rapidly. I made, also, three important observations. The first was, that as a general rule, the larger the bodies were, the more rapid their descent;—the second, that, between two masses of equal extent, the one spherical, and the other *of any other shape*, the superiority in speed of descent was with the sphere;—the third, that, between two masses of equal size, the one cylindrical, and the other of any other shape, the cylinder was absorbed the more slowly.

"Since my escape, I have had several conversations on this subject with an old school-master of the district; and it was from him that I learned the use of the words 'cylinder' and 'sphere.' He explained to me—although I have forgotten the explanation—how what I observed was, in fact, the natural consequence of the forms of the floating fragments—and showed me how it happened that a cylinder, swimming in a vortex, offered more resistance to its suction, and was drawn in with greater difficulty than an equally bulky body, of any form whatever.*

"There was one startling circumstance which went a great way in en-forcing these observations, and rendering me anxious to turn them to account, and this was that, at every revolution, we passed something like a barrel, or else the broken yard or the mast of a vessel, while many of these things, which had been on our level when I first opened my eyes upon the wonders of the whirlpool, were now high up above us, and seemed to have moved but little from their original station.

"I no longer hesitated what to do. I resolved to lash myself securely to the water cask upon which I now held, to cut it loose from the counter, and to throw myself with it into the water. I attracted my brother's atten-tion by signs, pointed to the floating barrels that came near us, and did everything in my power to make him understand what I was about to do. I thought at length that he comprehended my design—but, whether this was the case or not, he shook his head despairingly, and refused to move from his station by the ring-bolt. It was impossible to force him; the emergency admitted no delay; and so, with a bitter struggle, I resigned him to his fate, fastened myself to the cask by means of the lashings which secured it to the counter, and precipitated myself with it into the sea, without another moment's hesitation.

"The result was precisely what I had hoped it might be. As it is myself who now tell you this tale—as you see that I *did* escape—and as you are already in possession of the mode in which this escape was effected, and must therefore anticipate all that I have farther to say—I will bring my story quickly to conclusion. It might have been an hour, or thereabout, after my quitting the smack, when, having descended to a vast distance beneath me, it made three or four wild gyrations in rapid succession, and, bearing my loved brother with it, plunged headlong, at once and forever, into the chaos of foam below. The barrel to which I was attached sunk very little farther than half the distance between the bottom of the gulf and the spot at which I leaped overboard, before a great change took

* See Archimedes, *De Incidentibus in Fluido*—lib. 2.

place in the character of the whirlpool. The slope of the sides of the vast funnel became momently less and less steep. The gyrations of the whirl grew, gradually, less and less violent. By degrees, the froth and the rainbow disappeared, and the bottom of the gulf seemed slowly to uprise. The sky was clear, the winds had gone down, and the full moon was setting radiantly in the west, when I found myself on the surface of the ocean, in full view of the shores of Lofoden, and above the spot where the pool of the Moskoe-ström *had been.* It was the hour of the slack—but the sea still heaved in mountainous waves from the effects of the hurricane. I was borne violently into the channel of the Ström, and in a few minutes, was hurried down the coast into the 'grounds' of the fishermen. A boat picked me up—exhausted from fatigue—and (now that the danger was removed) speechless from the memory of its horror. Those who drew me on board were my old mates and daily companions—but they knew me no more than they would have known a traveller from the spirit-land. My hair, which had been raven-black the day before, was as white as you see it now. They say too that the whole expression of my countenance had changed. I told them my story—they did not believe it. I now tell it to *you* —and I can scarcely expect you to put more faith in it than did the merry fishermen of Lofoden."

The Captain of the Pole-Star

Sir Arthur Conan Doyle

[Being an extract from the singular journal of
JOHN M'ALISTER RAY, student of medicine.]

EPTEMBER 11TH.—LAT. 81° 40' N.; LONG. 2° E. Still lying-to amid enormous ice fields. The one which stretches away to the north of us, and to which our ice-anchor is attached, can not be smaller than an English county. To the right and left unbroken sheets extend to the horizon. This morning the mate reported that there were signs of pack ice to the southward. Should this form of sufficient thickness to bar our return, we shall be in a position of danger, as the food, I hear, is already running somewhat short. It is late in the season, and the nights are beginning to reappear. This morning I saw a star twinkling just over the foreyard, the first since the beginning of May. There is considerable discontent among the crew, many of whom are anxious to get back home to be in time for the herring season, when labor always commands a high price upon the Scotch coast. As yet their displeasure is only signified by sullen countenances and black looks, but I heard from the second mate this afternoon that they contemplated sending a deputation to the captain to explain their grievance. I much doubt how he will receive it, as he is a man of fierce temper, and very sensitive about anything approaching to an infringement of his rights. I shall venture after dinner to say a few words to him upon the subject. I have always found that he will tolerate from me what he would resent from any other member of the crew. Amsterdam Island, at the northwest corner of Spitzbergen, is visible upon our starboard quarter—a rugged line of volcanic rocks, intersected by white seams, which represent glaciers. It is curious to think that at the present moment there is probably no human being nearer to us than the Danish settlements in the south of Greenland—a good nine hundred miles as the crow flies. A captain takes a great responsibility upon himself when he risks his vessel under such circumstances. No whaler has ever remained in these latitudes till so advanced a period of the year.

9 P.M.—I have spoken to Captain Craigie, and though the result has been hardly satisfactory, I am bound to say that he listened to what I had to say very quietly and even deferentially. When I had finished he put on that air of iron determination which I have frequently observed upon his face, and paced rapidly backward and forward across the narrow cabin for some minutes. At first I feared that I had seriously offended him, but he dispelled the idea by sitting down again and putting his hand upon my arm with a gesture which almost amounted to a caress. There was a depth of tenderness too in his wild dark eyes which surprised me considerably.

"Look here, doctor," he said, "I'm sorry I ever took you—I am indeed —and I would give fifty pounds this minute to see you standing safe upon the Dundee quay. It's hit or miss with me this time. There are fish to the north of us. How dare you shake your head, sir, when I tell you I saw them blowing from the masthead?"—this in a sudden burst of fury, though I was not conscious of having shown any signs of doubt. "Two-and-twenty fish in as many minutes, as I am a living man, and not one under ten feet. Now, doctor, do you think I can leave the country when there is only one infernal strip of ice between me and my fortune? If it came on to blow from the north tomorrow we could fill the ship and be away before the frost could catch us. If it came on to blow from the south —well, I suppose the men are paid for risking their lives, and as for myself it matters but little to me, for I have more to bind me to the other world than to this one. I confess that I am sorry for *you,* though. I wish I had old Angus Tait who was with me last voyage, for he was a man that would never be missed, and you—you said once that you were engaged, did you not?"

"Yes," I answered, snapping the spring of the locket which hung from my watch-chain, and holding up the little vignette of Flora.

"Curse you!" he yelled, springing out of his seat, with his very beard bristling with passion. "What is your happiness to me? What have I to do with her that you must dangle her photograph before my eyes?"

I almost thought that he was about to strike me in the frenzy of his rage, but with another imprecation he dashed open the door of the cabin and rushed out upon deck, leaving me considerably astonished at his extraordinary violence. It is the first time that he has ever shown me anything but courtesy and kindness. I can hear him pacing excitedly up and down overhead as I write these lines.

I should like to give a sketch of the character of this man, but it seems presumptuous to attempt such a thing upon paper, when the idea in my own mind is at best a vague and uncertain one. Several times I have thought that I grasped the clue which might explain it, but only to be disappointed by his presenting himself in some new light which would upset all my conclusions. It may be that no human eye but my own shall ever rest upon these lines, yet as a psychological study I shall attempt to leave some record of Captain Nicholas Craigie.

A man's outer case generally gives some indication of the soul within. The captain is tall and well formed, with dark, handsome face, and a curious way of twitching his limbs, which may arise from nervousness, or be simply an outcome of his excessive energy. His jaw and whole cast of countenance are manly and resolute, but the eyes are the distinctive feature of his face. They are of the very darkest hazel, bright and eager, with a singular mixture of recklessness in their expression, and of something else which I have sometimes thought was more allied with horror than any other emotion. Generally the former predominated, but on occasions, and more particularly when he was thoughtfully inclined, the look of fear would spread and deepen until it imparted a new character to his whole countenance. It is at these times that he is most subject to tempestuous fits of anger, and he seems to be aware of it, for I have known him to lock himself up so that no one might approach him until his dark hour was passed. He sleeps badly, and I have heard him shouting during the night, but his cabin is some little distance from mine, and I could never distinguish the words which he said.

This is one phase of his character, and the most disagreeable one. It is only through my close association with him, thrown together as we are day after day, that I have observed it. Otherwise he is an agreeable companion, well-read and entertaining, and as gallant a seaman as ever trod a deck. I shall not easily forget the way in which he handled the ship when we were caught by a gale among the loose ice at the beginning of April. I have never seen him so cheerful, and even hilarious, as he was that night, as he paced backward and forward upon the bridge amid the flashing of the lightning and the howling of the wind. He has told me several times that the thought of death is a pleasant one to him, which is a sad thing for a young man to say; he cannot be much more than thirty, though his hair and mustache are already slightly grizzled. Some great sorrow must have overtaken him and blighted his whole life. Perhaps I should be the same if I lost my Flora—God knows! I think if it were not for her that I should care very little whether the wind blew from the north or the south tomorrow. There, I hear him come down the companion, and he has locked himself up in his room, which shows that he is still in an unamiable mood. And so to bed, as old Pepys would say, for the candle is burning down (we have to use them now since the nights are closing in), and the steward has turned in, so there are no hopes of another one.

September 12th.—Calm, clear day, and still lying in the same position. What wind there is comes from the southeast, but it is very slight. Captain is in a better humor, and apologized to me at breakfast for his rudeness. He still looks somewhat distrait, however, and retains that wild look in his eyes which in a Highlander would mean that he was "fey"—at least so our chief engineer remarked to me, and he has some reputation among the Celtic portion of our crew as a seer and expounder of omens.

It is strange that superstition should have obtained such mastery over this hard-headed and practical race. I could not have believed to what an extent it is carried had I not observed it for myself. We have had a perfect epidemic of it this voyage, until I have felt inclined to serve out rations of sedatives and nerve tonics with the Saturday allowance of grog. The first symptom of it was that shortly after leaving Shetland the men at the wheel used to complain that they heard plaintive cries and screams in the wake of the ship, as if something were following it and were unable to overtake it. This fiction has been kept up during the whole voyage, and on dark nights at the beginning of the seal-fishing it was only with great difficulty that men could be induced to do their spell. No doubt what they heard was either the creaking of the rudder-chains, or the cry of some passing sea-bird. I have been fetched out of bed several times to listen to it, but I need hardly say that I was never able to distinguish anything unnatural. The men, however, are so absurdly positive upon the subject that it is hopeless to argue with them. I mentioned the matter to the captain once, but to my surprise he took it very gravely, and indeed seemed to be considerably disturbed by what I told him. I should have thought that he at least would have been above such vulgar delusions.

All this disquisition upon superstition leads me up to the fact that Mr. Manson, our second mate, saw a ghost last night—or, at least says that he did, which of course is the same thing. It is quite refreshing to have some new topic of conversation after the eternal routine of bears and whales which has served us for so many months. Manson swears the ship is haunted, and that he would not stay in her a day if he had any other place to go to. Indeed, the fellow is honestly frightened, and I had to give him some chloral and bromide of potassium this morning to steady him down. He seemed quite indignant when I suggested that he had been having an extra glass the night before, and I was obliged to pacify him by keeping as grave a countenance as possible during his story, which he certainly narrated in a very straightforward and matter-of-fact way.

"I was on the bridge," he said, "about four bells in the middle watch, just when the night was at its darkest. There was a bit of a moon, but the clouds were blowing across it so that you couldn't see far from the ship. John M'Leod, the harpooner, came aft from the foc'sle-head and reported a strange noise on the starboard bow. I went forrad and we both heard it, sometimes like a bairn crying and sometimes like a wench in pain. I've been seventeen years to the country and I never heard seal, old or young, make a sound like that. As we were standing there on the foc'sle head the moon came out from behind a cloud, and we both saw a sort of white figure moving across the ice field in the same direction that we had heard the cries. We lost sight of it for a while, but it came back on the port bow, and we could just make it out like a shadow on the ice. I sent a hand aft for the rifles, and M'Leod and I went down on to the pack, thinking that maybe it might be a bear. When we got on the ice I lost sight of M'Leod, but I pushed on in the direction where I could still hear the cries. I followed them for a mile or maybe more, and then running round a hummock I came right on to the top of it standing and waiting for me seemingly. I don't know what it was. It wasn't a bear anyway. It was tall and white and straight, and if it wasn't a man nor a woman, I'll stake my davy it was something worse. I made for the ship as hard as I could run, and precious glad I was to find myself aboard. I signed articles to do my duty by the ship, and on the ship I'll stay, but you don't catch me on the ice again after sundown."

That is his story, given as far as I can in his own words. I fancy what he saw must, in spite of his denial, have been a young bear erect upon its hind legs, an attitude which they often assume when alarmed. In the uncertain light this would bear a resemblance to a human figure, especially to a man whose nerves were already somewhat shaken. Whatever it may have been, the occurrence is unfortunate, for it has produced a most unpleasant effect upon the crew. Their looks are more sullen than before, and their discontent more open. The double grievance of being debarred from the herring fishing and of being detained in what they choose to call a haunted vessel, may lead them to do something rash. Even the harpooners, who are the oldest and steadiest among them, are joining in the general agitation.

Apart from this absurd outbreak of superstition, things are looking rather more cheerful. The pack which was forming to the south of us has partly cleared away, and the water is so warm as to lead me to believe that we are lying in one of those branches of the Gulf Stream which run up between Greenland and Spitzbergen. There are numerous small Medusæ and sea-lemons about the ship, with abundance of shrimps, so that there is every possibility of "fish" being sighted. Indeed, one was seen blowing about dinnertime but in such a position that it was impossible for the boats to follow it.

September 13th.—Had an interesting conversation with the chief mate, Mr. Milne, upon the bridge. It seems that our captain is as great an enigma to the seamen, and even to the owners of the vessel, as he has been to me. Mr. Milne tells me that when the ship is paid off, upon returning from a voyage, Captain Craigie disappears, and is not seen again until the approach of another season, when he walks quietly into the office of the company, and asks whether his services will be required. He has no friend in Dundee, nor does any one pretend to be acquainted with his early history. His position depends entirely upon his skill as a seaman and the name for courage and coolness which he had earned in the capacity of mate, before being trusted with a separate command. The unanimous opinion seems to be that he is not a Scotchman, and that his name is an assumed one. Mr. Milne thinks that he has devoted himself to whaling simply for the reason that it is the most dangerous occupation which he could select, and that he courts death in every possible manner. He mentioned several instances of this, one of which is rather curious, if true. It seems that on one occasion he did not put in an appearance at the office, and a substitute had to be selected in his place. That was at the time of the last Russian and Turkish war. When he turned up again next spring he had a puckered wound in the side of his neck which he used to endeavor to conceal with his cravat. Whether the mate's inference that he had been engaged in the war is true or not I can not say. It was certainly a strange coincidence.

The wind is veering round in an easterly direction, but is still very slight. I think the ice is lying closer than it did yesterday. As far as the eye can reach on every side there is one wide expanse of spotless white, only broken by an occasional rift or the dark shadow of a hummock. To the south there is the narrow lane of blue water which is our sole means of escape, and which is closing up every day. The captain is taking a heavy responsibility upon himself. I hear that the tank of potatoes has been finished, and even the biscuits are running short, but he preserves the same impassable countenance, and spends the greater part of the day at the crow's nest, sweeping the horizon with his glass. His manner is very variable, and he seems to avoid my society, but there has been no repetition of the violence which he showed the other night.

7:30 P.M.—My deliberate opinion is that we are commanded by a madman. Nothing else can account for the extraordinary vagaries of Captain Craigie. It is fortunate that I have kept this journal of our voyage, as it will serve to justify us in case we have to put him under any sort of restraint, a step which I should only consent to as a last resource. Curiously enough it was he himself who suggested lunacy and not mere eccentricity as the secret of his strange conduct. He was standing upon the bridge about an hour ago, peering as usual through his glass, while I was walking up and down the quarterdeck. The majority of the men were below at their tea, for the watches have not been regularly kept of late. Tired of walking, I leaned against the bulwarks, and admired the mellow glow cast by the sinking sun upon the great ice fields which surround us. I was suddenly aroused from the reverie into which I had fallen by a hoarse voice at my elbow, and starting round I found that the captain had descended and was standing by my side. He was staring out over the ice with an expression in which horror, surprise, and something approaching to joy were contending for the mastery. In spite of the cold, great drops of perspiration were coursing down his forehead, and he was evidently fearfully excited. His limbs twitched like those of a man upon the verge of an epileptic fit, and the lines about his mouth were drawn and hard.

"Look!" he gasped, seizing me by the wrist, but still keeping his eyes upon the distant ice, and moving his head slowly in a horizontal direction, as if following some object which was moving across the field of vision. "Look! There, man, there! Between the hummocks! Now coming out from behind the far one! You see her—you *must* see her! There still! Flying from me, by God, flying from me—and gone!"

He uttered the last two words in a whisper of concentrated agony which shall never fade from my remembrance. Clinging to the ratlines, he endeavored to climb upon the top of the bulwarks as if in the hope of obtaining a last glance at the departing object. His strength was not equal to the attempt, however, and he staggered back against the saloon skylights, where he leaned panting and exhausted. His face was so livid that I expected him to become unconscious, so lost no time in leading him down the companion, and stretching him upon one of the sofas in the cabin. I then poured him out some brandy, which I held to his lips, and which had a wonderful effect upon him, bringing the blood back into his white face and steadying his poor shaking limbs. He raised himself up upon his elbow, and looking round to see that we were alone, he beckoned to me to come and sit beside him.

"You saw it, didn't you?" he asked, still in the same subdued awesome tone so foreign to the nature of the man.

"No, I saw nothing."

His head sunk back again upon the cushions. "No, he wouldn't without the glass," he murmured. "He couldn't. It was the glass that showed her to me, and then the eyes of love—the eyes of love. I say, Doc, don't let the steward in! He'll think I'm mad. Just bolt the door, will you?"

I rose and did what he had commanded.

He lay quiet for a while, lost in thought apparently, and then raised himself up upon his elbow again, and asked for some more brandy.

"You don't think I am, do you, Doc?" he asked, as I was putting the bottle back into the after-locker. "Tell me now, as man to man, do you think that I am mad?"

"I think you have something on your mind," I answered, "which is exciting you and doing you a good deal of harm."

"Right there, lad!" he cried, his eyes sparkling from the effects of the brandy. "Plenty on my mind—plenty! But I can work out the latitude and the longitude, and I can handle my sextant and manage my logarithms. You couldn't prove me mad in a court of law, could you, now?" It was curious to hear the man lying back and coolly arguing out the question of his own sanity.

"Perhaps not," I said; "but still I think you would be wise to get home as soon as you can, and settle down to a quiet life for a while."

"Get home, eh?" he muttered, with a sneer upon his face. "One word for me and two for yourself, lad. Settle down with Flora—pretty little Flora. Are bad dreams signs of madness?"

"Sometimes," I answered.

"What else? What would be the first symptoms?"

"Pains in the head, noises in the ears, flashes before the eyes, delusions—"

"Ah! what about them?" he interrupted. "What would you call a delusion?"

"Seeing a thing which is not there is a delusion."

"But she *was* there!" he groaned to himself. "She *was* there!" and rising, he unbolted the door and walked with slow and uncertain steps to his own cabin, where I have no doubt that he will remain until tomorrow morning. His system seems to have received a terrible shock, whatever it may have been that he imagined himself to have seen. The man becomes a greater mystery every day, though I fear that the solution which he has himself suggested is the correct one, and that his reason is affected. I do not think that a guilty conscience has anything to do with his behavior. The idea is a popular one among the officers, and, I believe, the crew; but I have seen nothing to support it. He has not the air of a guilty man, but of one who has had terrible usage at the hands of fortune, and who should be regarded as a martyr rather than a criminal.

The wind is veering round to the south tonight. God help us if it blocks that narrow pass which is our only road to safety! Situated as we are on the edge of the main Arctic pack, or the "barrier" as it is called by the whalers, any wind from the north has the effect of shredding out the ice around us and allowing our escape, while a wind from the south blows up all the loose ice behind us and hems us in between two packs. God help us, I say again!

September 14th.—Sunday, and a day of rest. My fears have been confirmed, and the thin strip of blue water has disappeared from the southward. Nothing but the great motionless ice fields around us, with their weird hummocks and fantastic pinnacles. There is a deathly silence over their wide expanse which is horrible. No lapping of the waves now, no cries of seagulls or straining of sails, but one deep universal silence in which the murmurs of the seamen, and the creak of their boots upon the white shining deck, seem discordant and out of place. Our only visitor was an Arctic fox, a rare animal upon the pack, though common enough upon the land. He did not come near the ship, however, but after surveying us from a distance fled rapidly across the ice. This was curious conduct, as they generally know nothing of man, and being of an inquisitive nature, become so familiar that they are easily captured. Incredible as it may seem, even this little incident produced a bad effect upon the crew. "Yon puir beastie kens mair, ay, an sees mair nor you nor me!" was the comment of one of the leading harpooners, and the others nodded their acquiescence. It is vain to attempt to argue against such puerile superstition. They have made up their minds that there is a curse upon the ship, and nothing will ever persuade them to the contrary.

The captain remained in seclusion all day except for about half an hour in the afternoon, when he came out upon the quarterdeck. I observe that he kept his eye fixed upon the spot where the vision of yesterday had appeared, and was quite prepared for another outburst, but none such came. He did not seem to see me although I was standing close beside him. Divine service was read as usual by the chief engineer. It is a curious thing that in whaling vessels the Church of England Prayer book is always employed, although there is never a member of that Church among either officers or crew. Our men are all Roman Catholics or Presbyterians, the former predominating. Since a ritual is used which is foreign to both, neither can complain that the other is preferred to them, and they listen with all attention and devotion, so that the system has something to recommend it.

A glorious sunset which made the great fields of ice look like a lake of blood. I have never seen a finer and at the same time more weird effect. Wind is veering round. If it will blow twenty-four hours from the north all will yet be well.

September 15th.—Today is Flora's birthday. Dear lass! It is well that she can not see her boy, as she used to call me, shut up among the ice fields with a crazy captain and a few weeks' provisions. No doubt she scans the shipping list in the *Scotsman* every morning to see if we are reported from Shetland. I have set an example to the men and look cheery and unconcerned; but God knows, my heart is very heavy at times.

The thermometer is at nineteen Fahrenheit today. There is but little wind, and what there is comes from an unfavorable quarter. Captain is in an excellent humor; I think he imagines he has seen some other omen or vision, poor fellow, during the night, for he came into my room early in the morning, and stooping down over my bunk, whispered, "It wasn't a delusion, Doc; it's all right!" After breakfast he asked me to find out how much food was left, which the second mate and I proceeded to do. It is even less than we had expected. Forward they have half a tank full of biscuits, three barrels of salt meat, and a very limited supply of coffee beans and sugar. In the afterhold and lockers there are a good many luxuries, such as tinned salmon, soups, harricot mutton, etc., but they will go a very short way among a crew of fifty men. There are two barrels of flour in the storeroom, and an unlimited supply of tobacco. Altogether there is about enough to keep the men on half rations for eighteen or twenty days—certainly not more. When we reported the state of things to the captain, he ordered all hands to be piped, and addressed them from the quarterdeck. I never saw him to better advantage. With his tall, well-knit figure, and dark animated face, he seemed a man born to command, and he discussed the situation in a cool, sailor-like way which showed that while appreciating the danger he had an eye for every loophole of escape.

"My lads," he said, "no doubt you think I brought you into this fix, if it is a fix, and maybe some of you feel bitter against me on account of it. But you must remember that for many a season no ship that comes to the country has brought in as much oil-money as the old *Pole-Star,* and every one of you has had his share of it. You can leave your wives behind you in comfort while other poor fellows come back to find their lasses on the parish. If you have to thank me for the one you have to thank me for the other, and we may call it quits. We've tried a bold venture before this and succeeded, so now that we've tried one and failed we've no cause to cry out about it. If the worst comes to the worst, we can make the land across the ice, and lay in a stock of seals which will keep us alive until the spring. It won't come to that, though, for you'll see the Scotch coast again before three weeks are out. At present every man must go on half rations, share and share alike, and no favor to any. Keep up your hearts and you'll pull through this as you've pulled through many a danger before." These few simple words of his had a wonderful effect upon the crew. His former unpopularity was forgotten, and the old harpooner whom I have already mentioned for his superstition, led off three cheers, which were heartily joined in by all hands.

September 16th.—The wind has veered round to the north during the night, and the ice shows some symptoms of opening out. The men are in good humor in spite of the short allowance upon which they have been placed. Steam is kept up in the engine room, that there may be no delay should an opportunity for escape present itself. The captain is in exuberant spirits, though he still retains that wild "fey" expression which I have already remarked upon. This burst of cheerfulness puzzles me more than his former gloom. I can not understand it. I think I mentioned in an early part of this journal that one of his oddities is that he never permits any person to enter his cabin, but insists upon making his own bed, such as it is, and performing every other office for himself.

To my surprise he handed me the key today and requested me to go down there and take the time by his chronometer while he measured the altitude of the sun at noon. It was a bare little room, containing a washing-stand and a few books, but little else in the way of luxury, except some pictures upon the walls. The majority of these are small cheap oleographs, but there was one watercolor sketch of the head of a young lady which arrested my attention. It was evidently a portrait, and not one of those fancy types of female beauty which sailors particularly effect. No artist could have evolved from his own mind such a mixture of character and weakness. The languid, dreamy eyes, with their drooping lashes, and the broad, low brow, unruffled by thought or care, were in strong contrast with the clean-cut, prominent jaw, and the resolute set of the lower lip. Underneath it in one of the corners was written, "M. B., æt. 19." That any one in the short space of nineteen years of existence could develop such strength of will as was stamped upon her face seemed to me at the time to be well-nigh incredible. She must have been an extraordinary woman. Her features have thrown such a glamour over me that, though I had but a fleeting glance at them, I could, were I a draughtsman, reproduce them line for line upon this page of the journal. I wonder what part she has played in our captain's life. He has hung her picture at the end of his berth, so that his eyes continually rest upon it. Were he a less reserved man I should make some remark upon the subject. Of the other things in his cabin there was nothing worthy of mention—uniform coats, a camp-stool, small looking glass, tobacco box, and numerous pipes, including an Oriental hookah—which, by-the-by, gives some color to Mr. Milne's story about his participation in the war, though the connection may seem rather a distant one.

11:20 P.M.—Captain has just gone to bed after a long and interesting conversation on general topics. When he chooses he can be a most fascinating companion, being remarkably well read, and having the power of expressing his opinion forcibly without appearing to be dogmatic. I hate to have my intellectual toes trod upon. He spoke about the nature of the soul, and sketched out the views of Aristotle and Plato upon the subject in a masterly manner. He seems to have a leaning for metempsychosis and the doctrines of Pythagoras. In discussing them we touched upon modern spiritualism, and I made some joking allusion to the impostures of Slade, upon which, to my surprise, he warned me most impressively against confusing the innocent with the guilty, and argued that it would be as logical to brand Christianity as an error because Judas, who professed that religion, was a villain. He shortly afterward bid me goodnight and retired to his room.

The wind is freshening up, and blows steadily from the north. The nights are as dark now as they are in England. I hope tomorrow may set us free from our frozen fetters.

September 17th.—The bogie again. Thank Heaven that I have strong nerves! The superstition of these poor fellows, and the circumstantial accounts which they give, with the utmost earnestness and self-conviction, would horrify any man not accustomed to their ways. There are many versions of the matter, but the sum total of them all is that something uncanny has been flitting round the ship all night, and that Sandie Mc-Donald of Peterhead and "lang" Peter Williamson of Shetland saw it, as also did Mr. Milne on the bridge—so, having three witnesses, they can make a better case of it than the second mate did. I spoke to Milne after breakfast, and told him that he should be above such nonsense, and that as an officer he ought to set the men a better example. He shook his weatherbeaten head ominously, but answered with characteristic caution, "Mebbe aye, mebbe na, doctor," he said; "I didna ca'it a ghaist. I canna' say I preen my faith in sea-bogles an' the like, though there's a mony as claims to ha' seen a' that and waur. I'm no easy feared, but maybe your ain bluid would run a bit cauld, mun, if instead o' speerin' aboot it in daylicht ye were wi' me last night, an' seed an awfu' like shape, white an' grewsome, whiles here, whiles there, an' it greetin' and ca'ing in the darkness like a bit lambie that hae lost its mither. Ye would na' be sae ready to put it a' doon to auld wives' clavers then, I'm thinkin'." I saw it was hopeless to reason with him, so contented myself with begging him as a personal favor to call me up the next time the spectre appeared—a request to which he acceded with many ejaculations expressive of his hopes that such an opportunity might never arise.

As I had hoped, the white desert behind us has become broken by many thin streaks of water which intersect it in all directions. Our latitude today was 80° 52′ N., which shows that there is a strong southerly drift upon the pack. Should the wind continue favorable it will break up as rapidly as it formed. At present we can do nothing but smoke and wait and hope for the best. I am rapidly becoming a fatalist. When dealing with such uncertain factors as wind and ice a man can be nothing else. Perhaps it was the wind and sand of the Arabian deserts which gave the minds of the original followers of Mohammed their tendency to bow to kismet.

These spectral alarms have a very bad effect upon the captain. I feared that it might excite his sensitive mind, and endeavored to conceal the absurd story from him, but unfortunately he overheard one of the men making an allusion to it, and insisted upon being informed about it. As I had expected, it brought out all his latent lunacy in an exaggerated form. I can hardly believe that this is the same man who discoursed philosophy last night with the most critical acumen and coolest judgment. He is pacing backward and forward upon the quarterdeck like a caged tiger, stopping now and again to throw out his hands with a yearning gesture, and stare impatiently out over the ice. He keeps up a continual mutter to himself, and once he called out, "But a little time, love—but a little time!" Poor fellow, it is sad to see a gallant seaman and accomplished gentleman reduced to such a pass, and to think that imagination and delusion can cow a mind to which real danger was but the salt of life. Was ever a man in such a position as I, between a demented captain and a ghost-seeing mate? I sometimes think I am the only real sane man aboard the vessel—except, perhaps, the second engineer, who is a kind of ruminant, and would care nothing for all the fiends in the Red Sea so long as they would leave him alone and not disarrange his tools.

The ice is still opening rapidly, and there is every probability of our being able to make a start tomorrow morning. They will think I am inventing when I tell them at home all the strange things that have befallen me.

12 P.M.—I have been a good deal startled, though I feel steadier now, thanks to a stiff glass of brandy. I am hardly myself yet, however, as this handwriting will testify. The fact is that I have gone through a very strange experience, and am beginning to doubt whether I was justified in branding every one on board as madmen because they professed to have seen things which did not seem reasonable to my understanding. Pshaw! I am a fool to let such a trifle unnerve me; and yet, coming as it does, after all these alarms, it has an additional significance, for I can not doubt either Mr. Manson's story or that of the mate, now that I have experienced that which I used formerly to scoff at.

After all it was nothing very alarming—a mere sound, and that was all. I can not expect that any one reading this, if any one ever should read it, will sympathize with my feelings, or realize the effect which it produced upon me at the time. Supper was over, and I had gone on deck to have a quiet pipe before turning in. The night was very dark—so dark that, standing under the quarter-boat, I was unable to see the officer upon the bridge. I think I have already mentioned the extraordinary silence which prevails in these frozen seas. In other parts of the world, be they ever so barren, there is some slight vibration of the air—some faint hum, be it from the distant haunts of men, or from the leaves of the trees, or the wings of the birds, or even the faint rustle of the grass that covers the ground. One may not actively perceive the sound, and yet if it were withdrawn it would be missed. It is only here in these Arctic seas that stark, unfathomable stillness obtrudes itself upon you in all its gruesome reality. You find your tympanum straining to catch some little murmur, and dwelling eagerly upon every accidental sound within the vessel. In this state I was leaning against the bulwarks when there arose from the ice almost directly underneath me a cry, sharp and shrill, upon the silent air of the night, beginning, as it seemed to me, at a note such as prima donna never reached, and mounting from that ever higher and higher until it culminated in a long wail of agony, which might have been the last cry of a lost soul. The ghastly scream is still ringing in my ears. Grief, unutterable grief, seemed to be expressed in it, and a great longing, and yet through it all there was an occasional wild note of exultation. It shrilled out from close beside me, and yet as I glared into the darkness I could discern nothing. I waited some little time, but without hearing any repetition of the sound, so I came below, more shaken than I have ever been in my life before. As I came down the companion I met Mr. Milne coming up to relieve the watch. "Weel, doctor," he said, "maybe that's auld wives' clavers tae? Did ye no hear it skirling? Maybe that's a superstee-tion? What d'ye think o't noo?" I was obliged to apologize to the honest fellow, and acknowledge that I was as puzzled by it as he was. Perhaps tomorrow things may look different. At present I dare hardly write all that I think. Reading it again in days to come, when I have shaken off all these associations, I should despise myself for having been so weak.

September 18th.—Passed a restless and uneasy night still haunted by that strange sound. The captain does not look as if he had had much repose either, for his face is haggard and his eyes bloodshot. I have not told him of my adventure of last night, nor shall I. He is already restless and excited, standing up, sitting down, and apparently utterly unable to keep still.

A fine lead appeared in the pack this morning, as I had expected, and we were able to cast off our ice-anchor, and steam about twelve miles in a west-sou'-westerly direction. We were then brought to a halt by a great floe as massive as any which we have left behind us. It bars our progress completely, so we can do nothing but anchor again and wait until it breaks up, which it will probably do within twenty-four hours, if the wind holds. Several bladder-nosed seals were seen swimming in the water, and one was shot, an immense creature more than eleven feet long. They are fierce, pugnacious animals, and are said to be more than a match for a bear. Fortunately they are slow and clumsy in their movements, so there is little danger in attacking them upon the ice.

The captain evidently does not think we have seen the last of our troubles, though why he should take a gloomy view of the situation is more than I can fathom since every one else on board considers that we have had a miraculous escape, and are sure now to reach the open sea.

"I suppose you think it's all right now, doctor?" he said, as we sat together after dinner.

"I hope so," I answered.

"We mustn't be too sure—and yet no doubt you are right. We'll all be in the arms of our own true loves before long, lad, won't we? But we mustn't be too sure—we mustn't be too sure."

He sat silent a little, swinging his leg thoughtfully backward and forward.

"Look here," he continued; "it's a dangerous place this, even at its best —a treacherous, dangerous place. I have known men cut off very suddenly in a land like this. A slip would do it sometimes—a single slip, and down you go through a crack, and only a bubble on the green water to show where it was that you sank. It's a queer thing," he continued with a nervous laugh, "but all the years I've been in this country I never once thought of making a will—not that I have anything to leave in particular, but still when a man is exposed to danger he should have everything arranged and ready—don't you think so?"

"Certainly," I answered, wondering what on earth he was driving at.

"He feels better for knowing it's all settled," he went on. "Now if anything should ever befall me I hope that you will look after things for me. There is very little in the cabin, but such as it is I should like it to be sold, and the money divided in the same proportion as the oil-money among the crew. The chronometer I wish you to keep yourself as some slight remembrance of our voyage. Of course all this is a mere precaution, but I thought I would take the opportunity of speaking to you about it. I suppose I might rely upon you if there were any necessity?"

"Most assuredly," I answered; "and since you are taking this step, I may as well. . . ."

"You! you!" he interrupted. *"You're* all right. What the devil is the matter with *you?* There, I didn't mean to be peppery, but I don't like to hear a young fellow, that has hardly begun life, speculating about death. Go up on deck and get some fresh air into your lungs instead of talking nonsense in the cabin, and encouraging me to do the same."

The more I think of this conversation of ours the less do I like it. Why should the man be settling his affairs at the very time when we seem to be emerging from all danger? There must be some method in his madness. Can it be that he contemplates suicide? I remember that upon one occasion he spoke in a deeply reverent manner of the heinousness of the crime of self-destruction. I shall keep my eye upon him, however, and though I can not intrude upon the privacy of his cabin, I shall at least make a point of remaining on deck as long as he stays up.

Mr. Milne pooh-poohs my fears, and says it is only the "skipper's little way." He himself takes a very rosy view of the situation. According to him we shall be out of the ice by the day after tomorrow, pass Jan Meyen two days after that, and sight Shetland in little more than a week. I hope he may not be too sanguine. His opinion may be fairly balanced against the gloomy precautions of the captain, for he is an old and experienced seaman and weighs his words well before uttering them.

The long-impending catastrophe has come at last. I hardly know what to write about it. The captain is gone. He may come back to us again alive, but I fear me—I fear me. It is now seven o'clock in the morning of the 19th of September. I have spent the whole night traversing the great ice-floe in front of us with a party of seamen in the hope of coming upon some trace of him, but in vain. I shall try to give some account of the circumstances which attended upon his disappearance. Should any one ever chance to read the words which I put down, I trust they will remember that I do not write from conjecture or from hearsay, but that I, a sane and educated man, am describing accurately what actually occurred before my very eyes. My inferences are my own, but I shall be answerable for the facts.

The captain remained in excellent spirits after the conversation which I have recorded. He appeared to be nervous and impatient, however, frequently changing his position, and moving his limbs in an aimless way which is characteristic of him at times. In a quarter of an hour he went upon deck seven times, only to descend after a few hurried paces. I followed him each time, for there was something about his face which confirmed my resolution of not letting him out of my sight. He seemed to observe the effect which his movements had produced, for he endeavored by an over-done hilarity, laughing boisterously at the very smallest of jokes, to quiet my apprehensions.

After supper he went on to the poop once more, and I with him. The night was dark and very still, save for the melancholy soughing of the wind among the spars. A thick cloud was coming up from the northwest, and the ragged tentacles which it threw out in front of it were drifting across the face of the moon, which only shone now and again through a rift in the wrack. The captain paced rapidly backward and forward, and then seeing me still dogging him he came across and hinted that he thought I should be better below—which I need hardly say, had the effect of strengthening my resolution to remain on deck.

I think he forgot about my presence after this, for he stood silently leaning over the taffrail, and peering out across the great desert of snow, part of which lay in shadow, while part glittered mistily in the moonlight. Several times I could see by his movements that he was referring to his watch, and once he muttered a short sentence, of which I could only catch the one word, "ready." I confess to having felt an eerie feeling creeping over me as I watched the loom of his tall figure through the darkness, and noted how completely he fulfilled the idea of a man who is keeping a tryst. A tryst with whom? Some vague perception began to dawn upon me as I pieced one fact with another, but I was utterly unprepared for the sequel.

By the sudden intensity of his attitude I felt that he saw something. I crept up behind him. He was staring with an eager, questioning gaze at what seemed to be a wreath of mist, blown swiftly in a line with the ship. It was a dim, nebulous body, devoid of shape, sometimes more, sometimes less apparent, as the light fell on it. The moon was dimmed in its brilliancy at the moment by a canopy of thinnest cloud, like the coating of an anemone.

"Coming, lass, coming," cried the skipper, in a voice of unfathomable tenderness and compassion, like one who soothes a beloved one by some favor long looked for and as pleasant to bestow as to receive.

What followed happened in an instant. I had no power to interfere. He gave one spring to the top of the bulwarks, and another which took him on to the ice, almost to the feet of the pale misty figure. He held out his hands as if to clasp it, and so ran into the darkness with outstretched arms and loving words. I still stood rigid and motionless, straining my eyes after his retreating form, until his voice died away in the distance. I never thought to see him again, but at that moment the moon shone out brilliantly through a chink in the cloudy heaven, and illuminated the great field of ice. Then I saw his dark figure, already a very long way off, running with prodigious speed across the frozen plain. That was the last glimpse which we caught of him—perhaps the last we ever shall. A party was organized to follow him, and I accompanied it, but the men's hearts were not in the work, and nothing was found. Another will be formed within a few hours. I can hardly believe I have not been dreaming, or suffering from some hideous nightmare, as I write these things down.

7:30 P.M.—Just returned dead beat and utterly tired out from a second unsuccessful search for the captain. The floe is of enormous extent, for though we have traversed at least twenty miles of its surface, there has been no sign of its coming to an end. The frost has been so severe of late that the overlying snow is frozen as hard as granite, otherwise we might have had the footsteps to guide us. The crew are anxious that we should cast off and steam round the floe and so to the southward, for the ice has opened up during the night, and the sea is visible upon the horizon. They argue that Captain Craigie is certainly dead, and that we are all risking our lives to no purpose by remaining when we have an opportunity of escape. Mr. Milne and I have had the greatest difficulty in persuading them to wait until tomorrow night, and have been compelled to promise that we will not under any circumstances delay our departure longer than that. We propose therefore to take a few hours' sleep, and then to start upon a final search.

September 20th, evening.—I crossed the ice this morning with a party of men exploring the southern part of the floe, while Mr. Milne went off in a northerly direction. We pushed on for ten or twelve miles without seeing a trace of any living thing except a single bird, which fluttered a great way over our heads, and which by its flight I should judge to have been a falcon. The southern extremity of the ice field tapered away into a long narrow spit which projected out into the sea. When we came to the base of this promontory the men halted, but I begged them to continue to the extreme end of it, that we might have the satisfaction of knowing that no possible chance had been neglected.

We had hardly gone a hundred yards before McDonald of Peterhead cried out that he saw something in front of us, and began to run. We all got a glimpse of it and ran too. At first it was only a vague darkness against the white ice, but as we raced along together it took the shape of a man, and eventually of the man of whom we were in search. He was lying face downward upon a frozen bank. Many little crystals of ice and feathers of snow had drifted on to him as he lay, and sparkled upon his dark seaman's jacket. As we came up some wandering puff of wind caught these tiny flakes in its vortex and they whirled up into the air, partially descended again, and then, caught once more in the current, sped rapidly away in the direction of the sea. To my eyes it seemed but a snowdrift, but many of my companions averred that it started up in the shape of a woman, stooped over the corpse and kissed it, and then hurried away across the floe. I have learned never to ridicule any man's opinion, however strange it may seem. Sure it is that Captain Nicholas Craigie had met with no painful end, for there was a bright smile upon his blue, pinched features, and his hands were still outstretched as though grasping at the strange visitor which had summoned him away into the dim world that lies beyond the grave.

We buried him the same afternoon with the ship's ensign around him, and a thirty-two-pound shot at his feet. I read the burial service, while the rough sailors wept like children, for there were many who owed much to his kind heart, and who showed now the affection which his strange ways had repelled during his lifetime. He went off the grating with a dull, sullen splash, and as I looked into the green water I saw him go down, down, down until he was but a little flickering patch of white hanging upon the outskirts of eternal darkness. Then even that faded away, and he was gone. There he shall lie, with his secret and his sorrows and his mystery all still buried in his breast, until that great day when the sea shall give up its dead, and Nicholas Craigie come out from among the ice with the smile upon his face, and his stiffened arms outstretched in greeting. I pray that his lot may be a happier one in that life than it has been in this.

I shall not continue my journal. Our road to home lies plain and clear before us, and the great ice field will soon be but a remembrance of the past. It will be some time before I get over the shock produced by recent events. When I began this record of our voyage I little thought of how I should be compelled to finish it. I am writing these final words in the lonely cabin, still starting at times and fancying I hear the quick nervous step of the dead man upon the deck above me. I entered his cabin tonight, as was my duty, to make a list of his effects in order that they might be entered in the official log. All was as it had been upon my previous visit, save that the picture which I have described as having hung at the end of his bed had been cut out of its frame, as with a knife, and was gone. With this last link in a strange chain of evidence I close my diary of the voyage of the *Pole-Star*.

[NOTE by Dr. John M'Alister Ray, senior.—I have read over the strange events connected with the death of the captain of the *Pole-Star*, as narrated in the journal of my son. That everything occurred exactly as he describes it I have the fullest confidence, and, indeed, the most positive certainty, for I know him to be a strong-nerved and unimaginative man, with the strictest regard for veracity. Still, the story is, on the face of it, so vague and so improbable, that I was long opposed to its publication. Within the last few days, however, I have had independent testimony upon the subject which throws a new light upon it. I had run down to Edinburgh to attend a meeting of the British Medical Association, when I chanced to come across Dr. P—, an old college chum of mine, now practicing at Saltash, in Devonshire. Upon my telling him of this experience of my son's, he declared to me that he was familiar with the man, and proceeded, to my no small surprise, to give me a description of him, which tallied remarkably well with that given in the journal, except that he depicted him as a younger man. According to his account, he had been engaged to a young lady of singular beauty residing upon the Cornish coast. During his absence at sea his betrothed had died under circumstances of peculiar horror.]

The Upper Berth

F. Marion Crawford

I

SOMEBODY ASKED FOR the cigars. We had talked long, and the conversation was beginning to languish; the tobacco smoke had got into the heavy curtains, the wine had got into those brains which were liable to become heavy, and it was already perfectly evident that, unless somebody did something to rouse our oppressed spirits, the meeting would soon come to its natural conclusion, and we, the guests, would speedily go home to bed, and most certainly to sleep. No one had said anything very remarkable; it may be that no one had anything very remarkable to say. Jones had given us every particular of his last hunting adventure in Yorkshire. Mr Tompkins, of Boston, had explained at elaborate length those working principles, by the due and careful maintenance of which the Atchison, Topeka, and Santa Fé Railroad not only extended its territory, increased its departmental influence, and transported live stock without starving them to death before the day of actual delivery, but, also, had for years succeeded in deceiving those passengers who bought its tickets into the fallacious belief that the corporation aforesaid was really able to transport human life without destroying it. Signor Tombola had endeavoured to persuade us, by arguments which we took no trouble to oppose, that the unity of his country in no way resembled the average modern torpedo, carefully planned, constructed with all the skill of the greatest European arsenals, but, when constructed, destined to be directed by feeble hands into a region where it must undoubtedly explode, unseen, unfeared, and unheard, into the illimitable wastes of political chaos.

It is unnecessary to go into further details. The conversation had assumed proportions which would have bored Prometheus on his rock, which would have driven Tantalus to distraction, and which would have impelled Ixion to seek relaxation in the simple but instructive dialogues of

Herr Ollendorff, rather than submit to the greater evil of listening to our talk. We had sat at table for hours; we were bored, we were tired, and nobody showed signs of moving.

Somebody called for cigars. We all instinctively looked towards the speaker. Brisbane was a man of five-and-thirty years of age, and remarkable for those gifts which chiefly attract the attention of men. He was a strong man. The external proportions of his figure presented nothing extraordinary to the common eye, though his size was above the average. He was a little over six feet in height, and moderately broad in the shoulder; he did not appear to be stout, but, on the other hand, he was certainly not thin; his small head was supported by a strong and sinewy neck; his broad, muscular hands appeared to possess a peculiar skill in breaking walnuts without the assistance of the ordinary cracker, and, seeing him in profile, one could not help remarking the extraordinary breadth of his sleeves, and the unusual thickness of his chest. He was one of those men who are commonly spoken of among men as deceptive; that is to say, that though he looked exceedingly strong he was in reality very much stronger than he looked. Of his features I need say little. His head is small, his hair is thin, his eyes are blue, his nose is large, he has a small moustache, and a square jaw. Everybody knows Brisbane, and when he asked for a cigar everybody looked at him.

"It is a very singular thing," said Brisbane.

Everybody stopped talking. Brisbane's voice was not loud, but possessed a peculiar quality of penetrating general conversation, and cutting it like a knife. Everybody listened. Brisbane, perceiving that he had attracted their general attention, lit his cigar with great equanimity.

"It is very singular," he continued, "that thing about ghosts. People are always asking whether anybody has seen a ghost. I have."

"Bosh! What, you? You don't mean to say so, Brisbane? Well, for a man of his intelligence!"

A chorus of exclamations greeted Brisbane's remarkable statement. Everybody called for cigars, and Stubbs, the butler, suddenly appeared from the depths of nowhere with a fresh bottle of dry champagne. The situation was saved; Brisbane was going to tell a story.

I am an old sailor, said Brisbane, and as I have to cross the Atlantic pretty often, I have my favourites. Most men have their favourites. I have seen a man wait in a Broadway bar for three-quarters of an hour for a particular car which he liked. I believe the bar-keeper made at least one-third of his living by that man's preference. I have a habit of waiting for certain ships when I am obliged to cross that duck-pond. It may be a prejudice, but I was never cheated out of a good passage but once in my life. I remember it very well; it was a warm morning in June, and the

Custom House officials, who were hanging about waiting for a steamer already on her way up from the Quarantine, presented a peculiarly hazy and thoughtful appearance. I had not much luggage—I never have. I mingled with the crowd of passengers, porters, and officious individuals in blue coats and brass buttons, who seemed to spring up like mushrooms from the deck of a moored steamer to obtrude their unnecessary services upon the independent passenger. I have often noticed with a certain interest the spontaneous evolution of these fellows. They are not there when you arrive; five minutes after the pilot has called "Go ahead!" they, or at least their blue coats and brass buttons, have disappeared from deck and gangway as completely as though they had been consigned to that locker which tradition unanimously ascribes to Davy Jones. But, at the moment of starting, they are there, clean shaved, blue coated, and ravenous for fees. I hastened on board. The *Kamtschatka* was one of my favourite ships. I say was, because she emphatically no longer is. I cannot conceive of any inducement which could entice me to make another voyage in her. Yes, I know what you are going to say. She is uncommonly clean in the run aft, she has enough bluffing off in the bows to keep her dry, and the lower berths are most of them double. She has a lot of advantages, but I won't cross in her again. Excuse the digression. I got on board. I hailed a steward, whose red nose and redder whiskers were equally familiar to me.

"One hundred and five, lower berth," said I, in the business-like tone peculiar to men who think no more of crossing the Atlantic than taking a whisky cocktail at down-town Delmonico's.

The steward took my portmanteau, greatcoat, and rug. I shall never forget the expression of his face. Not that he turned pale. It is maintained by the most eminent divines that even miracles cannot change the course of nature. I have no hesitation in saying that he did not turn pale; but, from his expression, I judged that he was either about to shed tears, to sneeze, or to drop my portmanteau. As the latter contained two bottles of particularly fine old sherry presented to me for my voyage by my old friend Snigginson van Pickyns, I felt extremely nervous. But the steward did none of these things.

"Well, I'm d——d!" said he in a low voice, and led the way.

I supposed my Hermes, as he led me to the lower regions, had had a little grog, but I said nothing, and followed him. 105 was on the port side, well aft. There was nothing remarkable about the state-room. The lower berth, like most of those upon the *Kamtschatka,* was double. There was plenty of room; there was the usual washing apparatus, calculated to convey an idea of luxury to the mind of a North American Indian; there were the usual inefficient racks of brown wood, in which it is more easy to hang a large-sized umbrella than the common tooth-brush of commerce.

Upon the uninviting mattresses were carefully folded together those blankets which a great modern humorist has aptly compared to cold buckwheat cakes. The question of towels was left entirely to the imagination. The glass decanters were filled with a transparent liquid faintly tinged with brown, but from which an odour less faint, but not more pleasing, ascended to the nostrils, like a far-off sea-sick reminiscence of oily machinery. Sad-coloured curtains half closed the upper berth. The hazy June daylight shed a faint illumination upon the desolate little scene. Ugh! how I hate that state-room!

The steward deposited my traps and looked at me, as though he wanted to get away—probably in search of more passengers and more fees. It is always a good plan to start in favour with those functionaries, and I accordingly gave him certain coins there and then.

"I'll try and make yer comfortable all I can," he remarked, as he put the coins in his pocket. Nevertheless, there was a doubtful intonation in his voice which surprised me. Possibly his scale of fees had gone up, and he was not satisfied; but on the whole I was inclined to think that, as he himself would have expressed it, he was "the better for a glass." I was wrong, however, and did the man injustice.

¶¶

Nothing especially worthy of mention occurred during that day. We left the pier punctually, and it was very pleasant to be fairly under way, for the weather was warm and sultry, and the motion of the steamer produced a refreshing breeze. Everybody knows what the first day at sea is like. People pace the decks and stare at each other, and occasionally meet acquaintances whom they did not know to be on board. There is the usual uncertainty as to whether the food will be good, bad, or indifferent, until the first two meals have put the matter beyond a doubt; there is the usual uncertainty about the weather, until the ship is fairly off Fire Island. The tables are crowded at first, and then suddenly thinned. Pale-faced people spring from their seats and precipitate themselves towards the door, and each old sailor breathes more freely as his sea-sick neighbour rushes from his side, leaving him plenty of elbow-room and an unlimited command over the mustard.

One passage across the Atlantic is very much like another, and we who cross very often do not make the voyage for the sake of novelty. Whales and icebergs are indeed always objects of interest, but, after all, one whale is very much like another whale, and one rarely sees an iceberg at close quarters. To the majority of us the most delightful moment of the day on board an ocean steamer is when we have taken our last turn on deck, have smoked our last cigar, and having succeeded in tiring ourselves, feel at liberty to turn in with a clear conscience. On that first night of the voyage I felt particularly lazy, and went to bed in 105 rather earlier than I usually do. As I turned in, I was amazed to see that I was to have a companion. A portmanteau, very like my own, lay in the opposite corner, and in the upper berth had been deposited a neatly-folded rug, with a stick and umbrella. I had hoped to be alone, and I was disappointed; but I wondered who my room-mate was to be, and I determined to have a look at him.

Before I had been long in bed he entered. He was, as far as I could see, a very tall man, very thin, very pale, with sandy hair and whiskers and colourless grey eyes. He had about him, I thought, an air of rather dubious fashion; the sort of man you might see in Wall Street, without being able precisely to say what he was doing there—the sort of man who frequents the Café Anglais, who always seems to be alone and who drinks champagne; you might meet him on a racecourse, but he would never appear to be doing anything there either. A little over-dressed—a little odd. There are three or four of his kind on every ocean steamer. I made up my mind that I did not care to make his acquaintance, and I went to sleep saying to myself that I would study his habits in order to avoid him. If he rose early, I would rise late; if he went to bed late, I would go to bed early. I did not care to know him. If you once know people of that kind they are always turning up. Poor fellow! I need not have taken the trouble to come to so many decisions about him, for I never saw him again after the first night in 105.

I was sleeping soundly when I was suddenly waked by a loud noise. To judge from the sound, my room-mate must have sprung with a single leap from the upper berth to the floor. I heard him fumbling with the latch and bolt of the door, which opened almost immediately, and then I heard his footsteps as he ran at full speed down the passage, leaving the door open behind him. The ship was rolling a little, and I expected to hear him stumble or fall, but he ran as though he were running for his life. The door swung on its hinges with the motion of the vessel, and the sound annoyed me. I got up and shut it, and groped my way back to my berth in the darkness. I went to sleep again; but I have no idea how long I slept.

When I awoke it was still quite dark, but I felt a disagreeable sensation of cold, and it seemed to me that the air was damp. You know the peculiar smell of a cabin which has been wet with sea-water. I covered myself up as well as I could and dozed off again, framing complaints to be made the next day, and selecting the most powerful epithets in the language. I could hear my room-mate turn over in the upper berth. He had probably returned while I was asleep. Once I thought I heard him groan, and I argued that he was sea-sick. That is particularly unpleasant when one is below. Nevertheless I dozed off and slept till early daylight.

The ship was rolling heavily, much more than on the previous evening, and the grey light which came in through the porthole changed in tint with every movement according as the angle of the vessel's side turned the glass seawards or skywards. It was very cold—unaccountably so for the month of June. I turned my head and looked at the porthole, and saw to my surprise that it was wide open and hooked back. I believe I swore audibly. Then I got up and shut it. As I turned back I glanced at the upper berth. The curtains were drawn close together; my companion had probably felt cold as well as I. It struck me that I had slept enough. The state-room was uncomfortable, though, strange to say, I could not smell the dampness which had annoyed me in the night. My room-mate was still asleep—excellent opportunity for avoiding him, so I dressed at once and went on deck. The day was warm and cloudy, with an oily smell on the water. It was seven o'clock as I came out—much later than I had imagined. I came across the doctor, who was taking his first sniff of the morning air. He was a young man from the West of Ireland—a tremendous fellow, with black hair and blue eyes, already inclined to be stout; he had a happy-go-lucky, healthy look about him which was rather attractive.

"Fine morning," I remarked, by way of introduction.

"Well," said he, eyeing me with an air of ready interest, "it's a fine morning and it's not a fine morning. I don't think it's much of a morning."

"Well, no—it is not so very fine," said I.

"It's just what I call fuggly weather," replied the doctor.

"It was very cold last night, I thought," I remarked. "However, when I looked about, I found that the porthole was wide open. I had not noticed it when I went to bed. And the state-room was damp, too."

"Damp!" said he. "Whereabouts are you?"

"One hundred and five——"

To my surprise the doctor started visibly, and stared at me.

"What is the matter?" I asked.

"Oh—nothing," he answered; "only everybody has complained of that state-room for the last three trips."

"I shall complain too," I said. "It has certainly not been properly aired. It is a shame!"

"I don't believe it can be helped," answered the doctor. "I believe there is something—well, it is not my business to frighten passengers."

"You need not be afraid of frightening me," I replied. "I can stand any amount of damp. If I should get a bad cold I will come to you."

I offered the doctor a cigar, which he took and examined very critically.

"It is not so much the damp," he remarked. "However, I dare say you will get on very well. Have you a room-mate?"

"Yes; a deuce of a fellow, who bolts out in the middle of the night, and leaves the door open."

Again the doctor glanced curiously at me. Then he lit the cigar and looked grave.

"Did he come back?" he asked presently.

"Yes. I was asleep, but I waked up, and heard him moving. Then I felt cold and went to sleep again. This morning I found the porthole open."

"Look here," said the doctor quietly, "I don't care much for this ship. I don't care a rap for her reputation. I tell you what I will do. I have a good-sized place up here. I will share it with you, though I don't know you from Adam."

I was very much surprised at the proposition. I could not imagine why he should take such a sudden interest in my welfare. However, his manner as he spoke of the ship was peculiar.

"You are very good, doctor," I said. "But, really, I believe even now the cabin could be aired, or cleaned out, or something. Why do you not care for the ship?"

"We are not superstitious in our profession, sir," replied the doctor, "but the sea makes people so. I don't want to prejudice you, and I don't want to frighten you, but if you will take my advice you will move in here. I would as soon see you overboard," he added earnestly, "as know that you or any other man was to sleep in one hundred and five."

"Good gracious! Why?" I asked.

"Just because on the last three trips the people who have slept there actually have gone overboard," he answered gravely.

The intelligence was startling and exceedingly unpleasant, I confess. I looked hard at the doctor to see whether he was making game of me, but he looked perfectly serious. I thanked him warmly for his offer, but told him I intended to be the exception to the rule by which every one who slept in that particular state-room went overboard. He did not say much, but looked as grave as ever, and hinted that, before we got across, I should probably reconsider his proposal. In the course of time we went to breakfast, at which only an inconsiderable number of passengers assembled. I noticed that one or two of the officers who breakfasted with us looked grave. After breakfast I went into my state-room in order to get a book. The curtains of the upper berth were still closely drawn. Not a word was to be heard. My room-mate was probably still asleep.

As I came out I met the steward whose business it was to look after me.

He whispered that the captain wanted to see me, and then scuttled away down the passage as if very anxious to avoid any questions. I went towards the captain's cabin, and found him waiting for me.

"Sir," said he, "I want to ask a favour of you."

I answered that I would do anything to oblige him.

"Your room-mate has disappeared," he said. "He is known to have turned in early last night. Did you notice anything extraordinary in his manner?"

The question coming, as it did, in exact confirmation of the fears the doctor had expressed half an hour earlier, staggered me.

"You don't mean to say he has gone overboard?" I asked.

"I fear he has," answered the captain.

"This is the most extraordinary thing——" I began.

"Why?" he asked.

"He is the fourth, then?" I exclaimed. In answer to another question from the captain, I explained, without mentioning the doctor, that I had heard the story concerning 105. He seemed very much annoyed at hearing that I knew of it. I told him what had occurred in the night.

"What you say," he replied, "coincides almost exactly with what was told me by the room-mates of two of the other three. They bolt out of bed and run down the passage. Two of them were seen to go overboard by the watch; we stopped and lowered boats, but they were not found. Nobody, however, saw or heard the man who was lost last night—if he is really lost. The steward, who is a superstitious fellow, perhaps, and expected something to go wrong, went to look for him this morning, and found his berth empty, but his clothes lying about, just as he had left them. The steward was the only man on board who knew him by sight, and he has been searching everywhere for him. He has disappeared! Now, sir, I want to beg you not to mention the circumstance to any of the passengers; I don't want the ship to get a bad name, and nothing hangs about an ocean-goer like stories of suicides. You shall have your choice of any one of the officers' cabins you like, including my own, for the rest of the passage. Is that a fair bargain?"

"Very," said I; "and I am much obliged to you. But since I am alone, and have the state-room to myself, I would rather not move. If the steward will take out the unfortunate man's things, I would as lief stay where I am. I will not say anything about the matter, and I think I can promise you that I will not follow my room-mate."

The captain tried to dissuade me from my intention, but I preferred having a state-room alone to being the chum of any officer on board. I do not know whether I acted foolishly, but if I had taken his advice I should have had nothing more to tell. There would have remained the disagreeable coincidence of several suicides occurring among men who had slept in the same cabin, but that would have been all.

That was not the end of the matter, however, by any means. I obstinately made up my mind that I would not be disturbed by such tales, and I even went so far as to argue the question with the captain. There was something wrong about the state-room, I said. It was rather damp. The porthole had been left open last night. My room-mate might have been ill when he came on board, and he might have become delirious after he went to bed. He might even now be hiding somewhere on board, and might be found later. The place ought to be aired and the fastening of the port looked to. If the captain would give me leave, I would see that what I thought necessary were done immediately.

"Of course you have a right to stay where you are if you please," he replied, rather petulantly; "but I wish you would turn out and let me lock the place up, and be done with it."

I did not see it in the same light, and left the captain, after promising to be silent concerning the disappearance of my companion. The latter had had no acquaintances on board, and was not missed in the course of the day. Towards evening I met the doctor again, and he asked me whether I had changed my mind. I told him I had not.

"Then you will before long," he said, very gravely.

٩٩٩

We played whist in the evening, and I went to bed late. I will confess now that I felt a disagreeable sensation when I entered my state-room. I could not help thinking of the tall man I had seen on the previous night, who was now dead, drowned, tossing about in the long swell, two or three hundred miles astern. His face rose very distinctly before me as I undressed, and I even went so far as to draw back the curtains of the upper berth, as though to persuade myself that he was actually gone. I also bolted the door of the state-room. Suddenly I became aware that the porthole was open, and fastened back. This was more than I could stand. I hastily threw on my dressing-gown and went in search of Robert, the steward of my passage. I was very angry, I remember, and when I found him I dragged him roughly to the door of 105, and pushed him towards the open porthole.

"What the deuce do you mean, you scoundrel, by leaving that port open every night? Don't you know it is against the regulations? Don't you know that if the ship heeled and the water began to come in, ten men could not shut it? I will report you to the captain, you blackguard, for endangering the ship!"

I was exceedingly wroth. The man trembled and turned pale, and then began to shut the round glass plate with the heavy brass fittings.

"Why don't you answer me?" I said roughly.

"If you please, sir," faltered Robert, "there's nobody on board as can keep this 'ere port shut at night. You can try it yourself, sir. I ain't agoing to stop any longer on board o' this vessel, sir; I ain't, indeed. But if I was you, sir, I'd just clear out and go and sleep with the surgeon, or something, I would. Look 'ere, sir, is that fastened what you may call securely, or not, sir? Try it, sir, see if it will move a hinch."

I tried the port, and found it perfectly tight.

"Well, sir," continued Robert triumphantly, "I wager my reputation as a A-one steward that in 'arf an hour it will be open again; fastened back, too, sir, that's the horful thing—fastened back!"

I examined the great screw and the looped nut that ran on it.

"If I find it open in the night, Robert, I will give you a sovereign. It is not possible. You may go."

"Soverin' did you say, sir? Very good, sir. Thank ye, sir. Good-night, sir. Pleasant reepose, sir, and all manner of hinchantin' dreams, sir."

Robert scuttled away, delighted at being released. Of course, I thought he was trying to account for his negligence by a silly story, intended to frighten me, and I disbelieved him. The consequence was that he got his sovereign, and I spent a very peculiarly unpleasant night.

I went to bed, and five minutes after I had rolled myself up in my blankets the inexorable Robert extinguished the light that burned steadily behind the ground-glass pane near the door. I lay quite still in the dark trying to go to sleep, but I soon found that impossible. It had been some satisfaction to be angry with the steward, and the diversion had banished that unpleasant sensation I had at first experienced when I thought of the drowned man who had been my chum; but I was no longer sleepy, and I lay awake for some time, occasionally glancing at the porthole, which I could just see from where I lay, and which, in the darkness, looked like a faintly-luminous soup-plate suspended in blackness. I believe I must have lain there for an hour, and, as I remember, I was just dozing into sleep when I was roused by a draught of cold air, and by distinctly feeling the spray of the sea blown upon my face. I started to my feet, and not having allowed in the dark for the motion of the ship, I was instantly thrown violently across the state-room upon the couch which was placed beneath the porthole. I recovered myself immediately, however, and climbed upon my knees. The porthole was again wide open and fastened back!

Now these things are facts. I was wide awake when I got up, and I should certainly have been waked by the fall had I still been dozing. Moreover, I bruised my elbows and knees badly, and the bruises were there on the following morning to testify to the fact, if I myself had doubted it. The porthole was wide open and fastened back—a thing so unaccountable that I remember very well feeling astonishment rather than fear when I discovered it. I at once closed the plate again, and screwed down the loop nut with all my strength. It was very dark in the state-room. I reflected that the port had certainly been opened within an hour after Robert had at first shut it in my presence, and I determined to watch it, and see whether it would open again. Those brass fittings are very heavy and by no means easy to move; I could not believe that the clamp had been turned by the shaking of the screw. I stood peering out through the thick glass at the alternate white and grey streaks of the sea that foamed beneath the ship's side. I must have remained there a quarter of an hour.

Suddenly, as I stood, I distinctly heard something moving behind me in one of the berths, and a moment afterwards, just as I turned instinctively to look—though I could, of course, see nothing in the darkness—I heard a very faint groan. I sprang across the state-room, and tore the curtains of the upper berth aside, thrusting in my hands to discover if there were any one there. There was some one.

I remember that the sensation as I put my hands forward was as though I were plunging them into the air of a damp cellar, and from behind the curtains came a gust of wind that smelled horribly of stagnant sea-water. I laid hold of something that had the shape of a man's arm, but was smooth, and wet, and icy cold. But suddenly, as I pulled, the creature sprang violently forward against me, a clammy, oozy mass, as it seemed to me, heavy and wet, yet endowed with a sort of supernatural strength. I reeled across the state-room, and in an instant the door opened and the thing rushed out. I had not had time to be frightened, and quickly recovering myself, I sprang through the door and gave chase at the top of my speed, but I was too late. Ten yards before me I could see—I am sure I saw it—a dark shadow moving in the dimly lighted passage, quickly as the shadow of a fast horse thrown before a dog-cart by the lamp on a dark night. But in a moment it had disappeared, and I found myself holding on to the polished rail that ran along the bulkhead where the passage turned towards the companion. My hair stood on end, and the cold perspiration rolled down my face. I am not ashamed of it in the least: I was very badly frightened.

Still I doubted my senses, and pulled myself together. It was absurd, I thought. The Welsh rare-bit I had eaten had disagreed with me. I had been in a nightmare. I made my way back to my state-room, and entered it with an effort. The whole place smelled of stagnant sea-water, as it had when I had waked on the previous evening. It required my utmost strength to go in, and grope among my things for a box of wax lights. As I lighted a railway reading lantern which I always carry in case I want to read after the lamps are out, I perceived that the porthole was again open, and a sort of creeping horror began to take possession of me which I never felt before, nor wish to feel again. But I got a light and proceeded to examine the upper berth, expecting to find it drenched with sea-water.

But I was disappointed. The bed had been slept in, and the smell of the sea was strong; but the bedding was as dry as a bone. I fancied that Robert had not had the courage to make the bed after the accident of the previous night—it had all been a hideous dream. I drew the curtains back as far as I could and examined the place very carefully. It was perfectly dry. But the porthole was open again. With a sort of dull bewilderment of horror I closed it and screwed it down, and thrusting my heavy stick through the brass loop, wrenched it with all my might, till the thick metal began to bend under the pressure. Then I hooked my reading lantern into the red velvet at the head of the couch, and sat down to recover my senses if I could. I sat there all night, unable to think of rest—hardly able to think at all. But the porthole remained closed, and I did not believe it would now open again without the application of a considerable force.

The morning dawned at last, and I dressed myself slowly, thinking over all that had happened in the night. It was a beautiful day and I went on deck, glad to get out into the early, pure sunshine, and to smell the breeze from the blue water, so different from the noisome, stagnant odour of my state-room. Instinctively I turned aft, towards the surgeon's cabin. There he stood, with a pipe in his mouth, taking his morning airing precisely as on the preceding day.

"Good-morning," said he quietly, but looking at me with evident curiosity.

"Doctor, you were quite right," said I. "There is something wrong about that place."

"I thought you would change your mind," he answered, rather triumphantly. "You have had a bad night, eh? Shall I make you a pick-me-up? I have a capital recipe."

"No, thanks," I cried. "But I would like to tell you what happened."

I then tried to explain as clearly as possible precisely what had occurred, not omitting to state that I had been scared as I had never been scared in my whole life before. I dwelt particularly on the phenomenon of the porthole, which was a fact to which I could testify, even if the rest had been an illusion. I had closed it twice in the night, and the second time I had actually bent the brass in wrenching it with my stick. I believe I insisted a good deal on this point.

"You seem to think I am likely to doubt the story," said the doctor, smiling at the detailed account of the state of the porthole. "I do not doubt it in the least. I renew my invitation to you. Bring your traps here, and take half my cabin."

"Come and take half of mine for one night," I said. "Help me to get at the bottom of this thing."

"You will get to the bottom of something else if you try," answered the doctor.

"What?" I asked.

"The bottom of the sea. I am going to leave this ship. It is not canny."

"Then you will not help me to find out——"

"Not I," said the doctor quickly. "It is my business to keep my wits about me—not to go fiddling about with ghosts and things."

"Do you really believe it is a ghost?" I enquired, rather contemptuously. But as I spoke I remembered very well the horrible sensation of the supernatural which had got possession of me during the night. The doctor turned sharply on me.

"Have you any reasonable explanation of these things to offer?" he asked. "No; you have not. Well, you say you will find an explanation. I say that you won't, sir, simply because there is not any."

"But, my dear sir," I retorted, "do you, a man of science, mean to tell me that such things cannot be explained?"

"I do," he answered stoutly. "And, if they could, I would not be concerned in the explanation."

I did not care to spend another night alone in the state-room, and yet I was obstinately determined to get at the root of the disturbances. I do not believe there are many men who would have slept there alone, after passing two such nights. But I made up my mind to try it, if I could not get any one to share a watch with me. The doctor was evidently not inclined for such an experiment. He said he was a surgeon, and that in case any accident occurred on board he must be always in readiness. He could not afford to have his nerves unsettled. Perhaps he was quite right, but I am inclined to think that his precaution was prompted by his inclination. On enquiry, he informed me that there was no one on board who would be likely to join me in my investigations, and after a little more conversation I left him. A little later I met the captain, and told him my story. I said that, if no one would spend the night with me, I would ask leave to have the light burning all night, and would try it alone.

"Look here," said he, "I will tell you what I will do. I will share your watch myself, and we will see what happens. It is my belief that we can find out between us. There may be some fellow skulking on board, who steals a passage by frightening the passengers. It is just possible that there may be something queer in the carpentering of that berth."

I suggested taking the ship's carpenter below and examining the place; but I was overjoyed at the captain's offer to spend the night with me. He accordingly sent for the workman and ordered him to do anything I required. We went below at once. I had all the bedding cleared out of the upper berth, and we examined the place thoroughly to see if there was a board loose anywhere, or a panel which could be opened or pushed aside. We tried the planks everywhere, tapped the flooring, unscrewed the fittings of the lower berth and took it to pieces—in short, there was not a square inch of the state-room which was not searched and tested. Everything was in perfect order, and we put everything back in its place. As we were finishing our work, Robert came to the door and looked in.

"Well, sir—find anything, sir?" he asked, with a ghastly grin.

"You were right about the porthole, Robert," I said, and I gave him the promised sovereign. The carpenter did his work silently and skilfully, following my directions. When he had done he spoke.

"I'm a plain man, sir," he said. "But it's my belief you had better just turn out your things, and let me run half a dozen four-inch screws through the door of this cabin. There's no good never came o' this cabin yet, sir, and that's all about it. There's been four lives lost out o' here to my own remembrance, and that in four trips. Better give it up, sir—better give it up!"

"I will try it for one night more," I said.

"Better give it up, sir—better give it up! It's a precious bad job," repeated the workman, putting his tools in his bag and leaving the cabin.

But my spirits had risen considerably at the prospect of having the captain's company, and I made up my mind not to be prevented from going to the end of the strange business. I abstained from Welsh rare-bits and grog that evening, and did not even join in the customary game of whist. I wanted to be quite sure of my nerves, and my vanity made me anxious to make a good figure in the captain's eyes.

IV

The captain was one of those splendidly tough and cheerful specimens of seafaring humanity whose combined courage, hardihood, and calmness in difficulty leads them naturally into high positions of trust. He was not the man to be led away by an idle tale, and the mere fact that he was willing to join me in the investigation was proof that he thought there was something seriously wrong, which could not be accounted for on ordinary theories, nor laughed down as a common superstition. To some extent, too, his reputation was at stake, as well as the reputation of the ship. It is no light thing to lose passengers overboard, and he knew it.

About ten o'clock that evening, as I was smoking a last cigar, he came up to me, and drew me aside from the beat of the other passengers who were patrolling the deck in the warm darkness.

"This is a serious matter, Mr Brisbane," he said. "We must make up our minds either way—to be disappointed or to have a pretty rough time of it. You see I cannot afford to laugh at the affair, and I will ask you to sign your name to a statement of whatever occurs. If nothing happens tonight we will try it again tomorrow and next day. Are you ready?"

So we went below, and entered the state-room. As we went in I could see Robert the steward, who stood a little further down the passage, watching us, with his usual grin, as though certain that something dreadful was about to happen. The captain closed the door behind us and bolted it.

"Supposing we put your portmanteau before the door," he suggested. "One of us can sit on it. Nothing can get out then. Is the port screwed down?"

I found it as I had left it in the morning. Indeed, without using a lever, as I had done, no one could have opened it. I drew back the curtains of the upper berth so that I could see well into it. By the captain's advice I lighted my reading lantern, and placed it so that it shone upon the white sheets above. He insisted upon sitting on the portmanteau, declaring that he wished to be able to swear that he had sat before the door.

Then he requested me to search the state-room thoroughly, an operation very soon accomplished, as it consisted merely in looking beneath the lower berth and under the couch below the porthole. The spaces were quite empty.

"It is impossible for any human being to get in," I said, "or for any human being to open the port."

"Very good," said the captain calmly. "If we see anything now, it must be either imagination or something supernatural."

I sat down on the edge of the lower berth.

"The first time it happened," said the captain, crossing his legs and leaning back against the door, "was in March. The passenger who slept here, in the upper berth, turned out to have been a lunatic—at all events, he was known to have been a little touched, and he had taken his passage without the knowledge of his friends. He rushed out in the middle of the night, and threw himself overboard, before the officer who had the watch could stop him. We stopped and lowered a boat; it was a quiet night, just before that heavy weather came on; but we could not find him. Of course his suicide was afterwards accounted for on the ground of his insanity."

"I suppose that often happens?" I remarked, rather absently.

"Not often—no," said the captain; "never before in my experience, though I have heard of it happening on board of other ships. Well, as I was saying, that occurred in March. On the very next trip——What are you looking at?" he asked, stopping suddenly in his narration.

I believe I gave no answer. My eyes were riveted upon the porthole. It seemed to me that the brass loop-nut was beginning to turn very slowly upon the screw—so slowly, however, that I was not sure it moved at all. I watched it intently, fixing its position in my mind, and trying to ascertain whether it changed. Seeing where I was looking, the captain looked, too.

"It moves!" he exclaimed, in a tone of conviction. "No, it does not," he added, after a minute.

"If it were the jarring of the screw," said I, "it would have opened during the day; but I found it this evening jammed tight as I left it this morning."

I rose and tried the nut. It was certainly loosened, for by an effort I could move it with my hands.

"The queer thing," said the captain, "is that the second man who was lost is supposed to have got through that very port. We had a terrible time over it. It was in the middle of the night, and the weather was very heavy; there was an alarm that one of the ports was open and the sea running in. I came below and found everything flooded, the water pouring in every time she rolled, and the whole port swinging from the top bolts—not the porthole in the middle. Well, we managed to shut it, but the water did some damage. Ever since that the place smells of sea-water from time to time. We supposed the passenger had thrown himself out, though the Lord only knows how he did it. The steward kept telling me that he cannot keep anything shut here. Upon my word—I can smell it now, cannot you?" he enquired, sniffing the air suspiciously.

"Yes—distinctly," I said, and I shuddered as that same odour of stagnant sea-water grew stronger in the cabin. "Now, to smell like this, the place must be damp," I continued, "and yet when I examined it with the carpenter this morning everything was perfectly dry. It is most extraordinary—hallo!"

My reading lantern, which had been placed in the upper berth, was suddenly extinguished. There was still a good deal of light from the pane of ground glass near the door, behind which loomed the regulation lamp. The ship rolled heavily, and the curtain of the upper berth swung far out into the state-room and back again. I rose quickly from my seat on the edge of the bed, and the captain at the same moment started to his feet with a loud cry of surprise. I had turned with the intention of taking down the lantern to examine it, when I heard his exclamation, and immediately afterwards his call for help. I sprang towards him. He was wrestling with all his might with the brass loop of the port. It seemed to turn against his hands in spite of all his efforts. I caught up my cane, a heavy oak stick I always used to carry, and thrust it through the ring and bore on it with all my strength. But the strong wood snapped suddenly and I fell upon the couch. When I rose again the port was wide open, and the captain was standing with his back against the door, pale to the lips.

"There is something in that berth!" he cried, in a strange voice, his eyes almost starting from his head. "Hold the door, while I look—it shall not escape us, whatever it is!"

But instead of taking his place, I sprang upon the lower bed, and seized something which lay in the upper berth.

It was something ghostly, horrible beyond words, and it moved in my grip. It was like the body of a man long drowned, and yet it moved, and had the strength of ten men living; but I gripped it with all my might—the slippery, oozy, horrible thing—the dead white eyes seemed to stare at me out of the dusk; the putrid odour of rank sea-water was about it, and its shiny hair hung in foul wet curls over its dead face. I wrestled with the dead thing; it thrust itself upon me and forced me back and nearly broke my arms; it wound its corpse's arms about my neck, the living death, and overpowered me, so that I, at last, cried aloud and fell, and left my hold.

As I fell the thing sprang across me, and seemed to throw itself upon the captain. When I last saw him on his feet his face was white and his lips set. It seemed to me that he struck a violent blow at the dead being, and then he, too, fell forward upon his face, with an inarticulate cry of horror.

The thing paused an instant, seeming to hover over his prostrate body, and I could have screamed again for very fright, but I had no voice left. The thing vanished suddenly, and it seemed to my disturbed senses that it made its exit through the open port, though how that was possible, considering the smallness of the aperture, is more than any one can tell. I lay a long time upon the floor, and the captain lay beside me. At last I partially recovered my senses and moved, and instantly I knew that my arm was broken—the small bone of the left forearm near the wrist.

I got upon my feet somehow, and with my remaining hand I tried to raise the captain. He groaned and moved, and at last came to himself. He was not hurt, but he seemed badly stunned.

Well, do you want to hear any more? There is nothing more. That is the end of my story. The carpenter carried out his scheme of running half a dozen four-inch screws through the door of 105; and if ever you take a passage in the *Kamtschatka*, you may ask for a berth in that state-room. You will be told that it is engaged—yes—it is engaged by that dead thing.

I finished the trip in the surgeon's cabin. He doctored my broken arm, and advised me not to "fiddle about with ghosts and things" any more.

The captain was very silent, and never sailed again in that ship, though it is still running. And I will not sail in her either. It was a very disagreeable experience, and I was very badly frightened, which is a thing I do not like. That is all. That is how I saw a ghost—if it was a ghost. It was dead, anyhow.

The Brute

Joseph Conrad

ODGING IN FROM the rain-swept street, I exchanged a smile and a glance with Miss Blank in the bar of the Three Crows. This exchange was effected with extreme propriety. It is a shock to think that, if still alive, Miss Blank must be something over sixty now. How time passes!

Noticing my gaze directed enquiringly at the partition of glass and varnished wood, Miss Blank was good enough to say, encouragingly,

"Only Mr. Jermyn and Mr. Stonor in the parlour, with another gentleman I've never seen before."

I moved towards the parlour door. A voice discoursing on the other side (it was but a matchboard partition) rose so loudly that the concluding words became quite plain in all their atrocity:

"That fellow Wilmot fairly dashed her brains out, and a good job too!"

This inhuman sentiment, since there was nothing profane or improper in it, failed to do as much as to check the slight yawn Miss Blank was achieving behind her hand. And she remained gazing fixedly at the windowpanes, which streamed with rain.

As I opened the parlour door the same voice went on in the same cruel strain:

"I was glad when I heard she got the knock from somebody at last. Sorry enough for poor Wilmot, though. That man and I used to be chums at one time. Of course that was the end of him. A clear case if there ever was one. No way out of it. None at all."

The voice belonged to the gentleman Miss Blank had never seen before. He straddled his long legs on the hearthrug. Jermyn, leaning forward, held his pocket handkerchief spread out before the grate. He looked back dismally over his shoulder, and as I slipped behind one of the little wooden tables, I nodded to him. On the other side of the fire, imposingly calm and large, sat Mr. Stonor, jammed tight into a capacious Windsor armchair. There was nothing small about him but his short, white side-whiskers. Yards and yards of extra superfine blue cloth (made up into an overcoat) reposed on a chair by his side. And he must just have brought some liner from sea, because another chair was smothered under his black waterproof, ample as a pall, and made of three-fold oiled silk, double-stitched throughout. A man's handbag of the usual size looked like a child's toy on the floor near his feet.

I did not nod to him. He was too big to be nodded to in that parlour. He was a senior Trinity pilot and condescended to take his turn in the cutter only during the summer months. He had been many times in charge of royal yachts in and out of Port Victoria. Besides, it's no use nodding to a monument. And he was like one. He didn't speak, he didn't budge. He just sat there, holding his handsome old head up, immovable, and almost bigger than life. It was extremely fine. Mr. Stonor's presence reduced old Jermyn to a mere shabby wisp of a man, and made the talkative stranger in tweeds on the hearthrug look absurdly boyish. The latter must have been a few years over thirty, and was certainly not the sort of individual that gets abashed at the sound of his own voice, because gathering me in, as it were, by a friendly glance, he kept it going without a check.

"I was glad of it," he repeated emphatically. "You may be surprised at it, but then you haven't gone through the experience I've had of her. I can tell you, it was something to remember. Of course, I got off scot-free myself—as you can see. She did her best to break up my pluck for me tho'. She jolly near drove as fine a fellow as ever lived into a madhouse. What do you say to that—eh?"

Not an eyelid twitched in Mr. Stonor's enormous face. Monumental! The speaker looked straight into my eyes.

"It used to make me sick to think of her going about the world murdering people."

Jermyn approached the handkerchief a little nearer to the grate and groaned. It was simply a habit he had.

"I've seen her once," he declared, with mournful indifference. "She had a house. . . ."

The stranger in tweeds turned to stare down at him, surprised.

"She had three houses," he corrected authoritatively. But Jermyn was not to be contradicted.

"She had a house, I say," he repeated, with dismal obstinacy. "A great big, ugly white thing. You could see it from miles away—sticking up."

"So you could," assented the other readily. "It was old Colchester's notion, though he was always threatening to give her up. He couldn't stand her racket any more, he declared; it was too much of a good thing for him; he would wash his hands of her, if he never got hold of another—and so on. I daresay he would have chucked her, only—it may surprise you—his missus wouldn't hear of it. Funny, eh? But with women, you never know how they will take a thing, and Mrs. Colchester, with her moustaches and big eyebrows, set up for being as strong-minded as they make them. She used to walk about in a brown silk dress, with a great gold cable flopping about her bosom. You should have heard her snapping out: 'Rubbish!' or 'Stuff and nonsense!' I daresay she knew when she was well off. They had no children, and had never set up a home anywhere. When in England she just made shift to hang out anyhow in some cheap hotel or boardinghouse. I daresay she liked to get back to the comforts she was used to. She knew very well she couldn't gain by any change. And, moreover, Colchester, though a first-rate man, was not what you may call in his first youth, and, perhaps, she may have thought that he wouldn't be able to get hold of another (as he used to say) so easily. Anyhow, for one reason or another, it was 'Rubbish' and 'Stuff and nonsense' for the good lady. I overheard once young Mr. Apse himself say to her confidentially, 'I assure you, Mrs. Colchester, I am beginning to feel quite unhappy about the name she's getting for herself.' 'Oh,' says she, with her deep little hoarse laugh, 'if one took notice of all the silly talk,' and she showed Apse all her ugly false teeth at once. 'It would take more than that to make me lose my confidence in her, I assure you,' says she."

At this point, without any change of facial expression, Mr. Stonor emitted a short sardonic laugh. It was very impressive, but I didn't see the fun. I looked from one to another. The stranger on the hearthrug had an ugly smile.

"And Mr. Apse shook both Mrs. Colchester's hands, he was so pleased to hear a good word said for their favourite. All these Apses, young and old you know, were perfectly infatuated with that abominable, dangerous—"

"I beg your pardon," I interrupted, for he seemed to be addressing himself exclusively to me, "but who on earth are you talking about?"

"I am talking of the Apse family," he answered, courteously.

I nearly let out a damn at this. But just then the respected Miss Blank put her head in, and said that the cab was at the door, if Mr. Stonor wanted to catch the eleven-three up.

At once the senior pilot arose in his mighty bulk and began to struggle into his coat, with awe-inspiring upheavals. The stranger and I hurried impulsively to his assistance, and directly we laid our hands on him he became perfectly quiescent. We had to raise our arms very high, and to make efforts. It was like caparisoning a docile elephant. With a "Thanks, gentlemen," he dived under and squeezed himself through the door in a great hurry.

We smiled at each other in a friendly way.

"I wonder how he manages to hoist himself up a ship's side-ladder," said the man in tweeds; and poor Jermyn, who was a mere North Sea pilot, without official status or recognition of any sort, pilot only by courtesy, groaned.

"He makes eight hundred a year."

"Are you a sailor?" I asked the stranger, who had gone back to his position on the rug.

"I used to be till a couple of years ago when I got married," answered this communicative individual. "I even went to sea first in that very ship we were speaking of when you came in."

"What ship?" I asked, puzzled. "I never heard you mention a ship."

"I've just told you her name, my dear sir," he replied. "The *Apse Family*. Surely you've heard of the great firm of Apse & Sons, shipowners. They had a pretty big fleet. There was the *Lucy Apse,* and the *Harold Apse,* and *Anne, John, Malcolm, Clara, Juliet,* and so on—no end of *Apses*. Every brother, sister, aunt, cousin, wife—and grandmother too, for all I know—of the firm had a ship named after them. Good, solid, old-fashioned craft they were too, built to carry and to last. None of your new-fangled, labour-saving appliances in them, but plenty of men and plenty of good salt beef and hardtack put aboard—and off you go to fight your way out and home again."

The miserable Jermyn made a sound of approval, which sounded like a groan of pain. Those were the ships for him. He pointed out in doleful tones that you couldn't say to labour-saving appliances, "Jump lively now, my hearties." No labour-saving appliance would go aloft on a dirty night with the sands under your lee.

"No," assented the stranger, with a wink at me. "The Apses didn't believe in them either, apparently. They treated their people well—as people don't get treated nowadays, and they were awfully proud of their ships. Nothing ever happened to them. This last one, the *Apse Family,* was to be like the others, only she was to be still stronger, still safer, still more roomy and comfortable. I believe they meant her to last for ever. They had her built composite—iron, teak-wood, and greenheart, and her scantling was something fabulous. If ever an order was given for a ship in a spirit of pride this one was. Everything of the best. The commodore captain of the employ was to command her, and they planned the accommodation for him like a house on shore under a big, tall poop that went nearly to the mainmast. No wonder Mrs. Colchester wouldn't let the old man give her up. Why, it was the best home she ever had in all her married days. She had a nerve, that woman.

"The fuss that was made while that ship was building! Let's have this a little stronger, and that a little heavier; and hadn't that other thing better be changed· for something a little thicker. The builders entered into the spirit of the game, and there she was, growing into the clumsiest, heaviest ship of her size right before all their eyes, without anybody becoming aware of it somehow. She was to be 2,000 tons register, or a little over; no less on any account. But see what happens. When they came to measure her she turned out 1,999 tons and a fraction. General consternation! And they say old Mr. Apse was so annoyed, when they told him, that he took to his bed and died. The old gentleman had retired from the firm twenty-five years before, and was ninety-six years old if a day, so his death wasn't, perhaps, so surprising. Still Mr. Lucian Apse was convinced that his father would have lived to a hundred. So we may put him at the head of the list. Next comes the poor devil of a shipwright that brute caught and squashed as she went off the ways. They called it the launch of a ship, but I've heard people say that, from the wailing and yelling and scrambling out of the way, it was more like letting a devil loose upon the river. She snapped all her checks like pack-threads, and went for the tugs in attendance like a fury. Before anybody could see what she was up to she sent one of them to the bottom, and laid up another for three months' repairs. One of her cables parted, and then, suddenly—you couldn't tell why—she let herself be brought up with the other as quiet as a lamb.

"That's how she was. You could never be sure what she would be up to next. There are ships difficult to handle, but generally you can depend on them behaving rationally. With *that* ship, whatever you did with her, you never knew how it would end. She was a wicked beast. Or, perhaps, she was only just insane."

He uttered this supposition in so earnest a tone that I could not refrain from smiling. He left off biting his lower lip to apostrophize me.

"Eh! Why not? Why couldn't there be something in her build, in her lines corresponding to. . . . What's madness? Only something just a tiny bit wrong in the make of your brain. Why shouldn't there be a mad ship —I mean mad in a ship-like way, so that under no circumstances could you be sure she would do what any other sensible ship would naturally do for you. There are ships that steer wildly, and ships that can't be quite trusted always to stay; others want careful watching when running in a gale; and, again, there may be a ship that will make heavy weather of it in every little blow. But then you expect her to be always so. You take it as part of her character, as a ship, just as you take account of a man's peculiarities of temper when you deal with him. But with her you couldn't. She was unaccountable. If she wasn't mad, then she was the most evil-minded, underhand, savage brute that ever went afloat. I've seen her run in a heavy gale beautifully for two days, and on the third broach to twice in the same afternoon. The first time she flung the helmsman clean over the wheel, but as she didn't quite manage to kill him she had another try about three hours afterwards. She swamped herself fore and aft, burst all the canvas we had set, scared all hands into a panic, and even frightened Mrs. Colchester down there in those beautiful stern cabins that she was so proud of. When we mustered the crew there was one man missing. Swept overboard, of course, without being either seen or heard, poor devil! and I only wonder more of us didn't go.

"Always something like that. Always. I heard an old mate tell Captain Colchester once that it had come to this with him, that he was afraid to open his mouth to give any sort of order. She was as much of a terror in harbour as at sea. You could never be certain what would hold her. On the slightest provocation she would start snapping ropes, cables, wire hawsers, like carrots. She was heavy, clumsy, unhandy—but that does not quite explain that power for mischief she had. You know, somehow, when I think of her I can't help remembering what we hear of incurable lunatics breaking loose now and then."

He looked at me inquisitively. But, of course, I couldn't admit that a ship could be mad.

"In the ports where she was known," he went on, "they dreaded the sight of her. She thought nothing of knocking away twenty feet or so of solid stone facing off a quay or wiping off the end of a wooden wharf. She must have lost miles of chain and hundreds of tons of anchors in her time. When she fell aboard some poor offending ship it was the very devil of a job to haul her off again. And she never got hurt herself—just a few scratches or so, perhaps. They had wanted to have her strong. And so she was. Strong enough to ram Polar ice with. And as she began so she went on. From the day she was launched she never let a year pass without murdering somebody. I think the owners got very worried about it. But they were a stiff-necked generation, all these Apses; they wouldn't admit there could be anything wrong with the *Apse Family*. They wouldn't even change her name. 'Stuff and nonsense,' as Mrs. Colchester used to say. They ought at least to have shut her up for life in some dry dock or other, away up the river, and never let her smell salt water again. I assure you, my dear sir, that she invariably did kill some one every voyage she made. It was perfectly well known. She got a name for it, far and wide."

I expressed my surprise that a ship with such a deadly reputation could ever get a crew.

"Then, you don't know what sailors are, my dear sir. Let me just show you by an instance. One day in dock at home, while loafing on the fore-castle head, I noticed two respectable salts come along, one a middle-aged, competent, steady man, evidently, the other a smart, youngish chap.

They read the name on the bows and stopped to look at her. Says the elder man: '*Apse Family.* That's the sanguinary female dog' (I'm putting it in that way) 'of a ship, Jack, that kills a man every voyage. I wouldn't sign in her—not for Joe, I wouldn't.' And the other says: 'If she were mine, I'd have her towed on the mud and set on fire, blamme if I wouldn't.' Then the first man chimes in: 'Much do they care! Men are cheap, God knows.' The younger one spat in the water alongside. 'They won't have me—not for double wages.'

"They hung about for some time and then walked up the dock. Half an hour later I saw them both on our deck looking about for the mate, and apparently very anxious to be taken on. And they were."

"How do you account for this?" I asked.

"What would you say?" he retorted. "Recklessness! The vanity of boasting in the evening to all their chums: 'We've just shipped in that there *Apse Family.* Blow her. She ain't going to scare us.' Sheer sailor-like perversity! A sort of curiosity. Well—a little of all that, no doubt. I put the question to them in the course of the voyage. The answer of the elderly chap was:

" 'A man can die but once.' The younger assured me in a mocking tone that he wanted to see 'how she would do it this time.' But I tell you what; there was a sort of fascination about the brute."

Jermyn, who seemed to have seen every ship in the world, broke in sulkily:

"I saw her once out of this very window towing up the river; a great black ugly thing, going along like a big hearse."

"Something sinister about her looks, wasn't there?" said the man in tweeds, looking down at old Jermyn with a friendly eye. "I always had a sort of horror of her. She gave me a beastly shock when I was no more than fourteen, the very first day—nay, hour—I joined her. Father came up to see me off, and was to go down to Gravesend with us. I was his second boy to go to sea. My big brother was already an officer then. We got on board about eleven in the morning, and found the ship ready to drop out of the basin, stern first. She had not moved three times her own length when, at a little pluck the tug gave her to enter the dock gates, she made one of her rampaging starts, and put such a weight on the check rope—a new six-inch hawser—that forward there they had no chance to ease it round in time, and it parted. I saw the broken end fly up high in the air, and the next moment that brute brought her quarter against the pierhead with a jar that staggered everybody about her decks. She didn't hurt herself. Not she! But one of the boys the mate had sent aloft on the mizzen to do something, came down on the poop-deck—thump—right in front of me. He was not much older than myself. We had been grinning at each other only a few minutes before. He must have been handling himself carelessly, not expecting to get such a jerk. I heard his startled cry—Oh!—in a high treble as he felt himself going, and looked up in time to see him go limp all over as he fell. Ough! Poor father was remarkably white about the gills when we shook hands in Gravesend. 'Are you all right?' he says, looking hard at me. 'Yes, father.' 'Quite sure?' 'Yes, father.' 'Well, then, good-bye, my boy.' He told me afterwards that for half a word he would have carried me off home with him there and then. I am the baby of the family—you know," added the man in tweeds, stroking his moustache with an ingenuous smile.

I acknowledged this interesting communication by a sympathetic murmur. He waved his hand carelessly.

"This might have utterly spoiled a chap's nerve for going aloft, you know—utterly. He fell within two feet of me, cracking his head on a mooring-bit. Never moved. Stone dead. Nice-looking little fellow, he was. I had just been thinking we would be great chums. However, that wasn't yet the worst that brute of a ship could do. I served in her three years of my time, and then I got transferred to the *Lucy Apse,* for a year. The sailmaker we had in the *Apse Family* turned up there, too, and I remember him saying to me one evening, after we had been a week at sea: 'Isn't she a meek little ship?' No wonder we thought the *Lucy Apse* a dear, meek little ship after getting clear of that big rampaging savage brute. It was like heaven. Her officers seemed to me the restfullest lot of men on earth. To me who had known no ship but the *Apse Family*, the *Lucy* was like a sort of magic craft that did what you wanted her to do of her own accord. One evening we got caught aback pretty sharply from right ahead. In about ten minutes we had her full again, sheets aft, tacks down, decks cleared, and the officer of the watch leaning against the weather rail peacefully. It seemed simply marvellous to me. The other would have stuck for half an hour in irons, rolling her decks full of water, knocking the men about—spars cracking, braces snapping, yards taking charge, and a confounded scare going on after because of her beastly rudder, which she had a way of flapping about fit to raise your hair on end. I couldn't get over my wonder for days.

"Well, I finished my last year of apprenticeship in that jolly little ship—she wasn't so little either, but after that other heavy devil she seemed but a plaything to handle. I finished my time and passed; and then just as I was thinking of having three weeks of real good time on shore I got at breakfast a letter asking me the earliest day I could be ready to join the *Apse Family* as third mate. I gave my plate a shove that shot it into the middle of the table; dad looked up over his paper; mother raised her hands in astonishment, and I went out bare-headed into our bit of garden, where I walked round and round for an hour.

"When I came in again mother was out of the diningroom, and dad had shifted berth into his big armchair. The letter was lying on the mantelpiece.

" 'It's very creditable to you to get the offer, and very kind of them to make it,' he said. 'And I see also that Charles has been appointed chief mate of that ship for one voyage.'

"There was overleaf a PS. to that effect in Mr. Apse's own handwriting, which I had overlooked. Charley was my big brother.

" 'I don't like very much to have two of my boys together in one ship,' father goes on, in his deliberate solemn way. 'And I may tell you that I would not mind writing Mr. Apse a letter to that effect.'

"Dear old dad! He was a wonderful father. What would you have done? The mere notion of going back (and as an officer, too), to be worried and bothered, and kept on the jump night and day by that brute, made me feel sick. But she wasn't a ship you could afford to fight shy of. Besides, the most genuine excuse could not be given without mortally offending Apse & Sons. The firm, and I believe the whole family down to the old unmarried aunts in Lancashire, had grown desperately touchy about that accursed ship's character. This was the case for answering 'Ready now' from your very deathbed if you wished to die in their good grace. And that's precisely what I did answer—by wire, to have it over and done with at once.

"The prospect of being shipmates with my big brother cheered me up considerably, though it made me a bit anxious, too. Ever since I remember myself as a little chap he had been very good to me, and I looked upon him as the finest fellow in the world. And so he was. No better officer ever walked the deck of a merchant ship. And that's a fact. He was a fine, strong, upstanding, suntanned young fellow, with his brown hair curling a little, and an eye like a hawk. He was just splendid. We hadn't seen each other for many years, and even this time, though he had been in England three weeks already, he hadn't showed up at home yet, but had spent his spare time in Surrey somewhere making up to Maggie Colchester, old Captain Colchester's niece. Her father, a great friend of dad's, was in the sugar-broking business, and Charley made a sort of second home of their house. I wondered what my big brother would think of me. There was a sort of sternness about Charley's face which never left it, not even when he was larking in his rather wild fashion.

"He received me with a great shout of laughter. He seemed to think my joining as an officer the greatest joke in the world. There was a difference of ten years between us, and I suppose he remembered me best in pinafores. I was a kid of four when he first went to sea. It surprised me to find how boisterous he could be.

" 'Now we shall see what you are made of,' he cried. And he held me off by the shoulders, and punched my ribs, and hustled me into his berth. 'Sit down, Ned. I am glad of the chance of having you with me. I'll put the finishing touch to you, my young officer, providing you're worth the trouble. And, first of all, get it well into your head that we are not going to let this brute kill anybody this voyage. We'll stop her racket.'

"I perceived he was in dead earnest about it. He talked grimly of the ship, and how we must be careful and never allow this ugly beast to catch us napping with any of her damned tricks.

"He gave me a regular lecture on special seamanship for the use of the *Apse Family;* then changing his tone, he began to talk at large, rattling off the wildest, funniest nonsense, till my sides ached with laughing. I could see very well he was a bit above himself with high spirits. It couldn't be because of my coming. Not to that extent. But, of course, I wouldn't have dreamt of asking what was the matter. I had a proper respect for my big brother, I can tell you. But it was all made plain enough a day or two afterwards, when I heard that Miss Maggie Colchester was coming for the voyage. Uncle was giving her a sea trip for the benefit of her health.

"I don't know what could have been wrong with her health. She had a beautiful colour, and a deuce of a lot of fair hair. She didn't care a rap for wind, or rain, or spray, or sun, or green seas, or anything. She was a blue-eyed, jolly girl of the very best sort, but the way she cheeked my big brother used to frighten me. I always expected it to end in an awful row. However, nothing decisive happened till after we had been in Sydney for a week. One day, in the men's dinner hour, Charley sticks his head into my cabin. I was stretched out on my back on the settee, smoking in peace.

" 'Come ashore with me, Ned,' he says, in his curt way.

"I jumped up, of course, and away after him down the gangway and up George Street. He strode along like a giant, and I at his elbow, panting. It was confoundedly hot. 'Where on earth are you rushing me to, Charley?' I made bold to ask.

" 'Here,' he says.

" 'Here' was a jeweller's shop. I couldn't imagine what he could want there. It seemed a sort of mad freak. He thrusts under my nose three rings, which looked very tiny on his big, brown palm, growling out, 'For Maggie! Which!'

"I got a kind of scare at this. I couldn't make a sound, but I pointed at the one that sparkled white and blue. He put it in his waistcoat pocket, paid for it with a lot of sovereigns, and bolted out. When we got on board I was quite out of breath. 'Shake hands, old chap,' I gasped out. He gave me a thump on the back. 'Give what orders you like to the boatswain when the hands turn-to,' says he; 'I am off duty this afternoon.'

"Then he vanished from the deck for a while, but presently he came out of the cabin with Maggie, and these two went over the gangway publicly, before all hands, going for a walk together on that awful, blazing, hot day, with clouds of dust flying about. They came back after a few hours looking very staid, but didn't seem to have the slightest idea where they had been. Anyway that's the answer they both made to Mrs. Colchester's question at tea-time.

"And didn't she turn on Charley, with her voice like an old night cabman's. 'Rubbish. Don't know where you've been! Stuff and nonsense. You've walked the girl off her legs. Don't do it again.'

"It's surprising how meek Charley could be with that old woman. Only on one occasion he whispered to me, 'I'm jolly glad she isn't Maggie's aunt, except by marriage. That's no sort of relationship.' But I think he let Maggie have too much of her own way. She was hopping all over that ship in her yachting skirt and a red tam-o'-shanter like a bright bird on a dead black tree. The old salts used to grin to themselves when they saw her coming along, and offered to teach her knots or splices. I believe she liked the men, for Charley's sake, I suppose.

"As you may imagine, the diabolic propensities of that cursed ship were never spoken of on board. Not in the cabin, at any rate. Only once on the homeward passage Charley said, incautiously, something about bringing all her crew home this time. Captain Colchester began to look uncomfortable at once, and that silly, hardbitten old woman flew out at Charley as though he had said something indecent. I was quite confounded myself; as to Maggie, she sat completely mystified, opening her blue eyes very wide. Of course, before she was a day older she wormed it all out of me. She was a very difficult person to lie to.

" 'How awful,' she said, quite solemn. 'So many poor fellows. I am glad the voyage is nearly over. I won't have a moment's peace about Charley now.'

"I assured her Charley was all right. It took more than that ship knew to get over a seaman like Charley. And she agreed with me.

"Next day we got the tug off Dungeness; and when the tow-rope was fast Charley rubbed his hands and said to me in an undertone, 'We've baffled her, Ned.'

" 'Look's like it,' I said, with a grin at him. It was beautiful weather, and the sea as smooth as a millpond. We went up the river without a shadow of trouble except once, when off Hole Haven the brute took a sudden sheer and nearly had a barge anchored just clear of the fairway. But I was aft, looking after the steering, and she did not catch me napping that time. Charley came up on the poop, looking very concerned. 'Close shave,' says he.

" 'Never mind, Charley,' I answered, cheerily. 'You've tamed her.'

"We were to tow right up to the dock. The river pilot boarded us below Gravesend, and the first words I heard him say were: 'You may just as well take your port anchor inboard at once, Mr. Mate.'

"This had been done when I went forward. I saw Maggie on the fore-castle head enjoying the bustle, and I begged her to go aft, but she took no notice of me, of course. Then Charley, who was very busy with the head gear, caught sight of her and shouted in his biggest voice: 'Get off the forecastle head, Maggie. You're in the way here.' For all answer she made a funny face at him, and I saw poor Charley turn away, hiding a smile. She was flushed with the excitement of getting home again, and her blue eyes seemed to snap electric sparks as she looked at the river. A collier brig had gone round just ahead of us, and our tug had to stop her engines in a hurry to avoid running into her.

"In a moment, as is usually the case, all the shipping in the reach seemed to get into a hopeless tangle. A schooner and a ketch got up a small collision all to themselves right in the middle of the river. It was exciting to watch, and, meantime, our tug remained stopped. Any other ship than that brute could have been coaxed to keep straight for a couple of minutes—but not she! Her head fell off at once, and she began to drift down, taking her tug along with her. I noticed a cluster of coasters at anchor within a quarter of a mile of us, and I thought I had better speak to the pilot. 'If you let her get amongst that lot,' I said quietly, 'she will grind some of them to bits before we get her out again.'

" 'Don't I know her!' cries he, stamping his foot in a perfect fury. And he out with his whistle to make that bothered tug get the ship's head up again as quick as possible. He blew like mad, waving his arm to port, and presently we could see that the tug's engines had been set going ahead. Her paddles churned the water, but it was as if she had been trying to tow a rock—she couldn't get an inch out of that ship. Again the pilot blew his whistle, and waved his arms to port. We could see the tug's paddles turn-ing faster and faster away, broad on our bow.

"For a moment tug and ship hung motionless in a crowd of moving shipping, and then the terrific strain that evil, stony-hearted brute would always put on everything tore the towing-chock clean out. The tow-rope surged over, snapping the iron stanchions of the headrail one after an-other as if they had been sticks of sealing-wax. It was only then I noticed that in order to have a better view over our heads, Maggie had stepped upon the port anchor as it lay flat on the forecastle deck.

"It had been lowered properly into its hardwood beds, but there had been no time to take a turn with it. Anyway, it was quite secure as it was, for going into dock; but I could see directly that the tow-rope would sweep under the fluke in another second. My heart flew up right into my throat, but not before I had time to yell out, 'Jump clear of that anchor!'

"But I hadn't time to shriek out her name. I don't suppose she heard me at all. The first touch of the hawser against the fluke threw her down; she was up on her feet again as quick as lightning, but she was up on the wrong side. I heard a horrid, scraping sound, and then that anchor, tipping over, rose up like something alive; its great, rough iron arm caught Maggie round the waist, seemed to clasp her close with a dreadful hug, and flung itself with her over and down in a terrific clang of iron, followed by heavy ringing blows that shook the ship from stern to stem—because the ring stopper held!"

"How horrible!" I exclaimed.

"I used to dream for years afterwards of anchors catching hold of girls," said the man in tweeds, a little wildly. He shuddered. "With a most pitiful howl Charley was over after her almost on the instant. But, Lord! he didn't see as much as a gleam of her red tam-o'-shanter in the water. Nothing! Nothing whatever! In a moment there were half-a-dozen boats around us, and he got pulled into one. I, with the boatswain and the carpenter, let go the other anchor in a hurry and brought the ship up somehow. The pilot had gone silly. He walked up and down the forecastle head wringing his hands and muttering to himself, 'Killing women, now! Killing women now!' Not another word could you get out of him.

"Dusk fell, then a night black as pitch; and peering upon the river I heard a low, mournful hail, 'Ship ahoy!' Two Gravesend watermen came alongside. They had a lantern in their wherry, and looked up the ship's side, holding on to the ladder without a word. I saw in the patch of light a lot of loose, fair hair down there."

He shuddered again.

"After the tide turned poor Maggie's body had floated clear of one of them big mooring buoys," he explained. "I crept aft, feeling half-dead, and managed to send a rocket up—to let the other searchers know, on the river. And then I slunk away forward like a cur, and spent the night sitting on the heel of the bowsprit so as to be as far as possible out of Charley's way."

"Poor fellow!" I murmured.

"Yes. Poor fellow," he repeated musingly. "That brute wouldn't let him—not even him—cheat her of her prey. But he made her fast in dock next morning. He did. We hadn't exchanged a word—not a single look for that matter. I didn't want to look at him. When the last rope was fast he put his hands to his head and stood gazing down at his feet as if trying to remember something. The men waited on the main deck for the words that end the voyage. Perhaps that is what he was trying to remember. I spoke for him. 'That'll do, men.'

"I never saw a crew leave a ship so quietly. They sneaked over the rail one after another, taking care not to bang their sea chests too heavily. They looked our way, but not one had the stomach to come up and offer to shake hands with the mate as is usual.

"I followed him all over the empty ship to and fro, here and there, with no living soul about but the two of us, because the old shipkeeper had locked himself up in the galley—both doors. Suddenly poor Charley mutters, in a crazy voice, 'I'm done here,' and strides down the gangway with me at his heels, up the dock, out at the gate, on towards Tower Hill. He used to take rooms with a decent old landlady in America Square, to be near his work.

"All at once he stops short, turns round, and comes back straight at me. 'Ned,' says he, 'I am going home.' I had the good luck to sight a four-wheeler and got him in just in time. His legs were beginning to give way. In our hall he fell down on a chair, and I'll never forget father's and mother's amazed, perfectly still faces as they stood over him. They couldn't understand what had happened to him till I blubbered out, 'Maggie got drowned, yesterday, in the river.'

"Mother let out a little cry. Father looks from him to me, and from me to him, as if comparing our faces—for, upon my soul, Charley did not resemble himself at all. Nobody moved; and the poor fellow raises his big brown hands slowly to his throat, and with one single tug rips everything open—collar, shirt, waistcoat—a perfect wreck and ruin of a man. Father and I got him upstairs somehow, and mother pretty nearly killed herself nursing him through a brain fever."

The man in tweeds nodded at me significantly.

"Ah! there was nothing that could be done with that brute. She had a devil in her."

"Where's your brother?" I asked, expecting to hear he was dead. But he was commanding a smart steamer on the China coast, and never came home now.

Jermyn fetched a heavy sigh, and the handkerchief being now sufficiently dry, put it up tenderly to his red and lamentable nose.

"She was a ravening beast," the man in tweeds started again. "Old Colchester put his foot down and resigned. And would you believe it? Apse & Sons wrote to ask whether he wouldn't reconsider his decision!

Anything to save the good name of the *Apse Family!* Old Colchester went to the office then and said that he would take charge again but only to sail her out into the North Sea and scuttle her there. He was nearly off his chump. He used to be darkish iron-grey, but his hair went snow-white in a fortnight. And Mr. Lucian Apse (they had known each other as young men) pretended not to notice it. Eh? Here's infatuation if you like! Here's pride for you!

"They jumped at the first man they could get to take her, for fear of the scandal of the *Apse Family* not being able to find a skipper. He was a festive soul, I believe, but he stuck to her grim and hard. Wilmot was his second mate. A harum-scarum fellow, and pretending to a great scorn for all the girls. The fact is he was really timid. But let only one of them do as much as lift her little finger in encouragement, and there was nothing that could hold the beggar. As apprentice, once, he deserted abroad after a petticoat, and would have gone to the dogs then if his skipper hadn't taken the trouble to find him and lug him by the ears out of some house of perdition or other.

"It was said that one of the firm had been heard once to express a hope that this brute of a ship would get lost soon. I can hardly credit the tale, unless it might have been Mr. Alfred Apse, whom the family didn't think much of. They had him in the office, but he was considered a bad egg altogether, always flying off to race meetings and coming home drunk. You would have thought that a ship so full of deadly tricks would run herself ashore some day out of sheer cussedness. But not she! She was going to last for ever. She had a nose to keep off the bottom."

Jermyn made a grunt of approval.

"A ship after a pilot's own heart, eh?" jeered the man in tweeds. "Well, Wilmot managed it. He was the man for it, but even he, perhaps, couldn't have done the trick without that green-eyed governess, or nurse, or whatever she was to the children of Mr. and Mrs. Pamphilius.

"Those people were passengers in her from Port Adelaide to the Cape. Well, the ship went out and anchored outside for the day. The skipper—hospitable soul—had a lot of guests from town to a farewell lunch—as usual with him. It was five in the evening before the last shore boat left the side, and the weather looked ugly and dark in the gulf. There was no reason for him to get under way. However, as he had told everybody he was going that day, he imagined it was proper to do so anyhow. But as he had no mind after all these festivities to tackle the straits in the dark, with a scant wind, he gave orders to keep the ship under lower topsails and foresail as close as she would lie, dodging along the land till the morning. Then he sought his virtuous couch. The mate was on deck, having his face washed very clean with hard rain squalls. Wilmot relieved him at midnight.

"The *Apse Family* had, as you observed, a house on her poop. . . ."

"A big, ugly white thing, sticking up," Jermyn murmured sadly, at the fire.

"That's it: a companion for the cabin stairs and a sort of chartroom combined. The rain drove in gusts on the sleepy Wilmot. The ship was then surging slowly to the southward, close hauled, with the coast within three miles or so to windward. There was nothing to look out for in that part of the gulf, and Wilmot went round to dodge the squalls under the lee of that chartroom, whose door on that side was open. The night was black, like a barrel of coal-tar. And then he heard a woman's voice whispering to him.

"That confounded green-eyed girl of the Pamphilius people had put the kids to bed a long time ago, of course, but it seems couldn't get to sleep herself. She heard eight bells struck, and the chief mate come below to turn in. She waited a bit, then got into her dressing-gown and stole across the empty saloon and up the stairs into the chartroom. She sat down on the settee near the open door to cool herself, I daresay.

"I suppose when she whispered to Wilmot it was as if somebody had struck a match in the fellow's brain. I don't know how it was they had got so very thick. I fancy he had met her ashore a few times before. I couldn't make it out, because, when telling the story, Wilmot would break off to swear something awful at every second word. We had met on the quay in Sydney, and he had an apron of sacking up to his chin, a big whip in his hand. A wagon-driver. Glad to do anything not to starve. That's what he had come down to.

"However, there he was, with his head inside the door, on the girl's shoulder as likely as not—officer of the watch! The helmsman, on giving his evidence afterwards, said that he shouted several times that the binnacle lamp had gone out. It didn't matter to him, because his orders were to 'sail her close.' 'I thought it funny,' he said, 'that the ship should keep on falling off in squalls, but I luffed her up every time as close as I was able. It was so dark I couldn't see my hand before my face, and the rain came in bucketfuls on my head.'

"The truth was that at every squall the wind hauled aft a little, till gradually the ship came to be heading straight for the coast, without a single soul in her being aware of it. Wilmot himself confessed that he had not been near the standard compass for an hour. He might well have confessed! The first thing he knew was the man on the lookout shouting blue murder forward there.

"He tore his neck free, he says, and yelled back at him: 'What do you say?'

" 'I think I hear breakers ahead, sir,' howled the man and came rushing aft with the rest of the watch, in the 'awfullest blinding deluge that ever fell from the sky,' Wilmot says. For a second or so he was so scared and bewildered that he could not remember on which side of the gulf the ship was. He wasn't a good officer, but he was a seaman all the same. He pulled himself together in a second, and the right orders sprang to his lips without thinking. They were to hard up with the helm and shiver the main and mizzen-topsails.

"It seems that the sails actually fluttered. He couldn't see them, but he heard them rattling and banging above his head. 'No use! She was too slow in going off,' he went on, his dirty face twitching, and the damn'd carter's whip shaking in his hand. 'She seemed to stick fast.' And then the flutter of the canvas above his head ceased. At this critical moment the wind hauled aft again with a gust, filling the sails, and sending the ship with a great way upon the rocks on her lee bow. She had overreached herself in her last little game. Her time had come—the hour, the man, the black night, the treacherous gust of wind—the right woman to put an end to her. The brute deserved nothing better. Strange are the instruments of Providence. There's a sort of poetical justice. . . ."

The man in tweeds looked hard at me.

"The first ledge she went over stripped the false keel off her. Rip! The skipper, rushing out of his berth, found a crazy woman, in a red flannel dressing-gown, flying round and round the cuddy, screeching like a cockatoo.

"The next bump knocked her clean under the cabin table. It also started the sternpost and carried away the rudder, and then that brute ran up a shelving, rocky shore, tearing her bottom out, till she stopped short, and the foremast dropped over the bows like a gangway."

"Anybody lost?" I asked.

"No one, unless that fellow Wilmot," answered the gentleman, unknown to Miss Blank, looking round for his cap. "And his case was worse than drowning for a man. Everybody got ashore all right. Gale didn't come on till next day, dead from the West, and broke up that brute in a surprisingly short time. It was as though she had been rotten at heart. . . ." He changed his tone. "Rain left off. I must get my bike and rush home to dinner. I live in Herne Bay—came out for a spin this morning."

He nodded at me in a friendly way, and went out with a swagger.

"Do you know who he is, Jermyn?" I asked.

The North Sea pilot shook his head, dismally. "Fancy losing a ship in that silly fashion! Oh dear! oh dear!" he groaned in lugubrious tones, spreading his damp handkerchief again like a curtain before the glowing grate.

On going out I exchanged a glance and a smile (strictly proper) with the respectable Miss Blank, barmaid of the Three Crows.

The Boats of the Glen Carrig

William Hope Hodgson

Being an account of their Adventures in the Strange Places of the Earth, after the foundering of the good ship Glen Carrig *through striking upon a hidden rock in the unknown seas to the Southward. As told by John Winterstraw, Gent., to his Son James Winterstraw, in the year 1757, and by him committed very properly and legibly to manuscript.*

MADRE MIA
People may say thou art no longer young
And yet, to me, thy youth was yesterday,
A yesterday that seems
Still mingled with my dreams.
Ah! how the years have o'er thee flung
Their soft mantilla, grey.

And e'en to them thou art not over old;
How could'st thou be! Thy hair
Hast scarcely lost its deep old glorious dark:
Thy face is scarcely lined. No mark
Destroys its calm serenity. Like gold
Of evening light, when winds scarce stir,
The soul-light of they face is pure as prayer.

9
The Land of Lonesomeness

OW WE HAD BEEN five days in the boats, and in all this time made no discovering of land. Then upon the morning of the sixth day came there a cry from the bo'sun, who had the command of the lifeboat, that there was something which might be land afar upon our larboard bow; but it was very low lying, and none could tell whether it was land or but a morning cloud. Yet, because there was the beginning of hope within our breasts, we pulled wearily towards it, and thus, in about an hour, discovered it to be indeed the coast of some flat country.

Then, it might be a little after the hour of midday, we had come so close to it that we could distinguish with ease what manner of land lay beyond the shore, and thus we found it to be of an abominable flatness, desolate beyond all that I could have imagined. Here and there it appeared to be covered with clumps of queer vegetation; though whether they were small trees or great bushes, I had no means of telling; but this I know, that they were like unto nothing which ever I had set eyes upon before.

So much as this I gathered as we pulled slowly along the coast, seeking an opening whereby we could pass inward to the land; but a weary time passed or ere we came upon that which we sought. Yet, in the end, we found it—a slimy-banked creek, which proved to be the estuary of a great river, though we spoke of it always as a creek. Into this we entered, and proceeded at no great pace upwards along its winding course; and as we made forward, we scanned the low banks upon each side, perchance there might be some spot where we could make to land; but we found none—the banks being composed of a vile mud which gave us no encouragement to venture rashly upon them.

Now, having taken the boat something over a mile up the great creek, we came upon the first of that vegetation which I had chanced to notice from the sea, and here, being within some score yards of it, we were the better able to study it. Thus I found that it was indeed composed largely of a sort of tree, very low and stunted, and having what might be described as an unwholesome look about it. The branches of this tree, I perceived to be the cause of my inability to recognize it from a bush, until I had come close upon it; for they grew thin and smooth through all their length, and hung towards the earth; being weighted thereto by a single, large cabbage-like plant which seemed to sprout from the extreme tip of each.

Presently, having passed beyond this first clump of the vegetation, and the banks of the river remaining very low, I stood me upon a thwart, by which means I was enabled to scan the surrounding country. This I discovered, so far as my sight could penetrate, to be pierced in all directions with innumerable creeks and pools, some of these latter being very great of extent; and, as I have before made mention, everywhere the country was low set—as it might be a great plain of mud; so that it gave me a sense of dreariness to look out upon it. It may be, all unconsciously, that my spirit was put in awe by the extreme silence of all the country around; for in all that waste I could see no living thing, neither bird nor vegetable, save it be the stunted trees, which, indeed, grew in clumps here and there over all the land, so much as I could see.

This silence, when I grew fully aware of it, was the more uncanny; for my memory told me that never before had I come upon a country which contained so much quietness. Nothing moved across my vision—not even a lone bird soared up against the dull sky; and, for my hearing, not so much as the cry of a sea-bird came to me—no! nor the croak of a frog, nor the plash of a fish. It was as though we had come upon the Country of Silence, which some have called the Land of Lonesomeness.

Now three hours had passed whilst we ceased not to labour at the oars, and we could no more see the sea; yet no place fit to our feet had come to view, for everywhere the mud, grey and black, surrounded us—encompassing us veritably by a slimy wilderness. And so we were fain to pull on, in the hope that we might come ultimately to firm ground.

Then, a little before sundown, we halted upon our oars, and made a scant meal from a portion of our remaining provisions; and as we ate, I could see the sun sinking away over the wastes, and I had some slight diversion in watching the grotesque shadows which it cast from the trees into the water upon our larboard side; for we had come to a pause opposite a clump of the vegetation. It was at this time, as I remember, that it was borne in upon me afresh how very silent was the land; and that this was not due to my imagination, I remarked that the men both in our own and in the bo'sun's boat, seemed uneasy because of it; for none spoke save in undertones, as though they had fear of breaking it.

And it was at this time, when I was awed by so much solitude, that there came the first telling of life in all that wilderness. I heard it first in the far distance, away inland—a curious, low, sobbing note it was, and the rise and the fall of it was like to the sobbing of a lonesome wind through a great forest. Yet was there no wind. Then, in a moment, it had died, and the silence of the land was awesome by reason of the contrast. And I looked about me at the men, both in the boat in which I was and that which the bo'sun commanded; and not one was there but held himself in a posture of listening. In this wise a minute of quietness passed, and then one of the men gave out a laugh, born of the nervousness which had taken him.

The bo'sun muttered to him to hush, and, in the same moment, there came again the plaint of that wild sobbing. And abruptly it sounded away on our right, and immediately was caught up, as it were, and echoed back from some place beyond us afar up the creek. At that, I got me upon a thwart, intending to take another look over the country about us; but the banks of the creek had become higher; moreover the vegetation acted as a screen, even had my stature and elevation enabled me to overlook the banks.

And so, after a little while, the crying died away, and there was another silence. Then, as we sat each one harking for what might next befall, George, the youngest 'prentice boy, who had his seat beside me, plucked me by the sleeve, inquiring in a troubled voice whether I had any knowledge of that which the crying might portend; but I shook my head, telling him that I had no knowing beyond his own; though, for his comfort, I said that it might be the wind. Yet, at that, he shook his head; for indeed, it was plain that it could not be by such agency for there was a stark calm.

Now, I had scarce made an end of my remark, when again the sad crying was upon us. It appeared to come from far up the creek, and from far down the creek, and from inland and the land between us and the sea. It filled the evening air with its doleful wailing, and I remarked that there was in it a curious sobbing, most human in its despairful crying. And so awesome was the thing that no man of us spoke; for it seemed that we harked to the weeping of lost souls. And then, as we waited fearfully, the sun sank below the edge of the world, and the dusk was upon us.

And now a more extraordinary thing happened; for, as the night fell with swift gloom, the strange wailing and crying was hushed, and another sound stole out upon the land—a far, sullen growling. At the first, like the crying, it came from far inland; but was caught up speedily on all sides of us, and presently the dark was full of it. And it increased in volume, and strange trumpetings fled across it. Then, though with slowness, it fell away to a low, continuous growling, and in it there was that which I can only describe as an insistent, hungry snarl. Aye! no other word of which I have knowledge so well describes it as that—a note of *hunger*, most awesome to the ear. And this, more than all the rest of those incredible voicings, brought terror into my heart.

Now as I sat listening, George gripped me suddenly by the arm, declaring in a shrill whisper that something had come among the clump of trees upon the left-hand bank. Of the truth of this, I had immediately a proof; for I caught the sound of a continuous rustling among them, and then a nearer note of growling, as though a wild beast purred at my elbow. Immediately upon this, I caught the bo'sun's voice, calling in a low tone to Josh, the eldest 'prentice, who had the charge of our boat, to come alongside of him; for he would have the boats together. Then got we out the oars and laid the boats together in the midst of the creek; and so we watched through the night, being full of fear, so that we kept our speech low; that is, so low as would carry our thoughts one to the other through the noise of the growling.

And so the hours passed, and naught happened more than I have told, save that once, a little after midnight, the trees opposite to us seemed to be stirred again, as though some creature, or creatures, lurked among them; and there came, a little after that, a sound as of something stirring the water up against the bank; but it ceased in a while and the silence fell once more.

Thus, after a weariful time, away Eastwards the sky began to tell of the coming of the day; and, as the light grew and strengthened, so did that insatiable growling pass hence with the dark and the shadows. And so at last came the day, and once more there was borne to us the sad wailing that had preceded the night. For a certain while it lasted, rising and falling most mournfully over the vastness of the surrounding wastes, until the sun was risen some degrees above the horizon; after which it began to fail, dying away in lingering echoes, most solemn to our ears. And so it passed, and there came again the silence that had been with us in all the daylight hours.

Now, it being day, the bo'sun bade us make such sparse breakfast as our provender allowed; after which, having first scanned the banks to discern if any fearful thing were visible, we took again to our oars, and proceeded on our upward journey; for we hoped presently to come upon a country where life had not become extinct, and where we could put foot to honest earth. Yet, as I have made mention earlier, the vegetation, where it grew, did flourish most luxuriantly; so that I am scarce correct when I speak of life as being extinct in that land. For, indeed, now I think of it, I can remember that the very mud from which it sprang seemed veritably to have a fat, sluggish life of its own, so rich and viscid was it.

Presently it was midday; yet was there but little change in the nature of the surrounding wastes; though it may be that the vegetation was something thicker, and more continuous along the banks. But the banks were still of the same thick, clinging mud; so that nowhere could we effect a landing; though, had we, the rest of the country beyond the banks seemed no better.

And all the while, as we pulled, we glanced continuously from bank to bank; and those who worked not at the oars were fain to rest a hand by their sheath-knives; for the happenings of the past night were continually in our minds, and we were in great fear; so that we had turned back to the sea but that we had come so nigh to the end of our provisions.

99
The Ship in the Creek

Then, it was nigh on to evening, we came upon a creek opening into the greater one through the bank upon our left. We had been like to pass it—as, indeed, we had passed many throughout the day—but that the bo'sun, whose boat had the lead, cried out that there was some craft lying-up, a little beyond the first bend. And, indeed, so it seemed; for one of the masts of her—all jagged, where it had carried away—stuck up plain to our view.

Now, having grown sick with so much lonesomeness, and being in fear of the approaching night, we gave out something near to a cheer, which, however, the bo'sun silenced, having no knowledge of those who might occupy the stranger. And so, in silence, the bo'sun turned his craft towards the creek, whereat we followed, taking heed to keep quietness, and working the oars warily. So, in a little, we came to the shoulder of the bend, and had plain sight of the vessel some little way beyond us. From the distance she had no appearance of being inhabited; so that after some small hesitation, we pulled towards her, though still being at pains to keep silence.

The strange vessel lay against that bank of the creek which was upon our right, and over above her was a thick clump of the stunted trees. For the rest, she appeared to be firmly imbedded in the heavy mud, and there was a certain look of age about her which carried to me a doleful suggestion that we should find naught aboard of her fit for an honest stomach.

We had come to a distance of maybe some ten fathoms from her starboard bow—for she lay with her head down towards the mouth of the little creek—when the bo'sun bade his men to back water, the which Josh did regarding our own boat. Then, being ready to fly if we had been in danger, the bo'sun hailed the stranger; but got no reply, save that some echo of his shout seemed to come back at us. And so he sung out again to her, chance there might be some below decks who had not caught his first hail; but, for the second time, no answer came to us, save the low echo—naught, but that the silent trees took on a little quivering, as though his voice had shaken them.

At that, being confident now within our minds, we laid alongside, and, in a minute had shinned up the oars and so gained her decks. Here, save that the glass of the skylight of the main cabin had been broken, and some portion of the framework shattered, there was no extraordinary litter; so that it appeared to us as though she had been no great while abandoned.

So soon as the bo'sun had made his way up from the boat, he turned aft towards the scuttle, the rest of us following. We found the leaf of the scuttle pulled forward to within an inch of closing, and so much effort did it require of us to push it back, that we had immediate evidence of a considerable time since any had gone down that way.

However, it was no great while before we were below, and here we found the main cabin to be empty, save for the bare furnishings. From it there opened off two state-rooms at the forrard end, and the captain's cabin in the after part, and in all of these we found matters of clothing and sundries such as proved that the vessel had been deserted apparently in haste. In further proof of this we found, in a drawer in the captain's room, a considerable quantity of loose gold, the which it was not to be supposed would have been left by the free-will of the owner.

Of the state-rooms, the one upon the starboard side gave evidence that it had been occupied by a woman—no doubt a passenger. The other, in which there were two bunks, had been shared, so far as we could have any certainty, by a couple of young men; and this we gathered by observation of various garments which were scattered carelessly about.

Yet it must not be supposed that we spent any great time in the cabins; for we were pressed for food, and made haste—under the directing of the bo'sun—to discover if the hulk held victuals whereby we might be kept alive.

To this end, we removed the hatch which led down to the lazarette, and, lighting two lamps which we had with us in the boats, went down to make a search. And so, in a little while, we came upon two casks which the bo'sun broke open with a hatchet. These casks were sound and tight, and in them was ship's biscuit, very good and fit for food. At this, as may be imagined, we felt eased in our minds, knowing that there was no immediate fear of starvation. Following this, we found a barrel of molasses; a cask of rum; some cases of dried fruit—these were mouldy and scarce fit to be eaten; a cask of salt beef, another of pork; a small barrel of vinegar; a case of brandy; two barrels of flour—one of which proved to be damp-struck; and a bunch of tallow dips.

In a little while we had all these things up in the big cabin, so that we might come at them the better to make choice of that which was fit for our stomachs, and that which was otherwise. Meantime, whilst the bo'sun overhauled these matters, Josh called a couple of the men, and went on deck to bring up the gear from the boats, for it had been decided that we should pass the night aboard the hulk.

When this was accomplished, Josh took a walk forrard to the fo'cas'le; but found nothing beyond two seamen's chests; a sea-bag, and some odd gear. There were, indeed, no more than ten bunks in the place; for she was but a small brig, and had no call for a great crowd. Yet Josh was more than a little puzzled to know what had come to the odd chests; for it was not to be supposed that there had been no more than two—and a sea-bag —among ten men. But to this, at that time, he had no answer, and so, being sharp for supper, made a return to the deck, and thence to the main cabin.

Now while he had been gone, the bo'sun had set the men to clearing out the main cabin; after which, he had served out two biscuits apiece all round, and a tot of rum. To Josh, when he appeared, he gave the same, and, in a little, we called a sort of council; being sufficiently stayed by the food to talk.

Yet, before we came to speech, we made shift to light our pipes; for the bo'sun had discovered a case of tobacco in the captain's cabin, and after this we came to the consideration of our position.

We had provender, so the bo'sun calculated, to last us for the better part of two months, and this without any great stint; but we had yet to prove if the brig held water in her casks, for that in the creek was brackish, even so far as we had penetrated from the sea; else we had not been in need. To the charge of this, the bo'sun set Josh, along with two of the men. Another, he told to take charge of the galley, so long as we were in the hulk. But for that night, he said we had no need to do aught; for we had sufficient of water in the boats' breakers to last us till the morrow. And so, in a little, the dusk began to fill the cabin; but we talked on, being greatly content with our present ease and the good tobacco which we enjoyed.

In a little while, one of the men cried out suddenly to us to be silent, and, in that minute, all heard it—a far, drawn-out wailing; the same which had come to us in the evening of the first day. At that we looked at one another through the smoke and the growing dark, and, even as we looked, it became plainer heard, until, in a while, it was all about us— aye! it seemed to come floating down through the broken framework of the skylight as though some weariful, unseen thing stood and cried upon the decks above our heads.

Now through all that crying, none moved; none, that is, save Josh and the bo'sun, and they went up into the scuttle to see whether anything was in sight; but they found nothing, and so came down to us; for there was no wisdom in exposing ourselves, unarmed as we were, save for our sheath-knives.

And so, in a little, the night crept down upon the world, and still we sat within the dark cabin, none speaking, and knowing of the rest only by the glows of their pipes.

All at once there came a low, muttered growl, stealing across the land; and immediately the crying was quenched in its sullen thunder. It died away, and there was a full minute of silence; then, once more it came, and it was nearer and more plain to the ear. I took my pipe from my mouth; for I had come again upon the great fear and uneasiness which the happenings of the first night had bred in me, and the taste of the smoke brought me no more pleasure. The muttered growl swept over our heads and died away into the distance, and there was a sudden silence.

Then, in that quietness, came the bo'sun's voice. He was bidding us haste every one into the captain's cabin. As we moved to obey him, he ran to draw over the lid of the scuttle; and Josh went with him, and, together, they had it across; though with difficulty. When we had come into the captain's cabin, we closed and barred the door, piling two great sea-chests up against it; and so we felt near safe; for we knew that no thing, man nor beast, could come at us there. Yet, as may be supposed, we felt not altogether secure; for there was that in the growling which now filled the darkness, that seemed demoniac, and we knew not what horrid Powers were abroad.

And so through the night the growling continued, seeming to be mighty near unto us—aye! almost over our heads, and of a loudness far surpassing all that had come to us on the previous night; so that I thanked the Almighty that we had come into shelter in the midst of so much fear.

999
The Thing That Made Search

Now at times, I fell upon sleep, as did most of the others; but, for the most part, I lay half sleeping and half waking—being unable to attain to true sleep by reason of the everlasting growling above us in the night, and the fear which it bred in me. Thus, it chanced that just after midnight, I caught a sound in the main cabin beyond the door, and immediately I was fully waked. I sat me up and listened, and so became aware that something was fumbling about the deck of the main cabin. At that, I got to my feet and made my way to where the bo'sun lay, meaning to waken him, if he slept; but he caught me by the ankle, as I stooped to shake him, and whispered to me to keep silence; for he too had been aware of that strange noise of something fumbling beyond in the big cabin.

In a little, we crept both of us so close to the door as the chests would allow, and there we crouched, listening; but could not tell what manner of thing it might be which produced so strange a noise. For it was neither shuffling, nor treading of any kind, nor yet was it the whirr of a bat's wings, the which had first occurred to me, knowing how vampires are said to inhabit the nights in dismal places. Nor yet was it the slurr of a snake; but rather it seemed to us to be as though a great wet cloth were being rubbed everywhere across the floor and bulkheads. We were the better able to be certain of the truth of this likeness, when, suddenly, it passed across the further side of the door behind which we listened: at which, you may be sure, we drew backwards both of us in fright; though the door, and the chests, stood between us and that which rubbed against it.

Presently, the sound ceased, and, listen as we might, we could no longer distinguish it. Yet, until the morning, we dozed no more; being troubled in mind as to what manner of thing it was which had made search in the big cabin.

Then in time the day came, and the growling ceased. For a mournful while the sad crying filled our ears, and then at last the eternal silence that fills the day hours of that dismal land fell upon us.

So, being at last in quietness, we slept, being greatly awearied. About seven in the morning, the bo'sun waked me, and I found that they had opened the door into the big cabin; but though the bo'sun and I made careful search, we could nowhere come upon anything to tell us aught concerning the thing which had put us so in fright. Yet, I know not if I am right in saying that we came upon nothing; for, in several places, the bulkheads had a *chafed* look; but whether this had been there before that night, we had no means of telling.

Of that which we had heard, the bo'sun bade me make no mention, for he would not have the men put more in fear than need be. This I conceived to be wisdom, and so held my peace. Yet I was much troubled in my mind to know what manner of thing it was which we had need to fear, and more—I desired greatly to know whether we should be free of it in the daylight hours; for there was always with me, as I went hither and thither, the thought that IT—for that is how I designated it in my mind— might come upon us to our destruction.

Now after breakfast, at which we had each a portion of salt pork, besides rum and biscuit (for by now the fire in the caboose had been set going), we turned-to at various matters, under the directing of the bo'sun. Josh and two of the men made examination of the water casks, and the rest of us lifted the main hatch-covers, to make inspection of her cargo; but lo! we found nothing, save some three feet of water in her hold.

By this time, Josh had drawn some water off from the casks; but it was most unsuitable for drinking, being vile of smell and taste. Yet the bo'sun bade him draw some into buckets, so that the air might haply purify it; but though this was done, and the water allowed to stand through the morning, it was but little better.

At this, as might be imagined, we were exercised in our minds as to the manner in which we should come upon suitable water; for by now we were beginning to be in need of it. Yet though one said one thing, and another said another, no one had wit enough to call to mind any method by which our need should be satisfied. Then, when we had made an end of dining, the bo'sun sent Josh, with four of the men, up stream, perchance after a mile or two the water should prove of sufficient freshness to meet our purpose. Yet they returned a little before sundown having no water; for everywhere it was salt.

Now the bo'sun, foreseeing that it might be impossible to come upon water, had set the man whom he had ordained to be our cook, to boiling the creek water in three great kettles. This he had ordered to be done soon after the boat left; and over the spout of each, he had hung a great pot of iron, filled with cold water from the hold—this being cooler than that from the creek—so that the steam from each kettle impinged upon the cold surface of the iron pots, and being by this means condensed, was caught in three buckets placed beneath them upon the floor of the caboose. In this way, enough water was collected to supply us for the evening and the following morning; yet it was but a slow method, and we had sore need of a speedier, were we to leave the hulk so soon as I, for one, desired.

We made our supper before sunset, so as to be free of the crying which we had reason to expect. After that, the bo'sun shut the scuttle, and we went every one of us into the captain's cabin, after which we barred the door, as on the previous night; and well was it for us that we acted with this prudence.

By the time that we had come into the captain's cabin, and secured the door, it was upon sunsetting, and as the dusk came on, so did the melancholy wailing pass over the land; yet, being by now somewhat inured to so much strangeness, we lit our pipes, and smoked; though I observed that none talked; for the crying without was not to be forgotten.

Now, as I have said, we kept silence; but this was only for a time, and our reason for breaking it was a discovery made by George, the younger apprentice. This lad, being no smoker, was fain to do something to while away the time, and with this intent, he had raked out the contents of a small box, which had lain upon the deck at the side of the forrard bulkhead.

The box had appeared filled with odd small lumber of which a part was a dozen or so grey paper wrappers, such as are used, I believe, for carrying samples of corn; though I have seen them put to other purposes, as, indeed, was now the case. At first George had tossed these aside; but it growing darker the bo'sun lit one of the candles which we had found in the lazarette. Thus, George, who was proceeding to tidy back the rubbish which was cumbering the place, discovered something which caused him to cry out to us his astonishment.

Now, upon hearing George call out, the bo'sun bade him keep silence, thinking it was but a piece of boyish restlessness; but George drew the candle to him, and bade us to listen; for the wrappers were covered with fine handwriting after the fashion of a woman's.

Even as George told us of that which he had found we became aware that the night was upon us; for suddenly the crying ceased, and in place thereof there came out of the far distance the low thunder of the night-growling, that had tormented us through the past two nights. For a space, we ceased to smoke, and sat—listening; for it was a very fearsome sound. In a very little while it seemed to surround the ship, as on the previous nights; but at length, using ourselves to it, we resumed our smoking, and bade George to read out to us from the writing upon the paper wrappers.

Then George, though shaking somewhat in his voice, began to decipher that which was upon the wrappers, and a strange and awesome story it was, and bearing much upon our own concerns:—

"Now, when they discovered the spring among the trees that crown the bank, there was much rejoicing; for we had come to have much need of water. And some, being in fear of the ship (declaring, because of all our misfortune and the strange disappearances of their messmates and the brother of my lover, that she was haunted by a devil), declared their intention of taking their gear up to the spring, and there making a camp. This they conceived and carried out in the space of one afternoon; though our Captain, a good and true man, begged of them, as they valued life, to stay within the shelter of their living-place. Yet, as I have remarked, they would none of them hark to his counselling, and, because the Mate and the bo'sun were gone he had no means of compelling them to wisdom—"

At this point, George ceased to read, and began to rustle among the wrappers, as though in search for the continuation of the story.

Presently he cried out that he could not find it, and dismay was upon his face.

But the bo'sun told him to read on from such sheets as were left; for, as he observed, we had no knowledge if more existed; and we were fain to know further of that spring which, from the story, appeared to be over the bank near to the vessel.

George, being thus adjured, picked up the topmost sheet; for they were, as I heard him explain to the bo'sun, all oddly numbered, and having but little reference one to the other. Yet we were mightily keen to know even so much as such odd scraps might tell unto us. Whereupon, George read from the next wrapper, which ran thus:—

"Now, suddenly, I heard the Captain cry out that there was something in the main cabin, and immediately my lover's voice calling to me to lock my door, and on no condition to open it. Then the door of the Captain's cabin slammed, and there came a silence, and the silence was broken by a *sound*. Now, this was the first time that I had heard the Thing make search through the big cabin; but, afterwards, my lover told me it had happened aforetime, and they had told me naught, fearing to frighten me needlessly; though now I understood why my lover had bidden me never to leave my state-room door unbolted in the night-time. I remember also, wondering if the noise of breaking glass that had waked me somewhat from my dreams a night or two previously, had been the work of this indescribable Thing; for on the morning following that night, the glass in the skylight had been smashed. Thus it was that my thoughts wandered out to trifles, while yet my soul seemed ready to leap out from my bosom with fright.

"I had, by reason of usage, come to ability to sleep despite of the fearsome growling; for I had conceived its cause to be the mutter of spirits in the night, and had not allowed myself to be unnecessarily frightened with doleful thoughts; for my lover had assured me of our safety, and that we should yet come to our home. And now, beyond my door, I could hear that fearsome sound of the Thing searching—"

George came to a sudden pause; for the bo'sun had risen and put a great hand upon his shoulder. The lad made to speak; but the bo'sun beckoned to him to say no word, and at that we, who had grown to nervousness through the happenings in the story, began every one to listen. Thus we heard a sound which had escaped us in the noise of the growling without the vessel, and the interest of the reading.

For a space we kept very silent, no man doing more than let the breath go in and out of his body, and so each one of us knew that something moved without, in the big cabin. In a little, something touched upon our door, and it was, as I have mentioned earlier, as though a great swab rubbed and scrubbed at the woodwork. At this, the men nearest unto the door came backwards in a surge, being put in sudden fear by reason of the Thing being so near; but the bo'sun held up a hand, bidding them, in a low voice, to make no unneedful noise. Yet, as though the sounds of their moving had been heard, the door was shaken with such violence that we waited, everyone, expecting to see it torn from its hinges; but it stood, and we hasted to brace it by means of the bunk boards, which we placed between it and the two great chests, and upon these we set a third chest, so that the door was quite hid.

Now, I have no remembrance whether I have put down that when we came first to the ship, we had found the stern window upon the larboard side to be shattered; but so it was, and the bo'sun had closed it by means of a teak-wood cover which was made to go over it in stormy weather, with stout battens across, which were set tight with wedges. This he had done upon the first night, having fear that some evil thing might come upon us through the opening, and very prudent was this same action of his, as shall be seen. Then George cried out that something was at the cover of the larboard window, and we stood back, growing ever more fearful because that some evil creature was so eager to come at us. But the bo'sun, who was a very courageous man, and calm withal, walked over to the closed window, and saw to it that the battens were secure; for he had knowledge sufficient to be sure, if this were so, that no creature with strength less than that of a whale could break it down, and in such case its bulk would assure us from being molested.

Then, even as he made sure of the fastenings, there came a cry of fear from some of the men; for there had come at the glass of the unbroken window, a reddish mass, which plunged up against it, sucking upon it, as it were. Then Josh, who was nearest to the table, caught up the candle, and held it towards the Thing; thus I saw that it had the appearance of a many-flapped thing shaped as it might be, out of raw beef—*but it was alive.*

At this, we stared, everyone being too bemused with terror to do aught to protect ourselves, even had we been possessed of weapons. And as we remained thus, an instant, like silly sheep awaiting the butcher, I heard the framework creak and crack, and there ran splits all across the glass. In another moment, the whole thing would have been torn away, and the cabin undefended, but that the bo'sun, with a great curse at us for our land-lubberly lack of use, seized the other cover, and clapped it over the window. At that, there was more help than could be made to avail, and the battens and wedges were in place in a trice. That this was no sooner accomplished than need be, we had immediate proof; for there came a rending of wood and a splintering of glass, and after that a strange yowling out in the dark, and the yowling rose above and drowned the continuous growling that filled the night. In a little, it died away, and in the brief silence that seemed to ensue, we heard a slobby fumbling at the teak cover; but it was well secured, and we had no immediate cause for fear.

IV
The Two Faces

Of the remainder of that night, I have but a confused memory. At times we heard the door shaken behind the great chests; but no harm came to it. And, odd whiles, there was a soft thudding and rubbing upon the decks over our heads, and once, as I recollect, the Thing made a final try at the teak covers across the windows; but the day came at last, and found me sleeping. Indeed, we had slept beyond the noon, but that the bo'sun, mindful of our needs, waked us, and we removed the chests. Yet, for perhaps the space of a minute, none durst open the door, until the bo'sun bid us stand to one side. We faced about at him then, and saw that he held a great cutlass in his right hand.

He called to us that there were four more of the weapons, and made a backward motion with his left hand towards an open locker. At that, as might be supposed, we made some haste to the place to which he pointed, and found that, among some other gear, there were three more weapons such as he held; but the fourth was a straight cut-and-thrust, and this I had the good fortune to secure.

Being now armed, we ran to join the bo'sun; for by this he had the door open, and was scanning the main cabin. I would remark here how a good weapon doth seem to put heart into a man; for I, who but a few, short hours since had feared for my life, was now right full of lustiness and fight; which, mayhap, was no matter for regret.

From the main cabin, the bo'sun led up on to the deck, and I remember some surprise at finding the lid of the scuttle even as we had left it the previous night; but then I recollected that the skylight was broken, and there was access to the big cabin that way. Yet, I questioned within myself as to what manner of thing it could be which ignored the convenience of the scuttle, and descended by way of the broken skylight.

We made a search of the decks and fo'cas'le, but found nothing, and, after that, the bo'sun stationed two of us on guard, whilst the rest went about such duties as were needful. In a little, we came to breakfast, and, after that, we prepared to test the story upon the sample wrappers and see perchance whether there was indeed a spring of fresh water among the trees.

Now between the vessel and the trees, lay a slope of the thick mud, against which the vessel rested. To have scrambled up this bank had been next to impossible, by reason of its fat richness; for, indeed, it looked fit to crawl; but that Josh called out to the bo'sun that he had come upon a ladder, lashed across the fo'cas'le head. This was brought, also several hatch covers. The latter were placed first upon the mud, and the ladder laid upon them; by which means we were enabled to pass up to the top of the bank without contact with the mud.

Here, we entered at once among the trees; for they grew right up to the edge; but we had no trouble in making a way; for they were nowhere close together; but standing, rather, each one in a little open space by itself.

We had gone a little way among the trees, when, suddenly, one who was with us cried out that he could see something away on our right, and we clutched everyone his weapon the more determinedly, and went towards it. Yet it proved to be but a seaman's chest, and a space further off, we discovered another. And so, after a little walking, we found the camp; but there was small semblance of a camp about it; for the sail of which the tent had been formed, was all torn and stained, and lay muddy upon the ground. Yet the spring was all we had wished, clear and sweet, and so we knew we might dream of deliverance.

Now, upon our discovery of the spring, it might be thought that we should set up a shout to those upon the vessel; but this was not so; for there was something in the air of the place which cast a gloom upon our spirits, and we had no disinclination to return unto the vessel.

Upon coming to the brig, the bo'sun called to four of the men to go down into the boats, and pass up the breakers: also, he collected all the buckets belonging to the brig, and forthwith each of us was set to our work. Some, those with the weapons, entered into the wood, and gave down the water to those stationed upon the bank, and these, in turn, passed it to those in the vessel. To the man in the galley, the bo'sun gave command to fill a boiler with some of the most select pieces of the pork and beef from the casks and get them cooked so soon as might be, and so we were kept at it; for it had been determined—now that we had come upon water—that we should stay not an hour longer in that monster-ridden craft, and we were all agog to get the boats revictualled, and put back to the sea, from which we had too gladly escaped.

So we worked through all that remainder of the morning, and right on into the afternoon; for we were in mortal fear of the coming dark. Towards four o'clock, the bo'sun sent the man, who had been set to do our cooking, up to us with slices of salt meat upon biscuits, and we ate as we worked, washing our throats with water from the spring, and so, before the evening, we had filled our breakers, and near every vessel which was convenient for us to take in the boats. More, some of us snatched the chance to wash our bodies; for we were sore with brine, having dipped in the sea to keep down thirst as much as might be.

Now, though it had not taken us so great a while to make a finish of our water-carrying if matters had been more convenient; yet because of the softness of the ground under our feet, and the care with which we had to pick our steps, and some little distance between us and the brig, it had grown later than we desired, before we had made an end. Therefore, when the bo'sun sent word that we should come aboard, and bring our gear, we made all haste. Thus, as it chanced, I found that I had left my sword beside the spring, having placed it there to have two hands for the carrying of one of the breakers. At my remarking my loss, George, who stood near, cried out that he would run for it, and was gone in a moment, being greatly curious to see the spring.

Now, at this moment, the bo'sun came up, and called for George; but I informed him that he had run to the spring to bring me my sword. At this, the bo'sun stamped his foot, and swore a great oath, declaring that he had kept the lad by him all the day; having a wish to keep him from any danger which the wood might hold, and knowing the lad's desire to adventure there. At this, a matter which I should have known, I reproached myself for so gross a piece of stupidity, and hastened after the bo'sun, who had disappeared over the top of the bank. I saw his back as he passed into the wood, and ran until I was up with him; for, suddenly, as it were, I found that a sense of chilly dampness had come among the trees; though a while before the place had been full of the warmth of the sun. This, I put to the account of evening, which was drawing on apace; and also, it must be borne in mind, that there were but the two of us.

We came to the spring; but George was not to be seen, and I saw no sign of my sword. At this, the bo'sun raised his voice, and cried out the lad's name. Once he called, and again; then at the second shout we heard the boy's shrill halloo, from some distance ahead among the trees. At that, we ran towards the sound, plunging heavily across the ground, which was everywhere covered with a thick scum, that clogged the feet in walking. As we ran, we hallooed, and so came upon the boy, and I saw that he had my sword.

The bo'sun ran towards him, and caught him by the arm, speaking with anger, and commanding him to return with us immediately to the vessel.

But the lad, for reply, pointed with my sword, and we saw that he pointed at what appeared to be a bird against the trunk of one of the trees. This, as I moved closer, I perceived to be a part of the tree, and no bird; but it had a very wondrous likeness to a bird; so much so that I went up to it, to see if my eyes had deceived me. Yet it seemed no more than a freak of nature, though most wondrous in its fidelity; being but an excrescence upon the trunk. With a sudden thought that it would make me a curio, I reached up to see whether I could break it away from the tree; but it was above my reach, so that I had to leave it. Yet, one thing I discovered; for, in stretching towards the protuberance, I had placed a hand upon the tree, and its trunk was soft as pulp under my fingers, much after the fashion of a mushroom.

As we turned to go, the bo'sun inquired of George his reason for going beyond the spring, and George told him that he had seemed to hear someone calling to him among the trees, and there had been so much pain in the voice that he had run towards it; but been unable to discover the owner. Immediately afterwards he had seen the curious, bird-like excrescence upon a tree nearby. Then we had called, and of the rest we had knowledge.

We had come nigh to the spring on our return journey, when a sudden low whine seemed to run among the trees. I glanced towards the sky, and realized that the evening was upon us. I was about to remark upon this to the bo'sun, when, abruptly, he came to a stand, and bent forward to stare into the shadows to our right. At that, George and I turned ourselves about to perceive what matter it was which had attracted the attention of the bo'sun; thus we made out a tree some twenty yards away, which had all its branches wrapped about its trunk, much as the lash of a whip is wound about its stock. Now this seemed to us a very strange sight, and we made all of us towards it, to learn the reason of so extraordinary a happening.

Yet, when we had come close upon it, we had no means of arriving at a knowledge of that which it portended; but walked each of us around the tree, and were more astonished, after our circumnavigation of the great vegetable than before.

Now, suddenly, and in the distance, I caught the far wailing that came before the night, and abruptly, as it seemed to me, the tree wailed at us. At that I was vastly astonished and frightened; yet, though I retreated, I could not withdraw my gaze from the tree; but scanned it the more intently; and, suddenly, I saw a brown, human face peering at us from between the wrapped branches. At this, I stood very still, being seized with that fear which renders one shortly incapable of movement. Then, before I had possession of myself, I saw that it was of a part with the trunk of the tree; for I could not tell where it ended and the tree began.

Then I caught the bo'sun by the arm, and pointed; for whether it was a part of the tree or not, it was a work of the devil; but the bo'sun, on seeing it, ran straightway so close to the tree that he might have touched it with his hand, and I found myself beside him. Now, George, who was on the bo'sun's other side, whispered that there was another face, not unlike to a woman's, and, indeed, so soon as I perceived it, I saw that the tree had a second excrescence, most strangely after the face of a woman. Then the bo'sun cried out with an oath, at the strangeness of the thing, and I felt the arm, which I held, shake somewhat, as it might be with a deep emotion. Then, far away, I heard again the sound of the wailing and, immediately, from among the trees about us, there came answering wails and a great sighing. And before I had time to be more than aware of these things, the tree wailed again at us. And at that, the bo'sun cried out suddenly that he knew; though of what it was that he *knew*, I had at that time no knowledge. And, immediately, he began with his cutlass to strike at the tree before us, and to cry upon God to blast it; and lo! at his smiting

a very fearsome thing happened; for the tree did bleed like any live creature. Thereafter, a great yowling came from it, and it began to writhe.
And, suddenly, I became aware that all about us the trees were a-quiver.

Then George cried out, and ran round upon my side of the bo'sun, and
I saw that one of the great cabbage-like things pursued him upon its stem,
even as an evil serpent; and very dreadful it was, for it had become blood
red in colour; but I smote it with the sword, which I had taken from the
lad, and it fell to the ground.

Now from the brig I heard them hallooing, and the trees had become
like live things, and there was a vast growling in the air, and hideous
trumpetings. Then I caught the bo'sun again by the arm, and shouted to
him that we must run for our lives; and this we did, smiting with our
swords as we ran; for there came things at us, out from the growing dusk.

Thus we made the brig, and, the boats being ready, I scrambled after
the bo'sun into his, and we put straightway into the creek, all of us,
pulling with so much haste as our loads would allow. As we went I looked
back at the brig, and it seemed to me that a multitude of things hung over
the bank above her, and there seemed a flicker of things moving hither
and thither aboard of her. And then we were in the great creek up which
we had come, and so, in a little, it was night.

All that night we rowed, keeping very strictly to the centre of the big
creek, and all about us bellowed the vast growling, being more fearsome
than ever I had heard it, until it seemed to me that we had waked all that
land of terror to a knowledge of our presence. But, when the morning
came, so good a speed had we made, what with our fear, and the current
being with us, that we were nigh upon the open sea; whereat each one of
us raised a shout, feeling like freed prisoners.

And so, full of thankfulness to the Almighty, we rowed outward to the
sea.

V
The Great Storm

Now, as I have said, we came at last in safety to the open sea, and so for a
time had some degree of peace; though it was long ere we threw off all of
the terror which the Land of Lonesomeness had cast over our hearts.

And one more matter there is regarding that land, which my memory
recalls. It will be remembered that George found certain wrappers upon
which there was writing. Now, in the haste of our leaving, he had given
no thought to take them with him; yet a portion of one he found within
the side pocket of his jacket, and it ran somewhat thus:—

"But I hear my lover's voice wailing in the night, and I go to find him; for my loneliness is not to be borne. May God have mercy upon me!"

And that was all.

For a day and a night we stood out from the land towards the North, having a steady breeze to which we set our lug sails, and so made very good way, the sea being quiet, though with a slow, lumbering swell from the Southward.

It was on the morning of the second day of our escape that we met with the beginnings of our adventure into the Silent Sea, the which I am about to make so clear as I am able.

The night had been quiet, and the breeze steady until near on to the dawn, when the wind slacked away to nothing, and we lay there waiting, perchance the sun should bring the breeze with it. And this it did; but no such wind as we did desire; for when the morning came upon us, we discovered all that part of the sky to be full of a fiery redness, which presently spread away down to the South, so that an entire quarter of the heavens was, as it seemed to us, a mighty arc of blood-coloured fire.

Now, at the sight of these omens, the bo'sun gave orders to prepare the boats for the storm which we had reason to expect, looking for it in the South, for it was from that direction that the swell came rolling upon us. With this intent, we roused out so much heavy canvas as the boats contained, for we had gotten a bolt and a half from the hulk in the creek; also the boat covers which we could lash down to the brass studs under the gunnels of the boats. Then, in each boat, we mounted the whaleback— which had been stowed along the tops of the thwarts—also its supports, lashing the same to the thwarts below the knees. Then we laid two lengths of the stout canvas the full length of the boat over the whaleback, over-lapping and nailing them to the same, so that they sloped away down over the gunnels upon each side as though they had formed a roof to us. Here, whilst some stretched the canvas, nailing its lower edges to the gunnel, others were employed in lashing together the oars and the mast, and to this bundle they secured a considerable length of new three-and-a-half-inch hemp rope, which we had brought away from the hulk along with the canvas. This rope was then passed over the bows and in through the painter ring, and thence to the forrard thwarts, where it was made fast, and we gave attention to parcel it with odd strips of canvas against danger of chafe. And the same was done in both of the boats, for we could not put our trust in the painters, besides which they had not sufficient length to secure safe and easy riding.

Now by this time we had the canvas nailed down to the gunnel around our boat, after which we spread the boat-cover over it, lacing it down to the brass studs beneath the gunnel. And so we had all the boat covered in, save a place in the stern where a man might stand to wield the steering oar, for the boats were double bowed. And in each boat we made the same preparation, lashing all movable articles, and preparing to meet so great a storm as might well fill the heart with terror; for the sky cried out to us that it would be no light wind, and further, the great swell from the South grew more huge with every hour that passed; though as yet it was without virulence, being slow and oily and black against the redness of the sky.

Presently we were ready, and had cast over the bundle of oars and the mast, which was to serve as our sea-anchor, and so we lay waiting. It was at this time that the bo'sun called over to Josh certain advice with regard to that which lay before us. And after that the two of them sculled the boats a little apart; for there might be a danger of their being dashed together by the first violence of the storm.

And so came a time of waiting, with Josh and the bo'sun each of them at the steering oars, and the rest of us stowed away under the coverings. From where I crouched near the bo'sun, I had sight of Josh away upon our port side: he was standing up black as a shape of night against the mighty redness, when the boat came to the foamless crowns of the swells, and then gone from sight in the hollows between.

Now midday had come and gone, and we had made shift to eat so good a meal as our appetites would allow; for we had no knowledge how long it might be ere we should have chance of another, if, indeed, we had ever need to think more of such. And then, in the middle part of the afternoon, we heard the first cryings of the storm—a far-distant moaning, rising and falling most solemnly.

Presently, all the Southern part of the horizon so high up, maybe, as some seven to ten degrees, was blotted out by a great black wall of cloud, over which the red glare came down upon the great swells as though from the light of some vast and unseen fire. It was about this time, I observed that the sun had the appearance of a great full moon, being pale and clearly defined, and seeming to have no warmth nor brilliancy; and this, as may be imagined, seemed most strange to us, the more so because of the redness in the South and East.

And all this while the swells increased most prodigiously; though without making broken water: yet they informed us that we had done well to take so much precaution; for surely they were raised by a very great storm. A little before evening, the moaning came again, and then a space of silence; after which there rose a very sudden bellowing, as of wild beasts, and then once more the silence.

About this time, the bo'sun making no objection, I raised my head above the cover until I was in a standing position; for, until now, I had taken no more than occasional peeps; and I was very glad of the chance to stretch my limbs; for I had grown mightily cramped. Having stirred the sluggishness of my blood, I sat me down again; but in such position that I could see every part of the horizon without difficulty. Ahead of us, that is to the South, I saw now that the great wall of cloud had risen some further degrees, and there was something less of the redness; though, indeed, what there was left of it was sufficiently terrifying; for it appeared to crest the black cloud like red foam, seeming, it might be, as though a mighty sea made ready to break over the world.

Towards the West, the sun was sinking behind a curious red-tinted haze, which gave it the appearance of a dull red disk. To the North, seeming very high in the sky, were some flecks of cloud lying motionless, and of a very pretty rose colour. And here I may remark that all the sea to the North of us appeared as a very ocean of dull red fire; though, as might be expected, the swells, coming up from the South, against the light were so many exceeding great hills of blackness.

It was just after I had made these observations that we heard again the distant roaring of the storm, and I know not how to convey the exceeding terror of that sound. It was as though some mighty beast growled far down towards the South; and it seemed to make very clear to me that we were but two small craft in a very lonesome place. Then, even while the roaring lasted, I saw a sudden light flare up, as it were from the edge of the Southern horizon. It had somewhat the appearance of lightning; yet vanished not immediately, as is the wont of lightning; and more, it had not been my experience to witness such spring up from out of the sea, but, rather, down from the heavens. Yet I have little doubt but that it was a form of lightning; for it came many times after this, so that I had chance to observe it minutely. And frequently, as I watched, the storm would shout at us in a most fearsome manner.

Then, when the sun was low upon the horizon, there came to our ears a very shrill, screaming noise, most penetrating and distressing, and, immediately afterwards the bo'sun shouted out something in a hoarse voice, and commenced to sway furiously upon the steering oar. I saw his stare fixed upon a point a little on our larboard bow, and perceived that in that direction the sea was all blown up into vast clouds of dust-like froth, and I knew that the storm was upon us. Immediately afterwards a cold blast struck us; but we suffered no harm, for the bo'sun had gotten the boat bows-on by this. The wind passed us, and there was an instant of calm. And now all the air above us was full of a continuous roaring, so very loud and intense that I was like to be deafened. To windward, I perceived an enormous wall of spray bearing down upon us, and I heard again the shrill screaming, pierce through the roaring. Then the bo'sun whipped in his oar under the cover, and, reaching forward, drew the canvas aft, so that it covered the entire boat, and he held it down against the gunnel upon the starboard side, shouting in my ear to do likewise upon the larboard. Now had it not been for this forethought on the part of the bo'sun we had been all dead men; and this may be the better believed when I explain that we felt the water falling upon the stout canvas overhead, tons and tons; though so beaten to froth as to lack solidity to sink or crush us. I have said "felt"; for I would make it so clear as may be, here once and for all, that so intense was the roaring and screaming of the elements, there could no sound have penetrated to us, no! not the pealing of mighty thunders. And so for the space of maybe a full minute the boat quivered and shook most vilely, so that she seemed like to have been shaken in pieces, and from a dozen places between the gunnel and the covering canvas, the water spurted in upon us. And here one other thing I would make mention of: During that minute, the boat had ceased to rise and fall upon the great swell, and whether this was because the sea was flattened by the first rush of the wind, or that the excess of the storm held her steady, I am unable to tell; and can put down only that which we felt.

Now, in a little, the first fury of the blast being spent, the boat began to sway from side to side, as though the wind blew now upon the one beam, and now upon the other; and several times we were stricken heavily with the blows of solid water. But presently this ceased, and we returned once again to the rise and fall of the swell, only that now we received a cruel jerk every time that the boat came upon the top of a sea. And so a while passed.

Towards midnight, as I should judge, there came some mighty flames of lightning, so bright that they lit up the boat through the double covering of canvas; yet no man of us heard aught of the thunder; for the roaring of the storm made all else a silence.

And so to the dawn, after which, finding that we were still, by the mercy of God, possessed of our lives, we made shift to eat and drink; after which we slept.

Now, being extremely wearied by the stress of the past night, I slumbered through many hours of the storm, waking at some time between noon and evening. Overhead, as I lay looking upwards, the canvas showed of a dull leadenish colour, blackened completely at whiles by the dash of spray and water. And so, presently, having eaten again, and feeling that all things lay in the hands of the Almighty, I came once more upon sleep.

Twice through the following night was I wakened by the boat being hurled upon her beam-ends by the blows of the seas; but she righted easily, and took scarce any water, the canvas proving a very roof of safety. And so the morning came again.

Being now rested, I crawled after to where the bo'sun lay, and, the noise of the storm lulling odd instants, shouted in his ear to know whether the wind was easing at whiles. To this he nodded, whereat I felt a most joyful sense of hope pulse through me, and ate such food as could be gotten, with a very good relish.

In the afternoon, the sun broke out suddenly, lighting up the boat most gloomily through the wet canvas; yet a very welcome light it was, and bred in us a hope that the storm was near to breaking. In a little, the sun disappeared; but, presently, it coming again, the bo'sun beckoned to me to assist him, and we removed such temporary nails as we had used to fasten down the after part of the canvas, and pushed back the covering a space sufficient to allow our heads to go through into the daylight. On looking out, I discovered the air to be full of spray, beaten as fine as dust, and then, before I could note aught else, a little gout of water took me in the face with such force as to deprive me of breath; so that I had to descend beneath the canvas for a little while.

So soon as I was recovered, I thrust forth my head again, and now I had some sight of the terrors around us. As each huge sea came towards us, the boat shot up to meet it, right up to its very crest, and there, for the space of some instants, we would seem to be swamped in a very ocean of foam, boiling up on each side of the boat to the height of many feet. Then, the sea passing from under us, we would go swooping dizzily down the great, black, froth-splotched back of the wave, until the oncoming sea caught us up most mightily. Odd whiles, the crest of a sea would hurl forward before we had reached the top, and though the boat shot upward like a veritable feather, yet the water would swirl right over us, and we would have to draw in our heads most suddenly; in such cases the wind flapping the cover down so soon as our hands were removed. And, apart from the way in which the boat met the seas, there was a very sense of terror in the air: the continuous roaring and howling of the storm; the *screaming* of the foam, as the frothy summits of the briny mountains hurled past us, and the wind that tore the breath out of our weak human throats, are things scarce to be conceived.

Presently, we drew in our heads, the sun having vanished again, and nailed down the canvas once more, and so prepared for the night.

From here on until the morning, I have very little knowledge of any happenings; for I slept much of the time, and, for the rest, there was little to know, cooped up beneath the cover. Nothing save the interminable, thundering swoop of the boat downwards, and then the halt and upward hurl, and the occasional plunges and surges to larboard or starboard, occasioned, I can only suppose, by the indiscriminate might of the seas.

I would make mention here, how that I had little thought all this while for the peril of the other boat, and, indeed, I was so very full of our own that it is no matter at which to wonder. However, as it proved, and as this is a most suitable place in which to tell it, the boat that held Josh and the rest of the crew came through the storm with safety; though it was not until many years afterwards that I had the good fortune to hear from Josh himself how that, after the storm, they were picked up by a homeward-bound vessel, and landed in the Port of London.

And now, to our own happenings.

VI
The Weed-Choked Sea

It was some little while before midday that we grew conscious that the sea had become very much less violent; and this despite the wind roaring with scarce abated noise. And, presently, everything about the boat, saving the wind, having grown indubitably calmer, and no great water breaking over the canvas, the bo'sun beckoned me again to assist him lift the after part of the cover. This we did, and put forth our heads to inquire the reason of the unexpected quietness of the sea; not knowing but that we had come suddenly under the lee of some unknown land. Yet, for a space, we could see nothing, beyond the surrounding billows; for the sea was still very furious, though no matter to cause us concern, after that through which we had come.

Presently, however, the bo'sun, raising himself, saw something, and, bending, cried in my ear that there was a low bank which broke the force of the sea; but he was full of wonder to know how that we had passed it without shipwreck. And whilst he was still pondering the matter I raised myself, and took a look on all sides of us, and so I discovered that there lay another great bank upon our larboard side, and this I pointed out to him. Immediately afterwards, we came upon a great mass of seaweed swung up on the crest of a sea, and, presently, another. And so we drifted on, and the seas grew less with astonishing rapidity, so that, in a little, we stript off the cover so far as the midship thwart; for the rest of the men were sorely in need of the fresh air, after so long a time below the canvas covering.

It was after we had eaten, that one of them made out that there was another low bank astern upon which we were drifting. At that, the bo'sun stood up and made an examination of it, being much exercised in his mind to know how we might come clear of it with safety. Presently, however, we had come so near to it that we discovered it to be composed of seaweed, and so we let the boat drive upon it, making no doubt but that the other banks, which we had seen, were of a similar nature.

In a little, we had driven in among the weed; yet, though our speed was greatly slowed, we made some progress, and so in time came out upon the other side, and now we found the sea to be near quiet, so that we hauled in our sea anchor—which had collected a great mass of weed about it—and removed the whaleback and canvas coverings, after which we stepped the mast, and set a tiny storm-foresail upon the boat; for we wished to have her under control, and could set no more than this, because of the violence of the breeze.

Thus we drove on before the wind, the bo'sun steering, and avoiding all such banks as showed ahead, and ever the sea grew calmer. Then, when it was near on to evening, we discovered a huge stretch of the weed that seemed to block all the sea ahead, and, at that, we hauled down the foresail, and took to our oars, and began to pull, broadside on to it, towards the West. Yet so strong was the breeze, that we were being driven down rapidly upon it. And then, just before sunset, we opened out the end of it, and drew in our oars, very thankful to set the little foresail, and run off again before the wind.

And so, presently, the night came down upon us, and the bo'sun made us take turn and turn about to keep a look-out; for the boat was going some knots through the water, and we were among strange seas; but *he* took no sleep all that night, keeping always to the steering oar.

I have memory, during my time of watching, of passing odd floating masses, which I make no doubt were weed, and once we drove right atop of one; but drew clear without much trouble. And all the while, through the dark to starboard, I could make out the dim outline of that enormous weed extent lying low upon the sea, and seeming without end. And so, presently, my time to watch being at an end, I returned to my slumber, and when next I waked it was morning.

Now the morning discovered to me that there was no end to the weed upon our starboard side; for it stretched away into the distance ahead of us so far as we could see; while all about us the sea was full of floating masses of the stuff. And then, suddenly, one of the men cried out that there was a vessel in among the weed. At that, as may be imagined, we were very greatly excited, and stood upon the thwarts that we might get a better view of her. Thus I saw her a great way in from the edge of the weed, and I noted that her foremast was gone near to the deck, and she had no main top-mast; though, strangely enough, her mizzen stood unharmed. And beyond this, I could make out but little, because of the distance; though the sun, which was upon our larboard side, gave me some sight of her hull, but not much, because of the weed in which she was deeply embedded; yet it seemed to me that her sides were very weatherworn, and in one place some glistening brown object, which may have been a fungus, caught the rays of the sun, sending off a wet sheen.

There we stood, all of us, upon the thwarts, staring and exchanging opinions, and were like to have overset the boat; but that the bo'sun ordered us down. And after this we made our breakfast, and had much discussion regarding the stranger, as we ate.

Later, towards midday, we were able to set our mizzen; for the storm had greatly modified, and so, presently, we hauled away to the West, to escape a great bank of the weed which ran out from the main body. Upon rounding this, we let the boat off again, and set the main lug, and thus made very good speed before the wind. Yet though we ran all that afternoon parallel with the weed to starboard, we came not to its end. And three separate times we saw the hulks of rotting vessels, some of them having the appearance of a previous age, so ancient did they seem.

Now, towards evening, the wind dropped to a very little breeze, so that we made but slow way, and thus we had better chance to study the weed. And now we saw that it was full of crabs; though for the most part so very minute as to escape the casual glance; yet they were not all small, for in a while I discovered a swaying among the weed, a little way in from the edge, and immediately I saw the mandible of a very great crab stir amid the weed. At that, hoping to obtain it for food, I pointed it out to the bo'sun, suggesting that we should try and capture it. And so, there being by now scarce any wind, he bade us get out a couple of the oars, and back the boat up to the weed. This we did, after which he made fast a piece of salt meat to a bit of spun yarn, and bent this on to the boat-hook. Then he made a running bowline, and slipped the loop on to the shaft of the boat-hook, after which he held out the boat-hook, after the fashion of a fishing-rod, over the place where I had seen the crab. Almost immediately, there swept up an enormous claw, and grasped the meat, and at that, the bo'sun cried out to me to take an oar and slide the bowline along the boat-hook, so that it should fall over the claw; and this I did, and immediately some of us hauled upon the line, taughtening it about the great claw. Then the bo'sun sung out to us to haul the crab aboard, that we had it most securely; yet on the instant we had reason to wish that we had been less successful; for the creature, feeling the tug of our pull upon it, tossed the weed in all directions, and thus we had full sight of it, and discovered it to be so great a crab as is scarce conceivable—a very monster. And further, it was apparent to us that the brute had no fear of us, nor intention to escape; but rather made to come at us; whereat the bo'sun, perceiving our danger, cut the line, and bade us put weight upon the oars, and so in a moment we were in safety, and very determined to have no more meddlings with such creatures.

Presently, the night came upon us, and, the wind remaining low, there was everywhere about us a great stillness, most solemn after the continuous roaring of the storm which had beset us in the previous days. Yet now and again a little wind would rise and blow across the sea, and where it met the weed, there would come a low, damp rustling, so that I could her the passage of it for no little time after the calm had come once more all about us.

Now it is a strange thing that I, who had slept amid the noise of the past days, should find sleeplessness amid so much calm; yet so it was, and presently I took the steering oar, proposing that the rest should sleep, and to this the bo'sun agreed, first warning me, however, most particularly to have care that I kept the boat off the weed (for we had still a little way on us), and, further, to call him should anything unforeseen occur. And after that, almost immediately he fell asleep, as indeed did the most of the men.

From the time that I relieved the bo'sun, until midnight, I sat upon the gunnel of the boat, with the steering oar under my arm, and watched and listened, most full of a sense of the strangeness of the seas into which we had come. It is true that I had heard tell of seas choked up with weed— seas that were full of stagnation, having no tides; but I had not thought to come upon such an one in my wanderings; having, indeed, set down such tales as being bred of imagination, and without reality in fact.

Then, a little before the dawn, and when the sea was yet full of darkness, I was greatly startled to hear a prodigious splash amid the weed, mayhaps at a distance of some hundred yards from the boat. Then, as I stood full of alertness, and knowing not what the next moment might bring forth, there came to me across the immense waste of weed, a long, mournful cry, and then again the silence. Yet, though I kept very quiet, there came no further sound, and I was about to re-seat myself, when, afar off in that strange wilderness, there flashed out a sudden flame of fire.

Now upon seeing fire in the midst of so much lonesomeness, I was as one mazed, and could do naught but stare. Then, my judgment returning to me, I stooped and waked the bo'sun; for it seemed to me that this was a matter for his attention. He, after staring at it awhile, declared that he could see the shape of a vessel's hull beyond the flame; but, immediately, he was in doubt, as, indeed, I had been all the while. And then, even as we peered, the light vanished, and though we waited for the space of some minutes, watching steadfastly, there came no further sight of that strange illumination.

From now until the dawn, the bo'sun remained awake with me, and we talked much upon that which we had seen; yet could come to no satisfac-

tory conclusion; for it seemed impossible to us that a place of so much
desolation could contain any living being. And then, just as the dawn was
upon us, there loomed up a fresh wonder—the hull of a great vessel
maybe a couple or three score fathoms in from the edge of the weed. Now
the wind was still very light, being no more than an occasional breath, so
that we went past her at a drift; thus the dawn had strengthened sufficiently to give to us a clear sight of the stranger, before we had gone more
than a little past her. And now I perceived that she lay full broadside on to
us, and that her three masts were gone close down to the deck. Her side
was streaked in places with rust, and in others a green scum overspread
her; but it was no more than a glance that I gave at any of those matters;
for I had spied something which drew all my attention—great leathery
arms splayed all across her side, some of them crooked in-board over the
rail, and then, low down, seen just above the weed, the huge, brown,
glistening bulk of so great a monster as ever I had conceived. The bo'sun
saw it in the same instant and cried out in a hoarse whisper that it was a
mighty devil-fish, and then, even as he spoke, two of the arms flickered up
into the cold light of the dawn, as though the creature had been asleep,
and we had waked it. At that, the bo'sun seized an oar, and I did likewise,
and, so swiftly as we dared, for fear of making any unneedful noise, we
pulled the boat to a safer distance. From there and until the vessel had
become indistinct by reason of the space we put between us, we watched
that great creature clutched to the old hull, as it might be a limpet to a
rock.

Presently, when it was broad day, some of the men began to rouse up,
and in a little we broke our fast, which was not displeasing to me, who
had spent the night watching. And so through the day we sailed with a
very light wind upon our larboard quarter. And all the while we kept the
great waste of weed upon our starboard side, and apart from the mainland of the weed, as it were, there were scattered about an uncountable
number of weed islets and banks, and there were thin patches of it that
appeared scarce above the water, and through these later we let the boat
sail; for they had not sufficient density to impede our progress more than
a little.

And then, when the day was far spent, we came in sight of another
wreck amid the weeds. She lay in from the edge perhaps so much as the
half of a mile, and she had all three of her lower masts in, and her lower
yards squared. But what took our eyes more than aught else was a great
superstructure which had been built upward from her rails, almost half-
way to her main tops, and this, as we were able to perceive, was supported by ropes let down from the yards; but of what material the superstructure was composed, I have no knowledge; for it was so over-grown

with some form of green stuff—as was so much of the hull as showed above the weed—as to defy our guesses. And because of this growth, it was borne upon us that the ship must have been lost to the world a very great age ago. At this suggestion, I grew full of solemn thought; for it seemed to me that we had come upon the cemetery of the oceans.

Now, in a little while after we had passed this ancient craft, the night came down upon us, and we prepared for sleep, and because the boat was making some little way through the water, the bo'sun gave out that each of us should stand our turn at the steering-oar, and that he was to be called should any fresh matter transpire. And so we settled down for the night, and owing to my previous sleeplessness, I was full weary, so that I knew nothing until the one whom I was to relieve shook me into wakefulness. So soon as I was fully waked, I perceived that a low moon hung above the horizon, and shed a very ghostly light across the great weed world to starboard. For the rest, the night was exceeding quiet, so that no sound came to me in all that ocean, save the rippling of the water upon our bends as the boat forged slowly along. And so I settled down to pass the time ere I should be allowed to sleep; but first I asked the man whom I had relieved, how long a time had passed since moon-rise; to which he replied that it was no more than the half of an hour, and after that I questioned whether he had seen aught strange amid the weed during his time at the oar; but he had seen nothing, except that once he had fancied a light had shown in the midst of the waste; yet it could have been naught save a humor of the imagination; though apart from this, he had heard a strange crying a little after midnight, and twice there had been great splashes among the weed. And after that he fell asleep, being impatient at my questioning.

Now it so chanced that my watch had come just before the dawn; for which I was full of thankfulness, being in that frame of mind when the dark breeds strange and unwholesome fancies. Yet, though I was so near to the dawn, I was not to escape free of the dread influence of that place; for, as I sat, running my gaze to and fro over its grey immensity, it came to me that there were strange movements among the weed, and I seemed to see vaguely, as one may see things in dreams, dim white faces peer out at me here and there; yet my commonsense assured me that I was but deceived by the uncertain light and the sleep in my eyes; yet for all that, it put my nerves on the quiver.

A little later, there came to my ears the noise of a very great splash amid the weed; but though I stared with intentness, I could nowhere discern aught as likely to be the cause thereof. And then, suddenly, between me and the moon, there drove up from out of that great waste a vast bulk, flinging huge masses of weed in all directions. It seemed to be no more than a hundred fathoms distant, and, against the moon, I saw the outline of it most clearly—a mighty devil-fish. Then it had fallen back once more with a prodigious splash, and so the quiet fell again, finding me sore afraid, and no little bewildered that so monstrous a creature could leap with such agility. And then (in my fright I had let the boat come near to the edge of the weed) there came a subtle stir opposite to our starboard bow, and something slid down into the water. I swayed upon the oar to turn the boat's head outward, and with the same movement leant forward and sideways to peer, bringing my face near to the boat's rail. In the same instant, I found myself looking down into a white demoniac face, human save that the mouth and nose had greatly the appearance of a beak. The thing was gripping at the side of the boat with two flickering hands—gripping the bare, smooth outer surface, in a way that woke in my mind a sudden memory of the great devil-fish which had clung to the side of the wreck we had passed in the previous dawn. I saw the face come up towards me, and one misshapen hand fluttered almost to my throat, and there came a sudden, hateful reek in my nostrils—foul and abominable. Then, I came into possession of my faculties, and drew back with great haste and a wild cry of fear. And then I had the steering-oar by the middle, and was smiting downward with the loom over the side of the boat; but the thing was gone from my sight. I remember shouting out to the bo'sun and to the men to awake, and then the bo'sun had me by the shoulder, was calling in my ear to know what dire thing had come about. At that, I cried out that I did not know, and, presently, being somewhat calmer, I told them of the thing that I had seen; but even as I told of it, there seemed to be no truth in it, so that they were all at a loss to know whether I had fallen asleep, or that I had indeed seen a devil.

And presently the dawn was upon us.

VIII
The Island in the Weed

It was as we were all discussing the matter of the devil face that had peered up at me out of the water, that Job, the ordinary seaman, discovered the island in the light of the growing dawn, and, seeing it, sprang to his feet, with so loud a cry that we were like for the moment to have thought he had seen a second demon. Yet when we made discovery of that which he had already perceived, we checked our blame at his sudden shout; for the sight of land, after so much desolation, made us very warm in our hearts.

Now at first the island seemed but a very small matter; for we did not know at that time that we viewed it from its end; yet despite this, we took to our oars and rowed with all haste towards it, and so, coming nearer, were able to see that it had a greater size than we had imagined. Presently, having cleared the end of it, and keeping to that side which was further from the great mass of the weed-continent, we opened out a bay that curved inward to a sandy beach, most seductive to our tired eyes. Here, for the space of a minute, we paused to survey the prospect, and I saw that the island was of a very strange shape, having a great hump of black rock at either end, and dipping down into a steep valley between them. In this valley there seemed to be a deal of a strange vegetation that had the appearance of mighty toadstools; and down nearer the beach there was a thick grove of a kind of very tall reed, and these we discovered afterwards to be exceeding tough and light, having something of the qualities of the bamboo.

Regarding the beach, it might have been most reasonably supposed that it would be very thick with the driftweed; but this was not so, at least, not at that time; though a projecting horn of the black rock which ran out into the sea from the upper end of the island, was thick with it.

And now, the bo'sun having assured himself that there was no appearance of any danger, we bent to our oars, and presently had the boat aground upon the beach, and here, finding it convenient, we made our breakfast. During this meal, the bo'sun discussed with us the most proper thing to do, and it was decided to push the boat off from the shore, leaving Job in her, whilst the remainder of us made some exploration of the island.

And so, having made an end of eating, we proceeded as we had determined, leaving Job in the boat, ready to scull ashore for us if we were pursued by any savage creature, while the rest of us made our way towards the nearer hump, from which, as it stood some hundred feet above the sea, we hoped to get a very good idea of the remainder of the island. First, however, the bo'sun handed out to us the two cutlasses and the cut-and-thrust (the other two cutlasses being in Josh's boat) and, taking one himself, he passed me the cut-and-thrust, and gave the other cutlass to the biggest of the men. Then he bade the others keep their sheath-knives handy, and was proceeding to lead the way, when one of them called out to us to wait a moment, and, with that, ran quickly to the clump of reeds. Here, he took one with both his hands and bent upon it; but it would not break, so that he had to notch it about with his knife, and thus, in a little, he had it clear. After this, he cut off the upper part, which was too thin and lissom for his purpose, and then thrust the handle of his knife into the end of the portion which he had retained, and in this wise he had a most serviceable lance or spear. For the reeds were very strong, and hollow after the fashion of bamboo, and when he had bound some yarn about the end into which he had thrust his knife, so as to prevent it splitting, it was a fit enough weapon for any man.

Now the bo'sun, perceiving the happiness of the fellow's idea, bade the rest make to themselves similar weapons, and whilst they were busy thus, he commended the man very warmly. And so, in a little, being now most comfortably armed, we made inland towards the nearer black hill, in very good spirits. Presently, we were come to the rock which formed the hill, and found that it came up out of the sand with great abruptness, so that we could not climb it on the seaward side. At that, the bo'sun led us round a space towards that side where lay the valley, and here there was under-foot neither sand nor rock; but ground of strange and spongy texture, and then suddenly, rounding a jutting spur of the rock, we came upon the first of the vegetation—an incredible mushroom; nay, I should say toadstool; for it had no healthy look about it, and gave out a heavy, mouldy odour. And now we perceived that the valley was filled with them, all, that is, save a great circular patch where nothing appeared to be growing; though we were not yet at a sufficient height to ascertain the reason of this.

Presently, we came to a place where the rock was split by a great fissure running up to the top, and showing many ledges and convenient shelves upon which we might obtain hold and footing. And so we set-to about climbing, helping one another so far as we had ability, until, in about the space of some ten minutes, we reached the top, and from thence had a very fine view. We perceived now that there was a beach upon that side of the island which was opposed to the weed; though, unlike that upon which we had landed, it was greatly choked with weed which had drifted ashore. After that, I gave notice to see what space of water lay between the island and the edge of the great weed-continent, and guessed it to be no more than maybe some ninety yards, at which I fell to wishing that it had been greater, for I was grown much in awe of the weed and the strange things which I conceived it to contain.

Abruptly, the bo'sun clapped me upon the shoulder, and pointed to some object that lay out in the weed at a distance of not much less than the half of a mile from where we stood. Now, at first, I could not conceive what manner of thing it was at which I stared, until the bo'sun, remarking my bewilderment, informed me that it was a vessel all covered in, no doubt as a protection against the devil-fish and other strange creatures in the weed. And now I began to trace the hull of her amid all that hideous growth; but of her masts, I could discern nothing; and I doubted not but that they had been carried away by some storm ere she was caught by the weed; and then the thought came to me of the end of those who had built up that protection against the horrors which the weed-world held hidden amid its slime.

Presently, I turned my gaze once more upon the island, which was very plain to see from where we stood. I conceived, now that I could see so much of it, that its length would be near to half a mile, though its breadth was something under four hundred yards; thus it was very long in proportion to its width. In the middle part it had less breadth than at the ends, being perhaps three hundred yards at its narrowest, and a hundred yards wider at its broadest.

Upon both sides of the island, as I have made already a mention, there was a beach, though this extended no great distance along the shore, the remainder being composed of the black rock of which the hills were formed. And now, having a closer regard to the beach upon the weed-side of the island, I discovered amid the wrack that had been cast ashore, a portion of the lower mast and topmast of some great ship, with rigging attached; but the yards were all gone. This find, I pointed out to the bo'sun, remarking that it might prove of use for firing; but he smiled at me, telling me that the dried weed would make a very abundant fire, and this without going to the labour of cutting the mast into suitable logs.

And now, he, in turn, called my attention to the place where the huge fungi had come to a stop in their growing, and I saw that in the centre of the valley there was a great circular opening in the earth, like to the mouth of a prodigious pit, and it appeared to be filled to within a few feet of the mouth with water, over which spread a brown and horrid scum. Now, as may be supposed, I stared with some intentness at this; for it had the look of having been made with labour, being very symmetrical; yet I could not conceive but that I was deluded by the distance, and that it would have a rougher appearance when viewed from a nearer standpoint.

From contemplating this, I looked down upon the little bay in which our boat floated. Job was sitting in the stern, sculling gently with the steering-oar and watching us. At that, I waved my hand to him in friendly fashion, and he waved back, and then, even as I looked, I saw something in the water under the boat—something dark coloured that was all of a-move. The boat appeared to be floating over it as over a mass of sunk weed, and then I saw that, whatever it was, it was rising to the surface. At this a sudden horror came over me, and I clutched the bo'sun by the arm, and pointed, crying out that there was something under the boat. Now the bo'sun, so soon as he saw the thing, ran forward to the brow of the hill and, placing his hands to his mouth after the fashion of a trumpet, sang out to the boy to bring the boat to the shore and make fast the painter to a large piece of rock. At the bo'sun's hail, the lad called out "I, I," and, standing up, gave a sweep with his oar that brought the boat's head round towards the beach. Fortunately for him he was no more than some thirty yards from the shore at this time, else he had never come to it in this life; for the next moment the moving brown mass beneath the boat shot out a great tentacle and the oar was torn out of Job's hands with such power as to throw him right over on to the starboard gunnel of the boat. The oar itself was drawn down out of sight, and for the minute the boat was left untouched. Now the bo'sun cried out to the boy to take another oar, and get ashore while still he had chance, and at that we all called out various things, one advising one thing, and another recommending some other; yet our advice was vain, for the boy moved not, at which some cried out that he was stunned. I looked now to where the brown thing had been, for the boat had moved a few fathoms from the spot, having got some way upon her before the oar was snatched, and thus I discovered that the monster had disappeared, having, I conceived, sunk again into the depths from which it had risen; yet it might re-appear at any moment, and in that case the boy would be taken before our eyes.

At this juncture, the bo'sun called to us to follow him, and led the way to the great fissure up which we had climbed, and so, in a minute, we were, each of us, scrambling down with what haste we could make towards the valley. And all the while as I dropped from ledge to ledge, I was full of torment to know whether the monster had returned.

The bo'sun was the first man to reach the bottom of the cleft, and he set off immediately round the base of the rock to the beach, the rest of us following him as we made safe our footing in the valley. I was the third man down; but, being light and fleet of foot, I passed the second man and caught up with the bo'sun just as he came upon the sand. Here, I found that the boat was within some five fathoms of the beach, and I could see Job still lying insensible; but of the monster there was no sign.

And so matters were, the boat nearly a dozen yards from the shore, and Job lying insensible in her; with, somewhere near under her keel (for all that we knew) a great monster, and we helpless upon the beach.

Now I could not imagine how to save the lad, and indeed I fear he had been left to destruction—for I had deemed it madness to try to reach the boat by swimming—but for the extraordinary bravery of the bo'sun, who, without hesitating, dashed into the water and swam boldly out to the boat, which, by the grace of God, he reached without mishap, and climbed in over the bows. Immediately, he took the painter and hove it to us, bidding us tail on to it and bring the boat to shore without delay, and by this method of gaining the beach he showed wisdom; for in this wise he escaped attracting the attention of the monster by uneedful stirring of the water, as he would surely have done had he made use of an oar.

Yet, despite his care, we had not finished with the creature; for, just as the boat grounded, I saw the lost steering-oar shoot up half its length out of the sea, and immediately there was a mighty splather in the water astern, and the next instant the air seemed full of huge, whirling arms. At that, the bo'sun gave one look behind, and, seeing the thing upon him, snatched the boy into his arms, and sprang over the bows on to the sand. Now, at sight of the devil-fish, we had all made for the back of the beach at a run, none troubling even to retain the painter, and because of this, we were like to have lost the boat; for the great cuttle-fish had its arms all splayed about it, seeming to have a mind to drag it down into the deep water from whence it had risen, and it had possibly succeeded, but that the bo'sun brought us all to our senses; for, having laid Job out of harm's way, he was the first to seize the painter, which lay trailed upon the sand, and, at that, we got back our courage and ran to assist him.

Now there happened to be convenient a great spike of rock, the same, indeed, to which the bo'sun had bidden Job tie the boat, and to this we ran the painter, taking a couple of turns about it and two half-hitches, and now, unless the rope carried away, we had no reason to fear the loss of the boat; though there seemed to us to be a danger of the creature's crushing it. Because of this, and because of a feeling of natural anger against the thing, the bo'sun took up from the sand one of the spears which had been cast down when we hauled the boat ashore. With this, he went down so far as seemed safe, and prodded the creature in one of its tentacles—the weapon entering easily, at which I was surprised, for I had understood that these monsters were near to invulnerable in all parts save their eyes. At receiving this stab, the great fish appeared to feel no hurt, for it showed no signs of pain, and, at that, the bo'sun was further emboldened to go nearer, so that he might deliver a more deadly wound; yet scarce had he taken two steps before the hideous thing was upon him, and, but for an agility wonderful in so great a man, he had been destroyed. Yet, spite of so narrow an escape from death, he was not the less determined to wound or destroy the creature, and, to this end, he despatched some of us to the grove of reeds to cut half a dozen of the strongest, and when we returned with these, he bade two of the men lash their spears securely to them, and by this means they had now spears of a length of between thirty and forty feet. With these, it was possible to attack the devil-fish without coming within reach of its tentacles. And now, being ready, he took one of the spears, telling the biggest of the men to take the other. Then he directed him to aim for the right eye of the huge fish whilst he would attack the left.

Now since the creature had so nearly captured the bo'sun, it had ceased to tug at the boat, and lay silent, with its tentacles spread all about it, and its great eyes appearing just over the stern, so that it presented an appearance of watching our movements; though I doubt if it saw us with any clearness; for it must have been dazed with the brightness of the sunshine.

And now the bo'sun gave the signal to attack, at which he and the man ran down upon the creature with their lances, as it were, in rest. The bo'sun's spear took the monster truly in its left eye; but the one wielded by the men was too bendable, and sagged so much that it struck the stern-post of the boat, the knife-blade snapping off short. Yet it mattered not; for the wound inflicted by the bo'sun's weapon was so frightful, that the giant cuttle-fish released the boat, and slid back into deep water, churning it into foam, and gouting blood.

For some minutes we waited to make sure that the monster had indeed gone, and after that, we hastened to the boat, and drew her up so far as we were able; after which we unloaded the heaviest of her contents, and so were able to get her right clear of the water.

And for an hour afterwards the sea all about the little beach was stained black, and in places red.

VIII
The Noises in the Valley

Now, so soon as we had gotten the boat into safety, the which we did with a most feverish haste, the bo'sun gave his attention to Job; for the boy had not yet recovered from the blow which the loom of the oar had dealt him beneath the chin when the monster snatched at it. For awhile, his attentions produced no effect; but presently, having bathed the lad's face with water from the sea, and rubbed rum into his breast over the heart, the youth began to show signs of life, and soon opened his eyes, whereupon the bo'sun gave him a stiff jorum of the rum, after which he asked him how he seemed in himself. To this Job replied in a weak voice that he was dizzy and his head and neck ached badly; on hearing which, the bo'sun bade him keep lying until he had come more to himself. And so we left him in quietness under a little shade of canvas and reeds; for the air was warm and the sand dry, and he was not like to come to any harm there.

At a little distance, under the directing of the bo'sun, we made to prepare dinner; for we were now very hungry, it seeming a great while since we had broken our fast. To this end, the bo'sun sent two of the men across the island to gather some of the dry seaweed; for we intended to cook some of the salt meat, this being the first cooked meal since ending the meat which we had boiled before leaving the ship in the creek.

In the meanwhile, and until the return of the men with the fuel, the bo'sun kept us busied in various ways. Two he sent to cut a faggot of the reeds, and another couple to bring the meat and the iron boiler, the latter being one that we had taken from the old brig.

Presently, the men returned with the dried seaweed, and very curious stuff it seemed, some of it being in chunks near as thick as a man's body; but exceeding brittle by reason of its dryness. And so in a little, we had a very good fire going, which we fed with the seaweed and pieces of the reeds; though we found the latter to be but indifferent fuel, having too much sap, and being troublesome to break into convenient size.

Now when the fire had grown red and hot, the bo'sun half filled the boiler with sea water, in which he placed the meat; and the pan, having a stout lid, he did not scruple to place it in the very heart of the fire, so that soon we had the contents boiling merrily.

Having gotten the dinner under way, the bo'sun set about preparing our camp for the night, which we did by making a rough framework with the reeds, over which we spread the boat's sails and the cover, pegging the canvas down with tough splinters of the reed. When this was completed, we set-to and carried there all our stores, after which the bo'sun took us over to the other side of the island to gather fuel for the night, which we did, each man bearing a great double armful.

Now by the time that we had brought over, each of us, two loads of the fuel, we found the meat to be cooked, and so, without more to-do, set ourselves down and made a very good meal off it and some biscuits, after which we had each of us a sound tot of the rum. Having made an end of eating and drinking, the bo'sun went over to where Job lay, to inquire how he felt, and found him lying very quiet, though his breathing had a heavy touch about it. However, we could conceive of nothing by which he might be bettered, and so left him, being more hopeful that Nature would bring him to health than any skill of which we were possessed.

By this time it was late afternoon, so that the bo'sun declared we might please ourselves until sunset, deeming that we had earned a very good right to rest; but that from sunset till the dawn we should, he told us, have each of us to take turn and turn about to watch; for though we were no longer upon the water, none might say whether we were out of danger or not, as witness the happening of the morning; though, certainly, he apprehended no danger from the devil-fish so long as we kept well away from the water's edge.

And so from now until dark most of the men slept; but the bo'sun spent much of that time in overhauling the boat, to see how it might chance to have suffered during the storm, and also whether the struggles of the devil-fish had strained it in any way. And, indeed, it was speedily evident that the boat would need some attention; for the plank in her bottom next but one to the keel, upon the starboard side, had been burst inwards; this having been done, it would seem, by some rock in the beach hidden just beneath the water's edge, the devil-fish having, no doubt, ground the boat down upon it. Happily, the damage was not great; though it would most certainly have to be carefully repaired before the boat would be again seaworthy. For the rest, there seemed to be no other part needing attention.

Now I had not felt any call to sleep, and so had followed the bo'sun to the boat, giving him a hand to remove the bottom-boards, and finally to slue her bottom a little upwards, so that he might examine the leak more closely. When he had made an end with the boat, he went over to the stores, and looked closely into their condition, and also to see how they were lasting. And, after that, he sounded all the water-breakers; having done which, he remarked that it would be well for us if we could discover any fresh water upon the island.

By this time it was getting on towards evening, and the bo'sun went across to look at Job, finding him much as he had been when we visited him after dinner. At that, the bo'sun asked me to bring across one of the longer of the bottom-boards, which I did, and we made use of it as a stretcher to carry the lad into the tent. And afterwards, we carried all the loose woodwork of the boat into the tent, emptying the lockers of their contents, which included some oakum, a small boat's hatchet, a coil of one-and-a-half-inch hemp line, a good saw, an empty, colza-oil tin, a bag of copper nails, some bolts and washers, two fishing-lines, three spare tholes, a three-pronged grain without the shaft, two balls of spun yarn, three hanks of roping-twine, a piece of canvas with four roping-needles stuck in it, the boat's lamp, a spare plug, and a roll of light duck for making boat's sails.

And so, presently, the dark came down upon the island, at which had bo'sun waked the men, and bade them throw more fuel on to the fire, which had burned down to a mound of glowing embers much shrouded in ash. After that, one of them part filled the boiler with fresh water, and soon we were occupied most pleasantly upon a supper of cold, boiled salt-meat, hard biscuits, and rum mixed with hot water. During supper, the bo'sun made clear to the men regarding the watches, arranging how they should follow, so that I found I was set down to take my turn from midnight until one of the clock. Then, he explained to them about the burst plank in the bottom of the boat, and how that it would have to be put right before we could hope to leave the island, and that after that night we should have to go most strictly with the victuals; for there seemed to be nothing upon the island, that we had up till then discovered, fit to satisfy our bellies. More than this, if we could find no fresh water, he should have to distil some to make up for that which we had drunk, and this must be done before leaving the island.

Now by the time that the bo'sun had made an end of explaining these matters, we had ceased from eating, and soon after this we made each one of us a comfortable place in the sand within the tent, and lay down to sleep. For a while, I found myself very wakeful, which may have been because of the warmth of the night, and, indeed, at last, I got up and went out of the tent, conceiving that I might the better find sleep in the open air. And so it proved; for, having lain down at the side of the tent, a little way from the fire, I fell soon into a deep slumber, which at first was dreamless. Presently, however, I came upon a very strange and unsettling dream; for I dreamed that I had been left alone on the island, and was sitting very desolate upon the edge of the brown-scummed pit. Then I was aware suddenly that it was very dark and very silent, and I began to shiver; for it seemed to me that something which repulsed my whole being had come quietly behind me. At that I tried mightily to turn and look into the shadows among the great fungi that stood all about me; but I had no power to turn. And the thing was coming nearer, though never a sound came to me, and I gave out a scream, or tried to; but my voice made no stir in the rounding quiet; and then something wet and cold touched my face, and slithered down and covered my mouth, and paused there for a vile, breathless moment. It passed onward and fell to my throat—and stayed there. . . .

Some one stumbled and fell over my feet, and at that, I was suddenly awake. It was the man on watch taking a walk round the back of the tent, and he had not known of my presence till he fell over my boots. He was somewhat shaken and startled, as might be supposed; but steadied himself on learning that it was no wild creature crouched there in the shadow; and all the time, as I answered his inquiries, I was full of a strange, horrid feeling that something had left me at the moment of my awakening. There was a slight, hateful odour in my nostrils that was not altogether unfamiliar, and then, suddenly, I was aware that my face was damp and that there was a curious sense of tingling at my throat. I put up my hand and felt my face, and the hand when I brought it away was slippery with slime, and at that, I put up my other hand, and touched my throat, and there it was the same, only, in addition, there was a slight swelled place a little to one side of the wind-pipe, the sort of place that the bite of a mosquito will make; but I had no thought to blame any mosquito.

Now the stumbling of the man over me, my awakening, and the discovery that my face and throat were be-slimed, were but the happenings of some few, short instants; and then I was upon my feet, and following him round to the fire; for I had a sense of chilliness and a great desire not to be alone. Now, having come to the fire, I took some of the water that had been left in the boiler, and washed my face and neck, after which I felt more my own man. Then I asked the man to look at my throat, so that he might give me some idea of what manner of place the swelling seemed, and he, lighting a piece of the dry seaweed to act as a torch, made examination of my neck; but could see little, save a number of small ring-like marks, red inwardly, and white at the edges, and one of them was bleeding slightly. After that, I asked him whether he had seen anything moving round the tent; but he had seen nothing during all the time that he had been on watch; though it was true that he had heard odd noises; but nothing very near at hand. Of the places on my throat he seemed to think but little, suggesting that I had been bitten by some sort of sand-fly; but at that, I shook my head, and told him of my dream, and after that, he was as anxious to keep near me as I to him. And so the night passed onward, until my turn came to watch.

For a little while, the man whom I had relieved sat beside me; having, I conceived, the kindly intent of keeping me company; but so soon as I perceived this, I entreated him to go and get his sleep, assuring him that I had no longer any feelings of fear—such as had been mine upon awakening and discovering the state of my face and throat—; and, upon this, he consented to leave me, and so, in a little, I sat alone beside the fire.

For a certain space, I kept very quiet, listening; but no sound came to me out of the surrounding darkness, and so, as though it were a fresh thing, it was borne in upon me how that we were in a very abominable place of lonesomeness and desolation. And I grew very solemn.

Thus as I sat, the fire, which had not been replenished for a while, dwindled steadily until it gave but a dullish glow around. And then, in the direction of the valley, I heard suddenly the sound of a dull thud, the noise coming to me through the stillness with a very startling clearness. At that, I perceived that I was not doing my duty to the rest, nor to myself, by sitting and allowing the fire to cease from flaming; and immediately reproaching myself, I seized and cast a mass of the dry weed upon the fire, so that a great blaze shot up into the night, and afterwards I glanced quickly to right and to left, holding my cut-and-thrust very readily, and most thankful to the Almighty that I had brought no harm to any by reason of my carelessness, which I incline me to believe was that strange inertia which is bred by fear. And then, even as I looked about me, there came to me across the silence of the beach a fresh noise, a continual soft slithering to and fro in the bottom of the valley, as though a multitude of creatures moved stealthily. At this, I threw yet more fuel upon the fire, and after that I fixed my gaze in the direction of the valley: thus in the following instant it seemed to me that I saw a certain thing, as it might be a shadow, move on the outer borders of the firelight. Now the man who had kept watch before me had left his spear stuck upright in the sand convenient to my grasp, and, seeing something moving, I seized the weapon and hurled it with all my strength in its direction; but there came no answering cry to tell that I had struck anything living, and immediately afterwards there fell once more a great silence upon the island, being broken only by a far splash out upon the weed.

It may be conceived with truth that the above happenings had put a very considerable strain upon my nerves, so that I looked to and fro continually, with ever and anon a quick glance behind me; for it seemed to me that I might expect some demoniac creature to rush upon me at any moment. Yet, for the space of many minutes, there came to me neither any sight nor sound of living creature; so that I knew not what to think, being near to doubting if I had heard aught beyond the common.

And then, even as I made halt upon the threshold of doubt, I was assured that I had not been mistaken; for, abruptly, I was aware that all the valley was full of a rustling, scampering sort of noise, through which there came to me occasional soft thuds, and anon the former slithering sounds. And at that, thinking a host of evil things to be upon us, I cried out to the bo'sun and the men to awake.

Immediately upon my shout, the bo'sun rushed out from the tent, the men following, and every one with his weapon, save the man who had left his spear in the sand, and that lay now somewhere beyond the light of the fire. Then the bo'sun shouted, to know what thing had caused me to cry out; but I replied nothing, only held up my hand for quietness, yet when this was granted, the noises in the valley had ceased; so that the bo'sun turned to me, being in need of some explanation; but I begged him to hark a little longer, which he did, and, the sounds re-commencing almost immediately, he heard sufficient to know that I had not waked them all without due cause. And then, as we stood each one of us staring into the darkness where lay the valley, I seemed to see again some shadowy thing upon the boundary of the firelight; and, in the same instant, one of the men cried out and cast his spear into the darkness. But the bo'sun turned upon him with a very great anger; for in throwing his weapon, the man had left himself without, and thus brought danger to the whole; yet, as will be remembered, I had done likewise but a little since.

Presently, there coming again a quietness within the valley, and none knowing what might be toward, the bo'sun caught up a mass of the dry weed, and, lighting it at the fire, ran with it towards that portion of the beach which lay between us and the valley. Here he cast it upon the sand, singing out to some of the men to bring more of the weed, so that we might have a fire there, and thus be able to see if anything made to come at us out of the deepness of the hollow.

Presently, we had a very good fire, and by the light of this the two spears were discovered, both of them stuck in the sand, and no more than a yard one from the other, which seemed to me a very strange thing.

Now, for a while after the lighting of the second fire, there came no further sounds from the direction of the valley; nothing indeed to break the quietness of the island, save the occasional lonely splashes that sounded from time to time out in the vastness of the weed-continent. Then, about an hour after I had waked the bo'sun, one of the men who had been tending the fires came up to him to say that we had come to the end of our supply of weed-fuel. At that, the bo'sun looked very blank, the which did the rest of us, as well we might; yet there was no help for it, until one of the men bethought him of the remainder of the faggot of reeds which we had cut, and which, burning but poorly, we had discarded for the weed. This was discovered at the back of the tent, and with it we fed the fire that burned between us and the valley; but the other we suffered to die out, for the reeds were not sufficient to support even the one until the dawn.

At last, and whilst it was still dark, we came to the end of our fuel, and as the fire died down, so did the noises in the valley re-commence. And there we stood in the growing dark, each one keeping a very ready weapon, and a more ready glance. And at times the island would be mightily quiet, and then again the sounds of things crawling in the valley. Yet, I think the silences tried us the more.

And so at last came the dawn.

IX
What Happened in the Dusk

Now with the coming of the dawn, a lasting silence stole across the island and into the valley, and, conceiving that we had nothing more to fear, the bo'sun bade us get some rest, whilst he kept watch. And so I got at last a very substantial little spell of sleep, which made me fit enough for the day's work.

Presently, after some hours had passed, the bo'sun roused us to go with him to the further side of the island to gather fuel, and soon we were back with each a load, so that in a little we had the fire going right merrily.

Now for breakfast, we had a hash of broken biscuit, salt meat and some shellfish which the bo'sun had picked up from the beach at the foot of the further hill; the whole being right liberally flavoured with some of the vinegar, which the bo'sun said would help keep down any scurvy that might be threatening us. And at the end of the meal he served out to us each a little of the molasses, which we mixed with hot water, and drank.

The meal being ended, he went into the tent to take a look at Job, the which he had done already in the early morning; for the condition of the lad preyed somewhat upon him; he being, for all his size and top-roughness, a man of surprisingly tender heart. Yet the boy remained much as on the previous evening, so that we knew not what to do with him to bring him into better health. One thing we tried, knowing that no food had passed his lips since the previous morning, and that was to get some little quantity of hot water, rum, and molasses down his throat; for it seemed to us he might die from very lack of food; but though we worked with him for more than the half of an hour, we could not get him to come-to sufficiently to take anything, and without that we had fear of suffocating him. And so, presently, we had perforce to leave him within the tent, and go about our business; for there was very much to be done.

Yet, before we did aught else, the bo'sun led us all into the valley, being determined to make a very thorough exploration of it, perchance there might be any lurking beast or devil-thing waiting to rush out and destroy us as we worked, and more, he would make search that he might discover what manner of creatures had disturbed our night.

Now in the early morning, when we had gone for the fuel, we had kept to the upper skirt of the valley where the rock of the nearer hill came down into the spongy ground; but now we struck right down into the middle part of the vale, making a way amid the mighty fungi to the pit-like opening that filled the bottom of the valley. Now though the ground was very soft, there was in it so much of springiness that it left no trace of our steps after we had gone on a little way, none, that is, save that in odd places, a wet patch followed upon our treading. Then, when we got ourselves near to the pit, the ground became softer, so that our feet sank into it, and left very real impressions; and here we found tracks most curious and bewildering; for amid the slush which edged the pit—which I would mention here had less the look of a pit now that I had come near to it—were multitudes of markings which I can liken to nothing so much as the tracks of mighty slugs amid the mud, only that they were not altogether like to that of slugs'; for there were other markings such as might have been made by bunches of eels cast down and picked up continually, at least, this is what they suggested to me, and I do but put it down as such.

Apart from the markings which I have mentioned, there was everywhere a deal of slime, and this we traced all over the valley among the great toadstool plants; but, beyond that which I have already remarked, we found nothing. Nay, but I was near to forgetting, we found a quantity of this thin slime upon those fungi which filled the end of the little valley nearest to our encampment, and here also we discovered many of them fresh broken or uprooted, and there was the same mark of the beast upon them all, and now I remember the dull thuds that I had heard in the night, and made little doubt but that the creatures had climbed the great toad-stools so that they might spy us out; and it may be that many climbed upon one, so that their weight broke the fungi, or uprooted them. At least, so the thought came to me.

And so we made an end of our search, and after that, the bo'sun set each one of us to work. But first he had us all back to the beach to give a hand to turn over the boat, so that he might get to the damaged part. Now, having the bottom of the boat full to his view, he made discovery that there was other damage beside that of the burst plank; for the bottom plank of all had come away from the keel, which seemed to us a very serious matter; though it did not show when the boat was upon her bilges. Yet the bo'sun assured us that he had no doubts but that she could be made seaworthy; though it would take a greater while than hitherto he had thought needful.

Having concluded his examination of the boat, the bo'sun sent one of the men to bring the bottom-boards out of the tent; for he needed some planking for the repair of the damage. Yet when the boards had been brought, he needed still something which they could not supply, and this was a length of very sound wood of some three inches in breadth each way, which he intended to bolt against the starboard side of the keel, after he had gotten the planking replaced so far as was possible. He had hopes that by means of this device he would be able to nail the bottom plank to this, and then caulk it with oakum, so making the boat almost so sound as ever.

Now hearing him express his need for such a piece of timber, we were all adrift to know from whence such a thing could be gotten, until there came suddenly to me a memory of the mast and topmast upon the other side of the island, and at once I made mention of them. At that, the bo'sun nodded, saying that we might get the timber out of it, though it would be a work requiring some considerable labour, in that we had only a hand-saw and a small hatchet. Then he sent us across to be getting it clear of the weed, promising to follow when he had made an end of trying to get the two displaced planks back into position.

Having reached the spars, we set-to with a very good will to shift away the weed and wrack that was piled over them, and very much entangled with the rigging. Presently we had laid them bare, and so we discovered them to be in remarkably sound condition, the lowermast especially being a fine piece of timber. All the lower and topmast standing rigging was still attached, though in places the lower rigging was stranded so far as half way up the shrouds; yet there remained much that was good and all of it quite free from rot, and of the very finest quality of white hemp, such as is to be seen only in the best found vessels.

About the time that we had finished clearing the weed, the bo'sun came over to us, bringing with him the saw and the hatchet. Under his directions, we cut the lanyards of the topmast rigging, and after that sawed through the topmast just above the cap. Now this was a very tough piece of work, and employed us a great part of the morning, even though we took turn and turn at the saw, and when it was done we were mightily glad that the bo'sun bade one of the men go over with some weed and make up the fire for dinner, after which he was to put on a piece of the salt meat to boil.

In the meanwhile, the bo'sun had started to cut through the topmast, about fifteen feet beyond the first cut, for that was the length of the batten he required; yet so wearisome was the work, that we had not gotten more than half through with it before the man whom the bo'sun had sent, returned to say that the dinner was ready. When this was dispatched, and we had rested a little over our pipes, the bo'sun rose and led us back; for he was determined to get through with the topmast before dark.

Presently, relieving each other frequently, we completed the second cut, and after that the bo'sun set us to saw a block about twelve inches deep from the remaining portion of the topmast. From this, when we had cut it, he proceeded to hew wedges with the hatchet. Then he notched the end of the fifteen-foot log, and into the notch he drove the wedges, and so, towards evening, as much, maybe, by good luck as good management, he had divided the log into two halves—the split running very fairly down the centre.

Now, perceiving how that it drew near to sundown, he bade the men haste and gather weed and carry it across to our camp; but one he sent along the shore to make a search for shell-fish among the weed; yet he himself ceased not to work at the divided log, and kept me with him as helper. Thus, within the next hour, we had a length, maybe some four inches in diameter, split off the whole length of one of the halves, and with this he was very well content; though it seemed but a very little result for so much labour.

By this time the dusk was upon us, and the men, having made an end of weed carrying, were returned to us, and stood about, waiting for the bo'sun to go into camp. At this moment, the man the bo'sun had sent to gather shell-fish, returned, and he had a great crab upon his spear, which he had spitted through the belly. This creature could not have been less than a foot across the back, and had a very formidable appearance; yet it proved to be a most tasty matter for our supper, when it had been placed for a while in boiling water.

Now so soon as this man was returned, we made at once for the camp, carrying with us the piece of timber which we had hewn from the top-mast. By this time it was quite dusk, and very strange amid the great fungi as we struck across the upper edge of the valley to the opposite beach. Particularly, I noticed that the hateful, mouldy odour of these monstrous vegetables was more offensive than I had found it to be in the daytime; though this may be because I used my nose the more, in that I could not use my eyes to any great extent.

We had gotten half way across the top of the valley, and the gloom was deepening steadily, when there stole to me upon the calmness of the eve-ning air, a faint smell; something quite different from that of the sur-rounding fungi. A moment later I got a great whiff of it, and was near sickened with the abomination of it; but the memory of that foul thing which had come to the side of the boat in the dawn-gloom, before we discovered the island, roused me to a terror beyond that of the sickness of my stomach; for, suddenly, I knew what manner of thing it was that had beslimed my face and throat upon the previous night, and left its hideous stench lingering in my nostrils. And with the knowledge, I cried out to the bo'sun to make haste, for there were demons with us in the valley. And at that, some of the men made to run; but he bade them, in a very grim voice, stay where they were, and keep well together, else would they be attacked and overcome, straggled all among the fungi in the dark. And this, being, I doubt not, as much in fear of the rounding dark as of the bo'sun, they did, and so we came safely out of the valley; though there seemed to follow us a little lower down the slope an uncanny slithering.

Now, so soon as we reached the camp, the bo'sun ordered four fires to be lit—one on each side of the tent, and this we did, lighting them at the embers of our old fire, which we had most foolishly allowed to die down. When the fires had been got going, we put on the boiler, and treated the great crab as I have already mentioned, and so fell-to upon a very hearty supper; but, as we ate, each man had his weapon stuck in the sand beside him; for we had knowledge that the valley held some devilish thing, or maybe many; though the knowing did not spoil our appetites.

And so, presently, we came to an end of eating, whereat each man pulled out his pipe, intending to smoke; but the bo'sun told one of the men to get him upon his feet and keep watch, else might we be in danger of surprise, with every man lolling upon the sand; and this seemed to me very good sense; for it was easy to see that the men, too readily, deemed themselves secure, by reason of the brightness of the fires about them.

Now whilst the men were taking their ease within the circle of the fires, the bo'sun lit one of the dips which we had out of the ship in the creek, and went in to see how Job was, after the day's rest. At that, I rose up, reproaching myself for having forgotten the poor lad, and followed the bo'sun into the tent. Yet, I had but reached the opening, when he gave out a loud cry, and held the candle low down to the sand. At that, I saw the reason for his agitation; for, in the place where we had left Job, there was nothing. I stepped into the tent, and, in the same instant, there came to my nostrils the faint odour of the horrible stench which had come to me in the valley, and before then from the thing that came to the side of the boat. And, suddenly, I knew that Job had fallen prey of those foul things, and, knowing this, I called out to the bo'sun that *they* had taken the boy, and then my eyes caught the smear of slime upon the sand, and I had proof that I was not mistaken.

Now, so soon as the bo'sun knew all that was in my mind; though indeed it did but corroborate that which had come to his own, he came swiftly out from the tent, bidding the men to stand back; for they had come all about the entrance, being very much discomposed at that which the bo'sun had discovered. Then the bo'sun took from a faggot of the reeds, which they had cut at the time when he had bidden them gather fuel, several of the thickest, and to one of these he bound a great mass of the dry weed; whereupon the men, divining his intention, did likewise with the others, and so we had each of us the wherewithal for a mighty torch.

So soon as we had completed our preparations, we took each man his weapon, and, plunging our torches into the fires, set off along the track which had been made by the devil-things and the body of poor Job; for now that we had suspicion that harm had come to him, the marks in the sand, and the slime, were very plain to be seen, so that it was wonderful that we had not discovered them earlier.

Now the bo'sun led the way, and, finding the marks lead direct to the valley, he broke into a run, holding his torch well above his head. At that, each of us did likewise; for we had a great desire to be together, and further than this, I think with truth I may say, we were all fierce to avenge Job, so that we had less of fear in our hearts than otherwise had been the case.

In less than the half of a minute we had reached the end of the valley; but here, the ground being of a nature not happy in the revealing of tracks, we were at fault to know in which direction to continue. At that, the bo'sun set up a loud shout to Job, perchance he might be yet alive; but there came no answer to us, save a low and uncomfortable echo. Then the bo'sun, desiring to waste no more time, ran straight down towards the centre of the valley, and we followed, and kept our eyes very open about us. We had gotten perhaps half way, when one of the men shouted that he saw something ahead; but the bo'sun had seen it earlier; for he was running straight down upon it, holding his torch high and swinging his great cutlass. Then, instead of smiting, he fell upon his knees beside it, and the following instant we were up with him, and in that same moment it seemed to me that I saw a number of white shapes melt swiftly into the shadows further ahead; but I had no thought for these when I perceived that by which the bo'sun knelt; for it was the stark body of Job, and no inch of it but was covered with the little ringed marks that I had discovered upon my throat, and from every place there ran a trickle of blood, so that he was a most horrid and fearsome sight.

At the sight of Job so mangled and be-bled, there came over us the sudden quiet of a mortal terror, and in that space of silence, the bo'sun placed his hand over the poor lad's heart; but there was no movement, though the body was still warm. Immediately upon that, he rose to his feet, a look of vast wrath upon his great face. He plucked his torch from the ground, into which he had plunged the haft, and stared round into the silence of the valley; but there was no living thing in sight, nothing save the giant fungi and the strange shadows cast by our great torches, and the loneliness.

At this moment, one of the men's torches, having burnt near out, fell all to pieces, so that he held nothing but the charred support, and immediately two more came to a like end. Upon this, we became afraid that they would not last us back to the camp, and we looked to the bo'sun to know his wish; but the man was very silent, and peering everywhere into the shadows. Then a fourth torch fell to the ground in a shower of embers, and I turned to look. In the same instant there came a great flare of light behind me, accompanied by the dull thud of a dry matter set suddenly alight. I glanced swiftly back to the bo'sun, and he was staring up at one of the giant toadstools which was in flames all along its nearer edge, and burning with an incredible fury, sending out spirits of flame, and anon giving out sharp reports, and at each report a fine powder was belched in thin streams; which, getting into our throats and nostrils, set us sneezing and coughing most lamentably; so that I am convinced, had any enemy come upon us at that moment, we had been undone by reason of our uncouth helplessness.

Now whether it had come to the bo'sun to set alight this first of the fungi, I know not; for it may be that his torch coming by chance against it, set it afire. However it chanced, the bo'sun took it as a veritable hint from Providence, and was already setting his torch to one a little further off, whilst the rest of us were near to choking with our coughings and sneezings. Yet, for all that we were so suddenly overcome by the potency of the powder, I doubt if a full minute passed before we were each one busied after the manner of the bo'sun; and those whose torches had burned out, knocked flaming pieces from the burning fungus, and with these impaled upon their torch-sticks, did so much execution as any.

And this it happened that within five minutes of the discovery of Job's body, the whole of that hideous valley sent up to heaven the reek of its burning; whilst we, filled with murderous desires, ran hither and thither with our weapons, seeking to destroy the vile creatures that had brought the poor lad to so unholy a death. Yet nowhere could we discover any brute or creature upon which to ease our vengeance, and so, presently, the valley becoming impassable by reason of the heat, the flying sparks and the abundance of the acrid dust, we made back to the body of the boy, and bore him thence to the shore.

And during all that night no man of us slept, and the burning of the fungi sent up a mighty pillar of flame out of the valley, as out of the mouth of a monstrous pit; and when the morning came it still burned. Then when it was daylight, some of us slept, being greatly awearied; but some kept watch.

And when we waked there was a great wind and rain upon the island.

X
The Light in the Weed

Now the wind was very violent from the sea, and threatened to blow down our tent, the which, indeed, it achieved at last as we made an end of a cheerless breakfast. Yet, the bo'sun bade us not trouble to put it up again; but spread it out with the edges raised upon props made from the reeds, so that we might catch some of the rain water; for it was become imperative that we should renew our supply before putting out again to sea. And whilst some of us were busied about this, he took the others and set up a small tent made of the spare canvas, and under this he sheltered all of our matters like to be harmed by the rain.

In a little, the rain continuing very violent, we had near a breaker-full of water collected in the canvas, and were about to run it off into one of the breakers, when the bo'sun cried out to us to hold, and first taste the water before we mixed it with that which we had already. At that, we put down our hands and scooped up some of the water to taste, and thus we discovered it to be brackish and quite undrinkable, at which I was amazed, until the bo'sun reminded us that the canvas had been saturated for many days with salt water, so that it would take a great quantity of fresh before all the salt was washed out. Then he told us to lay it flat upon the beach, and scour it well on both sides with the sand, which we did, and afterwards let the rain rinse it well, whereupon the next water that we caught we found to be near fresh; though not sufficiently so for our purpose. Yet when we had rinsed it once more, it became clear of the salt, so that we were able to keep all that we caught further.

And then, something before noon, the rain ceased to fall, though coming again at odd times in short squalls; yet the wind died not, but blew steadily, and continued so from that quarter during the remainder of the time that we were upon the island.

Upon the ceasing of the rain, the bo'sun called us all together, that we might make a decent burial of the unfortunate lad, whose remains had lain during the night upon one of the bottom-boards of the boat. After a little discussion, it was decided to bury him in the beach; for the only part where there was soft earth was in the valley, and none of us had a stomach for that place. Moreover, the sand was soft and easy to dig, and as we had no proper tools, this was a great consideration. Presently, using the bottom-boards and the oars and the hatchet, we had a place large and deep enough to hold the boy, and into this we placed him. We made no prayer over him; but stood about the grave for a little space, in silence. Then, the bo'sun signed to us to fill in the sand; and, therewith, we covered up the poor lad, and left him to his sleep.

And, presently, we made our dinner; after which the bo'sun served out to each one of us a very sound tot of the rum; for he was minded to bring us back again to a cheerful state of mind.

After we had sat awhile, smoking, the bo'sun divided us into two parties to make a search through the island among the rocks, perchance we should find water, collected from the rain, among the hollows and crevasses; for though we had gotten some, through our device with the sail, yet we had by no means caught sufficient for our needs. He was especially anxious for haste, in that the sun had come out again; for he was feared that such small pools as we should find would be speedily dried up by its heat.

Now the bo'sun headed one party, and set the big seaman over the other, bidding all to keep their weapons very handy. Then he set out to the rocks about the base of the nearer hill, sending the others to the farther and greater one, and in each party we carried an empty breaker slung from a couple of the stout reeds, so that we might put all such driblets as we should find, straight away into it, before they had time to vanish into the hot air; and for the purpose of bailing up the water, we had brought with us our tin pannikins, and one of the boat's bailers.

In a while, and after much scrambling amid the rocks, we came upon a little pool of water that was remarkably sweet and fresh, and from this we removed near three gallons before it became dry; and after that we came across, maybe, five or six others; but not one of them near so big as the first; yet we were not displeased; for we had near three parts filled the breaker, and so we made back to the camp, having some wonder as to the luck of the other party.

When we came near to the camp, we found the others returned before us, and seeming in a very high content with themselves; so that we had no need to call to them as to whether they had filled their breaker. When they saw us, they set out to us at a run to tell us that they had come upon a great basin of fresh water in a deep hollow a third of the distance up the side of the far hill, and at this the bo'sun bade us put down our breaker and make all of us to the hill, so that he might examine for himself whether their news was so good as it seemed.

Presently, being guided by the other party, we passed around to the back of the far hill, and discovered it to go upward to the top at an easy slope, with many ledges and broken places, so that it was scarce more difficult than a stair to climb. And so, having climbed perhaps ninety or a hundred feet, we came suddenly upon the place which held the water, and found that they had not made too much of their discovery; for the pool was near twenty feet long by twelve broad, and so clear as though it had come from a fountain; yet it had considerable depth, as we discovered by thrusting a spear shaft down into it.

Now the bo'sun, having seen for himself how good a supply of water there was for our needs, seemed very much relieved in his mind, and declared that within three days at the most we might leave the island, at which we felt none of us any regret. Indeed, had the boat escaped harm, we had been able to leave that same day; but this could not be; for there was much to be done before we had her seaworthy again.

Having waited until the bo'sun had made complete his examination, we turned to descend, thinking that this would be the bo'sun's intention; but he called to us to stay, and, looking back, we saw that he made to finish the ascent of the hill. At that, we hastened to follow him; though we had no notion of his reason for going higher. Presently, we were come to the top, and here we found a very spacious place, nicely level save that in one or two parts it was crossed by deepish cracks, maybe half a foot to a foot wide, and perhaps three to six fathoms long; but, apart from these and some great boulders, it was, as I have mentioned, a spacious place; moreover it was bone dry and pleasantly firm under one's feet, after so long upon the sand.

I think, even thus early, I had some notion of the bo'sun's design; for I went to the edge that overlooked the valley, and peered down, and, finding it nigh a sheer precipice, found myself nodding my head, as though it were in accordance with some part formed wish. Presently, looking about me, I discovered the bo'sun to be surveying that part which looked over towards the weed, and I made across to join him. Here, again, I saw that the hill fell away very sheer, and after that we went across to the seaward edge, and there it was near as abrupt as on the weed side.

Then, having by this time thought a little upon the matter, I put it straight to the bo'sun that here would make indeed a very secure camping place, with nothing to come at us upon our sides or back; and our front, where was the slope, could be watched with ease. And this I put to him with great warmth; for I was mortally in dread of the coming night.

Now when I had made an end of speaking, the bo'sun disclosed to me that this was, as I had suspicioned, his intent, and immediately he called to the men that we should haste down, and ship our camp to the top of the hill. At that, the men expressed their approbation, and we made haste every one of us to the camp, and began straightway to move our gear to the hill-top.

In the meanwhile, the bo'sun, taking me to assist him, set-to again upon the boat, being intent to get his batten nicely shaped and fit to the side of the keel, so that it would bed well to the keel, but more particularly to the plank which had sprung outward from its place. And at this he laboured the greater part of that afternoon, using the little hatchet to shape the wood, which he did with surprising skill; yet when the evening was come, he had not brought it to his liking. But it must not be thought that he did naught but work at the boat; for he had the men to direct, and once he had to make his way to the top of the hill to fix the place for the tent. And after the tent was up, he set them to carry the dry weed to the new camp, and at this he kept them until near dusk; for he had vowed never again to be without a sufficiency of fuel. But two of the men he sent to collect shell-fish—putting two of them to the task, because he would not have one alone upon the island, not knowing but that there might be danger, even though it were bright day; and a most happy ruling it proved; for, a little past the middle of the afternoon, we heard them shouting at the other end of the valley, and, not knowing but that they were in need of assistance, we ran with all haste to discover the reason of their calling, passing along the right-hand side of the blackened and sodden vale. Upon reaching the further beach, we saw a most incredible sight; for the two men were running towards us through the thick masses of the weed, while, no more than four or five fathoms behind, they were pursued by an enormous crab. Now I had thought the crab we had tried to capture before coming to the island, a prodigy unsurpassed; but this creature was more than treble its size, seeming as though a prodigious table were a-chase of them, and moreover, spite of its monstrous bulk, it made better way over the weed than I should have conceived to be possible—running almost sideways, and with one enormous claw raised near a dozen feet into the air.

Now whether, omitting accidents, the men would have made good their escape to the firmer ground of the valley, where they could have attained to a greater speed, I do not know; but suddenly one of them tripped over a loop of the weed, and the next instant lay helpless upon his face. He had been dead the following moment, but for the pluck of his companion, who faced round manfully upon the monster, and ran at it with his twenty-foot spear. It seemed to me that the spear took it about a foot below the overhanging armour of the great back shell, and I could see that it penetrated some distance into the creature, the man having, by the aid of Providence, stricken it in a vulnerable part. Upon receiving this thrust, the mighty crab ceased at once its pursuit, and clipped at the haft of the spear with its great mandible, snapping the weapon more easily than I had done the same thing to a straw. By the time we had raced up to the men, the one who had stumbled was again upon his feet, and turning to assist his comrade; but the bo'sun snatched his spear from him, and leapt forward himself; for the crab was making now at the other man. Now the bo'sun did not attempt to thrust the spear into the monster; but instead he made two swift blows at the great protruding eyes, and in a moment the creature had curled itself up, helpless, save that the huge claw wavered about aimlessly. At that, the bo'sun drew us off; though the man who had attacked the crab desired to make an end of it, averring that we should get some very good eating out of it; but to this the bo'sun would not listen, telling him that it was yet capable of very deadly mischief, did any but come within reach of its prodigious mandible.

And after this, he bade them look no more for shell-fish; but take out the two fishing-lines which we had, and see if they could catch aught from some safe ledge on the further side of the hill upon which we had made our camp. Then he returned to his mending of the boat.

It was a little before the evening came down upon the island, that the bo'sun ceased work; and, after that, he called to the men, who, having made an end of their fuel carrying, were standing near, to place the full breakers—which we had not thought needful to carry to the new camp on account of their weight—under the upturned boat, some holding up the gunnel whilst the others pushed them under. Then the bo'sun laid the unfinished batten along with them, and we lowered the boat again over all, trusting to its weight to prevent any creature from meddling with aught.

After that, we made at once to the camp, being wearifully tired, and with a hearty anticipation of supper. Upon reaching the hill-top, the men whom the bo'sun had sent with the lines, came to show him a very fine fish, something like to a huge king-fish, which they had caught a few minutes earlier. This, the bo'sun, after examining, did not hesitate to pronounce fit for food; whereupon they set-to and opened and cleaned it. Now, as I have said, it was not unlike a great king-fish, and like it, had a mouth full of very formidable teeth; the use of which I understood the better when I saw the contents of its stomach, which seemed to consist of nothing but the coiled tentacles of squid or cuttle-fish, with which, as I have shown, the weed-continent swarmed. When these were upset upon the rock, I was confounded to perceive the length and thickness of some of them; and could only conceive that this particular fish must be a very desperate enemy to them, and able successfully to attack monsters of a bulk infinitely greater than its own.

After this, and whilst the supper was preparing, the bo'sun called to some of the men to put up a piece of the spare canvas upon a couple of the reeds, so as to make a screen against the wind, which up there was so fresh that it came near at times to scattering the fire abroad. This they found not difficult; for a little on the windward side of the fire there ran one of the cracks of which I have made previous mention, and into this they jammed the supports, and so in a very little time had the fire screened.

Presently, the supper was ready, and I found the fish to be very fair eating; though somewhat coarse; but this was no great matter for concern with so empty a stomach as I contained. And here I would remark, that we made our fishing save our provisions through all our stay on the island. Then, after we had come to an end of our eating, we lay down to a most comfortable smoke; for we had no fear of attack, at that height, and with precipices upon all sides save that which lay in front. Yet, so soon as we had rested and smoked a while, the bo'sun set the watches; for he would run no risk through carelessness.

By this time the night was drawing on apace; yet it was not so dark but that one could perceive matters at a very reasonable distance. Presently, being in a mood that tended to thoughtfulness, and feeling a desire to be alone for a little, I strolled away from the fire to the leeward edge of the hill-top. Here, I paced up and down awhile, smoking and meditating. Anon, I would stare out across the immensity of the vast continent of weed and slime that stretched its incredible desolation out beyond the darkening horizon, and there would come the thought to me of the terror of men whose vessels had been entangled among its strange growths, and so my thoughts came to the lone derelict that lay out there in the dusk, and I fell to wondering what had been the end of her people, and at that I grew yet more solemn in my heart. For it seemed to me that they must have died at last by starvation, and if not by that, then by the act of some one of the devil-creatures which inhabited that lonely weed-world. And then, even as I fell upon this thought, the bo'sun clapt me upon the shoulder, and told me in a very hearty way to come to the light of the fire, and banish all melancholy thoughts; for he had a very penetrating discernment, and had followed me quietly from the camping place, having had reason once or twice before to chide me for gloomy meditations. And for this, and many other matters, I had grown to like the man, the which I could almost believe at times, was his regarding of me; but his words were too few for me to gather his feelings; though I had hope that they were as I surmised.

And so I came back to the fire, and presently, it not being my time to watch until after midnight, I turned into the tent for a spell of sleep, having first arranged a comfortable spread of some of the softer portions of the dry weed to make me a bed.

Now I was very full of sleep, so that I slept heavily, and in this wise heard not the man on watch call the bo'sun; yet the rousing of the others waked me, and so I came to myself and found the tent empty, at which I ran very hurriedly to the doorway, and so discovered that there was a clear moon in the sky, the which, by reason of the cloudiness that had prevailed, we had been without for the past two nights. Moreover, the sultriness had gone, the wind having blown it away with the clouds; yet though, maybe, I appreciated this, it was but in a half-conscious manner; for I was put about to discover the whereabouts of the men, and the reason of their leaving the tent. With this purpose, I stepped out from the entrance, and the following instant discovered them all in a clump beside the leeward edge of the hill-top. At that, I held my tongue; for I knew not but that silence might be their desire; but I ran hastily over to them, and inquired of the bo'sun what manner of thing it was which called them from their sleep, and he, for answer, pointed out into the greatness of the weed-continent.

At that, I stared out over the breadth of the weed, showing very ghostly in the moonlight; but, for the moment, I saw not the thing to which he purposed to draw my attention. Then, suddenly, it fell within the circle of my gaze—a little light out in the lonesomeness. For the space of some moments, I stared with bewildered eyes; then it came to me with abruptness that the light shone from the lone derelict lying out in the weed, the same that, upon that very evening, I had looked with sorrow and awe, because of the end of those who had been in her—and now, behold, a light burning, seemingly within one of her after cabins; though the moon was scarce powerful enough to enable the outline of the hulk to be seen clear of the rounding wilderness.

And from this time, until the day, we had no more sleep; but made up the fire, and sat round it, full of excitement and wonder, and getting up continually to discover if the light still burned. This it ceased to do about an hour after I had first seen it; but it was the more proof that some of our kind were no more than the half of a mile from our camp.

And at last the day came.

XI
The Signals from the Ship

Now so soon as it was clearly light, we went all of us to the leeward brow of the hill to stare upon the derelict, which now we had cause to believe no derelict, but an inhabited vessel. Yet though we watched her for upwards of two hours, we could discover no sign of any living creature, the which, indeed, had we been in cooler minds, we had not thought strange, seeing that she was all so shut in by the great superstructure; but we were hot to see a fellow creature, after so much lonesomeness and terror in strange lands and seas, and so could not by any means contain ourselves in patience until those aboard the hulk should choose to discover themselves to us.

And so, at last, being wearied with watching, we made it up together to shout when the bo'sun should give us the signal, by this means making a good volume of sound which we conceived the wind might carry down to the vessel. Yet though we raised many shouts, making as it seemed to us a very great noise, there came no response from the ship, and at last we were fain to cease from our calling, and ponder some other way of bringing ourselves to the notice of those within the hulk.

For awhile we talked, some proposing one thing, and some another; but none of them seeming like to achieve our purpose. And after that we fell to marvelling that the fire which we had lit in the valley had not awakened them to the fact that some of their fellow creatures were upon the island; for, had it, we could not suppose but that they would have kept a perpetual watch upon the island until such time as they should have been able to attract our notice. Nay! more than this, it was scarce credible that they should not have made an answering fire, or set some of their bunting above the superstructure, so that our gaze should be arrested upon the instant we chanced to glance towards the hulk. But so far from this, there appeared even a purpose to shun our attention; for that light which we had viewed in the past night was more in the way of an accident, than of the nature of a purposeful exhibition.

And so, presently, we went to breakfast, eating heartily; our night of wakefulness having given us mighty appetites; but, for all that, we were so engrossed by the mystery of the lonesome craft, that I doubt if any of us knew what manner of food it was with which we filled our bellies. For first one view of the matter would be raised, and when this had been combated, another would be broached, and in this wise it came up finally that some of the men were falling in doubt whether the ship was inhabited by anything human, saying rather that it might be held by some demoniac creature of the great weed-continent. At this proposition, there came among us a very uncomfortable silence; for not only did it chill the warmth of our hopes; but seemed like to provide us with a fresh terror, who were already acquainted with too much. Then the bo'sun spoke, laughing with a hearty contempt at our sudden fears, and pointed out that it was just as like that they aboard the ship had been put in fear by the great blaze from the valley, as that they should take it for a sign that fellow creatures and friends were at hand. For, as he put it to us, who of us could say what fell brutes and demons the weed-continent did hold, and if we had reason to know that there were very dread things among the weed, how much the more must they, who had, for all that we knew, been many years beset around by such. And so, as he went on to make clear, we might suppose that they were very well aware there had come some creatures to the island; yet, maybe, they desired not to make themselves known until they had been given sight of them, and because of this, we must wait until they chose to discover themselves to us.

Now when the bo'sun had made an end, we felt each one of us greatly cheered; for his discourse seemed very reasonable. Yet still there were many matters that troubled our company; for, as one put it, was it not mightily strange that we had not had previous sight of their light, or, in the day, of the smoke from their galley fire? But to this the bo'sun replied that our camp hitherto had lain in a place where we had not sight, even of the great world of weed, leaving alone any view of the derelict. And more, that at such times as we had crossed to the opposite beach, we had been occupied too sincerely to have much thought to watch the hulk, which, indeed, from that position showed only her great superstructure. Further, that, until the preceding day, we had but once climbed to any height; and that from our present camp the derelict could not be viewed, and to do so, we had to go near to the leeward edge of the hill-top.

And so, breakfast being ended, we went all of us to see if there were yet any signs of life in the hulk; but when an hour had gone, we were no wiser. Therefore, it being folly to waste further time, the bo'sun left one man to watch from the brow of the hill, charging him very strictly to keep in such position that he could be seen by any aboard the silent craft, and so took the rest down to assist him in the repairing of the boat. And from thence on, during the day, he gave the men a turn each at watching, telling them to wave to him should there come any sign from the hulk. Yet, excepting the watch, he kept every man so busy as might be, some bringing weed to keep up a fire which he had lit near the boat; one to help him turn and hold the batten upon which he laboured; and two he sent across to the wreck of the mast, to detach one of the futtock shrouds, which (as is most rare) were made of iron rods. This, when they brought it, he bade me heat in the fire, and afterwards beat out straight at one end, and when this was done, he set me to burn holes with it through the keel of the boat, at such places as he had marked, these being for the bolts with which he had determined to fasten on the batten.

In the meanwhile, he continued to shape the batten until it was a very good and true fit according to his liking. And all the while he cried out to this man and to that one to do this or that; and so I perceived that, apart from the necessity of getting the boat into a seaworthy condition, he was desirous to keep the men busied; for they were become so excited at the thought of fellow creatures almost within hail, that he could not hope to keep them sufficiently in hand without some matter upon which to employ them.

Now, it must not be supposed that the bo'sun had no share of our excitement; for I noticed that he gave ever and anon a glance to the crown of the far hill, perchance the watchman had some news for us. Yet the morning went by, and no signal came to tell us that the people in the ship had design to show themselves to the man upon watch, and so we came to dinner. At this meal, as might be supposed, we had a second discussion upon the strangeness of the behaviour of those aboard the hulk; yet none could give any more reasonable explanation than the bo'sun had given in the morning, and so we left it at that.

Presently, when we had smoked and rested very comfortably, for the bo'sun was no tyrant, we rose at his bidding to descend once more to the beach. But at this moment, one of the men having run to the edge of the hill to take a short look at the hulk, cried out that a part of the great superstructure over the quarter had been removed, or pushed back, and that there was a figure there, seeming, so far as his unaided sight could tell, to be looking through a spy-glass at the island. Now it would be difficult to tell of all our excitement at this news, and we ran eagerly to see for ourselves if it could be as he informed us. And so it was; for we could see the person very clearly; though remote and small because of the distance. That he had seen us, we discovered in a moment; for he began suddenly to wave something, which I judged to be the spy-glass, in a very wild manner, seeming also to be jumping up and down. Yet, I doubt not but that we were as much excited; for suddenly I discovered myself to be shouting with the rest in a most insane fashion, and moreover I was waving my hands and running to and fro upon the brow of the hill. Then,

I observed that the figure on the hulk had disappeared; but it was for no more than a moment, and then it was back and there were near a dozen with it, and it seemed to me that some of them were females; but the distance was over great for surety. Now these, all of them, seeing us upon the brow of the hill, where we must have shown up plain against the sky, began at once to wave in a very frantic way, and we, replying in like manner, shouted ourselves hoarse with vain greetings. But soon we grew wearied of the unsatisfactoriness of this method of showing our excitement, and one took a piece of the square canvas, and let it stream out into the wind, waving it to them, and another took a second piece and did likewise, while a third man rolled up a short bit into a cone and made use of it as a speaking trumpet; though I doubt if his voice carried any the further because of it. For my part, I had seized one of the long bamboo-like reeds which were lying about near the fire, and with this I was making a very brave show. And so it may be seen how very great and genuine was our exaltation upon our discovery of these poor people shut off from the world within that lonesome craft.

Then, suddenly, it seemed to come to us to realize that *they* were among the weed, and *we* upon the hill-top, and that we had no means of bridging that which lay between. And at this we faced one another to discuss what we should do to effect the rescue of those within the hulk. Yet it was little that we could even suggest; for though one spoke of how he had seen a rope cast by means of a mortar to a ship that lay off shore, yet this helped us not, for we had no mortar; but here the same man cried out that they in the ship might have such a thing, so that they would be able to shoot the rope to us, and at this we thought more upon his saying; for if they had such a weapon, then might our difficulties be solved. Yet we were greatly at a loss to know how we should discover whether they were possessed of one, and further to explain our design to them. But here the bo'sun came to our help, and bade one man go quickly and char some of the reeds in the fire, and whilst this was doing he spread out upon the rock one of the spare lengths of canvas; then he sung out to the man to bring him one of the pieces of charred reed, and with this he wrote our question upon the canvas, calling for fresh charcoal as he required it. Then, having made an end of writing, he bade two of the men take hold of the canvas by the ends, and expose it to the view of those in the ship, and in this manner we got them to understand our desires. For, presently, some of them went away, and came back after a little, and held up for us to see, a very great square of white, and upon it a great "NO," and at this were we again at our wits' ends to know how it would be possible to rescue those within the ship; for, suddenly, our whole desire to leave the island, was changed into a determination to rescue the people in the hulk, and, indeed, had our intentions not been such we had been veritable curs; though I am happy to tell that we had no thought at this juncture but for those who were now looking to us to restore them once more to the world to which they had been so long strangers.

Now, as I have said, we were again at our wits' ends to know how to come at those within the hulk, and there we stood all of us, talking together, perchance we should hit upon some plan, and anon we would turn and wave to those who watched us so anxiously. Yet, a while passed, and we had come no nearer to a method of rescue. Then a thought came to me (waked perchance by the mention of shooting the rope over to the hulk by means of a mortar) how that I had read once in a book, of a fair maid whose lover effected her escape from a castle by a similar artifice, only that in his case he made use of a bow in place of a mortar, and a cord instead of a rope, his sweetheart hauling up the rope by means of the cord.

Now it seemed to me a possible thing to substitute a bow for the mortar, if only we could find the material with which to make such a weapon, and with this in view, I took up one of the lengths of the bamboo-like reed, and tried the spring of it, which I found to be very good; for this curious growth, of which I have spoken hitherto as a reed, had no resemblance to that plant, beyond its appearance; it being extraordinarily tough and woody, and having considerably more nature than a bamboo. Now, having tried the spring of it, I went over to the tent and cut a piece of sampson-line which I found among the gear, and with this and the reed I contrived a rough bow. Then I looked about until I came upon a very young and slender reed which had been cut with the rest, and from this I fashioned some sort of an arrow, feathering it with a piece of one of the broad, stiff leaves, which grew upon the plant, and after that I went forth to the crowd about the leeward edge of the hill. Now when they saw me thus armed, they seemed to think that I intended a jest, and some of them laughed, conceiving that it was a very odd action on my part; but when I explained that which was in my mind, they ceased from laughter, and shook their heads, making that I did but waste time; for, as they said, nothing save gunpowder could cover so great a distance. And after that they turned again to the bo'sun with whom some of them seemed to be in argument. And so for a little space I held my peace, and listened; thus I discovered that certain of the men advocated the taking of the boat—so soon as it was sufficiently repaired—and making a passage through the weed to the ship, which they proposed to do by cutting a narrow canal. But the bo'sun shook his head, and reminded them of the great devil-fish and crabs, and the worse things which the weed concealed, saying that those in the ship would have done it long since had it been

possible, and at that the men were silenced, being robbed of their unreasoning ardour by his warnings.

Now just at this point there happened a thing which proved the wisdom of that which the bo'sun contended; for, suddenly, one of the men
cried out to us to look, and at that we turned quickly, and saw that there
was a great commotion among those who were in the open place in the
superstructure; for they were running this way and that, and some were
pushing to the slide which filled the opening. And then, immediately, we
saw the reason for their agitation and haste; for there was a stir in the
weed near to the stern of the ship, and the next instant, monstrous tentacles were reached up to the place where had been the opening; but the
door was shut, and those aboard the hulk in safety. At this manifestation,
the men about me who had proposed to make use of the boat, and the
others also, cried out their horror of the vast creature, and, I am convinced, had the rescue depended upon their use of the boat, then had
those in the hulk been forever doomed.

Now, conceiving that this was a good point at which to renew my
importunities, I began once again to explain the probabilities of my plan
succeeding, addressing myself more particularly to the bo'sun. I told how
that I had read that the ancients made mighty weapons, some of which
could throw a great stone so heavy as two men, over a distance surpassing
a quarter of a mile; moreover, that they compassed huge catapults which
threw a lance, or great arrow, even further. On this, he expressed much
surprise, never having heard of the like; but doubted greatly that we
should be able to construct such a weapon. Yet, I told him that I was
prepared; for I had the plan of one clearly in my mind, and further I
pointed out to him that we had the wind in our favour, and that we were
a great height up, which would allow the arrow to travel the farther
before it came so low as the weed.

Then I stepped to the edge of the hill, and, bidding him watch, fitted
my arrow to the string, and, having bent the bow, loosed it, whereupon,
being aided by the wind and the height on which I stood, the arrow
plunged into the weed at a distance of near two hundred yards from
where we stood, that being about a quarter of the distance on the road to
the derelict. At that, the bo'sun was won over to my idea; though, as he
remarked, the arrow had fallen nearer had it been drawing a length of
yarn after it, and to this I assented; but pointed out that my bow-and-
arrow was but a rough affair, and, more, that I was no archer; yet I
promised him, with the bow that I should make, to cast a shaft clean over
the hulk, did he but give me his assistance, and bid the men to help.

Now, as I have come to regard it in the light of greater knowledge, my promise was exceeding rash; but I had faith in my conception, and was very eager to put it to the test; the which, after much discussion at supper, it was decided I should be allowed to do.

Xqq
The Making of the Great Bow

The fourth night upon the island was the first to pass without incident. It is true that a light showed from the hulk out in the weed; but now that we had made some acquaintance with her inmates, it was no longer a cause for excitement, so much as contemplation. As for the valley where the vile things had made an end of Job, it was very silent and desolate under the moonlight; for I made a point to go and view it during my time on watch; yet, for all that it lay empty, it was very dree, and a place to conjure up uncomfortable thoughts, so that I spent no great time pondering it.

This was the second night on which we had been free from the terror of the devil-things, and it seemed to me that the great fire had put them in fear of us and driven them away; but of the truth or error of this idea, I was to learn later.

Now it must be admitted that, apart from a short look into the valley, and occasional starings at the light out in the weed, I gave little attention to aught but my plans for the great bow, and to such use did I put my time, that when I was relieved, I had each particular and detail worked out, so that I knew very well just what to set the men doing so soon as we should make a start in the morning.

Presently, when the morning had come, and we had made an end of breakfast, we turned-to upon the great bow, the bo'sun directing the men under my supervision. Now, the first matter to which I bent attention, was the raising, to the top of the hill, of the remaining half of that portion of the topmast which the bo'sun had split in twain to procure the batten for the boat. To this end, we went down, all of us, to the beach where lay the wreckage, and, getting about the portion which I intended to use, carried it to the foot of the hill; then we sent a man to the top to let down the rope by which we had moored the boat to the sea anchor, and when we had bent this on securely to the piece of timber, we returned to the hill-top, and tailed on to the rope, and so, presently, after much weariful pulling, had it up.

The next thing I desired was that the split face of the timber should be dubbed straight, and this the bo'sun understood to do, and whilst he was about it, I went with some of the men to the grove of reeds, and here, with great care, I made a selection of some of the finest, these being for the bow, and after that I cut some which were very clean and straight, intending them for the great arrows. With these we returned once more to the camp, and there I set-to and trimmed them of their leaves, keeping these latter, for I had a use for them. Then I took a dozen reeds and cut them each to a length of twenty-five feet, and afterwards notched them for the strings. In the meanwhile, I had sent two men down to the wreckage of the masts to cut away a couple of the hempen shrouds and bring them to the camp, and they, appearing about this time, I set to work to unlay the shrouds, so that they might get out the fine white yarns which lay beneath the outer covering of tar and blacking. These, when they had come at them, we found to be very good and sound, and this being so, I bid them make three-yarn sennit; meaning it for the strings of the bows. Now, it will be observed that I have said bows, and this I will explain. It had been my original intention to make one great bow, lashing a dozen of the reeds together for the purpose; but this, upon pondering it, I conceived to be but a poor plan; for there would be much life and power lost in the rendering of each piece through the lashings, when the bow was released. To obviate this, and further, to compass the bending of the bow, the which had, at first, been a source of puzzlement to me as to how it was to be accomplished, I had determined to make twelve separate bows, and these I intended to fasten at the end of the stock one above the other, so that they were all in one plane vertically, and because of this conception, I should be able to bend the bows one at a time, and slip each string over the catch-notch, and afterwards frap the twelve strings together in the middle part so that they would be but one string to the butt of the arrow. All this, I explained to the bo'sun, who, indeed, had been exercised in his own mind as to how we should be able to bend such a bow as I intended to make, and he was mightily pleased with my method of evading this difficulty, and also one other, which, else, had been greater than the bending, and that was the *stringing* of the bow, thich would have proved a very awkward work.

Presently, the bo'sun called out to me that he had got the surface of the stock sufficiently smooth and nice; and at that I went over to him; for now I wished him to burn a slight groove down the centre, running from end to end, and this I desired to be done very exactly; for upon it depended much of the true flight of the arrow. Then I went back to my own work; for I had not yet finished notching the bows. Presently, when I had made an end of this, I called for a length of the sennit, and, with the aid of another man, contrived to string one of the bows. This, when I had finished, I found to be very springy, and so stiff to bend that I had all that I could manage to do so, and at this I felt very satisfied.

Presently, it occurred to me that I should do well to set some of the men to work upon the line which the arrow was to carry; for I had determined that this should be made also from the white hemp yarns, and, for the sake of lightness, I conceived that one thickness of yarn would be sufficient; but so that it might compass enough of strength, I bid them split the yarns and lay the two halves up together, and in this manner they made me a very light and sound line; though it must not be supposed that it was finished at once; for I needed over half a mile of it, and thus it was later finished than the bow itself.

Having now gotten all things in train, I set me down to work upon one of the arrows; for I was anxious to see what sort of a fist I should make of them, knowing how much would depend upon the balance and truth of the missile. In the end, I made a very fair one, feathering it with its own leaves, and trueing and smoothing it with my knife; after which I inserted a small bolt in the forrard end, to act as a head, and, as I conceived, give it balance; though whether I was right in this latter, I am unable to say. Yet, before I had finished my arrow, the bo'sun had made the groove, and called me over to him, that I might admire it, the which I did; for it was done with a wonderful neatness.

Now I have been so busy with my description of how we made the great bow, that I have omitted to tell of the flight of time, and how we had eaten our dinner this long while since, and how that the people in the hulk had waved to us, and we had returned their signals, and then written upon a length of the canvas the one word, "WAIT." And, besides all this, some had gathered our fuel for the coming night.

And so, presently, the evening came upon us; but we ceased not to work; for the bo'sun bade the men to light a second great fire, beside our former one, and by the light of this we worked another long spell; though it seemed short enough, by reason of the interest of the work. Yet, at last, the bo'sun bade us to stop and make supper, which we did, and after that, he set the watches, and the rest of us turned in; for we were very weary.

In spite of my previous weariness, when the man whom I relieved called me to take my watch, I felt very fresh and wide awake, and spent a great part of the time, as on the preceding night, in studying over my plans for completing the great bow, and it was then that I decided finally in what manner I would secure the bows athwart the end of the stock; for until then I had been in some little doubt, being divided between several methods. Now, however, I concluded to make twelve grooves across the sawn end of the stock, and fit the middles of the bows into these, one above the other, as I have already mentioned; and then to lash them at each side to bolts driven into the sides of the stock. And with this idea I was very well pleased; for it promised to make them secure, and this without any great amount of work.

Now, though I spent much of my watch in thinking over the details of my prodigious weapon, yet it must not be supposed that I neglected to perform my duty as watchman; for I walked continually about the top of the hill, keeping my cut-and-thrust ready for any sudden emergency. Yet my time passed off quietly enough; though it is true that I witnessed one thing which brought me a short spell of disquiet thought. It was in this wise:—I had come to that part of the hill-top which overhung the valley, and it came to me, abruptly, to go near to the edge and look over. Thus, the moon being very bright, and the desolation of the valley reasonably clear to the eye, it appeared to me, as I looked that I saw a movement among certain of the fungi which had not burnt, but stood up shrivelled and blackened in the valley. Yet by no means could I be sure that it was not a sudden fancy, born of the eeriness of that desolate-looking vale; the more so as I was like to be deceived because of the uncertainty which the light of the moon gives. Yet, to prove my doubts, I went back until I had found a piece of rock easy to throw, and this, taking a short run, I cast into the valley, aiming at the spot where it had seemed to me that there had been a movement. Immediately upon this, I caught a glimpse of some moving thing, and then, more to my right, something else stirred, and at this, I looked towards it; but could discover nothing. Then, looking back at the clump at which I had aimed my missile, I saw that the slime-covered pool, which lay near, was all a-quiver, or so it seemed. Yet the next instant I was just as full of doubt; for, even as I watched it, I perceived that it was quite still. And after that, for some time, I kept a very strict gaze into the valley; yet could nowhere discover aught to prove my suspicions, and, at last, I ceased from watching it; for I feared to grow fanciful, and so wandered to that part of the hill which overlooked the weed.

Presently, when I had been relieved, I returned to sleep, and so till the morning. Then, when we had made each of us a hasty breakfast—for all were grown mightily keen to see the great bow completed—we set-to upon it, each at our appointed task. Thus, the bo'sun and I made it our work to make the twelve groves athwart the flat end of the stock, into which I proposed to fit and lash the bows, and this we accomplished by means of the iron futtock-shroud, which we heated in its middle part, and then, each taking an end (protecting our hands with canvas), we went one on each side and applied the iron until at length we had the groves burnt out very nicely and accurately. This work occupied us all the morning; for the groves had to be deeply burnt; and in the meantime the men had completed near enough sennit for the stringing of the bows; yet those who were at work on the line which the arrow was to carry, had scarce made more than half, so that I called off one man from the sennit to turn-to and give them a hand with the making of the line.

When dinner was ended, the bo'sun and I set-to about fitting the bows into their places, which we did, and lashed them to twenty-four bolts, twelve a side, driven into the timber of the stock, about twelve inches in from the end. After this, we bent and strung the bows, taking very great care to have each bent exactly as the one below it; for we started at the bottom. And so, before sunset, we had that part of our work ended.

Now, because the two fires which we had lit on the previous night had exhausted our fuel, the bo'sun deemed it prudent to cease work, and go down all of us to bring up a fresh supply of the dry seaweed and some faggots of the reeds. This we did, making an end of our journeyings just as the dusk came over the island. Then, having made a second fire, as on the preceding night, we had first our supper, and after that another spell of work, all the men turning-to upon the line which the arrow was to carry, whilst the bo'sun and I set-to, each of us, upon the making of a fresh arrow; for I had realized that we should have to make one of two flights before we could hope to find our range and make true our aim.

Later, maybe about nine of the night, the bo'sun bade us all to put away our work, and then he set the watches, after which the rest of us went into the tent to sleep; for the strength of the wind made the shelter a very pleasant thing.

That night, when it came my turn to watch, I minded me to take a look into the valley; but though I watched at intervals through the half of an hour, I saw nothing to lead me to imagine that I had indeed seen aught on the previous night, and so I felt more confidence in my mind that we should be troubled no further by the devil-things which had destroyed poor Job. Yet I must record one thing which I saw during my watch; though this was from the edge of the hill-top which overlooked the weed-continent, and was not in the valley, but in the stretch of clear water which lay between the island and the weed. As I saw it, it seemed to me that a number of great fish were swimming across from the island, diagonally towards the great continent of weed: they were swimming in one wake, and keeping a very regular line; but not breaking the water after the manner of porpoises or black fish. Yet, though I have mentioned this, it must not be supposed that I saw any very strange thing in such a sight, and indeed, I thought nothing more of it than to wonder what sort of fish they might be; for, as I saw them indistinctly in the moonlight, they made a queer appearance, seeming each of them to be possessed of two tails, and further, I could have thought I perceived a flicker as of tentacles just beneath the surface; but of this I was by no means sure.

Upon the following morning, having hurried our breakfast, each of us set-to again upon our tasks; for we were in hopes to have the great bow at work before dinner. Soon, the bo'sun had finished his arrow, and mine was completed very shortly after, so that there lacked nothing now to the completion of our work, save the finishing of the line, and the getting of the bow into position. This latter, assisted by the men, we proceeded now to effect, making a level bed of rocks near the edge of the hill which overlooked the weed. Upon this we placed the great bow, and then, having sent the men back to their work at the line, we proceeded to the aiming of the huge weapon. Now, when we had gotten the instrument pointed, as we conceived, straight over the hulk, the which we accomplished by squinting along the groove which the bo'sun had burnt down the centre of the stock, we turned-to upon the arranging of the notch and trigger, the notch being to hold the strings when the weapon was set, and the trigger—a board bolted on loosely at the side just below the notch—to push them upwards out of this place when we desired to discharge the bow. This part of the work took up no great portion of our time, and soon we had all ready for our first flight. Then we commenced to set the bows, bending the bottom one first, and then those above in turn, until all were set; and, after that, we laid the arrow very carefully in the groove. Then I took two pieces of spunyarn and frapped the strings together at each end of the notch, and by this means I was assured that all the strings would act in unison when striking the butt of the arrow. And so we had all things ready for the discharge; whereupon, I placed my foot upon the trigger, and, bidding the bo'sun watch carefully the flight of the arrow, pushed downwards. The next instant, with a mighty twang, and a quiver that made the great stock stir on its bed of rocks, the bow sprang to its lesser tension, hurling the arrow outwards and upwards in a vast arc. Now, it may be conceived with what mortal interest we watched its flight, and so in a minute discovered that we had aimed too much to the right; for the arrow struck the weed ahead of the hulk—but *beyond* it. At that, I was filled near to bursting with pride and joy, and the men who had come forward to witness the trial, shouted to acclaim my success, whilst the bo'sun clapt me twice upon the shoulder to signify his regard, and shouted as loud as any.

And now it seemed to me that we had but to get the true aim, and the rescue of those in the hulk would be but a matter of another day or two; for, having once gotten a line to the hulk, we should haul across a thin rope by its means, and with this a thicker one; after which we should set this up so taut as possible, and then bring the people in the hulk to the island by means of a seat and block which we should haul to and fro along the supporting-line.

Now, having realized that the bow would indeed carry so far as the wreck, we made haste to try our second arrow, and at the same time we bade the men go back to their work upon the line; for we should have need of it in a very little while. Presently, having pointed the bow more to the left, I took the frappings off the strings, so that we could bend the bows singly, and after that we set the great weapon again. Then, seeing that the arrow was straight in the groove, I replaced the frappings, and immediately discharged it. This time, to my very great pleasure and pride, the arrow went with a wonderful straightness towards the ship, and, clearing the superstructure, passed out of our sight as it fell behind it. At this, I was all impatience to try to get the line to the hulk before we made our dinner; but the men had not yet laid-up sufficient; there being then only four hundred and fifty fathoms (which the bo'sun measured off by stretching it along his arms and across his chest). This being so, we went to dinner, and made very great haste through it; and, after that, every one of us worked at the line, and so in about an hour we had sufficient; for I had estimated that it would not be wise to make the attempt with a less length than five hundred fathoms.

Having now completed a sufficiency of the line, the bo'sun set one of the men to flake it down very carefully upon the rock beside the bow, whilst he himself tested it at all such parts as he thought in any way doubtful, and so, presently, all was ready. Then I bent it on to the arrow, and, having set the bow whilst the men were flaking down the line, I was prepared immediately to discharge the weapon.

Now, all the morning, a man upon the hulk had observed us through a spy-glass, from a position that brought his head just above the edge of the superstructure, and, being aware of our intentions—having watched the previous flights—he understood the bo'sun, when he beckoned to him, that we had made ready for a third shot, and so, with an answering wave of his spy-glass, he disappeared from our sight. At that, having first turned to see that all were clear of the line, I pressed down the trigger, my heart beating very fast and thick, and so in a moment the arrow was sped. But now, doubtless because of the weight of the line, it made nowhere near so good a flight as on the previous occasion, the arrow striking the weed some two hundred yards short of the hulk, and at this, I could near have wept with vexation and disappointment.

Immediately upon the failure of my shot, the bo'sun called to the men to haul in the line very carefully, so that it should not be parted through the arrow catching in the weed; then he came over to me, and proposed that we should set-to at once to make a heavier arrow, suggesting that it had been lack of weight in the missile which had caused it to fall short. At that, I felt once more hopeful, and turned-to at once to prepare a new arrow; the bo'sun doing likewise; though in his case he intended to make a lighter one than that which had failed; for, as he put it, though the heavier one fell short, yet might the lighter succeed, and if neither, then we could only suppose that the bow lacked power to carry the line, and in that case we should have to try some other method.

Now, in about two hours, I had made my arrow, the bo'sun having finished his a little earlier; and so (the men having hauled in all the line and flaked it down ready) we prepared to make another attempt to cast it over the hulk. Yet, a second time we failed, and by so much that it seemed hopeless to think of success; but, for all that it appeared useless, the bo'sun insisted on making a last try with the light arrow, and, presently, when we had gotten the line ready again, we loosed upon the wreck; but in this case so lamentable was our failure, that I cried out to the bo'sun to set the useless thing upon the fire and burn it; for I was sorely irked by its failure, and could scarce abide to speak civilly of it.

Now the bo'sun, perceiving how I felt, sung out that we would cease troubling about the hulk for the present, and go down all of us to gather reeds and weed for the fire; for it was drawing nigh to evening. And this we did, though all in a disconsolate condition of mind; for we had seemed so near to success, and now it appeared to be further than ever from us. And so, in a while, having brought up a sufficiency of fuel, the bo'sun sent two of the men down to one of the ledges which overhung the sea, and bade them see whether they could not secure a fish for our supper. Then, taking our places about the fire, we fell-to upon a discussion as to how we should come at the people in the hulk.

Now, for a while there came no suggestion worthy of notice, until at last there occurred to me a notable idea, and I called out suddenly that we should make a small fire balloon, and float off the line to them by such means. At that, the men about the fire were silent a moment; for the idea was new to them, and moreover they needed to comprehend just what I meant. Then, when they had come fully at it, the one who had proposed that they should make spears of their knives, cried out to know why a kite would not do, and at that I was confounded, in that so simple an expedient had not occurred to any before; for, surely, it would be but a little matter to float a line to them by means of a kite, and, further, such a thing would take no great making.

And so, after a space of talk, it was decided that upon the morrow we should build some sort of kite, and with it fly a line over the hulk, the which should be a task of no great difficulty with so good a breeze as we had continually with us.

And, presently, having made our supper off a very fine fish, which the two fishermen had caught whilst we talked, the bo'sun set the watches, and the rest turned-in.

XLIV
The Weed Men

Now, on that night, when I came to my watch, I discovered that there was no moon, and, save for such light as the fire threw, the hill-top was in darkness; yet this was no great matter to trouble me; for we had been unmolested since the burning of the fungi in the valley, and thus I had lost much of the haunting fear which had beset me upon the death of Job. Yet, though I was not so much afraid as I had been, I took all precautions that suggested themselves to me, and built up the fire to a goodly height, after which I took my cut-and-thrust, and made the round of the camping place. At the edges of the cliffs which protected us on three sides, I made some pause, staring down into the darkness, and listening; though this latter was of but small use because of the strength of the wind which roared continually in my ears. Yet though I neither saw nor heard anything, I was presently possessed of a strange uneasiness, which made me return twice or thrice to the edge of the cliffs; but always without seeing or hearing anything to justify my superstitions. And so, presently, being determined to give way to no fancifulness, I avoided the boundary of cliffs, and kept more to that part which commanded the slope, up and down which we made our journeys to and from the island below.

Then, it would be near half way through my time of watching, there came to me out of the immensity of weed that lay to leeward, a far distant sound that grew upon my ear, rising and rising into a fearsome screaming and shrieking, and then dying away into the distance in queer sobs, and so at last to a note below that of the wind's. At this, as might be supposed, I was somewhat shaken in myself to hear so dread a noise coming out of all that desolation, and then, suddenly, the thought came to me that the screaming was from the ship to leeward of us, and I ran immediately to the edge of the cliff overlooking the weed, and stared into the darkness; but now I perceived, by a light which burned in the hulk, that the screaming had come from some place a great distance to the right of her, and more, as my sense assured me, it could by no means have been possible for those in her to have sent their voices to me against such a breeze as blew at that time.

And so, for a space, I stood nervously pondering, and peering away into the blackness of the night; thus, in a little, I perceived a dull glow upon the horizon, and, presently, there rose into view the upper edge of the moon, and a very welcome sight it was to me; for I had been upon the point of calling the bo'sun to inform him regarding the sound which I had heard; but I had hesitated, being afraid to seem foolish if nothing should befall. Then, even as I stood watching the moon rise into view, there came again to me the beginning of that screaming, somewhat like to the sound of a woman sobbing with a giant's voice, and it grew and strengthened until it pierced through the roar of the wind with an amazing clearness, and then slowly, and seeming to echo and echo, it sank away into the distance, and there was again in my ears no sound beyond that of the wind.

At this, having looked fixedly in the direction from which the sound had proceeded, I ran straightway to the tent and roused the bo'sun; for I had no knowledge of what the noise might portend, and this second cry had shaken from me all my bashfulness. Now the bo'sun was upon his feet almost before I had made an end of shaking him, and catching up his great cutlass which he kept always by his side, he followed me swiftly out on to the hill-top. Here, I explained to him that I had heard a very fearsome sound which had appeared to proceed out of the vastness of the weed-continent, and that, upon a repetition of the noise, I had decided to call him; for I knew not but that it might signal to us of some coming danger. At that, the bo'sun commended me; though chiding me in that I had hesitated to call him at the first occurrence of the crying, and then, following me to the edge of the leeward cliff, he stood there with me, waiting and listening, perchance there might come again a recurrence of the noise.

For perhaps something over an hour we stood there very silent and listening; but there came to us no sound beyond the continuous noise of the wind, and so, by that time, having grown somewhat impatient of waiting, and the moon being well risen, the bo'sun beckoned to me to make the round of the camp with him. Now, just as I turned away, chancing to look downward at the clear water directly below, I was amazed to see that an innumerable multitude of great fish, like unto those which I had seen on the previous night, were swimming from the weed-continent towards the island. At that, I stepped nearer the edge; for they came so directly towards the island that I expected to see them close in-shore; yet I could not perceive one; for they seemed all of them to vanish at a point some thirty yards distant from the beach, and at that, being amazed both by the numbers of the fish and their strangeness, and the way in which they came on continually, yet never reached the shore, I called to the bo'sun to come and see; for he had gone on a few paces. Upon hearing my call, he came running back; whereat I pointed into the sea below. At that, he stooped forward and peered very intently, and I with him; yet neither one of us could discover the meaning of so curious an exhibition, and so for a while we watched, the bo'sun being quite so much interested as I.

Presently, however, he turned away, saying that we did foolishly to stand here peering at every curious sight, when we should be looking to the welfare of the camp, and so we began to go the round of the hill-top. Now, whilst we had been watching and listening, we had suffered the fire to die down to a most unwise lowness, and consequently, though the moon was rising, there was by no means the same brightness that should have made the camp light. On perceiving this, I went forward to throw some fuel on to the fire, and then, even as I moved, it seemed to me that I saw something stir in the shadow of the tent. And at that, I ran towards the place, uttering a shout, and waving my cut-and-thrust; yet I found nothing, and so, feeling somewhat foolish, I turned to make up the fire, as had been my intention, and whilst I was thus busied, the bo'sun came running over to me to know what I had seen, and in the same instant there ran three of the men out of the tent, all of them waked by my sudden cry. But I had naught to tell them, save that my fancy had played me a trick, and had shown me something where my eyes could find nothing, and at that, two of the men went back to resume their sleep; but the third, the big fellow to whom the bo'sun had given the other cutlass, came with us, bringing his weapon; and, though he kept silent, it seemed to me that he had gathered something of our uneasiness; and for my part I was not sorry to have his company.

Presently, we came to that portion of the hill which overhung the valley, and I went to the edge of the cliff, intending to peer over; for the valley had a very unholy fascination for me. Yet, no sooner had I glanced down than I started, and ran back to the bo'sun and plucked him by the sleeve, and at that, perceiving my agitation, he came with me in silence to see what matter had caused me so much quiet excitement. Now, when he looked over, he also was astounded, and drew back instantly; then, using great caution, he bent forward once more, and stared down, and, at that, the big seaman came up behind, walking upon his toes, and stooped to see what manner of thing we had discovered. Thus we each of us stared down upon a most unearthly sight; for the valley all beneath us was a-swarm with moving creatures, white and unwholesome in the moonlight, and their movements were somewhat like the movements of monstrous slugs; though the things themselves had no resemblance to such in their contours; but minded me of naked humans, very fleshy and crawling upon their stomachs; yet their movements lacked not a surprising rapidity. And now, looking a little over the bo'sun's shoulder, I discovered that these hideous things were coming up out from the pit-like pool in the bottom of the valley, and, suddenly, I was minded of the multitudes of strange fish which we had seen swimming towards the island; but which had all disappeared before reaching the shore, and I had no doubt but that they entered the pit through some natural passage known to them beneath the water. And now I was made to understand my thought of the previous night, that I had seen the flicker of tentacles; for these things below us had each two short and stumpy arms; but the ends appeared divided into hateful and wriggling masses of small tentacles, which slid hither and thither as the creatures moved about the bottom of the valley, and at their hinder ends, where they should have grown feet, there seemed other flickering bunches; but it must not be supposed that we saw these things clearly.

Now it is scarcely possible to convey the extraordinary disgust which the sight of these human slugs bred in me; nor, could I, do I think I would; for were I successful, then would others be like to retch even as I did, the spasm coming on without premonition, and born of very horror. And then, suddenly, even as I stared, sick with loathing and apprehension, there came into view, not a fathom below my feet, a face like to the face which had peered up into my own on that night, as we drifted beside the weed-continent. At that, I could have screamed, had I been in less terror; for the great eyes, so big as crown pieces, the bill like to an inverted parrot's, and the slug-like undulating of its white and slimy body, bred in me the dumbness of one mortally stricken. And, even as I stayed there, my helpless body bent and rigid, the bo'sun spat a mighty curse into my ear, and, leaning forward, smote at the thing with his cutlass; for in the instant that I had seen it, it had advanced upward by so much as a yard. Now, at this action of the bo'sun's, I came suddenly into possession of myself, and thrust downward with so much vigour that I was like to have followed the brute's carcass; for I overbalanced, and danced giddily for a moment upon the edge of eternity; and then the bo'sun had me by the waistband, and I was back in safety; but in that instant through which I had struggled for my balance, I had discovered that the face of the cliff was near hid with the number of the things which were making up to us, and I turned to the bo'sun, crying out to him that there were thousands of them swarming up to us. Yet, he was gone already from me, running towards the fire, and shouting to the men in the tent to haste to our help for their very lives, and then he came racing back with a great armful of the weed, and after him came the big seaman, carrying a burning tuft from the camp fire, and so in a few moments we had a blaze, and the men were bringing more weed; for we had a very good stock upon the hill-top; for which the Almighty be thanked.

Now, scarce had we lit one fire, when the bo'sun cried out to the big seaman to make another, further along the edge of the cliff, and, in the same instant, I shouted, and ran over to that part of the hill which lay towards the open sea; for I had seen a number of moving things about the edge of the seaward cliff. Now here there was a deal of shadow; for there were scattered certain large masses of rock about this part of the hill, and these held off both the light of the moon, and that from the fires. Here, I came abruptly upon three great shapes moving with stealthiness towards the camp, and, behind these, I saw dimly that there were others. Then, with a loud cry for help, I made at the three, and, as I charged, they rose up on end at me, and I found that they overtopped me, and their vile tentacles were reached out at me. Then I was smiting, and gasping, sick with a sudden stench, the stench of the creatures which I had come already to know. And then something clutched at me, something slimy and vile, and great mandibles champed in my face; but I stabbed upward, and the thing fell from me, leaving me dazed and sick, and smiting weakly. Then there came a rush of feet behind, and a sudden blaze, and the bo'sun crying out encouragement, and, directly, he and the big seaman thrust themselves in front of me, hurling from them great masses of burning weed, which they had borne, each of them, upon a long reed. And immediately the things were gone, slithering hastily down over the cliff edge.

And so, presently, I was more my own man, and made to wipe from my throat the slime left by the clutch of the monster: and afterwards I ran from fire to fire with weed, feeding them, and so a space passed, during which we had safety; for by that time we had fires all about the top of the hill, and the monsters were in mortal dread of fire, else had we been dead, all of us, that night.

Now, a while before the dawn, we discovered, for the second time since we had been upon the island, that our fuel could not last us the night at the rate at which we were compelled to burn it, and so the bo'sun told the men to let out every second fire, and thus we staved off for a while the time when we should have to face a spell of darkness, and the things which, at present, the fires held off from us. And so at last, we came to the end of the weed and the reeds, and the bo'sun called out to us to watch the cliff edges very carefully, and smite on the instant that any thing showed; but that, should he call, all were to gather by the central fire for a last stand. And, after that, he blasted the moon which had passed behind a great bank of cloud. And thus matters were, and the gloom deepened as the fires sank lower and lower. Then I heard a man curse, on that part of the hill which lay towards the weed-continent, his cry coming up to me against the wind, and the bo'sun shouted to us all to have a care, and directly afterwards I smote at something that rose silently above the edge of the cliff opposite to where I watched.

Perhaps a minute passed, and then there came shouts from all parts of the hill-top, and I knew that the weed men were upon us, and in the same instant there came two above the edge near me, rising with a ghostly quietness, yet moving lithely. Now the first, I pierced somewhere in the throat, and it fell backward; but the second, though I thrust it through, caught my blade with a bunch of its tentacles, and was like to have snatched it from me; but that I kicked it in the face, and at that, being, I believe, more astonished than hurt, it loosed my sword, and immediately fell away out of sight. Now this had taken, in all, no more than some ten seconds; yet already I perceived so many as four others coming into view a little to my right, and at that it seemed to me that our deaths must be very near, for I knew not how we were to cope with the creatures, coming as they were so boldly and with such rapidity. Yet, I hesitated not, but ran at them, and now I thrust not; but cut at their faces, and found this to be very effectual; for in this wise I disposed of three in as many strokes; but the fourth had come right over the cliff edge, and rose up at me upon its hinder parts, as had done those others when the bo'sun had succoured me. At that, I gave way, having a very lively dread; but, hearing all about me the cries of conflict, and knowing that I could expect no help, I made at the brute: then as it stooped and reached out one of its bunches of tentacles, I sprang back, and slashed at them, and immediately I followed this up by a thrust in the stomach, and at that it collapsed into a writhing white ball, that rolled this way and that, and so, in its agony, coming to the edge of the cliff, it fell over, and I was left, sick and near helpless with the hateful stench of the brutes.

Now by this time all the fires about the edges of the hill were sunken into dull glowing mounds of embers; though that which burnt near to the entrance of the tent was still of a good brightness; yet this helped us but little, for we fought too far beyond the immediate circle of its beams to have benefit of it. And still the moon, at which now I threw a despairing glance, was no more than a ghostly shape behind the great bank of cloud which was passing over it. Then, even as I looked upward, glancing as it might be over my left shoulder, I saw, with a sudden horror, that something had come anigh me, and upon the instant, I caught the reek of the thing, and leapt fearfully to one side, turning as I sprang. Thus was I saved in the very moment of my destruction; for the creature's tentacles smeared the back of my neck as I leapt, and then I had smitten, once and again, and conquered.

Immediately after this, I discovered something to be crossing the dark space that lay between the dull mound of the nearest fire, and that which lay further along the hill-top, and so, wasting no moment of time, I ran towards the thing, and cut it twice across the head before ever it could get upon its hind parts, in which position I had learned greatly to dread them. Yet, no sooner had I slain this one, than there came a rush of maybe a dozen upon me; these having climbed silently over the cliff edge in the meanwhile. At this, I dodged, and ran madly towards the glowing mound of the nearest fire, the brutes following me almost so quick as I could run; but I came to the fire the first, and then, a sudden thought coming to me, I thrust the point of my cut-and-thrust among the embers and switched a great shower of them at the creatures, and at that I had a momentary clear vision of many white, hideous faces stretched out towards me, and brown, champing mandibles which had the upper beak shutting into the lower; and the clumped, wriggling tentacles were all a-flutter. Then the gloom came again; but immediately, I switched another and yet another shower of the burning embers towards them, and so, directly, I saw them give back, and then they were gone. At this, all about the edges of the hill-top, I saw the fires being scattered in like manner; for others had adopted this device to help them in their sore straits.

For a little after this, I had a short breathing space, the brutes seeming to have taken fright; yet I was full of trembling, and I glanced hither and thither, not knowing when some one or more of them would come upon me. And ever I glanced towards the moon, and prayed the Almighty that the clouds would pass quickly, else should we be all dead men; and then, as I prayed, there rose a sudden very terrible scream from one of the men, and in the same moment there came something over the edge of the cliff fronting me; but I cleft it or ever it could rise higher, and in my ears there echoed still the sudden scream which had come from that part of the hill which lay to the left of me: yet I dared not to leave my station; for to have done so would have been to have risked all, and so I stayed, tortured by the strain of ignorance, and my own terror.

Again, I had a little spell in which I was free from molestation; nothing coming into sight so far as I could see to right or left of me; though others were less fortunate, as the curses and sounds of blows told to me, and then, abruptly, there came another cry of pain, and I looked up again to the moon, and prayed aloud that it might come out to show some light before we were all destroyed; but it remained hid. Then a sudden thought came into my brain, and I shouted at the top of my voice to the bo'sun to set the great cross-bow upon the central fire; for thus we should have a big blaze—the wood being very nice and dry. Twice I shouted to him, saying: —"Burn the bow! Burn the bow!" And immediately he replied, shouting to all the men to run to him and carry it to the fire; and this we did, and bore it to the centre fire, and then ran back with all speed to our places. Thus in a minute we had some light, and the light grew as the fire took hold of the great log, the wind fanning it to a blaze. And so I faced outwards, looking to see if any vile face showed above the edge before me, or to my right or left. Yet, I saw nothing, save, as it seemed to me, once a fluttering tentacle came up, a little to my right; but nothing else for a space.

Perhaps it was near five minutes later, that there came another attack, and, in this, I came near to losing my life, through my folly in venturing too near to the edge of the cliff; for, suddenly, there shot up out from the darkness below, a clump of tentacles, and caught me about the left ankle, and immediately I was pulled to a sitting posture, so that both my feet were over the edge of the precipice, and it was only by the mercy of God that I had not plunged head foremost into the valley. Yet, as it was, I suffered a mighty peril; for the brute that had my foot, put a vast strain upon it, trying to pull me down; but I resisted, using my hands and seat to sustain me, and so, discovering that it could not compass my end in this wise, it slacked somewhat of the stress, and bit at my boot, shearing through the hard leather, and nigh destroying my small toe; but now, being no longer compelled to use both hands to retain my position, I slashed down with great fury, being maddened by the pain and the mortal fear which the creature had put upon me; yet I was not immediately free of the brute; for it caught my sword blade; but I snatched it away before it could take a proper hold, mayhaps cutting its feelers somewhat thereby; though of this I cannot be sure, for they seemed not to grip around a thing, but to *suck* to it; then, in a moment, by a lucky blow, I maimed it, so that it loosed me, and I was able to get back into some condition of security.

And from this onwards, we were free from molestation; though we had no knowledge but that the quietness of the weed men did but portend a fresh attack, and so, at last, it came to the dawn; and in all this time the moon came not to our help, being quite hid by the clouds which now covered the whole arc of the sky, making the dawn of a very desolate aspect.

And so soon as there was a sufficiency of light, we examined the valley; but there were nowhere any of the weed men, no! nor even any of their dead for it seemed that they had carried off all such and their wounded, and so we had no opportunity to make an examination of the monsters by daylight. Yet, though we could not come upon their dead, all about the edges of the cliffs was blood and slime, and from the latter there came ever the hideous stench which marked the brutes; but from this we suffered little, the wind carrying it far away to leeward, and filling our lungs with sweet and wholesome air.

Presently, seeing that the danger was past, the bo'sun called us to the centre fire, on which burnt still the remnants of the great bow, and here we discovered for the first time that one of the men was gone from us. At that, we made search about the hill-top, and afterwards in the valley and about the island; but found him not.

XIV
In Communication

Now of the search which we made through the valley for the body of Tompkins, that being the name of the lost man, I have some doleful memories. But first, before we left the camp, the bo'sun gave us all a very sound tot of the rum, and also a biscuit apiece, and thereafter we hasted down, each man holding his weapon readily. Presently, when we were come to the beach which ended the valley upon the seaward side, the bo'sun led us along to the bottom of the hill, where the precipices came down into the softer stuff which covered the valley, and here we made a careful search, perchance he had fallen over, and lay dead or wounded near to our hands. But it was not so, and after that, we went down to the mouth of the great pit, and here we discovered the mud all about it to be covered with multitudes of tracks, and in addition to these and the slime, we found many traces of blood; but nowhere any signs of Tompkins. And so, having searched all the valley, we came out upon the weed which strewed the shore nearer to the great weed-continent; but discovered nothing until we had made up towards the foot of the hill, where it came down sheer into the sea. Here, I climbed on to a ledge—the same from which the men had caught their fish—thinking that, if Tompkins had fallen from above, he might lie in the water at the foot of the cliff, which was here, maybe, some ten to twenty feet deep; but, for a little space, I saw nothing. Then, suddenly, I discovered that there was something white, down in the sea away to my left, and, at that, I climbed farther out along the ledge.

In this wise I perceived that the thing which had attracted my notice was the dead body of one of the weed men. I could see it but dimly, catching odd glimpses of it as the surface of the water smoothed at whiles. It appeared to me to be lying curled up, and somewhat upon its right side, and in proof that it was dead, I saw a mighty wound that had come near to shearing away the head; and so, after a further glance, I came in, and told what I had seen. At that, being convinced by this time that Tompkins was indeed done to death, we ceased our search; but first, before we left the spot, the bo'sun climbed out to get a sight of the dead weed man and after him the rest of the men for they were greatly curious to see clearly what manner of creature it was that had attacked us in the night. Presently, having seen so much of the brute as the water would allow, they came in again to the beach, and afterwards we returned to the opposite side of the island, and so, being there, we crossed over to the boat, to see whether it had been harmed; but found it to be untouched. Yet, that the creatures had been all about it, we could perceive by the marks of slime upon the sand, and also by the strange trail which they had left in the soft surface. Then one of the men called out that there had been something at Job's grave, which, as will be remembered, had been made in the sand some little distance from the place of our first camp. At that, we looked all of us, and it was easy to see that it had been disturbed, and so we ran hastily to it, knowing not what to fear; thus we found it to be empty; for the monsters had digged down to the poor lad's body, and of it we could discover no sign. Upon this, we came to a greater horror of the weed men than ever; for we knew them now to be foul ghouls who could not let even the dead body rest in the grave.

Now after this, the bo'sun led us all back to the hill-top, and there he looked to our hurts; for one man had lost two fingers in the night's fray; another had been bitten savagely in the left arm; whilst a third had all the skin of his face raised in wheals where one of the brutes had fixed its tentacles. And all of these had received but scant attention, because of the stress of the fight, and, after that, through the discovery that Tompkins was missing. Now, however, the bo'sun set-to upon them, washing and binding them up, and for dressings he made use of some of the oakum which we had with us, binding this on with strips torn from the roll of spare duck, which had been in the locker of the boat.

For my part, seizing this chance to make some examination of my wounded toe, the which, indeed, was causing me to limp, I found that I had endured less harm than seemed to me; for the bone of the toe was untouched, though showing bare; yet when it was cleansed, I had not overmuch pain with it; though I could not suffer to have the boot on, and so bound some canvas about my foot, until such time as it should be healed.

Presently, when our wounds were all attended to, the which had taken time, for there was none of us altogether untouched, the bo'sun bade the man whose fingers were damaged, to lie down in the tent, and the same order he gave also to him that was bitten in the arm. Then, the rest of us he directed to go down with him and carry up fuel; for that the night had shown him how our very lives depended upon a sufficiency of this; and so all that morning we brought fuel to the hill-top, both weed and reeds, resting not until midday, when he gave us a further tot of the rum, and after that set one of the men upon the dinner. Then he bade the man, Jessop by name, who had proposed to fly a kite over the vessel in the weed, to say whether he had any craft in the making of such a matter. At that, the fellow laughed, and told the bo'sun that he would make him a kite that would fly very steadily and strongly, and this without the aid of a tail. And so the bo'sun bade him set-to without delay; for that we should do well to deliver the people in the hulk, and afterwards make all haste from the island, which was no better than a nesting place of ghouls.

Now, hearing the man say that his kite would fly without a tail, I was mightily curious to see what manner of thing he would make; for I had never seen the like, nor heard that such was possible. Yet he spoke of no more than he could accomplish; for he took two of the reeds and cut them to a length of about six feet; then he bound them together in the middle so that they formed a Saint Andrew's cross, and after that he made two more such crosses, and when these were completed, he took four reeds maybe a dozen feet long, and bade us stand them upright in the shape of a square, so that they formed the four corners, and after that he took one of the crosses, and laid it in the square so that its four ends touched the four uprights, and in this position he lashed it. Then he took the second cross and lashed it midway between the top and bottom of the uprights, and after that he lashed the third at the top, so that the three of them acted as spreaders to keep the four longer reeds in their places as though they were for the uprights of a little square tower. Now, when he had gotten so far as that, the bo'sun called out to us to make our dinners, and this we did, and afterwards had a short time in which to smoke, and whilst we were thus at our ease the sun came out, the which it had not done all the day, and at that we felt vastly brighter; for the day had been very gloomy with clouds until that time, and what with the loss of Tompkins, and our own fears and hurts, we had been exceeding doleful; but now, as I have said, we became more cheerful, and went very alertly to the finishing of the kite.

At this point it came suddenly to the bo'sun that we had made no provision of cord for the flying of the kite, and he called out to the man to know what strength the kite would require, at which Jessop answered him that maybe ten-yarn sennit would do, and this being so, the bo'sun led three of us down to the wrecked mast upon the further beach, and from this we stripped all that was left of the shrouds, and carried them to the top of the hill, and so, presently, having unlaid them, we set-to upon the sennit, using ten yarns; but plaiting two as one, by which means we progressed with more speed than if we had taken them singly.

Now, as we worked, I glanced occasionally towards Jessop, and saw that he stitched a band of the light duck around each end of the framework which he had made, and these bands I judged to be about four feet wide, in this wise leaving an open space between the two, so that now the thing looked something like to a Punchinello show, only that the opening was in the wrong place, and there was too much of it. After that he bent on a bridle to two of the uprights, making this of a piece of good hemp rope which he found in the tent, and then he called out to the bo'sun that the kite was finished. At that, the bo'sun went over to examine it, the which did all of us; for none of us had seen the like of such a thing, and, if I misdoubt not, few of us had much faith that it would fly; for it seemed so big and unwieldy. Now, I think that Jessop gathered something of our thoughts; for, calling to one of us to hold the kite, lest it should blow away, he went into the tent, and brought out the remainder of the hemp line, the same from which he had cut the bridle. This, he bent on to it, and, giving the end into our hands, bade us go back with it until all the slack was taken up, he, in the meanwhile, steadying the kite. Then, when we had gone back to the extent of the line, he shouted to us to take a very particular hold upon it, and then, stooping, caught the kite by the bottom, and threw it into the air, whereupon, to our amazement, having swooped somewhat to one side, it steadied and mounted upwards into the sky like a very bird.

Now at this, as I have made mention, we were astonished; for it appeared like a miracle to us to see so cumbrous a thing fly with so much grace and persistence, and further, we were mightily surprised at the manner in which it pulled upon the rope, tugging with such heartiness that we were like to have loosed it in our first astonishment, had it not been for the warning which Jessop called to us.

And now, being well assured of the properness of the kite, the bo'sun bade us to draw it in, the which we did only with difficulty, because of its bigness and the strength of the breeze. And when we had it back again upon the hill-top, Jessop moored it very securely to a great piece of rock, and, after that, having received our approbation, he turned-to with us upon the making of the sennit.

Presently, the evening drawing near, the bo'sun set us to the building of fires about the hill-top, and after that, having waved our good-nights to the people in the hulk, we made our suppers, and lay down to smoke, after which, we turned-to again at our plaiting of the sennit, the which we were in very great haste to have done. And so, later, the dark having come down upon the island, the bo'sun bade us take burning weed from the centre fire, and set light to the heaps of weed that we had stacked round the edges of the hill for that purpose, and so in a few minutes the whole of the hill-top was very light and cheerful, and afterwards, having put two of the men to keep watch and attend to the fires, he sent the rest of us back to our sennit making, keeping us at it until maybe about ten of the clock, after which he arranged that two men at a time should be on watch throughout the night, and then he bade the rest of us turn-in, so soon as he had looked to our various hurts.

Now, when it came to my turn to watch, I discovered that I had been chosen to company the big seaman, at which I was by no means displeased; for he was a most excellent fellow, and moreover a very lusty man to have near, should anything come upon one unawares. Yet, we were happy in that the night passed off without trouble of any sort, and so at last came the morning.

So soon as we had made our breakfast, the bo'sun took us all down to the carrying of fuel; for he saw very clearly that upon a good supply of this depended our immunity from attack. And so for the half of the morning we worked at the gathering of weed and reeds for our fires. Then, when we had obtained a sufficiency for the coming night, he set us all to work again upon the sennit, and so until dinner, after which we turned-to once more upon our plaiting. Yet it was plain that it would take several days to make a sufficient line for our purpose, and because of this, the bo'sun cast about in his mind for some way in which he could quicken its production. Presently, as a result of some little thought, he brought out from the tent the long piece of hemp rope with which we had moored the boat to the sea anchor, and proceeded to unlay it, until he had all three strands separate. Then he bent the three together, and so had a very rough line of maybe some hundred and eighty fathoms in length; yet, though so rough, he judged it strong enough, and thus we had this much the less sennit to make.

Now, presently, we made our dinner, and after that for the rest of the day we kept very steadily to our plaiting, and so, with the previous day's work, had near two hundred fathoms completed by the time that the bo'sun called us to cease and come to supper. Thus it will be seen that counting all, including the piece of hemp line from which the bridle had ben made, we may be said to have had at this time about four hundred fathoms towards the length which we needed for our purpose, this having been reckoned at five hundred fathoms.

After supper, having lit all the fires, we continued to work at the plaiting, and so, until the bo'sun set the watches, after which we settled down for the night, first, however, letting the bo'sun see to our hurts. Now this night, like to the previous, brought us no trouble; and when the day came, we had first our breakfast, and then set-to upon our collecting of fuel, after which we spent the rest of the day at the sennit, having manufactured a sufficiency by the evening, the which the bo'sun celebrated by a very rousing tot of the rum. Then, having made our supper, we lit the fires, and had a very comfortable evening, after which, as on the preceding nights, having let the bo'sun attend our wounds, we settled for the night, and on this occasion the bo'sun let the man who had lost his fingers, and the one who had been bitten so badly in the arm, take their first turn at the watching since the night of the attack.

Now when the morning came we were all of us very eager to come to the flying of the kite; for it seemed possible to us that we might effect the rescue of the people in the hulk before the evening. And, at the thought of this, we experienced a very pleasurable sense of excitement; yet, before the bo'sun would let us touch the kite, he insisted that we should gather our usual supply of fuel, the which order, though full of wisdom, irked us exceedingly, because of our eagerness to set about the rescue. But at last this was accomplished, and we made to get the line ready, testing the knots, and seeing that it was all clear for running. Yet, before setting the kite off, the bo'sun took us down to the further beach to bring up the foot of the royal and t'gallant mast, which remained fast to the topmast, and when we had this upon the hill-top, he set its ends upon two rocks, after which he piled a heap of great pieces around them, leaving the middle part clear. Round this he passed the kite line a couple or three times, and then gave the end to Jessop to bend on to the bridle of the kite, and so he had all ready for paying out to the wreck.

And now, having nothing to do, we gathered round to watch, and, immediately, the bo'sun giving the signal, Jessop cast the kite into the air, and, the wind catching it, lifted it strongly and well, so that the bo'sun could scarce pay out fast enough. Now, before the kite had been let go, Jessop had bent to the forward end of it a great length of the spunyarn, so that those in the wreck could catch it as it trailed over them, and, being eager to witness whether they would secure it without trouble, we ran all of us to the edge of the hill to watch. Thus, within five minutes from the time of the loosing of the kite, we saw the people in the ship wave to us to cease veering, and immediately afterwards the kite came swiftly downwards, by which we knew that they had the tripping-line, and were hauling upon it, and at that we gave out a great cheer, and afterwards we sat about and smoked, waiting until they had read our instructions, which we had written upon the covering of the kite.

Presently, maybe the half of an hour afterwards, they signalled to us to haul upon our line, which we proceeded to do without delay, and so, after a great space, we had hauled in all of our rough line, and come upon the end of theirs, which proved to be a fine piece of three-inch hemp, new and very good; yet we could not conceive that this would stand the stress necessary to lift so great a length clear of the weed, as would be needful, or ever we could hope to bring the people of the ship over it in safety. And so we waited some little while, and, presently, they signalled again to us to haul, which we did, and found that they had bent on a much greater rope to the bight of the three-inch hemp, having merely intended the latter for a hauling-line by which to get the heavier rope across the weed to the island. Thus, after a wear4ul time of pulling, we got the end of the bigger rope up to the hill-top, and discovered it to be an extraordinarily sound rope of some four inches diameter, and smoothly laid of fine yarns round and very true and well spun, and with this we had ever reason to be satisfied.

Now to the end of the big rope they had tied a letter, in a bag of oilskin, and in it they said some very warm and grateful things to us, after which they set out a short code of signals by which we should be able to understand one another on certain general matters, and at the end they asked if they should send us any provision ashore; for, as they explained, it would take some little while to get the rope set up taut enough for our purpose, and the carrier fixed and in working order. Now, upon reading this letter, we called out to the bo'sun that he should ask them if they would send us some soft bread; the which he added thereto a request for lint and bandages and ointment for our hurts. And this he bade me write upon one of the great leaves from off the reeds, and at the end he told me to ask if they desired us to send them any fresh water. And all of this, I wrote with a sharpened splinter of reed, cutting the words into the surface of the leaf. Then, when I had made an end of writing, I gave the leaf to the bo'sun, and he enclosed it in the oilskin bag, after which he gave the signal for those in the hulk to haul on the smaller line, and this they did.

Presently, they signed to us to pull in again, the which we did, and so, when we had hauled in a great length of their line, we came to the little, oilskin bag, in which we found lint and bandages and ointment, and a further letter, which set out that they were baking bread, and would send us some as soon as it was out from the oven.

Now, in addition to the matters for the healing of our wounds, and the letter, they had included a bundle of paper in loose sheets, some quills and an inkhorn, and at the end of their epistle, they begged very earnestly of us to send them some news of the outer world; for they had been shut up in that strange continent of weed for something over seven years. They told us then that there were twelve of them in the hulk, three of them being women, one of whom had been the captain's wife; but he had died soon after the vessel became entangled in the weed, and along with him more than half of the ship's company, having been attacked by giant devil-fish, as they were attempting to free the vessel from the weed, and afterwards they who were left had built the superstructure as a protection against the devil-fish, and the *devil-men,* as they termed them; for, until it had been built, there had been safety about the decks, neither day nor night.

To our question as to whether they were in need of water, the people in the ship replied that they had a sufficiency, and, further, that they were very well supplied with provisions; for the ship had sailed from London with a general cargo, among which there was a vast quantity of food in various shapes and forms. At this news we were greatly pleased, seeing that we need have no more anxiety regarding a lack of victuals, and so in the letter which I went into the tent to write, I put down that we were in no great plentitude of provisions, at which hint I guessed they would add somewhat to the bread when it should be ready. And after that I wrote down such chief events as my memory recalled as having occurred in the course of the past seven years, and then, a short account of our own adventures, up to that time, telling them of the attack which we had suffered from the weed men, and asking such questions as my curiosity and wonder prompted.

Now whilst I had been writing, sitting in the mouth of the tent, I had observed, from time to time, how that the bo'sun was busied with the men in passing the end of the big rope round a mighty boulder, which lay about ten fathoms in from the edge of the cliff which overlooked the hulk. This he did, parcelling the rope where the rock was in any way sharp, so as to protect it from being cut; for which purpose he made use of some of the canvas. And by the time that I had the letter completed, the rope was made very secure to the great piece of rock, and, further, they had put a large piece of chafing gear under that part of the rope where it took the edge of the cliff.

Now having, as I have said, completed the letter, I went out with it to the bo'sun; but, before placing it in the oilskin bag, he bade me add a note at the bottom, to say that the big rope was all fast, and that they could heave on it so soon as it pleased them, and after that we dispatched the letter by means of the small line, the men in the hulk hauling it off to them so soon as they perceived our signals.

By this, it had come well on to the latter part of the afternoon, and the bo'sun called us to make some sort of a meal, leaving one man to watch the hulk, perchance they should signal to us. For we had missed our dinner in the excitement of the day's work, and were come now to feel the lack of it. Then, in the midst of it, the man upon the look-out cried out that they were signalling to us from the ship, and, at that, we ran all of us to see what they desired, and so, by the code which we had arranged between us, we found that they waited for us to haul upon the small line. This did we, and made out presently that we were hauling something across the weed, of a very fair bulk, at which we warmed to our work, guessing that it was the bread which they had promised us, and so it proved, and done up with great neatness in a long roll of tarpaulin, which had been wrapped around both the loaves and the rope, and lashed very securely at the ends, thus producing a taper shape convenient for passing over the weed without catching. Now, when we came to open this parcel, we discovered that my hint had taken very sound effect; for there were in the parcel, besides the loaves, a boiled ham, a Dutch cheese, two bottles of port well padded from breakage, and four pounds of tobacco in plugs. And at this coming of good things, we stood all of us upon the edge of the hill, and waved our thanks to those in the ship, they waving back in all good will, and after that we went back to our meal, at which we sampled the new victuals with very lusty appetites.

There was in the parcel, one other matter, a letter, most neatly indited, as had been the former epistles, in a feminine hand-writing, so that I guessed they had one of the women to be their scribe. This epistle answered some of my queries, and, in particular, I remember that it informed me as to the probable cause of the strange crying which preceded the attack by the weed men, saying that on each occasion when they in the ship had suffered their attacks, there had been always this same crying, being evidently a summoning call or signal to the attack, though how given, the writer had not discovered; for the weed *devils*—this being how they in the ship spoke always of them—made never a sound when attacking, not even when wounded to the death, and, indeed, I may say here, that we never learnt the way in which that lonesome sobbing was produced, nor, indeed, did they, or we, discover more than the merest tithe of the mysteries which that great continent of weed holds in its silence.

Another matter to which I had referred was the consistent blowing of the wind from one quarter, and this the writer told me happened for as much as six months in the year, keeping up a very steady strength. A further thing there was which gave me much interest; it was that the ship had not been always where we had discovered her; for at one time they had been so far within the weed, that they could scarce discern the open sea upon the far horizon; but that at times the weed opened in great gulfs that went yawning through the continent for scores of miles, and in this way the shape and coasts of the weed were being constantly altered; these happenings being for the most part at the change of the wind.

And much more there was that they told us then and afterwards, how that they dried weed for their fuel, and how the rains, which fell with great heaviness at certain periods, supplied them with fresh water; though, at times, running short, they had learnt to distil sufficient for their needs until the next rains.

Now, near to the end of the epistle, there came some news of their present actions, and thus we learnt that they in the ship were busy at staying the stump of the mizzen-mast, this being the one to which they proposed to attach the big rope, taking it through a great iron-bound snatch-block, secured to the head of the stump, and then down to the mizzen-capstan, by which, and a strong tackle, they would be able to heave the line so taut as was needful.

Now, having finished our meal, the bo'sun took out the lint, bandages, and ointment, which they had sent us from the hulk, and proceeded to dress our hurts, beginning with him who had lost his fingers, which, happily, were making a very healthy heal. And afterwards we went all of us to the edge of the cliff, and sent back the look-out to fill such crevices in his stomach as remained yet empty; for we had passed him already some sound hunks of the bread and ham and cheese, to eat whilst he kept watch, and so he had suffered no great harm.

It may have been near an hour after this, that the bo'sun pointed out to me that they in the ship had commenced to heave upon the great rope, and so I perceived, and stood watching it; for I knew that the bo'sun had some anxiety as to whether it would take-up sufficiently clear of the weed to allow those in the ship to be hauled along it, free from molestation by the great devil-fish.

Presently, as the evening began to draw on, the bo'sun bade us go and build our fires about the hill-top, and this we did, after which we returned to learn how the rope was lifting, and now we perceived that it had come clear of the weed, at which we felt mightily rejoiced, and waved encouragement, chance there might be any who watched us from the hulk. Yet, though the rope was up clear of the weed, the bight of it had to rise to a much greater height, or ever it would do for the purpose for which we intended it, and already it suffered a vast strain, as I discovered by placing my hand upon it; for, even to lift the slack of so great a length of line meant the stress of some tons. And later I saw that the bo'sun was growing anxious; for he went over to the rock around which he had made fast the rope, and examined the knots, and those places where he had parcelled it, and after that he walked to the place where it went over the edge of the cliff, and here he made a further scrutiny; but came back presently, seeming not dissatisfied.

Then, in a while, the darkness came down upon us, and we lighted our fires and prepared for the night, having the watches arranged as on the preceding nights.

XV
Aboard the Hulk

Now when it came to my watch, the which I took in company with the big seaman, the moon had not yet risen, and all the island was vastly dark, save the hill-top, from which the fires blazed in a score of places, and very busy they kept us, supplying them with fuel. Then, when maybe the half of our watch had passed, the big seaman, who had been to feed the fires upon the weed side of the hill-top, came across to me, and bade me come and put my hand upon the lesser rope; for that he thought they in the ship were anxious to haul it in so that they might send some message across to us. At his words, I asked him very anxiously whether he had perceived them waving a light, the which we had arranged to be our method of signalling in the night, in the event of such being needful; but, to this, he said that he had seen naught; and, by now, having come near the edge of the cliff, I could see for myself, and so perceived that there was none signalling to us from the hulk. Yet, to please the fellow, I put my hand upon the line, which we had made fast in the evening to a large piece of rock, and so, immediately, I discovered that something was pulling upon it, hauling and then slackening, so that it occurred to me that the people in the vessel might be indeed wishful to send us some message, and at that, to make sure, I ran to the nearest fire, and, lighting a tuft of weed, waved it thrice; but there came not any answering signal from those in the ship, and at that I went back to feel at the rope, to assure myself that it had not been the pluck of the wind upon it; but I found that it was something very different from the wind, something that plucked with all the sharpness of a hooked fish, only that it had been a mighty great fish to have given such tugs, and so I knew that some vile thing out in the darkness of the weed was fast to the rope, and at this there came the fear that it might break it, and then a second thought that something might be climbing up to us along the rope, and so I bade the big seaman stand ready with his great cutlass, whilst I ran and waked the bo'sun. And this I did, and explained to him how that something meddled with the lesser rope, so that he came immediately to see for himself how this might be, and when he had put his hand upon it, he bade me go and call the rest of the men, and let them stand round by the fires; for that there was something abroad in the night, and we might be in danger of attack; but he and the big seaman stayed by the end of the rope, watching, so far as the darkness would allow, and ever and anon feeling the tension upon it.

Then, suddenly, it came to the bo'sun to look to the second line, and he ran, cursing himself for his thoughtlessness; but because of its greater weight and tension, he could not discover for certain whether anything meddled with it or not; yet he stayed by it, arguing that if aught touched the smaller rope then might something do likewise with the greater, only that the small line lay along the weed, whilst the greater one had been some feet above it when the darkness had fallen over us, and so might be free from any prowling creatures.

And thus, maybe, an hour passed, and we kept watch and tended the fires, going from one to another, and, presently, coming to that one which was nearest to the bo'sun, I went over to him, intending to pass a few minutes in talk; but as I drew nigh to him, I chanced to place my hand upon the big rope, and at that I exclaimed in surprise; for it had become much slacker than when last I had felt it in the evening, and I asked the bo'sun whether he had noticed it, whereat he felt the rope, and was almost more amazed than I had been; for when last he had touched it, it had been taut, and humming in the wind. Now, upon this discovery, he was in much fear that something had bitten through it, and called to the men to come all of them and pull upon the rope, so that he might discover whether it was indeed parted; but when they came and hauled upon it, they were unable to gather in any of it, whereat we felt all of us mightily relieved in our minds; though still unable to come at the cause of its sudden slackness.

And so, a while later, there rose the moon, and we were able to examine the island and the water between it and the weed-continent, to see whether there was anything stirring; yet neither in the valley, nor on the faces of the cliffs, nor in the open water could we perceive aught living, and as for anything among the weed, it was small use trying to discover it among all that shaggy blackness. And now, being assured that nothing was coming at us, and that, so far as our eyes could pierce, there climbed nothing upon the ropes, the bo'sun bade us get turned-in, all except those whose time it was to watch. Yet, before I went into the tent, I made a careful examination of the big rope, the which did also the bo'sun, but could perceive no cause for its slackness; though this was quite apparent in the moonlight, the rope going down with greater abruptness than it had done in the evening. And so we could but conceive that they in the hulk had slacked it for some reason; and after that we went to the tent and a further spell of sleep.

In the early morning we were waked by one of the watchmen, coming into the tent to call the bo'sun; for it appeared that the hulk had moved in the night, so that its stern was now pointed somewhat towards the island. At this news, we ran all of us from he tent to the edge of the hill, and found it to be indeed as the man had said, and now I understood the reason of that sudden slackening of the rope; for, after withstanding the stress upon it for some hours, the vessel had at last yielded, and slewed its stern towards us, moving also to some extent bodily in our direction.

And now we discovered that a man in the look-out place in the top of the structure was waving a welcome to us, at which we waved back, and then the bo'sun bade me haste and write a note to know whether it seemed to them likely that they might be able to heave the ship clear of the weed, and this I did, greatly excited within myself at this new thought, as, indeed, was the bo'sun himself and the rest of the men. For could they do this, then how easily solved were every problem of coming to our own country. But it seemed too good a thing to have come true, and yet I could but hope. And so, when my letter was completed, we put it up in the little oilskin bag, and signalled to those in the ship to haul in upon the line. Yet, when they went to haul, there came a mighty splather amid the weed, and they seemed unable to gather in any of the slack, and then, after a certain pause, I saw the man in the look-out point something, and immediately afterwards there belched out in front of him a little puff of smoke, and, presently, I caught the report of a musket, so that I knew that he was firing at something in the weed. He fired again, and yet once more, and after that they were able to haul in upon the line, and so I perceived that his fire had proved effectual; yet we had no knowledge of the thing at which he had discharged his weapon.

Now, presently, they signalled to us to draw back the line, the which we could do only with great difficulty, and then the man in the top of the superstructure signed to us to vast hauling, which we did, whereupon he began to fire again into the weed; though with what effect we could not perceive. Then, in a while, he signalled to us to haul again, and now the rope came more easily; yet still with much labour, and a commotion in the weed over which it lay and, in places, sank. And so, at last, as it cleared the weed because of the lift of the cliff, we saw that a great crab had clutched it, and that we hauled it towards us; for the creature had too much obstinacy to let go.

Perceiving this, and fearing that the great claws of the crab might divide the rope, the bo'sun caught up one of the men's lances, and ran to the cliff edge, calling to us to pull in gently, and put no more strain upon the line than need be. And so, hauling with great steadiness, we brought the monster near to the edge of the hill, and there, at a wave from the bo'sun, stayed our pulling. Then he raised the spear, and smote at the creature's eyes, as he had done on a previous occasion, and immediately it loosed its hold, and fell with a mighty splash into the water at the foot of the cliff. Then the bo'sun bade us haul in the rest of the rope, until we should come to the packet, and, in the meantime, he examined the line to see whether it had suffered harm through the mandibles of the crab; yet, beyond a little chafe, it was quite sound.

And so we came to the letter, which I opened and read, finding it to be written in the same feminine hand which had indited the others. From it we gathered that the ship had burst through a very thick mass of the weed which had compacted itself about her, and that the second mate, who was the only officer remaining to them, thought there might be good chance to heave the vessel out; though it would have to be done with great slowness, so as to allow the weed to part gradually, otherwise the ship would but act as a gigantic rake to gather up weed before it, and so form its own barrier to clear water. And after this there were kind wishes and hopes that we had spent a good night, the which I took to be prompted by the feminine heart of the writer, and after that I fell to wondering whether it was the captain's wife who acted as scribe. Then I was waked from my pondering, by one of the men crying out that they in the ship had commenced to heave again upon the big rope, and, for a time, I stood and watched it rise slowly, as it came to tautness.

I had stood there awhile, watching the rope, when, suddenly, there came a commotion amid the weed, about two-thirds of the way to the ship, and now I saw that the rope had freed itself from the weed, and, clutching it, were, maybe, a score of giant crabs. At this sight, some of the men cried out their astonishment, and then we saw that there had come a number of men into the look-out place in the top of the superstructure, and, immediately, they opened a very brisk fire upon the creatures, and so, by ones and twos they fell back into the weed, and after that, the men in the hulk resumed their heaving, and so, in a while, had the rope some feet clear of the surface.

Now, having tautened the rope so much as they thought proper, they left it to have its due effect upon the ship, and proceeded to attach a great block to it; then they signalled to us to slack away on the little rope until they had the middle part of it, and this they hitched around the neck of the block, and to the eye in the strop of the block they attached a bo'sun's chair, and so they had ready a carrier, and by this means we were able to haul stuff to and from the hulk without having to drag it across the surface of the weed; being, indeed, the fashion in which we had intended to haul ashore the people in the ship. But now we had the bigger project of salving the ship herself, and, further, the big rope, which acted as support for the carrier, was not yet of a sufficient height above the weed-continent for it to be safe to attempt to bring any ashore by such means; and now that we had hopes of saving the ship, we did not intend to risk parting the big rope, by trying to attain such a degree of tautness as would have been necessary at this time to have raised its bight to the desired height.

Now, presently, the bo'sun called out to one of the men to make breakfast, and when it was ready we came to it, leaving the man with the wounded arm to keep watch; then when we had made an end, he sent him, that had lost his fingers, to keep a look-out whilst the other came to the fire and ate his breakfast. And in the meanwhile, the bo'sun took us down to collect weed and reeds for the night, and so we spent the greater part of the morning, and when we had made an end of this, we returned to the top of the hill, to discover how matters were going forward; thus we found, from the one at the look-out, that they, in the hulk, had been obliged to heave twice upon the big rope to keep it off the weed, and by this we knew that the ship was indeed making a slow sternway towards the island—slipping steadily through the weed, and as we looked at her, it seemed almost that we could perceive that she was nearer; but this was no more than imagination; for, at most, she could not have moved more than some odd fathoms. Yet it cheered us greatly, so that we waved our congratulations to the man who stood in the look-out in the superstructure, and he waved back.

Later, we made dinner, and afterwards had a very comfortable smoke, and then the bo'sun attended to our various hurts. And so through the afternoon we sat about upon the crest of the hill overlooking the hulk, and thrice had they in the ship to heave upon the big rope, and by evening they had made near thirty fathoms towards the island, the which they told us in reply to a query which the bo'sun desired me to send them, several messages having passed between us in the course of the afternoon, so that we had the carrier upon our side. Further than this, they explained that they would tend the rope during the night, so that the strain would be kept up, and, more, this would keep the ropes off the weed.

And so, the night coming down upon us, the bo'sun bade us light the fires about the top of the hill, the same having been laid earlier in the day, and thus, our supper having been dispatched, we prepared for the night. And all through it there burned lights aboard the hulk, the which proved very companionable to us in our times of watching; and so, at last came the morning, the darkness having passed without event. And now, to our huge pleasure, we discovered that the ship had made great progress in the night; being now so much nearer that none could suppose it a matter of imagination; for she must have moved nigh sixty fathoms nearer to the island, so that now we seemed able almost to recognize the face of the man in the look-out; and many things about the hulk we saw with greater clearness, so that we scanned her with a fresh interest. Then the man in the look-out waved a morning greeting to us, the which we returned very heartily, and, even as we did so, there came a second figure beside the man, and waved some white matter, perchance a handkerchief, which is like enough, seeing that it was a woman, and at that, we took off our head coverings, all of us, and shook them at her, and after this we went to our breakfast; having finished which, the bo'sun dressed our hurts, and then, setting the man, who had lost his fingers, to watch, he took the rest of us, excepting him that was bitten in the arm, down to collect fuel, and so the time passed until near dinner.

When we returned to the hill-top, the man upon the look-out told us that they in the ship had heaved not less than four separate times upon the big rope, the which, indeed, they were doing at that present minute; and it was very plain to see that the ship had come nearer even during the short space of the morning. Now, when they had made an end of tautening the rope, I perceived that it was, at last, well clear of the weed through all its length, being at its lowest part nigh twenty feet above the surface, and, at that, a sudden thought came to me which sent me hastily to the bo'sun; for it had occurred to me that there existed no reason why we should not pay a visit to those aboard the hulk. But when I put the matter to him, he shook his head, and, for awhile, stood out against my desire; but, presently, having examined the rope, and considering that I was the lightest of any in the island, he consented, and at that I ran to the carrier which had been hauled across to our side, and got me into the chair. Now, the men, so soon as they perceived my intention, applauded me very heartily, desiring to follow; but the bo'sun bade them be silent, and, after that, he lashed me into the chair, with his own hands, and then signalled to those in the ship to haul upon the small rope; he, in the meanwhile, checking my descent towards the weeds, by means of our end of the hauling-line.

And so, presently, I had come to the lowest part, where the bight of the rope dipped downward in a bow towards the weed, and rose again to the mizzen-mast of the hulk. Here I looked downward with somewhat fearful eyes; for my weight on the rope made it sag somewhat lower than seemed to me comfortable, and I had a very lively recollection of some of the horrors which that quiet surface hid. Yet I was not long in this place; for they in the ship, perceiving how the rope let me nearer to the weed than was safe, pulled very heartily upon the hauling-line, and so I came quickly to the hulk.

Now, as I drew nigh to the ship, the men crowded upon a little platform which they had built in the superstructure somewhat below the broken head of the mizzen, and here they received me with loud cheers and very open arms, and were so eager to get me out of the bo'sun's chair, that they cut the lashings, being too impatient to cast them loose. Then they led me down to the deck, and here, before I had knowledge of aught

else, a very buxom woman took me into her arms, kissing me right heartily, at which I was greatly taken aback; but the men about me did naught
but laugh, and so, in a minute, she loosed me, and there I stood, not
knowing whether to feel like a fool or a hero; but inclining rather to the
latter. Then, at this minute, there came a second woman, who bowed to
me in a manner most formal, so that we might have been met in some
fashionable gathering, rather than in a cast-away hulk in the lonesomeness and terror of that weed-choked sea; and at her coming all the mirth
of the men died out of them, and they became very sober, whilst the
buxom woman went backward for a piece, and seemed somewhat
abashed. Now, at all this, I was greatly puzzled, and looked from one to
another to learn what it might mean; but in the same moment the woman
bowed again, and said something in a low voice touching the weather,
and after that she raised her glance to my face, so that I saw her eyes, and
they were so strange and full of melancholy, that I knew on the instant
why she spoke and acted in so unmeaning a way; for the poor creature
was out of her mind, and when I learnt afterwards that she was the
captain's wife, and had seen him die in the arms of a mighty devil-fish, I
grew to understand how she had come to such a pass.

Now for a minute after I had discovered the woman's madness, I was
so taken aback as to be unable to answer her remark; but for this there
appeared no necessity; for she turned away and went aft towards the
saloon stairway, which stood open, and here she was met by a maid very
bonny and fair, who led her tenderly down from my sight. Yet, in a
minute, this same maid appeared, and ran along the decks to me, and
caught my two hands, and shook them, and looked up at me with such
roguish, playful eyes, that she warmed my heart, which had been
strangely chilled by the greeting of the poor mad woman. And she said
many hearty things regarding my courage, to which I knew in my heart I
had no claim; but I let her run on, and so, presently, coming more to
possession of herself, she discovered that she was still holding my hands,
the which, indeed, I had been conscious of the while with a very great
pleasure; but at her discovery she dropped them with haste, and stood
back from me a space, and so there came a little coolness into her talk: yet
this lasted not long; for we were both of us young, and, I think, even thus
early we attracted one the other; though, apart from this, there was so
much that we desired each to learn, that we could not but talk freely,
asking question for question, and giving answer for answer. And thus a
time passed, in which the men left us alone, and went presently to the
capstan, about which they had taken the big rope, and at this they toiled
awhile; for already the ship had moved sufficiently to let the line fall slack.

Presently, the maid, whom I had learnt was niece to the captain's wife, and named Mary Madison, proposed to take me the round of the ship, to which proposal I agreed very willingly; but first I stopped to examine the mizzen stump, and the manner in which the people of the ship had stayed it, the which they had done very cunningly, and I noted how that they had removed some of the superstructure from about the head of the mast, so as to allow passage for the rope, without putting a strain upon the super-structure itself. Then when I had made an end upon the poop, she led me down on to the main-deck, and here I was very greatly impressed by the prodigious size of the structure which they had built about the hulk, and the skill with which it had been carried out, the supports crossing from side to side and to the decks in a manner calculated to give great solidity to that which they upheld. Yet, I was very greatly puzzled to know where they had gotten a sufficiency of timber to make so large a matter; but upon this point she satisfied me by explaining that they had taken up the 'tween decks, and used all such bulkheads as they could spare, and, fur-ther, that there had been a good deal among the dunnage which had proved usable.

And so we came at last to the galley, and here I discovered the buxom woman to be installed as cook, and there were in with her a couple of fine children, one of whom I guessed to be a boy of maybe some five years, and the second a girl, scarce able to do more than toddle. At this I turned and asked Mistress Madison whether these were her cousins; but in the next moment I remembered that they could not be; for, as I knew, the captain had been dead some seven years; yet it was the woman in the galley who answered my question; for she turned and, with something of a red face, informed me that they were hers, at which I felt some surprise; but supposed that she had taken passage in the ship with her husband; yet in this I was not correct; for she proceeded to explain that, thinking they were cut off from the world for the rest of this life, and falling very fond of the carpenter, they had made it up together to make a sort of marriage, and had gotten the second mate to read the service over them. She told me then, how that she had taken passage with her mistress, the captain's wife, to help her with her niece, who had been but a child when the ship sailed; for she had been very attached to them both, and they to her. And so she came to an end of her story, expressing a hope that she had done no wrong by her marriage, as none had been intended. And to this I made answer, assuring her that no decent-minded man could think the worse of her; but that I, for my part, thought rather the better, seeing that I liked the pluck which she had shown. At that she cast down the soup ladle, which she had in her fist, and came towards me, wiping her hands; but I gave back, for I shamed to be hugged again, and before Mistress Mary Madison, and at that she came to a stop and laughed very heartily; but, all the same, called down a very warm blessing upon my head; for which I had no cause to feel the worse. And so I passed on with the captain's niece.

Presently, having made the round of the hulk, we came aft again to the poop, and discovered that they were heaving once more upon the big rope, the which was very heartening, proving, as it did, that the ship was still a-move. And so, a little later, the girl left me, having to attend to her aunt. Now whilst she was gone, the men came all about me, desiring news of the world beyond the weed-continent, and so for the next hour I was kept very busy, answering their questions. Then the second mate called out to them to take another heave upon the rope, and at that they turned to the capstan, and I with them, and so we hove it taut again, after which they got about me once more, questioning; for so much seemed to have happened in the seven years in which they had been imprisoned. And then, after a while, I turned-to and questioned them on such points as I had neglected to ask Mistress Madison, and they discovered to me their terror and sickness of the weed-continent, its desolation and horror, and the dread which had beset them at the thought that they should all of them come to their ends without sight of their homes and countrymen.

Now, about this time, I became conscious that I had grown very empty; for I had come off to the hulk before we had made our dinner, and had been in such interest since, that the thought of food had escaped me; for I had seen none eating in the hulk, they, without doubt, having dined earlier than my coming. But now, being made aware of my state by the grumbling of my stomach, I inquired whether there was any food to be had at such a time, and, at that, one of the men ran to tell the woman in the galley that I had missed my dinner, at which she made much ado, and set-to and prepared me a very good meal, which she carried aft and set out for me in the saloon, and after that she sent me down to it.

Presently, when I had come near to being comfortable, there chanced a lightsome step upon the floor behind me, and, turning, I discovered that Mistress Madison was surveying me with a roguish and somewhat amused air. At that, I got hastily to my feet; but she bade me sit down, and therewith she took a seat opposite, and so bantered me with a gentle playfulness that was not displeasing to me, and at which I played so good a second as I had ability. Later, I fell to questioning her, and, among other matters, discovered that it was she who acted as scribe for the people in the hulk, at which I told her that I had done likewise for those on the island. After that, our talk became somewhat personal, and I learnt that she was near on to nineteen years of age, whereat I told her that I had passed my twenty-third. And so we chatted on, until, presently, it occurred to me that I had better be preparing to return to the island, and I rose to my feet with this intention; yet feeling that I had been very much happier to have stayed, the which I thought, for a moment, had not been displeasing to her, and this I imagined, noting somewhat in her eyes when I made mention that I must be gone. Yet it may be that I flattered myself.

Now when I came out on deck, they were busied again in heaving taut the rope, and, until they had made an end, Mistress Madison and I filled the time with such chatter as is wholesome between a man and maid who have not long met, yet find one another pleasing company. Then, when at last the rope was taut, I went up to the mizzen staging, and climbed into the chair, after which some of the men lashed me in very securely. Yet when they gave the signal to haul me to the island, there came for awhile no response, and then signs that we could not understand; but no movement to haul me across the weed. At that, they unlashed me from the chair, bidding me get out, whilst they sent a message to discover what might be wrong. And this they did, and, presently, there came back word that the big rope had stranded upon the edge of the cliff, and that they must slacken it somewhat at once, the which they did, with many expressions of dismay. And so, maybe an hour passed, during which we watched the men working at the rope, just where it came down over the edge of the hill, and Mistress Madison stood with us and watched; for it was very terrible, this sudden thought of failure (though it were but temporary) when they were so near to success. Yet, at last there came a signal from the island for us to loose the hauling-line, the which we did, allowing them to haul across the carrier, and so, in a little while, they signalled back to us to pull in, which, having done, we found a letter in the bag lashed to the carrier, in which the bo'sun made it plain that he had strengthened the rope, and placed fresh chafing-gear about it, so that he thought it would be so safe as ever to heave upon; but to put it to a less strain. Yet he refused to allow me to venture across upon it, saying that I must stay in the ship until we were clear of the weed; for if the rope had stranded in one place, then had it been so cruelly tested that there might be some other points at which it was ready to give. And this final note of the bo'sun's made us all very serious; for, indeed, it seemed possible that it was as he suggested; yet they reassured themselves by pointing out that, like enough, it had been the chafe upon the cliff edge which had frayed the strand, so that it had been weakened before it parted; but I, remembering the chafing-gear which the bo'sun had put about it in the first instance, felt not so sure; yet I would not add to their anxieties.

And so it came about that I was compelled to spend the night in the hulk; but, as I followed Mistress Madison into the big saloon, I felt no regret, and had near forgotten already my anxiety regarding the rope.

And out on deck there sounded most cheerily the clack of the capstan.

XVI
Freed

Now, when Mistress Madison had seated herself, she invited me to do likewise, after which we fell into talk, first touching upon the matter of the stranding of the rope, about which I hastened to assure her, and later to other things, and so, as is natural enough with a man and maid, to ourselves, and here we were very content to let it remain.

Presently, the second mate came in with a note from the bo'sun, which he laid upon the table for the girl to read, the which she beckoned me to do also, and so I discovered that it was a suggestion, written very rudely and ill-spelt, that they should send us a quantity of reeds from the island, with which we might be able to ease the weed somewhat from around the stern of the hulk, thus aiding her progress: And to this the second mate desired the girl to write a reply, saying that we should be very happy for the reeds, and would endeavour to act upon his hint, and this Mistress Madison did, after which she passed the letter to me, perchance I desired to send any message. Yet I had naught that I wished to say, and so handed it back, with a word of thanks, and, at once, she gave it to the second mate, who went, forthwith, and dispatched it.

Later, the stout woman from the galley came aft to set out the table, which occupied the centre of the saloon, and whilst she was at this, she asked for information on many things, being very free and unaffected in her speech, and seeming with less of deference to my companion, than a certain motherliness; for it was very plain that she loved Mistress Madison, and in this my heart did not blame her. Further, it was plain to me that the girl had a very warm affection for her old nurse, which was but natural, seeing that the old woman had cared for her through all the past years, besides being companion to her, and a good and cheerful one, as I could guess.

Now awhile I passed in answering the buxom woman's questions, and odd times such occasional ones as were slipt in by Mistress Madison; and then, suddenly there came the clatter of men's feet overhead, and, later, the thud of something being cast down upon the deck, and so we knew that the reeds had come. At that, Mistress Madison cried out that we should go and watch the men try them upon the weed; for that if they proved of use in easing that which lay in our path, then should we come the more speedily to the clear water, and this without the need of putting so great a strain upon the hawser, as had been the case hitherto.

When we came to the poop, we found the men removing a portion of the superstructure over the stern, and after that they took some of the stronger reeds, and proceeded to work at the weed that stretched away in a line with our taffrail. Yet that they anticipated danger, I perceived; for there stood by them two of the men and the second mate, all armed with muskets, and these three kept a very strict watch upon the weed, knowing, through much experience of its terrors, how that there might be a need for their weapons at any moment. And so a while passed, and it was plain that the men's work upon the weed was having effect; for the rope grew slack visibly, and those at the capstan had all that they could do, taking fleet and fleet with the tackle, to keep it anywhere near to tautness, and so, perceiving that they were kept so hard at it, I ran to give a hand, the which did Mistress Madison, pushing upon the capstan-bars right merrily and with heartiness. And thus a while passed, and the evening began to come down upon the lonesomeness of the weed-continent. Then there appeared the buxom woman, and bade us come to our suppers, and her manner of addressing the two of us was the manner of one who might have mothered us; but Mistress Madison cried out to her to wait, that we had found work to do, and at that the big woman laughed, and came towards us threateningly, as though intending to remove us hence by force.

And now, at this moment, there came a sudden interruption which checked our merriment; for, abruptly, there sounded the report of a musket in the stern, and then came shouts, and the noise of the two other weapons, seeming like thunder, being pent by the over-arching superstructure. And, directly, the men about the taffrail gave back, running here and there, and so I saw that great arms had come all about the opening which they had made in the superstructure, and two of these flickered in-board, searching hither and thither; but the stout woman took a man near to her, and thrust him out of danger, and after that, she caught Mistress Madison up in her big arms, and ran down on to the main-deck with her, and all this before I had come to a full knowledge of our danger. But now I perceived that I should do well to get further back from the stern, the which I did with haste, and, coming to a safe position, I stood and stared at the huge creature, its great arms, vague in the growing dusk, writhing about in vain search for a victim. Then returned the second mate, having been for more weapons, and now I observed that he armed all the men, and had brought up a spare musket for my use, and so we commenced, all of us, to fire at the monster, whereat it began to lash about most furiously, and so, after some minutes, it slipped away from the opening and slid down into the weed. Upon that several of the men rushed to replace those parts of the superstructure which had been removed, and I with them; yet there were sufficient for the job, so that I had no need to do aught; thus, before they had made up the opening, I had been given chance to look out upon the weed, and so discovered that all the surface which lay between our stern and the island, was moving in vast ripples, as though mighty fish were swimming beneath it, and then, just before the men put back the last of the great panels, I saw the weed all tossed up like to a vast pot a-boil, and then a vague glimpse of thousands of monstrous arms that filled the air, and came towards the ship.

And then the men had the panel back in its place, and were hasting to drive the supporting struts into their positions. And when this was done, we stood awhile and listened; but there came no sound above that of the wail of the wind across the extent of the weed-continent. And at that, I turned to the men, asking how it was that I could hear no sounds of the creatures attacking us, and so they took me up into the look-out place, and from there I stared down at the weed; but it was without movement, save for the stirring of the wind, and there was nowhere any sign of the devil-fish. Then, seeing me amazed, they told me how that anything which moved the weed seemed to draw them from all parts; but that they seldom touched the hulk unless there was something visible to them which had movement. Yet, as they went on to explain, there would be hundreds and hundreds of them lying all about the ship, hiding in the weed; but that, if we took care not to show ourselves within their reach, they would have gone most of them by the morning. And this the men told me in a very matter-of-fact way; for they had become inured to such happenings.

Presently, I heard Mistress Madison calling to me by name, and so descended out of the growing darkness, to the interior of the superstructure, and here they had lit a number of rude slush-lamps, the oil for which, as I learned later, they obtained from a certain fish which haunted the sea, beneath the weed, in very large schools, and took near any sort of bait with great readiness. And so, when I had climbed down into the light, I found the girl waiting for me to come to supper, for which I discovered myself to be in a mightily agreeable humour.

Presently, having made an end of eating, she leaned back in her seat and commenced once more to bait me in her playful manner, the which appeared to afford her much pleasure, and in which I joined with no less, and so we fell presently to more earnest talk, and in this wise we passed a great space of the evening. Then there came to her a sudden idea, and what must she do but propose that we should climb to the look-out, and to this I agreed with a very happy willingness. And to the look-out we went. Now when we had come there, I perceived her reason for this freak; for away in the night, astern the hulk, there blazed half way between the heaven and the sea, a mighty glow, and suddenly, as I stared, being dumb with admiration and surprise, I knew that it was the blaze of our fires upon the crown of the bigger hill; for, all the hill being in shadow, and hidden by the darkness, there showed only the glow of the fires, hung, as it were, in the void, and a very striking and beautiful spectacle it was. Then, as I watched, there came, abruptly a figure into view upon the edge of the glow, showing black and minute, and this I knew to be one of the men come to the edge of the hill to take a look at the hulk, or test the strain on the hawser. Now, upon my expressing admiration of the sight to Mistress Madison, she seemed greatly pleased, and told me that she had been up many times in the darkness to view it. And after that we went down again into the interior of the superstructure, and here the men were taking a further heave upon the big rope, before settling the watches for the night, the which they managed, by having one man at a time to keep awake and call the rest whenever the hawser grew slack.

Later, Mistress Madison showed me where I was to sleep, and so, having bid one another a very warm good-night, we parted, she going to see that her aunt was comfortable, and I out on to the main-deck to have a chat with the man on watch. In this way, I passed the time until midnight, and in that while we had been forced to call the men thrice to heave upon the hawser, so quickly had the ship begun to make way through the weed. Then, having grown sleepy, I said good-night, and went to my berth, and so had my first sleep upon a mattress, for some weeks.

Now when the morning was come, I waked, hearing Mistress Madison calling upon me from the other side of my door, and rating me very saucily for a lie-a-bed, and at that I made good speed at dressing, and came quickly into the saloon, where she had ready a breakfast that made me glad I had waked. But first, before she would do aught else, she had me out to the look-out place, running up before me most merrily and singing in the fullness of her glee, and so, when I had come to the top of the superstructure, I perceived that she had very good reason for so much merriment, and the sight which came to my eyes, gladdened me most mightily, yet at the same time filling me with a great amazement; for, behold! in the course of that one night, we had made near unto two hundred fathoms across the weed, being now, with what we had made previously, no more than some thirty fathoms in from the edge of the weed. And there stood Mistress Madison beside me, doing somewhat of a dainty step-dance upon the flooring of the look-out, and singing a quaint old lilt that I had not heard that dozen years, and this little thing, I think, brought back more clearly to me than aught else how that this winsome maid had been lost to the world for so many years, having been scarce of the age of twelve when the ship had been lost in the weed-continent. Then, as I turned to make some remark, being filled with many feelings, there came a hail, from far above in the air, as it might be, and, looking up, I discovered the men upon the hill to be standing along the edge, and waving to us, and now I perceived how that the hill towered a very great way above us, seeming, as it were, to overhang the hulk though we were yet some seventy fathoms distant from the sheer sweep of its nearer precipe. And so, having waved back our greeting, we made down to breakfast, and, having come to the saloon, set-to upon the good victuals, and did very sound justice thereto.

Presently, having made an end of eating, and hearing the clack of the capstan-pawls, we hurried out on deck, and put our hands upon the bars, intending to join in that last heave which should bring the ship free out of her long captivity, and so for a time we moved round about the capstan, and I glanced at the girl beside me; for she had become very solemn, and indeed it was a strange and solemn time for her; for she, who had dreamed of the world as her childish eyes had seen it, was now, after many hopeless years, to go forth once more to it—to live in it, and to learn how much had been dreams, and how much real; and with all these thoughts I credited her; for they seemed such as would have come to me at such a time, and, presently, I made some blundering effort to show to her that I had understanding of the tumult which possessed her, and at that she smiled up at me with a sudden queer flash of sadness and merriment, and our glances met, and I saw something in hers, which was but new-born, and though I was but a young man, my heart interpreted it for me, and I was all hot suddenly with the pain and sweet delight of this new thing; for I had not dared to think upon that which already my heart had made bold to whisper to me, so that even thus soon I was miserable out of her presence. Then she looked downward at her hands upon the bar; and, in the same instant, there came a loud, abrupt cry from the second mate, to vast heaving, and at that all the men pulled out their bars and cast them upon the deck, and ran, shouting, to the ladder that led to the look-out, and we followed, and so came to the top, and discovered that at last the ship was clear of the weed, and floating in the open water between it and the island.

Now at the discovery that the hulk was free, the men commenced to cheer and shout in a very wild fashion, as, indeed, is no cause for wonder, and we cheered with them. Then, suddenly, in the midst of our shouting, Mistress Madison plucked me by the sleeve and pointed to the end of the island where the foot of the bigger hill jutted out in a great spur, and now I perceived a boat, coming round into view, and in another moment I saw that the bo'sun stood in the stern, steering; thus I knew that he must have finished repairing her whilst I had been on the hulk. By this, the men about us had discovered the nearness of the boat, and commenced shouting afresh, and they ran down, and to the bows of the vessel, and got ready a rope to cast. Now when the boat came near, the men in her scanned us very curiously; but the bo'sun took off his head-gear, with a clumsy grace that well became him; at which Mistress Madison smiled very kindly upon him, and, after that, she told me with great frankness that he pleased her, and, more, that she had never seen so great a man, which was not strange seeing that she had seen but few since she had come to years when men become of interest to a maid.

After saluting us the bo'sun called out to the second mate that he would tow us round to the far side of the island, and to this the officer agreed, being, I surmised, by no means sorry to put some solid matter between himself and the desolation of the great weed-continent; and so, having loosed the hawser, which fell from the hill-top with a prodigious splash, we had the boat ahead, towing. In this wise we opened out, presently, the end of the hill; but feeling now the force of the breeze, we bent a kedge to the hawser, and, the bo'sun carrying it seawards, we warped ourselves to windward of the island, and here, in forty fathoms, we vast heaving, and rode to the kedge.

Now when this was accomplished they called to our men to come aboard, and this they did, and spent all of that day in talk and eating; for those in the ship could scarce make enough of our fellows. And then, when it had come to night, they replaced that part of the superstructure which they had removed from about the head of the mizzen-stump, and so, all being secure, each one turned-in and had a full night's rest, of the which, indeed, many of them stood in sore need.

The following morning, the second mate had a consultation with the bo'sun, after which he gave the order to commence upon the removal of the great superstructure, and to this each one of us set himself with vigour. Yet it was a work requiring some time, and near five days had passed before we had the ship stripped clear. When this had been accomplished, there came a busy time of routing out various matter of which we should have need in jury rigging her; for they had been so long in disuse, that none remembered where to look for them. At this a day and half was spent, and after that we set-to about fitting her with such jury-masts as we could manage from our material.

Now, after the ship had been dismasted, all those seven years gone, the crew had been able to save many of her spars, these having remained attached to her, through their inability to cut away all of the gear; and though this had put them in sore peril at the time, of being sent to the bottom with a hole in their side, yet now had they every reason to be thankful; for, by this accident, we had now a foreyard, a topsail-yard, a main t'gallant-yard, and the fore-topmast. They had saved more than these; but had made use of the smaller spars to shore up the superstructure, sawing them into lengths for that purpose. Apart from such spars as they had managed to secure, they had a spare topmast lashed along under the larboard bulwarks, and a spare t'gallant and royal-mast lying along the starboard side.

Now, the second mate and the bo'sun set the carpenter to work upon the spare topmast, bidding him make for it some trestle-trees and bolsters, upon which to lay the eyes of the rigging; but they did not trouble him to shape it. Further, they ordered the same to be fitted to the fore-topmast and the spare t'gallant and royal-mast. And in the meanwhile, the rigging was prepared, and when this was finished, they made ready the shears to hoist the spare topmast, intending this to take the place of the main lower-mast. Then, when the carpenter had carried out their orders, he was set to make three partners with a step cut in each, these being intended to take the heels of the three masts, and when these were completed, they bolted them securely to the decks at the fore part of each one of the stumps of the three lower-masts. And so, having all ready, we hove the main-mast into position, after which we proceeded to rig it. Now, when we had made an end of this, we set-to upon the foremast, using for this the fore-topmast which they had saved, and after that we hove the mizzen-mast into place, having for this the spare t'gallant and royal-mast.

Now the manner in which we secured the masts, before ever we came to the rigging of them, was by lashing them to the stumps of the lower-masts, and after we had lashed them, we drove dunnage and wedges between the masts and the lashings, thus making them very secure. And so, when we had set up the rigging, we had confidence that they would stand all such sail as we should be able to set upon them. Yet, further than this, the bo'sun bade the carpenter make wooden caps of six-inch oak, these caps to fit over the *squared* heads of the lower-mast stumps, and having a hole, each of them, to embrace the jury-mast, and by making these caps in two halves, they were abled to bolt them on after the masts had been hove into position.

And so, having gotten in our three jury lower-masts, we hoisted up the foreyard to the main, to act as our mainyard, and did likewise with the topsail-yard to the fore, and after that, we sent up the t'gallant-yard to the mizzen. Thus we had her sparred, all but a bowsprit and jibboom; yet this we managed by making a stumpy, spike bowsprit from one of the smaller spars which they had used to shore up the superstructure, and because we feared that it lacked strength to bear the strain of our fore and aft stays, we took down two hawsers from the fore, passing them in through the hawse-holes and setting them up there. And so we had her rigged, and, after that, we bent such sail as our gear abled us to carry, and in this wise had the hulk ready for sea.

Now, the time that it took us to rig the ship, and fit her out, was seven weeks, saving one day. And in all this time we suffered no molestation from any of the strange habitants of the weed-continent; though this may have been because we kept fires of dried weed going all the night about the decks, these fires being lit on big flat pieces of rock which we had gotten from the island. Yet, for all that we had not been troubled, we had more than once discovered strange things in the water swimming near to the vessel; but a flare of weed, hung over the side, on the end of a reed, had sufficed always to scare away such unholy visitants.

And so at last we came to the day on which we were in so good a condition that the bo'sun and the second mate considered the ship to be in a fit state to put to sea—the carpenter having gone over so much of her hull as he could get at, and found her everywhere very sound; though her lower parts were hideously overgrown with weed, barnacles and other matters; yet this we could not help, and it was not wise to attempt to scrape her, having consideration to the creatures which we knew to abound in those waters.

Now in those seven weeks, Mistress Madison and I had come very close to one another, so that I had ceased to call her by any name save Mary, unless it were a dearer one than that; though this would be one of my own invention, and would leave my heart too naked did I put it down here.

Of our love one for the other, I think yet, and ponder how that mighty man, the bo'sun, came so quickly to a knowledge of the state of our hearts; for he gave me a very sly hint one day that he had a sound idea of the way in which the wind blew, and yet, though he said it with a half-jest, methought there was something wistful in his voice, as he spoke, and at that I just clapt my hand in his, and he gave it a very huge grip. And after that he ceased from the subject.

XVII
How We Came to Our Own Country

Now when the day came on which we made to leave the nearness of the island, and the waters of that strange sea, there was great lightness of heart among us, and we went very merrily about such tasks as were needful. And so, in a little, we had the kedge tripped, and had cast the ship's head to starboard, and presently, had her braced up upon the larboard tack, the which we managed very well; though our gear worked heavily, as might be expected. And after that we had gotten under way, we went to the lee side to witness the last of that lonesome island, and with us came the men of the ship, and so, for a space, there was a silence among us; for they were very quiet, looking astern and saying naught; but we had sympathy with them, knowing somewhat of those past years.

And now the bo'sun came to the break of the poop, and called down to the men to muster aft, the which they did, and I with them; for I had come to regard them as my very good comrades; and rum was served out to each of them, and to me along with the rest, and it was Mistress Madison herself who dipped it out to us from the wooden bucket; though it was the buxom woman who had brought it up from the lazarette. Now, after the rum, the bo'sun bade the crew to clear up the gear about the decks, and get matters secured, and at that I turned to go with the men, having become so used to work with them; but he called to me to come up to him upon the poop, the which I did, and there he spoke respectfully, remonstrating with me, and reminding me that now there was need no longer for me to toil; for that I was come back to my old position of passenger, such as I had been in the *Glen Carrig,* ere she foundered. But to this talk of his, I made reply that I had as good a right to work my passage home as any other among us; for though I had paid for a passage in the *Glen Carrig,* I had done no such thing regarding the *Seabird*—this being the name of the hulk—and to this, my reply, the bo'sun said little; but I perceived that he liked my spirit, and so from thence until we reached the Port of London, I took my turn and part in all seafaring matters, having become by this quite proficient in the calling. Yet, in one matter, I availed myself of my former position; for I chose to live aft, and by this was abled to see much of my sweetheart, Mistress Madison.

Now after dinner upon the day on which we left the island, the bo'sun and the second mate picked the watches, and thus I found myself chosen to be in the bo'sun's, at which I was mightily pleased. And when the watches had been picked, they had all hands to 'bout ship, the which, to the pleasure of all, she accomplished; for under such gear and with so much growth upon her bottom, they had feared that we should have to veer, and by this we should have lost much distance to leeward, whereas we desired to edge so much to windward as we could, being anxious to put space between us and the weed-continent. And twice more that day we put the ship about, though the second time it was to avoid a great bank of weed that lay floating athwart our bows; for all the sea to windward of the island, so far as we had been able to see from the top of the higher hill, was studded with floating masses of the weed, like unto thousands of islets, and in places like to far-spreading reefs. And, because of these, the sea all about the island remained very quiet and unbroken, so that there was never any surf, no, nor scarce a broken wave upon its shore, and this, for all that the wind had been fresh for many days.

When the evening came, we were again upon the larboard tack, making, perhaps, some four knots in the hour; though, had we been in proper rig, and with a clean bottom, we had been making eight or nine, with so good a breeze and so calm a sea. Yet, so far, our progress had been very reasonable; for the island lay, maybe, some five miles to leeward, and about fifteen astern. And so we prepared for the night. Yet, a little before dark, we discovered that the weed-continent trended out towards us; so that we should pass it, maybe, at a distance of something like half a mile, and, at that, there was talk between the second mate and the bo'sun as to whether it was better to put the ship about, and gain a greater sea-room before attempting to pass this promontory of weed; but at last they decided that we had naught to fear; for we had fair way through the water, and further, it did not seem reasonable to suppose that we should have aught to fear from the habitants of the weed-continent, at so great a distance as the half of a mile. And so we stood on; for, once past the point, there was much likelihood of the weed trending away to the Eastward, and if this were so, we could square-in immediately and get the wind upon our quarter, and so make better way.

Now it was the bo'sun's watch from eight of the evening until midnight, and I, with another man, had the look-out until four bells. Thus it chanced that, coming abreast of the point during our time of watching, we peered very earnestly to leeward; for the night was dark, having no moon until nearer the morning; and we were full of unease in that we had come so near again to the desolation of that strange continent. And then, suddenly, the man with me clutched my shoulder, and pointed into the darkness upon our bow, and thus I discovered that we had come nearer to the weed than the bo'sun and the second mate had intended; they, without doubt, having miscalculated our leeway. At this, I turned and sung out to the bo'sun that we were near to running upon the weed, and, in the same moment, he shouted to the helmsman to luff, and directly afterwards our starboard side was brushing against the great outlying tufts of the point, and so, for a breathless minute, we waited. Yet the ship drew clear, and so into the open water beyond the point; but I had seen something as we scraped against the weed, a sudden glimpse of white, gliding among the growth, and then I saw others, and, in a moment, I was down on the main-deck, and running aft to the bo'sun; yet midway along the deck a horrid shape came above the starboard rail, and I gave out a loud cry of warning. Then I had a capstan-bar from the rack near, and smote with it at the thing, crying all the while for help, and at my blow the thing went from my sight, and the bo'sun was with me, and some of the men.

Now the bo'sun had seen my stroke, and so sprang upon the t'gallant rail, and peered over; but gave back on the instant, shouting to me to run and call the other watch, for that the sea was full of the monsters swimming off to the ship, and at that I was away at a run, and when I had waked the men, I raced aft to the cabin and did likewise with the second mate, and so returned in a minute, bearing the bo'sun's cutlass, my own cut-and-thrust, and the lantern that hung always in the saloon. Now when I had gotten back, I found all things in a mighty scurry—men running about in their shirts and drawers, some in the galley bringing fire from the stove, and others lighting a fire of dry weed to leeward of the galley, and along the starboard rail there was already a fierce fight, the men using capstan-bars, even as I had done. Then I thrust the bo'sun's cutlass into his hand, and at that he gave a great shout, part of joy, and part of approbation, and after that he snatched the lantern from me, and had run to the larboard side of the deck, before I was well aware that he had taken the light; but now I followed him, and happy it was for all of us in the ship that he had thought to go at that moment; for the light of the lantern showed me the vile faces of three of the weed men climbing over the larboard rail; yet the bo'sun had cleft them or ever I could come near; but in a moment I was full busy; for there came nigh a dozen heads above the rail a little aft of where I was, and at that I ran at them, and did good execution; but some had been aboard, if the bo'sun had not come to my help. And now the decks were full of light, several fires having been lit, and the second mate having brought out fresh lanterns; and now the men had gotten their cutlasses, the which were more handy than the capstan-bars; and so the fight went forward, some having come over to our side to help us, and a very wild sight it must have seemed to any onlooker; for all about the decks burned the fires and the lanterns, and along the rails ran the men, smiting at hideous faces that rose in dozens into the wild glare of our fighting lights. And everywhere drifted the stench of the brutes. And up on the poop, the fight was as brisk as elsewhere; and here, having been drawn by a cry for help, I discovered the buxom woman smiting with a gory meat-axe at a vile thing which had gotten a clump of its tentacles upon her dress; but she had dispatched it, or ever my sword could help her, and then, to my astonishment, even at that time of peril, I discovered the captain's wife, wielding a small sword, and the face of her was like to the face of a tiger; for her mouth was drawn, and showed her teeth clenched; but she uttered no word nor cry, and I doubt not but that she had some vague idea that she worked her husband's vengeance.

Then, for a space, I was as busy as any, and afterwards I ran to the buxom woman to demand the whereabouts of Mistress Madison, and she, in a very breathless voice, informed me that she had locked her in her room out of harm's way, and at that I could have embraced the woman; for I had been sorely anxious to know that my sweetheart was safe.

And, presently, the fight diminished, and so, at last, came to an end, the ship having drawn well away from the point, and being now in the open. And after that I ran down to my sweetheart, and opened her door, and thus, for a space, she wept, having her arms about my neck; for she had been in sore terror for me, and for all the ship's company. But, soon, drying her tears, she grew very indignant with her nurse for having locked her into her room, and refused to speak to that good woman for near an hour. Yet I pointed out to her that she could be of very great use in dressing such wounds as had been received, and so she came back to her usual brightness, and brought out bandages, and lint, and ointment, and thread, and was presently very busy.

Now it was later that there rose a fresh commotion in the ship; for it had been discovered that the captain's wife was a-missing. At this, the bo'sun and the second mate instituted a search; but she was nowhere to be found, and, indeed, none in the ship ever saw her again, at which it was presumed that she had been dragged over by some of the weed men, and so come upon her death. And at this, there came a great prostration to my sweetheart so that she would not be comforted for the space of nigh three days, by which time the ship had come clear of those strange seas, having left the incredible desolation of the weed-continent far under our starboard counter.

And so, after a voyage which lasted for nine and seventy days since getting under weigh, we came to the Port of London, having refused all offers of assistance on the way.

Now here, I had to say farewell to my comrades of so many months and perilous adventures; yet, being a man not entirely without means, I took care that each of them should have a certain gift by which to remember me.

And I placed monies in the hands of the buxom woman, so that she could have no reason to stint my sweetheart, and she having—for the comfort of her conscience—taken her good man to the church, set up a little house upon the borders of my estate; but this was not until Mistress Madison had come to take her place at the head of my hall in the County of Essex.

Now one further thing there is of which I must tell. Should any, chancing to trespass upon my estate, come upon a man of very mighty proportions, albeit somewhat bent by age, seated comfortably at the door of his little cottage, then shall they know him for my friend the bo'sun; for to this day do he and I fore-gather, and let our talk drift to the desolate places of this earth, pondering upon that which we have seen—the weed-continent, where reigns desolation and the terror of its strange habitants. And, after that, we talk softly of the land where God hath made monsters after the fashion of trees. Then, maybe, my children come about me, and so we change to other matters; for the little ones love not terror.

ᗡhe Song of the Sirens

Edward Lucas White

I FIRST CAUGHT SIGHT of him as he sat on the wharf. He was seated on a rather large seaman's chest that was painted green and very much battered. He wore gray, his shirt was navy-blue flannel, his necktie a flaring red bandana handkerchief knotted loosely under an ill-fitting lop-sided collar, his hat was soft, gray felt and he held it in his hands on his knees. His hair was fine, straight and lightish, his eyes china-blue, his nose straight, his skin tanned. His features were those of an intelligent face, but there was in it no expression of intelligence, in fact no expression at all. It was this absence of expression that caught my eye. His face was blank, not with the blankness of vacuity, but with the insensibility of abstraction. He sat there amid the voluble loafers, the hurrying stevedores, the shouting wharf-hands, the chattering tackles, the creaking shears and all the hurry and bustle of unloading or loading four vessels, as imperturbable as a bronze statue of Buddha in meditation. His gaze was fixed unvaryingly straight before him and he seemed to notice and observe more distant objects; the larger panorama of moving craft in the harbor, the fussy haste of the scuttling tugboats tugging nothing, the sullen reluctance of the urged scows, the outgoing and incoming pungies and schooners, the interwoven pattern they all formed together, the break in it now and again from the dignified passage of a towed bark or ship or from the stately progress of a big steamer. Of all this he seemed aware, but of what went on about him he seemed not only unaware but unconscious, with an impassivity not as if intentionaly aloof nor absorbingly preoccupied but as if utterly unconscious or totally insensible to it all. During my long, fidgety wait that first morning I watched him at intervals a good part of the time. Once a pimply, bloated boarding-master, patrolling the wharf, stopped full in front of him, caught his eye and exchanged a few words with him, otherwise no one seemed to notice him, and he scarcely moved, bare-headed all the while in the June sunlight. When I was at last notified that the *Medorus* would not sail that day, went over her side, and left the pier, I saw him sitting as when I first caught sight of him.

Next morning I found him in almost the same spot, in precisely the same attitude and with the same demeanor. He might have been there all night.

Soon after I reached the *Medorus* the second morning the bloated boarding-master came on board with that rarity, a native American seaman. I was sitting on the cabin-deck by the saloon-skylight, Griswold on one side of me and Mr. Collins on the other. Captain Benson, puffy, pasty-faced and shifty-eyed, was sitting on the booby-hatch, whistling in an exasperatingly monotonous, tuneless and meaningless fashion. As soon as the Yankee came up the companion-ladder, he halted, turned to the boarding-master, who was following him and blurted out:

"What! Beast Benson! Me ship with Beast Benson!" And back he went down the ladder and off up the pier.

Benson said never a word, but recommenced his whistling. It was part of his undignified shiftlessness that he aired his shame on deck. Almost any captain, fool or knave or both, would have kept his cabin or sat by his saloon table. Benson advertised his helplessness to crew, loafers and passers-by alike.

The boarding-master walked up to Mr. Collins and said:

"You see, sir. I can't do anything. You're lucky enough to be only two hands short for a crew and luckier to have gotten a second mate to sign. Wilson's the best I can do for first mate. He's willing and he's the only man I can get. Not another boarding-master will so much as try for you."

Mr. Collins kept his irritating set smile, his mean little eyes peering out of his narrow face, his stubby scrubbing-brush pepper-and-salt mustache bristling against his nose. He made no reply to the boarding-master but turned to Griswold.

"You're a doctor, aren't you?" he queried.

"Not yet," Griswold replied.

"Well," said Mr. Collins impatiently, "you know pretty much what doctors know?"

"Pretty much, I trust," Griswold answered cheerfully.

"Can you tell whether a man is deaf or not?" Mr. Collins pursued.

"I fancy I could," Griswold declared, gaily.

"Would you mind testing that man over there for me?" Mr. Collins jerked his thumb toward the impassive figure on the seaman's chest.

Griswold stared.

"He looks deaf enough from here," he asserted.

"Try him nearer," Mr. Collins insisted.

* * *

Griswold swung off the cabin-deck, lounged over to the companion ladder went down it leisurely and sauntered toward the seated mariner. Griswold had a taking way with him, a jaunty manner, an agreeable smile, a charming demeanor and plenty of self-confidence. He usually got on immediately with strangers. So now you could see him win at once the confidence of the man. He looked up at him with a sentient and interested personal glance. They talked some little time and then Griswold sauntered back. He did not speak but seated himself by me as before, lit a fresh cigarette and smoked reflectively.

"Is he deaf?" Mr. Collins inquired.

"Deaf is no word for it," Griswold declared, "an adder is nothing to him. I'll bet he has neither tympanum, malleus, incus nor stapes in either ear, and that both cochleas are totally ossified; that the middle ear is annihilated and the inner ear obliterated on both sides of his head. His hearing is not defective, it is abolished, non-existent. I never saw or heard of a man who impressed me as being so totally deaf."

"What did I tell you?" broke in Captain Benson from the booby-hatch.

"Benson, shut up," said Mr. Collins. Benson took it without any change of expression or attitude.

"You seemed to talk to him," Mr. Collins said to Griswold.

"He can read lips cleverly," Griswold replied. "Only once did I have to repeat anything."

"Did you ask him if he was deaf?" Mr. Collins inquired.

"I did," said Griswold, "and he told the truth instanter."

"Impressed you as truthful, did he?" Mr. Collins queried.

"Notably," Griswold said. "There is a gentlemanly something about him. He is the kind of man you respect from the first and truthful as possible."

"You hear that, Benson?" Mr. Collins asked.

"What's truthfulness of a pitch-dark night in a gale of wind!" Benson snorted. "The man's stone deaf."

Mr. Collins flared up.

"You may take your choice of three ways," he said, "the *Medorus* tows you out at noon. If you can find a first mate to suit you by then, or if you take Wilson as first mate, you take her out. If not, I'll find another master for her and you can find another ship."

Benson lumbered off the booby-hatch and disappeared down the cabin companion-way. The cabin-boy came up whistling, went briskly over the side and scampered some little distance up the pier to where three boarding-masters stood chatting. One of them came back with him, three or four half sober sailors tagging after him. These he left by the deaf man's sea chest. Its owner came aboard with him and together they went down into the cabin.

"Look here, Mr. Collins," I said, "I've half a mind to back out of this and stay ashore!"

"Why?" he queried, his little gray eyes like slits in his face.

"I heard this captain called Beast Benson, I see he had difficulty in getting a crew and before me you force him to take a deaf mate. An unwilling crew, a defective officer and an unpopular captain seem to me to make a risky combination."

"All combinations are risky at sea, as far as that goes," said Mr. Collins easily. "Most crews are unwilling and few captains popular. Benson is not half a bad captain. He always has bother getting a crew because he is economical of food with them. But you'll find good eating in the cabin. He has never had any trouble with a crew, once at sea. He is cautious, takes better care of his sails, rigging and tackle than any man I know, is a natural genius at seamanship, humoring his ship, coaxing the wind and all that. And he is a precious sharp hand to sell flour and buy coffee, I can tell you. You'll be safe with him. I should feel perfectly safe with him. I'm sorry I can't go, I can tell you."

"But the deaf mate," I persisted.

"He has good discharges," said Mr. Collins, "and is well spoken of. He's all right."

At that moment the boarding-master came out of the cabin and went over the side. Two of the sailors picked up the first-mate's chest and it was soon aboard. The two men went down into the cabin to sign articles. As they went down and as they came up I had a good look at them. One was a Mecklenburger, a lout of a hulking boy, with an ugly face made uglier by loathsome swellings under his chin. The other was a big, stout Irishman, his curly hair tousled, his fat face flushed, his eyes wild and rolling with the after-effects of a shore debauch. His eyes were notable, one bright enamel-blue, the other skinned-over with an opaque, white film. He lurched against the companion-hatch, as he came up, and half rolled, half stumbled forward. He was still three-quarters drunk.

The *Medorus* towed us at noon. Mr. Collins and Griswold stayed aboard till the tug cast loose, about dusk. After that he worked down the bay under our own sail. Even in the bay I was seasick and for some days I took little interest in anything. I had made some attempt to eat, but beyond calling the first mate Mr. Wilson and the second mate Mr. Olsen, my brief stays at the table had profited me little. I had brought a steamer-chair with me and lolled in it most of the daylight, too limp to notice much of anything.

I couldn't help noticing Captain Benson's undignified behavior. A merchant captain, beyond taking the sun each morning and noon and being waked at midnight by the mate just off watch to hear his report, plotting his course on his chart and keeping his log, concerns himself not at all with the management of his ship, except when he takes the wheel at the critical moment of tacking, or of box-hauling, if the wind changes suddenly or when a dangerous storm makes it incumbent upon him to take charge continually. Otherwise he leaves all routine matters to the mate on watch.

Benson transgressed sea-etiquette continually in this respect. He was forever nosing about and interfering with one or the other mate in respect to matters too small for a self-respecting captain's notice. His mate's contempt for him was plain enough, but was discreetly veiled behind silent lips, expressionless face and far-off eyes. The men were more open and exchanged sneering glances. The captain would sit on the edge of the cabin-deck, his feet dangling over the poop-deck, and continually nag the steersman, keeping it up for hours.

"Keep her up to the wind," he would say, "keep that royal lifting."

"Aye, aye, sir," would come from the man at the wheel.

Next moment, the captain would shout:

"Let her off, you damn fool. You'll have her aback!"

"Let her go off, sir," the victim would reply.

Presently again Benson would snarl:

"Where are you lettin' her go to? Keep her up to the wind."

"Keep her up to wind, sir," would come the reply and so on in maddening reiteration.

A day or two after we cleared the capes the big one-eyed Irishman had the wheel. His name, I found afterwards, was Terence Burke and he was from Five Rivers, Canada. He had been a mariner all his life; knew most of the seas and ports of the world. He was especially proud of having been in the United States Navy and of his Civil War record. He had been one of the seamen on the *Congress* or the *Cumberland,* I forget which, and graphic were his descriptions of his sensations while the *Merrimac*'s shells were tearing through the helpless ship, the men lying flat in rows on the farther side of the decks and the six-foot live-oak splinters, deadly as the bits of shell themselves, flying murderously about as each shell burst; of how they took to their boats after dark, and reached the shore, expecting to be captured every moment; of how they saw the *Ericsson*'s lights (Burke always called the *Monitor* the *Ericsson*) coming in from the sea, and took heart. Burke was justly proud that he had been one of the men detailed, as biggest and strongest, to work the *Ericsson*'s guns, and that he had helped fight her big turret guns in her famous first battle.

All this about Burke I did not learn till many days later. But it was plain to be seen, even by a seasick land-lubber, that he was an able seaman, seasoned, competent and self-respecting. All that was manifest all over him as he stood at the wheel. Likewise it was plain that he had brought liquor aboard with him, for he was still half drunk, and quarrelsome drunk. Even I could see that in his attitude, in his florid face, in his boiled eye. But Captain Benson did not see it when presently he came on deck and seated himself on the edge of the cabin-deck. He cocked his eye up the main-mast and presently growled:

"Let her go off."

Burke shifted the wheel a quarter of a spoke, his jaws clenched, his lips tight shut.

Benson chewed on his quid and kept his eye aloft. Again he growled:

"Keep her up to the wind."

Burke shifted the wheel back a quarter of a spoke, again without any word.

"I'll learn ye sea-manners," Benson snarled. "I'll learn ye to repeat after me what I say. Do ye hear me?"

"Aye, aye, sor," Burke replied, smartly enough.

Shortly Benson came at him again, shouting:

"Let her go off, you damn fool."

"Let her go off, you damn fool, sor," Burke sang out in a rasping Celtic roar which carried to the jibboom.

It was Olsen's watch and the big Norseman was standing by the weather-rigging, his hand on one of the main shrouds. He grinned broadly, full in Captain Benson's face and then looked away to windward. Burke was clutching the spokes as if he were ready to tear them out of the wheel. He looked fighting mad all over. Captain Benson looked aft at him, looked forward, looked aloft and then rose and went below without a word. Henceforward he worried the steersman no more, unless it were Dutch Charlie, the big loutish boy with the ulcerated chin, or Pomeranian Emil, a timid Baltic waif. Burke and the other full-grown men he let alone.

Next day Burke looked drunker and more belligerent than ever. I noted it, even in my half daze of flabby nauseated weakness, which subdued me so totally that not even a beautiful and novel spectacle revived me. It was just before noon. The captain and the first mate had come on deck with their sextants to determine our latitude. The day was fine with a gentle steady breeze, a clear sky and unclouded sunlight, over all the white-capped blue waters. Smoke sighted a little before turned out to be that of a British man-of-war.

Just as the captain told the man at the wheel to make it eight-bells, the man-of-war crossed our bows, all white paint and gliding, her ensign spread, flags everywhere, her band playing and her crew manning the yards. The cabin-boy said it was an English bank-holiday, and that she was bound for Bermuda. I was too flaccid to ask further or to care. I made no attempt to go below for the noon meal. I lay at length in my chair. While the captain and mates were at their dinner I could hear loud voices from the forecastle, or perhaps around the galley door.

Presently the first-mate came on deck. He walked to starboard, which was to windward, and stood staring after the far-off smoke of the vanished man-of-war. He was a tall, clean-built, square-shouldered man, English in every detail of movement, attitude and demeanor. He interested me, for in spite of his expressionless face he looked far too intelligent for his calling. I was watching him when I was aware of Burke puffing and snorting aft along the main-deck. He puffed and snorted up the port companion-ladder to the poop-deck. His face was redder than ever and his eyes redder than his face. He carried a pan of scouse or biscuit-hash or some such mess. He approached the first-mate from behind and hailed him.

"Luke at thot, sor," he said. "Uz thot fit fude fur min?"

The mate, unaware of his presence, did not move or speak.

"Luke at thot, Oi say," Burke roared. "Uz thot fit to fade min on?"

The mate remained immobile.

Burke gave a sort of snarling howl, hurled at the mate the pannikin, which hit him on the back of the head, its contents going all over his neck and down his collar. As he threw it Burke leaped at the officer. He whirled round before he was seized and met the attack with a short, right-hand jab on Burke's jaw. There was not enough swing in the blow to down the sailor. He clutched both lapels of the mate's open pea jacket and pulled him forward. The force the mate had put into the blow, and the impetus it had imparted to Burke, besides his sideways wrench, took the mate half off his feet. He got in a second jab, this time with his left hand, but again too short to be effective. Both men lurched toward the booby-hatch and the inside breast-pockets of the mate's jolted jacket cascaded a shower of letters upon the deck, which blew hither and thither to port. My chair was out on the cabin-deck just above the port companion-ladder. The booky man's instinct to save written paper shook me out of my lethargy. In an instant I was out of my chair, down the ladder and picking up the scattered envelopes. Not one, I think, went overboard. I saved three by the port rail and a half a dozen more further inboard.

As I scrambled out from one to the other I glanced again and again at the men struggling on the other side of the booby-hatch. The mate had not lost his footing. His short-arm jabs had pushed Burke back till he lost hold of the pea jacket. The Irishman gathered himself for a rush, the mate squared off, in perfect form, met the rush with a left-hand upper cut on the seaman's chin, calculated his swing and planted a terribly accurate right-hand drive full in Burke's face. He went backward over the starboard companion-ladder down into the main deck.

Paying no more attention to him the mate turned to pick up his letters. He found several on the deck against the booby-hatch, and one by the break of the cabin. Then he looked about for more. I stepped unsteadily toward him and handed him those I had gathered up. In gathering them it had been impossible for me to help noting the address, and the stamps and by the postmarks, which on several were English, on two or three French, on two Italian, on one German, on one Egyptian and on one Australian. The address the same on all, was:

Geoffrey Cecil, Esq.
c/o Alexander Brown & Son,
Baltimore, Maryland
U. S. A.

Instinctively I turned the packet face down as I handed it to him. He took it gracefully and in his totally toneless voice said:

"Thank you very much."

As he said the words Captain Benson appeared in the cabin companion-way, his revolver in his hands. The mate in the act of stowing with his left hand the letters in his inner breast-pocket, pointed his extended index finger at the pistol.

"Put that thing away!" he commanded.

The voice was as toneless as before, but far otherwise than the blurred British evenness of his acknowledgment to me, these words rang hard and sharp. Benson took the rebuke as if he had been the mate and the other his captain, turned and shuffled fumblingly back down the companionway. As he passed the pantry door the cabin-boy whipped out of it and popped up the companion-way to see, and the big Norse mate emerged deliberately behind him.

By this time the fat steward and most of the crew had come aft and gathered about the prostrate Burke.

The first-mate cleared the scouse from his neck and collar, took some tarred marline from an outside pocket of his pea jacket and in a leisurely way went down into the waist. He had the men turn Burke over and tie his hands behind him and his ankles together. Then he had buckets of sea-water dashed over him. Burke soon regained consciousness.

"Carry him forward and put him in his bunk," the mate commanded. "When he says he will behave cut him loose."

Captain Benson had come on deck and was standing by the booby-hatch.

"That man ought to be put in irons," he said as the mate turned.

The mate's eyes were on his face as he said it.

"He needs no iron," he retorted crisply. "Why make a mountain out of a molehill?"

I had been hoping that I was getting used to the sea, for I was only passively uncomfortable and mildly wretched. But sometime that night it came on to blow fresh and I waked acutely sea-sick and suffering violently from horrible urging qualms in every joint. I clambered out of my bunk, struggled into some clothes and crawled across the cabin and up the after companion-way to the wheel-deck. There I collapsed at full length into four inches of warm rain-water against the lee-rail.

At first the baffling breeze was comforting after the stuffy cabin, smelling of stale coffee, damp sea-biscuit, prunes, oilskins and what not. But I was soon too cold, for I was vestless and coatless, and before long my teeth were chattering and I had a general chill to add to my misery. It was the first-mate's watch and coming aft on his eternal round he found me there.

He at once went below and brought me not only vest and jacket but my mackintosh also. I was wet to the skin all over, but the mackintosh was gratefully warm. Forgetting that he could not hear I thanked him inarticulately, and relapsed into my shifting pond, where I slipped into oblivion, my head on the outer timber, the tearing dawn-wind across my face.

Sometime before noon I was again in my chair, as on the day before, and it was again the first-mate's watch. Again I saw Burke come aft. He was not puffing and snorting this time but very silent. His florid face was a sort of gray-brown. His head was tied up and the bandage tilted sideways over his bad eye. He came up the port companion-ladder half way from the waist of the poop-deck. There he stood holding on to the top of the rail, looking very humble and abashed. It was some time before the first-mate noticed him or deigned to notice him. In that interval Burke said a score of times:

"Mr. Wilson, sor."

Each time he realized he was ignored he waited meekly for a chance to try again. Finally the mate saw him speak and asked:

"What is it, Burke?"

Burke began to pour out a torrent of speech.

"Come here," said the mate.

When Burke was close to him he said:

"Speak slow."

"Shure, sor," he said, "ye wudn't go fur to call ut mut'ny when a man's droonk an' makes a fule of himsilf?"

"Perhaps not," the mate replied, his steady eyes on Burke's face.

"Ye wudn't, I know," Burke went on confidently. "Ye see, sor, Oi was half-droonk when Oi cum aboord. An' Oi had licker tu, more fule Oi. Mr. Olsen, he cum forrard in the dog-watch afther ye'd taat me me place, and he routed ut out an' hove ut overboord. Oi'm sobered now, sor, with the facer ye giv me an' the cowld wather an' the slape. Oi'm sobered, an' Oi'm sobered for the voyage, sor. Ye'll foind me quoite and rispectful, sor. Oi was droonk, sor, an' the scouse misloiked me, an' Oi made a fule ov mesilf. Ye'll foind me quoite and rispectful, sor, indade ye will. Ye wudn't go for to log me for mut'ny for makin' a fule ov mesilf, sor, wud ye now, sor?"

"No, Burke," said the mate. "I shall not log you. Go forward."

Burke went.

Some days later I was forward on the forecastle deck, ensconced against the big canvas-covered anchor, leaning over the side and watching the foam about the cut-water and the upspurted coveys of sudden flying fish, darting out of the waves, at the edge of the bark's shadows and veering erratically in their unpredictable flights. Burke, barefoot and chewing a large quid, was going about with a tar-bucket, swabbing mats and other such devices. He approached me.

"Mr. Ferris, sor," he said, "ye wudn't have a bit of washin' a man cud du for ye? Ye'll be strange loike aboord ship, an' this yer foorst voyge, an' yer the only passenger, an' this a sailin' ship, tu. Ye'll be thinkin' ov a hotel, Mr. Ferris, sor. An' there's no wan to du washin' here for ye, sor. The cuke is no manner ov use tu ye. Ye give me any bits ye want washed an Oi'll wash 'em nate fur ye. A man-o'-war's man knows a dale ov washin' an' ye'll pay me wut ye loike. Thin I'll not be set ashore in Rio wudout a cint, sor."

"You'll have your wages," I hazarded.

"Not with Beast Benson," he replied; "little duh ye know Beast Benson. Oi know um. Wut didn't go into me advances ull go into the schlopchest. Oi may have a millrace or maybe tu at Rio, divil a cint moor."

This was the beginning of many chats with Burke. He told me of Five Rivers, of his life on men-of-war, of his participation in the battle between the *Merrimac* and the *Ericsson,* as he called the *Monitor,* of unholy adventures in a hundred ports, of countless officers he had served under.

"An' niver wan uz foine a gintlemin uz Mr. Willson," he would wind up. "Niver wan ov them all. Shure, he's no Willson. He ships as John Willson, Liverpool. Now all the seas knows John Willson ov Liverpool. There's thousands ov him. He's afloat all over the wurruld. He's always the same, short and curly-headed, black-haired and dark-faced, ivery John Willson is loike ivery other wan. Ivery Liverpool Portugee uz John Willson whin he cooms to soign articles. But Mr. Willson's no Liverpool man at all.

"He's a gintlemin, British all over, an' a midlander at thot an' no seaman be naature at all. But he's the gintlemin. Not a midshipman or liftenant did iver Oi see a foiner gintlemin than him, and how sinsible he uz. Haff the officers Oi've served under wuz lunies, sinsible on this or thot, but half luny on most things and luny all over on this or thot. But luke at Mr. Willson. Sinsible all over he uz, sinsible all thru. Luke at the discipline he huz. An' no wunder. Luke at huz oi!

"He cudn't du a mane thing av he wanted tu, he cudn't tell a loi av he wanted tu, he cudn't tell a loi av he throid, thrust me, sor, Oi know, the min knows. It's loike byes at skule wid a tacher, or min in the army wid their orficers. You can't fule thim, they knows, an' wull they knows a man whin they say wan. Oi'd thrust Mr. Willson annywhere and annyhow. So wud anny other sailor man or anny man. Deef he us, deef as an anchor fouled on a rock bottom. But he hears wid huz eyes, wid huz fingers, wid the hull skin av him. He's all sinse an' trewth an' koindness."

Not any other of the sailors besides Burke did I find sociable or communicative or capable, apparently, of intelligent intercourse. Of the captain I saw and heard enough, and more than enough, at meal times. He deserved his nickname and I avoided him with detestation.

The second mate, a big Norwegian named Olaf Olsen, was a kindly soul, but dull and uncommunicative. He had a companionable eye, but neither any need of converse nor any prompting toward it. Speech he never volunteered, questions he answered monosyllabically. One Sunday indeed he so far unbent to ask if he might borrow one of my books. I told him, I doubted if any would please him. He looked them over disappointedly.

"Have you any books of Doomuses?" he queried.

"Doomus?" I repeated after him reflectively.

"You're a scholar, aren't you?" he demanded.

"I aim to be," I said.

"How do you pronounce, D-u-m-a-s?" he inquired.

"I am no Frenchman," I told him, "but Dumas is pretty close to it."

"That's what I said," he shouted, "and they all laughed at me and said 'Doomus, ye damn fool.' Have you any of his books?"

"No," I confessed and he ceased to regard me as worth borrowing from.

Not so Mr. Wilson. Before we ran into the doldrums I had found my sea-legs and exhausted the diversion of learning the name of every bit of rope, metal and wood on the bark, and also the amusement of climbing the rigging. I settled down to luxurious days of reading. The first Sunday afterwards Mr. Wilson asked for a book. I took him into my cabin and showed him my stock, one-volume poets mostly, the Iliad, the Odyssey, the Greek Anthology, Dante, Carducci, Goethe, Heine, Shakespeare, Milton, Shelley, Keats, Tennyson, Browning, Swinburne and Rossetti, and a dozen volumes of Hugo's lyrics. I watched him as he conned them over and thought I saw his eyes light over the Greek volumes, though I saw in them both desire and resignation. He took Milton to begin on and afterward borrowed my English books in series. I believe he read each entire, certainly he read much during his watches below.

At first I felt equal only to the English myself. But after we entered the glorious south-east trades, I read first Faust, then the Divina Commedia, then the Iliad, and, as our voyage neared its end gave myself up to the delights of the Odyssey.

Meanwhile I had come to feel very well acquainted with the deaf mate. Generally we had spent part of each fair Sunday in conversation. He read lips so instantly and accurately that if I faced the sun and he was close to me we talked almost as easily as if he had heard perfectly. The conversations were all of his making. He was not a man whom one would question, whereas he questioned me freely after he had made sure, but very delicately managed tentative beginnings, that I did not at all object to being questioned. He was a little stiff at first, half timid, half wary.

After we grew to know each other he would patrol the deck only at intervals, spending most of his watch seated on the cabin-deck at the break, on the rail or on the booby-hatch, according to the position of my chair. He mostly began:

"Have you ever read——?" Or, "Did you ever read——?"

Sometimes I had read the book, oftener I had not. In either case I was fascinated by his sane, cool judgment, equally trenchant and subtle, and by the even flow of his well-chosen words.

Our voyage neared its end sooner than I had anticipated. The southeast trades had been almost head winds for us and we had tacked through them close-hauled, a long leg on the port tack and a short leg on the starboard. Then the proximity of the land blurred the unalterable perpetuity of the trade winds and on a Sunday morning the wind came fair. It was my first experience of running before the wind and it intoxicated me with elation. We were out of sight of land, even of its loom, yet no longer in blue water, but over that enormous sixty-fathom shelf which juts out more than a hundred miles into the Atlantic between Bahia and Rio de Janeiro, or to be more precise, between Canavieiras and Itapemirim. The day was bright and the sky sufficiently diversified with clouds to vary pleasingly its insistent blue, the sea a pale, golden green all torn by racing white-caps and dappled with the scurrying shadows of the clouds. The bark leapt joyously, the combers overtaking her charged in smothers of foam past each counter, the delight of merely living in such a glorious day infected even the crew.

I had my chair amidships by the break of the deck, just abaft the booby-hatch. There I was reading the Odyssey. The mate came and sat down by me on the booby-hatch.

"What are you reading?" he asked as usual.

"About the Sirens," I answered.

The strangest alteration came over his expression.

"Did you ever notice," he asked, "how little Homer really tells about them?"

"I was meditating on just that," I replied. "He tells only that there were two of them and that they sang. I was wondering where the popular notions of their appearance came from."

"What is your idea of the popular notions of their appearance?" he demanded.

"I have a very vague idea," I confessed. "They are generally supposed to have had bird's feet. It seems to me I have seen figures of them as so depicted on Greek tombs and coins. And there is Boecklin's picture."

"Boecklin?" he ruminated. "The Munich man? The morbid man?"

"If you choose to call him so," I assented. "I shouldn't call him morbid."

"His ugly idea is a mere personal conception," he said.

"I grant you that," I agreed, "as far as the age and the ugliness go. But the bird's feet of some kind are in the general conception."

"The general conception is wrong," he asserted, with something more like an approach to heat than anything I had seen in him.

"You seem to feel very sure of it," I replied.

"I do not feel," he answered, "I know."

"How do you know?" I inquired.

"I have seen them," he asserted.

"Seen them?" I puzzled.

"Yes, seen them," he asseverated. "Seen the twin Sirens under the golden sun, under the silver moon, under the countless stars; watched them singing as they are singing now!"

"What!" I exclaimed.

My face must have painted my amazement, my tone must have betrayed my startled bewilderment.

His face went scarlet and then pale. He sprang up and strode off to the weather rail. There he stood for a long time. Presently he wheeled, crossed the deck, the booby-hatch between us, and plunged down the cabin companion-way without looking at me.

He did not once meet my eye during the remaining days of the voyage, let alone approach me. He was again the impassive, inscrutable figure I had first seen him on the wharf at Baltimore.

We drew near Rio harbor, late of a perfect tropic September day, just too late to enter before sunset. In the brief tropic dusk we anchored under the black beetling shoulder of Itaipu inside the little islands of Mai and Pai. There we lay wobbling at anchor, there I watched the cloudless sky fill with the infinite multitudes of tropic stars, and gazed at the lights of the city, plainly visible through the harbor mouth between Morro de Sao Joao and the Sugar Loaf, twinkling brighter than the stars, not three miles away.

It must have been somewhere toward midnight when he approached me. My chair was by the rail on which he half sat, leaning down to me. So placed he began such a monologue as I had often heard from him, a monologue I could neither question nor modify, which I must listen to entire or break off completely.

"You were astonished," he said, "when I told you I had seen the Sirens, but I have. It was about six years ago. I was then in New York and I had my usual difficulty getting a ship on account of my deafness. My boarding-master tried a Captain George Andrews of the *Joyous Castle*. Andrews looked me over and said he liked me. Then he talked to me alone.

" 'We are bound on an adventure,' he said, 'and I want a man who will obey orders and keep his mouth shut.'

"I told him I was his man for whatever risk. With a light mixed cargo, hardly more than half a cargo, hardly more than ballast, we cleared for Guam and a market. I was second mate. The first mate was a big Swede named Gustave Obrink. The very first meal I ever sat down to with him he made an impression on me as one of the greediest men I had ever seen. He not only ate enormously, but he seemed more than half unsatisfied after he had stuffed himself with an amazing quantity of food. He seemed to possess an unbluntable zest in the act of swallowing, an ever fresh gusto for any and every food flavor.

"I never saw a man relish his food so. He was an equally inordinate drinker, the quantity of coffee he could swill at one meal was amazing. Between meals he was always thirsty and drank incredible quantities of water. He was forever going to the butt by the galley door and drinking from it. And he would smack his lips over it and enjoy it as a connoisseur would a rare wine.

"When we came to choose watches Captain Andrews told us to choose a bo'sun for each watch. Obrink wanted to know why.

"The captain told him it was none of his business to ask questions. The Swede assented and backed down. We chose each an Irishman. Obrink, a tall, loose-jointed man named Pat Ryan and I, a compact stocky fellow named Mike Leary. Next day the captain had the boatswains shift their dunnage and bunk and mess aft. They were nearly as great gluttons as Obrink. They fed like animals and the subject of food and drink was the backbone of their conversation.

"The crew were hearty eaters as well and Captain Andrews catered to their likings. The *Joyous Castle* was amazingly well found, the cabin fare very abundant and varied, the forecastle food plenty and good.

"Soon after Captain Andrews was sure that the crew had entirely sobered up from their shore-drinking he called them aft one noon and announced that the steward was to serve grog daily until further notice. Naturally they cheered. After that we had a good, cheap wine daily in the cabin. When Captain Andrews had made up his mind that both mates and both boatswains were sober men he had a bottle of whisky placed on the rack over the table and kept filled. It was a curiosity to watch Obrink, Ryan and Leary patronize that bottle. Not one of the three but was cautious, not one of the three but could have drunk three times as much as he did. But the way they savored every drop they took, the affectionate satisfaction they exhibited over each nip, their eager anticipation of the next made a spectacle.

"Captain Andrews kept good discipline, we crossed the line and rounded the Cape of Good Hope without any event.

"When we were off Madagascar, Obrink, going below to get his sextant, missed it from its place. The ship was searched and Captain Andrews held an inquisition. But the sextant was never found, nor any light thrown on how it had disappeared. After that the captain alone took the observations.

"Then began a series of erratic changes of our course. We kept on dodging about for six weeks, until the crew talked of nothing else and openly said the captain was trying to lose us; certainly not one of us except the captain could have designated our position. We knew we were south of the line, not ten degrees south of it, and between 50 and 110 east longitude, but within those limits we might be almost anywhere.

"We had had nothing that could be called a storm since we left New York. When a storm struck us it was a storm indeed. When it blew over it left us making water fast. After a day and a night at the pumps, we took to our boats. Captain Andrews had the cook and the cabin-boy in his boat, gave each boatswain a dory and two men, and directed us to steer north by east. When Obrink and I asked for our latitude and longitude he said that was his business. He had had the boats provisioned while we pumped and they were well supplied. We left the ship under a clear sky, the wind light after the storm, the ground-swell running heavy and slow. We lowered near sunset.

"Next morning the Captain's boat had vanished, and there we were, two whaleboats, two dories, twenty men in all and no idea of our position.

"The third day we sighted land. It was a low atoll, not much more than a mile across, nearly circular as far as we could make out, with the usual cocoa palms all along its ring, the surf breaking on interrupted reefs off shore and, as we drew nearer, a channel into the lagoon facing us. As we threaded it we saw about the center of the lagoon a steep narrow, pinkish crag, maybe fifty feet high, with a bit of flat island showing behind it. Otherwise the lagoon was unbroken.

"We made a landing on the atoll near the channel where we had entered, found good water, cocoanuts in abundance and hogs running wild all about, but no traces of human beings. I shot a hog and the men roasted it at once. As they ate they talked of nothing but the short rations they had had in the boats. They were all docile enough and good natured, but I believe every man of them said a dozen times how much he missed his grog, and Obrink, who had kept himself and his boatload well in hand, said a score of times how much he would like to serve out grog, but must take care of his small supply. They talked a great deal of their hunger in the boats and of their relish of the pork; they ate an astonishing number of cocoanuts. It seemed to me that they were as greedy a set of men as could be met with.

"We cut down five palm-trees, and on supports made of the others set one horizontally as a ridge pole. Over this we stretched the sails of the whaleboats. So we camped on the sandbeach of the lagoon. I slept utterly. But when I waked I understood the men one and all to complain of light and broken sleep, of dreams, of dreaming they heard a queer noise like music, of seeming to continue to hear it after they woke. They breakfasted on another hog and on more cocoanuts.

"Then Obrink told me to take charge of the camp. I agreed. He had everything removed from his whaleboat and into it piled all the men, except a little Frenchman who went by no name save 'Frenchy,' a New Englander named Peddicord, a short red-headed Irishman named Mullen, Ryan, my boatswain and myself. Those of my watch who wanted to go I let go. They rowed off, across the lagoon toward the pink crag.

"After Obrink and the men were gone I meant to take stock of our stores. I sent Ryan with Frenchy around the atoll in one direction and Peddicord, who had sense for a foremast hand, with Mullen in the other direction. I then went over the stores. Fairly promising for twenty men they were, even a random boat-voyage in the Indian Ocean. With unlimited cocoanuts and abundant hogs they were a handsome provision, and need only be safeguarded from the omnipresent rats.

"Very shortly my four men returned, the two parties nearly at the same time. It was nearly noon, and no sign of Obrink or the boat. I had followed the whaleboat with my glass till it rounded the pink crag, a short half mile away, and had disappeared. Ryan asked my permission to take one dory and go join the rest on the crag. I readily agreed, for I had not yet cached the spirits. They rowed off as the others had.

"I made use of their welcome absence to conceal the liquor in four different places, carefully writing, in my notebook, the marks by which I was to find the caches again. I did the like with most of the ammunition. I had no idea of trying to get the upper hand of Obrink. I meant to tell him of my proceedings and expected him to approve.

"I expected the men back about two hours before sunset. No sign of them appeared. No sign of them near sunset, nor at sunset. Of course I waited inactive until it was too late for me to venture alone on the unknown lagoon at night, and there would have been no sense in one man going to look for nineteen anyhow. Moreover I must protect our stores from hogs and rats. I turned over in my mind a thousand conjectures and slept little.

"Next morning I slung what I could of our stores from our jury-ridge-pole, out of the reach of hogs and rats, made sure that the remaining whaleboat would not get adrift, prepared the remaining dory with cocoanuts, biscuits, a keg of water, liquor, some miscellaneous stores, medicine, ammunition, repeating rifle, my glass and my compass. I carried two revolvers. I knew by this time something was wrong and I rowed warily across the placid lagoon toward the pink crag.

"As I approached it I could not but remark the peacefulness and beauty of my surroundings. The sky was deep tropic blue, the sun not an hour high, the wind a mild breeze, hardly more than rippling the lagoon, my horizon was all the tops of palms on the atoll except the one glimpse of white surf on the reef beyond the channel where we had entered.

"I rowed slowly, for the dory was heavy, and kept looking over my shoulder.

"The crag rose sheer out of deep water. It might have been granite, but I could not tell what sort of stone it was. It was very pink and nothing grew on it, not anything whatever. It was just sheer naked rock. As I rounded it I could see the flattish island beyond. There was not a tree on it and I could see nothing but the even beach of it rising some six or eight feet above high-water mark. Nothing was visible beyond the crest of the beach. I knew our men had meant to land on it and I stopped and considered. Then I rowed around the base of the crag. Facing the flat islet was a sort of a shelf of the pink rock, half submerged, half out of the water, sloping very gently and just the place to make a landing.

"I rowed the dory carefully till its bottom grated on the flat top of this shelf, the bow in say a foot of water, the stern over water maybe sixty fathom deep, for I could see no bottom to its limpid blue. I stepped out and drew the dory well up on the shelf. Then I essayed to climb the crag. I succeeded at once, but it was none too easy and I had no leisure to look behind me till I reached the top. Once on the fairly flat top, which might have been thirty feet across, I turned and looked over the islet.

"Then I sat down heavily and took out my flask. I took a big drink, shut my eyes, said a prayer, I think, and looked again. I saw just what I seen before.

"There was about a ship's-length of water between the crag and the islet, which might have been four ship's-lengths across and was nearly circular. All round it was a white beach of clean coral-sand sloping evenly and rising perhaps ten feet at most above high-water mark. The rest of the island was a meadow, nearly level but cupping ever so little from the crest of the beach. It was covered with short, soft-looking grass, of a bright pale green, a green like that of an English lawn in spring.

"In the center of the island and of the meadow it was an oval slab of pinkish stone, the same stone, apparently, as made up the crag on which I sat. On it were two shapes of living creatures, but shapes which I rubbed my eyes to look at. Midway between the slab and the crest of the beach a long windrow heap of something white swept in a circle around the slab, maybe ten fathom from it. I did not surely make out what the windrow was composed of until I took my glasses to it.

"But it needed no glass to see our men, all nineteen of them, all sitting, some just inside the white windrow, some just outside of it, some on it, or in it. Their faces were turned to the slab.

"I took my glass out of my pocket, trembling so I could hardly adjust it. With it I saw clearly the windrow as I had guessed, the shapes on the slab as I had seemed to see them with my unaided eyes.

"The windrow was all of human bones. I could see them clearly through the glass.

"The two creatures on the slab were shaped like full-bodied young women. Except their faces, nothing of their flesh was visible. They were clad in something close-fitting, and pearly gray, which clung to every part of them, and revealed every curve of their forms; as it were a tight-fitting envelopment of fine moleskin or chinchilla. But it shimmered in the sunlight more like elder-down.

"And their hair! I rubbed my eyes. I took out my handkerchief and rubbed the lenses of my glasses. I looked again. I saw as before. Their hair was abundant, and fell in curly waves to their hips. But it seemed a deep dark blue, or a dull intense shot-green or both at once or both together. I could not see it any other way.

"And their faces!

"Their faces were those of European women, of young handsome gentlewomen.

"One of them lay on the slab half on her side, her knees a little drawn up, her head on one bent arm, her face toward me, as if asleep. The other sat, supporting herself by one straight arm. Her mouth was open, her lips moved, her face was the face of a woman singing. I dared not look any more. It was so real and so incredible.

"I scanned our men through my glass. I could see their shoulders heave as they breathed, otherwise not one moved a muscle while I looked at him.

"I shut my glass and put it in my pocket. I shouted. Not a man turned. I fixed my gaze so as to observe the whole group at once. I shouted again. Not a man moved. I took my revolver from its holster and fired in the air. Not a single man turned.

"Then I started to clamber down the crag. I had to turn my back on the islet, regard the far horizon, fix my gaze on the camp, discernible by the white patch, where the white sails were stretched over the palm trunk, and try to realize the reality of things before I could gather myself together to climb down.

"I made it, but I nearly lost my hold a dozen times.

"I pushed off the dory, rowed to the islet and beached the dory between the other and the whaleboat. Both were half adrift and I hauled them up as well as I could.

"Then I went up the beach. When I came to its crest and saw the backs of our men I shouted again. Not a man turned his head. I approached them: their faces were set immovably toward the rock and the two appearances on it.

"Peddicord was nearest to me, the windrow of bones in front of him was not wide nor high. He stared across it. I caught him by the shoulders and shook him, then he did turn his head and look up at me, just a glance, the glance of a peevish, protesting child disturbed at some absorbing play, an unintelligent vacuous glance, unrecognizing and uncomprehending.

"The glance startled me enough, for Peddicord had been a hard-headed, sensible Yankee. But the change in his face, since yesterday, startled me more. Of a sudden I realized that Peddicord, Ryan, Mullen and Frenchy had been without food or water since I last saw them, that they had been just where I found them since soon after they left me, had been exposed the day before to a tropical sun for some six hours, had sat all night also without moving or sleeping. At the same instant I realized that the rest had been in the same state for some hours longer, some hours of a burning, morning tropical sun. The realization of it lost my head completely. I ran from man to man, I yelled, I pulled them, I struck them.

"Not one struck back, or answered or looked at me twice. Each shook me off impatiently and relapsed into his intent posture, even Obrink.

"Obrink, it is true, partially opened his mouth, as if to speak.

"I saw his tongue!

"I ran to the boat, took a handful of ship-biscuit and a pan of water, with these I returned to the men.

"Not one would notice the biscuit, not one showed any interest in the water, not one looked at it as if he saw it when I held it before his face, not one tried to drink, not one would drink when I tried to force it on him.

"I emptied my flask into the water; with that I went from man to man. Not even the smell of the whisky roused them. Each pushed the pan from before his face, each resisted me, each shoved me away.

"I went back to the boat, filled a tin cup with raw whisky and went the round with that. Not one would regard it, much less swallow it.

"Then I myself turned to the slab of stone.

"There sat the sirens. Well I recognized now what they were. Both were awake now and both singing. What I had seen through the glass was visible more clearly, more intelligibly. They were indeed shaped like young, healthy women; like well-matured Caucasian women. They were covered all over with close, soft plumage, like the breast of a dove, colored like the breast of a dove, a pale, delicate, iridescent, pinkish gray. As a woman's long hair might trail to her hips, there trailed from their heads a mass of long dark strands. Imagine single strands of ostrich feathers, a yard long or more, curling spirally or at random, colored the deep, shot, blue-green of the eye of a peacock feather, or of a gamecock's hackles. That was what grew from their heads, as I seemed to see it.

"I stepped over the windrow of bones. Some were mere dust; some bleached gray by sun, wind and rain; some white. Skulls were there, five or six I saw in as many yards of the windrow near me and more beyond. In some places the windrow was ten feet wide and three feet deep in the middle. It was made up of the skeletons of hundreds of thousands of victims.

"I took out my other revolver, spun the cylinder and strode toward the slab.

"Forty feet from it I stopped. I was determined to abolish the superhuman monsters. I was resolute. I was not afraid. But I stopped. Again and again I strove to go nearer, I braced my resolutions. I tried to go nearer. I could not.

"Then I tried to go sideways. I was able to step. I made the circuit of the slab, some forty feet from it. Nearer I could not go. It was as if a glass wall were between me and the sirens.

"Standing at my distance, once I found I could go no nearer, I essayed to aim my revolver at them. My muscles, my nerves refused to obey me. I tried in various ways. I might have been paralyzed. I tried other movements. I was capable of any other movement. But aim at them I could not.

"I regarded them. Especially their faces, their wonderful faces.

"Their investiture of opalescent plumelets covered their throats. Between it and the deep, dark chevelure above, their faces showed ivory-smooth, delicately tinted. I could see their ears too, shell-like ears, entirely human in form, peeping from under the glossy shade of their miraculous tresses.

"They were as alike as any twin sisters.

"Their faces were oval, their features small, clean-cut, regular and shapely, their foreheads were wide and low, their brows were separate, arched, penciled and definite, not of hair, but of tiny feathers, of gold-shot, black, blue-green, like the color of their ringlets, but far darker. I took out my binoculars and conned their brows. Their eyes were dark blue-gray, bright and young, their noses were small and straight, low between the eyes, neither wide nor narrow, and with molded nostrils, rolled and fine.

"Their upper lips were short, both lips crimson red and curved about their small mouths, their teeth were very white, their chins round and babyish. They were beautiful and the act of singing did not mar their beauty. Their mouths did not strain open, but their lips parted easily into an opening. Their throats seemed to ripple like the throat of a trilling canary-bird. They sang with zest and the zest made them all the more beautiful. But it was not so much their beauty that impressed me, it was the nobility of their faces.

"Some years before I had been an officer on the private steam-yacht of a very wealthy nobleman. He was of a family fanatically devoted to the church of Rome and all its interests. Some Austrian nuns, of an order made up exclusively of noblewomen, were about to go to Rome for an audience with the Pope. My employer placed his yacht at their disposal and we took them on at Trieste. They several times sat on deck during the voyage and the return. I watched them as much as I could, for I never had seen such human faces, and I had seen many sorts. Their faces seemed to tell of a long lineage of men all brave and honorable, women gentle and pure. There was not a trace on their faces of any sort of evil in themselves or in anything that had ever really influenced them. They were really saintly faces, the faces of ideal nuns.

"Well, the sirens' faces were like that, only more ineffably perfect. There was no guile or cruelty in them, no delight in the exercise of their power, no consciousness of my proximity, or of the spell-bound men or of the uncountable skeletons of their myriad victims. Their faces expressed but one emotion: utter absorption in the ecstasy of singing, the infinite preoccupation of artists in their art.

"I walked all round them, gazing now with all my eyes, now through my short-focused glass. Their coat of feathers was as if very short and close like seal-skin fur and covered them entirely from the throat down, to the ends of their fingers and the soles of their feet. They did not move except to sit up to sing or lie down to sleep. Sometimes both sang together, sometimes alternately, but if one slept the other sang on and on without ceasing.

"I of course could not hear their music, but the mere sight of them fascinated me so that I forgot my weariness from anxiety and loss of sleep, forgot the vertical sun, forgot food and drink, forgot everything.

"But as I could not hear, this state was transitory. I began to look elsewhere than at the sirens. My gaze turned again upon the men. Again I made futile efforts to reach the sirens, to shoot at them, to aim at them. I could not.

"I returned to my dory and drank a great deal of water. I ate a ship-biscuit or two. I then made the round of the men, and tried on each, food, water and spirits. They were oblivious to everything except the longing to listen, to listen, to listen.

"I walked around the windrow of bones. With the skulls and collapsing rib-arches I found leather boots, several leather belts, case-knives, kreeses, guns of various patterns, pistols, watches, gold and jeweled finger rings and coins, many coins, copper, silver and gold. The grass was short, and the earth under it smooth as a rolled lawn.

"The bones were of various ages, but all old, except two skeletons, entire, side by side, just beyond the windrow at the portion opposite where the men sat. There was long fine golden hair on one skull. Women too!

"I went back to the dory, rowed to the camp, shot a hog, roasted it, wrapped the steaming meat in fresh leaves and rowed back to the islet. It was not far from sunset.

"Not a man heeded the savory meat, still warm. They just sat and gazed and listened.

"I was free of the spell. I could do them no good by staying. I rowed back to camp before sunset and slept, yes I slept all night long.

"The sun woke me. I shot and cooked another hog, took every bit of rope or marline I could find and rowed back to the islet.

"You are to understand that the men had by then been more than forty hours, all of them, without moving or swallowing anything. If I was to save any it must be done quickly.

"I found them as they had been, but with an appalling change in themselves. The day before they had been uncannily unaware of their sufferings, today they were hideously conscious of them.

"Once I had a pet terrier, a neat, trim, intelligent, little beast. He ran under a moving train and had both his hind legs cut off. He dragged himself to me, and the appealing gaze of his eyes expressed his dumb wonder that I did not help him.

"Well, out of the staring, blood-shot eyes of those bewitched men I saw the same look of helpless wonderment and mute appeal.

"Strange, but I never thought of knocking them senseless. I had an idea of tying them one by one, carrying or dragging them to the dory and ferrying my captives to camp.

"I began on Frenchy, he was the smallest.

"He fought like a demon. After all that sleeplessness and fasting he was stronger than I. Our tussle wore me out, but moved him not at all.

"I tried them with the warm, juicy, savory pork. They paid not heed to it and pushed me away. I tried them with biscuit, water and liquor. Not one heeded. I tried Obrink particularly. Again he opened his lips. His tongue was black, hard and swelled till it filled his mouth.

"Then I lost count of time, of what I did, of what happened. I do not know whether it was on that day or the next that the first man died. He was Jack Register, a New York wharf-rat. The next died a few hours later, a Philadelphia seaman he was, named Tom Smith.

"They putrefied with rapidity surpassing anything I ever saw, even in a horse dropped dead of over-driving.

"The rest sat there by the carrion of their comrades, rocking with weakness, crazed by sleeplessness, racked by tortures inexpressible, the gray of death deepening on their faces, listening, listening, listening.

"As I said, I had lost consciousness of time. I do not know how many days Obrink lived, and he was the last to die. I do not know how long it was after his death before I came to myself.

"When I was myself I made haste to leave the accursed isle. I made ready the second whaleboat with the best stores she could carry and spare sails. I stepped the mast and steered across the lagoon.

"As I passed the islet, I could see nothing but the white sandbeach that ringed it. For all my horror I could not resist landing once more for one last look.

"Under the afternoon sun I saw the green meadow, the white curve of bones, the rotting corpses, the pink slab, the feathered sirens, their sweet serene faces uplifted, singing on in a rapt trance.

"I took but one look. I fled. The whaleboat passed the outlet of the lagoon.

"I had been at sea alone for twenty-one days when I was rescued, not three hundred miles from Ceylon, by a tramp steamer out of Colombo bound for Adelaide."

Here he broke off, stood up and for the rest of the watch maintained his sentry-go by the break of the poop.

Next day we towed into the harbor of Rio de Janeiro; then still the capital of an empire, and mildly enthusiastic for Dom Pedro. I hastened to go ashore. When my boat was ready the deaf mate was forward, superintending the sealing of the hatches.

After some days of discomfort at the Hotel des Etrangers and of worse at Young's Hotel I found a harborage with five jolly bachelors housekeeping in a delightful villa up on Rua do Jonquillos on Santa Theresa. The *Nipsic* was in the harbor and I thought I knew a lieutenant on her and went off one day to visit her. After my visit my boatman landed me at the Red Steps. As I trod up the steps a man came down. He was English all over, irreproachably shod, trousered, coated, gloved, hatted and monocled. Behind him two porters carried big, new portmanteaux. I recognized the man whom I had known as John Wilson of Liverpool, second mate on the *Medorus*, the man who had seen the sirens.

Not only did I recognize him, but he recognized me.

"I am going home," he said, nodding toward a steamer at anchor. "I am glad we met. I enjoyed our talks. Perhaps, we may meet again."

He shook hands without any more words. I stood at the top of the steps and watched his boat put off, watched it as it receded. As I watched a bit of paper on a lower step caught my eye. I went down and picked it up. It was an empty envelope, with an English stamp and postmark, addressed:

> **Geoffrey Cecil, Esq.,**
> **c/o Swanwick & Co.**
> **54 Rua de Alfandega**
> **Rio de Janeiro, Brazil.**

Naturally I asked every Englishman I ever met if he had ever heard of a deaf man named Geoffrey Cecil. For more than ten years I elicited no response. Then at lunch, in the Hotel Victoria at Interlaken, I happened to be seated opposite a stout, elderly Briton. He perceived that I was an American and became affable and agreeable. I never saw him after that lunch and never learned his name.

At a suitable opportunity I put my usual query.

"Geoffrey Cecil?" he said. "Deaf Geoffrey Cecil? Of course I know of him. Knew him too. He was or is Earl of Aldersmere."

"Was or is?" I queried.

"It was this way," my interlocutor explained. "The ninth Earl of Aldersmere had three sons. All pre-deceased him and each left one son. Geoffrey was the heir. He had wanted to go into the Navy, but his deafness cut him off from that. When he quarreled with his father he naturally ran away to sea. Track of him was lost. He was supposed dead. That was years before his father's death.

"When his father died nothing had been heard of him for ten years. But when his grandfather died and his cousin Roger supposed himself Earl, some firm of solicitors interposed, claiming that Geoffrey was alive.

"When Geoffrey turned up in six months Roger was disappointed. Geoffrey paid no attention to anything but buying or chartering a steam-yacht. She sailed as soon as possible, passed the canal, touched at Aden, and has never been heard of since.

"That was nine years ago."

"Is Roger Cecil alive?" I asked.

"Very much alive," affirmed my informant.

"You may tell him from me," I declared, "that he is now the Eleventh Earl of Aldersmere."

The Ship of Silent Men

Philip M. Fisher

1
The Electric Storm

THE STEAMSHIP *LANOA*, Carden Line of San Francisco, with nine thousand tons of raw sugar in her holds and a deck load of bananas and pines, was two days out from Honolulu when the electric storm broke upon us. We were still in the warm belt and would not expect bad weather or cold for at least another forty-eight hours. That was the rule—and even when this nature's rule was transgressed, the weather was only moderate, the temperature simply low enough to suggest the possibility of donning one's light coat. Neither heat nor cold came in extreme.

Yet suddenly, on this second day out, at about ten-twenty in the morning and without barometic warning, a blanketing chill dropped over the ship, enveloped us with searching aggressiveness, and literally froze our tropic-acclimated selves, body and soul.

Every man on board piled into his coast underwear and war-time sweater and socks—but it did no good. Every man's nose and cheeks were hard-looking and purple-gray—every man's breath exhaled in a cloud of fog. And we three passengers, half-hid in coats and rugs, were yet forced to the engine-room for comfort.

This was the first symptom of the strange meteorological condition that was to harry us for the next two days. And it was, in the annals of marine history, unlogged, unprecedented.

The next indication of extraordinary weather conditions was the sudden failure of the radio. This started perhaps an hour after the falling of the mercury. The apparatus worked intermittently—one moment normally registering the Press Association News, the next moment, tune it as the operator would, he could send, or receive, nothing. The transmitter hashed its spark—the receivers were absolutely dead.

Then, without warning, the code would come singing in the puzzled man's ears once more—as though nothing at all had occurred; as though —paradoxically—the wires had been cut, held apart for some minutes, then put in contact again. Then the whole thing would be repeated again —and again. This went on for the next two days—along with that deathly chill—went on until there came, as a climax, that final beautiful yet awe-inspiring occurrence which brought us to that thing which will, I fear, for all time haunt my dreams, the thing that is the seaman's nightmare, of all seas, the seaman's ghost.

The electric lights worked badly, too, dimming unaccountably at times, then flaring up until one expected momentarily that the filament would go to pieces. The engine crew and the firemen did not like it at all—especially with the triple expansion Corliss turning over her usual eighty-seven, and the generator turbine steady as a clock.

They were a superstitious lot, too—Belgians and Swedes and Welsh— and I found myself colder yet as I listened to the yarns they told. At sea, with the illimitable waste about one, and the loneliness of it all, stories of the strange and unexplainable always thrill more than they do on land. And when they are told when the actual conditions then existent are strange and unexplainable, too, and the nearest land is a mere speck seven hundred miles back, the thrill changes into something more like a spine-prickling uneasiness. The crew were that way—and the passengers three.

The cold became more penetrating. The bridge officer—wool-wrapped —paced stumblingly. The radio had lapses of an hour long—the wireless operator was frantic. The shadows below decks became as of the dead alive, and the black gang forgot its tales, and cursed softly.

Then came darkness, and with it a doubled phosphorescence in our wake. The air was permeated with that weird sea feel, hardly to be called an odor, or ozone. And at about seven bells of the first watch, just before midnight, the steel rigging was alive with bluish flickering—electric streamlets, running, pausing, dancing, now quiescent and dying dim— now pulsingly alive, now peacefully aglow—now madly, enthusiastically, and at times almost malevolently, rampant.

The deck watch shivered a bit from more than the cold—the below-decks crew, about to come on watch and up for a breath of air, stared thoughtfully and stowed back their half-filled pipes, and felt their way down to the comfort of their still steady engines.

Eight bells, and midnight came. The chill reached the marrow of our bones. The electricity on the rigging silently threatened. The shadows blacked and grayed with a hundred shifting, shapeless things that stared and kept one's chin on one's shoulder in breathless moments when the lights went nearly out.

* * *

On my way to my cabin I stopped at the wireless-room.

"Lights still out," growled the operator, "since four bells not a snitch or a buzz. Two hours—"

He adjusted and readjusted his headgear.

"But what *is* the matter?" I whispered, half to myself.

"How the hell do I know!" the man snapped.

I shrugged my shoulders and went on.

Grahame and Stevenot, the two other passengers, grinned weakly as the globes in our room slowly came to life.

"Queer combination," grunted Grahame, as he crawled into the double lower berth, and I followed.

"Humph!" came from Stevenot above our heads. "Turn out that footlight."

I crawled out again.

"What's the use?" muttered Grahame, then: "Damn peculiar—cursed if it ain't!"

"Shut up," said Stevenot. "Shut up—and go to sleep."

"An' the stars," Grahame doggedly continued. "I'd swear I saw the masthead knock one off an' it ran down the forestay there, an'—"

"Drowned itself in the sea," shouted Stevenot. "Go to sleep."

The next morning things were the same. And the crew was getting itchy—and silent. One of the wipers, when I went below for warmth, whispered to me that he'd seen something in the starboard alley that beckoned to him. He'd thrown a monkey wrench at it, and then climbed around the steering engine and felt his way for'ard along the port alley. And when he'd gone below again, there was his wrench in its regular place in the rack under the revolution indicator. What did I think of that?

Then came the first breath of real trouble.

At three in the afternoon, one of the men came below and told us that the wireless had worked for a few minutes, and the operator had picked up an S.O.S. The gang eyed each other silently.

I climbed top side.

Grahame and Stevenot were in the radio office. The mate was there, too. The operator was penciling on his tablet—a bit white in the face.

"God!" muttered the mate. "If the damn thing will only hold out—hold out—"

He peered at the operator's pencil point as the letters slowly, spasmodically, jerked out.

Grahame pressed my arm, and pointed.

I read the message so far written.

"S.O.S.—S.O.S."—the letters were just scrawled—"S.O.S.—" Then a word, evidently the name of the ship in distress—"Karnak." Then again: "S.O.S., Lat. 52—19—" Then there was a break—then the same thing repeated.

"Must have been sending that for an hour," Grahame whispered. "Been several breaks, you know—each time got as far as the latitude the poor devil's in. But no longitude—an' how can they tell where to go? The mate says the old man'll order the ship about if he can tell where to head her, but he'll be cursed if he'll play hide and seek on the forty-second parallel with the bit of frozen mystery we're in now. If they can only get the longitude, they'll be fixed, but so far—"

He stopped abruptly. The pencil had begun to move. Every man of us grew tense. The operator's corded hand was white despite the blue chill of his office.

"S.O.S.—S.O.S. S.O.S.—Karnak—Lat. 52—19—" Here the operator hunched suddenly, and a wild oath escaped his tight lips. His hand jerked. "Long.," he wrote—and a sigh came from the mate—from all of us— "152—37—"

The mate, jaw set, elbowed out. He had the pleading vessel's location at last.

Stevenot grinned.

"Gee!" he said thickly. "I'm glad we picked it all up at last. Got on my nerves."

Grahame pulled his mustache.

"Blame queer, I'd say," he murmured.

The wireless operator still hunched, one hand on his tuning lever, the other repeating on paper the same call for aid.

"Let's get out in the air," said Stevenot.

99
S·O·S·

The helmsman already had wheel orders for an approximate course, and the ship's head was swinging. The three of us, lone passengers, had been given access to all parts of the *Lanoa*, so stayed now on the bridge—still wrapped, even though the sun was blindingly on high, in all our sweaters and robes.

The skipper, pulling violently on the Manila man-killer he chewed, and quite oblivious to the fact that it was unlit, waved his arms and clapped his mittened hands before and behind him as he paced. In the wheelhouse the steersman showed a pale and thoughtful countenance.

The mate was bending over a chart, and the second was wildly turning the pages of his Bowditch. For several minutes they figured—then checked their work. Then the mate brought out the chart and the figures to the skipper, who nodded with a glance about the awning, at the sun; the mate nodded to the second and the latter stood beside the wheelsman and gave the exact course which would bring the *Lanoa* to the ship that, out of all this mysterious and unprecedented weather, on a smooth sea, and beneath a bright sun, cried so persistently for help.

The *Lanoa* straightened out on the northerly course that should bring her to the *Karnak*—and a half-dozen revolutions were added to the turn of the screw.

Again that night did the blue flame flicker ghostily in the rigging. Still did the shadows below decks rise and fall as spasmodically, as slowly, as terribly in their awful hesitation, as the breath of a dying man. Still was the wireless a practically useless thing and our ship cut off from all the world in all this sea of mystery. Still the chill of the cold crept into our hearts, and chilled our very souls.

Once, just after nine o'clock, out of the crystal-starred blackness of the night came the same cry for help from the *Karnak*. "S.O.S." it called—"Karnak—Lat. 52—19—Long. 152—37—" Then repeated the same.

But when our operator sent our word that rescue was coming—there came again no answer except the same repeated plea.

The mate and skipper, when they heard this, stared at each other. Then the mate shook his head. And Stevenot evidently voiced the officer's thought—for he started and stared again when Stevenot said:

"And here a whole day has passed and they send the same latitude and the same longitude. Even with engines broken down, I should think they'd drift a good many minutes just in the Japan current. Yet here—the same—"

And that's when the mate seized the skipper's arm and abruptly dragged him from the radio office.

Grahame grunted. "Blame peculiar," he muttered.

And Stevenot, without a word, led us out to the open deck. The stars were a comfort—one had but to stand on tiptoe and he might pluck the brightest out, one by one. But that weirdly running blue flame on ratlines and stays and cargo booms—we didn't like.

Yet we stayed on deck—and smoked a bit—and said nothing—only thought and stared—and wondered what was yet to come—and shivered in the cold.

Then suddenly—deep away in the sparkling blue-black bowl that capped the oily sea—appeared a moving glow. It grew in size; it flashed across the zenith in northerly flight. It changed in color from ghostly white to yellow flame. It changed in form from nebulous shapelessness to clear cut crystal.

Even though its flight was over us, and away, toward the north, it grew to a vastness that colored all the sea—and gleamed on the faces and eyes of my two companions as they stared.

A great humming filled the air—changed slowly to an ear-straining hissing sound—then to a vast droning roar as it fell away toward the line where the starry heavens, dimmed to almost nothingness now, met the sea.

Then even as the shape itself rushed beyond our sight, there came a blinding flash of yellow light—and as we stiffly leaned against the rail, a thunderlike detonation that rattled everything on board the ship and all but threw us off our feet.

Stevenot seized my arm, and clung there like a frightened child. Grahame, mouth open, pointed tensely northward.

"The *Karnak*," he cried hoarsely. "The *Karnak*—it fell—it fell— toward the *Karnak*."

Then suddenly rang a cry from the bridge—and the mate came running down the gangway to the maindeck.

"The cold—" he cried, "the cold!" And he sped by us into the radio room.

Stevenot's grasp relaxed.

"By Heaven!" he gasped, tearing off his blanket—"it's warm as—as toast"—ending with most innocuous comparison.

"And the blue flame—gone!" I cried as my senses returned. "Gone—"

"And the lights," gasped Stevenot.

I peeled my coat, for the cold, even as the great electric mass seemed to burst, was lifted from us, and the gentle warmth of the semi-tropic sea dropped in its place. And the air smelled clean again. And the dancing electricity on the rigging had vanished—the lights glowed steady white— and even as we stood in wonder the motor of the radio turned up its crescendo hum, and the regulated yet intermittent crashing of the spark told us that once again the wireless was in commission.

In that flash, things were back to normal—and we breathed. The strangeness was gone—the tenseness was gone—and we breathed.

Then even as our pulse became regular, our breathing even, the mate came out of the radio office.

"All right again," he said stiffly. "And the machine is working all right. But—well," he nodded toward the office—"he can't seem to connect."

Stevenot jumped.

"That meteor—or electric bolt—whatever it was," he jerked out, "toward the north toward the *Karnak*—"

The mate nodded silently. There was a solemn pause.

Then the officer muttered.

"And the instruments are O.K., too. But the *Karnak*—"

"No answer?" cried Stevenot.

The mate shook his head: "Not a jot," he said briefly, and with a tenseness I well remember, a tenseness that brought to me a reminiscence of the chill which had gripped us for the past two days. And then he left and climbed up the ladder to the bridge deck.

I called after him.

"But you're not going to—"

He turned.

"We're going on to—to find the *Karnak*," he said.

My heart jolted once—and I felt a great relief. We were going to help—if help were yet of any avail. I wondered if it would be.

And Grahame, as he felt in the dark for the single sheet beneath which we now tried to sleep, gave vent to his feelings, too.

"Peculiar," he muttered. "Blamed peculiar, I'd say."

999
The Silence of the Ship

So on we steamed.

Our wireless continued to stay in proper order—but we could get no word from the *Karnak*. For all we knew she had vanished from the surface of the seas—and Heaven knew in what manner, and Heaven knew where.

And when we spoke with other ships, none had received her call. Nor were there other vessels now nearer to the location the *Karnak* had given to render her, did she yet need it, a quicker assistance than would be ours. So on we steamed.

The sea was smooth—conditions were normal. Peace and tranquillity were over all, even as had been that blanketing chill before and the fearsome uneasiness it laid upon us. And as the sun beamed down upon us with all its old genial warmth, and the blue sea sparkled so happily about, we nearly forgot that we were hundreds of miles off our course—nearly forgot the strange, the sad errand that might yet be ours.

The nights, too, were calm and full of gentle comfort. Slightly cooler, of course, for we were northing, and the Japan current had but little warming effect as yet. Yet the rigging was untouched by even a hint of dancing blue—the electric globes pulsed steadily under the dynamos humming below decks—the radio operators were at peace with the world.

Yet still no news of the *Karnak*—no answer from the stricken ship.

Then came the mate—next morning.

"We ought to sight her around eleven o'clock," he said quietly.

He accepted my cigar—then added:

"Yes—we ought to."

Stevenot—we three passengers were as one, ever together, and had been companions in travel and adventure since long before the war—we and one other, the dear fellow who had been number four—Stevenot, ever quick to sense a thing out of order, asked:

"Then you do not expect—"

The mate, match rising under his palm as he held it to his cigar, shook his head vehemently.

"I didn't say that—no! I simply said we *ought* to sight her about eleven. Maybe we will—maybe not. But I know where we are—and the point where she said she was. Ought to—that's all."

This was at eight-thirty.

And yet not ten minutes had passed before the bridge lookout sighted a smudge of smoke to the northward.

We wirelessed at once—and received no answer. And we knew that all steamers must carry wireless—yet here, a steamer, and no answer to our call. Perhaps its apparatus was out of order—perhaps not. We conjectured as to possibilities—could it be the *Karnak*—this early?

Gradually we drew upon it—and finally the ship's hull came up. With glasses we made her out to be a vessel of perhaps seventy-five hundred tons, high-pooped, and high-bowed, with bridge deck midships, and two black funnels. And that to a "T" was the Ship's Register description of the *Karnak*—the vessel that had called for help. We had sighted her some three hours before expected.

And she had way on her, too, heading as near as we could make out, southeast.

We wirelessed again—no answer.

So, knowing they could see us as plainly as we could see them, we broke out the International Code pennant, and ran up a line of flags.

The mate and skipper, glasses glued to their eyes, cursed softly. The *Karnak* did not answer our visual signal.

Visions of mutiny aboard arose before me. I pictured a crew of grim fellows doing away with their officers, determined on making one rich haul, and then a quick getaway. Here they signaled for help in order to get some vessel to come to them—faked trouble—and when the rescuer came close enough, with some war-time gun mounted behind falling bulwarks, hold it up and practice a bit of modern piracy.

The *Karnak* continued silent. We headed in to cross her close stern—

and made ready the little signal gun on the observation deck above the bridge.

The gun boomed—if the *Karnak* had for some inexplicable cause not seen us, this would speedily wake her up.

We waited tensely—for hours it seemed. The *Karnak* did not answer.

She did not answer wireless. She did not answer our flag hoist. She did not answer the roar of our signal gun.

The mate and skipper stared. The wheelsman's eyes popped.

"What in hell's the matter?" growled the old man. "Look at the dodgin' she's doing."

We stared at the vessel, now not a quarter mile away.

"Steers most peculiar I ever saw," muttered Grahame. "Zigzaggin' for subs—looks like."

We shot the gun again.

With glasses—without glasses—we could see movement—the crew on board—working on the decks.

Yet the *Karnak* did not answer.

The captain cursed—broke out the United States ensign—ordered the second mate to take the wheel. "Get her close, and stick by her," he ordered.

Then he took the megaphone.

"Ahoy there, *Karnak*!" he roared across the fifty-fathom stretch of blue that now separated us. He roared again. Visible members of the crew did not even look up. An officer pacing the bridge above did not alter his step, nor move a hand. The skipper bellowed once more—still the *Karnak* did not answer.

"By gosh!" cried the captain, "I'm going aboard to wake 'em up. Get out the motor launch," he ordered. "Six men and rifles! Run up the rags for her to heave to; and load that damn pea shooter with a bit of solid iron. I'll stand for no monkey business. The sea's goin' to the dogs these days, anyhow!"

Grahame and Stevenot and I, ever one when adventure was in the air, looked at each other with the same question in our eyes. Then, as one, we nodded. I, as usual, was the spokesman.

I turned to the skipper, who had just come out of his cabin buckling a forty-five automatic about his bulgy waist.

"Captain—" I started.

"Yes, yes, yes!" he cried explosively. "Get your guns and come along. My cursed crew are seein' yellow as it is—don't know a bowline from a binnacle! Jump!"

We jumped. There were times during the next few days when I dearly wished we had not. But we did—and I don't regret it now. Yet in my dreams—

Stevenot remarked casually—he was generally casual when real concrete danger was at hand, or when we thought it was at hand:

"Old man seems a bit excited—wot?"

"Blame peculiar, I'd say," muttered Grahame.

I said nothing, though in my heart I felt both to be right.

The *Lanoa* had slowed down a bit so we might get off safely. The *Karnak* was forging ahead. We climbed into the fast motor launch which was ready to be swung out. The new signal was up—the *Karnak* still held her erratic course—still was silent.

"Yellow-looking gang," said the skipper quietly to me, as I sat on the thwart beside him. "And wearing sweaters and heavy rags, too. Ain't cold to-day, is it?"

I shook my head. It was not cold now—it was warm.

I stared across at a couple of the *Karnak*'s crew muffled in sweaters, wiping her starboard rail. Their appearance, even from the distance, was decidedly peculiar. Faces and hands were pasty yellow—sickly yellow—of a yellow that was ghastly and sickening to see.

A sudden thought came to me.

"Disease?" I whispered to the old man. "Yellow fever—or some—"

"Don't get that at sea, man," the captain replied. "And they ain't too sick to work, are they?"

They certainly were not. Yet as I watched the two it seemed that they worked strangely, mechanically, spasmodically—as if each move were not that of a smoothly regulated and continuous thought, but prompted each by a single jerky impulse.

We dropped to the smooth running water to the squeal of seldom used blocks—the after falls were released, the motor started, then—I remember the delightful thrill of being cut off from the great ship—we released the forward falls and cut across to the silent *Karnak*.

A small grapnel was brought along so that we might get a line over the rail and board her. But as we rounded the stern and came up on the *Karnak*'s lee, what should we find there but the two dangling blocks from a pair of davits on the high deck midships!

The skipper growled something under his breath.

Stevenot whispered to me.

"Why should a boat have left that ship? And the rest of the crew left her lines a-dangling? That's not seamanship."

We ran alongside.

The skipper, with jaw set, seized the after falls himself and bent the painter about its four parts. Then, with a growl: "You four aft stand by the launch—and your guns. Rest of you—come on—" He climbed hand over hand up the standing part of the fall, swung himself over the davit head, and slid to the *Karnak*'s deck—crouched, gun in hand.

Stevenot, crowding ahead of the mate, was at his side in a moment—and watchful, too—and ready.

The mate followed with three rifles slung over his shoulder; and he hauled up the rope ladder and hooked it over the rail. Up this I clambered, and the others followed.

19
Aboard the Karnak

Even as I drew my gun and stood leaning expectantly forward beside the rest, an officer came aft along the deck. Every one of us was instantly stiffly tense—wondering, and ready.

The man's face was of the same awful yellow as those of the two seamen on the starboard side. I wondered, too, at this officer, pacing so smartly toward us, that he should be so unshaven—and so thickly muffled in clothes. And then—this all happened in ten seconds, you must know— the man, eyes straight ahead, passed by us without a look or a word. Passed as though we, strangers on board his ship, were not even there.

I gasped—the man's cap had the device "Second Mate" upon it, and on board ship a second mate is supposed to be all eyes. Yet the man had not even noticed us. A sigh breathed from my companions.

The skipper sprang into life.

"Mate!" he cried after the man. "Just a moment!"

The officer did not turn a fraction of an inch, or falter a second in his quick, jerky step. Then he wheeled to the left and entered an open passage.

The old man gasped again—hunched forward with automatic raised.

Grahame, coming to my side—on tiptoe—nodded toward the passage into which the man had disappeared.

"Notice his shoes?" he whispered.

I shook my head.

"One black—one tan." Grahame's voice trembled a bit with excitement. "And he wore a sweater under his coat. And he didn't take a rap of notice of us, either. Blame peculiar, I'd say."

The skipper shook himself savagely. Then turned to us.

"Keep together and follow me. Don't shoot unless I give the order." He leaned against the davit a moment and called down to those in the motor launch. "Keep the engine turning," he cried, "and be ready to cast off."

Then to us: "Come on!" And he started forward. "We'll make a round of the decks first."

The captain led. On his left stepped the eager mate—but warily, gun in hand. At his right Stevenot had pushed in—ever quick-scented when on a trail, despite the apprehension he so often voiced. Grahame and I held the flanks, and behind us were four of the crew—tiptoeing softly and quick-eyed.

The other two members of the gang were the two oilers who stayed with the boat. Our party thus was nine, all armed, all mystified, all a bit scared deep within our secret selves—but all eager and all ready.

We stepped as though over a mined field.

We watched for a sudden descent upon us of a piratical, knife-slinging crew of mutinied cut-throats. We expected every moment for some silent yellow-skinned something to spring upon our backs out of the silent nothingness about us and claw, and rip, and rend, and tear.

The silence continued. We peered into passageways and cabin ports—and saw nothing—heard nothing. My skin began to prickle slightly. The four men behind us stepped upon our heels. The old man cursed softly as he peered about.

Grahame spoke—startling us.

"A man aloft polishing the flute," he said briefly.

We looked up at the forward funnel.

A seaman in dungarees, with one leg hooked over the rungs of the iron ladder that ran up to the lip of the funnel, was industriously scrubbing the great brass whistle. In his left hand he held a glass bottle, of polish I suppose, and his body was twisted to the left as he reached with his right hand about the big tube of the thing.

Suddenly he lost his balance, grabbed at the rungs—and the glass bottle crashed on the deck below. He righted himself carefully—and went right on polishing.

He acted strangely, it seemed to me. Made peculiar motions.

Grahame spoke again.

"Why, he's mad! Look—he makes the same motion with his left hand as though he still had that bottle of polish in it. Shakes it up—and pours it on his rag—and *nothing there!*

We stared.

The captain, after a pause, shouted. His voice seemed a trifle high to me.

"Aloft there! You at the flute!"

The man continued to shake and polish—he made no sign of hearing or answer.

After a moment the skipper cursed again.

"Crazy—or deaf!"

Stevenot shook his head.

"But they ought to *see* us, even if they can't hear—or if they are mad."

The captain and mate both grunted.

"Come on," jerked the old man then.

We followed him to the bridge—where from our ship we had seen an officer pacing. That officer was still there, still pacing.

The skipper went up to him—met him as he wheeled at the starboard end of the bridge and stood directly in his path—holding out his right hand, gun in left behind his back.

We held our breaths—I know not why.

The yellow-faced officer, jerky-stepped, head turned slightly toward the bows and eyes there, too, without the slightest pause or notice of the captain's presence, ignored the proffered hand. And before the skipper could sidestep, the man walked straight into him, knocked him down by sheer mechanical momentum, staggered a bit, then continued on his way to the port end of the bridge.

As they collided the skipper's gun went off with a bang—from nervousness, or accident, or in what he thought was self-defense, I know not. But it startled us all—the captain himself, too. And Stevenot whispered:

"Now we get it—ready!"

But naught followed that ringing shot.

The captain leaped to his feet—pale and shaky.

"Walked right over me," he sputtered. "As if I wasn't there—into me—knocked me down—what in hell's the matter—" He shivered a bit—the officer had wheeled at the bridge end and was jerkily pacing back, face turned toward the bows, now on his left, eyes cast ahead as well. "By Heaven!" the captain swore, "I'll show him—"

And he seized the officer by his right hand and neck—and instantly with a startled cry jerked his hands away and rubbed them on his trousers.

"What's the matter?" cried the mate.

"Cold!" muttered the skipper, rubbing his hands still on his trouser legs, and staring at the retreating figure. "Cold—his hand—his neck—cold as ice."

"Cold!" cried Stevenot.

And he ran forward and touched the officer's hand—and dropped it with a cry.

"It *is*—cold as ice!" he whispered tensely.

The officer himself took no notice of either the skipper's touch or Stevenot's. He swayed lightly as each touched him, but kept on pacing.

Stevenot and the captain stared at each other.

"Let him alone," the skipper then ordered huskily. "Try the wheel-house."

He glanced again at the pacing officer, and shivered slightly once more.

As we entered, the man at the wheel was spinning her for a left rudder.

"What's he doin' that for?" demanded the captain. "What's his course?"

A clipped paper hung near the binnacle. On it was the course—172°.

I leaned over the binnacle—the man at the wheel took no notice of me. The lubber's line of the compass showed that the ship was swinging toward 215°. The course should have been, according to the navigator's slip hanging in sight, a few degrees east of south. And yet here was the man at the wheel holding the *Karnak* almost southwest—43° off her course.

I showed the skipper. Even as I did so, the wheelsman spun the gear for a right rudder and straightened her out on 215°.

For some minutes we watched.

Then the mate burst out:

"He's crazy—he's holding her against yawing when she's not yawing an inch! And he let's her go when she swings clear off. Look at him spin her there—he's off, I tell you. Here—"

He seized the man's hand and started to tear it from the spokes—then snatched his own hand away and looked at us with sudden consternation in his eyes.

V
Something Wrong!

The skipper and Stevenot and he exchanged glances.

"Cold—as ice—that man—cold!" muttered the mate. Stevenot nodded.

"Like the officer outside," he said.

Grahame leaned forward and touched the wheelsman's hand.

"Ugh!" he exclaimed. "Blamed peculiar, I'd say. Let's see somethin' else."

At that moment came a rush of feet outside—and loud cries.

"Good!" cried the skipper, relief in his voice. "Now they're coming. Wait till I give—"

Then he stopped. It was not an attacking party. It was the four men we'd left in the launch.

"We heard a shot," one of the oilers started. "We thought—" Then he stared at the wheelsman, yellow-faced, besweatered. Then to the old man: "If you say, sir, we'll—we'll go back."

The captain tapped his teeth thoughtfully. Then nodded. Then turned to the four men with rifles.

"You, too—if you wish."

Without a word the whole eight of them, huddled closely, left the house. Outside the door they stepped slowly at first, on tiptoe, and with chins upon their shoulders. Then as a flock of sheep they broke and ran— and in a moment slid out of sight overside.

The skipper, watching, grunted. Stevenot, with a wry smile, muttered something I did not get.

"Let's get on," Grahame suggested.

It seemed that we all were open to suggestion—the captain started for the door and had one foot over the raised sill when he stopped and backed in again, one hand up for silence.

The same officer we had seen when we first climbed aboard stepped high over the sill, and entered. He went straight for the chart table on the starboard and opened a case and took out a sextant. This he wiped perfunctorily—then left, as oblivious to our presence as though we had not been there.

The captain's eyes followed him.

"A sight?" he questioned us all. "Is he going to take a sight at this hour in the morning—at sea? What time is it?"

I looked at my watch.

"Almost ten-thirty, captain," I said.

"Why in hell at ten-thirty?" he complained. "Didn't he get his morning shot at eight—it's clear enough! Your watch right?"

I nodded—and Grahame and the mate examining theirs, confirmed the accuracy of mine.

"Ten-thirty," they said as one.

The captain wheeled to the chart table. On it was pinned a Mercator chart. A series of courses was drawn from a point in Alaska to San Francisco Bay, and several lightly penciled marks showed where the navigator had marked each day's progress. And between the marks were the dates for each run. We huddled about the table—for the captain had stared at the chart as though half hypnotized.

After a minute or more the old man pointed pudgily at the last run marked.

"What's the date to-day?" he asked.

"August 24," the mate replied.

"Humph!" grunted the captain. "Look at the last date that was written down there."

With wonder we looked.

The date for the last run made was that of three days before—August 21.

Stevenot bent close. Then straightened and his eye shifted about to each of us. He shook his head.

"I don't quite get all this," he said quietly. "The last date there is August 21, and if you'll look closely you'll see it's been repeated, almost over the first date, twice. As if it had been gone over to make it clearer, though Heaven knows it's never done.

"And there"—he put his finger where the last criss-cross marked the end of the August 21 run—"that's been crossed twice again, too. It's just as if—"

He hesitated. Then shrugged his shoulders.

"As if what?" snapped the captain, his eye piercing Stevenot's.

"Well," said Stevenot. "I don't know exactly myself. But these men are all—all—oh, but that's utter nonsense. Let's see more first."

The old man glared.

"But I want to know just what you mean," he demanded.

Stevenot stared.

"I'm not quite sure myself," he answered stiffly. "I can't quite—"

He stopped short.

"Back!" he cried curtly. "Back!" And he spread his arms wide and pushed us from the table.

The officer, yellow-faced, sweater-clad, and with the odd-colored shoes upon his feet, returned with the sextant. He held it carefully in his hand, adjusted the reading glass, and held it beneath the electric globe so that the light shown upon the vernier. He examined this closely—pulled a sheet of coordinate paper from a pigeonhole on the bulkhead, and set down the sextant reading—the altitude of the sun above the horizon.

The mate leaned forward and read it. Then bent down and picked up a similar piece of paper which lay on the floor near the littered wastebasket. He looked at the figures on this, and grunted. I peered over his shoulder. The first figures on it were those of the same sextant altitude as the officer had just put down. Identical.

The man had sat down in the chair before the desk, and was now working out his latitude from a form he had taken from another pigeon-hole.

The mate leaned across and picked up the instrument—adjusted the focus of the eyepiece—and then drew a long, sharp whistle.

"What's a matter!" snapped the skipper.

"Read the thing," said the mate. "Then see what this fellow's put down."

The captain read—then seized the paper from the mate's hand. He stared at the reading set down there, then at the one the officer had just jotted down—then again glued his eye to the glass over the vernier of the sextant. Then he said under his breath:

"Well, I'll be damned!"

The mate nodded.

"So will I," he said quietly.

"What—" I started.

The captain turned quickly—he always did when I started to question. I don't know why.

"The man just put down a reading that's several full degrees off what the sextant here indicates. Look for yourself." He thrust the sextant at me, and I, having tried the thing on the *Lanoa*'s bridge before, read, and saw for myself. The captain ran on:

"And that other paper, that old one—it must be yesterday's or 'twould have been swept out—the same handwriting has put down the same reading there—the same identical reading to a quarter of a minute. And yet the sextant reads—you saw yourself."

I nodded dumbly. Vague thoughts began to run through my mind. Theories. And conjectures. And I began at last to associate more and more the strange meteorological conditions of the past few days, the coldness and all, with this ship and the strange men who ran her—or, second thought prompted this, who appeared to run her—who went through all the motions, but—

And there I had to stop. As I stopped I felt a sudden thrill crawl from my toes to my head and creep chillily over my skin—for I thought I glimpsed what the captain had tried to get Stevenot to say. And to tell the truth, I liked it not. No man would. It was just a bit too gruesome. And too uncannily close.

I watched, with the others, that yellow and overwarmly clad man at the table as he plied his pencil.

The mate, eyes alternately on the paper he held, and that on which the man was working, followed every figure with an intentness that was almost hypnotic. I began to watch, too—and started before I had got halfway down—the figures were identical—even one error that was made on each and crossed out and the figuring redone.

And then a thing happened that was small in itself, but so fearsome in all that it might indicate, that I cannot help but set it down with all the rest I saw and heard and felt on board that awful ship.

As the officer wrote—his pencil point suddenly snapped, and flew against the bulkhead. But he, apparently unaware that what he now figured with made not a mark or jot, continued to work on. The thrill I'd felt before came now again—and left me cold.

And when the man reached for his log-book, and opened up at a mark ready placed, and began to put down, with a pencil that made no mark, figures identical with those we now could see had been already retraced twice before, my confidence in what I had believed possible and impossible gave way.

This was too much. I shivered, and seized Stevenot's arm. He started violently, and I noticed that his forehead showed damp in the yellow glow of the bulb.

"Let's get out on deck," I suggested.

Stevenot nodded.

We left.

And as one, the rest followed—the captain, the mate, and Grahame—into the open, beneath the warming sun, where we could breathe.

"The same figures—same mistakes," ejaculated Grahame, "the same. Darned peculiar, I'd say."

The mate nodded.

"And the wrong reading at that," he added.

"Humph!" grunted the skipper, as he stared back into the wheelhouse at the steersman who again was spinning for rudder to counteract a yawing that was not there.

"And it's so warm here, yet they—sweaters and all—" started Stevenot. Then he shuddered a bit.

Then looked at his hand, and rubbed it on his sleeve. When he glanced up I caught his eye. He reddened slightly. It was the hand with which he had seized that of the silent, yellow, heavily clad officer who even yet was pacing the bridge. The officer who had so callously, so coldly, so mechanically, walked into, knocked down, and stepped upon our own captain. The officer who, like these others of the *Karnak*'s crew, was so uncanny in appearance, so icy to the touch.

There was a long silence. Instinctively the captain and the mate drew together and slightly apart from us. And as instinctively, too—or was it from the gravitation of mutual interest?—Grahame and Stevenot and I had grouped, too.

Apart from the officers, Stevenot spoke:

"I've my notions of this," he said. "But I'd like to see more—first."

Grahame nodded and looked at me. I met his questioning eye.

Stevenot went on, whispering.

"Something's dead wrong—with ship and crew," he declared. "And the old man has sense. It's scary—and he's scared himself though Lord knows he's been to sea long enough to know that it's never done with mystery, and probably never will be.

"But he's got sense—and a nose for finance. And he'll dope it out as salvage—the situation I mean. He's scared—but not scared of money. And if he can get this ship to port it'll mean—" Stevenot broke off abruptly. Then, with a vague glance inside where the officer still vainly penciled, he muttered: "I wonder what the cargo is—from Alaska."

He started for the door.

The captain wheeled.

"Hey! Where you going?" His voice a bit high-pitched. He was not as calm as a captain should be.

Stevenot's chin went up a moment. Then with a slight smile he answered.

"To get the log-book."

"Oh," answered the skipper, and fell back to talking to his mate again.

VI
With a Cargo of Ore

Stevenot was in the house for some minutes. I glanced after him, naturally, and saw him reach for the log and take it from under the officer's hands. Then he pulled open a little drawer under the pigeonholes, puttered in it. Then another—and from this he drew something I could not make out.

Then he bent over the officer and gingerly picked up the latter's right hand. A full minute thus—then he took up the book, and came out rubbing his hands as before, alternately, on his trousers.

His face was very sober now.

Yet he opened the book at once, and fingered for the first page of the *Karnak*'s trip. There, as our own officers listened, he read the date the vessel had cleared, various other routine remarks, then:

" 'With a cargo of ore,' " he said, and stopped.

The captain's eyes and the mate's met for a second.

"Ore," repeated Stevenot—with a glance at Grahame and me.

The old man coughed slightly.

"She's salvage," he jerked out. "We'll take her in to port—salvage."

Stevenot eyed him.

"But the crew's still running her," he said with a slight upward intonation in his voice—and a nod at the wheelsman.

The captain shook his head.

"Dead men can't run a ship," he grunted, watching Stevenot's face.

"Dead men!" cried Stevenot.

"You said it," grunted the skipper again. "An' it's salvage. We'll put a gang on board, an' take her in. These—*things*—now on ship—they'll have to be—I'll—"

Stevenot held him with his eye.

"Dead men?" he questioned again. "And you'll—"

The skipper flushed up.

"Well maybe they are—maybe not. But we'll fix 'em up some way. And I'll get a gang aboard, and take her in."

The mate nodded with him.

"I've seen enough to be satisfied," said the skipper, as he led us to the davits below which was the launch. "The ship's out of gear—and the crew's—it ain't worth a cent. It's salvage. I'll send a gang—"

He stopped short, and his breath wheezed.

"By the Lord!" cried the mate. "The launch is gone!"

It was indeed. On a ship that was as near a tomb as a ship might be, and with a crew of men who might as well be dead, we five were marooned. My heart gave a great jolt as two seamen with mops and buckets stepped mechanically up the gangway from the after-waist of the ship, and started to swab about the decks.

They, too, were yellow, and muffled up in sweaters though the sun was hot above them, gleaming hot. They, too, looked cold and lifeless. Yet they, too, went at once to work—and swabbed, and squeezed, and wiped. I shuddered—how like men from the grave they looked! Did the captain really think—

We ran across decks to the starboard side. The launch was just coming under the *Lanoa*'s lee. A moment more, even as we frantically waved, the launch was hove up, and we saw the crew move in a body up decks to the bridge.

They disappeared in chart house and cabins—and a few moments more came out again.

Then the *Lanoa*'s propeller churned white under the stern, and slowly she drew away.

What had happened? Had our own officers, those left on board, deserted us? A chill ran through me, as I glanced back at the yellow, frigid-looking seamen at their labors, twenty feet away. Then hot anger, as the *Lanoa* still forged ahead.

The captain, with a curse, ran to the wheelhouse, and immediately afterward the *Karnak*'s whistle gave four feeble toots. This was answered by four mocking blasts from the *Lanoa*'s deep bass; and on the *Lanoa* steamed.

We were dumfounded. The skipper was white. The mate was biting his lower lip. But Stevenot grinned with gusto, and cried:

"With a ship of dead men—this is sport!"

"Sport, hell!" snapped the skipper, apparently ignoring Stevenot's insinuation regarding the Karnak's crew. "Wait'll you're with this gang a week. Ugh! What will we do now?"

"You're the boss," hinted Stevenot.

The captain flushed.

"Why not use the wireless, and get help?" Grahame suggested.

The office was at the after end of the bridge deck—I imagine so that the varying currents used might not interfere with the compass. The captain threw open the door with an oath—and stared once more.

Over his shoulder I could see the operator sitting at his instrument—yellow, and muffled as from cold. Silent he was—and but for his right hand, motionless. But the hand upon the key was moving—and, from what knowledge I had gleaned while serving in our war-time navy, I caught one familiar grouping of sound among all the rest.

Three shorts, three longs, three shorts—three dots, three dashes, three dots—S.O.S. of the International Code. Then came more I could not make out—then breaking in again: S.O.S.—S.O.S.

Thus the key clicked on—and on—and on—as we watched in frozen silence.

The captain gasped.

"The machine isn't working! It's not working! But he—he—"

"You're right—it's useless—dead!" affirmed Stevenot in a whisper.

And he was right. The spark of the old-fashioned apparatus was not working. The machine was quite dead. And yet the operator, apparently quite oblivious to the fact that it was vain labor, was steadily tapping his key, still sending out his call for help.

"Machine's dead, I tell you," cried the skipper. "Machine's dead—and by Heaven, so's the man." He peered wildly about him, then backed away. "And here we're stuck," he cursed soulfully. "And my ship—gone. And these dead—"

"Nonsense!" muttered Stevenot. "Dead? And yet working the ship?"

The skipper turned on him.

"What did you say?" he demanded. "It's salvage, I tell you!"

The mate seized him by the shoulder.

"Come on, Cap," he exclaimed bruskly, but with a certain quaver in his voice. "We're all a bit nervous now. Let's run through below decks, and see what we can see. We're stuck—let's make the most of it."

The captain frowned a moment at Stevenot. Then turned and stared at the *Lanoa,* now fast dropping in the swells about us. Then with a short grunt he started for the gangway leading to the after waist.

We followed, closely bunched.

And of what we saw below decks, and forward later in the fo'c'sle, a book might well be written. Suffice it here to say that the crew was at its regular routine. The firemen—the *Karnak* burned oil—were watching by the boilers—yellow and cold, they, too.

In the engine-room the second assistant engineer was on watch, and his wipers and oilers were about their tasks, caring for the ponderously moving iron and steel that was their charge—all yellow, and chilled, and silent, too.

And none took notice of us.

Yet to watch them, the mechanical manner in which each moved about; the strange errors they made; how they would wipe where no wiping was needed; how they would oil where the oil already overflowed; how they would pick up bits of stuff where no stuff was, and carry them over to the waste can and there deposit them—nothing—solemnly, with painstaking care—that would make the book.

VII
Bound for Seattle

Keeping close together we climbed the slippery ladders to the open air, again, and went forward. In the fo'c'sle were three seamen lying in their tiered bunks, shoes off, arms flung about their heads—apparently asleep, or resting—yellow, cold-looking, as were all.

And on a bench before the door of his tiny quarters sat the bosun, pipe —long since dead, in hand, staring before him at the fo'c'sle's high-silled entrance. And he, too, was yellow and hard-skinned, and muffled up in woolen stuffs.

We retreated to the bridge deck, and held a conference.

And we decided to stick by the ship. The captain himself was vehement for it. It meant money—good money to him. And we were even more enthusiastic—whole-souledly so. This was adventure—and adventure was our life.

It was Stevenot who showed us the way.

"All that is needed," he declared, "is for us to take turn about at the wheel. The captain here can dope out a course to Seattle, say, and we can follow it. If these—*men*—continue to fire ship and tend the engines, that's enough. We'll steer and get the *Karnak* in."

And so it was decided.

We wondered how we could relieve the man now at the wheel—but that turned out to be easy enough. We simply took his hands off the thing, and led him to one of the cabins, and laid him on the bunk, and locked the door upon him.

I drew first watch—and was glad it came in daylight.

Grahame drew the next. Then Stevenot. Then the mate. Then the skipper.

We decided at first on two-hour shifts—thus each man had two on, and eight off. No one on the bridge.

But the skipper objected to this. He was in command now, he said, and he demanded a bridge lookout, as well as a man at the wheel. I had my own opinion why, and Stevenot's eyes showed that he had one, too. So we had to shift things so as to have two go on at a time, and changed over thuswise: We kept the order of watches as we had drawn, but when each of us first went on he was to take the wheel two hours, then the bridge for another two, while the next man in order took the wheel. This made four hours on, and only six off—but the man at the wheel would always be fairly fresh, and six hours rest a couple times out of each twenty-four would not be bad.

Then we chose cabins.

The skipper and mate naturally fell together—and commenced a great cleaning up.

And the rest of us found one, on the port side, that would take in three —it was the engineer officers' cabin, but we carried the chief and the first assistant to one of the others, laid them out, and locked them in as we had the steersman.

We went below and washed mightily. Then invaded the galley, where the cooks puttered mechanically, and took up enough of tinned stuff and fruit and bread to withstand a siege.

At noon we started our routine—I on the bridge for only two hours, Grahame at the wheel.

I believe the captain and mate sat in their cabin most of the time. Stevenot went exploring about ship.

Then Grahame took the deck, and Stevenot the wheel.

Then Stevenot the deck, and the mate the wheel.

Then the mate had the deck, and the old man steered. And so on it went.

We had no difficulty with the men of the *Karnak*'s crew when dutifully, and wrapped in their warmest togs, and yellow and cold and tight-skinned, they came to relieve the watch. We simply treated them as we had the others—steered them to a cabin and locked them in. The below decks force, of course, we did not touch—as long as they made steam and

did not blow up the boilers we worried not. We simply wanted no interference with our steering.

The *Lanoa* slowly sank out of sight.

Night came down, and a great loneliness seized us. At eight I came on
again, the skipper on deck.

Five men we were—on a great ship. Five men—and some forty others
who were men and yet not men, alive and yet—I hesitate to say—not
alive. I felt as the blackness grew that my nerves were getting a bit on
edge, too—like those of the captain. And I wondered what had happened
to these men—and what might happen to us during the long days I knew
must drift past before we sighted solid land.

Those hours of blackness passed slowly indeed. Ofttimes I fancied I
heard footsteps about me, and would start violently and swing about. But
naught occurred.

However, I felt continually a-tingle as though every nerve fiber of me
were vibrating with involuntary fear. This grew and grew until finally I
found myself in a sudden chill and 'twas all I could do to stand there at
the wheel, or hold the lubber's line to the degree we steered. Now and
again the bulky shadow of the old man crossed the glass before me, yet
strange to say, the captain's presence gave me but little confidence.

He certainly had not inspired any during the day—even though at first
he had so boldly led the way. Bold enough—yet when, just where he
tramped so loudly now, and puffed so strenuously at the cigar he'd taken
from the box in the cabin of the *Karnak*'s captain—who by the way we'd
found there lying on his bunk, evidently off watch, and locked in as per
usual—when, I say, in so peculiar a manner he had been trod upon by the
icy mate and then felt that terrible iciness itself, that boldness had been
sapped away.

Then Grahame relieved me at the wheel—and I took the deck while the
captain sought the seclusion that his cabin granted.

I felt better with Grahame at the wheel—and occasionally stepped in
for a chat.

Grahame could not account for the appearance and actions of the
Karnak's crew. I hinted of my theory—and he listened, but did not com-
mit himself.

I reminded him that the captain swore they were all dead men. He
asked if I thought the captain had ever read the "Ancient Mariner"—and
grinned. Ask Stevenot, he said—he'd a theory that was near right. Meanwhile go back to your job and step lively, too. I went out on the bridge
again—and listened to the lap of black waters alongside, and the dash of
spray ahead against the bows.

Then I was relieved and went to our cabin.

And there, an hour later, I was suddenly awakened by someone trying to crawl into my bunk—I had a double lower. It was quite dark, but I figured it was one of my mates just off watch.

"Tired?" I muttered.

There was no answer.

And a second later a chill touch sent my nerves flying and my hair a-prickle. With a wild yell I dashed out of the cabin. I heard Grahame, who had evidently taken the upper as I slept, give a cry, too—and a moment later the light flashed upon the second assistant engineer, whom we had entirely forgotten, and who must have just come off watch to get a bit of rest and sleep. As if those—*men*—needed sleep!

There he lay on the lower berth—yellow, and icy cold—he'd crawled in with *me!*

Picture if you can the whiteness of my face, the condition of my nerves, the crawling of my flesh, when Grahame and I carried that awful thing to the cabin where we'd locked the others.

VIII
The Second Day

And picture again my consternation, when at six o'clock I went to relieve the captain at the wheel, I could find neither the captain nor the mate anywhere about.

I aroused the others.

We made search.

And on the starboard side another lifeboat was gone. Some time in the night the captain and mate had deserted us—somewhere even now, they floated on the blackness of the heaving sea, preferring it to the terror and mystery and the yellow, icy, mechanical human *things* aboard the *Karnak*.

We held a conference—low-voiced.

We changed the method of our watch—just a man at the wheel—four hours on, four off. Our navigators were gone, but we knew the general course—anywhere east would bring us to land, and with slight knowledge of the sextant, and care in lookout, we could pilot the *Karnak* to some harbor along the coast.

Little did we know then that the *Karnak* was destined never again to see the land. Had we known that, we might have deserted her and that crew of strange and silent men even as had the old man and his first. And when we did see, did understand—the shock on our nerves of what *might* have been was a fiber-shattering thing.

I, for one, believe its effect on me will never wear off. Even when now it comes upon me, that recollection, my whole body goes a-tremble, and a coldness seizes me even as chill as that which, for those first two days of electric storm and extraordinary cold, held the *Lanoa*, and the *Karnak*.

During the day naught occurred but the now usual actions of the strange men yet about the decks.

Yet here we did note a curious thing. The man who had been polishing the whistle when first we came aboard repeated every action of the day before. He lost his balance, his hands jerked as though the bottle had fallen, he regained his equilibrium, and commenced again to use the bottle when he had none in his hands.

Every motion was almost identical with that he'd made the day before. His every move a repetition—a duplicate—of what, the day before, we had seen him do.

Another thing: The second mate had not been locked up with the rest. Around nine-thirty he took another shot at the sun. Then he came down to the chart table and read the vernier. Then, exactly as he'd done the day before, and I suppose for three days before that, he set down the same sextant altitude of the sun—absolutely wrong, absolutely *not* that which the sextant showed—but the same identical figures that he'd set down before. And when he figured he made the same error as he had before. He, too, was repeating himself—every move, every act.

To test him I drew the paper from beneath the pencil—the skipper had sharpened it when he'd worked out our course—and the yellow-faced man kept penciling on the table top. He did not know the paper was not there—or knowing, heeded the omission not one whit.

Then he drew out the log-book which we had replaced—and over the old entries, at the page marked, he penciled the same figures again.

As I stared, I wondered just what he was—what had happened to him —what he *was now*.

And then, queerly enough, I wondered what Stevenot had done to him, or discovered about him, when the day before he had gone into the wheel-house to get the log-book and ascertain the *Karnak*'s cargo. Why had he looked so doubly serious when he came out?

By noon that day we had made 192.7 miles—as near as I could figure from the Negus log trailing aft and the revolution indicator in the engine-room. We had yet many days of slow steaming ahead—provided our strange crew held out. I recalled my old war-navy school work—and practical navigation.

And already our engine-room counter had dropped ten revolutions a minute.

We tried to find out why—but knowing little of the *Karnak*'s machinery, our investigations came to naught. We shivered a bit, too, watching the yellow, staring-eyed men perform at their tasks.

We shivered more during the next night.

IX
The Third Day

Grahame, awakening me next morning to relieve Stevenot at the wheel, mentioned it to me.

"I felt a queer tingling all last night," he complained. "My back—whole spine. Oh, it wasn't fear—although I don't like the situation at all, I admit. It was something different. I rolled over, too, in my sleep, and awoke to find my whole side a-tingle, as though it were asleep."

I started.

"That's exactly what I felt," I said.

We mentioned it to Stevenot.

He nodded.

"Me, too," he answered. "As if that part of me were asleep."

"It's blame peculiar," muttered Grahame.

Stevenot nodded quietly.

Maybe it is—maybe it isn't," he said thoughtfully.

Then I took the wheel.

The lights were acting poorly now, too—as they had on the *Lanoa* during those two eerie days.

And as I tried to keep the compass steady, the dim thought worked up within me, that perhaps the captain and mate had not been such great fools when they had deserted the *Karnak*.

This thought took hold of me, somehow, up there in the loneliness of the wheelhouse. The sea sparkled so happily about, the sun was so whitely bright outside—yet this ship—this crew! Why had I awakened the night before, even before that icy engineer had started to crawl into his old bunk by my side, and been so singularly alarmed by the persistent tingling that was upon me?

And by what strange coincidence, then, other than the preying of a subconscious fear, had each of us three felt the same sensation? And then, too, the sudden little chills that, nervelike, shot now and again through me. Surely I was not that deeply frightened.

I held my hand out. It was as steady as the chronometers in their soft racks beneath the chart table's hinged top. I was not afraid. Mystified, yes —but not afraid.

Then why that curious and softly alarming sensation—as of part of me asleep? And why those chilling waves that swept my body—when the night was warm, and I a well man?

I wondered if I were quite well.

When I went off, I searched among the captain's effects and found a clinical thermometer.

And then I was thoroughly frightened—my temperature, even though I now felt quite warm, was some *eight degrees below normal.* In sudden anxiety, I ran out up to Grahame, now at the wheel.

His temperature had dropped, too—to 94°, and 98.5° is normal.

In palpitating fear I sought Stevenot, who as usual, fearless, curious, was prowling around below.

He nodded when I told him—but was almost precipitous in putting the thermometer under his tongue. And his temperature was even lower than mine—88°.

"Good God!" he cried softly, and stared at me.

"Well?" I queried.

He stared steadily at the yellow, thick-clad man puttering about the deck. And when he saw the fellow stoop and make all the motions of picking up something that was not there, and carry it to the rail and toss it lightly overboard, he started, and his eyes found mine.

"They—they are very cold—very cold—themselves!" he muttered half to himself. "And now—"

"I don't like it," I burst out.

He stared at me.

"And do you know," he said, "that this ship rides at least two feet lower in the water than when we boarded her?"

"What?" I exclaimed.

"I've been around her more than you two," he nodded quietly. "And been investigating. And she's loaded with ore—ore won't float, you know."

"Let's tell Grahame," I whispered.

We all whispered—the silence of all these men about seemed to literally force us to.

Grahame took it calmly enough.

"We haven't been using the pumps," he said, exhaling smoke from one of the *Karnak*'s cigars.

Stevenot's answer chilled me.

"They've been working full power ever since we've been aboard. I've been looking around, you know."

"What'll we do?" I queried.

"It might be well to provision another lifeboat," Stevenot replied quietly. "The pumps are still working—there's plenty of time. And every mile we stay with the *Karnak*— Also, we can't tell—these fellows—these cold —they may yet—" He shrugged his shoulders.

Grahame nodded, then stopped and furtively picked up his cigar. He'd bitten it through.

In half an hour No. 3 lifeboat, next to the swinging falls where had hung the whaleboat the captain and mate had taken, was ready for sea. And we were overjoyed at finding beneath her canvas cover a small portable motor. We clamped this on the stern—it made us feel nearer home. Of provisions we put in enough to last a dozen men a month.

I felt foolish as I worked at this. Then the sudden appearance of one of the yellow crew doubled my efforts.

That night the tingling was decidedly pronounced—all over me now, not simply on the side that was beneath. And alternately I was swept by great surging waves of chill and heat.

The sweat broke out on me—cold sweat. I felt sudden nausea. And then a black juggernaut of fear almost paralyzed me. I struggled against it —and, almost fainting, cried aloud to Grahame above me.

At once he answered.

"Let's get out," he cried—and his voice was weak—his words sharp, spasmodic.

We seized clothes and tumbled out on the deck. And there we met Stevenot—deserted from the wheel.

"The lights are out," he cried. "And the ship—the ship."

And then I noted for the first time that every bit of metal on the *Karnak* was faintly aglow—not with the blue electric flame that had danced on the *Lanoa*'s rigging before the great electric bolt had fallen—but half-luminous with quiet, almost menacing, phosphorescence.

Again a wave of icy chill clutched at me—and then, with terrifying coincidence, in the moony radiance of all about me, there passed as silently as a ghost, a staring-eyed member of the crew.

As one we madly dashed for the lifeboat. And five minutes later, our motor chugging hopefully, we were floating a hundred yards away from the weirdly glowing *Karnak*, that followed us with slowly turning wheel.

We had deserted the *Karnak*, too.

And perhaps a half hour later, Stevenot, who sat in the bow facing aft, pointed and cried out: "The *Karnak*—the *Karnak*!"

We turned—and even as we turned, the great vessel, glowing as though impregnated in every part with eerie moonlight, looming like a vast ghost of the sea, dropped with all her crew, and as silently as her crew had labored, beneath the surface of the sea.

And to tell the truth, a sigh of vast relief breathed from us all.

We were free—we were safe, in a small open boat on the great northern sea. But the *Karnak*—we were not with her.

And three days later, yet some hundreds of miles from land, we were picked up by one of the salmon ships bound with her thousands of cases for San Francisco Bay. We were safe! But the *Karnak* and her fearsome crew were at the bottom of the sea—hid deep away—even as they well should be—and as are many others of ocean's mysteries and ocean's tragedies, too—even as they well should be—and safe.

X
Why?

The first night out, under the stars that now watched with such twingling comfort upon us, Stevenot gave us his explanation of the thing. I myself like puzzles solved, and all puzzles, it must be remembered, do have their solutions.

Stevenot's solution may be the right one, may not be. Yet does, in my estimation, untwist every thread of the *Karnak*'s strange tangle. And I, for one, even out there on the deep, with the strange ship and crew perhaps yet plunging deeper into the abysmal black beneath us, heard and was satisfied. So, with the account of the mystery itself, I offer my companion's explanation here.

"Why, you ask?" questioned Stevenot from the bows. "Why was it so —and how—and what? Simple enough, I think.

"I'd call it conincidence—and one that never yet has been brought to man's attention—and that man live. It may have happened before—ships disappear, you know—but none lived to tell the tale.

"We saw the thing start on the *Lanoa*—only the *Lanoa* was loaded with sugar, not with ore. We were chilled by the same cold as was the *Karnak*. The blue flowing electricity was as rampant on our rigging as it must have been upon the *Karnak*'s. Our wireless was off and on, even as was that of the unfortunate ship just gone to its destined end.

"But we were farther from the influence of the great electric masses of the north. We were far to the south of that place whence the *Karnak* pleaded for help. And we were loaded with raw sugar; we did not have a steel hull packed with metallic ore—ore that attracted electricity, ore that was imbued with electric action itself, ore that perhaps was lightly radioactive, as are many of the mineral products of the countries of the north.

"What happened, you ask? Again I say 'tis simple—again; coincidence.

"The electric storm descended, and with it, or as a consequence, the cold. With us it was a matter of temporary inconvenience. With the *Karnak*, the stuff took permanent and relentless hold. We were a simple ship laden with vegetable produce—the *Karnak* was a huge electro-magnet. The electricity literally soaked into her—we shed it as a duck sheds water —she soaked it up as a sponge.

"I believe her master realized this—and so called for help while his radio would allow. He himself felt the tingling and the same evil chills as we did—and realized what their portent was. He knew with what his holds were full—and how the electricity would work upon the iron plates of the hull itself, and rot, and rot, and rot, until the seams would open up, the bottom of the ship fall out beneath them all, and the *Karnak*, plummetlike, would drop from the ken of man as we just have seen it do.

"The *Karnak*'s captain knew this all, I say, and called for men to help. But others felt it, too, perhaps; and thus did one boatload desert before there came that final electric blast—which on the *Lanoa* we saw and heard—which fell upon the *Karnak*, and overwhelmed it and all the crew —and sapped the life out of every man. Sapped it out, sucked it out, with terrible, unthinking, relentless malevolence—and in its place put part of its own self, its own electric mass, its own electric energizing power."

Stevenot paused a moment, his hands folded about his knees—huddled beneath the blanket he'd thrown about his shoulders.

"The *Karnak* called for help—until the bolt came that killed the wireless—and even then the radio operator stuck on the job. Why? You wonder why these men, yellow, and icy, and yet wrapped in the thick woolens they donned when the chill fell upon them all, why they continued, though dead men in every sense of the word, to go about their routine tasks?

"Simply because the electricity about them and in them, impregnating every cell of their flesh and bone and blood, had crystallized, in the last day of its vast intensity, the brain fibers regulating every act they had performed—crystallized their brains—even, to put it crudely, as sound waves are crystallized on a phonographic record.

"At the same time every nerve, every cell, though the real soul, the real man, was dead, was yet alive with electricity. *Rigor mortis,* under such stimulus, could not set in. And so under the electric impulse—perhaps, too, forced on by the slight radioactivity of the thousands of tons of ore in the holds—the crystallized routine thought continued to impel—continued to operate the messages along the nerves—the muscles reacted to the electric impulse—the body performed all its functions—mechanically, automatically, regularly.

"Thus, when we landed, the mate did not see us, or hear us call. His action was simply a *motographic,* if I may use the word, reproduction, of his *thought action of the day before.* He turned in at the passage, without noticing us, because he had done the same the day before. And were we there the day before?

"You see now?

"It was the same with the man polishing up the whistle—losing his balance, dropping the bottle. It was the same with the officer on the bridge—knocking the captain down—the wonder that he regained his balance and paced on.

"It was the same with the man at the wheel—who steered to avoid a yawing that affected the ship the last day when he really was alive, when his brain was actually recording thought and being crystallized by the surging electricity in him, and the cold about. So, too, with the mate taking observations—he set down what he had read when last he had read the vernier, *alive* and *thinking*.

"It was watching him that gave me my first real clue. And surreptitiously, knowing it was a test for death, I pricked his hand with a pin I found in a drawer by the chart table—no blood came forth—the man was not alive then—but dead, *dead*. Yet I didn't want to scare the captain out yet.

"So in dressing—they still clothed themselves to withstand cold. And some, groping, found odd clothing—even as did the second mate with his shoes.

"And thus with every man on board—even him who crawled, dead and icy cold, into the berth with you. All, from the captain who lay sleeping, exhausted from his watching, I suppose—down to the humblest of the crew, from fire-room to fo'c'sle—all were dead men, but put in jerky action by the energizing power of the electricity in which they had been drenched.

"And the great bolt, when it came, attracted by the metallic cargo the *Karnak* held, overwhelmed them all, struck out what real life was yet left, finally crystallized their thought action, and set them into machinelike motion—made of live men, dead—automatons.

"Then we arrived—you know the rest."

Stevenot paused again, and even in the darkness I felt his eyes on mine. Grahame at my side, the tiller of the chugging little boat under his arm, coughed slightly. I gazed deep into the unfathomable mystery of the myriad of twinkling stars above—worlds and suns, like ours, all; and with our troubles, our mysteries, our joys, too.

"You see now—you understand?" Stevenot's voice drifted quietly to us again.

Grahame's answer came with mine—softly, too, for the influence of the days before, and of this night, was on him, too.

"Yes," we answered as one, "I do understand."

And, in all faith, I believe Stevenot had hit upon the truth.

It was simple after all—as most mysteries are. Simple—and yet how awful during that time the thing was mystery.

I have many times since awakened in the night in cold sweat, dreaming that that icy engineer was crawling between my sheets as I lay asleep. I have many times since felt the icy tingling run through me—an actual physical reminiscence, I do believe, of those electric chills we felt aboard the *Karnak*, chills which would have made us in time, too, even as were those unfortunate members of the *Karnak*'s crew—yellow, icy, machine-like, as had been the *Karnak*'s second mate, the officer of the bridge, the man at the wheel, and all the rest. And, too, walking alone in the lonely shadow of a moonlit road—I still start with sudden fright—seeing in the shadow's rise and fall the movement of those men, the dead-alive.

I have often wondered, too, if those dead-alive—deep beneath the sea went on, and on, and on—I hope not. And I believe not.

Fate, Nature, is too kind to allow such tragedy. And the good old sea, too, has given them burial, and will give them peace. Nature, in the end, is kind. And the *Karnak*, and those silent men, are finally at rest—at peace!

The Temple

H. P. Lovecraft

(Manuscript found on the coast of Yucatan.)

ON AUGUST 20, 1917, I, Karl Heinrich, Graf von Altberg-Ehrenstein, Lieutenant-Commander in the Imperial German Navy and in charge of the submarine U-29, deposit this bottle and record in the Atlantic Ocean at a point to me unknown but probably about N. Latitude 20 degrees, W. Longitude 35 degrees, where my ship lies disabled on the ocean floor. I do so because of my desire to set certain unusual facts before the public; a thing I shall not in all probability survive to accomplish in person, since the circumstances surrounding me are as menacing as they are extraordinary, and involve not only the hopeless crippling of the U-29, but the impairment of my iron German will in a manner most disastrous.

On the afternoon of June 18, as reported by wireless to the U-61, bound for Kiel, we torpedoed the British freighter *Victory*, New York to Liverpool, in N. Latitude 45° 16′, W. Longitude 28° 34′; permitting the crew to leave in boats in order to obtain a good cinema view for the admiralty records. The ship sank quite picturesquely, bow first, the stern rising high out of the water whilst the hull shot down perpendicularly to the bottom of the sea. Our camera missed nothing, and I regret that so fine a reel of film should never reach Berlin. After that we sank the lifeboats with our guns and submerged.

When we rose to the surface about sunset a seaman's body was found on the deck, hands gripping the railing in curious fashion. The poor fellow was young, rather dark, and very handsome; probably an Italian or Greek, and undoubtedly of the *Victory*'s crew. He had evidently sought refuge on the very ship which had been forced to destroy his own—one more victim of the unjust war of aggression which the English pig-dogs are waging upon the Fatherland. Our men searched him for souvenirs, and found in his coat pocket a very odd bit of ivory carved to represent a youth's head crowned with laurel. My fellow-officer, Lieut. Klenze, believed that the thing was of great age and artistic value, so took it from the men for himself. How it had ever come into the possession of a common sailor, neither he nor I could imagine.

As the dead man was thrown overboard there occurred two incidents which created much disturbance amongst the crew. The fellow's eyes had been closed; but in the dragging of his body to the rail they were jarred open, and many seemed to entertain a queer delusion that they gazed steadily and mockingly at Schmidt and Zimmer, who were bent over the corpse. The Boatswain Müller, an elderly man who would have known better had he not been a superstitious Alsatian swine, became so excited by this impression that he watched the body in the water; and swore that after it sank a little it drew its limbs into a swimming position and sped away to the south under the waves. Klenze and I did not like these displays of peasant ignorance, and severely reprimanded the men, particularly Müller.

The next day a very troublesome situation was created by the indisposition of some of the crew. They were evidently suffering from the nervous strain of our long voyage, and had had bad dreams. Several seemed quite dazed and stupid; and after satisfying myself that they were not feigning their weakness, I excused them from their duties. The sea was rather rough, so we descended to a depth where the waves were less troublesome. Here we were comparatively calm, despite a somewhat puzzling southward current which we could not identify from our oceanographic charts. The moans of the sick men were decidedly annoying; but since they did not appear to demoralise the rest of the crew, we did not resort to extreme measures. It was our plan to remain where we were and intercept the liner *Dacia*, mentioned in information from agents in New York.

In the early evening we rose to the surface, and found the sea less heavy. The smoke of a battleship was on the northern horizon, but our distance and ability to submerge made us safe. What worried us more was the talk of Boatswain Müller, which grew wilder as night came on. He was in a detestably childish state, and babbled of some illusion of dead bodies drifting past the undersea portholes; bodies which looked at him intensely, and which he recognised in spite of bloating as having seen dying during some of our victorious German exploits. And he said that the young man we had found and tossed overboard was their leader. This was very gruesome and abnormal, so we confined Müller in irons and had him soundly whipped. The men were not pleased at his punishment, but discipline was necessary. We also denied the request of a delegation headed by Seaman Zimmer, that the curious carved ivory head be cast into the sea.

On June 20, Seamen Bohm and Schmidt, who had been ill the day before, became violently insane. I regretted that no physician was included in our complement of officers, since German lives are precious; but the constant ravings of the two concerning a terrible curse were most subversive of discipline, so drastic steps were taken. The crew accepted the event in a sullen fashion, but it seemed to quiet Müller; who thereafter gave us no trouble. In the evening we released him, and he went about his duties silently.

In the week that followed we were all very nervous, watching for the *Dacia*. The tension was aggravated by the disappearance of Müller and Zimmer, who undoubtedly committed suicide as a result of the fears which had seemed to harass them, though they were not observed in the act of jumping overboard. I was rather glad to be rid of Müller, for even his silence had unfavourably affected the crew. Everyone seemed inclined to be silent now, as though holding a secret fear. Many were ill, but none made a disturbance. Lieut. Klenze chafed under the strain, and was annoyed by the merest trifles—such as the school of dolphins which gathered about the U-29 in increasing numbers, and the growing intensity of that southward current which was not on our chart.

It at length became apparent that we had missed the *Dacia* altogether. Such failures are not uncommon, and we were more pleased than disappointed; since our return to Wilhelmshaven was now in order. At noon June 28 we turned northeastward, and despite some rather comical entanglements with the unusual masses of dolphins were soon under way.

The explosion in the engine room at 2 p.m. was wholly a surprise. No defect in the machinery or carelessness in the men had been noticed, yet without warning the ship was racked from end to end with a colossal shock. Lieut. Klenze hurried to the engine room, finding the fuel-tank and most of the mechanism shattered, and Engineers Raabe and Schneider instantly killed. Our situation had suddenly become grave indeed; for though the chemical air regenerators were intact, and though we could use the devices for raising and submerging the ship and opening the hatches as long as compressed air and storage batteries might hold out, we were powerless to propel or guide the submarine. To seek rescue in the lifeboats would be to deliver ourselves into the hands of enemies unreasonably embittered against our great German nation, and our wireless had failed ever since the *Victory* affair to put us in touch with a fellow U-boat of the Imperial Navy.

From the hour of the accident till July 2 we drifted constantly to the south, almost without plans and encountering no vessel. Dolphins still encircled the U-29, a somewhat remarkable circumstance considering the distance we had covered. On the morning of July 2 we sighted a warship flying American colours, and the men became very restless in their desire to surrender. Finally Lieut. Klenze had to shoot a seaman named Traube, who urged this un-German act with especial violence. This quieted the crew for the time, and we submerged unseen.

The next afternoon a dense flock of sea-birds appeared from the south, and the ocean began to heave ominously. Closing our hatches, we awaited developments until we realised that we must either submerge or be swamped in the mounting waves. Our air pressure and electricity were diminishing, and we wished to avoid all unnecessary use of our slender mechanical resources; but in this case there was no choice. We did not descend far, and when after several hours the sea was calmer, we decided to return to the surface. Here, however, a new trouble developed; for the ship failed to respond to our direction in spite of all that the mechanics could do. As the men grew more frightened at this undersea imprisonment, some of them began to mutter again about Lieut. Klenze's ivory image, but the sight of an automatic pistol calmed them. We kept the poor devils as busy as we could, tinkering at the machinery even when we knew it was useless.

Klenze and I usually slept at different times; and it was during my sleep, about 5 a.m., July 4, that the general mutiny broke loose. The six remaining pigs of seamen, suspecting that we were lost, had suddenly burst into a mad fury at our refusal to surrender to the Yankee battleship two days before; and were in a delirium of cursing and destruction. They roared like the animals they were, and broke instruments and furniture indiscriminately; screaming about such nonsense as the curse of the ivory image and the dark dead youth who looked at them and swam away. Lieut. Klenze seemed paralysed and inefficient, as one might expect of a soft, womanish Rhinelander. I shot all six men, for it was necessary, and made sure that none remained alive.

We expelled the bodies through the double hatches and were alone in the U-29. Klenze seemed very nervous, and drank heavily. It was decided that we remain alive as long as possible, using the large stock of provisions and chemical supply of oxygen, none of which had suffered from the crazy antics of those swine-hound seamen. Our compasses, depth gauges, and other delicate instruments were ruined; so that henceforth our only reckoning would be guesswork, based on our watches, the calendar, and our apparent drift as judged by any objects we might spy through the portholes or from the conning tower. Fortunately we had storage batteries still capable of long use, both for interior lighting and for the searchlight. We often cast a beam around the ship, but saw only dolphins, swimming parallel to our own drifting course. I was scientifically interested in those dolphins; for though the ordinary *Delphinus delphis* is a cetacean mammal, unable to subsist without air, I watched one of the swimmers closely for two hours, and did not see him alter his submerged condition.

With the passage of time Klenze and I decided that we were still drifting south, meanwhile sinking deeper and deeper. We noted the marine fauna and flora, and read much on the subject in the books I had carried with me for spare moments. I could not help observing, however, the inferior scientific knowledge of my companion. His mind was not Prussian, but given to imaginings and speculations which have no value. The fact of our coming death affected him curiously, and he would frequently pray in remorse over the men, women, and children we had sent to the bottom; forgetting that all things are noble which serve the German state. After a time he became noticeably unbalanced, gazing for hours at his ivory image and weaving fanciful stories of the lost and forgotten things under the sea. Sometimes, as a psychological experiment, I would lead him on in these wanderings, and listen to his endless poetical quotations and tales of sunken ships. I was very sorry for him, for I dislike to see a German suffer; but he was not a good man to die with. For myself I was proud, knowing how the Fatherland would revere my memory and how my sons would be taught to be men like me.

On August 9, we espied the ocean floor, and sent a powerful beam from the searchlight over it. It was a vast undulating plain, mostly covered with seaweed, and strown with the shells of small molluscs. Here and there were slimy objects of puzzling contour, draped with weeds and encrusted with barnacles, which Klenze declared must be ancient ships lying in their graves. He was puzzled by one thing, a peak of solid matter, protruding above the ocean bed nearly four feet at its apex; about two feet thick, with flat sides and smooth upper surfaces which met at a very obtuse angle. I called the peak a bit of outcropping rock, but Klenze thought he saw carvings on it. After a while he began to shudder, and turned away from the scene as if frightened; yet could give no explanation save that he was overcome with the vastness, darkness, remoteness, antiquity, and mystery of the oceanic abysses. His mind was tired, but I am always a German, and was quick to notice two things; that the U-29 was standing the deep-sea pressure splendidly, and that the peculiar dolphins were still about us, even at a depth where the existence of high organisms is considered impossible by most naturalists. That I had previously overestimated our depth, I was sure; but none the less we must still be deep enough to make these phenomena remarkable. Our southward speed, as gauged by the ocean floor, was about as I had estimated from the organisms passed at higher levels.

It was at 3:15 p.m., August 12, that poor Klenze went wholly mad. He had been in the conning tower using the searchlight when I saw him bound into the library compartment where I sat reading, and his face at once betrayed him. I will repeat here what he said, underlining the words he emphasised: "_He_ is calling! _He_ is calling! I hear him! We must go!" As he spoke he took his ivory image from the table, pocketed it, and seized my arm in an effort to drag me up the companionway to the deck. In a moment I understood that he meant to open the hatch and plunge with me into the water outside, a vagary of suicidal and homicidal mania for which I was scarcely prepared. As I hung back and attempted to soothe him he grew more violent, saying: "Come now—do not wait until later; it is better to repent and be forgiven than to defy and be condemned." Then I tried the opposite of the soothing plan, and told him he was mad—pitifully demented. But he was unmoved, and cried: "If I am mad, it is mercy! May the gods pity the man who in his callousness can remain sane to the hideous end! Come and be mad whilst _he_ still calls with mercy!"

This outburst seemed to relieve a pressure in his brain; for as he finished he grew much milder, asking me to let him depart alone if I would not accompany him. My course at once became clear. He was a German, but only a Rhinelander and a commoner; and he was now a potentially dangerous madman. By complying with his suicidal request I could immediately free myself from one who was no longer a companion but a menace. I asked him to give me the ivory image before he went, but this request brought from him such uncanny laughter that I did not repeat it. Then I asked him if he wished to leave any keepsake or lock of hair for his family in Germany in case I should be rescued, but again he gave me that strange laugh. So as he climbed the ladder I went to the levers, and allowing proper time-intervals operated the machinery which sent him to his death. After I saw that he was no longer in the boat I threw the searchlight around the water in an effort to obtain a last glimpse of him; since I wished to ascertain whether the water-pressure would flatten him as it theoretically should, or whether the body would be unaffected, like those extraordinary dolphins. I did not, however, succeed in finding my late companion, for the dolphins were massed thickly and obscuringly about the conning tower.

That evening I regretted that I had not taken the ivory image surreptitiously from poor Klenze's pocket as he left, for the memory of it fascinated me. I could not forget the youthful, beautiful head with its leafy crown, though I am not by nature an artist. I was also sorry that I had no one with whom to converse. Klenze, though not my mental equal, was much better than no one. I did not sleep well that night, and wondered exactly when the end would come. Surely, I had little enough chance of rescue.

The next day I ascended to the conning tower and commenced the customary searchlight explorations. Northward the view was much the same as it had been all the four days since we had sighted the bottom, but I perceived that the drifting of the U-29 was less rapid. As I swung the beam around to the south, I noticed that the ocean floor ahead fell away in a marked declivity, and bore curiously regular blocks of stone in certain places, disposed as if in accordance with definite patterns. The boat did not at once descend to match the greater ocean depth, so I was soon forced to adjust the searchlight to cast a sharply downward beam. Owing to the abruptness of the change a wire was disconnected, which necessitated a delay of many minutes for repairs; but at length the light streamed on again, flooding the marine valley below me.

I am not given to emotion of any kind, but my amazement was very great when I saw what lay revealed in that electrical glow. And yet as one reared in the best *Kultur* of Prussia I should not have been amazed, for geology and tradition alike tell us of great transpositions in oceanic and continental areas. What I saw was an extended and elaborate array of ruined edifices; all of magnificent though unclassified architecture, and in various stages of preservation. Most appeared to be of marble, gleaming whitely in the rays of the searchlight, and the general plan was of a large city at the bottom of a narrow valley, with numerous isolated temples and villas on the steep slopes above. Roofs were fallen and columns were broken, but there still remained an air of immemorially ancient splendour which nothing could efface.

Confronted at last with the Atlantis I had formerly deemed largely a myth, I was the most eager of explorers. At the bottom of that valley a river once had flowed; for as I examined the scene more closely I beheld the remains of stone and marble bridges and sea-walls, and terraces and embankments once verdant and beautiful. In my enthusiasm I became nearly as idiotic and sentimental as poor Klenze, and was very tardy in noticing that the southward current had ceased at last, allowing the U-29 to settle slowly down upon the sunken city as an aëroplane settles upon a town of the upper earth. I was slow, too, in realising that the school of unusual dolphins had vanished.

In about two hours the boat rested in a paved plaza close to the rocky wall of the valley. On one side I could view the entire city as it sloped from the plaza down to the old river-bank; on the other side, in startling proximity, I was confronted by the richly ornate and perfectly preserved facade of a great building, evidently a temple, hollowed from the solid rock. Of the original workmanship of this titanic thing I can only make conjectures. The facade, of immense magnitude, apparently covers a continuous hollow recess; for its windows are many and widely distributed. In the centre yawns a great open door, reached by an impressive flight of steps, and surrounded by exquisite carvings like the figures of Bacchanals in relief. Foremost of all are the great columns and frieze, both decorated with sculptures of inexpressible beauty; obviously portraying idealised pastoral scenes and processions of priests and priestesses bearing strange ceremonial devices in adoration of a radiant god. The art is of the most phenomenal perfection, largely Hellenic in idea, yet strangely individual. It imparts an impression of terrible antiquity, as though it were the remotest rather than the immediate ancestor of Greek art. Nor can I doubt that every detail of this massive product was fashioned from the virgin hillside rock of our planet. It is palpably a part of the valley wall, though how the vast interior was ever excavated I cannot imagine. Perhaps a cavern or series of caverns furnished the nucleus. Neither age nor submersion has corroded the pristine grandeur of this awful fane—for fane indeed it must be—and today after thousands of years it rests untarnished and inviolate in the endless night and silence of an ocean chasm.

I cannot reckon the number of hours I spent in gazing at the sunken city with its buildings, arches, statues, and bridges, and the colossal temple with its beauty and mystery. Though I knew that death was near, my curiosity was consuming; and I threw the searchlight's beam about in eager quest. The shaft of light permitted me to learn many details, but refused to shew anything within the gaping door of the rock-hewn temple; and after a time I turned off the current, conscious of the need of conserving power. The rays were now perceptibly dimmer than they had been during the weeks of drifting. And as if sharpened by the coming deprivation of light, my desire to explore the watery secrets grew. I, a German, should be the first to tread those aeon-forgotten ways!

I produced and examined a deep-sea diving suit of joined metal, and experimented with the portable light and air regenerator. Though I should have trouble in managing the double hatches alone, I believed I could overcome all obstacles with my scientific skill and actually walk about the dead city in person.

On August 16 I effected an exit from the U-29, and laboriously made my way through the ruined and mud-choked streets to the ancient river. I found no skeletons or other human remains, but gleaned a wealth of archaeological lore from sculptures and coins. Of this I cannot now speak save to utter my awe at a culture in the full noon of glory when cave-dwellers roamed Europe and the Nile flowed unwatched to the sea. Others, guided by this manuscript if it shall ever be found, must unfold the mysteries at which I can only hint. I returned to the boat as my electric batteries grew feeble, resolved to explore the rock temple on the following day.

On the 17th, as my impulse to search out the mystery of the temple waxed still more insistent, a great disappointment befell me; for I found that the materials needed to replenish the portable light had perished in the mutiny of those pigs in July. My rage was unbounded, yet my German sense forbade me to venture unprepared into an utterly black interior which might prove the lair of some indescribable marine monster or a labyrinth of passages from whose windings I could never extricate myself. All I could do was to turn on the waning searchlight of the U-29, and with its aid walk up the temple steps and study the exterior carvings. The shaft of light entered the door at an upward angle, and I peered in to see if I could glimpse anything, but all in vain. Not even the roof was visible; and though I took a step or two inside after testing the floor with a staff, I dared not go farther. Moreover, for the first time in my life I experienced the emotion of dread. I began to realise how some of poor Klenze's moods had arisen, for as the temple drew me more and more, I feared its aqueous abysses with a blind and mounting terror. Returning to the submarine, I turned off the lights and sat thinking in the dark. Electricity must now be saved for emergencies.

Saturday the 18th I spent in total darkness, tormented by thoughts and memories that threatened to overcome my German will. Klenze had gone mad and perished before reaching this sinister remnant of a past unwholesomely remote, and had advised me to go with him. Was, indeed, Fate preserving my reason only to draw me irresistibly to an end more horrible and unthinkable than any man has dreamed of? Clearly, my nerves were sorely taxed, and I must cast off these impressions of weaker men.

I could not sleep Saturday night, and turned on the lights regardless of the future. It was annoying that the electricity should not last out the air and provisions. I revived my thoughts of euthanasia, and examined my automatic pistol. Toward morning I must have dropped asleep with the lights on, for I awoke in darkness yesterday afternoon to find the batteries dead. I struck several matches in succession, and desperately regretted the improvidence which had caused us long ago to use up the few candles we carried.

After the fading of the last match I dared to waste, I sat very quietly without a light. As I considered the inevitable end my mind ran over preceding events, and developed a hitherto dormant impression which would have caused a weaker and more superstitious man to shudder. *The head of the radiant god in the sculptures on the rock temple is the same as that carven bit of ivory which the dead sailor brought from the sea and which poor Klenze carried back into the sea.*

I was a little dazed by this coincidence, but did not become terrified. It is only the inferior thinker who hastens to explain the singular and the complex by the primitive short cut of supernaturalism. The coincidence was strange, but I was too sound a reasoner to connect circumstances which admit of no logical connexion, or to associate in any uncanny fashion the disastrous events which had led from the *Victory* affair to my present plight. Feeling the need of more rest, I took a sedative and secured some more sleep. My nervous condition was reflected in my dreams, for I seemed to hear the cries of drowning persons, and to see dead faces pressing against the portholes of the boat. And among the dead faces was the living, mocking face of the youth with the ivory image.

I must be careful how I record my awaking today, for I am unstrung, and much hallucination is necessarily mixed with fact. Psychologically my case is most interesting, and I regret that it cannot be observed scientifically by a competent German authority. Upon opening my eyes my first sensation was an overmastering desire to visit the rock temple; a desire which grew every instant, yet which I automatically sought to resist through some emotion of fear which operated in the reverse direction. Next there came to me the impression of *light* amidst the darkness of dead batteries, and I seemed to see a sort of phosphorescent glow in the water through the porthole which opened toward the temple. This aroused my curiosity, for I knew of no deep-sea organism capable of emitting such luminosity. But before I could investigate there came a third impression which because of its irrationality caused me to doubt the objectivity of anything my senses might record. It was an aural delusion; a sensation of rhythmic, melodic sound as of some wild yet beautiful chant or choral hymn, coming from the outside through the absolutely sound-proof hull of the U-29. Convinced of my psychological and nervous abnormality, I lighted some matches and poured a stiff dose of sodium bromide solution, which seemed to calm me to the extent of dispelling the illusion of sound. But the phosphorescence remained, and I had difficulty in repressing a childish impulse to go to the porthole and seek its source. It was horribly realistic, and I could soon distinguish by its aid the familiar objects around me, as well as the empty sodium bromide glass of which I had had no former visual impression in its present location. This last circumstance made me ponder, and I crossed the room and touched the glass. It was indeed in the place where I had seemed to see it. Now I knew that the light was either real or part of an hallucination so fixed and consistent that I could not hope to dispel it, so abandoning all resistance I ascended to the conning tower to look for the luminous agency. Might it not actually be another U-boat, offering possibilities of rescue?

It is well that the reader accept nothing which follows as objective truth, for since the events transcend natural law, they are necessarily the subjective and unreal creations of my overtaxed mind. When I attained the conning tower I found the sea in general far less luminous than I had expected. There was no animal or vegetable phosphorescence about, and the city that sloped down to the river was invisible in blackness. What I did see was not spectacular, not grotesque or terrifying, yet it removed my last vestige of trust in my consciousness. *For the door and windows of the undersea temple hewn from the rocky hill were vividly aglow with a flickering radiance, as from a mighty altar-flame far within.*

Later incidents are chaotic. As I stared at the uncannily lighted door and windows, I became subject to the most extravagant visions—visions so extravagant that I cannot even relate them. I fancied that I discerned objects in the temple—objects both stationary and moving—and seemed to hear again the unreal chant that had floated to me when first I awaked. And over all rose thoughts and fears which centred in the youth from the sea and the ivory image whose carving was duplicated on the frieze and columns of the temple before me. I thought of poor Klenze, and wondered where his body rested with the image he had carried back into the sea. He had warned me of something, and I had not heeded—but he was a soft-headed Rhinelander who went mad at troubles a Prussian could bear with ease.

The rest is very simple. My impulse to visit and enter the temple has now become an inexplicable and imperious command which ultimately cannot be denied. My own German will no longer controls my acts, and volition is henceforward possible only in minor matters. Such madness it was which drove Klenze to his death, bareheaded and unprotected in the ocean; but I am a Prussian and man of sense, and will use to the last what little will I have. When first I saw that I must go, I prepared my diving suit, helmet, and air regenerator for instant donning; and immediately commenced to write this hurried chronicle in the hope that it may some day reach the world. I shall seal the manuscript in a bottle and entrust it to the sea as I leave the U-29 forever.

I have no fear, not even from the prophecies of the madman Klenze. What I have seen cannot be true, and I know that this madness of my own will at most lead only to suffocation when my air is gone. The light in the temple is a sheer delusion, and I shall die calmly, like a German, in the black and forgotten depths. This daemoniac laughter which I hear as I write comes only from my own weakening brain. So I will carefully don my diving suit and walk boldly up the steps into that primal shrine; that silent secret of unfathomed waters and uncounted years.

Bells of Oceana

Arthur J. Burks

I T WAS ON a heavily laden troopship, westward heading. Hours before, the sun had gone down toward China, trailing ebon night behind her. For a full week, since dropping the California coast behind us, there had been nothing in all the wild waste of waters for us to see save ourselves. No ship's funnels broke the lowering horizon, no sign of land, for our skipper had chosen a passage lying somewhere in between the usual steamer lanes. The nearest land, save that which stretched in eternal darkness some three miles below us, was more than a thousand miles beyond the southern horizon. We were just a single ship, burdened with a precious freight of souls, upon an ocean that seemed endless. The first day out had been squally, and everyone had been sick, save those of us who had gone down to the sea in ships before. But with the dawning of the second morning the sea had calmed down, and our vessel rode through the blue, toward the horizon bowl which ever crept before us, in the golden wake of the setting sun. The voyage, if the old salts spoke truly, would be uneventful; but, with that strange premonitory feeling which comes to all of us at times, I did not believe them.

Something, from the very first, warned me that our voyage was ill-fated. I couldn't explain my feeling. It wasn't a feeling of dread, exactly, nor of fear. Just a strange feeling of unease, much like that which comes to people on their first voyage, when a ship is rolling slightly under their feet, and everything, until they get their sealegs, seems strangely out of focus. That doesn't explain it, I know; but it is as near as I can put my feeling into words.

I knew, when the sun went down ahead of us, with the hundred and eightieth meridian less than twenty-four hours ahead, that we were on the eve of strange, momentous happenings. To add to my feeling of unease, and as though it had been all planned out by some invisible *something* or *somebody,* in the vague beginning, the officer who should have had the watch that night fell suddenly ill, and I was called upon to take his place. I knew, as I donned my belt, holster, and pistol, that I obeyed the will of some invisibile prompter—a prompter without a name.

We had seven sentries out at various important places about the ship, and I made the routine inspections before turning in, less than an hour before midnight. When I entered my stateroom and turned on the light, that feeling of unease was more pronounced than it had been at any time previously. I had the feeling, though I had locked my door when I had last quitted my stateroom, that I had entered again immediately *after* someone had left it. Yet that was impossible. I had carried the key in my pocket all the time, and my cabin-boy was not provided with one. There was no way that anyone, or anything, could have entered my stateroom in my absence, save—

Still as though my every move had been ordered by some invisible prompter, my eyes darted to the port-hole beside my bed. It was quite too small for the passage of a human body. If anyone had gone out through the port-hole, that one had fallen, or plunged into the sea, for had the port-hole been ever so big, there was absolutely no way one could have left my stateroom by that way and still remained upon the ship—unless that one had gone out and were even now hanging by his hands along the ship's side. So strongly had the feeling of an alien presence intruded itself upon me that, in spite of knowing myself an utter fool for entertaining any doubt whatsoever, I strode to the port-hole and looked out. There was nothing, of course, save water, now black and forbidding, stretching away to the south, to a horizon that, since night had fallen, seemed to have crept quite close to us to watch our passing.

Still unsatisfied, in spite of arguing with myself, condemning myself for a fool, I deliberately closed the glass which masked the port, took my seat in a chair beside the bunk, facing the round glass—which resembled, to an imagination suddenly fevered, the eye of a huge one-eyed giant—of the port-hole, and began to undress. Mechanically I lifted first one foot and then the other, removing shoes and stockings.

But I kept my eyes upon the closed port-hole—and that feeling of an unseen presence in the room was stronger as the moments fled. My undressing completed, I stood erect to turn out the lights, and paused in the very act, a cry of terror smothered in my throat by a sheer act of will.

For, for the most fleeting of seconds, I had seen a dead-white face outside the glass which covered the port-hole! It was the face of a person who had drowned, I told myself wildly, and the dripping hair wore a coronet of fluttering seaweed. The eyes of this strange outsider stared straight into mine, devoid of expression, totally unwinking, and the lips, which seemed blue as though with icy cold long endured, smiled a thin and ironic smile. It took all the courage I possessed, which is little enough in the face of the unknown, to hurl myself across the bed, right hand extended toward the heavy screw which held the circular piece of glass in place. In the instant my hand would have touched the glass, the ship rode into the edge of the storm that was to fill the remainder of the night, and the stern of the steamer rose dizzily on the crest of a mighty wave, dragging all the vessel with it—and the face slid slowly out of sight below the port-hole, the bluish lips still smiling!

I admit that I was trembling, that my fingers were unsteady as I fumbled with the screw to unloose the glass. When the port-hole was open once more, and the cold breeze of this latitude came in to fan my fevered face, I thrust my head out of the port and gazed right and left, and up and down, along the curving side of the ship. But there was nothing—save straight ahead, on our port side. And even there there was nothing but black water, huge mountainous waves touched with whitecaps at their crests, like flying shrouds, or like lacy streamers created as a fringe for the mantle of night.

I watched several of the waves sweep under the vessel, which rose and fell sluggishly. The waves seemed to be traveling in no certain direction, but broke into a veritable welter of warring forces, roaring as they came together with the bellowing of maddened, deep-throated bulls. Valleys with darkness on their floors, mountain-tops touched with snow that shifted eerily in the breeze.

I was about to close the port when, many yards away from the ship, as though born of the womb of old ocean, I heard the bells!

Like the tiny bells which the bell-wether wears to signal the ewes and the lambs, was the tinkling of the bells—like those bells, yet not like them, totally out of place in mid-ocean, and I felt a strange prickling of the scalp as I listened. Hurriedly, driven by a fear I could not have explained then, nor can I now explain, I closed the port-hole again. And whirled about with another scream, which this time came forth from my quivering lips in spite of all I could do to prevent.

Just inside my stateroom door stood my sergeant of the guard, and his lips were trembling more wildly than my own, his eyes protruded horribly, his face was chalk-white, and he was striving with all his power to speak! As I watched his manful struggle, I dreaded for him to speak—for I knew that what he had come to tell me would be something strange and terrible, something hitherto entirely outside my experience.

"Sir," he managed at last, when I stiffly nodded permission for him to speak, "I just made the rounds of the sentries!"

Here the poor fellow stopped, unable to go on, and his knees knocked together audibly.

"Yes, sergeant," I managed to mutter, "you went the usual rounds of the sentries, and then?"

"The sentry who should be on duty on the main deck, forward of the bridge, is missing!"

Of course I knew on the instant that there might be many reasons for the failure of the sergeant of the guard to find the sentry, many logical reasons. The sentry might have quitted his post (a violation of regulations, true) for a quiet cigarette in the lee of a lifeboat; he might have been walking his post in the direction taken by the sergeant, so that the latter had not overtaken him, even with a complete circling of the main deck; he might—oh, there were many logical explanations; but I guessed instinctively that none of these reasons fitted the case. For one thing, the sergeant of the guard was an old-timer, had spent many years of his life at sea—yet he was frightened half out of his wits, and I knew he held as many decorations for bravery as any other officer or man in the Marine Corps. There was something terrible, something—if you will—uncanny behind this disappearance of the sentry.

I muttered an oath, more to prod my own flagging courage than for any other reason, and started toward the door, motioning the sergeant to precede me. But he shook his head stubbornly and barred my way. I halted, for it was evident that he had not completed his report.

"You'll maybe think me daft," he said; "but I couldn't let you go out there, sir, without telling you everything. The corporal on watch at the head of the promenade gangway told me a strange story just before I made my rounds. He opened the door leading onto the starboard promenade, for a look at the weather outside, and just as he was about to close it again, the ship lifted on the crest of a huge wave—and out beyond the wave, many yards away from the ship, he heard something which he likened to the tinkling of little bells!"

"Good God!" I exclaimed.

"And," the sergeant continued, "all the time I was looking for the missing sentry, I had the idea there was someone behind me, following me every step of the way; yet when I whirled to look, the deck behind me was empty!"

"And you found no sign of the sentry?" I said stupidly.

The sergeant shook his head.

"Nothing," he said, "except—except—well, sir, you'll maybe think me daft, as I said before; but on the spot where the sentry had stood to wait for me on my last round, I found wet marks on the deck floor—the marks, as near as I could tell with my flashlight, of bare feet!"

Mechanically, as the sergeant spoke, I had been donning my clothes, leaving my shoes, however, unlaced. I felt an icy chill along my spine as the sergeant continued, and I dreaded, as I had never dreaded anything before, to ask him further about those wet footprints on the deck.

"The wet footprints," he went on, and he was talking wildly now, his words tripping over one another, so rapidly were they uttered, as though he wished to finish his report before I could interrupt again, "led away where the sentry should have been standing, straight to the starboard rail! Right at the rail I stooped to examine the prints more closely. They were the footprints of a human being, I was sure, and the marks of the toes were blurred, and very wide, as though whoever—or whatever—had made them had been carrying a burden in his arms!"

"Good God, sergeant!" I said again; "what are you driving at?"

"Just this, sir. There's something terribly wrong with this ship! *Something took that sentry bodily over the side!*"

I believe that putting a name, however meaningless, to what was in my own mind, caused a little of my courage to return, for I did not find it difficult now to bring myself to leave the stateroom. The sergeant almost trod on my heels as I hurried to the main deck, starboard side, where the wind wrapped icy fingers around me, chilling me to the bone.

As I hurried forward I looked over the side, into the welter of water—and stopped short!

Behind me the sergeant groaned—hollowly, like a man who has been mortally wounded. For out of the waters, away to starboard, came the sound of tinkling bells! I darted to the rail and leaned far outboard, striving to pierce the gloom. But there was nothing save the watery wastes, mountains and valleys—and two spots of greenish phosphorescence, far out, like serpent's eyes which watched the passing ship. But when I looked at them closely, straining my eyes, seeking the form below the eyes, the twin balls of eery flame vanished, a wall of water intruding itself between!

Well, we found the sentry, sprawled on his face, where the sergeant should have found him on his rounds. I turned the body over, and it was quite cold—with excellent reason! The corpse was dripping wet, entirely nude, and the lips and cheeks as coldly blue as though the corpse had been dragged for hours on a line in the wake of the ship!

No matter how secluded one's life may have been, no matter how carefully one may have been guarded during one's lifetime, there come into the lives of most of us certain inexplicable happenings which may never be forgotten. This matter of the dead sentry was one of these for me, and I shall go to my grave with the memory of his cold cheeks and bluish lips limned upon the retina of my very soul. So many strange circumstances—thank God that, at the moment, I could not look into the two hours or more of terror which even then stretched before me, else I should most surely have gone entirely mad!—were there connected with this matter that, taken altogether, it is little wonder that I have been unable to forget. The roaring of the wind which was lashing all the ocean into fury, a maelstrom in mid-ocean, ghostly whitecaps stretching away into darkness, into seeming infinity; the frightened sergeant behind me, his teeth chattering with fear; the dead sentry at my feet, his body blue with cold, entirely nude as I have said; the marks on the deck of huge bare feet, wet as though the feet had come up out of the sea; the eery sound of bells between our vessel and the lowering horizon—and that dead-white face which I had seen beyond the port-hole of my own cabin a half-hour before.

What was the explanation of it all? What was the cause of the bells, if bells there were? What had come up out of the sea to stride barefooted across the promenade deck of the slumbering troopship? Had my sentry seen whatever had come for him before he had been taken?

Add to all these circumstances the fact that all hell was loose in the watery wastes, that it was now after midnight, and you will understand a little of my feelings. Never before or since have I been as frightened as I was then. I don't regard myself as a coward, nor am I ordinarily superstitious; but show me the man who is without fear in the presence of the unknown, the utterly uncanny, and I will show you a man who has no soul.

I whirled, bumping into the sergeant, who manfully muffled a scream at my unexpected movement, and started, almost blindly, toward the stern of the troopship. As I strode along, with the sergeant at my heels once more, strange images fled across my mind. I remembered the tale of *Die Lorelei*, the maiden who lured sailors to their death with her eery singing, and strained my eyes through the gloom, seeking shapes I feared to see. Then my mind went farther back, to the years before I could read, years in which, thirsty for knowledge, I studied pictures out of old histories to satisfy my longing for wisdom. One of these pictures came back to my mind as I hurried aft: a picture of a hideous monster of unbelievable proportions, who had come up from behind the ocean's horizon, blotting out the sunlight, long arms extended into the picture's foreground, the right hand holding aloft a medieval sailing vessel which had been lifted bodily from the ocean. A fantastic picture, I knew now, drawn to prove the existence of terrible monsters beyond the horizon to which, as yet, no caravel or galleon had dared travel. I wondered, as I strode aft, why this old picture should return to my mind at this time, and fear was at my throat again as I walked.

"I am coming, oh, my beloved!"

The words, high-pitched with ecstasy, came from straight ahead of me, and out of the heavy shadow cast by a huge funnel stepped one of my sentries. Just for a second, as he strode toward the starboard rail, I could see his face—and the face was transfigured, as though the man gazed into the very soul of the Perfect Sweetheart somewhere beyond the rail. Slowly, step by step, as though he would prolong the joy of anticipation, the sentry, who had hurled his rifle aside, approached the rail, still with his eyes fixed on the welter of waters overside, while I halted spellbound to watch what he would do. From out of the waters there came once more the tinkling of bells! And with the sound, as though the sound had been a signal, a huge shadow detached itself from the shadow whence the sentry had stepped but a moment ago, and loomed high above the luckless youth. At the same time the ship climbed high upon a monster wave, so that her starboard side went down, down, until white water came over the side—and when she straightened again, shuddering through all of her, the sentry had vanished! From well rearward of where the man had disappeared, from out of the smother of waters, there came a single long-drawn cry—and it was not a cry of terror, not a cry of pain, but a scream of ecstasy!

"He's gone, sergeant," I said stupidly, "but what took him? Not the wave: he had only to seize the rail to save himself."

"Did you see the shadow, Lieutenant?" the sergeant replied.

I did not answer. *He knew* I had seen it.

We strode on again, heading toward the stern—and all about us now, over the ship, on either side of her—but never on her—there tinkled the eery, unexplainable bells!

We stood at last in the very stern of the troopship, gazing into the ghostly wake far below our coign of vantage, and with certain care, I followed the wake rearward with my eyes. But one could not follow it far! That was the circumstance which impressed itself upon me almost at once. The wake died away, short off, within less than a dozen yards of the ship's stern—as though at the very moment of birth, it had been ignominiously smothered!

In a trice I understood the reason, and thought I understood many things besides. For, like a monster raft, stretching away rearward as far as I could see, and into the darkness beyond my vision to right and left, there followed us, close to, an undulating mass of odorless seaweed! Acres and acres of it there were, rising and falling sluggishly, but keeping pace with the troopship through the night and the storm! Came again that sound of bells, and my hair stiffened at the base of my skull when I saw, watching the seaweed, the result of the tinkling of the bells. The seaweed, when the bells sounded, seemed imbued suddenly with life that was utterly and completely rampant. Long tendrils of the stuff drew away to right and left below us, as though endowed with will of their own, and these tendrils, countless thousands of them, collided with other tendrils in the mass, and slithered over them so that all the mass of the seaweed writhed as though in torment, resembling countless hordes of serpents gathered together from all the evil places of the earth—and where the tendrils had drawn aside I could see black water in the rift as though the tendrils had drawn aside so that I *might* see. Some terrible fascination held me, my eyes fixed on that space of black water, for several moments after the tendrils of seaweed had drawn away to right and left—and up from the depths, into the opening, came two who filled all my being with abject terror—and something else.

One of the two was dead, I knew on the instant, for I could see his face, all white and drawn, yet with the blue lips smiling, of the ill-fated sentry who had gone over the side before my very eyes! And he had been brought up from the depths in the arms of—I hesitate to give the creature a name. A woman? I scarcely know; yet this I do know: in the instant I looked into her eyes, I understood the ecstacy I had read in the face of the sentry whom she now held in her arms. Her breasts, nude and unashamed, were the breasts of a buxom woman, her lips as red as full-blown roses, her hair as black as the wings of a crow, a mantle of loveliness all about her wondrous body, whipping this way and that in the storm.

Her eyes swerved away from mine, and one arm, shapely and snowy, raised aloft from the water—and to my ears came again the sound of tinkling bells! Once more the seaweed writhed and twisted, pressed forward about the ship; but a single mass of it detached itself from the larger mass, pressed close to the—should I call her "woman"—and swerved away again; and the arms of the beautiful creature were empty. Instinctively I whirled about, knowing somehow that I must move my head before I met this creature's eyes again, and stared forward to the shadowy portion of the promenade whence the sentry had emerged before his plunge over the side. Up the starboard side of the ship crept a veritable wall of seaweed; up to the rail, pausing there for a moment, then to the deck, where it squirmed for a moment or two, taking a weird distorted shape that made me think of a man. From out of the heart of this monstrosity there dropped soggily a white, cold figure! The second sentry had returned, as the first had done!

I knew, as I searched through all my experience, seeking the key to this uncanny enigma, that we were heading westward outside the usually traveled sea-lanes; that ships seldom, if ever, came this way; that in seven days we had seen not one vessel, nor even the smoke of one upon the horizon. Why did not vessels come this way?

But I could not answer my many questions. I could only ask them, and hope within me that they be not answered, ever. Nauseated by the return of the dead sentry, nude as the first had been, I closed my eyes for a moment, and when I opened them again, there was no seaweed, no monstrous shape, upon the promenade; but even from where I stood I could see the wet footprints—and wondered whom next the creature of the deep would claim from aboard our ill-fated vessel.

I drew my pistol and returned once more toward the stern of the vessel. This creature of the depths, whatever it was, had taken life—twice. Whatever it was, it was mortal, and whatever is mortal a bullet will slay. But, in the very act of whirling, I stopped short—for between me and the stern of the vessel, smiling dreamily, water rippling over her nude and glorious body to splash upon the deck, stood the creature who had come up from the depths in the wake of the ship, bearing the dead man in her arms! My arm fell to my side, my weapon clattered to the deck, and as I moved forward once more, slowly, a step at a time as the sentry had done, the wondrous creature held out her dripping arms, and my eyes drank in all the glorious wonder of her—from head to—*but she had no feet!*

Where the feet should have been, and the legs, there were neither legs nor feet; but a scaly column, wet and dripping, like a serpent with a woman's body; I screamed in terror and unbelief; but it was too late, and her arms were about me, preventing all escape! But, with the touch of those arms, I did not wish to struggle. I knew what had happened to the two sentries; knew the same was the prospect for me; yet at the moment there seemed nothing in all the world more worth-while than to slip over the side, into the depths, with the arms of this wondrous creature about me.

"Lieutenant! Lieutenant! For the love of God what is happening to you?"

It was the voice of the sergeant of the guard, freighted with abysmal terror; but I did not care. The shapely, strangely warm arms of the sea-creature were about me, and the sound of the bells, unbelievably sweet now, was in my ears. For me the world had ceased to exist, save for knowledge that these two things were true. I was carried to the rail, and went over slowly, without commotion, as comfortably as though I had been riding on a couch of eiderdown—and came to myself to know myself lost indeed!

I was deep down, whirling over and over behind the whirling screws of the ship, holding my breath until my lungs were nigh to bursting, swimming with all my might, striving to reach the surface, and life-giving air, when I hadn't the slightest idea which way was upward. With all my power I fought toward the surface; but my progress was slow and dragging, for there was a weight about my knees, as though arms were clasped about them, striving to hold me down. A wordless voice was in my ears—begging, beseeching, and there was something in the voice which made my struggles seem foolish and unnecessary, so that I desired never to reach the air I needed. I closed my eyes, which I had opened instinctively upon striking the water, and two lips pressed firmly against my own—and those lips saved my life, and my reason; for they were the cold lips of a corpse, with neither love nor challenge in them. I flailed out once more, and my hand caught in the line which the steamer dragged over her stern to measure the knots she traveled. All about me as I was hurled forward, now under water, now with nostrils out for a brief breathing space, the mass of seaweed rose and fell on the heavy seas.

God knows how I ever got back aboard the troopship; but I awoke at mess-call in the morning, and sent immediately for the sergeant of the guard.

"What happened after I came back aboard last night, sergeant?" I asked abruptly.

The sergeant of the guard stared at me as though he thought me insane.

"I don't understand you," he managed finally.

"Have we finally passed through the area of seaweed?"

"Seaweed? Is the lieutenant making sport of me? We're two thousand miles from any land, save the ocean bottom, and there ain't any seaweed anywhere! I don't understand you!"

"Let it pass," I said. "When did you last visit the sentries last night?"

"Just before midnight, sir."

"And were all of them at their post of duty?"

"Yes sir."

"And what about the bells?"

Again the sergeant's puzzlement was so genuine that I knew he did not understand my meaning. How much of my experience had been real, how much fantasy? I tried another tack.

"Did you make a round of the sentries after midnight?"

The sergeant shook his head sheepishly—it is one of the rules of guard duty that one visit to all sentries must take place between midnight and morning.

"Then the guard hasn't been mustered this morning? Is everyone present? You don't know? Then go at once and find out!"

Ten minutes later the sergeant returned, chalk-white of face, to report that two of the guards were missing, and could not be found anywhere aboard. He told me their names—and instantly my mind went back to the night of uncanny happenings just past, and the two nude bodies brought back from the deep in the arms of—whom? Or what?

I never knew, and to this day the questions I have propounded have never been answered.

But this I know: there are strange things, and sounds, in the sea near the hundred and eightieth meridian, a thousand miles north of Honolulu —and this is the strangest incident in my night of terror: the clothing which I donned next morning was entirely dry; but my hair was stiff with salt water, and there was the tang of seaweed in my room when I awoke!

I looked, too, at the glass which covered the port-hole beside my bed—

Outside that glass were the smudged prints of thin lips, the blur above them which told of a face pressed against the glass from outside—as though somebody, or *something*, had tried to peer in, between nightfall and morning!

And the bells? I still can hear them, in memory, when sometimes I waken at sea after midnight, and the rolling and the plunging of the ship tell me that a storm is making.

Second Night Out

Frank Belknap Long

T WAS PAST MIDNIGHT when I left my stateroom. The upper promenade deck was entirely deserted and thin wisps of fog hovered
about the deck chairs and curled and uncurled about the gleaming
rails. There was no air stirring. The ship moved forward sluggishly
through a quiet, fog-enshrouded sea.

But I did not object to the fog. I leaned against the rail and inhaled the
damp, murky air with a positive greediness. The almost unendurable nausea, the pervasive physical and mental misery had departed, leaving me
serene and at peace. I was again capable of experiencing sensuous delight,
and the aroma of the brine was not to be exchanged for pearls and rubies.
I had paid in exorbitant coinage for what I was about to enjoy—for the
five brief days of freedom and exploration in glamorous, sea-splendid
Havana which I had been promised by an enterprising and, I hoped,
reasonably honest tourist agent. I am in all respects the antithesis of a
wealthy man, and I had drawn so heavily upon my bank balance to satisfy
the greedy demands of The Loriland Tours, Inc., that I had been compelled to renounce such really indispensable amenities as after-dinner cigars and ocean-privileged sherry and chartreuse.

But I was enormously content. I paced the deck and inhaled the moist,
pungent air. For thirty hours I had been confined to my cabin with a sea-
illness more debilitating than bubonic plague or malignant sepsis, but
having at length managed to squirm from beneath its iron heel I was free
to enjoy my prospects. They were enviable and glorious. Five days in
Cuba, with the privilege of driving up and down the sun-drenched
Malecon in a flamboyantly upholstered limousine, and an opportunity to
feast my discerning gaze on the pink walls of the Cabanas and the Colum-
bus Cathedral and La Fuerza, the great storehouse of the Indies. Opportunity, also, to visit sunlit *patios,* and saunter by iron-barred *rejas,* and to
sip *refrescos* by moonlight in open-air cafés, and to acquire, incidentally,
a Spanish contempt for Big Business and the Strenuous Life. Then on to

Haiti, dark and magical, and the Virgin Islands, and the quaint, incredible Old World harbor of Charlotte Amalie, with its chimneyless, red-roofed houses rising in tiers to the quiet stars—the natural Sargasso, the inevitable last port of call for rainbow fishes, diving boys and old ships with sun-bleached funnels and incurably drunken skippers. A flaming opal set in an amphitheater of malachite—its allure blazed forth through the gray fog and dispelled my northern spleen. I leaned against the rail and dreamed also of Martinique, which I would see in a few days, and of the Indian and Chinese wenches of Trinidad. And then, suddenly, a dizziness came upon me. The ancient and terrible malady had returned to plague me.

Sea-sickness, unlike all other major afflictions, is a disease of the individual. No two people are ever afflicted with precisely the same symptoms. The manifestations range from a slight malaise to a devastating impairment of all one's faculties. I was afflicted with the gravest symptoms imaginable. Choking and gasping, I left the rail and sank helplessly down into one of the three remaining deck chairs.

Why the steward had permitted the chairs to remain on deck was a mystery I couldn't fathom. He had obviously shirked a duty, for passengers did not habitually visit the promenade deck in the small hours, and foggy weather plays havoc with the wicker-work of steamer chairs. But I was too grateful for the benefits which his negligence had conferred upon me to be excessively critical. I lay sprawled at full length, grimacing and gasping and trying fervently to assure myself that I wasn't nearly as sick as I felt. And then, all at once, I became aware of an additional source of discomfiture.

The chair exuded an unwholesome odor. It was unmistakable. As I turned about, as my cheek came to rest against the damp, varnished wood my nostrils were assailed by an acrid and alien odor of a vehement, cloying potency. It was at once stimulating and indescribably repellent. In a measure, it assuaged my physical unease, but it also filled me with the most overpowering revulsion, with a sudden, hysterical, and almost frenzied distaste.

I tried to rise from the chair, but the strength was gone from my limbs. An intangible presence seemed to rest upon me and weigh me down. And then the bottom seemed to drop out of everything. I am not being facetious. Something of the sort actually occurred. The *base* of the sane, familiar world vanished, was swallowed up. I sank down. Limitless gulfs seemed open beneath me, and I was immersed, lost in a gray void. The ship, however, did not vanish. The ship, the deck, the chair continued to support me, and yet, despite the retention of these outward symbols of reality, I was afloat in an unfathomable void. I had the illusion of falling, of sinking helplessly down through an eternity of space. It was as though the chair which supported me had passed into another dimension without ceasing to leave the familiar world—as though it floated simultaneously both in our three-dimensional world and in another world of alien, unknown dimensions. I became aware of strange shapes and shadows all about me. I gazed through illimitable dark gulfs at continents and islands, lagoons, atolls, vast gray waterspouts. I sank down into the great deep. I was immersed in dark slime. The boundaries of sense were dissolved away, and the breath of an active corruption blew through me, gnawing at my vitals and filling me with extravagant torment. I was alone in the great deep. And the shapes that accompanied me in my utter abysmal isolation were shriveled and black and dead, and they cavorted deliriously with little monkey-heads with streaming, sea-drenched viscera and putrid, pupilless eyes.

And then, slowly, the unclean vision dissolved. I was back again in my chair and the fog was as dense as ever, and the ship moved forward steadily through the quiet sea. But the odor was still present—acrid, overpowering, revolting. I leapt from the chair, in profound alarm. . . . I experienced a sense of having emerged from the bowels of some stupendous and unearthly *encroachment,* of having in a single instant exhausted the resources of earth's malignity, and drawn upon untapped and intolerable reserves.

I have gazed without flinching at the turbulent, demon-seething, utterly benighted infernos of the Italian and Flemish primitives. I have endured with calm vision the major inflictions of Hieronymus Bosch, and Lucas Cranach, and I have not quailed even before the worst perversities of the elder Breughel, whose outrageous gargoyles and ghouls and cacodemons are so self-contained that they fester with an over-brimming malignancy, and seem about to burst asunder and dissolve hideously in a black and intolerable froth. But not even Signorelli's *Soul of the Damned,* or Goya's *Los Caprichos,* or the hideous, ooze-encrusted sea-shapes with half-assembled bodies and dead, pupilless eyes which drag themselves sightlessly through Segrelles' blue worlds of fetor and decay were as unnerving and ghastly as the flickering visual sequence which had accompanied my perception of the odor. I was vastly and terribly shaken.

I got indoors somehow, into the warm and steamy interior of the upper saloon, and waited, gasping, for the deck steward to come to me. I had pressed a small button labeled "Deck Steward" in the wainscoting adjoining the central stairway, and I frantically hoped that he would arrive before it was too late, before the odor outside percolated into the vast, deserted saloon.

The steward was a daytime official, and it was a cardinal crime to fetch him from his berth at one in the morning, but I had to have some one to talk to, and as the steward was responsible for the chairs I naturally thought of him as the logical target for my interrogations. He would *know*. He would be able to explain. The odor would not be unfamiliar to him. He would be able to explain about the chairs . . . about the chairs . . . about the chairs. . . . I was growing hysterical and confused.

I wiped the perspiration from my forehead with the back of my hand, and waited with relief for the steward to approach. He had come suddenly into view above the top of the central stairway, and he seemed to advance toward me through a blue mist.

He was extremely solicitous, extremely courteous. He bent above me and laid his hand concernedly upon my arm. "Yes, sir. What can I do for you, sir? A bit under the weather, perhaps. What can I do?"

Do? Do? It was horribly confusing. I could only stammer: "The chairs, steward. On the deck. Three chairs. Why did you leave them there? Why didn't you take them inside?"

It wasn't what I had intended asking him. I had intended questioning him about the odor. But the strain, the shock had confused me. The first thought that came into my mind on seeing the steward standing above me, so solicitous and concerned, was that he was a hypocrite and a scoundrel. He pretended to be concerned about me and yet out of sheer perversity he had prepared the snare which had reduced me to a pitiful and helpless wreck. He had left the chairs on deck deliberately, with a cruel and crafty malice, knowing all the time, no doubt, that *something* would occupy them.

But I wasn't prepared for the almost instant change in the man's demeanor. It was ghastly. Befuddled as I had become I could perceive at once that I had done him a grave, a terrible injustice. *He hadn't known.* All the blood drained out of his cheeks and his mouth fell open. He stood immobile before me, completely inarticulate, and for an instant I thought he was about to collapse, to sink helplessly down upon the floor.

"You saw—chairs?" he gasped at last.

I nodded.

The steward leaned toward me and gripped my arm. The flesh of his face was completely destitute of luster. From the parchment-white oval his two eyes, tumescent with fright, stared wildly down at me.

"It's the black, dead thing," he muttered. "The monkey-face. I *knew* it would come back. It always comes aboard at midnight on the second night out."

He gulped and his hand tightened on my arm.

"It's always on the second night out. It knows where I keep the chairs, and it takes them on deck and sits in them. I *saw* it last time. It was squirming about in the chair—lying stretched out and squirming horribly.

Like an eel. It sits in all three of the chairs. When it saw me it got up and started toward me. But I got away. I came in here, and shut the door. But I saw it through the window."

The steward raised his arm and pointed.

"There. Through that window there. Its face was pressed against the glass. It was all black and shriveled and eaten away. A monkey-face, sir. So help me, the face of a dead, shriveled monkey. And wet—dripping. I was so frightened I couldn't breath. I just stood and groaned, and then it went away."

He gulped.

"Doctor Blodgett was mangled, clawed to death at ten minutes to one. We heard his shrieks. The thing went back, I guess, and sat in the chairs for thirty or forty minutes after it left the window. Then it went down to Doctor Blodgett's stateroom and took his clothes. It was horrible. Doctor Blodgett's legs were missing, and his face was crushed to a pulp. There were claw-marks all over him. And the curtains of his berth were drenched with blood.

"The captain told me not to talk. But I've got to tell some one. I can't help myself, sir. I'm afraid—I've got to talk. This is the third time it's come aboard. It didn't take anybody the first time, but it sat in the chairs. It left them all wet and slimy, sir—all covered with black stinking slime."

I stared in bewilderment. What was the man trying to tell me? Was he completely unhinged? Or was I too confused, too ill myself to catch all that he was saying?

He went on wildly: "It's hard to explain, sir, but this boat is *visited*. Every voyage, sir—on the second night out. And each time it sits in the chairs. Do you understand?"

I didn't understand, clearly, but I murmured a feeble assent. My voice was appallingly tremulous and it seemed to come from the opposite side of the saloon.

"Something out there," I gasped. "It was awful. Out there, you hear? An awful odor. My brain. I can't imagine what's come over me, but I feel as though something were pressing on my brain. Here."

I raised my fingers and passed them across my forehead.

"Something here—something—"

The steward appeared to understand perfectly. He nodded and helped me to my feet. He was still self-engrossed, still horribly wrought up, but I could sense that he was also anxious to reassure and assist me.

"Stateroom 16 D? Yes, of course. Steady, sir."

The steward had taken my arm and was guiding me toward the central stairway. I could scarcely stand erect. My decrepitude was so apparent, in fact, that the steward was moved by compassion to the display of an almost heroic attentiveness. Twice I stumbled and would have fallen had not the guiding arm of my companion encircled my shoulders and levitated my sagging bulk.

"Just a few more steps, sir. That's it. Just take your time. There isn't anything will come of it, sir. You'll feel better when you're inside, with the fan going. Just take your time, sir."

At the door of my stateroom I spoke in a hoarse whisper to the man at my side. "I'm all right now. I'll ring if I need you. Just—let me—get inside. I want to lie down. Does this door lock from the inside?"

"Why, yes. Yes, of course. But maybe I'd better get you some water."

"No, don't bother. Just leave me—please."

"Well—all right, sir." Reluctantly the steward departed, after making certain that I had a firm grip on the handle of the door.

The stateroom was extremely dark. I was so weak that I was compelled to lean with all my weight against the door to close it. It shut with a slight click and the key fell out upon the floor. With a groan I went down on my knees and grovelled apprehensively with my fingers on the soft carpet. But the key eluded me.

I cursed and was about to rise when my hand encountered something fibrous and hard. I started back, gasping. Then, frantically, my fingers slid over it, in a hectic effort at appraisal. It was—yes, undoubtedly a shoe. And sprouting from it, an ankle. The shoe reposed firmly on the floor of the stateroom. The flesh of the ankle, beneath the sock which covered it, was very cold.

In an instant I was on my feet, circling like a caged animal about the narrow dimensions of the stateroom. My hands slid over the walls, the ceiling. If only, dear God, the electric light button would not continue to elude me!

Eventually my hands encountered a rubbery excrescence on the smooth panels. I pressed, resolutely, and the darkness vanished to reveal a man sitting upright on a couch in the corner—a stout, well-dressed man holding a grip and looking perfectly composed. Only his face was invisible. His face was concealed by a handkerchief—a large handkerchief which had obviously been placed there intentionally, perhaps as a protection against the rather chilly air currents from the unshuttered port. The man was obviously asleep. He had not responded to the tugging of my hands on his ankles in the darkness, and even now he did not stir. The glare of the electric light bulbs above his head did not appear to annoy him in the least.

I experienced a sudden and overwhelming relief. I sat down beside the intruder and wiped the sweat from my forehead. I was still trembling in every limb, but the calm appearance of the man beside me was tremendously reassuring. A fellow-passenger, no doubt, who had entered the wrong compartment. It should not be difficult to get rid of him. A mere tap on the shoulder, followed by a courteous explanation, and the intruder would vanish. A simple procedure, if only I could summon the strength to act with decision. I was so horribly enfeebled, so incredibly weak and ill. But at last I mustered sufficient energy to reach out my hand and tap the intruder on the shoulder.

"I'm sorry, sir," I murmured, "but you've got into the wrong stateroom. If I wasn't a bit under the weather I'd ask you to stay and smoke a cigar with me, but you see I"—with a distorted effort at a smile I tapped the stranger again nervously—"I'd rather be alone, so if you don't mind—sorry I had to wake you."

Immediately I perceived that I was being premature. I had not waked the stranger. The stranger did not budge, did not so much as agitate by his breathing the handkerchief which concealed his features.

I experienced a resurgence of my alarm. Tremulously I stretched forth my hand and seized a corner of the handkerchief. It was an outrageous thing to do, but I had to know. If the intruder's face matched his body, if it was composed and familiar all would be well, but if for any reason—

The fragment of physiognomy revealed by the uplifted corner was not reassuring. With a gasp of affright I tore the handkerchief completely away. For a moment, a moment only, I stared at the dark and repulsive visage, with its stary, corpse-white eyes, viscid and malignant, its flat simian nose, hairy ears, and thick black tongue that seemed to leap up at me from out of the mouth. The face *moved* as I watched it, wriggled and squirmed revoltingly, while the head itself shifted its position, turning slightly to one side and revealing a profile more bestial and gangrenous and unclean than the brunt of its countenance.

I shrank back against the door, in frenzied dismay. I suffered as an animal suffers. My mind, deprived by shock of all capacity to form concepts, agonized instinctively, at a brutish level of consciousness. Yet through it all one mysterious part of myself remained horribly observant. I saw the tongue snap back into the mouth; saw the lines of the features shrivel and soften until presently from the slavering mouth and white sightless eyes there began to trickle thin streams of blood. In another moment the mouth was a red slit in a splotched horror of countenance—a red slit rapidly widening and dissolving in an amorphous crimson flood. The horror was hideously and repellently dissolving into the basal sustainer of all life.

It took the steward nearly ten minutes to restore me. He was compelled to force spoonfuls of brandy between my tightly-locked teeth, to bathe my forehead with ice-water and to massage almost savagely my wrists and ankles. And when, finally, I opened my eyes he refused to meet them. He quite obviously wanted me to rest, to remain quiet, and he appeared to distrust his own emotional equipment. He was good enough, however, to enumerate the measures which had contributed to my restoration, and to enlighten me in respect to the *remnants:*

"The clothes were all covered with blood—*drenched,* sir. I burned them."

On the following day he became more loquacious. "It was wearing the clothes of the gentleman who was killed last voyage, sir—it was wearing Doctor Blodgett's things. I recognized them instantly."

"But why—"

The steward shook his head. "I don't know, sir. Maybe your going up on deck saved you. Maybe it couldn't wait. It left a little after one the last time, sir, and it was later than that when I saw you to your stateroom. The ship may have passed out of its *zone,* sir. Or maybe it fell asleep and couldn't get back in time, and that's why it—dissolved. I don't think it's gone for good. There was blood on the curtains in Doctor Blodgett's cabin, and I'm afraid it always *goes* that way. It will come back next voyage, sir. I'm sure of it."

He cleared his throat.

"I'm glad you rang for me. If you'd gone right down to your stateroom it might be wearing your clothes next voyage."

Havana failed to restore me. Haiti was a black horror, a repellent quagmire of menacing shadows and alien desolation, and in Martinique I did not get a single hour of undisturbed sleep in my room at the hotel.

The Black Kiss

Robert Bloch and
Henry Kuttner

They rise in green robes roaring from the green hells of the sea,
Where fallen skies and evil hues and eyeless creatures be.
—CHESTERTON: *Lepanto*

1
The Thing in the Waters

GRAHAM DEAN NERVOUSLY crushed out his cigarette and met Doctor Hedwig's puzzled eyes.

"I've never been troubled like this before," he said. "These dreams are so oddly persistent. They're not the usual haphazard nightmares. They seem—I know it sounds ridiculous—they seem *planned*."

"Dreams planned? Nonsense." Doctor Hedwig looked scornful. "You, Mr. Dean, are an artist, and naturally of impressionable temperament. This house at San Pedro is new to you, and you say you've heard wild tales. The dreams are due to imagination and overwork."

Dean glanced out of the window, a frown on his unnaturally pale face.

"I hope you're right," he said, softly. "But dreams shouldn't make me look like this. Should they?"

A gesture indicated the great blue rings beneath the young artist's eyes. His hands indicated the bloodless pallor of his gaunt cheeks.

"Overwork has done that, Mr. Dean. I know what has happened to you better than you do yourself."

The white-haired physician picked up a sheet covered with his own scarcely decipherable notes and scrutinized it in review.

"You inherited this house at San Pedro a few months ago, eh? And you moved in alone to do some work."

"Yes. The seacoast there has some marvelous scenes." For a moment Dean's face looked youthful once more as enthusiasm kindled its ashy fires. Then he continued, with a troubled frown. "But I haven't been able to paint, lately—not seascapes, anyway. It's very odd. My sketches don't seem quite right any more. There seems to be a quality in them that I don't put there——"

"A quality, did you say?"

"Yes. A quality of *malignness,* if I can call it that. It's indefinable. Something *behind* the picture takes all the beauty out. And I haven't been overworking these last weeks, Doctor Hedwig."

The doctor glanced again at the paper in his hand.

"Well, I disagree with you there. You might be unconscious of the effort you expend. These dreams of the sea that seem to worry you are meaningless, save as an indication of your nervous condition."

"You're wrong." Dean rose, suddenly. His voice was shrill.

"That's the dreadful part of it. The dreams are *not* meaningless. They seem cumulative; cumulative and planned. Each night they grow more vivid, and I see more of that green, shining place under the sea. I get closer and closer to those black shadows swimming there; those shadows that I know aren't shadows but something worse. I see more each night. It's like a sketch I'd block out, gradually adding more and more until——"

Hedwig watched his patient keenly. He suggested "Until——?"

But Dean's tense face relaxed. He had caught himself just in time. "No, Doctor Hedwig. You must be right. It's overwork and nervousness, as you say. If I believed what the Mexicans had told me about Morella Godolfo —well, I'd be mad and a fool."

"Who is this Morella Godolfo? Some woman who has been filling you with foolish tales?"

Dean smiled. "No need to worry about Morella. She was my great-great-grand-aunt. She used to live in the San Pedro house and started the legends, I think."

Hedwig had been scribbling on a slip of paper. "Well, I see, young man! You heard these legends; your imagination ran riot; you dreamed. This prescription will fix you up."

"Thanks."

Dean took the paper, lifted his hat from the table, and started for the door. In the doorway he paused, smiling wryly.

"But you're not quite correct in thinking the legends started me dreaming, Doctor. I began to dream before I learned the history of the house."

And with that he went out.

Driving back to San Pedro, Dean tried to understand what had happened to him. But always he came up against a blank wall of impossibility. Any logical explanation wandered off into a tangle of fantasy. The one thing he could not explain—which Doctor Hedwig had not been able to explain—was the dreams.

The dreams started soon after he came into his legacy; this ancient house north of San Pedro, which had so long stood deserted. The place was picturesquely old, and that attracted Dean from the first. It had been built by one of his ancestors when the Spaniards still ruled California. One of the Deans—the name was Dena, then—had gone to Spain and returned with a bride. Her name was Morella Godolfo, and it was this long-vanished woman about whom all the subsequent legends centered.

Even yet there were wrinkled, toothless Mexicans in San Pedro who whispered incredible tales of Morella Godolfo—she who had never grown old and who had a weirdly evil power over the sea. The Godolfos had been among the proudest families of Granada, but furtive legends spoke of their intercourse with the terrible Moorish sorcerers and necromancers. Morella, according to these same hinted horrors, had learned uncanny secrets in the black towers of Moorish Spain, and when Dena had brought her as his bride across the sea she had already sealed a pact with dark Powers and had undergone a *change*.

So ran the tales, and they further told of Morella's life in the old San Pedro house. Her husband had lived for ten years or more after the marriage, but rumors said that he no longer possessed a soul. It is certain that his death was very mysteriously hushed up by Morella Godolfo, who went on living alone in the great house beside the sea.

The whispers of the peons were hereafter monstrously augmented. They had to do with the *change* in Morella Godolfo; the sorcerous change which caused her to swim far out to sea on moonlit nights so that watchers saw her white body gleaming amidst the spray. Men bold enough to gaze from the cliffs might catch glimpses of her then, sporting with queer sea-creatures that gamboled about her in the black waters, nuzzling her with shockingly deformed heads. These creatures were not seals, or any known form of submarine life, it was averred; although sometimes bursts of chuckling, gobbling laughter could be heard. It is said that Morella Godolfo had swum out there one night, and that she never came back. But thereafter the laughter was louder from afar, and the sporting amidst the black rocks continued, so that the tales of the early peons had been nourished down to the present day.

Such were the legends known to Dean. The facts were sparse and in-conclusive. The old house had fallen into decrepitude, and was only occa-sionally rented through the years. These rentals had been as short as they were infrequent. There was nothing definitely wrong with the house be-tween White's Point and Point Fermin, but those who had lived there said that the crashing of the surf sounded subtly different when heard through windows that overlooked the sea, and, too, they dreamed unpleasantly. Sometimes the occasional tenants had mentioned with peculiar horror the moonlit nights, when the sea became altogether too clearly visible. At any rate, occupants often vacated the house hastily.

Dean had moved in immediately after inheriting, because he had thought the place ideal for painting the scenes he loved. He had learned the legend and the facts behind it later, and by this time his dreams had started.

At first they had been conventional enough, though, oddly, all centered about the sea which he so loved. But it was not the sea he loved that he knew in sleep.

The Gorgons lived in his dreams. Scylla writhed hideously across dark and surging waters, where harpies flew screaming. Weird creatures crawled sluggishly up from the black, inky depths where eyeless, bloated sea-beasts dwelt. Gigantic and terrible leviathans leapt and plunged, while monstrous serpents squirmed a strange obeisance to a mocking moon. Foul and hidden horrors of the sea's depths engulfed him in sleep.

This was bad enough, but it was only a prelude. The dreams began to change. It was almost as though the first few formed a definite setting for the greater terrors to come. From the mythic images of old sea-gods another vision emerged. It was inchoate at first, taking definite form and meaning very slowly over a period of several weeks. And it was this dream which Dean now feared.

It had occurred generally just before he awoke—a vision of green, translucent light, in which dark shadows swam slowly. Night after night the limpid emerald glow grew brighter, and the shadows twisted into a more visible horror. These were never clearly seen, although their amorphous heads held a strangely repellent recognizable quality for Dean.

Presently, in this dream of his, the shadow-creatures would move aside as though to permit the passage of another. Swimming into the green haze would come a coiling shape—whether similar to the rest or not Dean could not tell, for his dream always ended there. The approach of this last shape always caused him to awake in a nightmare paroxysm of terror.

He dreamt of being somewhere under the sea, amidst swimming shadows with deformed heads; and each night one particular shadow was coming closer and closer.

Each day, now, when he awoke with the cold sea-wind of early dawn blowing through the windows, he would lie in a lazy, languid mood till long past daybreak. When he rose these days he felt inexplicably tired, and he could not paint. This particular morning the sight of his haggard face in the mirror had forced him to visit a physician. But Doctor Hedwig had not been helpful.

Nevertheless Dean filled the prescription on the way home. A swallow of the bitter, brownish tonic strengthened him somewhat, but as he parked his car the feeling of depression settled down on him again. He walked up to the house still puzzled and strangely afraid.

Under the door was a telegram. Dean read it with a puzzled frown.

JUST LEARNED YOU ARE LIVING IN SAN PEDRO HOUSE STOP VITALLY IMPORTANT YOU VACATE IMMEDIATELY STOP SHOW THIS CABLE TO DOCTOR MAKOTO YAMADA 17BUENA STREET SAN PEDRO STOP AM RETURNING VIA AIRPLANE STOP SEE YAMADA TODAY

MICHAEL LEIGH

Dean read the message again, and a flash of remembrance came to him. Michael Leigh was his uncle, but he had not seen the man for years. Leigh had been a puzzle to the family; he was an occultist, and spent most of his time delving in far corners of the earth. Occasionally he dropped from sight for long periods of time. The cable Dean held was sent from Calcutta, and he supposed that Leigh had recently emerged from some spot in the interior of India to learn of Dean's inheritance.

Dean searched his mind. He recalled now, that there had been some family quarrel about this very house years ago. The details were no longer clear, but he remembered that Leigh had demanded the San Pedro house be razed. Leigh had given no sane reasons, and when the request was refused he had dropped out of sight for a time. And now came this inexplicable cablegram.

Dean was tired from his long drive, and the unsatisfactory interview with the doctor had irritated him more than he had realized. Nor was he in the mood to follow his uncle's cabled request and undertake the long journey to Buena Street, which was miles away. The drowsiness which he felt, however, was normal healthy exhaustion, unlike the languor of recent weeks. The tonic he had taken was of some value after all.

He dropped into his favorite chair by the window that overlooked the sea, rousing himself to watch the flaming colors of the sunset. Presently the sun dropped below the horizon, and gray dusk crept in. Stars appeared, and far to the north he could see the dim lights of the gambling-ships off Venice. The mountains shut off his view of San Pedro, but a diffused pale glow in that direction told him that the New Barbary was wakening into roaring, brawling life. Slowly the face of the Pacific brightened. A full moon was rising above the San Pedro hills.

*   *   *

For a long time Dean sat quietly by the window, his pipe forgotten in his hand, staring down at the slow swells of the ocean, which seemed to pulse with a mighty and alien life. Gradually drowsiness crept up and overwhelmed him. Just before he dropped into the abyss of sleep there flashed into his mind da Vinci's saying, "The two most wonderful things in the world are a woman's smile and the motion of mighty waters."

He dreamed, and this time it was a different dream. At first only blackness, and a roaring and thundering as of angry seas, and oddly mingled with this was the hazy thought of a woman's smile . . . and a woman's lips . . . pouting lips, softly alluring . . . but strangely the lips were not red—no! They were very pale, bloodless, like the lips of a thing that had long rested beneath the sea. . . .

The misty vision changed, and for a flashing instant Dean seemed to see the green and silent place of his earlier visions. The shadowy black shapes were moving more quickly behind the veil, but this picture was of but a second's duration. It flashed out and vanished, and Dean was standing alone on a beach; a beach he recognized in his dream—the sandy cove beneath the house.

The salt breeze blew coldly across his face, and the sea glistened like silver in the moonlight. A faint splash told of a sea-thing that broke the surface of the waters. To the north the sea washed against the rugged surface of the cliff, barred and speckled with black shadows. Dean felt a sudden, inexplicable impulse to move in that direction. He yielded.

As he clambered over the rocks he was suddenly conscious of a strange sensation, as though keen eyes were focussed upon him—eyes that watched and warned! Vaguely in his mind rose up the gaunt face of his uncle, Michael Leigh, the deep-set eyes glowing. But swiftly this was gone, and he found himself before a deeper niche of blackness in the cliff face. Into it he knew he must go.

He squeezed himself between two jutting points of rock, and found himself in utter, dismal darkness. Yet somehow he was conscious that he was in a cave, and he could hear water lapping near by. All about him was a musty salt odor of sea-decay, the fetid smell of sunless ocean caves and holds of ancient ships. He stepped forward, and, as the floor shelved sharply downward, stumbled and fell headlong into icy, shallow water. He felt, rather than saw, a flicker of swift movement, and then abruptly hot lips were pressed against his.

Human lips, Dean thought, at first.

He lay on his side in the chill water, his lips against those responsive ones. He could see nothing, for all was lost in the blackness of the cave. The unearthly lure of those invisible lips thrilled through him.

He responded to them, pressed them fiercely, gave them what they were avidly seeking. The unseen waters crawled against the rocks, whispering warning.

And in that kiss strangeness flooded him. He felt a shock and a tingling go through him, and then a thrill of sudden ecstasy, and swift on its heels came horror. Black loathsome foulness seemed to wash his brain, indescribable but fearfully real, making him shudder with nausea. It was as though unutterable evil were pouring into his body, his mind, his very soul, through the blasphemous kiss on his lips. He felt loathsome, contaminated. He fell back. He sprang to his feet.

And Dean saw, for the first time, the ghastly thing he had kissed, as the sinking moon sent a pale shaft of radiance creeping through the cave mouth. For something rose up before him, a serpentine and seal-like bulk that coiled and twisted and moved toward him, glistening with foul slime; and Dean screamed and turned to flee with nightmare fear tearing at his brain, hearing behind him a quiet splashing as though some bulky creature had slid back into the water. . . .

99
A Visit from Doctor Yamada

He awoke. He was still in his chair before the window, and the moon was paling before the grayness of dawn. He was shaken with nausea, sick and shuddering with the shocking realism of his dream. His clothing was drenched with perspiration, and his heart hammered furiously. An immense lethargy seemed to have overwhelmed him, making it an intense effort to rise from the chair and stagger to a couch, on which he flung himself to doze fitfully for several hours.

A sharp pealing of the door-bell roused him. He still felt weak and dizzy, but the frightening lethargy had somewhat abated. When Dean opened the door, a Japanese standing on the porch began a bobbing little bow, a gesture that was abruptly arrested as the sharp black eyes focussed on Dean's face. A little hiss of indrawn breath came from the visitor.

Dean said irritably, "Well? Do you want to see me?"

The other was still staring, his thin face sallow beneath a stiff thatch of gray hair. He was a small, slender man, with his face covered with a finespun web of wrinkles. After a pause he said, "I am Doctor Yamada."

Dean frowned, puzzled. Abruptly he remembered his uncle's cable of the day before. An odd, unreasonable irritation began to mount within him, and he said, more bruskly than he had intended, "This isn't a professional call, I hope. I've already——"

"Your uncle—you are Mr. Dean?—cabled me. He was rather worried." Doctor Yamada glanced around almost furtively.

Dean felt distaste stir within him, and his irritation increased.

"My uncle is rather eccentric, I'm afraid. There's nothing for him to worry about. I'm sorry you had your trip for nothing."

Doctor Yamada did not seem to take offense at Dean's attitude. Rather, a strange expression of sympathy showed for a moment on his small face.

"Do you mind if I come in?" he asked, and moved forward confidently.

Short of barring his way, Dean had no means of stopping him, and ungraciously led his guest to the room where he had spent the night, motioning him to a chair while he busied himself with a coffee-pot.

Yamada sat motionless, silently watching Dean. Then without preamble he said, "Your uncle is a great man, Mr. Dean."

Dean made a noncommittal gesture. "I have seen him only once."

"He is one of the greatest occultists of this day. I, too, have studied psychic lore, but beside your uncle I am a novice."

Dean said, "He is eccentric. Occultism, as you term it, has never interested me."

The little Japanese watched him impassively. "You make a common error, Mr. Dean. You consider occultism a hobby for cranks. No"—he held up a slender hand—"your disbelief is written in your face. Well, it is understandable. It is an anachronism, an attitude handed down from the earliest times, when scientists were called alchemists and sorcerers and burned for making pacts with the devil. But actually there are no sorcerers, no—witches. Not in the sense that man understands these terms. There are men and women who have acquired mastery over certain sciences which are not wholly subject to mundane physical laws."

There was a little smile of disbelief on Dean's face. Yamada went on quietly. "You do not believe because you do not understand. There are not many who can comprehend, or who wish to comprehend, this greater science which is not bound by earthly laws. But here is a problem for you, Mr. Dean." A little spark of irony flickered in the black eyes. "Can you tell me how I know you have suffered from nightmares recently?"

Dean jerked around and stood staring. Then he smiled.

"As it happens, I know the answer, Doctor Yamada. You physicians have a way of hanging together—and I must have let something slip to Doctor Hedwig yesterday." His tone was offensive, but Yamada merely shrugged slightly.

"Do you know your Homer?" he asked, apparently irrelevantly, and at Dean's surprised nod went on, "And Proteus? You remember the Old Man of the Sea who possessed the power of changing his shape? I do not wish to strain your credulity, Mr. Dean, but for a long time students of the dark lore have known that behind this legend there exists a very terrible truth. All the tales of spirit-possession, of reincarnation, even the comparatively innocuous experiments in thought-transference, point to the truth. Why do you suppose folklore abounds with tales of men who have been able to change themselves into beasts—werewolves, hyenas, tigers, the seal-men of the Eskimos? Because these tales are founded on truth!

"I do not mean," he went on, "that the actual physical metamorphosis of the body is possible, so far as we know. But it has long been known that the intelligence—the mind—of an adept can be transferred to the brain and body of a satisfactory subject. Animals' brains are weak, lacking the power of resistance. But men are different, unless there are certain circumstances——"

As he hesitated, Dean proffered the Japanese a cup of coffee—coffee was generally brewing in the percolator these days—and Yamada accepted it with a formal little bow of acknowledgment. Dean drank his coffee in three hasty gulps, and poured more. Yamada, after a polite sip, put the cup aside and leaned forward earnestly.

"I must ask you to make your mind receptive, Mr. Dean. Don't allow your conventional ideas of life to influence you in this matter. It is vitally to your interest that you listen carefully to me, and understand. Then—perhaps——"

He hesitated, and again threw that oddly furtive glance at the window.

"Life in the sea has followed different lines from life on land. Evolution has followed a different course. In the great deeps of the ocean, life utterly alien to ours has been discovered—luminous creatures which burst when exposed to the lighter pressure of the air—and in those tremendous depths forms of life completely inhuman have been developed, life forms that the uninitiated mind may think impossible. In Japan, an island country, we have known of these sea-dwellers for generations. Your English writer, Arthur Machen, has told a deep truth in his statement that man, afraid of these strange beings, has attributed to them beautiful or pleasantly grotesque forms which in reality they do not possess. Thus we have the nereids and oceanids—but nevertheless man could not fully disguise the true foulness of these creatures. Therefore there are legends of the Gorgons, of Scylla and the harpies—and, significantly, of the mermaids and their soullessness. No doubt you know the mermaid tale—how they long to steal the soul of a man, and draw it out by means of their kiss."

Dean was at the window now, his back to the Japanese. As Yamada paused he said tonelessly, "Go on."

"I have reason to believe," Yamada went on very quietly, "that

Morella Godolfo, the woman from Alhambra, was not fully—human. She left no issue. These things never have children—they cannot."

"What do you mean?" Dean had turned and was facing the Japanese, his face a ghastly white, the shadows beneath his eyes hideously livid. He repeated harshly, "What do you mean? You can't frighten me with your tales—if that's what you're trying to do. You—my uncle wants me out of this house, for some reason of his own. You're taking this means of getting me out—aren't you? Eh?"

"You must leave this house," Yamada said. "Your uncle is coming, but he may not be in time. Listen to me: these creatures—the sea-dwellers—envy man. Sunlight, and warm fires, and the fields of earth—things which the sea-dwellers cannot normally possess. These things—and *love*. You remember what I said about mind-transference—the possession of a brain by an alien intelligence. That is the only way these things can attain that which they desire, and know the love of man or woman. Sometimes—not very often—one of these creatures succeeds in possessing itself of a human body. They watch always. When there is a wreck, they go there, like vultures to a feast. They can swim phenomenally fast. When a man is drowning, the defenses of his mind are down, and sometimes the sea-dwellers can thus acquire a human body. There have been tales of men saved from wrecks who ever after were oddly changed.

"Morella Godolfo was one of these creatures! The Godolfos knew much of the dark lore, but used it for evil purposes—the so-called black magic. And it was, I think, through this that sea-dweller gained power to usurp the brain and body of the woman. A transference took place. The mind of the sea-dweller took possession of Morella Godolfo's body, and the intelligence of the original Morella was forced into the terrible form of that creature of the abyss. In time the human body of the woman died, and the usurping mind returned to its original shell. The intelligence of Morella Godolfo was then ejected from its temporary prison, and left homeless. That is true death."

Dean shook his head slowly, as though in denial, but did not speak. And inexorably Yamada kept on.

"For years, generations, since then she has dwelt in the sea, waiting. Her power is strongest here, where she once lived. But, as I told you, only under unusual circumstances can this—transference take place. The tenants of this house might be troubled with dreams, but that would be all. The evil being had no power to steal their bodies. Your uncle knew that, or he would have insisted that the place be immediately destroyed. He did not foresee that you would ever live here."

The little Japanese bent forward, and his eyes were twin points of black light.

"You do not need to tell me what you have undergone in the past month. I know. The sea-dweller has power over you. For one thing, there are bonds of blood, even though you are not directly descended from her. And your love for the ocean—your uncle spoke of that. You live here alone with your paintings and your imaginative fancies; you see no one else. You are an ideal victim, and it was easy for that sea horror to become *en rapport* with you. Even now you show the stigmata."

Dean was silent, his face a pale shadow amidst the darker ones in the corners of the room. What was the man trying to tell him? What were these hints leading up to?

"Remember what I have said." Doctor Yamada's voice was fanatically earnest. "That creature wants you for your youth—your soul. She has lured you in sleep, with visions of Poseidonis, the twilight grottoes in the deep. She has sent you beguiling visions at first, to hide what she was doing. She has drained your life forces, weakened your resistance, waiting until she is strong enough to take possession of your brain.

"I have told you what she wants—what all these hybrid horrors raven for. She will reveal herself to you in time, and when her will is strong upon you in slumber, you will do her bidding. She will take you down into the deep, and show you the kraken-fouled gulfs where these things bide. You will go willingly, and that will be your doom. She may lure you to their feasts there—the feasts they hold upon the drowned things they find floating from wrecked ships. And you will live such madness in your sleep because she rules you. And then—then, when you have become weak enough, she will have her desire. The sea-thing will usurp your body and walk once more on earth. And you will go down into the darkness where once you dwelt in dreams, for ever. Unless I am mistaken, you have already seen enough to know that I speak truth. I think that this terrible moment is not so far off, and I warn you that alone you cannot hope to resist the evil. Only with the aid of your uncle and me——"

Doctor Yamada stood up. He moved forward and confronted the dazed youth face to face. In a low voice he asked, "In your dreams—*has the thing kissed you?*"

For a heart-beat there was utter silence. Dean opened his mouth to speak, and then a curious little warning note seemed to sound in his brain. It rose, like the quiet roaring of a conch-shell, and a vague nausea assailed him.

Almost without volition he heard himself saying, "No."

Dimly, as though from an incredibly far distance, he heard Yamada suck in his breath, as if surprised. Then the Japanese said, "That is good.

Very good. Now listen: your uncle will be here soon. He has chartered a special plane. Will you be my guest until he arrives?"

The room seemed to darken before Dean's eyes. The form of the Japanese was receding, dwindling. Through the window the surf-sound came crashing, and it rolled on in waves through Dean's brain. In its thunder a thin, insistent whispering penetrated.

"Accept," it murmured. "Accept!" And Dean heard his own voice accept Yamada's invitation.

He seemed incapable of coherent thought. That last dream haunted him . . . and now Doctor Yamada's disturbing story . . . he was ill—that was it!—very ill. He wanted very much to sleep, now. A flood of darkness seemed to wash up and engulf him. Gratefully he allowed it to sweep through his tired head. Nothing existed but the dark, and a restless lapping of unquiet waters.

Yet he seemed to know, in an odd way, that he was still—some outer part of him—conscious. He strangely realized that he and Doctor Yamada had left the house, were entering a car, and driving a long way. He was—with that strange, external other self—talking casually to the doctor; entering his house in San Pedro; drinking; eating. And all the while his soul, his real being, was buried in waves of blackness.

Finally a bed. From below, the surf seemed to blend into the blackness that engulfed his brain. It spoke to him now, as he rose stealthily and clambered out of the window. The fall jarred his outer self considerably, but he was on the ground outside without injury. He kept in the shadows as he crept away down to the beach—the black, hungry shadows that were like the darkness surging through his soul.

¶¶¶
Three Dreadful Hours

With a shock, he was himself once more—completely. The cold water had done it; the water in which he found himself swimming. He was in the ocean, borne on waves as silver as the lightning that occasionally flashed overhead. He heard thunder, felt the sting of rain. Without wondering about the sudden transition, he swam on, as though fully aware of some planned destination. For the first time in over a month he felt fully alive, actually himself. There was a surge of wild elation in him that defied the facts; he no longer seemed to care about his recent illness, the weird warnings of his uncle and Doctor Yamada, and the unnatural darkness that had previously shadowed his mind. In fact, he no longer had to think —it was as though he were being *directed* in all his movements.

He was swimming parallel with the beach now, and with curious detachment he observed that the storm had subsided. A pale, fog-like glow hovered over the lashing waters, and it seemed to beckon.

The air was chill, as was the water, and the waves high; yet Dean experienced neither cold nor fatigue. And when he saw the things that waited for him on the rocky beach just ahead, he lost all perception of himself in a crescendo of mounting joy.

This was inexplicable, for they were the creatures of his last and wildest nightmares. Even now he did not see them plainly as they sported in the surf, but there were dim suggestions of past horror in their tenebrous outlines. The things were like seals; great, fish-like, bloated monsters with pulpy, shapeless heads. These heads rested on columnar necks that undulated with serpentine ease, and he observed, without any sensation other than curious familiarity, that the heads and bodies of the creatures were a sea-bleached white.

Soon he was swimming in among them—swimming with peculiar and disturbing ease. Inwardly he marveled, with a touch of his former feeling, that he was not now horrified by the sea-beasts in the least. Instead, it was almost with a feeling of kinship that he listened to their strange low gruntings and cackles—listened *and understood.*

He *knew* what they were saying, and he was not amazed. He was not frightened by what he heard, though the words would have sent abysmal horror through his soul in the previous dreams.

He knew where they were going and what they meant to do when the entire group swam out into the water once more, yet he did not fear. Instead, he felt a strange hunger at the thought of what was to come, a hunger that impelled him to take the lead as the things, with undulant swiftness, glided through the inky waters to the north. They swam with incredible speed, yet it was hours before a seacoast loomed up through the murk, lit by a blinding flare of light from offshore.

Twilight deepened to true darkness over the water, but the offshore light burned brightly. It seemed to come from a huge wreck in the waves just off the coast, a great hulk floating on the waters like a crumpled beast. There were boats gathered around it, and floating flares of light that revealed the scene.

As though by instinct, Dean, with the pack behind him, headed for the spot. Swiftly and silently they sped, their slimy heads blurred in the shadows to which they clung as they circled the boats and swam in toward the great crumpled shape. Now it was looming above him, and he could see arms flailing desperately as man after man sank below the surface. The colossal bulk from which they leaped was a wreck of twisted girders in which he could trace the warped outline of a vaguely familiar shape.

And now, with curious disinterest, he swam lazily about, avoiding the lights bobbing over the water as he watched the actions of his companions. They were hunting their prey. Leering muzzles gaped for the drowning men, and lean talons raked bodies from the darkness. Whenever a man was glimpsed in shadows not yet invaded by rescue-boats, one of the sea-things craftily snared his victim.

In a little while they turned and slowly swam away. But now many of the creatures clutched a grisly trophy at their squamous breasts. The pale white limbs of drowning men trailed in the water as they were dragged off into the darkness by their captors. To the accompaniment of low, carrion laughter the beasts swam away, back down the coast.

Dean swam with the rest. His mind was again a blur of confusion. He knew what that thing in the water was, and yet he could not name it. He had watched those hateful horrors snare doomed men and drag them off to the deep, yet he had not intervened. What was wrong? Even now, as he swam with frightening agility, he felt a call he could not fully understand —a call that his body was answering.

The hybrid things were gradually dispersing. With eery splashings they disappeared below the surface of the gelid black waters, pulling with them the dreadfully limp bodies of the men, pulling them down to the blackness biding beneath.

They were hungry. Dean knew it without thinking. He swam on, along the coast, impelled by his curious urge. That was it—he was hungry.

And now he was going for food.

Hours of steady swimming southward. Then the familiar beach, and above it a lighted house which Dean recognized—his own house on the cliff. There were figures descending the slope now; two men with torches were coming down to the beach. He must not let them see him—why, he did not know, but they must not. He crawled along the beach, keeping close to the water's edge. Even so, he seemed to move very swiftly.

The men with the torches were some distance behind him now. Ahead loomed another familiar outline—a cave. He had clambered over these rocks before, it seemed. He knew the pits of shadow that speckled the cliff rock, and knew the narrow passage of stone through which he now squeezed his prostrate body.

Was that someone shouting, far away? . . .

Darkness, and a lapping pool. He crawled forward, felt chill waters creep over his body. Muffled by distance came an insistent shouting from outside the cave.

"Graham! Graham Dean!"

Then the smell of dank sea-foulness was in his nostrils—a familiar, pleasant smell. He knew where he was, now. It was the cave where in his dream he had kissed the sea-thing. It was the cave in which——

He remembered now. The black blur lifted from his brain, and he remembered all. His mind bridged the gap, and he once again recalled coming here earlier this very evening, before he had found himself in the water.

Morella Godolfo had called him here; here her dark whispers had guided him at twilight, when he had come from the bed at Doctor Yamada's house. It was the siren song of the sea-creature that had lured him in dreams.

He remembered how she had coiled about his feet when he entered, flung her sea-bleached body up until its inhuman head had loomed close to his own. And then the hot pulpy lips had pressed against his—the loathsome, slimy lips had kissed him again. Wet, dank, horribly avid kiss! His senses had drowned in its evil, for he knew that this second kiss meant doom.

"The sea-dweller will take your body," Doctor Yamada had said. . . . And the second kiss meant doom.

All this had happened hours ago!

Dean shifted around in the rocky chamber to avoid wetting himself in the pool. As he did so, he glanced down at his body for the first time that night—glanced down with an undulating neck at the shape he had worn for three hours in the sea. He saw the fish-like scales, the scabrous whiteness of the slimy skin; saw the veined gills. He stared into the waters of the pool then, so that the reflection of his face was visible in the dim moonlight that filtered through fissures in the rocks.

He saw all. . . .

His head rested on the long, reptilian neck. It was an anthropoid head with flat contours that were monstrously inhuman. The eyes were white and protuberant; they bulged with the glassy stare of a drowning thing. There was no nose, and the center of the face was covered with a tangle of wormy blue feelers. The mouth was worst of all. Dean saw pale white lips in a dead face—human lips. Lips that had kissed his own. And now—*they were his own!*

He was in the body of the evil sea-thing—the evil sea-thing that had once harbored the soul of Morella Godolfo!

At that moment Dean would gladly have welcomed death, for the stark, blasphemous horror of his discovery was too much to bear. He knew about his dreams now, and the legends; he had learned the truth, and paid a hideous price. He recalled, vividly, how he had recovered consciousness in the water and swum out to meet those—others. He recalled the great black hulk from which drowning men had been taken in boats—the shattered wreck on the water. What was it Yamada had told him? "When there is a wreck they go there, like vultures to a feast." And now, at last, he remembered what had eluded him that night—what that familiar shape on the waters had been. It was a crashed zeppelin. He had gone swimming into the wreckage with those things, and they had taken men. . . . Three hours—God! Dean wanted very much to die. He was in the sea-body of Morella Godolfo, and it was too evil for further life.

Morella Godolfo! Where was *she?* And his own body, the shape of Graham Dean?

A rustling in the shadowy cavern behind him proclaimed the answer. Graham Dean saw *himself* in the moonlight—saw his body, line for line, hunching furtively past the pool in an attempt to creep away unobserved.

Dean's flippered fins moved swiftly. His own body turned.

It was ghastly for Dean to see himself reflected where no mirror existed; ghastlier still to see that in his face there no longer were *his* eyes. The sly, mocking stare of the sea-creature peered out at him from behind their fleshy mask, and they were ancient, evil. The pseudo-human snarled at him and tried to dodge off into the darkness. Dean followed, on all fours.

He knew what he must do. That sea-thing—Morella—she had taken his body during that last black kiss, just as he had been forced into hers. But she had not yet recovered enough to go out into the world. That was why he had found her still in the cave. Now, however, she would leave, and his uncle Michael would never know. The world would never know, either, what horror stalked its surface—until it was too late. Dean, his own tragic form hateful to him now, knew what he must do.

Purposefully he maneuvered the mocking body of himself into a rocky corner. There was a look of fright in those gelid eyes. . . .

A sound caused Dean to turn, pivoting his reptilian neck. Through glazed fish-eyes he saw the faces of Michael Leigh and Doctor Yamada. Torches in hand, they were entering the cave.

Dean knew what they would do, and he no longer cared. He closed in on the human body that housed the soul of the sea-beast; closed in with the beast's own flailing flippers; seized it in its own arms and menaced it with its own teeth near the creature's white, human neck.

From behind him he heard shouts and cries at his very back, but Dean did not care. He had a duty to perform; an atonement. Through the corner of his eye, he saw the barrel of a revolver as it glinted in Yamada's hand.

Then came two bursts of stabbing flame, and the oblivion Dean craved. But he died happy, for he had atoned for the black kiss.

Even as he sank into death, Graham Dean had bitten with animal fangs into his own throat, and his heart was filled with peace as, dying, he saw himself die. . . .

His soul mingled in the third black kiss of Death.

The Sea Thing

A. E. van Vogt

HE THING SCRAMBLED out of the water and stood for a moment swaying gently on its human legs, as if intoxicated. Odd how blurred everything was; its mind blackened by mist, it fought to adjust itself to its human body and to the cool, wet feel of the sand under its feet.

Behind it, the waves whispered against the moonlit beach. And ahead—

It felt a queer uncertainty as it stared into the shadow world ahead; an unwillingness, a vast melancholy reluctance to leave the edge of the water. A dragging uneasiness writhed along the fish nerves of its human body, as it realized that its deadly yet all-necessary purpose left no alternative but to go ahead. No fear could ever touch that cold fish brain, and yet—

The thing quivered, as the deep, hoarse guffaw of a man jarred the sullen night air. The sound carried on the slow, warm, trade wind, queerly distorted by distance—a disembodied bellow of laughter that stabbed from the other side of the coral island through semidarkness of the moon-filled night. A raucous, arrogant laugh, it was, that brought an answering thickness to the creature's throat. An icy, ruthless sneer squeezed the lines of the thing's human face until, for a brief, horrible moment, it was a tiger shark's face that grimaced there, a hard, ferocious head that barely held its human shape. Steely teeth clicked with the metallic snap of a shark lashing forth at its prey.

With a quivering gasp, the creature drew breath into its human mouth and down its human throat. The air felt suddenly, strangely, unpleasantly dry and hot after that brief moment of semireversion to a fish state—a harsh, strangling sensation that brought a racking paroxysm of cough choking up in a mist of white foam. It clutched at its neck with its hard human fingers, and stood for a horrible moment fighting the darkness out of its brain.

Stinging rage against this human body it had put on burned a shivering course along its cold fish nerves. It *hated* this new form—this helpless thing of legs and arms, small, horrible construction of globular head and snakelike neck, fastened precariously to an almost solid chunk of weak flesh and bone. Not only was it almost useless in water, but it seemed useless for any other purpose as well.

The thought fled as, with muscles tensed, it stared across the dim reaches of the island. In the near distance, blackness piled up fantastically into deeper blackness—trees! There were other clumps of blackness in the farther distance, but it was too hard to see whether they were trees or hills —or buildings!

One was unmistakably a building. A pale, yellow-orange light gleamed from an opening in its low, spreading bulk. As the thing watched with grim eyes, a shadow passed before the light. The shadow of a man!

These white men were a hardy lot, incredibly different from the brown natives of the nearby islands. It was not yet dawn, yet they were risen from sleep, preparing for the labors of the day.

The thing spat with a sudden ferocity of hate, as the thought of those labors poured like molten fire through its brain. Its human lips parted in a hideous grin of uncontrollable rage at these human beings who dared to hunt and kill sharks.

Let them keep to the land and live on the land where they belonged. The sea—this wild and great sea—was not for their kind; and of all the things of the sea, the shark lords were the sacred, the untouchables. Nothing else mattered, but *they* must not be systematically hunted. Self-defense was the first law of nature!

With a snarl of unutterable fury, the thing strode along the stretching away of gray-dark shore, then headed inland, straight toward where the yellow light blinked palely out into the false dawn of early, early morning.

The sinking, bloated moon rode the waters to the west, as Corliss heaved his square-built body up the sharp embankment that led from the water's edge, where he had washed himself, to the cook's building. The man ahead of him, Progue, the Dutchman, stepped into the shack's doorway, and his thick body almost blotted out the sickly yellow lamp glow that came from within.

Corliss heard the deep bellow that burst from Progue's throat: "Isn't breakfast ready yet? You've been sleeping in again, you lily-livered slob!"

Corliss swore to himself. In a kind of a way, he liked the tremendous Dutchman, but the man could be annoying in his swift and terrific tempers. The leader called sharply: "Shut up, Progue!"

Progue turned in the doorway and grunted: "When I'm hungry, Corliss, I'm hungry; and blast his cockney soul for keeping me waiting. I—"

He stopped, and Corliss could see his head jerk sideways. The man's eyes glowed with a faint, yellow light, as he stared at the pale, bloodless ball of moon. His voice held a queer, urgent pitch when he spoke:

"Corliss, we're all here, the whole sixteen of us, aren't we? On this side of the island, I mean!"

"We were a minute ago," the leader replied wonderingly. "I saw the whole gang pile out of the bunkhouse and start washing up. Why?"

Progue snapped tensely: "Just watch that moon. Maybe he'll do it again."

The Dutchman's vast body grew so rigid with the intentness of his stare that, briefly, Corliss throttled down his questions. He followed the man's gaze.

The seconds dragged by; an eerie sense of unreality crept over Corliss. The island in the immediate foreground was a dark mass, except where the gloomy, white moon path lay in a thick, somber swath across the silent, dark land.

Beyond the island, he could see the dark glint of the lagoon waters, the darker ocean beyond, and the way the white, mysterious moonbeams made a road of light into the remote distance of that immensity of water.

Incredible vista it was in that night under that blue-dark southern sky. The *lap, lap* of the water against the sand of the shore; the faint, distant, sullen roar of the breakers, when the waves pounded their tireless strength against the shallow line of rocks that formed a jagged, guardian ring around the island. The breakers themselves, visible in the darkness, a long scatter of glittering white, like broken glass, that swirled and plunged, and broke and fought, and roared and smashed the eternal, bitter battle of the sea against the land.

And over everything hung the brooding night sky; the moon, so bright and white and sated-looking, sinking sluggishly behind the ocean to the west.

With an effort, Corliss tore his mind back to the Dutchman, as Progue half whispered:

"I could have sworn—I do swear I saw a man silhouetted against the moon!"

Corliss threw off the spell of that early, early morning. He snapped: "You're crazy! A man here, in this the loneliest waste of the lonely Pacific. You're seeing things!"

"Maybe I am!" Progue muttered. "The way you put it, it does sound crazy."

He turned reluctantly, and Corliss followed him in to breakfast.

*   *   *

The creature slowed instinctively, as the yellow-orange glow from the doorway washed across its feet. Men's voices spilled out the door, a low, deep murmur of conversation. There was a clatter of other sounds and the blurred scent of strange foods.

The thing hesitated the barest moment, then walked full into the sickly glow of that light. Tensely, it stepped through the open doorway, and stood blinking with fish eyes at the scene that spread before it.

Sixteen men sat around a large table, their needs being served by a seventeenth.

It was this serving man, a scrawny, horrible caricature of a man in a greasy white apron, who looked up straight into the creature's eyes.

"Blimey!" he ejaculated. "If 'tain't a bloomin' stranger! Where the devil are you from?"

Sixteen heads bobbed up. And thirty-two eyes, cold and hard with surprise and speculation, stared at the thing. Under that alert scrutiny, it felt a vague unease, a distant sense of alarm, a cold premonition that these men were going to be more difficult to murder than it had anticipated.

The moment lengthened into seconds; and the thing suddenly had the weird impression that, not a few, but a million eyes swayed and gleamed there before it—a million searching, suspicious eyes that blurred and wavered, and yet held a hard, glittery stare. The thing fought off the feeling; and it was then that, from deep within itself, came the first disturbing reaction to the question the little cockney had asked. Even as the unpleasant glimmer of thought quivered at the doors of its brain, another man asked the question:

"Where did you come from?"

Come from! The question beat a vague path in the thing's brain. Why, from the sea, of course! Where else? In all these wild, dark miles, there was only the sea, and the waves that rose and fell in their ceaseless rhythm —glittering like cut gems in the eternity of sunlit days, turgid and morose in the nights! The primeval sea that whispered and rippled and hinted blackly of things indescribable.

"Well!" rapped Progue, before Corliss could speak, "haven't you got a tongue? Who are you? Where're you from?"

"I—" the creature began lamely. "I—"

A stunned dismay was creeping along those icy fish nerves. It seemed suddenly incredible that it had prepared no explanation. Where *had* it come from that would satisfy the harsh, shrewd minds of these men?

"Why, I—" it started again hopelessly. Frantically, it searched its memory for things it had heard could happen to men. A picture came of a boat, and of what a boat could experience. Its voice stabbed forth eagerly: "M-my boat . . . overturned. I was rowing and—"

"A rowboat!" Progue snorted. The big Dutchman sounded to Corliss as if his intelligence had been utterly outraged by such an explanation. "Why, you dirty liar. A rowboat a thousand miles from the nearest port! What're you up to? What're you tryin' to put over? Who do you think you're fooling?"

"Pipe down, Progue!" Corliss snapped. "Can't you see what's happened to this chap?"

He lifted his magnificent and commanding bulk of body out of his chair and came around the table. He grabbed a towel from the towel rack and tossed it to the creature. "Here, stranger, dry the chill off your body with this!"

He faced the table of men, half-accusingly. "Can't you see, he's been through hell! Think of swimming out there in these shark-infested waters and accidentally hitting this island. He must have gone nearly crazy. His mind did go a little, his memory snapped. Amnesia, they call it. Here are some dry togs, stranger!"

Corliss jerked an old pair of trousers and a rough gray shirt from a hook, and watched as the creature gingerly climbed into them.

"Hey," said a man, "he's putting the pants on backwards."

"You can see," said Corliss grimly, as the thing hesitantly corrected its mistake, "how far gone he was. Doesn't even know any more how to dress. At least, he understands. Here, stranger, sit down here, and stow some hot food under your belt. It ought to go good after what you've been through."

The only vacant space was across from Progue; the thing sank hesitantly into the chair and—as hesitantly—tackled the plateful of food the cook set before it, using the fork and knife, as it had seen the others do.

Progue grumbled: "I don't like the looks of this guy! Those eyes! He may be a weak-minded baby now, but I'll bet he was so tough he was tossed overboard from a passing ship. Those eyes give me the shivers!"

"Shut up!" Corliss roared in abrupt fury. "None of us are to blame for our appearance, for which you should be damned thankful."

"Bah!" said Progue. He went on, muttering words that came to Corliss in a disconnected stream. "If I was boss . . . believe me, this outfit . . . a damned crime . . . when I don't trust a man it's a cinch . . . probably the mate on some tramp steamer . . . so tough he was heaved over—"

"That's impossible!" said Corliss flatly. "No tramp steamers pass this way. There'll not be a steamer until ours arrives five months from now. This fellow's explanation, though blurred, is clear enough. He was in a rowboat; and you know as well as I do there are some larger islands to the south of us, with small native populations and some whites. He could have come from there."

"Yaah!" snarled Progue, his beefy face aflame with ugly color. Corliss recognized the stubborn streak that sometimes made the big Dutchman unmanageable. "Well, I don't like him, see! Do you hear that, you?"

The thing looked up, a vague yet burning rage pulsing through its alien brain. It saw, in this man's hostility, the danger to its purpose, a suspicious mind, questioning its every action. The creature's throat thickened and drooled forth a snarl of feral hate.

"Yes," it snapped from its human mouth. "I hear!"

With a single lunge, it was on its feet. All in one incredibly swift movement, it reached across the table, caught Progue's shirt where it bulged open at his great neck—and jerked!

The Dutchman bellowed his fury, as that steel strength tore him clear off the floor, smashed his body across the table, and flung him in a single, sweeping motion headfirst out of the door.

Half a dozen dishes clattered to the cement floor, but they were made of tough clay and none broke.

A man said in an awed voice: "He may be weak-minded, but now I can understand how he could swim maybe miles."

Amid dead silence, then, the creature sat down, and began to eat again. Its brain was swirling with the murderous desire to leap after the stunned man and tear him to bits. With a horrible effort, it controlled that wild and flaming lust. It recognized that it had made a good impression on these hard men.

To Corliss, the silence was a weighted thing. The yellow-orange light that flooded from the lamps which hung down from the ceiling did queer, ghastly things to the strained faces around the rough table. It was only with half his mind that he noticed the light of dawn was trickling through the window at his left, spilling in a dingy pool on the floor.

From outside came the scraping sound of Progue furiously picking himself off the packed dirt. It was an angry noise, fraught with a sense of violence, the rage of a violent, unruly nature frenzied by humiliation. And yet, Corliss knew, the big Dutchman was unpredictable. Anything could happen.

Briefly, Corliss held his breath, as Progue's scowling face peered in at the door. Then the man came in, his whole great body towering there. Corliss said sharply, his voice deep with command:

"Progue, don't start anything if you want to keep my respect."

The Dutchman flashed a terrible look at him, his face dark and glowering: "I'm starting nothing. I had that coming to me. But I still don't like his eyes. That's all."

He went around the table; and it was odd, Corliss thought, that in spite of the ease with which the stranger had handled him, the big man had lost none of the respect of the others. There was no feeling that Progue had backed down from fear, for it was only too obvious that fear was not in him.

He grunted into his chair and began to shovel food into his mouth at a mad pace. Corliss echoed the sigh that went up from the men—an audible noise like a faint hiss. He had had visions of a cook shack smashed to a shambles.

One of the men—the swarthy Frenchman, Perratin—said hastily, and the very haste suggested that he was as much anxious to ease the tense atmosphere as to say what he had to say:

"Boss, I think a couple of us ought to go see if that monster we saw yesterday has come to the surface yet. I'll absolutely swear, and *le bon Dieu* be my witness, that I got him right between the eyes."

"Monster!" a tall, thin-faced, thin-bodied man exclaimed from the end of the table. "What's all this?"

"Seen from boat number two!" Corliss explained succinctly. "Perratin was telling me about it last night, but I was rather sleepy. Something about a big creature with flippers like a devilfish."

"*Sacré du Nom!*" cried Perratin. "The devilfish is a harmless baby compared to this fellow. He was all gray-blue, hard to see, I mean, and had a shark's head and tail, both long and vicious—" He broke off abruptly. "What's the matter with you, Brains? The way your eyes are goggling means you've seen one of these before."

"Not seen, but heard of!" the tall, thin-bodied Englishman said slowly.

There was something so queer in the way he spoke that Corliss looked at him sharply. He had a deep respect for Brains Stapley. The man was reputed to be a university graduate; his past was a mystery, but that was nothing unusual; everyone in the room had a past of some kind.

Stapley went on: "You may not realize it, Perratin, but what you're describing is the natural form of the mythical shark god. I never thought to hear of such a thing actually existing—"

"For Heaven's sake," somebody cut in, "are we gonna listen to a bunch of native superstitions? Go on, Perratin."

Perratin looked at the thin-bodied Stapley with the quiet respect that he and some of the others had for the man; then, as Stapley was silent, apparently lost in thought, he said:

"It was Denton who saw him first. You tell 'em, Denton."

Denton was a smallish man with lively black eyes and a quick, jerky voice. He took up the refrain in his choppy way:

"Like Perratin said, Corliss, we were sittin' there in the boat, the big chunk of meat bait dangling well into the water. We had to take the dark meat yesterday, you know, and you know how scary sharks act with the dark stuff. Well, that's the way it was. They just cruised around, almost mad with the smell of the meat, but scared because it was dark. I guess there were fifteen of 'em when I saw the flash in the water—and this creature came up.

"He wasn't alone, either. Had a bunch of hammerheads with him— biggest, most dangerous-looking sharks I've ever laid eyes on. Great, big, long fellows, with those wicked heads, you know, and torpedo bodies— we shot a couple of 'em, so you saw 'em, too. Anyway, this big flipper fellow was swimming in the center of 'em like a king.

"Well, there was nothing really surprising about that. We've seen swordfish cruising around with sharks, and all kinds of sharks hanging around together, just as if they knew they was related; though, come to think of it, I've never seen a devilfish with sharks; and the devilfish belongs to the shark family.

"Anyway, there he was, big as life. He stopped and looked at that bait we had in the water; and then, just as if to say, 'What are you fellows scared of?' he just dived right at it, and that was that. The whole pack made a beeline for the meat and starts chawing away like merry hell—just what we'd been waitin' for."

Corliss noticed that the stranger was staring at Denton with an intent, fascinated stare. For the briefest moment, he understood Progue's repelled feeling at the man's eyes. He fought the emotion down and said:

"Denton means that we've found, once sharks attack, they lose all fear, no matter how many of their fellows are killed thereafter. Our whole industry here—we want their amazingly tough hides—is built on that fact."

The stranger looked at him, as if to indicate that he understood.

Denton went on: "Well, that's what happened. As soon as the water stopped boiling from their movements, we started picking them off with—"

Perratin broke in eagerly: "It was then I noticed the big fellow had moved off to one side and was just watching us—that's the way it looked to me, anyway. I tell you he just lay there, his eyes cold and hard and calm —and he watched what we were doing; so I let him have it right between the eyes. He jumped like a mule that's been stung, and then dropped into the depths like a lead weight.

"I tell you I got him, boss, and he'll be floating on the surface by now; a couple of us ought to go out and tow him in."

"Hm-m-m!" frowned Corliss, his strong, tanned face dark with thought. "We can't really spare more than one man. You'd have to take the small boat."

The creature was quivering, a deep, internal throb of unutterable ferocity, as it stared at Perratin. This was the man who had fired the weapon that had struck it such a staggering blow. Its every nerve shrank in brief, horrible memory of the stunning pain of that one smash in the head. Its mind soared with the awful hunger of rage to leap at the man. Only by sheer physical effort did it fight down that ravening eagerness, and it said in a thin voice:

"I'll be only too glad to go along and help him. I might as well be earning what I eat here. I can help in any of the physical work."

"Why, thanks!" said Corliss, and he hoped that Progue felt properly ashamed of his suspicions of the stranger, after such a good-will offer. "And, incidentally, seeing as we can't find out your real name, we'll call you Jones. Now, let's get going. Hard day ahead!"

As the thing followed the men into the muggy gloom of early dawn, it thought rapaciously: "It's easier than I expected!" And it retched a little from the flaming fever of its desire. Its steel muscles vibrated tautly with hellish glee at the very idea of what was going to happen to the man when the two of them were alone in the small boat.

Shaking with the pure, unadulterated passion of its blood hunger, it followed the men—followed them over the spongy grass, through a dim shadowland toward where a projection of land jutted out into the gray waters of the lagoon. A building loomed there, a long, low bulk that dissolved itself presently into a one-story wooden structure with a platform running out into the water.

From this building, there came a stench. As the first wave of that incredible, piercing smell struck the thing, it stopped short. Dead shark! The tart odor of decaying fish. The thing started dizzily forward again. Its brain was whirling with a mad surge of flaming thoughts, and as that stink grew stronger and stronger, that unwholesome stream of thoughts grew wilder and more violent with each passing moment.

It stared at the men's backs with hot, glittering eyes, fighting the devil impulse to leap at the nearest man and sink razor-sharp teeth into his soft neck, and then slash at the next man with a ferocious, murder strength, tearing him to bits before the others could even realize what was going on.

And when they did realize—the monster's lips parted in a silent snarl of inhuman hate. For a bare instant, it almost succumbed to the fury of its lust to kill; it throbbed in every nerve with horrible fascination at the thought of smashing in among the men and ripping the life from each weak body.

Surging memory stopped that insane impulse. Remembrance that its body, too, was human now, and correspondingly weak. An attack against these hard, experienced men would be pure suicide at this stage.

With a start, the thing saw that Perratin had fallen back level with it. He was saying: "You and me go this way, Jones. That's a good name, Jones is. Covers up a lot—like Perratin! Anyway, you and me take this little boat here. We've got a hard row ahead of us. We'll just cruise straight west. That's the best way to get out, too. Some pretty dangerous rock splits the lagoon into several sections; we'll have to edge along the shore for a ways to get by them, and then out through the break in the breakers that surround the island. Ha, that's funny, isn't it? Break in the breakers! Get it, Jones?"

Funny!—thought the thing. Funny! What was funny, and why? It wondered if it was supposed to make some answer to what was obviously at least half a question. It grew tense with the thought that, if it did not answer, this man might become suspicious—just now when he was walking into a trap. Slowly, the creature relaxed, as the swarthy little man put the oars in the boat and cried:

"Get in! Get in!"

Out in the water, it was still dark, but the waves were turning a strangely beautiful blue shade, as the dawn crept forward toward sunrise, and the eastern sky grew brighter and brighter until the whole horizon was a dazzle of brilliance.

Abruptly, the first blaze of sun sparkled across the waters, and Perratin said:

"How about you takin' the oars for a while? Two hours is a long row for one guy!"

As they crowded past each other in the narrow confines of the boat, the thing thought with burning intensity: "Now!"

Then it paused. They were too close to the island. The island lay behind them on its bed of water, glistening like an emerald in a platinum setting, with the sun directly behind it. The whole world of ocean was a shining, gorgeous spectacle, dominated by that ball of red fire resting its full circle now on the heaving horizon of water.

Perratin exclaimed: *"Mon Dieu,* but there are a lot of sharks around! I've seen two dozen in the last two minutes. The men should have come out this way again today."

He fingered the long gun he held. "Maybe I ought to ping a few, and we could tow 'em in. I got plenty of rope."

A surging shock stabbed through the monster, as it realized the man had a gun. Swift alarm burned along its alien nerves. The gun made a difference. A damnable difference! The thing was conscious of a brief wave of fury that it had so readily taken over the oars, leaving the man's hands free. Somehow, their present positions dimmed the certainty of the man being easy prey.

The sun was hours higher in the sky, the island a dark spot on that living waste of water, when Perratin said:

"Should be about here. Keep your eyes peeled, Jones. If those blasted sharks haven't eaten it. Hey, you're shaking the boat!"

His voice, shrill with anxiety, seemed to come from a great distance. And his body, too, seemed farther away, isolated there at the rear of the boat. Yet the thing could see everything with preternatural clearness.

The swarthy face of the little, thick-built man, cheeks grown strangely pale under their sunburn, eyes wide and wild. Arms and hands tensed, but still holding the gun.

"What the devil you trying to do? This place is alive with sharks. *Sacré du Nom,* say something, and quit staring with those horrible eyes. I—"

He dropped the gun and grabbed wildly at the gunwale. With a snarl, the creature launched at him, and in one swift jerk of irresistible muscles threw him overboard. There was a boiling of movement, as long, dark bodies shaped like cigars darted up from the depths. Blood mingled with the blue waters, and the thing picked up the oars.

It was shaking in every nerve with horrible excitement, a burning sense of satisfaction. But now—there were explanations to think of. Cold with thoughtful speculation, it rowed toward where the island lay slumbering in the warm brilliance of the peaceful morning sun.

It got back to the island too soon! The sun hung in midsky over a silent, deserted land. The cook was around somewhere, but no noises came from him. The boats of the men were beyond vision, beyond the blue watery horizon that quivered ever so gently against the background of blue haze of sky.

It was the waiting that was hard. The seconds and minutes of the eternity of the afternoon dragged their deadly course. The thing walked along the shore, tensely; it lay restlessly in the lush green grass under the cool of the palm trees, and in every moment of every hour its mind was fuming with a mad chaos of plans, of wild emotion tides turgid with murder lust, and of a ceaseless, anxious mental reiteration of the explanation it had prepared.

Once, it heard a clatter of dishes from the cook's shack. Its pulses leaped, and its first deadly desire was to rush over and destroy him. But cunning stopped that surging thrust of ferine eagerness. It would go over, instead, and try its story on him—but it dismissed that plan, too, as useless.

At last, the men came, their boats pulling long rows of dead sharks. The creature watched with glowing, remorseless eyes, its body so tortured by fury that for a crazy moment it wanted only to leap down on the boat and smash the men to death with battering blows.

And then Corliss was climbing out of the boat, and the thing heard itself saying something in a choked voice, and Corliss was exclaiming incredulously:

"Attacked you! The flipper thing attacked the boat and killed Perratin!"

Corliss was vaguely aware of the other men hurrying up from the boats muttering questions. The sun, low in the western sky, speared slanting rays into his eyes; and he kept squinting them, as he stood there on the wooden, makeshift dock. Instinctively, his feet planted apart, as if he had to brace his body against a stunning blow. He stared at the lean, dark face of the stranger with its queer eyes, rugged line of powerful jaw and aquiline features; and a curious chill followed an abnormal path up his spinal column, lodging finally like a cake of ice in his brain.

It wasn't the death. He had seen death before, horrible death, and heard of things that had happened to men he knew; mind-shaking things. And always he had felt that some day the laws of chance would write an agonizing conclusion to his own life. More than once he had felt the thrill touch, when it seemed as if that some day had come.

No, it wasn't the death. It was the sense of unreality, of stark disbelief, of slow, sick distrust of this—this Jones, that grew and grew until it was a dry ache within him. His voice, when he forced himself to speak again, sounded harsh and rasping to his own ears:

"Why didn't Perratin shoot the damned beast? A couple of bullets could have—"

"He did shoot!" the creature said hurriedly, adjusting its mind to this new twist. It hadn't thought again of the gun until this moment, but if Corliss wanted Perratin to have fired a gun, then he could have that, too. It went on swiftly: "But we didn't have a chance. The monster just struck the boat so hard that Perratin was knocked out. I tried to pull him in, but I was far too late. The creature pulled Perratin under, and I was so scared that it might come at the boat again that I grabbed the oars and pulled for the island. The cook will tell you I arrived about noon."

* * *

From behind Corliss, Progue uttered a jarring laugh, a deep, mirthless guffaw that split the late-afternoon air. He said:

"Of all the weak stories I've ever heard, the ones this guy pulls are lousiest. I tell you, Corliss, there's something damn funny when, the first time this here stranger goes out with one of our men, there's a murder. Yeah, I said murder!"

Corliss stared at the big Dutchman, and for a moment it seemed to him his own face must have looked very like Progue's: dark and grim and suspicious. And then—it was odd how Progue, putting into words the very thoughts that were in his own mind, made him realize how mad and preposterous the very idea of such a thing was. Murder! Utterly ridiculous!

"Progue," Corliss snapped, "you've got to learn to control your tongue! The thing is absolutely absurd."

The thing looked at the Dutchman, its body stiff. Strangely, its only emotion was egotistical consciousness of its control of the situation; the feeling was so strong that, for the moment, it was incapable even of anger. It said: "I don't want to quarrel with you, and I realize it looks bad, what happened, but just remember we were going out after what Perratin himself described as a new and dangerous type of shark. And why should I want to murder a perfect stranger. I—"

Its voice trailed off, for Progue had turned away and was staring down at the rowboat it and Perratin had used. The boat was moored to the end of the dock, and Progue just stood there, looking down at it. Suddenly, he jumped down into the boat, and the thing held its breath as the Dutchman stooped out of its sight beyond the edge of the dock. Its impulse was to run forward and see what the man was doing, but it didn't dare.

Corliss was saying: "That's right, Progue. You're altogether too damn free with your accusations. What possible motives could—"

The creature heard no more. Its brain was a black swirl of chaos as it stared aghast at Progue. The Dutchman had straightened, and in his hands he held Perratin's shining rifle. He had taken something from the gun, a glittery metal thing that shone in his hands; he said softly:

"How many bullets did you say Perratin fired?"

A strange blur of horror swirled through the thing's mind. It knew there must be meaning to such a question, for there was meaning to the hard, expectant expression on the tough, muscular face of the Dutchman. A trap! But what, how? It stammered:

"Why . . . two . . . three." With a dreadful effort, it caught itself. "I mean two. Yes, two! Then the flipper fish hit the boat, and Perratin dropped the gun and—"

It stopped! It stopped because Progue was smiling, a dangerous, nasty, triumphant, sneering smile. His voice came, a deep, liquid, caressing sound:

"Then how come that not one bullet in the clip of this automatic rifle has been fired? Explain that, Mr. Clever Stranger Jones—" His voice exploded abruptly into a burst of rage: "You damned murderer!"

It was strange the way the comforting world of the island seemed suddenly to fade away into remoteness. To Corliss, the effect was utterly curious and grim, ultimately cold and unpleasant, as if the little group of men seemed abruptly to be, not on the island at all, but on that bare, wooden, unprotected platform in the middle of a vast, unfriendly sea. The sickening sensation was heightened by the way the long, low-built building blotted out the green security of the island. Only the shaking shadows of darkening water remained on all sides; and into his brain pulsed the indescribable melancholy of its ceaseless, insistent lapping against the wooden girders that held up the platform.

It didn't make sense, what Progue had said. The big body of the Dutchman towered before him, and on the man's face was the tigerish smile of certainty, grim and unyielding. For a moment, then, in his mind's eye, Corliss saw the horror of the swarthy little Frenchman, Perratin, being ripped to pieces by an armored monster of the deep. But the rest didn't make sense. He jerked out:

"You're crazy, Progue. Why, in the name of all the gods of this ocean, should Jones kill any of us?"

The thing's whirling mind snatched ravenously at the refuge offered by those words. It asked, in bewilderment:

"A clip! I don't know what you mean!"

The Dutchman's beefy face thrust forward until it was only about a foot from the thing's lean, hard, puzzled face.

"Yaah!" he snarled. "That's exactly what caught you—not knowing what an automatic rifle was. Well, it has a clip in it, a clip of bullets—twenty-five, this one's got, and not one of 'em's been fired."

The full force of the trap into which it had thrust itself closed like steel jaws on the creature's mind. But now the danger was here, uncertainty and confusion fell away from its brain. Caution remained, and a raging chagrin; it spat in an ugly voice:

"I don't know how it happened, but it did. He fired two shots, and if you can't think of how he could have done it, I can't help you. I repeat, what reason could I have for killing anybody here? I—"

"I think I can explain this business." The tall, thin body of Brains Stapley forced itself to the front of the body of men who stood there in grim silence. "Suppose Perratin did fire twice—with the two bullets that remained from his last clip. Before he could more than insert another clip, it was too late. Jones could have been so excited that he didn't even notice what Perratin was doing."

"Jones ain't the excitable type!" Progue grunted, yet there was a grudging acceptance of the explanation in his voice.

"But there's something else not so easily explained." Stapley went on in a stiff voice. "Considering that a shark can travel up to seventy miles an hour, it isn't possible that they found this creature in approximately the same place as yesterday. In other words, Jones is lying when he says they saw the creature, unless—"

He hesitated, and Corliss broke in: "Unless what?"

Brains still hesitated, but at last he said almost reluctantly: "I'm back on my subject, the shark god!"

He went on hastily, before anybody could speak: "Don't say it's far-fetched. I know it. But we've all been in the South Seas for years, and we've all seen inexplicable things. Our minds have taken curious, irrational twists in that period. I know that, according to the scientific outlook, I've become a superstitious yokel, but I've reached the point where I question that verdict. I think in reality I've become attuned to the mystery that's here. I can see things, feel things, *know* things that have no meaning for the westerner.

"For years now, I've been in lonely places, listening to the tide whisper against a hundred remote shores. I've watched the southern moon, and been saturated with a sense of the timelessness of this world of water; the primeval, incredible timelessness of it.

"We white men have come here in our boisterous way, and we've brought motor-driven ships, and we've built cities on the edge of the water. Unreal cities! They suggest time in the midst of the timeless, and you know that they're not here to stay. Some day, there'll be no white men in this part of the world; there'll only be the islands and the men of the islands, the sea and the things of the sea.

"Here's what I'm getting at: I've sat around native fires and listened to the old, old stories of the shark gods, and of the form of the shark god when he was in the water. It fitted; I tell you, Corliss, it fitted with this creature that Perratin described. At first, it just struck me as curious that there actually could be a shark of that description. And then I began to think about it, and the more I thought about it, the more alarmed I became.

"Because, you see, a shark god can take the form of a man. And there really isn't any other explanation of a man coming to this island, a thousand hopeless miles from the nearest port. Jones is—"

A deep, disgusted voice interrupted him—to Corliss' amazement, Progue's voice, biting, sharp with sarcasm: "Of all the damned crazy, superstitious junk! Brains, you'd better go soak your head. I still don't like this guy's manner; I don't like his eyes; I don't like anything about him. But when the day comes that I swallow that kind of rot—"

"You can both stop talkin'," said the little Englishman, Denton. Corliss saw that the man had moved to the edge of the building, from where the island was partly visible. "If you'll come here, and see what I see, you'll both quit spoutin' rot. There's a native in a canoe, and he's already inside the breakers, coming along the shore toward us. He's proof that Jones could have come in a boat."

The native was a splendid young man in his prime, brown-skinned, handsome, magnificently muscled. As he came forward from where he had drawn his canoe up onto the shore, rocky at the point, he was grinning with the easy good nature of a friendly man of the islands in the presence of white men. Corliss grinned in return, but when he spoke it was to Progue and to the thing:

"Denton's right—and Jones, believe me, I'm sorry for all the trouble we've been making for you."

The thing acknowledged the apology with a slight nod of its head. But there was no relaxing of its body or mind. It stared at the approaching native with every muscle tensed, conscious of a cold dismay as it remembered that those men of the islands had within them the special sense.

Almost sick with anxiety, it half turned away, as the native stopped a few feet from Corliss. Partly concealed by the little group of men, it knelt and fumbled with the shoelace of one shoe. It heard Corliss say in one of the island dialects:

"And what brings you here, friend?"

The young man answered in the low, musical voice of his people: "A storm comes, white man, and I was far out to sea. The storm approaches from the direction of my own land, so I have come seeking refuge where it is to be found. I—"

His voice trailed off curiously, and Corliss saw that the native was staring with widening eyes at Jones. "Hello," the leader said, "do you know him?"

The thing rose to its feet, like a tiger at bay; there was a swift, ruthless, unconquerable ferocity in the chill gaze with which it bored into the brown man's eyes. The incredible fury hate in that icy fish brain bridged the gap between the native and the creature. The man opened his mouth, tried to speak, licked dry lips, and then turned blindly and started to run back toward his boat.

"What the devil!" Corliss ejaculated. "Hey, come back here."

The native did not even look around. At top speed, he reached his boat. All in one movement, he jerked it into the water and leaped into it. And in the gathering gloom of falling night began to paddle with a furious disregard of danger along the devious path of deep water that wound in and out among the rocks that made the lagoon at this point a trap for the unwary.

Corliss snapped: "Progue, take the rest of the men and get those dead sharks into the warehouse!" He raised his voice in a shrill shout: "Hey, you fool! You can't go out in that storm. We'll protect you!"

The native must have heard. But in the darkness it was impossible to see whether he so much as looked back. Corliss whirled on the thing, his face hard with suspicion.

"That was rather obvious," he said coldly. "The man knew you. That means you're from his island or from around there. He's afraid of you, so extraordinarily afraid that he immediately thought that he had fallen in with your gang. Progue was quite right. You're a tough customer. Well, let me warn you! We're the toughest outfit you've ever run across. You'll never be alone with one of us again, though I must admit that I still don't believe you killed Perratin. It doesn't make sense. As soon as this storm is over, we'll take you to the islands and find out what all this is about."

Abruptly, he walked away. But the thing was scarcely aware, except that he was gone. It was thinking flamingly: "The man of the islands will be driven back this way by the storm. He will remember what Corliss said about protecting him, and will remember that white men, too, are strong. In his terror, he will expose me. There is only one thing to do!"

It was darker now, and the native was barely visible in the dusk that was pressing down upon the island and the water. The thing walked swiftly to where a gill of turgid water cascaded down into the lagoon. The lagoon was deep here, sinking straight from the rock shore. The thing was so intent on the shark that swirled up in a rush of boiling water that the swirl and the noise of the tiny waterfall drowned out the approach of Corliss. Suddenly, with a gasp, it twisted on its heel; and there was Corliss, a few feet away, staring down at the black waters.

Corliss couldn't have explained the impulse that had made him turn and follow the thing. It was partly interest in watching the native, and then the movement in the water where Jones had gone, and the way Jones was bending toward the water.

A needle of horror pierced him now as he saw, by the light of day that remained, a long, dark, vicious shape, a torpedolike body that plunged into the shadows below and vanished. Abruptly, he glanced up at the thing, conscious of deadly danger.

The thing stood very still for a moment, glaring back at him. They were alone there, at the edge of the sea; and its every muscle grew taut and electric with the murder determination to drag this big, grim man into the water. It half crouched, to make one overpowering spring, when it caught the glint of metal in Corliss' hand, and its unholy desire evaporated like mist in sunlight before that weapon of death.

Corliss was saying: "By Heaven, that was a shark, and you were talking to it! I must be going crazy—"

"You are crazy!" the thing gasped. "I saw the shark and I drove it away. If the storm's over by morning, I want to take a swim here, and I don't want any sharks around. Get those ideas out of your head. I—"

It was interrupted by a shriek for help, a horrible, high-pitched sound that quivered on the dim, twilight air like a very devil's scream of agonized fear. It came from out over the water, where the native was a dim shape against the background of black water and dark, moonless sky. It was a sound that made Corliss' blood run cold.

The world of lowering darkness pressed down upon Corliss like an enveloping blanket, weighted yet without warmth. There, a few feet away, was—Jones—a lean, hard-built man with cold, inhuman eyes that glowed vaguely in the quarter light of approaching night. The sense that this ruthless-looking stranger might attack him was so strong that Corliss gripped his revolver with tight fingers, and for a moment dared no more than send one glance out toward the southwest, where the native was a blur on the black water.

Instinctively, he backed away from the water's edge, and from the stranger—and looked again out over that ebony sea. The native seemed to be fighting something that was attacking him from the water, striking at it with his oar, up and down, up and down, desperately, hopelessly. Three times, while Corliss looked, the man grasped at the gunwale of his canoe and simply hung on, trying to keep his tiny craft from turning over. With a rush, Corliss turned his gaze back to the thing, motioned menacingly with his weapon.

"Get going—ahead of me!" He raised his voice, a deep-bellowed command for the men on the wharf: "Hey, Progue, quick! Get the launch ready, start the engine! We've got to go after that native—and a couple of you come out here, give me a hand!"

Two men approached after a moment, and Corliss recognized Denton and a man called Tareyton, a blunt-nosed, blunt-minded American. Corliss snapped:

"Take this guy to the bunkhouse and keep him under guard till I get back. Denton, here's my gun!"

He thrust the weapon into the tough little Englishman's fingers, and the last thing he heard, as he sped off at a run, was Denton's harsh voice snarling: "Get a move on, you!"

The boat engine was throbbing as Corliss leaped aboard, and, under Progue's guiding fingers, moved away from the wharf immediately. Gasping, Corliss flung himself down beside Progue, who was at the steering wheel. The big Dutchman turned a dark, humorless face toward him.

"We're fools to risk those rocks in this darkness!"

Corliss ground out: "We've got to save that native from whatever is attacking him—to find out why he was so desperately afraid of Jones. I tell you, Progue, it's the most important thing in our lives right now."

It wasn't exactly dark. The beam of the motor launch's searchlight blazed a path along the black waters. Corliss watched tensely as the launch began at dead-slow pace to wind in and out along the rock-lined valley of deep water that was the only outlet to the larger, deeper part of the lagoon, where it was too dark now to see the native—too dark because of the black, ugly clouds that swam up out of the horizon and billowed monstrously over the night sky.

Abruptly, a sickening jar! The boat reeled, and Corliss was flung stunningly for several feet. Dizzily, he clawed for a hold, grabbed a brace pole of the steering gear, and pulled himself back. The boat was still tilting sharply, the motor screaming with speed, and then, somehow, they were going on again.

Corliss gasped: "We struck a rock!"

He waited for the rush of water that would drag them into the black depths. Progue's voice came to him, deep-toned, puzzled, alarmed. "It wasn't a rock. We've been out of the shallows for more than a minute. We're in deep water. I thought for a second we might have run into that native's canoe, but I would have seen it first!"

Corliss relaxed—and was flung with a jar that jerked him painfully against the gunwale. He clutched frantically, dizzily for support; and then his blurring vision saw that the launch was keeling over at a dismaying angle. With a shout, he clawed in the other direction, throwing his weight desperately to re-establish the balance. Alone, he couldn't have done it. He realized that and thanked his gods for the insight that had made him select hard-bitten, quick-witted men for his sharking crews—men who, like himself, had faced deadly danger in all its forms and needed no leader to tell them what to do in an emergency. As one man, they, too, flung their weight into that desperate balance.

And once again the boat righted itself and plowed on.

"Slow down!" Corliss yelled hoarsely. "And turn that searchlight into the water. We've got to see where we are."

Somebody manipulated the searchlight mechanism; the beam flashed down into the waters of the lagoon. For a moment, it sparkled and reflected so brilliantly that Corliss was dazzled. And then—

Then he flinched. Never in all his born days would he forget the horror, the spine-chilling terror of the nightmare shapes that turned and twisted, wriggled and churned in the nocturnal gloom below.

In that lurid spray of light, the water showed alive with sharks. Massive, twisting, writhing bodies, glittering triangular fins. Hundreds of long, vicious, torpedo shapes. *Thousands!*

Even as he stared with distended eyes, he realized that somewhere out there was the torn and tattered body of the native. Corliss felt the launch reel like a sick and living thing as it struck a wall of the giant fish. He saw the towering Dutchman twist the wheel like a flash, and dizzily the boat turned and righted itself.

"Back!" Corliss thundered. "Back for our lives! Head for the beach! Beach the boat on the sand! They're trying to turn us over!"

The water swirled and boiled; the motor snarled with power; the boat shuddered and squealed in every thin, hard plank, and overhead the reaching blackness of clouds swelled malignantly over the farthest sky. The first blast of wind, like a blow from a sledge hammer, spewed water at them as they frantically dragged the boat onto the upper heights of the sandy beach. Corliss shouted:

"We've got to hurry, hurry! Grab the loose stuff and head for the bunkhouse at top speed. We left Denton and Tareyton alone with the devil himself. They haven't a chance because they don't know what they're up against."

A solid sheet of rain struck his face and body, and nearly knocked him to the ground before he could turn his back to it. The rain and the wind lashed their backs with whiplike savagery as they ran, a long, thin line of men, desperately striving to escape that hell of raging storm.

The howling of the wind outside came to the thing as it sat with stiffened muscles and taut nerves in the bunkhouse. To its straining, infuriated senses, bent only on escape, the dim world of wooden bunks was an unreal, fantastic place. Weird yellow shadows flickered on the walls as the yellow light from the lamps that hung down from the ceiling waxed and waned in the raging drafts that squeezed through the cracks in the walls of the poorly constructed building.

And then the rain came, a battering roar of it that threatened to smash the very roof above them. But the roof, at least, was snugly built, and no leaks started. The seeking, frenzied mind of the creature flashed from the thought of the storm to the men who were out in that hideous tempest— who must be coming toward the cabin by now—if they had escaped. It felt no real hope that they had not escaped the peril of the water monsters.

That thought, too, was smashed aside; and, once again, the whole abnormal power of the thing's mind concentrated on the two men who stood between it and safety, two men who must die within two minutes, if the escape was to be made before Corliss and the others returned.

Two minutes! The monster turned its chill gaze on the two men appraising for the hundredth time in less than half an hour the situation they created.

The man Denton sat on the edge of his bunk, small, chunkily built, inordinately nervous, shifting his feet, twisting his body, his fingers manipulating with ceaseless energy the glinting revolver he held. He caught the measured gaze of the thing and stiffened; the words that barked from his lips only confirmed the creature in its opinion of the grim capabilities of this little Englishman.

"Yeah!" the man snapped. "There's a look in your eyes that says you want to start something. Well, don't! I've been around these seas for twenty years, and believe me I've handled tough customers in my time. I don't have to be told you've got the strength to tear me apart—I saw you handle Progue this morning and I know what you can do—but just remember this little piece of steel cuts you right down to my size."

He waved the revolver with an easy confidence, and the thing thought tensely: "If I changed to my true shape, I could kill him in spite of the gun, but I couldn't change back again and couldn't get out of this cabin. I'd be trapped!"

It grew aware that the American was speaking. "What Denton said goes double for me, see! There ain't nuthin' I ain't done in my time, an' to my way of thinkin' Perratin was a damn good fellow, and I don't like the way he died. I'm just achin' for you to start somethin' so Denton here— an' me—can watch the lead tearin' into your brain. You know, Denton" —he half turned, his brown eyes gleaming, his flattened nose dilating— "why not just make a target outa him, and tell Corliss he tried to escape?"

"Naw!" Denton shook his head. "Corliss ought to be here any minute with the gang. Besides, I don't go for straight murder."

"Bah!" Tareyton grunted ferociously. " 'Tain't murder to kill a murderer!"

The thing watched Denton uneasily. He had the revolver, and nothing else mattered. It said, with a horrible effort at casualness:

"You men must be fools, or cowards. Here we are, all of us, on an island. There's no way for any of us to get off. If I leave this cabin, I go out into the naked storm—and I'd spend a miserable, rotten night, and in the morning you'd find me, anyway. What're you going to do—sit up and watch me all night?"

"By golly!" snapped Tareyton. "There's an idea. Let's turn him out, lock the door from the inside, and we'll all get some sleep."

The thing's brain leaped high with hope, then sank leadenly as Denton shook his head. "Naw, I wouldn't do that to a mad dog. But what he said gave me an idea." His voice became mocking: "Tareyton, show the gentleman what we're gonna do with him. Take the rope from that nail behind you and tie him up. I'll watch the whole business with this little gun, so there'll be no funny business. Mind that, you, or I'll let you have it."

The thing rasped: "What a fool I'd be to attack Tareyton and have you put a bullet in my back—"

But with horrendous eagerness, it thought: The American would block the gun for one fraction of a second. Even if he didn't, it wouldn't matter. He'd be close, the first time either of them had come close, and that was all that was needed. Neither had the faintest inkling of the strength they faced and—

Now!

With tigerish speed, it leaped at Tareyton. It had a flashing vision of his distorted eyes, mouth gaping to cry out, and then it had ripped him from the floor and flung him, all in one lightning movement, straight at Denton.

The hoarse, startled bellow of Denton mingled with the dismayed, baritone cry of Tareyton in one blended scream of agony, as they smashed together sickeningly and crashed in a contorted heap against the nearest wall.

The thing ached to leap upon them and tear them to bits, but there was no time even to see if they were dead. Already the two minutes of grace were ages past. It was too late—too late for anything but instant flight.

It snatched open the door and bumped with headlong, body-jarring force into Corliss. It was flung back off its balance. And in that moment of dismay it saw the towering Progue beyond the leader. And there were other men crowding forward.

The moment seemed an eternity there in that night of mad storm. The yellow-orange light from inside the bunkhouse did crazy, ghastly things to the faces of the startled men who crouched low against the nightmare blasts of tempest; a jagged spur of lightning showed them the lean, dark, wolfish face of the thing as it struggled to right itself.

Surprise was equal, but the infinitely harder, steelier muscles recovered first. The thing struck at Corliss, one smashing, hate-driven blow that caught him glancingly and sent him staggering back against Progue—and then it was darting out into the night, out into the fury of unrelenting wind and rain.

One assault it made against the wild strength of the storm, head bent, body straining against that ferocious pressure, and then, in a flare of caution, as it realized its slow progress made it an easy target for rifles fired from the bunkhouse, it ceased bucking the wind and, instead, ran with it toward where the waters glinted black in the near east—black and boiling with unholy frenzy of wind-lashed waves.

As it ran, it began to tear off its clothes—shirt, trousers, shoes, stockings—and the men saw it for an instant silhouetted against a spasm of sheet lightning, tall and gleaming naked against the briefly brilliant sky.

They saw it once more after that, a shining, unconquerable shape, as it poised on the rocky brink of the Stygian sea. And then it was gone—a white flash diving into the pounding black waters beyond. Corliss found his voice.

"We've got him!" he bellowed above the shriek of the tempest. "We've got the damn thing where it can't get away."

Before he could speak further, he was swept into the bunkhouse by the tide of men that poured through the open doorway. The door was shut, and it was Progue who breathlessly snapped:

"What the devil do you mean—got him? The damn fool committed suicide. You bet your life it can't get away after that."

Corliss pulled himself together, but when he started to explain, a literal gush of words flooded from him. "I tell you," he finished, "that's proof! Brains was right. That damned thing out there is the shark god in human form—and I tell you we've got him—if we hurry!"

His voice took on a machine-gun quality: "Don't you see? There's no outlet to the sea where he jumped into the lagoon, except through the channel we use for our boats. At one point, that channel hugs the shore, and that's where we've got to stop him from getting to the safety of the open sea. Brains!"

"Yes, sir!" The tall, thin, intellectual-looking Englishman jumped forward briskly.

"Take a half dozen men, get a parcel of dynamite caps from the ammunition shack, take a searchlight, and station yourself on the shore beside the channel. Set off the dynamite at intervals *under* water—no fish or any living thing can stand the blast of sound made by an underwater explosion. Use the searchlight to probe the waters. It's narrow there. You can't and mustn't miss! Hurry!"

After the men were gone, Progue said: "You've forgotten one thing, boss. There *is* an outlet to the sea where that damned thing jumped into the lagoon. Remember the bottleneck of water between two towering stretches of rock. A shark could just slip out there."

Corliss shook his head grimly. "I didn't forget, and you're right—as far as you go. A shark could get out there. But this thing in its natural form has great, powerful flippers. And those flippers are too big for it to go through the narrow hell of water; they'd be torn off, cut to ribbons. Don't you see what that means? The thing has to retain its human form if it wants to go through that neck of deep water to the open sea; and in its human shape, it must be horribly vulnerable, or it wouldn't have been so cautious with us. It—"

A dull *boom* out of the night cut his voice off abruptly. A slow, hard smile of satisfaction twisted his heavy, powerful face.

"There went the first explosion. That may mean the damned thing tried to get through the regular channel. Well, it knows better now. We've got it cornered. Either it takes the risks of swimming that hell's gantlet in human form, or we kill it tomorrow morning, whatever its shape. And now, quick, everybody take torches and rifles and line the shore. It mustn't get ashore!

The sea was too strong, the waves too high, the night too dark! A sense of disaster, cold and deadly, throbbed along the thing's icy fish nerves as it struggled to keep its human body where its thin, helpless knob of human head could breathe air. It fought with bitter, ceaseless strength, but the sea thundered and roared, bellowed and churned.

The nightmare sea was a pressing wall of darkness on every side except one. And that one straight ahead, where the water glittered white—even in this darkness the white fury of the breakers was visible. In that white sea of foam-flecked death showed a single dark ribbon—the one way that was open to the safe, vast ocean beyond; a narrow ribbon of blackness, where the water was deep and twisting and incredibly fast.

And through that storm-frenzied channel, a shark was now pressing outward from the lagoon toward the ocean, showing the way.

The thing struggled to hold itself erect in the water, paddled furiously with its legs, slashed at the boiling, raging water with its arms—and strained its vision to the utmost limit, striving to follow the faint gleam of the flashing dark, triangular fin of the pilot shark as the shark made the test run of that demon channel.

The shark was struggling now, maneuvering frantically as it fought the roaring ferocity of the water that poured and belched through the writhing bottleneck to safety. The fin vanished, and then it was there again, vaguely visible against the gray-white waves.

It was through, safe, a dingy blur of fin that vanished instantly into the blackness of the thunderous ocean beyond.

The thing hesitated. It was its turn now, but there was no eagerness within it to storm those jagged, shaking waters in this frail human body that it wore.

It snarled in frustrated rage, a high, shrill, inhuman cry of unutterable hate—and half turned back to the shore, impelled by a wild, surging desperation to smash its way through the soft-bodied cordon of men, regardless of the danger they represented.

And then it snarled again and spat its ferocity as it saw the line of flaming torches that dotted the shore. Each torch cast a pale, flickering shadow of light even in that hell of rain and tempest, and beside each torch a man paced restlessly, carrying a rifle in alert, nervous fingers.

That way was blocked. The thing realized it even as the mad thoughts of rushing the shore stabbed through its brain. Only too well, now, it saw the trap that held it. This small section of the lagoon was blocked off as completely as if nature had waited through a million million years for this moment, to trap this deadly monster of the deep.

Escape was blocked, except—straight ahead!

Once again, the thing turned its cold, glittering fish eyes toward that deadly outlet. Steely teeth clicked in horrible defiance, lips tightened into a thin, sharkish line—and then it launched itself into those raging waters.

There was a sense of incredible velocity; instinctively it struggled to make a twist that sight of the shark's test run had seared into its mind. Water smashed down into its mouth; it spat, coughed, fought, and then it had a brief vision of dreadful doom—a wall of rock reared up straight ahead, yards high, black, grim, merciless rock. Frantically, it twisted and plunged aside with maddened, reaching arms. But no muscles could fight that irresistible sea.

One glimpse of its doom, one fearless snarl of astounded, unbelieving ferocity, and then a stab of pain unutterable as its human head crushed into a pulp against steel-hard rock. Bones broke, muscles tore, flesh mashed—a tormented body was flung out into the midnight ocean.

The pilot shark smelled the fresh meat and came circling back. In a moment, it was joined by a dozen other dark, struggling shapes.

The storm pounded all through that black night. It was a cold, wet dawn that broke finally over a cold, wet, weary group of men. As Corliss headed the first boat out into the quietened waters of the lagoon, toward that narrow, still-roaring funnel of death, his face was dark with the fatigue of the long vigil, but grim with determination.

"If the thing took the chance," he said, "we'll never find anything. But we'll know. There's an undercurrent where the channel twists that only a big fish could fight. Nothing else could prevent itself being smashed."

"Hey," yelled Denton in alarm, his face still white from the pain he had endured, "don't go too near that place. Tareyton and I have had enough smashing for one day."

It was noon before Corliss was convinced that no dangerous living thing remained in the lagoon. As they headed toward the shore, tired but relieved, the southern sun was sparkling down on an emerald isle that glittered and shone in its vast setting of sapphire ocean.

Sea Curse

Robert E. Howard

And some return by the failing light
And some in the waking dream,
For she hears the heels of the dripping ghosts
That ride the rough roofbeam.
—Kipling

THEY WERE THE BRAWLERS and braggarts, the loud boasters and hard drinkers, of Faring town, John Kulrek and his crony Lie-lip Canool. Many a time have I, a tousled-haired lad, stolen to the tavern door to listen to their curses, their profane arguments and wild sea songs; half fearful and half in admiration of these wild rovers. Aye, all the people of Faring town gazed on them with fear and admiration, for they were not like the rest of the Faring men; they were not content to ply their trade along the coasts and among the shark-teeth shoals. No yawls, no skiffs for them! They fared far, farther than any other man in the village, for they shipped on the great sailing-ships that went out on the white tides to brave the restless grey ocean and make ports in strange land.

Ah, I mind it was swift times in the little sea-coast village of Faring when John Kulrek came home, with the furtive Lie-lip at his side, swaggering down the gang-plank, in his tarry sea-clothes, and the broad leather belt that held his ever-ready dagger; shouting condescending greeting to some favored acquaintance, kissing some maiden who ventured too near; then up the street, roaring some scarcely decent song of the sea. How the cringers and the idlers, the hangers-on, would swarm about the two desperate heroes, flattering and smirking, guffawing hilariously at each nasty jest. For to the tavern loafers and to some of the weaker among the straight-forward villagers, these men with their wild talk and their brutal deeds, their tales of the Seven Seas and the far countries, these men, I say, were valiant knights, nature's noblemen who dared to be men of blood and brawn.

And all feared them, so that when a man was beaten or a woman insulted, the villagers muttered—and did nothing. And so when Moll Farrell's niece was put to shame by John Kulrek, none dared even to put into words what all thought. Moll had never married, and she and the girl lived alone in a little hut down close to the beach, so close that in high tide the waves came almost to the door.

The people of the village accounted old Moll something of a witch, and she was a grim, gaunt old dame who had little to say to anyone. But she minded her own business, and eked out a slim living by gathering clams, and picking up bits of driftwood.

The girl was a pretty, foolish little thing, vain and easily befooled, else she had never yielded to the shark-like blandishments of John Kulrek.

I mind the day was a cold winter day with a sharp breeze out of the east when the old dame came into the village street shrieking that the girl had vanished. All scattered over the beach and back among the bleak inland hills to search for her—all save John Kulrek and his cronies who sat in the tavern dicing and toping. All the while beyond the shoals, we heard the never-ceasing droning of the heaving, restless grey monster, and in the dim light of the ghostly dawn Moll Farrell's girl came home.

The tides bore her gently across the wet sands and laid her almost at her own door. Virgin-white she was, and her arms were folded across her still bosom; calm was her face, and the grey tides sighed about her slender limbs. Moll Farrell's eyes were stones, yet she stood above her dead girl and spoke no word till John Kulrek and his crony came reeling down from the tavern, their drinking-jacks still in their hands. Drunk was John Kulrek, and the people gave back for him, murder in their souls; so he came and laughed at Moll Farrell across the body of her girl.

"Zounds!" swore John Kulrek; "the wench has drowned herself, Lie-lip!"

Lie-lip laughed, with the twist of his thin mouth. He always hated Moll Farrell, for it was she that had given him the name of Lie-lip.

Then John Kulrek lifted his drinking-jack, swaying on his uncertain legs. "A health to the wench's ghost!" he bellowed, while all stood aghast.

Then Moll Farrell spoke, and the words broke from her in a scream which sent ripples of cold up and down the spines of the throng.

"The curse of the Foul Fiend upon you, John Kulrek!" she screamed. "The curse of God rest upon your vile soul throughout eternity! May you gaze on sights that shall sear the eyes of you and scorch the soul of you! May you die a bloody death and writhe in hell's flames for a million and a million and yet a million years! I curse you by sea and by land, by earth and by air, by the demons of the swamplands, the fiends of the forest and the goblins of the hills! And you"—her lean finger stabbed at Lie-lip

Canool and he started backward, his face paling—"you shall be the death of John Kulrek and he shall be the death of you! You shall bring John Kulrek to the doors of hell and John Kulrek shall bring you to the gallows-tree! I set the seal of death upon your brow, John Kulrek! You shall live in terror and die in horror far out upon the cold grey sea! But the sea that took the soul of innocence to her bosom shall not take you, but shall fling forth your vile carcass to the sands! Aye, John Kulrek"—and she spoke with such a terrible intensity that the drunken mockery on the man's face changed to one of swinish stupidity—"the sea roars for the victim it will not keep! There is snow upon the hills, John Kulrek, and ere it melts your corpse will lie at my feet. And I shall spit upon it and be content."

Kulrek and his crony sailed at dawn for a long voyage, and Moll went back to her hut and her clam gathering. She seemed to grow leaner and more grim than ever and her eyes smoldered with a light not sane. The days glided by and people whispered among themselves that Moll's days were numbered, for she faded to a ghost of a woman; but she went her way, refusing all aid.

That was a short, cold summer and the snow on the barren inland hills never melted; a thing very unusual, which caused much comment among the villagers. At dusk and at dawn Moll would come up on the beach, gaze up at the snow which glittered on the hills, then out to sea with a fierce intensity in her gaze.

Then the days grew shorter, the nights longer and darker, and the cold grey tides came sweeping along the bleak strands, bearing the rain and sleet of the sharp east breezes.

And upon a bleak day a trading-vessel sailed into the bay and anchored. And all the idlers and the wastrels flocked to the wharfs, for that was the ship upon which John Kulrek and Lie-Lip Canool had sailed. Down the gang-plank came Lie-lip, more furtive than ever, but John Kulrek was not there.

To shouted queries, Canool shook his head. "Kulrek deserted ship at a port of Sumatra," said he. "He had a row with the skipper, lads; wanted me to desert, too, but no! I had to see you fine lads again, eh, boys?"

Almost cringing was Lie-lip Canool, and suddenly he recoiled as Moll Farrell came through the throng. A moment they stood eyeing each other; then Moll's grim lips bent in a terrible smile.

"There's blood on your hand, Canool!" she lashed out suddenly—so suddenly that Lie-lip started and rubbed his right hand across his left sleeve.

"Stand aside, witch!" he snarled in sudden anger, striding through the crowd which gave back for him. His admirers followed him to the tavern.

* * *

Now, I mind that the next day was even colder; grey fogs came drifting out of the east and veiled the sea and the beaches. There would be no sailing that day, and so all the villagers were in their snug houses or matching tales at the tavern. So it came that Joe, my friend, a lad of my own age, and I, were the ones who saw the first of the strange thing that happened.

Being harum-scarum lads of no wisdom, we were sitting in a small rowboat, floating at the end of the wharfs, each shivering and wishing the other would suggest leaving, there being no reason whatever for our being there, save that it was a good place to build air-castles undisturbed.

Suddenly Joe raised his hand. "Say," he said, "d'ye hear? Who can be out on the bay upon a day like this?"

"Nobody. What d'ye hear?"

"Oars. Or I'm a lubber. Listen."

There was no seeing anything in that fog, and I heard nothing. Yet Joe swore he did, and suddenly his face assumed a strange look.

"Somebody rowing out there, I tell you! The bay is alive with oars from the sound! A score of boats at the least! Ye dolt, can ye not hear?"

Then, as I shook my head, he leaped and began to undo the painter.

"I'm off to see. Name me liar if the bay is not full of boats, all together like a close fleet. Are you with me?"

Yes, I was with him, though I heard nothing. Then out in the greyness we went, and the fog closed behind and before so that we drifted in a vague world of smoke, seeing naught and hearing naught. We were lost in no time, and I cursed Joe for leading us upon a wild goose chase that was like to end with our being swept out to sea. I thought of Moll Farrell's girl and shuddered.

How long we drifted I know not. Minutes faded into hours, hours into centuries. Still Joe swore he heard the oars, now close at hand, now far away, and for hours we followed them, steering our course toward the sound, as the noise grew or receded. This I later thought of, and could not understand.

Then, when my hands were so numb that I could no longer hold the oar, and the forerunning drowsiness of cold and exhaustion was stealing over me, bleak white stars broke through the fog which glided suddenly away, fading like a ghost of smoke, and we found ourselves afloat just outside the mouth of the bay. The waters lay smooth as a pond, all dark green and silver in the starlight, and the cold came crisper than ever. I was swinging the boat about, to put back into the bay, when Joe gave a shout, and for the first time I heard the clack of oar-locks. I glanced over my shoulder and my blood went cold.

A great beaked prow loomed above us, a weird, unfamiliar shape against the stars, and as I caught my breath, sheered sharply and swept by us, with a curious swishing I never heard any other craft make. Joe screamed and backed oars frantically, and the boat walled out of the way just in time; for though the prow missed us, still otherwise we had died. For from the sides of the ship stood long oars, bank upon bank which swept her along. Though I had never seen such a craft, I knew her for a galley. But what was she doing upon our coasts? They said, the far-farers, that such ships were still in use among the heathens of Barbary, but it was many a long, heaving mile to Barbary, and even so she did not resemble the ships described by those who had sailed far.

We started in pursuit, and this was strange, for though the waters broke about her prow, and she seemed fairly to fly through the waves, yet she was making little speed, and it was no time before we caught up with her. Making our painter fast to a chain far back beyond the reach of the swishing oars, we hailed those on deck. But there came no answer, and at last, conquering our fears, we clambered up the chain and found ourselves upon the strangest deck man has trod for many a long, roaring century.

"This is no Barbary rover!" muttered Joe fearsomely. "Look, how old it seems! Almost ready to fall to pieces. Why, 'tis fairly rotten!"

There was no one on deck, no one at the long sweep with which the craft was steered. We stole to the hold and looked down the stair. Then and there, if ever men were on the verge of insanity, it was we. For there were rowers there, it is true; they sat upon the rowers' benches and drove the creaking oars through the grey waters. *And they that rowed were skeletons!*

Shrieking, we plunged across the deck, to fling ourselves into the sea. But at the rail I tripped upon something and fell headlong, and as I lay, I saw a thing which vanquished my fear of the horrors below for an instant. The thing upon which I had tripped was a human body, and in the dim grey light that was beginning to steal across the eastern waves I saw a dagger hilt standing up between his shoulders. Joe was at the rail, urging me to haste, and together we slid down the chain and cut the painter.

Then we stood off into the bay. Straight on kept the grim galley, and we followed, slowly, wondering. She seemed to be heading straight for the beach beside the wharfs, and as we approached, we saw the wharfs thronged with people. They had missed us, no doubt, and now they stood, there in the early dawn light, struck dumb by the apparition which had come up out the night and the grim ocean.

Straight on swept the galley, her oars a-swish; then ere she reached the shallow water—crash!—a terrific reverberation shook the bay. Before our eyes the grim craft seemed to melt away; then she vanished, and the green waters seethed where she had ridden, but there floated no driftwood there, nor did there ever float any ashore. Aye, something floated ashore, but it was grim driftwood!

We made the landing amid a hum of excited conversation that stopped suddenly. Moll Farrell stood before her hut, limned gauntly against the ghostly dawn, her lean hand pointing seaward. And across the sighing wet sands, borne by the grey tide, something came floating; something that the waves dropped at Moll Farrell's feet. And there looked up at us, as we crowded about, a pair of unseeing eyes set in a still, white face. John Kulrek had come home.

Still and grim he lay, rocked by the tide, and as he lurched sideways, all saw the dagger hilt that stood from his back—the dagger all of us had seen a thousand times at the belt of Lie-lip Canool.

"Aye, I killed him!" came Canool's shriek, as he writhed and groveled before our gaze. "At sea on a still night in a drunken brawl I slew him and hurled him overboard! And from the far seas he has followed me"—his voice sank to a hideous whisper—"because—of—the—curse—the—sea—would—not—keep—his—body!"

And the wretch sank down, trembling, the shadow of the gallows already in his eyes.

"Aye!" Strong, deep, and exultant was Moll Farrell's voice. "From the hell of lost craft Satan sent a ship of bygone ages! A ship red with gore and stained with the memory of horrid crimes! None other would bear such a vile carcass! The sea has taken vengeance and has given me mine. See now, how I spit upon the face of John Kulrek."

And with a ghastly laugh, she pitched forward, the blood starting to her lips. And the sun came up across the restless sea.

A Vintage from Atlantis

Clark Ashton Smith

THANK YOU, friend, but I am no drinker of wine, not even if it be the rarest Canary or the oldest Amontillado. Wine is a mocker, strong drink is raging . . . and more than others, I have reason to know the truth that was writ by Solomon the Jewish king. Give ear, if ye will, and I shall tell you a story such as would halt the half-drained cup on the lips of the hardiest bibber.

We were seven-and-thirty buccaneers, who raked the Spanish Main under Barnaby Dwale, he that was called Red Barnaby for the spilling of blood that attended him everywhere. Our ship, the *Black Falcon,* could outfly and outstrike all other craft that flew the Jolly Roger. Full often, Captain Dwale was wont to seek a remote isle on the eastward verge of the West Indies, and lighten the vessel of its weight of ingots and doubloons.

The isle was far from the common course of maritime traffic, and was not known to maps or other mariners; so it suited our purpose well. It was a place of palms and sand and cliffs, with a small harbor sheltered by the curving outstretched arms of rugged reefs, on which the dark ocean climbed and gnashed its fangs of white foam without troubling the tranquil waters beyond. I know not how many times we had visited the isle; but the soil beneath many a coco-tree was heavy with our hidden trove. There we had stored the loot of bullion-laden ships, the massy plate and jewels of cathedral towns.

Even as to all mortal things, an ending came at last to our visits. We had gathered a goodly cargo, but might have stayed longer on the open main where the Spaniards passed, if a tempest had not impended. We were near the secret isle, as it chanced, when the skies began to blacken; and wallowing heavily in the rising seas we fled to placid harbor, reaching it by nightfall. Before dawn the hurricane had blown by; and the sun came up in cloudless amber and blue. We proceeded with the landing and burying of our chests of coin and gems and ingots, which was a task of some length; and afterward we refilled our water-casks at a cool sweet spring that ran from beneath the palmy hill not far inland.

It was now midafternoon. Captain Dwale was planning to weigh anchor shortly and follow the westering sun toward the Caribbees. There were nine of us, loading the last barrels into the boats, with Red Barnaby looking on and cursing us for being slower than mud-turtles; and we were bending knee-deep in the tepid, lazy water, when suddenly the captain ceased to swear, and we saw that he was no longer watching us. He had turned his back and was stooping over a strange object that must have drifted in with the tide, after the storm: a huge and barnacle-laden thing that lay on the sand, half in and half out of the shoaling water. Somehow, none of us had perceived it heretofore.

Red Barnaby was not silent long.

"Come here, ye chancre-eaten coistrels," he called to us. We obeyed willingly enough, and gathered around the beached object, which our captain was examining with much perplexity. We too were greatly bewondered when we saw the thing more closely; and none of us could name it offhand or with certainty.

The object had the form of a great jar, with a tapering neck and a deep, round, abdominous body. It was wholly encrusted with shells and corals that had gathered upon it as if through many ages in the ocean deeps, and was festooned with weeds and sea-flowers such as we had never before beheld; so that we could not determine the substance of which it was made.

At the order of Captain Dwale, we rolled it out of the water and beyond reach of the tide, into the shade of nearby palms; though it required the efforts of four men to move the unwieldy thing, which was strangely ponderous. We found that it would stand easily on end, with its top reaching almost to the shoulders of a tall man. While we were handling the great jar, we heard a swishing noise from within, as if it were filled with some sort of liquor.

Our captain, as it chanced, was a learned man.

"By the communion cup of Satan!" he swore. "If this thing is not an antique wine-jar, then I am a Bedlamite. Such vessels—though mayhap they were not so huge—were employed by the Romans to store the goodly vintages of Falernus and Cecuba. Indeed, there is today a Spanish wine—that Valdepeñas—which is kept in earthen jars. But this, if I mistake not, is neither from Spain nor olden Rome. It is ancient enough, by its look, to have come from that long-sunken isle, the Atlantis whereof Plato speaks. Truly, there should be a rare vintage within, a wine that was mellowed in the youth of the world, before the founding of Rome and Athens; and which, perchance, has gathered fire and strength with the centuries. Ho!

my rascal sea-bullies! We sail not from this harbor till the jar is broached. And if the liquor within be sound and potable, we shall make holiday this evening on the sands."

"Belike, 'tis a funeral urn, full of plaguey cinders and ashes," said the mate, Roger Aglone, who had a gloomy turn of thought.

Red Barnaby had drawn his cutlass and was busily prying away the crust of barnacles and quaint fantastic coral-growths from the top of the jar. Layer on layer of them he removed, and swore mightily at this increment of forgotten years. At last a great stopper of earthenware, sealed with a clear wax that had grown harder than amber, was revealed by his prying. The stopper was graven with queer letters of an unknown language, plainly to be seen; but the wax refused the cutlass-point. So, losing all patience, the captain seized a mighty fragment of stone, which a lesser man could scarce have lifted, and broke therewith the neck of the jar.

Now even in those days, I, Stephen Magbane, the one Puritan amid that Christless crew, was no bibber of wine or spirituous liquors, but a staunch Rechabite on all occasions. Therefore I held back, feeling little concern other than that of reprobation, while the others pressed about the jar and sniffed greedily at the contents. But, almost immediately with its opening, my nostrils were assailed by an odor of heathen spices, heavy and strange; and the very inhalation thereof caused me to feel a sort of giddiness, so that I thought it well to retreat still further. But the others were eager as midges around a fermenting-vat in autumn.

" 'Sblood! 'Tis a royal vintage!" roared the captain, after he had dipped a forefinger in the jar and sucked the purple drops that dripped from it. "Avast, ye slumgullions! Stow the water-casks on board, and summon all hands ashore, leaving only a watch there to ward the vessel. We'll have a gala night before we sack any more Spaniards."

We obeyed his order; and there was much rejoicing amid the crew of the *Black Falcon* at the news of our find and the postponement of the voyage. Three men, grumbling sorely at their absence from the revels, were left on board; though, in that tranquil harbor, such vigilance was virtually needless. We others returned to the shore, bringing a supply of pannikins in which to serve the wine, and provision for a feast. Then we gathered pieces of drift with which to build a great fire, and caught several tortoises along the sands, and unearthed their hidden eggs, so that we might have an abundance and variety of victuals.

In these preparations I took part with no special ardor. Knowing my habit of abstention, and being of a somewhat malicious and tormenting humor, Captain Dwale had expressly commanded my presence at the feast. However, I anticipated nothing more than a little ribaldry at my expense, as was customary at such times; and being partial to fresh tortoise-meat, I was not wholly unresigned to my lot as a witness of the Babylonian inebrieties of the others.

At nightfall, the feasting and drinking began; and the fire of driftwood, with eerie witch-colors of blue and green and white amid the flame, leapt high in the dusk while the sunset died to a handful of red embers far on purpling seas.

It was a strange wine that the crew and captain swilled from their pannikins. I saw that the stuff was thick and dark, as if it had been mingled with blood; and the air was filled with the reek of those pagan spices, hot and rich and unholy, that might have poured from a broken tomb of antique emperors. And stranger still was the intoxication of that wine; for those who drank it became still and thoughtful and sullen; and there was no singing of lewd songs, no playing of apish antics.

Red Barnaby had been drinking longer than the others, having begun to sample the vintage while the crew were making ready for their revel. To our wonderment, he ceased to swear at us after the first cupful, and no longer ordered us about or paid us any heed, but sat peering into the sunset with eyes that held the dazzlement of unknown dreams. And one by one, as they began to drink, the others were likewise affected, so that I marveled much at the unwonted power of the wine. I had never before beheld an intoxication of such nature; for they spoke not nor ate, and moved only to refill their cups from the mighty jar.

The night had grown dark as indigo beyond the flickering fire, and there was no moon; and the firelight blinded the stars. But one by one, after an interval, the drinkers rose from their places and stood staring into the darkness toward the sea. Unquietly they stood, and strained forward, peering intently as men who behold some marvelous thing; and queerly they muttered to one another, with unintelligible words. I knew not why they stared and muttered thus, unless it were because of some madness that had come upon them from the wine; for naught was visible in the dark, and I heard nothing, save the low murmur of wavelets lapping on the sand.

Louder grew the muttering; and some raised their hands and pointed seaward, babbling wildly as if in delirium. Noting their demeanor, and doubtful as to what further turn their madness might take, I bethought me to withdraw along the shore. But when I began to move away, those who were nearest me appeared to waken from their dream, and restrained me with rough hands. Then, with drunken, gibbering words, of which I could make no sense, they held me helpless while one of their number forced me to drink from a pannikin filled with the purple wine.

I fought against them, doubly unwilling to quaff that nameless vintage, and much of it was spilled. The stuff was sweet as liquid honey to the taste, but burned like hell-fire in my throat. I turned giddy; and a sort of dark confusion possessed my senses by degrees; and I seemed to hear and see and feel as in the mounting fever of calenture.

The air about me seemed to brighten, with a redness of ghostly blood that was everywhere; a light that came not from the fire nor from the nocturnal heavens. I beheld the faces and forms of the drinkers, standing without shadow, as if mantled with a rosy phosphorescence. And beyond them, where they stared in troubled and restless wonder, the darkness was illumed with the strange light.

Mad and unholy was the vision that I saw; for the harbor waves no longer lapped on the sand, and the sea had wholly vanished. The *Black Falcon* was gone, and where the reefs had been, great marble walls ascended, flushed as if with the ruby of lost sunsets. Above them were haughty domes of heathen temples, and spires of pagan palaces; and beneath were mighty streets and causeys where people passed in a neverending throng. I thought that I had gazed upon some immemorial city, such as had flourished in Earth's prime; and I saw the trees of its terraced gardens, fairer than the palms of Eden. Listening, I heard the sound of dulcimers that were sweet as the moaning of women; and the cry of horns that told forgotten glorious things; and the wild sweet singing of people who passed to some hidden, sacred festival within the walls.

I saw that the light poured upward from the city, and was born of its streets and buildings. It blinded the heavens above; and the horizon beyond was lost in a shining mist. One building there was, a high fane above the rest, from which the light streamed in a ruddier flood; and from its open portals music came, sorcerous and beguiling as the far voices of bygone years. And the revellers passed gaily into its portals, but none came forth. The weird music seemed to call me and entice me; and I longed to tread the streets of the alien city, and a deep desire was upon me to mingle with its people and pass into the flowing fane.

Verily I knew why the drinkers had stared at the darkness and had muttered among themselves in wonder. I knew that they also longed to descend into the city. And I saw that a great causey, built of marble and gleaming with the red luster, ran downward from their very feet over meadows of unknown blossoms to the foremost buildings.

Then, as I watched and listened, the singing grew sweeter, the music stranger, and the rosy luster brightened. Then, with no backward glance, no word or gesture of injunction to his men, Captain Dwale went slowly forward, treading the marble causey like a dreamer who walks in his dream. And after him, one by one, Roger Aglone and the crew followed in the same manner, going toward the city.

Haply I too should have followed, drawn by the witching music. For truly it seemed that I had trod the ways of that city in former time, and had known the things whereof the music told and the voices sang. Well did I remember why the people passed eternally into the fane, and why they came not forth; and there, it seemed, I should meet familiar and beloved faces, and take part in mysteries recalled from the foundered years.

All this, which the wine had remembered through its sleep in the ocean depths, was mine to behold and conceive for a moment. And well it was that I had drunk less of that evil and pagan vintage than the others, and was less besotted than they with its luring vision. For, even as Captain Dwale and his crew went toward the city, it appeared to me that rosy glow began to fade a little. The walls took on a wavering thinness, and the domes grew insubstantial. The rose departed, the light was pale as a phosphor of the tomb; and the people went to and fro like phantoms, with a thin crying of ghostly horns and a ghostly singing. Dimly above the sunken causey the harbor waves returned; and Red Barnaby and his men walked down beneath them. Slowly the waters darkened above the fading spires and walls; and the midnight blackened upon the sea; and the city was lost like the vanished bubbles of wine.

A terror came upon me, knowing the fate of those others. I fled swiftly, stumbling in darkness toward the palmy hill that crowned the isle. No vestige remained of the rosy light; and the sky was filled with returning stars. And looking oceanward as I climbed the hill, I saw a lantern that burned on the *Black Falcon*—in the harbor, and discerned the embers of our fire that smoldered on the sands. Then, praying with a fearful fervor, I waited for dawn.

Derelict

Hugh B. Cave

SEVEN BELLS. From habit, Bill Stillson reached for the key with his right hand, the starter button with his left, then remembered something and sat back soberly without touching either.

The smoldering cigarette in the porcelain dish (bought in Tocapilla for one American dime) lay neglected, as did his sister's letter and the matchstick darts on the operating table. The grimy deck of cards fanned out in a half-finished game of solitaire seemed somehow sacrilegious, because those cards bore prints of the same thin fingers which should now, but would never again, be batting out a message.

Seven bells. *"Blue Line schedule, Bill."* But there was no schedule to keep now, because Marty Andrews and the Blue Runner were gone. The sea alone knew their fate.

No schedule. But the call was there as always; the tenuous whine of Marty's old spark set rode with the wind's banshee howl at the ports. You *could* come back. So often Marty had done it, or half done it. So often Bill Stillson's phones had been on the last thin verge of tightening to Marty's tell-tale touch.

He groped for the cigarette and sat back in his chair. The eyes that smiled at him from the photograph on the wall were somehow magnetic, holding him motionless when the room's eerie emptiness strove to expel him. They were a little boy's eyes in a little boy's body that contained the heart and soul and courage of a man. Marty Andrews—gone now, yet always returning, never really away.

Bill Stillson swiped aside message blanks, pencils and headphones and strode across the room. The door was hooked open. The fog that licked at his tired face as he veered along the passageway to the bridge deck was a wet, dank shroud smothering the ship, the shadow-shapes upon it, and the viscous black sea swelling beneath. He leaned at the rail and stared vacantly into it, breathing it into eyes, lungs and empty soul. It drove out memories and then mockingly it brought them back.

Brought back Marty Andrews, frail, sickly brass-pounder of the vanished *Blue Runner*. There'd been fog that night, too—fog as thick and strangling as the winding-sheet that enveloped the sea tonight. Pals, Bill and Marty, the one a key-thumper aboard the *Blue Belle* en route to South America out of New York, the other a radio operator of the sister freighter *Blue Runner,* bound north from Tocapilla.

Signals had been good that night. With the *Blue Belle* just southeast of Trinidad, you could hear the bell-clear tones from Tuckerton, the swinging drone of Chatham, the squeaky whistle from the naval station at Norfolk. You could hear your own heart mumbling, hear low-powered stations from both coasts booming in like tons of bricks. A night crystal clear for the message that was to be Marty Andrew's last.

"SOS SOS SOS DE KOVA KOVA SS BLUE RUNNER LAT 39.21 N LONG 72.36 W—"

No more. The "W" of Marty Andrews' plaintive call for help had moaned into oblivion like the diminishing howl of a siren. Then silence, cold and black and frightening.

No more. No more of anything. Strait-jacketed by radio regulations, he had sat with leaden fingers aching to reach for the key before him. But you mustn't touch that key. Separated from the scene of disaster by hundreds of miles, you must remain silent while the SOS shrills its way through the ether to other ships close enough to render assistance. With your best friend hunched over those unseen instruments, his pale, slim fingers gripping the key with a touch so vividly familiar, you must sit and stare—and pray.

Even without the *Blue Runner*'s call letters you know the crisp bugling howl of Marty Andrews' 500 cycle spark set. It is a tocsin—you know it as you'd know the voice of Marty himself, clear and soft as a plucked banjo string.

"SOS SS BLUE RUNNER . . ." and you must not answer.

You sit there staring, trembling, ears ringing with the numbing cacophony of uncountable signals from ships near and far.

The signals fade. A warning hiss tells you a tropical static storm is nearly over you. For a few breathless seconds you hear the bleating and screeching transmitters inquiring, "WHO SENT SOS?" and "WHAT IS WRONG WITH SS BLUE RUNNER?" And you sit there, powerless, helpless beneath the elements. In a few more minutes all is gone. Even the powerful groan from the ancient spark set at Trinidad fades to a hissing grit, almost lost in the rain of static. Another minute and it, too, fades. Nothing is left but the static.

Alone in a room ugly with shadows of impending tragedy, Bill Stillson had waited, not daring to open up for fear that the frantic questions eating at his heart might, if sent out, interfere with rescue work. No more until two bells, when a single short news-flash had come in on the routine press.

"ITEM. NEW YORK JULY 8—AT NINE THIRTY P.M. LAST NIGHT THE BLUE LINE FREIGHTER SS BLUE RUNNER SENT A DISTRESS MESSAGE GIVING HIS POSITION AS LATITUDE 39.21 N AND LONGITUDE 72.36 W. MESSAGE WAS NOT COMPLETED OR REPEATED. THREE PASSENGER SHIPS ONE TANKER AND NUMEROUS COAST GUARD CUTTERS HAVE BEEN SEARCHING AROUND THIS POSITION BUT AS YET HAVE FAILED TO FIND ANY TRACE OF THE BLUE RUNNER OR ITS CREW."

No more. No more ever, except occasional lurid newspaper articles about the latest macabre mystery of the sea. There'd been the usual imaginative reports of a truant ship sighted on nights dark and dank; but darkness and fog were conducive to illusions and the long awaited howl of Marty Andrews' 500 cycle spark set—the slow, drawling swing of Marty's fist—had remained silent.

Bill Stillson, staring into fog, drew cold air between his teeth and swung abruptly when a hand nudged his shoulder. A sailor had approached soundlessly.

"Third mate wants you on the bridge, Sparks."

The *Blue Belle*'s third mate, big, husky, phlegmatic, was a mountainous black blob in the darkness of the wheelhouse.

"Please, Sparks," he boomed, "I want to put it in my log what ship is that passing. I think she is the *San Barton*. You find out for sure."

Bill stared a moment at the cluster of lights visible through the wheelhouse windows. Groping in the darkness, he found the heavy telegraph key in the box just beyond the door.

"WHAT SHIP IS THAT?" he blinked.

From her masthead the passing ship flashed a reply. "SS SAN BARTON WHAT SHIP IS THAT?"

"SS BLUE BELLE BON VOYAGE."

"THANKS THE SAME TO YOU."

Bill turned to the third mate. "It's the *San Barton*," he said. With cold fingers he stroked his scowling mouth. The *San Barton* was Anne's ship, wasn't it? Or had she and her new husband sailed on the *San Rafael*?

He returned to the radio shack and and looked again at Anne's letter, postmarked in New York and delivered to him weeks ago in Tocapilla. *"We're to be married Saturday, Bill—"* day before yesterday, that was— *"and will sail at midnight on the San Barton for Rio. Harry thinks we may pass your ship as you return from South America."*

So she and Harry were married now, and probably some of the tiny spots of light gleaming from the side of that passing ship came from the portholes of their bridal suite. A good egg, Harry, dependable and straight. He'd make Anne happy and they'd travel a bit. They'd have a nice home on Pelham Parkway; they'd have friends and children and get along fine.

But the wide, staring eyes in the photograph over Bill's desk seemed hurt, somehow. Seemed to know, and were infinitely sad. Squirming uncomfortably in his chair, Bill stared back into them and shook his head, frowning.

"It's best the way it is, Marty. You know that. Harry's an all-right guy. How could you expect to—well, Anne couldn't very well know you were in love with her when you never told her about it, could she? Why, when you and I were sailing all over this world on ships, she was just growing up. Maybe she would have been glad to know how you felt about her, Marty . . . Why didn't you tell her? Scared to, I guess, huh? Afraid she wouldn't care to marry a sailor and be left alone at home while her husband roamed all over?"

No answer, of course. The eyes couldn't answer.

Marty would understand. Marty's love for Anne had been the only big thing in his life, but with nothing to offer her he had kept it to himself. Only Bill knew. . . .

Bill shook himself and glanced back at the letter. *"And will sail at midnight."* Turning, he flipped the toggle switch on the bench at his left. A whining hum came from the room outside, then a click, then another. The hum increased to a shrill ringing sound. He reached for the key and rapped out the call letters of the San Barton, signing his own.

"KFYU KFYU DE KDZL RQ."

Almost immediately the ripping squish of the San Barton's tube set blasted into his ears. "KDZL KFYU K."

"KFYU KDZL GOOD EVENING OLD MAN MY SISTER IS PASSENGER ABOARD YOUR SHIP WILL YOU PLEASE TAKE A NOTE FOR HER?"

"SURE GA." (GO AHEAD)

"THANKS NOTE MRS. HARRY CRAIG CONGRATULATIONS AND LOVE TO YOU BOTH PASSED YOU FEW MINUTES AGO BILL."

"OK QRX MIN WL GET QSL." (WAIT A MINUTE WILL GET REPLY)

Bill lit a cigarette and in a few minutes heard his call letters being punched out by the operator on the *San Barton* "KDZL KFYU BQ."

"KFYU KDZL K."

"HERE'S YOUR ANSWER OLD MAN—BILL STILLSON SS BLUE BELLE MANY THANKS HAVING WONDERFUL TIME LOVE FROM US BOTH ANNE AND HARRY."

The eyes on the wall seemed sadly to approve as Bill acknowledged the message with thanks, flipped the toggle switch and turned off the receiver.

* * *

He hung up the phones and went on deck. The fog was thickening. Resounding blasts from the *Blue Belle*'s whistle threatened at two-minute intervals to shred his eardrums. Nothing weird, nothing ghostly about that sound at close range; it was a wheezy bellow ripping the darkness, capable of murdering a man's nerves.

He walked forward along the slippery steel deck in an effort to escape the whistle's withering blast, and the fog went with him, soaking through his faded blue sweater. A voice and a shape came at him together. "That you, Sparks?"

"Yeah. Hello, Chief."

The chief engineer's weathered face gleamed pink and wet behind the glow of his pipe. He leaned on the rail, looked up at the funnel midships and wearily stretched his legs.

"Nasty night, Sparks," he grumbled. "The owners'll squawk plenty when they get the fuel bill for this trip."

Bill breathed fog. "Matter? She a hog?"

"She's a hog when that whistle's blowin'! Listen to it! Gar! Every time the third mate pulls that cord, she sucks another barrel of oil and she rips my head apart!"

Bill shrugged his big shoulders and gazed into darkness. Somewhere out there, perhaps ten miles distant by now, was the *San Barton*, with Anne and her husband aboard. Anne would be frightened tonight. Fog had always terrified her, perhaps because he himself had told her tales of tragic happenings under the fog's gray veil. Tales of collisions, wrecks, ghost ships drifting . . .

The third assistant engineer came through the mist and said, "Better come down below, Chief. Another gasket just gone to hell." The chief growled a hasty good night and strode away.

Bill Stillson stayed at the rail until a fine spray of rain blinded him; then, cold and shivering, he felt his way along the starboard side of the ship, pulled open the door of his own room and entered.

The room was a relief. Small, warm, it contained a bunk, a desk, and a battered trunk up-ended against one wall. You could escape from the fog here and get away from sticky tentacles of dampness. You could scrub your wet face with a coarse towel and then stretch out with something to read.

The ship's clock clipped out two bells—nine P.M.—while Bill idly flipped the pages of a magazine. But reading was impossible tonight. That night eternities ago, when Marty's ship had vanished, had been a night like this.

He tossed the magazine aside and kicked it into a corner as he rolled off the bunk to pour himself a drink. It wasn't only the fog, the darkness, the night; something was wrong with Bill Stillson. Too much introspection, that was it. Too many gray memories.

The rain had become a vicious downpour, audible through the walls. It lashed the room's single port. And there'd been rain that night, too. He had run to the radio shack and—

The glass slid out of Bill's fingers. He stared at the door and realized that the ports in the radio shack were open again tonight; rain would be slanting in on sensitive instruments. Gripping the collar of his coat, he ran topside to the shack.

The door was open as he had left it. Rain had puddled the floor beneath the open ports and wet the spark gaps. He closed the ports, removed the gaps from their rack in front of the panel, and with one leg hooked around a leg of the bench braced himself in the chair and reached for a cloth.

His left knee poked the loud-speaker plug into its jack under the table. He rubbed the spark gaps vigorously. A sudden hiss of squall static screamed out at him. Machine-gun volleys of sparks jumped across the plates of the antenna condenser, their crackle filling the room for many minutes before gradually fading to permit the passage of code.

The air was clear then, clear as fine wine. You could taste the ozone. You could hear Trinidad, San Francisco, Colon and New York booming in with equal intensity.

Routine stuff. Mustn't forget the time signals and weather from Arlington at 10 P.M. Mustn't forget to listen on the half-hour for naval storm warnings. Gaps to clean. Six messages to abstract. New ribbon on the mill here. And wind the clock.

The clock's hands stood at nine-twenty. Bill scratched a match under the table, lit his pipe and went back to the job of cleaning gaps.

The speaker rattled with the raucous tones of a Telefunken transmitter from a German freighter. "DEUT DEUT DE DOAC DOAC QTC ANTWORT F BIT." Some operator with traffic for Germany calling a sister ship and requesting a reply on wave F or 730 meters. And then an Italian ship asking all nearby ships of his nationality if they had anything for him, and telling them—as if they cared—that he had nothing for them. "IAAC IAAC DA IAOB QRU? NIENTE."

His mind was impervious to the blur of messages that followed. The air was full of signals, a heterogeneous miscellany from everywhere. Funny, there'd been the same sort of hash the night the *Blue Runner*—but Marty's call of SOS had silenced it.

Bong-bong-bong. Bill Stillson's gaze focused on the clock in front of him. Three bells. Marty's SOS had come through at three bells, too, and every letter of that message was still crystal clear in Bill's brain. "SOS SOS DE KOVA—"

He stiffened suddenly and looked at the speaker. His hands gripped the edge of the table. No, it couldn't be. He was hearing things.

He felt foolish.

"Must be going nuts," he mumbled. "Need sleep, I guess. This rain . . . fog . . ."

He *was* hearing things, of course. The memory of that other night had acquired a voice and was plaguing him. Anne's marriage to Harry Craig had stirred up violent recollections of Marty, and because tonight was so like that ghastly night of months ago . . .

It came again, preceded by a growl of static as if the speaker were warningly clearing its throat. With din enough to shake the walls, it blared out: "SOS SOS SOS DE KFYU KFYU KFYU SS SAN BARTON LAT 39.48 N LONG 73.00 W RAMMED DRIFTING DERELICT TAKING WATER RAPIDLY MUST ABANDON SHIP REQUIRE IMMEDIATE ASSISTANCE."

Bill Stillson typed it automatically without shifting his stare from the speaker. It didn't register, didn't reach into him, even though his mind mechanically transposed the screaming code into words and his fingers tapped the message out on the keys of the typewriter. He had to read the words themselves before believing.

The *San Barton!* Anne's ship! Good Lord—!

His big body shook from head to foot. His lips, white and tight, mumbled incoherently, "Marty! You're kidding, Marty . . . kidding me. You've come back. . . ."

But it wasn't Marty. That wasn't Marty's tell-tale, drawling fist. The sheet of yellow paper in the typewriter was real, and the message on it was vividly, hideously authentic, no ghostly prank from a phantom ship's operator.

The *San Barton* was sinking, and Anne was aboard her!

The chair scraped backward on two legs and thudded against the wall as Bill tore paper from the typewriter. Got to get this to the old man! Got to—fast! The *San Barton* had been within arm's reach, almost, a short while ago. She'd still be close.

He ran to the bridge. "Call me if it gets thick" had been the captain's routine order for years, and it was plenty thick right now, rain whipping the wheelhouse windows, visibility almost nil. Bill almost ran into him as he stumbled in the darkness of the room.

"Steady, Sparks," he heard the skipper say. "What's up?"

Bill handed over the message without a word. The captain turned on a light in the chartroom. His leathery face darkened, eyes flashed as he read.

"About twenty miles astern of us," he said grimly, then rapped out: "Answer him, Sparks. Be there in about two hours."

Back in the radio shack, Bill jerked the chair to the table, flipped the toggle switch and waited impatiently for the generator to build up speed. Turning, he glanced at the transmitter. Only five gaps in. Need more power than that to cut through the static.

Fingers wet, he gripped the metal switch with his left hand, gave it one quarter turn and nervously tapped the key with his right. His head exploded. The shock was like a sledge-hammer blow between the eyes, hurling him across the room.

Dazed, he picked himself up, both arms numb, an ugly burn crimsoning his right palm. "Damn fool! Been in this business long enough to know better than that. Be committing suicide next thing."

He stumbled back to the table, again set the chair upright and slumped into it, his head ringing, eyes refusing to focus. The fingers of his injured hand gripped the key. Pain crept to every nerve-end as he rapped out: "KFYU KFYU DE KDZL AR."

Immediately he heard the screaming reply from the *San Barton*.

"KDZL KFYU K." (GO AHEAD)

"BE WITH YOU IN ABOUT TWO HOURS," Bill told him. "IS ANY OTHER SHIP NEARER?"

"NO OTHER SH—" The signals from the *San Barton* fluttered and died like a candle flame in a gust of wind.

"KFYU KDZL?" Bill queried anxiously.

No answer.

"KFYU KFYU KDZL ARE YOU THERE?" Bill rapped out, frowning.

Again no answer.

Bill sent blind. "KFYU KFYU KFYU DE KDZL KDZL KDZL PROCEEDING YOUR LAST POSITION ARRIVE ABOUT TWO HOURS."

Something had gone wrong in the *San Barton*'s radio shack. Power had failed, probably, or Sparks had been ordered to leave the ship. The crash had been serious, then. Two hours might be too late.

He felt the *Blue Belle* wallow as she changed course. Bells clanged on the bridge. The speaking tube from bridge to radio room whistled, and Bill removed it from its hook. "Yes, sir?"

The captain's voice came firmly. "What does he say, Sparks? Can you tune him in on the direction finder?"

"He answered me, sir, but his transmitter broke down before he finished."

"See if you can get him again. It will save a lot of time if we can follow his beam."

Bill shook his head glumly at the tube.

"Afraid the way that transmitter stopped, his power is gone, sir." The pain in his burned hand was getting him; he shifted the tube to his left. "Wait a minute. I—I think I hear him!"

He dropped the tube and clamped the headphones over his ears. Have to forget the pain in that hand now. Something was coming through those phones!

"KDZL KFYU POWER FAILED OK NOW," he heard. "ABANDONING SHIP BUT WILL KEEP TRANSMITTER ON AIR FOR DIRECTION FINDER YOUR END. PLEASE HURRY SHIP SINKING FAST."

It was not the message, it was the fist sending it that slugged Bill Stillson between the eyes and straightened him against the broken back of the chair. He felt blood fading from his face, hairs rising from his tingling scalp. His eyes stayed wide, but their stare shifted from the receiver to the photograph above.

"Marty!" he whispered.

It *was* Marty! No operator in the world could imitate that fist. No transmitter but the one last operated by Marty had a note like that.

The grave had given up its ghost. Marty Andrews and his transmitter were on the *San Barton!*

Bill's hand leaped to the key. "MARTY," he spelled out, "IS IT YOU?"

"PLEASE HURRY TAKING WATER FAST WILL SEND MO FOR DIRECTION FINDER—MO MO MO MO MO MO MO MO. . . ."

The dashes continued. Bewildered, Bill automatically reached for the speaking tube.

"You there, Captain?"

"What is it, Sparks?"

"Got him again now, sir. Be right up to tune him in."

He replaced the tube on its hook. The receiver droned an unceasing "MO MO MO MO MO MO" from Marty Andrews' inimitable fist—the fist of a man assumed months ago to be dead. Bill could not answer. Personalities had to be forgotten.

He hesitated a moment, then pulled the cord on the heavy antenna switch, grounding all his apparatus. The MO died behind him as he rushed up the stairway to the chartroom, where the captain was bending over a table, studying a map.

Anxiously Bill turned on the direction finder receiver, tuned it to six hundred meters and adjusted it to the *San Barton*'s MO. It came clearly. Expertly he cut the volume down until the MO was a faint whisper, then reached overhead, grasped the loop wheel and turned it slowly, carefully, until the signal again became strong.

"Got it, sir," he told the captain.

The old man did not reply. With pencil and pad he wrote down the figures of the indicator beneath the loop, then returned grimly to the table to make calculations.

Bill stood there. The MO continued droningly, mocking him—Marty's fist, Marty's antiquated spark set seeming so out of place on a modern luxury liner. Rain beat an endless accompaniment against the chartroom windows. The captain's breathing was a harsh, asthmatic wheeze.

"Got a cigarette, Sparks?" Obviously that was an attempt to remain calm in the face of frightening uncertainty. The fingers that took the cigarette shook a little, and the old man's face was haggard with anxiety. At two-minute intervals the fog whistle blared its lurid warning into the night, savagely twisting Bill's nerves.

He sat on the stairway railing, phones glued to his ears while he listened to the monotonous "MO MO MO MO MO MO." An occasional "QRT SOS" came from some ship out there in the fog as its helpful operator endeavored to silence other ships but succeeded only in adding to the interference.

A naval shore station blared out a storm warning in blissful ignorance of the existing emergency. But gradually the disturbance disappeared, the air became weirdly quiet, punctured only by Marty Andrews' undying "MO MO MO MO MO. . . ."

An hour of that. An hour of listening and wondering. Then half an hour of nerve-wracking silence.

No need for the direction finder now. Within a few minutes the *Blue Belle* should reach the scene of disaster. Bill hung up the phones and turned wearily to the skipper. "Apparently his power's gone again, Captain. I'll go back to the shack." The captain nodded.

Bill returned to the radio room, pulled the antenna cord back into working position and sat there. Funny, this business of Marty Andrews' being on the *San Barton,* especially with Anne and her husband there too. Had Marty done that deliberately, after hiding away for months?

You could reason that out, of course, but what of the transmitter? The *San Barton* was a new ship, equipped with modern tube apparatus. Queer, the whole business. But there'd be an answer presently, when the *Blue Belle* reached the end of its forced-draft race with time. Marty himself could answer—

The room's stillness was disturbed suddenly by a weak staccato fizz from the receiver. Bill strained to catch the scratchy characters, stiffened and held his breath.

The *San Barton* again!

"KDZL KFYU CAN SEE YOUR LIGHTS NOW WITHIN HALF MILE OF US CHANGE YOUR

COURSE A LITTLE EAST WATCH OUT FOR LIFEBOATS STANDING CLOSE BY. THIS IS 30 (FINAL TRANSMISSION) AND GOOD-BY."

And—good-by? Heart thumping, Bill feverishly started his transmitter and streaked out, "OK MARTY FB CUL." (FINE BUSINESS. SEE YOU LATER.) Then he sat back, anxiously awaiting a reply.

It came at last, faintly, tenuously, like the whisper of a dying breeze. Almost inaudible. Almost not there at all. "PLEASE . . . BILL . . . REMEMBER . . . ME . . . TO . . . ANNE."

Somehow Bill knew that was the end, knew that his own inability to press the key was not caused solely by the pain of his scorched hand. Marty was gone now. There'd be no more. The echoes of that last "Remember me to Anne" seemed to linger a while in the room's strained silence, and then were smothered by the night outside.

He turned in his chair and listened to the clanking of heavy chains, the buzzing of a windlass, the thudding of rope ladders against the side of the ship. Sharp voices issued commands as lifeboats were lowered.

He went on deck, stood mutely with unlighted cigarette between his lips and watched while men scurried about like drenched rats. Searchlights bored through the fog and rain, illuminating patches of the ugly, heaving waste on all sides. Somewhere out there, in one of the crowded boats bobbing on the inky surface, was Anne.

He could make out the huge bulk of the *San Barton* low in the water, her nose buried deep in the bowels of a half-submerged derelict. It would be over soon. At any moment the big liner would shudder and submerge, dragging the derelict with her.

Bill strained to get a better look at the derelict. She was long, low and ugly, uncannily similar to the ship on whose deck he was standing. Now and then the beam of a searchlight swept across her bow but failed to reveal her name.

"Old man wants you, Sparks."

He turned. The speaker was already a receding shape in the darkness. On the bridge the captain handed him a sheet of paper and said curtly. "Send this to the office. Stand by for an answer."

Once more Bill Stillson sat at the table in the radio shack, this time punching out slowly: "BLUELIN NEW YORK—CHANGED COURSE 9:35 PM ANSWERING DISTRESS SS SAN BARTON NOW STANDING BY PICKING UP SURVIVORS ARRIVED SCENE 11:24 PM MORE LATER—MASTER BLUE BELLE."

He leaned back after the OK flashed from Chatham, then reached for a blank and rolled it in the typewriter. For the next twenty minutes he was busy copying messages from the press associations, queries from anxious friends and relatives of the *San Barton*'s passengers, and answering numerous questions from the Coast Guard.

＊ ＊ ＊

The *San Barton*'s operators, drenched and shivering, had been taken aboard. Two of them came to the shack to offer assistance. Bill knew them both by name, got up and shook hands with them.

"Where's the third?" he asked quietly.

"Hurt trying to string up an emergency antenna," the chief mumbled. "Name's Benny Lang—you know him, don't you? I was afraid you hadn't got us, Stillson. Antenna came down while I was trying to answer you and we were ordered to abandon ship about five minutes later. Just got out that one SOS."

Bill Stillson heard none of the receiver's furious din calling him back to duty. He stared at the *San Barton*'s chief, licked his lips and said almost inaudibly, "Just that—one—SOS was all you sent?"

"Well, I got in a couple of words before the antenna came down, but—"

The skipper, red-eyed and exhausted, entered on heavy feet.

"You fellows better change into dry clothes," he said. Then, to Bill: "Came to tell you your sister's safe, Sparks. She and her husband are resting in your room." He shivered violently as a trickle of water from his cap ran down the back of his neck. "*San Barton* just went down. Ugly mess. Two passengers and four crew missing, and some of the others badly shaken up."

He stopped suddenly and turned a quizzical gaze on Bill's sober face. "That derelict was the *Blue Runner,* Sparks, sister to this wagon. Didn't you have a friend on there when she disappeared?"

Bill inclined his head slowly. "Yes, I had a friend on there. Marty Andrews."

The captain opened his mouth to speak, then, apparently sensing something, closed it again and walked out. Bill Stillson was looking at the photograph on the wall.

The eyes were the same strange, sad eyes, but somehow even in their sadness they seemed now to be smiling. For a moment Bill sat as if hypnotized. Then he whispered, "Okay, Marty . . . thanks!"

Sea-Tiger

Henry S. Whitehead

ARTHUR HEWITT'S FIRST INTIMATION of the terrific storm which struck the *Barbadian* off Hatteras, *en route* for the West Indies, was a crash which awakened him out of uneasy sleep in the narrow berth of his cabin. When he staggered up to the saloon-deck the next morning after an extremely uncomfortable, sleepless night, he looked out of the ports upon a sea which transcended anything he had ever seen. The *Barbadian,* heeling and hanging, wallowed in the trough of cross seas which wrenched her lofty bridge-deck.

A steward, who was having a rather difficult time keeping his feet, fetched him a sandwich and a cup of coffee. In a little while two other passengers appeared for breakfast: one a British salesman, and the other an American ship's officer, out of a professional berth and going to Antigua to help take off a sugar crop. The three men, warmed now by the coffee and the comfortable security of the lounge, snored and chattered intimately.

Nevertheless, a sinister foreboding seemed to hang over them. At last Matthews, the American, voiced it plainly:

"I hope she'll make St. Thomas! Well—I've always heard that Captain Baird knows his business; a good sailorman, they say."

"Do you think there'll be any let-up when we get into the Gulf Stream?" This was the Englishman, breaking a long, dreary silence.

"More likely a let-*down,* I'd say," replied the pessimistic Matthews. "She'll be worse, if anything, in my judgment."

This gloomy prediction justified itself the following morning. The *Barbadian* had entered the Gulf Stream, and the malevolent fury of the sea increased with daylight. Hewitt came on deck, and, leaning against the jamb of a partly opened hatch on the protected leeside, looked out upon a world of heaving gray-green water with that feeling of awe which the sea in all its many moods invariably awakened in him. A gust of wind caught his unbuttoned coat, and out of a pocket and onto the wet, heaving deck slid the morocco-bound Testament which his mother had given him years before.

He stepped out through the hatchway, cautiously, making his way precariously across the deck to where it lay caught in the metal scupper. He arrived safely against the rail, which he gripped firmly with one hand, while he stooped to recover the book with the other. As he bent forward the tail-end of an enormous overtopping wave which had caught the vessel under her weather-quarter, caught him and raised his body like a feather over the rail's top.

But Hewitt was not cast into the sea. With a frantic, instinctive movement, he clung to the rail as his body struck violently against the ship's side.

With the *Barbadian*'s righting herself he found himself hanging on like grim death, his body dangling perilously over the angry waters, the Testament clutched firmly in his other hand.

He attempted to set his feet against one of the lower railings, to hook his legs about a stanchion. He almost succeeded, and would doubtless have been back upon the deck in safety had not the crest of the following wave dislodged his one-hand hold on the rail. The angry sea took him to itself, while the laboring ship, bounding into the teeth of the gale, bore on, all unconcerned over his sudden, unceremonious departure.

The incidents of Hewitt's life marched through his consciousness with an incredible rapidity. He remembered his mother poignantly—his mother dead these eight years—and a salt tear mingled with the vast saltiness of this cold, inhospitable ocean which had taken him to its disastrous embrace.

Down and down into the watery inferno he sank, weighted down with his winter boots and heavy overcoat. Strangely enough, he was not afraid, but he responded to the major mechanical impulses of a drowning man— the rigid holding of his breath, the desperate attempts to keep his head toward the surface so as to stay the sinking process, the well-nigh mechanical prayer to God.

His lungs were bursting, it seemed! Hot pain seared him, the red pain of unendurable pressures. He must resist as long as he had consciousness. He clamped his jaws desperately together.

It was calm down here, and dark! Here was no trace of the raging tempest on the surface, that tumultuous surface of lashed fury. The water seemed constantly heavier, more opaque, a vast, pervading indigo.

The pain and the burning pressure were gone now. He seemed no longer to sink. Nor did he rise, apparently. Probably he could not exhale his breath now if he wanted to. Well, he did not want to. It was no longer cold. Here was a world of calm, of perfect peace. Drowning is an easy death, after all. . . .

He hoped the *Barbadian* would make St. Thomas. . . .

His last conscious sensation was of a gentle sinking through a vast, imponderable blueness, which seemed pervading the universe, a restful blueness to which one could yield readily. He relaxed, let himself go, with no desire to struggle. He sank and sank, it seemed. . . .

He lay now upon a beach, his chin propped in his cupped hands, his elbows deep in the warm sand. It was from this warmth that he derived his first conscious sensation. A soft sea-wind, invigorating from its long contact with illimitable expanses of tropic seas, blew freshly. He felt very weary, and, it seemed, he had newly awakened out of a very protracted sleep. He turned his head at some slight sound and looked into the face of a girl who lay on the sand beside him.

He realized, as the march of events passed through his mind, that he must have gone through the gate of death. This, then, was that next world of which he had heard vaguely, all his life long. It was puzzling, somewhat. He was dead. He knew he must be dead. Do the dead lie on tropical beaches, under faint moonlight, and think, and feel this fresh wind from the sea? The dead, surely, do not dream. Perhaps they do dream. He had no knowledge, no experience, of course. He had read tales of after-death. Most of them, he remembered, revealed the surprise of the hero at the unexpectedness of his surroundings.

The girl touched him gently on the shoulder, and her hand was unbelievably cool and soothing. As he turned and looked at her in a kind of terror, the faint moonlight abruptly faded. Then the rim of the sun broke, red and sharp, like a blazing scimitar blade, across the horizon. The leaves of many trees stirred, welcoming the tropic day. Little monkeys swung and chattered overhead. A great flaming macaw sped, arrow-like, across the scope of his vision. The girl spoke to him:

"We must be gone to the sea."

The girl moved delicately towards the place where, near at hand, the turquoise sea lapped softly against weed-strewn boulders and freshly gleaming white sand. As he, too, induced by some compelling impulse beyond the scope of his understanding, moved instinctively to seek the refuge of the sea, he saw his companion clearly for the first time. Stupefied, incredulous, he glanced down at his own body, and saw, glistening, iridescent in the new light of fresh dawn, a great flashing, gleaming tail like that of some fabled, stupendous denizen of enchanted deeps. Then, his wonderment losing itself in a great exultation, he followed his mermaid into the shining, welcoming waters. . . .

*   *   *

On an early afternoon—for the sun was high in the heavens—he emerged from the sea into the shallows of that sandy beach where he had awakened to amphibian existence seemingly ages ago. Slowly, painfully, he dragged himself upon the warm sand. He was very weary, for he had finished an enormous swim, away from the scene of a fearful combat which he had waged with a now dimly remembered monster of the great deeps of the warm sea. His companion, who, during these long, dimly remembered eras, had been dear to him, was gone. She had succumbed in the direful struggle with the sea-beast. His heartache transcended the immediate painfulness and fatigue of his bruised and weary body.

He had had his vengeance, though. Beside her body lay that of the sea-beast, crustaceous, horrible, slain by him after a titanic struggle, mangled in the imponderable ooze. . . .

He rested at last, prone upon the yielding, sun-soaked sand. The insistent light of the glaring sun troubled him, and he moved impatiently. A vague murmur, too, was disturbingly apparent. He decided, wearily, to shift his position to the nearby shade of a palm grove. He turned over, slowly, painfully.

Then the light from the sun smote his eyes, attuned to the cool dimness of the sea-deeps, and as he moved towards the palms he raised a hand to his brow. That disquieting murmur took form abruptly, became intelligible. It seemed, somehow, to take on the familiarity of a remembered human voice. He lowered his hand, puzzled, disturbed, and found himself looking at an electric-light bulb. In its light he saw three men sitting on a leather sofa. He rose on his elbow, still painfully, for he was very weary after that dire combat, and peered at them. He now fixed his dazed stare on Matthews, who was in the middle of the row, and mumbled some incoherent words. The man seated at the end of the sofa rose hastily, and came towards him. He saw that it was Hegeman, the *Barbadian*'s doctor.

"Back awake, eh?" It was Hegeman's cheerful voice. The doctor placed a hand on Hewitt's pulse. "You'll do," he announced confidently.

Matthews was standing beside the doctor. Over Matthews' shoulder Hewitt could see, peering, the spectacled face of the salesman. Matthews was speaking:

"We were through the Gulf Stream a day ago, and the sun's out. It was a narrow squeak! Old Baird should have the Board of Trade medal for getting you. Thought you'd never come up!"

"A bit battered but right as rain, what!" The Englishman had added his word of cheer.

"You'll be on your pins in a day or two," said the doctor. "Keep still for the present." Hewitt nodded. He did not want to talk. He had too much to get settled in his mind. Those experiences! Or what seemed to be experiences, the chimeras of the unconscious mind.

"One of the stewards saw you go," added Hegeman. "Two of your teeth are chipped, where you clamped your jaws to hold your breath. Plucky thing to do. It saved your life."

Hewitt held out a heavy hand. The doctor took it and placed it gently by his side. "Go back to sleep," he ordered, and the three filed out.

During the remainder of the voyage Hewitt slowly recovered from the severe shock of his long immersion in wintry seawater. He was chiefly occupied though, with the strange history of his experience, which continued to stand out quite sharply in his mind. He could not shake off the notion that it had been, somehow, a *real* experience. Why—he could remember the details of day after day of it. He seemed to have acquired some unique knowledge of the ways of the sea's great deeps: the barely luminous darkness of animal phosphorescence; the strange monsters; the incredible cold of that world of pressure and dead ooze; the effortless motion through the water; the strange grottoes; above all, the eery austere companionship of the mer-woman and the final dreadful battle. . . . His mind was filled to overflowing with intimate details of what seemed a long, definite, regulated, amphibian life, actually lived!

There remained, permanently, even after the process of time had done its work in rendering most of the details indistinct in his mind, the desire for the sea: the overwhelming urge to go into, under, the water; to swim for incalculable distances; to lie on dim, sandy depths, the light, blue and faint, from above, among the swarming, glowing, harmless parrot-fish. And, deeper than all, in this persistent urge of consciousness, was the half-buried, basic desire to rive and tear and rend—a curious, almost inexplicable, persistent set of wholly new instincts, which disturbed his mind when he allowed himself to dwell on them. He looked forward to the first swim in the Carribean, after landing at his port, St. Croix, in the Virgin Islands.

Fully restored to his ordinary physical vigor, he joined a swimming party on the afternoon following his arrival in Frederiksted. There had been rumors of sharks, but his hosts hastened to reassure their guests. No! Sharks were virtually negligible, anyhow. Sharks were cowardly creatures, easily frightened away from any group of swimmers. If it were a barracuda, now—that would be quite another matter. Over in Porto Rico, so report had it, there had been a case of a barracuda attacking an American school-teacher. Terribly injured—permanently, it was said. Months in the hospital, poor fellow.

But, barracuda rarely troubled the bathing beaches. Occasionally, yes, one would take the bait of one of the Negro fishermen, far out in their little boats, and then the fisherman, if he were agile, would cut his line and row, gray-faced, inshore, perhaps not to venture out again for days. They were the sea-tigers, the barracudas.

Their attack was a fiendish thing. With its eighteen-inch jaw, and its rows of rip-saw teeth, it would charge, and charge again, tearing its helpless victim to ribbons, stripping flesh from bones with relentless avidity. There was no escape, it seemed, once those lightning rushes had begun. They came in such rapid succession that unless the victim were almost on shore there was no escape. Yes, a kind Providence save us from a barracuda!

The party, a gay one, entered the water under the declining afternoon sun. The beach here shelved steeply, four or five steps being quite enough to reach swimming depth. The water was so clear, over its white, sandy bottom, that a swimmer, floating face downward, could see bottom clearly, and count the little parrot-fish, like flashing sunbeams, as they sported about, apparently near enough to be gathered up by extending the hand; a curious, amusing delusion.

Hewitt swam easily, lazily, revelling with satisfaction in the stimulating clear water which in these latitudes is like a sustained caress to the body.

He had never felt so much at ease in the water before. It seemed, however, quite natural to him now. It fitted, precisely, into what had grown to be his expectations during the past few days on the ship. It was as though latent, untried powers deep within him had been stimulated and released by the strange, mental experience he had undergone during those few hours of his unconsciousness. He dived deeply, and all the processes involved—the holding of the breath, the adjustment of muscular actions and reactions, the motions of underwater swimming—were as natural and effortless as though he had been, he told himself musingly, really amphibious.

Unnoticed by him, the remainder of the swimming party, only about half of whom he had met, retired to the beach and spread themselves in little sociable groups along the sandy edge. A few lingered in the shallows.

He was floating on his back, the little waves of that calm sea lapping against his cheeks, when he heard faintly the terrified, cutting scream of a girl. He treaded water, and looked towards the beach, where he saw the various members of the large party rushing towards a young girl whom he had not especially noticed before. The girl was one of those who had remained in the shallows, and as he looked he saw many hands extended towards her, and drawing her upon the sand, and he saw, too, a pinkish froth of fresh blood about the place from which she had emerged.

Something seemed to snap inside his brain. That terrible, atavistic, inexplicable sense of combat, the desire to rend and tear suffused him. In the grip of this strange, primitive, savage urge, he turned abruptly and dived straight down to where a flickering gray shadow passed; to where an enormous barracuda slowed to turn for its lightning rush at its second victim. Hewitt sped down like a plummet, exulting. . . .

A moment later the attention of the group on the beach was distracted from the young girl whose foot had been cruelly gashed by the sea-tiger's teeth, to a seething, foaming, writhing thing that rose from the calm surface of the sea a hundred feet out from the beach, struggled furiously on the lashed surface for a few seconds, and then as abruptly disappeared in a tortured mass of foam. A sunburned young Navy doctor went on binding up the girl's foot, but the rest, wonder-stricken, silent, scanned the surface eagerly for another glimpse of this strange, titanic combat. "What is it?" "What can it be?" The questions ran from mouth to mouth.

The barracuda rose again, this time within twenty feet of the beach, and Hewitt lay locked along the steel-gray back, his hands closed in a vise-like grip about the terrible jaws, his tensed muscles corded with the fearful strain. Over and over, sidewise, backwards, forward, moved fish and man as one, locked together in dives and turns and dashes so swift as to baffle the gaping eyes of the amazed onlookers, standing now in a wondering, intrigued row upon the edge of the sand. And always, with great, powerful lunges of feet and sweeps of elbows and hands and knees, now above, now beneath, but ever unrelaxed in that deadly grip, on the frothing surface or in the quiet depths, Hewitt forced his demon antagonist towards the beach.

In the course of their fourth emergence, the two, rolling over and over upon the bottom sand of the shore shallows, shot out upon the beach, and Hewitt, finding his feet, with a great wrench, raised the sea-tiger in his hands and with a great sweeping motion which bent the iron-like head and its cruel jaws towards the rigid, mackerel-like tail, cracked the giant killer's backbone, and flung the barracuda down on the sand where it lay, crushed and broken, writhing out its life in convulsive leaps.

Hewitt took several deep, restoring breaths, and the killing-lust passed from him, the strange urge satisfied by his successful struggle. The members of the swimming party slowly gathered about him. There was, it appeared, nothing much to say. One of the men cautiously rolled over the crushed barracuda with a tentative foot. Hewitt raised his eyes and looked towards the young girl, who was now standing lightly on the bandaged foot, supported by the Navy doctor.

She looked back at Hewitt, and there was a great wonder in her sea-blue eyes. The fresh wind moved her coppery hair, now released from the rubber bathing-cap.

Oblivious of the chorus of admiration and bewilderment of the rest of the swimming party, Hewitt gazed at her, awed, overcome, feeling suddenly weak. For—wonder of wonders!—leaning on the arm of the solicitous young doctor, there stood before him the perfect embodiment of his sea-companion, that strange, alluring, product of his recent subconscious experience, his extraordinary dream.

He drew several long breaths, to steady himself. Now the remarks of the swimmers began to break through his dazed consciousness, and he came to himself. He stepped towards the injured girl, fumbling in his rapidly clearing mind for some suitable expression of sympathy. . . .

Abruptly the members of the swimming party fell silent, realizing that they stood here in the presence of some inexplicable drama; of something subtle and vague, but something unmistakably finished, appropriate.

"I hope you were not hurt very badly," was all that Hewitt could manage.

The girl answered him not a word but looked steadily into his face, and Hewitt knew that here was the beginning of his real life.

The Women

Ray Bradbury

IT WAS AS IF a light came on in a green room.

The ocean burned. A white phosphorescence stirred like a breath of steam through the autumn morning sea, rising. Bubbles rose from the throat of some hidden sea ravine.

Like lightning in the reversed green sky of the sea it was, aware. It was old and beautiful. Out of the deeps it came, indolently. A shell, a wisp, a bubble, a weed, a glitter, a whisper, a gill. Suspended in its depths were brainlike trees of frosted coral, eyelike pips of yellow kelp, hairlike fluids of weed. Growing with the tides, growing with the ages, collecting and hoarding and saving unto itself identities and ancient dusts, octopus-inks and all the trivia of the sea.

Until now—it was aware.

It was a shining green intelligence, breathing in the autumn sea. Eyeless but seeing, earless but hearing, bodyless but feeling. It was of the sea. And being of the sea it was—feminine.

It in no way resembled man or woman. But it had a woman's ways, the silken, sly and hidden ways. It moved with a woman's grace. It was all the evil things of vain women.

Dark waters flowed through and by and mingled with her on the way to the gulf streams. In the water were carnival caps, horns, serpentine, confetti. They passed through her like wind through an ancient tree. Orange peels, napkins, papers, eggshells, and burnt kindling from nightfires on the beaches; all the flotsam of the gaunt high people who stalked on the lone sands of the continental islands, people from brick cities, people who shrieked in metal demons down concrete highways, gone.

She rose softly, shimmering, foaming, into cool morning airs. She lay in the swell after the long time of forming through darkness.

She perceived the shore.

The man was there.

He was a sun-darkened man with strong legs and a good chest.

Each day he should have come down to the water, to bathe, to swim, to be anywhere at all near. But he had never moved. There was a woman on the sand with him, a woman in a black bathing suit who lay next to him talking quietly, laughing. Sometimes they held hands, sometimes they listened to a little sounding machine that they dialed and out of which music came.

The phosphorescence hung quietly in the waves, anxiety returning. It was the end of the season. September. Things were shutting down.

Any day now he might go away and never return.

Today, he *must* come in the water.

They lay on the sand with the heat in them. The radio played softly and the woman in the black bathing suit stirred fitfully, eyes closed.

The man did not lift his head from where he cushioned it on his muscled left arm. He drank the sun with his face, his open mouth, his nostrils. "What's wrong?" he asked.

"A bad dream," said the woman in the black suit.

"Dreams in the daytime?" he asked.

"Don't *you* ever dream in the afternoon?"

"I *never* dream," he said. "I've never had a dream in my life."

She lay there, fingers twitching. "God, I had a horrible dream!"

"What about?"

"I don't know," she said, as if she really didn't. It was so bad she had forgotten. Now, eyes shut, she tried to remember.

"It was about me," he said, lazily, stretching.

"No," she said.

"Yes," he said, smiling to himself. "I was off with another woman, that's what."

"No," she said.

"I insist," he said. "There I was, off with another woman, and you discovered us, and somehow, in all the mix-up, I got shot or something."

She wrenched involuntarily. "Don't *talk* that way."

"Let's see now," he said. "What sort of woman was I with? Gentlemen prefer blondes, don't they?"

"Please don't joke," she said. "I don't feel well."

He opened his eyes. "Did it affect you that much?"

She nodded. "Whenever I dream in the daytime this way, it depresses me something terribly."

"I'm sorry." He took her hand. "Anything I can get you?"

"No."

"Ice cream cone? Eskimo pie? A coke?"

"You're a dear, but no. I'll be all right. It's just that, the last four days haven't been right. This isn't like it used to be early in the summer. Something's happened."

"Not between us," he said.

"Oh, no, of course not," she said, quickly. "But don't you feel that sometimes *places* change? Even a thing like a pier changes, and the merry-go-rounds, and all that. Even the hot dogs taste different this week."

"How do you mean?"

"They taste old and funny. It's hard to explain, but I've lost my appetite, and I wish this vacation was over. Really, what I want to do most of all is go home."

"Tomorrow's our last day; can't you stick it out? You know how much this extra week means to me."

"I'll try," she said. "If only this place didn't feel so funny and changed."

"I don't think it's changed. Places never do," he said. "But people or *things* change them. Maybe we're just tired of this beach and want to go somewhere else, some other beach?"

"I don't know. But all of a sudden I just had a feeling I wanted to get up and run."

"For why? Because of your dream? Me and my blonde and me dead all of a sudden."

"Don't," she said. "Don't talk about dying that way!"

She lay there very close to him. "If I only knew what it was."

"There, there," he petted her. "I'll protect you."

"It's not me, it's you," her breath whispered in his ear. "I had the feeling that you were tired of me and went away."

"I wouldn't do that; I love you."

"I'm silly." She forced a laugh. "God, what a silly thing I am!"

They lay quietly, the sun and sky over them like a lid.

"You know," he said, thoughtfully, "I get a little of that feeling you're talking about. This place has changed. There *is* something different."

"I'm glad you feel it, too."

He shook his head, drowsily, smiling softly, shutting his eyes, drinking the sun. "Both crazy. Both crazy." Murmuring. "Both."

The sea came in on the shore three times, softly.

The afternoon came on. The sun struck the skies a grazing blow. The yachts bobbed hot and shining white in the harbor swells. The fishermen spat and lined their baited lines off the pier. The smells of fried meat and burnt onion filled the wind. The sand whispered and stirred like an image in a vast, melting mirror.

The radio at their elbow murmured discreetly. They lay like dark arrows on the white sand. They did not move. Only their eyelids flickered with awareness, only their ears were alert. Now and again their tongues might slide along their baking lips. Sly prickles of moisture appeared on their brows to be burned away by the sun.

He lifted his head, blindly, listening in the heat.

The radio sighed.

He put his head down for a minute.

She felt him lift himself again. She opened one eye and he rested on one elbow looking around, at the pier, at the sky, at the water, at the sand.

"What's wrong?" she asked.

"Nothing," he said, lying down again.

"Something," she said.

"I thought I heard something."

"The radio."

"No, not the radio. Something else."

"Somebody *else's* radio."

He didn't answer. She felt his arm tense and relax, tense and relax. "Damn it," he said. "There it is, again."

They both lay listening.

"I don't hear anything—"

"Shh!" he cried. "For God's sake—"

The waves broke on the shore, silent mirrors, heaps of melting, whispering glass.

"Somebody singing."

"What?"

"I'd swear it was someone singing."

"Nonsense."

"No, listen."

They did that for a while.

"I don't hear a thing," she said, turning very cold.

He was on his feet. There was nothing in the sky, nothing on the pier, nothing on the sand, nothing in the hot dog stands. There was a staring silence, the wind blowing over his ears, the wind preening along the light, blowing hairs of his arms and legs.

He took a step toward the sea.

"Don't!" she said.

He looked down at her, oddly, as if she were not there. He was still listening.

She turned the portable radio up full, loud. It exploded words and rhythm and melody:

"—I found a million dollar baby—"

He made a wry face, raising his open palm violently. "Turn it off!"

"No, I like it!" She turned it louder. She snapped her fingers, rocking her body vaguely, trying to smile.

"in the five and ten cent store!"

It was two o'clock.

The sun steamed the waters. The ancient pier expanded with a loud groan in the heat. The birds were held in the hot sky, unable to move. The sun struck through the green liquors that poured about the pier; struck, caught and burnished an idle whiteness that drifted in the off-shore ripples.

The white foam, the frosted coral brain, the kelp-pip, the tide dust lay in the water, spreading, seeing.

The dark man still lay on the sand, the woman in the black suit beside him.

Music drifted up like mist from the water. It was a whispering music of deep tides and passed years, of salt and travel, of accepted and familiar strangenesses. The music sounded not unlike water on the shore, rain falling, the turn of a limb in the depths. It was very soft. It was a singing of a time-lost voice in a caverned sea shell. The hissing and sighing of tides in deserted holds of treasure ships. The sound the wind makes in an empty skull thrown out on the baked sand.

But the radio up on the blanket on the beach played louder.

The phosphorescence, light as a woman, sank down, tired, from sight. Only a few more hours. They might leave at any time. If only he would come in, for an instant, just an instant. The mists stirred silently, thinking of his face and his body in the water, deep under. She thought of him caught, held, as they sank ten fathoms down, on a sluice that bore them twisting and turning in frantic gesticulations, to the depths of a hidden gulf in the sea.

The heat of his body, the water taking fire from his warmth, and the frosted coral brain, the jeweled dusts, the salted mists feeding on his hot breath from his opened lips. The foam shivering with this thought now.

The waves moved the soft and changing thoughts into the shallows which were tepid as bath waters from the two o'clock sun.

He mustn't go away. If he goes now, he'll not return.

Now. The cold coral brain drifted, drifted. *Now.* Calling across the hot spaces of windless air in the early afternoon. *Come down to the water. Now,* said the music. *Now.*

*   *   *

The woman in the black bathing suit twisted the radio dial.

"Attention!" screamed the radio. "Now, today, you can buy a new car at—"

"For cripe's sake!" said the man, reaching over and tuning the scream down. "Must you have it so loud!"

"I like it loud," said the woman in the black bathing suit, looking over her shoulder at the sea.

It was three o'clock. The sky was all sun.

Sweating, he stood up. "I'm going in," he said.

"Get me a hot dog first, will you?" she said.

"Can't you wait until I come out? Must it be now?"

"Please." She pouted. *"Now."*

"Everything on it?"

"Yes, and bring *three* of them."

"Three? God, what an appetite!" He ran off to the small cafe.

She waited until he was gone. Then she turned the radio off. She lay listening a long time. She heard nothing. She looked at the water until the glints and shatters of sun stabbed through her head, like needles driven deep.

The sea had quieted. There was only a faint, far and fine net of ripples giving off sunlight in infinite repetition. She squinted again and again at the water, scowling.

He bounded back. "Damn, but the sand's hot; burns my feet off!" He flung himself on the blanket. "Eat 'em up!"

She took the three hot dogs and fed quietly on one of them. When she finished it, she handed him the remaining two. "Here, you finish them. My eyes are bigger than my stomach."

He eyed her petulantly. "All right." He swallowed the hot dogs in silence. "Next time," he said, finishing, don't order more than you can use. It's a helluva waste."

"Here," she said, unscrewing a thermos, "you must be thirsty. Finish our lemonade."

"Thanks." He drank. Then he slapped his hands together and said, "Well, I'll go jump in the water now." He looked anxiously at the bright sea.

"Just one more thing," she said, just remembering it. "Will you buy me a bottle of sun-tan oil? I'm all out."

"Haven't you some in your purse?"

"I used it all."

"I wish you'd told me when I was up there buying the hot dogs," he said, irritably. "But, okay." He ran back, loping steadily.

When he was gone, she took the sun-tan bottle from her purse, half full, unscrewed the cap, and poured the liquid into the sand, covering it over surreptitiously, looking out at the sea, and smiling. She rose then and went down to the edge of the sea and looked out, searching the innumerable small and insignificant waves.

You can't have him, she thought. Whoever or whatever you are, he's mine, and you can't have him. I don't know what's going on; I don't know anything, really. All I know is we're going on a train tonight at seven if I have to take him bodily along. And we won't be here tomorrow. So you can just stay here and wait, ocean, sea, or whatever it is that's wrong here today.

She wanted to say this out loud, because she knew it was right. But she said nothing, for others might think her blazed, ruined by the odd sunlight and the quiet waters.

Do your damnedest; you're no match for me, she thought. She picked up a stone and threw it at the sea.

"There!" she cried. "You."

He was standing beside her.

"Oh?" she jumped back.

"It's only me from over the sea," he sang. "Barnacle Bill the Sailor!" He bit her neck and she thrashed playfully in his grasp. "Hey, what gives? You standing here muttering?"

"Was I?" She was surprised at herself. "Where's the sun-tan oil? Will you put it on my back?"

He poured a yellow twine of oil and massaged it onto her golden back. She looked out at the water from time to time, eyes sly, nodding at the water as if to say, "Look! You see? Ah-ha!" She purred like a kitten.

"There." He gave her the bottle.

He was half into the water before she screamed.

"Where are you going! Come here!"

He turned as if she were someone he didn't know. "For God's sake, what's wrong?"

"Why, you just finished your hot dogs and lemonade—you can't go in the water now and get cramps!"

He scoffed. "Old wives' tales."

"Just the same, you come back up on the sand and wait an hour before you go in, do you hear? I won't have you getting a cramp and drowning."

"Ah," he said, disgusted.

"Come along." She turned, and he followed, looking back at the sea.

Three o'clock. Four.

The change came at four-ten. Lying on the sand, the woman in the black suit saw it coming and relaxed. The clouds had been forming since three. Now, with a sudden rush, the fog came in from off the bay. Where it had been warm, now it was cold. A wind blew up out of the nothing. Darker clouds moved in.

"It's going to rain," she said, proudly.

"You sound absolutely pleased," he observed, sitting with arms folded. "Maybe our last day, and you sound pleased because it's clouding up."

"The weather man," she confided, "said there'd be thunder showers all tonight and tomorrow. It might be a good idea to leave tonight."

"We'll stay, just in case it clears. I want to get one more day of swimming in, anyway," he said. "I haven't been in the water yet today."

"We've had so much fun talking and eating, time passes."

"Yeah," he said, looking at his hands.

The fog flailed across the sand in soft strips.

"There," she said. "That was a raindrop on my nose!" She laughed ridiculously at it. Her eyes were bright and young again. She was almost triumphant. "Good old rain."

"Why are you so pleased?" he demanded. "You're an odd duck!"

"Come on, rain!" she said. "Well, help me with these blankets. We'd better run!"

He picked up the blankets slowly, preoccupied. "Not even one last swim, damn it.

"I've a mind to take just one dive." He smiled at her. "Only a minute!"

"No." Her face paled. "You'll catch cold, and I'll have to nurse you!"

"Okay, okay." He turned away from the sea. Gentle rain began to fall.

Marching ahead of him, she headed for the hotel. She was singing softly to herself.

"Hold on!" he said.

She halted. She did not turn. She only listened to his voice far away.

"Why, there's someone out there, in the water!" he cried. "Drowning!"

She couldn't move. She heard his feet running.

"Wait here!" he shouted. "I'll be right back! There's someone there! A woman, I think!"

"Let the lifeguards get her!" cried the woman in the black suit, whirling.

"Aren't any! Off duty; late!" He ran down to the shore, the sea, the waves.

"Come back!" she screamed. "There's no one out there! Don't, oh, don't!"

"Don't worry, I'll be right back!" he called. "She's drowning out there, see?"

The fog came in, the rain pattered down, a white flashing light raised in the waves. He ran, and the woman in the black suit ran after him, scattering beach implements behind her, crying, tears rushing from her eyes. "Don't!" she said. She put out her hands.

He leaped into an onrushing dark wave.

The woman in the black bathing suit waited in the rain.

At six o'clock the sun set somewhere behind black clouds. The rain rattled softly on the water, a distant drum snare.

Under the sea, a move of illuminant white.

The soft shape, the foam, the weed lay in the shallows. Among the stirring glitter, deep under, was the man.

Fragile. The foam bubbled and broke. The frosted coral brain rang against a pebble with hidden thought. Fragile men. So fragile. Like dolls, they break. Nothing, nothing to them. A minute under water and they're sick and pay no attention and they vomit out and kick and then, suddenly, just lie there, doing nothing. Doing nothing at all. How strange and how disappointing, after all the days of waiting.

What to do with him now? His head lolls, his mouth opens, his eyelids loosen, his eyes stare, his skin pales. Silly man, wake up! Wake up!

The water raced about him.

The man hung limply, loosely, mouth agape.

The phosphorescence, the green hair weed withdrew.

He was released. A wave carried him back to the silent shore. Back to his wife, who was waiting for him there in the cold rain.

The rain poured over the black waters.

Distantly, under the leaden skies, from the twilight shore, a woman screamed.

Ah—the ancient dusts stirred sluggishly in the water—isn't that *like* a woman? Now, *she* doesn't want him, *either!*

At seven o'clock the rain fell thick. It was night and very cold and the hotels all along the sea had to turn on the heat.

The Doors of His Face, the Lamps of His Mouth

Roger Zelazny

'M A BAITMAN. No one is born a baitman, except in a French novel where everyone is. (In fact, I think that's the title, *We are All Bait.* Pfft!) How I got that way is barely worth the telling and has nothing to do with neo-exes, but the days of the beast deserve a few words, so here they are.

The Lowlands of Venus lie between the thumb and forefinger of the continent known as Hand. When you break into Cloud Alley it swings its silverblack bowling ball toward you without a warning. You jump then, inside that fire-tailed tenpin they ride you down in, but the straps keep you from making a fool of yourself. You generally chuckle afterwards, but you always jump first.

Next, you study Hand to lay its illusion and the two middle fingers become dozen-ringed archipelagoes as the outers resolve into greengray peninsulas; the thumb is too short, and curls like the embryo tail of Cape Horn.

You suck pure oxygen, sigh possibly, and begin the long topple to the Lowlands.

There, you are caught like an infield fly at the Lifeline landing area—so named because of its nearness to the great delta in the Eastern Bay—located between the first peninsula and "thumb." For a minute it seems as if you're going to miss Lifeline and wind up as canned seafood, but afterwards—shaking off the metaphors—you descend to scorched concrete and present your middle-sized telephone directory of authorizations to the short, fat man in the gray cap. The papers show that you are not subject to mysterious inner rottings and etcetera. He then smiles you a short, fat, gray smile and motions you toward the bus which hauls you to the Reception Area. At the R.A. you spend three days proving that, indeed, you are not subject to mysterious inner rottings and etcetera.

Boredom, however, is another rot. When your three days are up, you generally hit Lifeline hard, and it returns the compliment as a matter of reflex. The effects of alcohol in variant atmospheres is a subject on which the connoisseurs have written numerous volumes, so I will confine my remarks to noting that a good binge is worthy of at least a week's time and often warrants a lifetime study.

I had been a student of exceptional promise (strictly undergraduate) for going on two years when the *Bright Water* fell through our marble ceiling and poured its people like targets into the city.

Pause. The Worlds Almanac re Lifeline: ". . . Port city on the eastern coast of Hand. Employees of the Agency for Non-terrestrial Research comprise approximately 35% of its 100,000 population (2010 Census). Its other residents are primarily personnel maintained by several industrial corporations engaged in basic research. Independent marine biologists, wealthy fishing enthusiasts, and waterfront entrepreneurs make up the remainder of its inhabitants."

I turned to Mike Dabis, a fellow entrepreneur, and commented on the lousy state of basic research.

"Not if the mumbled truth be known."

He paused behind his glass before continuing the slow swallowing process calculated to obtain my interest and a few oaths, before he continued.

"Carl," he finally observed, poker playing, "they're shaping Tensquare."

I could have hit him. I might have refilled his glass with sulfuric acid and looked on with glee as his lips blackened and cracked. Instead, I grunted a noncommittal.

"Who's fool enough to shell out fifty grand a day? ANR?"

He shook his head.

"Jean Luharich," he said, "the girl with the violet contacts and fifty or sixty perfect teeth. I understand her eyes are really brown."

"Isn't she selling enough face cream these days?"

He shrugged.

"Publicity makes the wheels go 'round. Luharich Enterprises jumped sixteen points when she picked up the Sun Trophy. You ever play golf on Mercury?"

I had, but I overlooked it and continued to press.

"So she's coming here with a blank check and a fishhook?"

"*Bright Water,* today," he nodded. "Should be down by now. Lots of cameras. She wants an Ikky, bad."

"Hmm," I hmmed. "How bad?"

"Sixty day contract, Tensquare. Indefinite extension clause. Million and a half deposit," he recited.

"You seem to know a lot about it."

"I'm Personnel Recruitment. Luharich Enterprises approached me last month. It helps to drink in the right places."

"Or own them." He smirked, after a moment.

I looked away, sipping my bitter brew. After awhile I swallowed several things and asked Mike what he expected to be asked, leaving myself open for his monthly temperance lecture.

"They told me to try getting you," he mentioned. "When's the last time you sailed?"

"Month and a half ago. The *Corning.*"

"Small stuff," he snorted. "When have you been under, yourself?"

"It's been awhile."

"It's been over a year, hasn't it? That time you got cut by the screw, under the *Dolphin?*"

I turned to him.

"I was in the river last week, up at Angleford where the currents are strong. I can still get around."

"Sober," he added.

"I'd stay that way," I said, "on a job like this."

A doubting nod.

"Straight union rates. Triple time for extraordinary circumstances," he narrated. "Be at Hangar Sixteen with your gear, Friday morning, five hundred hours. We push off Saturday, daybreak."

"You're sailing?"

"I'm sailing."

"How come?"

"Money."

"Ikky guano."

"The bar isn't doing so well and baby needs new minks."

"I repeat—"

". . . And I want to get away from baby, renew my contact with basics—fresh air, exercise, make cash . . ."

"All right, sorry I asked."

I poured him a drink, concentrating on H_2SO_4, but it didn't transmute. Finally I got him soused and went out into the night to walk and think things over.

Around a dozen serious attempts to land *Ichthyform Leviosaurus Levianthus,* generally known as "Ikky," had been made over the past five years. When Ikky was first sighted, whaling techniques were employed. These proved either fruitless or disastrous, and a new procedure was inaugurated. Tensquare was constructed by a wealthy sportsman named Michael Jandt, who blew his entire roll on the project.

After a year on the Eastern Ocean, he returned to file bankruptcy. Carlton Davits, a playboy fishing enthusiast, then purchased the huge raft and laid a wake for Ikky's spawning grounds. On the nineteenth day out he had a strike and lost one hundred and fifty bills' worth of untested gear, along with one *Ichthyform Levianthus*. Twelve days later, using tripled lines, he hooked, narcotized, and began to hoist the huge beast. It awakened then, destroyed a control tower, killed six men, and worked general hell over five square blocks of Tensquare. Carlton was left with partial hemiplegia and a bankruptcy suit of his own. He faded into waterfront atmosphere and Tensquare changed hands four more times, with less spectacular but equally expensive results.

Finally, the big raft, built only for one purpose, was purchased at auction by ANR for "marine research." Lloyd's still won't insure it, and the only marine research it has ever seen is an occasional rental at fifty bills a day—to people anxious to tell Leviathan fish stories. I've been baitman on three of the voyages, and I've been close enough to count Ikky's fangs on two occasions. I want one of them to show my grandchildren, for personal reasons.

I faced the direction of the landing area and resolved a resolve.

"You want me for local coloring, gal. It'll look nice on the feature page and all that. But clear this— If anyone gets you an Ikky, it'll be me. I promise."

I stood in the empty Square. The foggy towers of Lifeline shared their mists.

Shoreline a couple eras ago, the western slope above Lifeline stretches as far as forty miles inland in some places. Its angle of rising is not a great one, but it achieves an elevation of several thousand feet before it meets the mountain range which separates us from the Highlands. About four miles inland and five hundred feet higher than Lifeline are set most of the surface airstrips and privately owned hangars. Hangar Sixteen houses Cal's Contract Cab, hop service, shore to ship. I do not like Cal, but he wasn't around when I climbed from the bus and waved to a mechanic.

Two of the hoppers tugged at the concrete, impatient beneath flywing haloes. The one on which Steve was working belched deep within its barrel carburetor and shuddered spasmodically.

"Bellyache?" I inquired.

"Yeah, gas pains and heartburn."

He twisted setscrews until it settled into an even keening, and turned to me.

"You're for out?"

I nodded.

"Tensquare. Cosmetics. Monsters. Stuff like that."

He blinked into the beacons and wiped his freckles. The temperature was about twenty, but the big overhead spots served a double purpose.

"Luharich," he muttered. "Then you *are* the one. There's some people want to see you."

"What about?"

"Cameras. Microphones. Stuff like that."

"I'd better stow my gear. Which one am I riding?"

He poked the screwdriver at the other hopper.

"That one. You're on video tape now, by the way. They wanted to get you arriving."

He turned to the hangar, turned back.

"Say 'cheese.' They'll shoot the close close-ups later."

I said something other than "cheese." They must have been using tele-lens and been able to read my lips, because that part of the tape was never shown.

I threw my junk in the back, climbed into a passenger seat, and lit a cigarette. Five minutes later, Cal himself emerged from the office Quonset, looking cold. He came over and pounded on the side of the hopper. He jerked a thumb back at the hangar.

"They want you in there!" he called through cupped hands. "Interview!"

"The show's over!" I yelled back. "Either that, or they can get themselves another baitman!"

His rustbrown eyes became nailheads under blond brows and his glare a spike before he jerked about and stalked off. I wondered how much they had paid him to be able to squat in his hangar and suck juice from his generator.

Enough, I guess, knowing Cal. I never liked the guy, anyway.

Venus at night is a field of sable waters. On the coasts, you can never tell where the sea ends and the sky begins. Dawn is like dumping milk into an inkwell. First, there are erratic curdles of white, then streamers. Shade the bottle for a gray colloid, then watch it whiten a little more. All of a sudden you've got day. Then start heating the mixture.

I had to shed my jacket as we flashed out over the bay. To our rear, the skyline could have been under water for the way it waved and rippled in the heatfall. A hopper can accommodate four people (five, if you want to bend Regs and underestimate weight), or three passengers with the sort of gear a baitman uses. I was the only fare, though, and the pilot was like his machine. He hummed and made no unnecessary noises. Lifeline turned a somersault and evaporated in the rear mirror at about the same time Tensquare broke the fore-horizon. The pilot stopped humming and shook his head.

I leaned forward. Feelings played flopdoodle in my guts. I knew every bloody inch of the big raft, but the feelings you once took for granted change when their source is out of reach. Truthfully, I'd had my doubts I'd ever board the hulk again. But now, now I could almost believe in predestination. There it was!

A tensquare football field of a ship. A-powered. Flat as a pancake, except for the plastic blisters in the middle and the "Rooks" fore and aft, port and starboard.

The Rook towers were named for their corner positions—and any two can work together to hoist, co-powering the graffles between them. The graffles—half gaff, half grapple—can raise enormous weights to near water level; their designer had only one thing in mind, though, which accounts for the gaff half. At water level, the Slider has to implement elevation for six to eight feet before the graffles are in a position to push upward, rather than pulling.

The Slider, essentially, is a mobile room—a big box capable of moving in any of Tensquare's crisscross groovings and "anchoring" on the strike side by means of a powerful electromagnetic bond. Its winches could hoist a battleship the necessary distance, and the whole craft would tilt, rather than the Slider come loose, if you want any idea of the strength of that bond.

The Slider houses a section operated control indicator which is the most sophisticated "reel" ever designed. Drawing broadcast power from the generator beside the center blister, it is connected by shortwave with the sonar room, where the movements of the quarry are recorded and repeated to the angler seated before the section control.

The fisherman might play his "lines" for hours, days even, without seeing any more than metal and an outline on the screen. Only when the beast is graffled and the extensor shelf, located twelve feet below waterline, slides out for support and begins to aid the winches, only then does the fisherman see his catch rising before him like a fallen Seraphim. Then, as Davits learned, one looks into the Abyss itself and is required to act. He didn't, and a hundred meters of unimaginable tonnage, undernarcotized and hurting, broke the cables of the winch, snapped a graffle, and took a half-minute walk across Tensquare.

We circled till the mechanical flag took notice and waved us on down. We touched beside the personnel hatch and I jettisoned my gear and jumped to the deck.

"Luck," called the pilot as the door was sliding shut. Then he danced into the air and the flag clicked blank.

I shouldered my stuff and went below.

Signing in with Malvern, the de facto captain, I learned that most of the others wouldn't arrive for a good eight hours. They had wanted me alone at Cal's so they could pattern the pub footage along twentieth-century cinema lines.

Open: landing strip, dark. One mechanic prodding a contrary hopper. Stark-o-vision shot of slow bus pulling in. Heavily dressed baitman descends, looks about, limps across field. Close-up: he grins. Move in for words: "Do you think this is the time? The time he *will* be landed?" Embarrassment, taciturnity, a shrug. Dub something. —"I see. And why do you think Miss Luharich has a better chance than any of the others? Is it because she's better equipped? [Grin.] Because more is known now about the creature's habits than when you were out before? Or is it because of her will to win, to be a champion? Is it any one of these things, or is it all of them?" Reply: "Yeah, all of them." "—Is that why you signed on with her? Because your instincts say, 'This one will be it'?" Answer: "She pays union rates. I couldn't rent that damned thing myself. And I want in." Erase. Dub something else. Fade-out as he moves toward hopper, etcetera.

"Cheese," I said, or something like that, and took a walk around Tensquare, by myself.

I mounted each Rook, checking out the controls and the underwater video eyes. Then I raised the main lift.

Malvern had no objections to my testing things this way. In fact, he encouraged it. We had sailed together before and our positions had even been reversed once upon a time. So I wasn't surprised when I stepped off the lift into the Hopkins Locker and found him waiting. For the next ten minutes we inspected the big room in silence, walking through its copper coil chambers soon to be Arctic.

Finally, he slapped a wall.

"Well, will we fill it?"

I shook my head.

"I'd like to, but I doubt it. I don't give two hoots and a damn who gets credit for the catch, so long as I have a part in it. But it won't happen. That gal's an egomaniac. She'll want to operate the Slider, and she can't."

"You ever meet her?"

"Yeah."

"How long ago?"

"Four, five years."

"She was a kid then. How do you know what she can do now?"

"I know. She'll have learned every switch and reading by this time. She'll be up on all theory. But do you remember one time we were together in the starboard Rook, forward, when Ikky broke water like a porpoise?"

"How could I forget?"

"Well?"

He rubbed his emery chin.

"Maybe she can do it, Carl. She's raced torch ships and she's scubaed in bad waters back home." He glanced in the direction of invisible Hand. "And she's hunted in the Highlands. She might be wild enough to pull that horror into her lap without flinching.

". . . For Johns Hopkins to foot the bill and shell out seven figures for the corpus," he added. "That's money, even to a Luharich."

I ducked through a hatchway.

"Maybe you're right, but she was a rich witch when I knew her.

"And she wasn't blonde," I added, meanly.

He yawned.

"Let's find breakfast."

We did that.

When I was young I thought that being born a sea creature was the finest choice Nature could make for anyone. I grew up on the Pacific coast and spent my summers on the Gulf or the Mediterranean. I lived months of my life negotiating coral, photographing trench dwellers, and playing tag with dolphins. I fished everywhere there are fish, resenting the fact that they can go places I can't. When I grew older I wanted bigger fish, and there was nothing living that I knew of, excepting a Sequoia, that came any bigger than Ikky. That's part of it. . . .

I jammed a couple of extra rolls into a paper bag and filled a thermos with coffee. Excusing myself, I left the galley and made my way to the Slider berth. It was just the way I remembered it. I threw a few switches and the shortwave hummed.

"That you, Carl?"

"That's right, Mike. Let me have some juice down here, you double-crossing rat."

He thought it over, then I felt the hull vibrate as the generators cut in. I poured my third cup of coffee and found a cigarette.

"So why am I a double-crossing rat this time?" came his voice again.

"You knew about the cameramen at Hangar Sixteen?"

"Yes."

"Then you're a double-crossing rat. The last thing I want is publicity.

'He who fouled up so often before is ready to try it, nobly, once more.' I can read it now."

"You're wrong. The spotlight's only big enough for one, and she's prettier than you."

My next comment was cut off as I threw the elevator switch and the elephant ears flapped above me. I rose, settling flush with the deck. Retracting the lateral rail, I cut forward into the groove. Amidships, I stopped at a juncture, dropped the lateral, and retracted the longitudinal rail.

I slid starboard, midway between the Rooks, halted, and threw on the coupler.

I hadn't spilled a drop of coffee.

"Show me pictures."

The screen glowed. I adjusted and got outlines of the bottom.

"Okay."

I threw a Status Blue switch and he matched it. The light went on.

The winch unlocked. I aimed out over the waters, extended the arm, and fired a cast.

"Clean one," he commented.

"Status Red. Call strike." I threw a switch.

"Status Red."

The baitman would be on his way with this, to make the barbs tempting.

It's not exactly a fishhook. The cables bear hollow tubes; the tubes convey enough dope for any army of hopheads; Ikky takes the bait, dandled before him by remote control, and the fisherman rams the barbs home.

My hands moved over the console, making the necessary adjustments. I checked the narco-tank reading. Empty. Good, they hadn't been filled yet. I thumbed the Inject button.

"In the gullet," Mike murmured.

I released the cables. I played the beast imagined. I let him run, swinging the winch to simulate his sweep.

I had the air conditioner on and my shirt off and it was still uncomfortably hot, which is how I knew that morning had gone over its noon. I was dimly aware of the arrivals and departures of the hoppers. Some of the crew sat in the "shade" of the doors I had left open, watching the operation. I didn't see Jean arrive or I would have ended the session and gotten below.

She broke my concentration by slamming the door hard enough to shake the bond.

"Mind telling me who authorized you to bring up the Slider?" she asked.

"No one," I replied. "I'll take it below now."

"Just move aside."

I did, and she took my seat. She was wearing brown slacks and a baggy shirt and she had her hair pulled back in a practical manner. Her cheeks were flushed, but not necessarily from the heat. She attacked the panel with a nearly amusing intensity that I found disquieting.

"Status Blue," she snapped, breaking a violet fingernail on the toggle.

I forced a yawn and buttoned my shirt slowly. She threw a side glance my way, checked the registers, and fired a cast.

I monitored the lead on the screen. She turned to me for a second.

"Status Red," she said levelly.

I nodded my agreement.

She worked the winch sideways to show she knew how. I didn't doubt she knew how and she didn't doubt that I didn't doubt, but then—

"In case you're wondering," she said, "you're not going to be anywhere near this thing. You were hired as a baitman, remember? Not a Slider operator! A baitman! Your duties consist of swimming out and setting the table for our friend the monster. It's dangerous, but you're getting well paid for it. Any questions?"

She squashed the Inject button and I rubbed my throat.

"Nope," I smiled, "but I am qualified to run that thingamajigger—and if you need me I'll be available, at union rates."

"Mister Davits," she said, "I don't want a loser operating this panel."

"Miss Luharich, there has never been a winner at this game."

She started reeling in the cable and broke the bond at the same time, so that the whole Slider shook as the big yo-yo returned. We skidded a couple of feet backwards. She raised the laterals and we shot back along the groove. Slowing, she transferred rails and we jolted to a clanging halt, then shot off at a right angle. The crew scrambled away from the hatch as we skidded onto the elevator.

"In the future, Mister Davits, do not enter the Slider without being ordered," she told me.

"Don't worry. I won't even step inside if I am ordered," I answered. "I signed on as a baitman. Remember? If you want me in here, you'll have to *ask* me."

"That'll be the day," she smiled.

I agreed, as the doors closed above us. We dropped the subject and headed in our different directions after the Slider came to a halt in its berth. She did say "good day," though, which I thought showed breeding as well as determination, in reply to my chuckle.

* * *

Later that night Mike and I stoked our pipes in Malvern's cabin. The winds were shuffling waves, and a steady spattering of rain and hail overhead turned the deck into a tin roof.

"Nasty," suggested Malvern.

I nodded. After two bourbons the room had become a familiar woodcut, with its mahogany furnishings (which I had transported from Earth long ago on a whim) and the dark walls, the seasoned face of Malvern, and the perpetually puzzled expression of Dabis set between the big pools of shadow that lay behind chairs and splashed in corners, all cast by the tiny table light and seen through a glass, brownly.

"Glad I'm in here."

"What's it like underneath on a night like this?"

I puffed, thinking of my light cutting through the insides of a black diamond, shaken slightly. The meteor-dart of a suddenly illuminated fish, the swaying of grotesque ferns, like nebulae—shadow, then green, then gone—swam in a moment through my mind. I guess it's like a spaceship would feel, if a spaceship could feel, crossing between worlds—and quiet, uncannily, preternaturally quiet; and peaceful as sleep.

"Dark," I said, "and not real choppy below a few fathoms."

"Another eight hours and we shove off," commented Mike.

"Ten, twelve days, we should be there," noted Malvern.

"What do you think Ikky's doing?"

"Sleeping on the bottom with Mrs. Ikky if he has any brains."

"He hasn't. I've seen ANR's skeletal extrapolation from the bones that have washed up—"

"Hasn't everyone?"

". . . Fully fleshed, he'd be over a hundred meters long. That right, Carl?"

I agreed.

". . . Not much of a brain box, though, for his bulk."

"Smart enough to stay out of our locker."

Chuckles, because nothing exists but this room, really. The world outside is an empty, sleet drummed deck. We lean back and make clouds.

"Boss lady does not approve of unauthorized fly fishing."

"Boss lady can walk north till her hat floats."

"What did she say in there?"

"She told me that my place, with fish manure, is on the bottom."

"You don't Slide?"

"I bait."

"We'll see."

"That's all I do. If she wants a Slideman she's going to have to ask nicely."

"You think she'll have to?"

"I think she'll have to."

"And if she does, can you do it?"

"A fair question," I puffed. "I don't know the answer, though."

I'd incorporate my soul and trade forty percent of the stock for the answer. I'd give a couple years off my life for the answer. But there doesn't seem to be a lineup of supernatural takers, because no one knows. Supposing when we get out there, luck being with us, we find ourselves an Ikky? Supposing we succeed in baiting him and get lines on him. What then? If we get him shipside, will she hold on or crack up? What if she's made of sterner stuff than Davits, who used to hunt sharks with poison-darted air pistols? Supposing she lands him and Davits has to stand there like a video extra.

Worse yet, supposing she asks for Davits and he still stands there like a video extra or something else—say, some yellowbellied embodiment named Cringe?

It was when I got him up above the eight-foot horizon of steel and looked out at all that body, sloping on and on till it dropped out of sight like a green mountain range. . . . And that head. Small for the body, but still immense. Fat, craggy, with lidless roulettes that had spun black and red since before my forefathers decided to try the New Continent. And swaying.

Fresh narco-tanks had been connected. It needed another shot, fast. But I was paralyzed.

It had made a noise like God playing a Hammond organ. . . .

And looked at me!

I don't know if seeing is even the same process in eyes like those. I doubt it. Maybe I was just a gray blur behind a black rock, with the plexi-reflected sky hurting its pupils. But it fixed on me. Perhaps the snake doesn't really paralyze the rabbit, perhaps it's just that rabbits are cowards by constitution. But it began to struggle and I still couldn't move, fascinated.

Fascinated by all that power, by those eyes, they found me there fifteen minutes later, a little broken about the head and shoulders, the Inject still unpushed.

And I dream about those eyes. I want to face them once more, even if their finding takes forever. I've got to know if there's something inside me that sets me apart from a rabbit, from notched plates of reflexes and instincts that always fall apart in exactly the same way whenever the proper combination is spun.

Looking down, I noticed that my hand was shaking. Glancing up, I noticed that no one else was noticing.

I finished my drink and emptied my pipe. It was late and no songbirds were singing.

I sat whittling, my legs hanging over the aft edge, the chips spinning down into the furrow of our wake. Three days out. No action.

"You!"

"Me?"

"You."

Hair like the end of the rainbow, eyes like nothing in nature, fine teeth.

"Hello."

"There's a safety rule against what you're doing, you know."

"I know. I've been worrying about it all morning."

A delicate curl climbed my knife then drifted out behind us. It settled into the foam and was plowed under. I watched her reflection in my blade, taking a secret pleasure in its distortion.

"Are you baiting me?" she finally asked.

I heard her laugh then, and turned, knowing it had been intentional.

"What, me?"

"I could push you off from here, very easily."

"I'd make it back."

"Would you push me off, then—some dark night, perhaps?"

"They're all dark, Miss Luharich. No, I'd rather make you a gift of my carving."

She seated herself beside me then, and I couldn't help but notice the dimples in her knees. She wore white shorts and a halter and still had an offworld tan to her which was awfully appealing. I almost felt a twinge of guilt at having planned the whole scene, but my right hand still blocked her view of the wooden animal.

"Okay, I'll bite. What have you got for me?"

"Just a second. It's almost finished."

Solemnly, I passed her the wooden jackass I had been carving. I felt a little sorry and slightly jackass-ish myself, but I had to follow through. I always do. The mouth was split into a braying grin. The ears were upright.

She didn't smile and she didn't frown. She just studied it.

"It's very good," she finally said, "like most things you do—and appropriate, perhaps."

"Give it to me." I extended a palm.

She handed it back and I tossed it out over the water. It missed the white water and bobbed for awhile like a pigmy seahorse.

"Why did you do that?"

"It was a poor joke. I'm sorry."

"Maybe you are right, though. Perhaps this time I've bitten off a little too much."

I snorted.

"Then why not do something safer, like another race?"

She shook her end of the rainbow.

"No. It has to be an Ikky."

"Why?"

"Why did you want one so badly that you threw away a fortune?"

"Man reasons," I said. "An unfrocked analyst who held black therapy sessions in his basement once told me, 'Mister Davits, you need to reinforce the image of your masculinity by catching one of every kind of fish in existence.' Fish are a very ancient masculinity symbol, you know. So I set out to do it. I have one more to go. —Why do you want to reinforce *your* masculinity?"

"I don't," she said. "I don't want to reinforce anything but Luharich Enterprises. My chief statistician once said, 'Miss Luharich, sell all the cold cream and face powder in the System and you'll be a happy girl. Rich, too.' And he was right. I am the proof. I can look the way I do and do anything, and I sell most of the lipstick and face powder in the System —but I have to be *able* to do anything."

"You do look cool and efficient," I observed.

"I don't feel cool," she said, rising. "Let's go for a swim."

"May I point out that we are making pretty good time?"

"If you want to indicate the obvious, you may. You said you could make it back to the ship, unassisted. Change your mind?"

"No."

"Then get us two scuba outfits and I'll race you under Tensquare.

"I'll win, too," she added.

I stood and looked down at her, because that usually makes me feel superior to women.

"Daughter of Lir, eyes of Picasso," I said, "you've got yourself a race. Meet me at the forward Rook, starboard, in ten minutes."

"Ten minutes," she agreed.

And ten minutes it was. From the center blister to the Rook took maybe two of them, with the load I was carrying. My sandals grew very hot and I was glad to shuck them for flippers when I reached the comparative cool of the corner.

We slid into harnesses and adjusted our gear. She had changed into a trim one-piece green job that made me shade my eyes and look away, then look back again.

I fastened a rope ladder and kicked it over the side. Then I pounded on the wall of the Rook.

"Yeah?"

"You talk to the port Rook, aft?" I called.

"They're all set up," came the answer. "There's ladders and draglines all over that end."

"You sure you want to do this?" asked the sunburnt little gink who was her publicity man, Anderson yclept.

He sat beside the Rook in a deckchair, sipping lemonade through a straw.

"It might be dangerous," he observed, sunken-mouthed. (His teeth were beside him, in another glass.)

"That's right," she smiled. "It *will* be dangerous. Not overly, though."

"Then why don't you let me get some pictures?" We'd have them back to Lifeline in an hour. They'd be in New York by tonight. Good copy."

"No," she said, and turned away from both of us.

She raised her hands to her eyes.

"Here, keep these for me."

She passed him a box full of her unseeing, and when she turned back to me they were the same brown that I remembered.

"Ready?"

"No," I said, tautly. "Listen carefully, Jean. If you're going to play this game there are a few rules. First," I counted, "we're going to be directly beneath the hull, so we have to start low and keep moving. If we bump the bottom, we could rupture an air tank. . . ."

She began to protest that any moron knew that and I cut her down.

"Second," I went on, "there won't be much light, so we'll stay close together, and we will *both* carry torches."

Her wet eyes flashed.

"I dragged you out of Govino without—"

Then she stopped and turned away. She picked up a lamp.

"Okay. Torches. Sorry."

". . . And watch out for the drive-screws," I finished. "There'll be strong currents for at least fifty meters behind them."

She wiped her eyes again and adjusted the mask.

"All right, let's go."

We went.

She led the way, at my insistence. The surface layer was pleasantly warm. At two fathoms the water was bracing; at five it was nice and cold. At eight we let go the swinging stairway and struck out. Tensquare sped forward and we raced in the opposite direction, tattooing the hull yellow at ten-second intervals.

The hull stayed where it belonged, but we raced on like two darkside satellites. Periodically, I tickled her frog feet with my light and traced her antennae of bubbles. About a five meter lead was fine; I'd beat her in the home stretch, but I couldn't let her drop behind yet.

Beneath us, black. Immense. Deep. The Mindanao of Venus, where eternity might eventually pass the dead to a rest in cities of unnamed fishes. I twisted my head away and touched the hull with a feeler of light; it told me we were about a quarter of the way along.

I increased my beat to match her stepped-up stroke, and narrowed the distance which she had suddenly opened by a couple meters. She sped up again and I did, too. I spotted her with my beam.

She turned and it caught on her mask. I never knew whether she'd been smiling. Probably. She raised two fingers in a V-for-Victory and then cut ahead at full speed.

I should have known. I should have felt it coming. It was just a race to her, something else to win. Damn the torpedoes!

So I leaned into it, hard. I don't shake in the water. Or, if I do it doesn't matter and I don't notice it. I began to close the gap again.

She looked back, sped on, looked back. Each time she looked it was nearer, until I'd narrowed it down to the original five meters.

Then she hit the jatoes.

That's what I had been fearing. We were about halfway under and she shouldn't have done it. The powerful jets of compressed air could easily rocket her upward into the hull, or tear something loose if she allowed her body to twist. Their main use is in tearing free from marine plants or fighting bad currents. I had wanted them along as a safety measure, because of the big suck-and-pull windmills behind.

She shot ahead like a meteorite, and I could feel a sudden tingle of perspiration leaping to meet and mix with the churning waters.

I swept ahead, not wanting to use my own guns, and she tripled, quadrupled the margin.

The jets died and she was still on course. Okay, I was an old fuddy-duddy. She *could* have messed up and headed toward the top.

I plowed the sea and began to gather back my yardage, a foot at a time. I wouldn't be able to catch her or beat her now, but I'd be on the ropes before she hit the deck.

Then the spinning magnets began their insistence and she wavered. It was an awfully powerful drag, even at this distance. The call of the meat grinder.

I'd been scratched up by one once, under the *Dolphin,* a fishing boat of the middle-class. I *had* been drinking, but it was also a rough day, and the thing had been turned on prematurely. Fortunately, it was turned off in time, also, and a tendon-stapler made everything good as new, except in the log, where it only mentioned that I'd been drinking. Nothing about it being off-hours when I had a right to do as I damn well pleased.

She had slowed to half her speed, but she was still moving crosswise, toward the port, aft corner. I began to feel the pull myself and had to slow down. She'd made it past the main one, but she seemed too far back. It's hard to gauge distances under water, but each red beat of time told me I was right. She was out of danger from the main one, but the smaller port screw, located about eighty meters in, was no longer a threat but a certainty.

She had turned and was pulling away from it now. Twenty meters separated us. She was standing still. Fifteen.

Slowly, she began a backward drifting. I hit my jatoes, aiming two meters behind her and about twenty back of the blades.

Straightline! Thankgod! Catching, softbelly, leadpipe on shoulder SWIMLIKEHELL! maskcracked, not broke though AND UP!

We caught a line and I remember brandy.

Into the cradle endlessly rocking I spit, pacing. Insomnia tonight and left shoulder sore again, so let it rain on me—they can cure rheumatism. Stupid as hell. What I said. In blankets and shivering. She: "Carl, I can't say it." Me: "Then call it square for that night in Govino, Miss Luharich. Huh?" She: nothing. Me: "Any more of that brandy?" She: "Give me another, too." Me: sounds of sipping. It had only lasted three months. No alimony. Many $ on both sides. Not sure whether they were happy or not. Wine-dark Aegean. Good fishing. Maybe he should have spent more time on shore. Or perhaps she shouldn't have. Good swimmer, though. Dragged him all the way to Vido to wring out his lungs. Young. Both. Strong. Both. Rich and spoiled as hell. Ditto. Corfu should have brought them closer. Didn't. I think that mental cruelty was a trout. He wanted to go to Canada. She: "Go to hell if you want!" He: "Will you go along?" She: "No." But she did, anyhow. Many hells. Expensive. He lost a monster or two. She inherited a couple. Lot of lightning tonight. Stupid as hell. Civility's the coffin of a conned soul. By whom?—Sounds like a bloody neo-ex. . . . But I hate you, Anderson, with your glass full of teeth and her new eyes. . . . Can't keep this pipe lit, keep sucking tobacco. Spit again!

Seven days out and the scope showed Ikky.

Bells jangled, feet pounded, and some optimist set the thermostat in the Hopkins. Malvern wanted me to sit it out, but I slipped into my harness and waited for whatever came. The bruise looked worse than it felt. I had exercised every day and the shoulder hadn't stiffened on me.

A thousand meters ahead and thirty fathoms deep, it tunneled our path. Nothing showed on the surface.

"Will we chase him?" asked an excited crewman.

"Not unless she feels like using money for fuel." I shrugged.

Soon the scope was clear, and it stayed that way. We remained on alert and held our course.

I hadn't said over a dozen words to my boss since the last time we went drowning together, so I decided to raise the score.

"Good afternoon," I approached. "What's new?"

"He's going north-northeast. We'll have to let this one go. A few more days and we can afford some chasing. Not yet."

Sleek head . . .

I nodded. "No telling where this one's headed."

"How's your shoulder?"

"All right. How about you?"

Daughter of Lir . . .

"Fine. By the way, you're down for a nice bonus."

Eyes of perdition!

"Don't mention it," I told her back.

Later that afternoon, and appropriately, a storm shattered. (I prefer "shattered" to "broke." It gives a more accurate idea of the behavior of tropical storms on Venus and saves lots of words.) Remember that inkwell I mentioned earlier? Now take it between thumb and forefinger and hit its side with a hammer. Watch yourself! Don't get splashed or cut—

Dry, then drenched. The sky one million bright fractures as the hammer falls. And sounds of breaking.

"Everyone below?" suggested loudspeakers to the already scurrying crew.

Where was I? Who do you think was doing the loudspeaking?

Everything loose went overboard when the water got to walking, but by then no people were loose. The Slider was the first thing below decks. Then the big lifts lowered their shacks.

I had hit it for the nearest Rook with a yell the moment I recognized the pre-brightening of the holocaust. From there I cut in the speakers and spent half a minute coaching the track team.

Minor injuries had occurred, Mike told me over the radio, but nothing serious. I, however, was marooned for the duration. The Rooks do not lead anywhere; they're set too far out over the hull to provide entry downwards, what with the extensor shelves below.

So I undressed myself of the tanks which I had worn for the past several hours, crossed my flippers on the table, and leaned back to watch the hurricane. The top was black as the bottom and we were in between, and somewhat illuminated because of all that flat, shiny space. The waters above didn't rain down—they just sort of got together and dropped.

The Rooks were secure enough—they'd weathered any number of these onslaughts—it's just that their positions give them a greater arc of rise and descent when Tensquare makes like the rocker of a very nervous grandma. I had used the belts from my rig to strap myself into the bolted-down chair, and I removed several years in purgatory from the soul of whoever left a pack of cigarettes in the table drawer.

I watched the water make teepees and mountains and hands and trees until I started seeing faces and people. So I called Mike.

"What are you doing down there?"

"Wondering what you're doing up there," he replied. "What's it like?"

"You're from the Midwest, aren't you?"

"Yeah."

"Get bad storms out there?"

"Sometimes."

"Try to think of the worst one you were ever in. Got a slide rule handy?"

"Right here."

"Then put a one under it, imagine a zero or two following after, and multiply the thing out."

"I can't imagine the zeros."

"Then retain the multiplicand—that's all you can do."

"So what are you doing up there?"

"I've strapped myself in the chair. I'm watching things roll around the floor right now."

I looked up and out again. I saw one darker shadow in the forest.

"Are you praying or swearing?"

"Damned if I know. But if this were the Slider—if only this were the Slider!"

"He's out there?"

I nodded, forgetting that he couldn't see me.

Big, as I remembered him. He'd only broken surface for a few moments, to look around. *There is no power on Earth that can be compared with him who was made to fear no one.* I dropped my cigarette. It was the same as before. Paralysis and an unborn scream.

"You all right, Carl?"

He had looked at me again. Or seemed to. Perhaps that mindless brute had been waiting half a millennium to ruin the life of a member of the most highly developed species in business. . . .

"You okay?"

. . . Or perhaps it had been ruined already, long before their encounter, and theirs was just a meeting of beasts, the stronger bumping the weaker aside, body to psyche. . . .

"Carl, dammit! Say something!"

He broke again, this time nearer. Did you ever see the trunk of a tornado? It seems like something alive, moving around in all that dark. Nothing has a right to be so big, so strong, and moving. It's a sickening sensation.

"Please answer me."

He was gone and did not come back that day. I finally made a couple of wisecracks at Mike, but I held my next cigarette in my right hand.

The next seventy or eighty thousand waves broke by with a monotonous similarity. The five days that held them were also without distinction. The morning of the thirteenth day out, though, our luck began to rise. The bells broke our coffee-drenched lethargy into small pieces, and we dashed from the galley without hearing what might have been Mike's finest punchline.

"Aft!" cried someone. "Five hundred meters!"

I stripped to my trunks and started buckling. My stuff is always within grabbing distance.

I flipflopped across the deck, girding myself with a deflated squiggler.

"Five hundred meters, twenty fathoms!" boomed the speakers.

The big traps banged upward and the Slider grew to its full height, m'lady at the console. It rattled past me and took root ahead. Its one arm rose and lengthened.

I breasted the Slider as the speakers called, "Four-eighty, twenty!"

"Status Red!"

A belch like an emerging champagne cork and the line arced high over the waters.

"Four-eighty, twenty!" it repeated, all Malvern and static. "Baitman, attend!"

I adjusted my mask and hand-over-handed it down the side. Then warm, then cool, then away.

Green, vast, down. Fast. This is the place where I am equal to a squiggler. If something big decides a baitman looks tastier than what he's carrying, then irony colors his title as well as the water about it.

I caught sight of the drifting cables and followed them down. Green to dark green to black. It had been a long cast, too long. I'd never had to follow one this far down before. I didn't want to switch on my torch.

But I had to.

Bad! I still had a long way to go. I clenched my teeth and stuffed my imagination into a straightjacket.

Finally the line came to an end.

I wrapped one arm about it and unfastened the squiggler. I attached it, working as fast as I could, and plugged in the little insulated connections which are the reason it can't be fired with the line. Ikky could break them, but by then it wouldn't matter.

My mechanical eel hooked up, I pulled its section plugs and watched it grow. I had been dragged deeper during this operation, which took about a minute and a half. I was near—too near—to where I never wanted to be.

Loath as I had been to turn on my light, I was suddenly afraid to turn it off. Panic gripped me and I seized the cable with both hands. The squiggler began to glow, pinkly. It started to twist. It was twice as big as I am and doubtless twice as attractive to pink squiggler-eaters. I told myself this until I believed it, then I switched off my light and started up.

If I bumped into something enormous and steel-hided my heart had orders to stop beating immediately and release me—to dart fitfully forever along Acheron, and gibbering.

Ungibbering, I made it to green water and fled back to the nest.

As soon as they hauled me aboard I made my mask a necklace, shaded my eyes, and monitored for surface turbulence. My first question, of course, was: "Where is he?"

"Nowhere," said a crewman; "we lost him right after you went over. Can't pick him up on the scope now. Musta dived."

"Too bad."

The squiggler stayed down, enjoying its bath. My job ended for the time being, I headed back to warm my coffee with rum.

From behind me, a whisper: "Could you laugh like that afterwards?"

Perceptive Answer: "Depends on what he's laughing at."

Still chuckling, I made my way into the center blister with two cupfuls. "Still hell and gone?"

Mike nodded. His big hands were shaking, and mine were steady as a surgeon's when I set down the cups.

He jumped as I shrugged off the tanks and looked for a bench.

"Don't drip on that panel! You want to kill yourself and blow expensive fuses?"

I toweled down, then settled down to watching the unfilled eye on the wall. I yawned happily; my shoulder seemed good as new.

The little box that people talk through wanted to say something, so Mike lifted the switch and told it to go ahead.

"Is Carl there, Mister Davis?"

"Yes, ma'am."

"Then let me talk to him."

Mike motioned and I moved.

"Talk," I said.

"Are you all right?"

"Yes, thanks. Shouldn't I be?"

"That was a long swim. I—I guess I overshot my cast."

"I'm happy," I said. "More triple-time for me. I really clean up on that hazardous duty clause."

"I'll be more careful next time," she apologized. "I guess I was too eager. Sorry—" Something happened to the sentence, so she ended it there, leaving me with half a bagful of replies I'd been saving.

I lifted the cigarette from behind Mike's ear and got a light from the one in the ashtray.

"Carl, she was being nice," he said, after turning to study the panels.

"I know," I told him. "I wasn't."

"I mean, she's an awfully pretty kid, pleasant. Headstrong and all that. But what's she done to you?"

"Lately?" I asked.

He looked at me, then dropped his eyes to his cup.

"I know it's none of my bus—" he began.

"Cream and sugar?"

Ikky didn't return that day, or that night. We picked up some Dixieland out of Lifeline and let the muskrat ramble while Jean had her supper sent to the Slider. Later she had a bunk assembled inside. I piped in "Deep Water Blues" when it came over the air and waited for her to call up and cuss us out. She didn't, though, so I decided she was sleeping.

Then I got Mike interested in a game of chess that went on until daylight. It limited conversation to several "checks," one "checkmate," and a "damn!" Since he's a poor loser it also effectively sabotaged subsequent talk, which was fine with me. I had a steak and fried potatoes for breakfast and went to bed.

Ten hours later someone shook me awake and I propped myself on one elbow, refusing to open my eyes.

"Whassamadder?"

"I'm sorry to get you up," said one of the younger crewmen, "but Miss Luharich wants you to disconnect the squiggler so we can move on."

I knuckled open one eye, still deciding whether I should be amused.

"Have it hauled to the side. Anyone can disconnect it."

"It's at the side now, sir. But she said it's in your contract and we'd better do things right."

"That's very considerate of her. I'm sure my Local appreciates her remembering."

"Uh, she also said to tell you to change your trunks and comb your hair, and shave, too. Mister Anderson's going to film it."

"Okay. Run along; tell her I'm on my way—and ask if she has some toenail polish I can borrow."

I'll save on details. It took three minutes in all, and I played it properly, even pardoning myself when I slipped and bumped into Anderson's white tropicals with the wet squiggler. He smiled, brushed it off; she smiled, even though Luharich Complectacolor couldn't completely mask the dark circles under her eyes; and I smiled, waving to all our fans out there in videoland. —Remember, Mrs. Universe, you, too, can look like a monster-catcher. Just use Luharich face cream.

I went below and made myself a tuna sandwich, with mayonnaise.

Two days like icebergs—bleak, blank, half-melting, all frigid, mainly out of sight, and definitely a threat to peace of mind—drifted by and were good to put behind. I experienced some old guilt feelings and had a few disturbing dreams. Then, I called Lifeline and checked my bank balance.

"Going shopping?" asked Mike, who had put the call through for me.

"Going home," I answered.

"Huh?"

"I'm out of the baiting business after this one, Mike. The Devil with Ikky! The Devil with Venus and Luharich Enterprises! And the Devil with you!"

Up eyebrows.

"What brought that on?"

"I waited over a year for this job. Now that I'm here, I've decided the whole thing stinks."

"You knew what it was when you signed on. No matter what else you're doing, you're selling face cream when you work for face cream sellers."

"Oh, that's not what's biting me. I admit the commercial angle irritates me, but Tensquare has always been a publicity spot, ever since the first time it sailed."

"What, then?"

"Five or six things, all added up. The main one being that I don't care any more. Once it meant more to me than anything else to hook that critter, and now it doesn't. I went broke on what started out as a lark and I wanted blood for what it cost me. Now I realize that maybe I had it coming. I'm beginning to feel sorry for Ikky."

"And you don't want him now?"

"I'll take him if he comes peacefully, but I don't feel like sticking out my neck to make him crawl into the Hopkins."

"I'm inclined to think it's one of the four or five other things you said you added."

"Such as?"

He scrutinized the ceiling.

I growled.

"Okay, but I won't say it, not just to make you happy you guessed right."

He, smirking: "That look she wears isn't just for Ikky."

"No good, no good." I shook my head. "We're both fission chambers by nature. You can't have jets on both ends of the rocket and expect to go anywhere—what's in the middle just gets smashed."

"That's how it *was*. None of my business, of course—"

"Say that again and you'll say it without teeth."

"Any day, big man"—he looked up—"any place . . ."

"So go ahead. Get it said!"

"She doesn't care about that bloody reptile, she came here to drag you back where you belong. You're not the baitman this trip."

"Five years is too long."

"There must be something under that cruddy hide of yours that people like," he muttered, "or I wouldn't be talking like this. Maybe you remind us humans of some really ugly dog we felt sorry for when we were kids. Anyhow, someone wants to take you home and raise you—also, something about beggars not getting menus."

"Buddy," I chuckled, "do you know what I'm going to do when I hit Lifeline?"

"I can guess."

"You're wrong. I'm torching it to Mars, and then I'll cruise back home, first class. Venus bankruptcy provisions do not apply to Martian trust funds, and I've still got a wad tucked away where moth and corruption enter not. I'm going to pick up a big old mansion on the Gulf and if you're ever looking for a job you can stop around and open bottles for me."

"You are a yellowbellied fink," he commented.

"Okay," I admitted, "but it's her I'm thinking of, too."

"I've heard the stories about you both," he said. "So you're a heel and a goofoff and she's a bitch. That's called compatibility these days. I dare you, baitman, try keeping something you catch."

I turned.

"If you ever want that job, look me up."

I closed the door quietly behind me and left him sitting there waiting for it to slam.

*   *   *

The day of the beast dawned like any other. Two days after my gutless flight from empty waters I went down to rebait. Nothing on the scope. I was just making things ready for the routine attempt.

I hollered a "good morning" from outside the Slider and received an answer from inside before I pushed off. I had reappraised Mike's words, sans sound, sans fury, and while I did not approve of their sentiment or significance, I had opted for civility anyhow.

So down, under, and away. I followed a decent cast about two hundred ninety meters out. The snaking cables burned black to my left and I paced their undulations from the yellowgreen down into the darkness. Soundless lay the wet night, and I bent my way through it like a cock-eyed comet, bright tail before.

I caught the line, slick and smooth, and began baiting. An icy world swept by me then, ankles to head. It was a draft, as if someone had opened a big door beneath me. I wasn't drifting downwards that fast either.

Which meant that something might be moving up, something big enough to displace a lot of water. I still didn't think it was Ikky. A freak current of some sort, but not Ikky. Ha!

I had finished attaching the leads and pulled the first plug when a big, rugged, black island grew beneath me. . . .

I flicked the beam downward. His mouth was opened.

I was rabbit.

Waves of the death-fear passed downward. My stomach imploded. I grew dizzy.

Only one thing, and one thing only. Left to do. I managed it, finally. I pulled the rest of the plugs.

I could count the scaly articulations ridging his eyes by then.

The squiggler grew, pinked into phosphorescence . . . squiggled!

Then my lamp. I had to kill it, leaving just the bait before him.

One glance back as I jammed the jatoes to life.

He was so near that the squiggler reflected on his teeth, in his eyes. Four meters, and I kissed his lambent jowls with two jets of backwash as I soared. Then I didn't know whether he was following or had halted. I began to black out as I waited to be eaten.

The jatoes died and I kicked weakly.

Too fast, I felt a cramp coming on. One flick of the beam, cried rabbit. One second, to know . . .

Or end things up, I answered. No, rabbit, we don't dart before hunters. Stay dark.

Green waters finally, to yellowgreen, then top.

Doubling, I beat off toward Tensquare. The waves from the explosion behind pushed me on ahead. The world closed in, and a screamed, "He's alive!" in the distance.

A giant shadow and a shock wave. The line was alive, too. Happy Fishing Grounds. Maybe I did something wrong. . . .

Somewhere Hand was clenched. What's bait?

A few million years. I remember starting out as a one-celled organism and painfully becoming an amphibian, then an air-breather. From somewhere high in the treetops I heard a voice.

"He's coming around."

I evolved back into homosapience, then a step further into a hangover.

"Don't try to get up yet."

"Have we got him?" I slurred.

"Still fighting, but he's hooked. We thought he took you for an appetizer."

"So did I."

"Breathe some of this and shut up."

A funnel over my face. Good. Lift your cups and drink. . . .

"He was awfully deep. Below scope range. We didn't catch him till he started up. Too late, then."

I began to yawn.

"We'll get you inside now."

I managed to uncase my ankle knife.

"Try it and you'll be minus a thumb."

"You need rest."

"Then bring me a couple more blankets. I'm staying."

I fell back and closed my eyes.

Someone was shaking me. Gloom and cold. Spotlights bled yellow on the deck. I was in a jury-rigged bunk, bulked against the center blister. Swaddled in wool, I still shivered.

"It's been eleven hours. You're not going to see anything now."

I tasted blood.

"Drink this."

Water. I had a remark but I couldn't mouth it.

"Don't ask how I feel," I croaked. "I know that comes next, but don't ask me. Okay?"

"Okay. Want to go below now?"

"No. Just get me my jacket."

"Right here."

"What's he doing?"

"Nothing. He's deep, he's doped but he's staying down."

"How long since last time he showed?"

"Two hours, about."

"Jean?"

"She won't let anyone in the Slider. Listen, Mike says come on in. He's right behind you in the blister."

I sat up and turned. Mike was watching. He gestured; I gestured back.

I swung my feet over the edge and took a couple of deep breaths. Pains in my stomach. I got to my feet and made it into the blister.

"Howza gut?" queried Mike.

I checked the scope. No Ikky. Too deep.

"You buying?"

"Yeah, coffee."

"You're ill. Also, coffee is all that's allowed in here."

"Coffee is a brownish liquid that burns your stomach. You have some in the bottom drawer."

"No cups. You'll have to use a glass."

"Tough."

He poured.

"You do that well. Been practicing for that job?"

"What job?"

"The one I offered you—"

A blot on the scope!

"Rising, ma'am! Rising!" he yelled into the box.

"Thanks, Mike. I've got it in here," she crackled.

"Jean!"

"Shut up! She's busy!"

"Was that Carl?"

"Yeah," I called. "Talk later," and I cut it.

Why did I do that?

"Why did you do that?"

I didn't know.

"I don't know."

Damned echoes! I got up and walked outside.

Nothing. Nothing.

Something?

Tensquare actually rocked! He must have turned when he saw the hull and started downward again. White water to my left, and boiling. An endless spaghetti of cable roared hotly into the belly of the deep.

I stood awhile, then turned and went back inside.

Two hours sick. Four, and better.

"The dope's getting to him."

"Yeah."

"What about Miss Luharich?"

"What about her?"

"She must be half dead."

"Probably."

"What are you going to do about it?"

"She signed the contract for this. She knew what might happen. It did."

"I think you could land him."

"So do I."

"So does she."

"Then let her ask me."

Ikky was drafting lethargically, at thirty fathoms.

I took another walk and happened to pass behind the Slider. She wasn't looking my way.

"Carl, come in here!"

Eyes of Picasso, that's what, and a conspiracy to make me Slide . . .

"Is that an order?"

"Yes—No! Please."

I dashed inside and monitored. He was rising.

"Push or pull?"

I slammed the "wind" and he came like a kitten.

"Make up your own mind now."

He balked at ten fathoms.

"Play him?"

"No!"

She wound him upwards—five fathoms, four . . .

She hit the extensors at two, and they caught him. Then the graffles.

Cries without and a heat lightning of flashbulbs.

The crew saw Ikky.

He began to struggle. She kept the cables tight, raised the graffles . . .

Up.

Another two feet and the graffles began pushing.

Screams and fast footfalls.

Giant beanstalk in the wind, his neck, waving. The green hills of his shoulders grew.

"He's big, Carl!" she cried.

And he grew, and grew, and grew uneasy . . .

"Now!"

He looked down.

He looked down, as the god of our most ancient ancestors might have looked down. Fear, shame, and mocking laughter rang in my head. Her head, too?

"Now!"

She looked up at the nascent earthquake.

"I can't!"

It was going to be so damnably simple this time, now the rabbit had died. I reached out.

I stopped.

"Push it yourself."

"I can't. You do it. Land him, Carl!"

"No. If I do, you'll wonder for the rest of your life whether you could have. You'll throw away your soul finding out. I know you will, because we're alike, and I did it that way. Find out now!"

She stared.

I gripped her shoulders.

"Could be that's me out there," I offered. "I am a green sea serpent, a hateful, monstrous beast, and out to destroy you. I am answerable to no one. Push the Inject."

Her hand moved to the button, jerked back.

"Now!"

She pushed it.

I lowered her still form to the floor and finished things up with Ikky.

It was a good seven hours before I awakened to the steady, sea-chewing grind of Tensquare's blades.

"You're sick," commented Mike.

"How's Jean?"

"The same."

"Where's the beast?"

"Here."

"Good." I rolled over. ". . . Didn't get away this time."

So that's the way it was. No one is born a baitman, I don't think, but the rings of Saturn sing epithalamium the sea-beast's dower.

The Wine-Dark Sea

Robert Aickman

O FF CORFU? Off Euboea? Off Cephalonia? Grigg would never say which it was. Beyond doubt it was an island relatively offshore from an enormously larger island which was relatively inshore from the mainland. On this bigger island was a town with a harbour, mainly for fishing-boats but also for the occasional caïque, and with, nowadays, also a big parking place for motor-coaches. From the waterfront one could see the offshore island, shaped like a whale with a building on its back, or, thought Grigg, like an elephant and castle.

Grigg had not come by motor-coach, and therefore had freedom to see the sights, such as they were; to clamber over the hot, rocky hills; and to sit at his ease every evening watching the splendid sunsets. He found the food monotonous, the noise incredible, and the women disappointing (in general, they seemed only to come to identity around the age of sixty, when they rapidly transmogrified into witches and seers); but drink was cheap and the distant past ubiquitous. The language was a difficulty, of course, but Grigg could still scramble a short distance on what remained to him of the ancient variety, which, now that a test had come, was more than he had supposed.

Most of the time it was straight, beating sunshine, something that had to be accommodated to by a steady act of will, like a Scandinavian winter (at least if there was any kind of serious enterprise on hand), but sometimes the air was green or blue or purple, and then the vast bay could be among the most beautiful places in the world, especially when the colour was purple. On his second or third evening, Grigg sat outside a café, an establishment patronized almost entirely by boring, noisy males, but unself-conscious and affable, none the less. He was drinking local drinks, and, despite the din, feeling himself almost to merge with the purple evening light. In the middle of the view appeared a smallish boat, with curving bow and stern, low freeboard, and a single square sail. If it had not risen from the depths, it must have sailed from behind the small offshore island. It seemed timeless in shape and handling. It added exactly the right kind of life to the sea, air, and evening.

But Grigg noticed at once that the other customers did not seem to think so. Not only did they stare at the beautiful boat, but they stared with expressions of direct hatred that an Englishman has no practice in adopting. They fell almost silent, which was a bad sign indeed. Even the white-coated waiters stopped running about and stood gazing out to sea like the customers. All that happened was that the boat put about and sailed on to the open waters. As she turned, Grigg thought that he could discern the shapes of sailors. They must have been good at their work, because the ship made off along a dead straight line in what seemed to Grigg to be very little breeze. Already she was merely a darker purple fleck in the perceptibly oncoming evening. The hubbub in the café soon worked up again. Grigg got the impression that the ship, though unpopular, was quite familiar.

Soon his waiter was removing his glass. Grigg ordered a renewal.

"What was that ship?"

He perceived that the waiter had a little English, but doubted whether it would suffice for this. It did suffice.

"She comes from the island." The waiter stood gazing out, either at the ship or at the island.

"Can I visit the island?"

"No. There is no boat."

"Surely I can hire one if I pay for it?"

"No. There is no boat." And the waiter departed.

When he returned with Grigg's ensuing *ouzo*, Grigg did not resume the subject. All the same, what the waiter said had been absurd. The island could hardly have been more than a mile away and lay in the center of the calm, sheltered bay. Grigg had not previously thought of the island as anything more than a point of emphasis in the view, an eye-catcher, as our ancestors termed it. Now he wanted to see more.

In the town was one of the state tourist offices, to which all foreign travellers are directed to go when in need. Grigg had not visited any of them before, but now was the time. He went next morning.

The pleasant young man who seemed in sole possession spoke pretty good English and received Grigg's enquiry with sophistication.

"The fishermen do not like the island," he said, smiling. "They give it, as you say, a wide berth."

"Why is that?"

"It is said to be a very *old* island."

"But surely this is a very old country?"

"Not as old as the island. Or so the fishermen say."

"Is that a *bad* thing? Being very old?"

"Yes," said the young man, with perceptibly less sophistication. "A bad thing." He sounded surprisingly firm. Grigg recollected that the tourist officials were recruited from the police.

"Then you think that no one will take me there?"

"I am sure of it," said the young man, again smiling. "No one."

"Then I shall have to swim," said Grigg. He spoke lightly, and he would have hated to have to do it. But the young man, who could not be sure of this, tried another tack.

"There's nothing to see on the island," he said a shade anxiously. "Nothing at all, I assure you. Let me give you our leaflet of tourist sights. All very nice."

"Thank you," said Grigg. "I've got one already."

The young man put the leaflet away, more obviously disappointed than an Englishman would have permitted of himself.

"Then you've been to the island yourself?" asked Grigg.

"No," said the young man. "As I told you, there is nothing to see."

"Last night I saw a ship sail from the island. Either someone must live there or there must be some reason for going there."

"I do not know about that," said the young man, slightly sulky but still trying. "I cannot imagine that anyone lives there or wants to go there." Grigg could not suppose that this was to be interpreted quite literally.

"Why shouldn't they?"

"The Turks. The Turks made the island unlucky."

Long before, Grigg had realized that throughout Hellas everything bad that cannot be attributed to the evil eye or other supernatural influence is blamed upon the Turks; even though the stranger is apt on occasion to suspect, however unworthily, that the Turks provided the last settled and secure government the region has known. And he had furthermore realized that it is a subject upon which argument is not merely useless but impossible. The Turks and their special graces have been expunged from Hellenic history; their mosques demolished or converted into cinemas.

"I see," said Grigg. "Thank you for your advice. But I must make it clear that I do not undertake to follow it."

The young man smiled him out, confident that the local brick wall would fully withstand the pounding of Grigg's unbalanced and middle-aged head.

And so it seemed. Contrary to legend, Grigg, as the day wore on, discovered that few of the fishermen seemed interested in his money: to be more precise, none of them, or none that he approached, and he had approached many. It did not seem to be that they objected to going to the

island, because in most cases he had not reached the point of even mentioning the island: they simply did not want to take him anywhere, even
for what Grigg regarded as a considerable sum. They appeared to be very
much preoccupied with their ordinary work. They would spend one entire
day stretching their saffron-coloured nets to dry on the stones of the quay.
Naturally the language barrier did not help, but Grigg got the impression
that, in the view of the fishermen, as of various others he had met, tourists
should adhere to their proper groove and not demand to wander among
the real toilers, the genuine and living ancestors. Tourists were not to be
comprehended among those strangers for whom, notoriously, the word is
the same as for guests.

None of the separate, discouraging negotiations had taken long, and by
the evening of that same day Grigg had combed the port and now found
time on his hands. Thinking about it all, over an early drink, he wondered
if word could have gone round as to the real destination of his proposed
excursion. He also wondered if the island could be an enclave of the
military, who were often to be found embattled in the most renowned and
unexpected corners of the land. It seemed unlikely: the young man would
have been proud to tell him so at once, as a young cowherd had told him
at the ancient castro above Thessalonika. Besides, the ship he had seen
could hardly have served for war since the Pericleans. It struck him to
wonder whether the ship had returned during the night. He felt sure that
it belonged to the island and not elsewhere. He even thought of buying a
pair of field-glasses, but desisted because they would have to be carried all
the way home.

Over his next *ouzo*, Grigg went on to consider why it mattered to him
about reaching the island, especially when so much difficulty seemed to be
involved. He decided that, in the first place, it had been the beautiful ship.
In the second place, it had been the hostility to her of the people in the
café. Grigg was one whose feelings were usually contrary to any that
might be expressed in mass emotion; and he was confirmed in this when
the popular feeling was so morally narrow and so uniform as, commonly,
among the Hellenes. In the third place, it was undoubtedly the mysterious
business about the island being bad because very old. A perceptive traveller in Hellas comes to think of the Parthenon as quite modern; to become
more and more absorbed by what came earlier. Soon, if truly perceptive,
he is searching seriously for centaurs.

All the same, Grigg quite surprised himself by what he actually did.
Walking along the hard road in the heat of the next mid-afternoon, with
almost no one else so foolish as to be about at all, apart from the usual
discontented coach trip, he observed a small boat with an outboard motor. She was attached, bow on, to a ring. He could borrow her, visit the

island, be back almost within an hour, and pay then, if anyone relevant had appeared. He was sure that it was now or never. He was able to untie the painter almost at his leisure, while the coach-party stared at him, welcoming the familiar activity and the familiar-looking man who was doing it. The engine started popping at the first pull. A miracle, thought Grigg, who had experience of outboards: fate is with me. In a matter of · hardly more than seconds in all, his hand was on the helm and he was off.

To anyone that loves the seas of Britain or the great sands of Belgium and Holland, there is something faintly repulsive about the tideless Mediterranean and Aegean, which on a calm day tend to be at once stagnant and a little uncanny. Dense weed often clogs the shallows, uncleaned by ebb and flow; and one speculates upon fathom five and millennia many of unshifting spoil. While he was still near the shore, Grigg's enjoyment was mitigated also by the smell, much more noticeable than from the land; but soon the pleasure of being afloat at all worked on him, and within minutes there was nothing in his heart but the sun, the breeze, the parting of the water at the prow of the boat, and the island ahead. After a spell, he did half look over his shoulder for a possible gesticulating figure on the quay. There was no one. Even the coach-party was re-embarked and poised to go elsewhere. And soon the lights that sparkled on the miniature waves were like downland flowers in spring.

Upon a closer view, the building on the island's back proved to be merely the central section, or keep, of saffron-coloured fortifications that included the whole area. In view of what the man at the tourist office had said, they had presumably been erected by the Turks, but one never quite knew whether there had not been contributions from the Venetians, or the Normans, or the Bulgars, or the Cyclops, or, at different times, from them all. Some of the present structures seemed far gone in decay, but all of them were covered with clusters and swags of large, brightly coloured flowers, so that the total effect was quite dazzling, especially when seen across a few hundred yards of radiant blue sea. Grigg perceived that the island was simply a rock; a dark brown, or reddish brown rock, which stood out everywhere quite distinctly from the lighter hue of the stonework.

Then he saw that the sunlight was glinting on glass in at least some of the windows, small and deepset though they were. To his right, moreover, an ornamental balustrade, hardly a part of the fortress, descended the sloping back of the island until it ended almost at sea-level. Grigg thought that the rock might continue to slope in the same gentle degree under the water, so that it would be as well to go cautiously and to keep well out; but it seemed, none the less, the likeliest end of the island for a landing. He rounded the island in this way without incident, and saw that on the far side there was a square stone harbour, though void alike of craft and of citizens. He cut off his noisy engine and drifted in. He marvelled more than ever at the number, the size, and the gorgeousness of the flowers. Already, still out at sea, he could even smell them: not the smell of one particular species, but a massed perfume, heavy and almost melodious, drifting across the limpid water to meet and enfold him. He sailed silently in like a coasting bird, and settled perfectly at the harbour steps, as one commonly does when not a soul is looking. Grigg sprang ashore, climbed the steps, which were made of marble, and made fast to one of the rings in the stonework at the top. He observed that here the ocean-verge was uncluttered with weed, so that he could look downwards many yards through the water and the shoals of fish to the sunny sand below.

Having but borrowed the boat, he meant, of course, to remain for only a matter of minutes; merely to make up his mind as to whether there was anything on the island to justify the difficulty of a renewed effort for a more conventional visit. At once, however, he realized how glad he was to be alone, how greatly a professional boatman would have spoiled his pleasure.

On this side of the long sloping balustrade were wide steps; a marble staircase leading from port to citadel. They were immaculate: even, level, and almost polished in their smoothness. Grigg ascended. On his right was the bare brown rock. He noticed that it was strikingly rough and gnarled, with hardly anywhere a flat area as big as a lace handkerchief. He put his hand on this rough rock. It was so hot that it almost burnt him. Still, soil had come from somewhere: as well as the wonderful flowers, there were fruit trees ahead and heavy creepers. Curiously coloured lizards lay about the steps watching him. He could not quite name the colour. Azure, perhaps; or cerulean. When he reached the citadel, there were nectarines hanging from the branches spread out against the yellow walls. They seemed much ahead of their time, Grigg thought, but supposed that so far south the seasons were different. He was feeling more and more a trespasser. The island was quite plainly inhabited and cared for. There was nothing about it which accorded with the impression given at the tourist office.

The citadel had wooden gates, but they were open. Grigg hesitated. There was nothing to be heard but the soft sea and the bees. He listened, and entered the citadel.

The structure ranged round three sides of a stone-paved courtyard. The fourth side, which faced away from the bigger island, had either fallen or been bombarded into ruin, and then perhaps been demolished, so that now there was nothing left but high, rough edges of yellow masonry framing the view of the open sea, vast, featureless, and the colour of the sky. Again there were flowers everywhere, with a big flowering tree near the centre of the court. The glazed windows stood open, and so did several doors. Grigg did not care to enter: the place was clearly lived in, and he had no justification for being there.

Still he did not feel as yet like returning.

On the far side of the courtyard was another open gateway. Grigg passed cautiously through it. There seemed nothing to worry about. As usual, no one was to be seen. There were not even the farm animals he had half expected. There was nothing but a tangle of collapsed defence structures from past centuries, starting with an irregular wall which ringed this entire end of the island at little above sea-level. Between the many ruined buildings was dense, sharp grass, reaching above Grigg's knees, and unpleasantly suggestive also of snakes. None the less, he ploughed on, convinced by now that this was his only chance, as he would never be able to find a reason for coming back.

A considerable garrison must have been installed at one time, or at least contemplated. The place was still like a maze, and also gave the impression, even now, of having been abandoned quite suddenly, doubtless when the Turks departed. There were still long guns, mounted and pointing out to sea, though drawn back. There were straggling, dangerous stacks of stone, and other obviously ancient heaps that might once have been heaps of anything. Grigg was far too hot and increasingly lacerated, but he determined to scramble on, as there was a circular tower at the end of the island, which, if climbable, might offer a more revealing panorama. Anyway, who that had imagination, could reach the island in the way Grigg had reached it, and not at least try to climb that tower?

When at long last attained, the tower seemed to be in almost perfect order. Grigg dragged open the parched door, and wound his way up and up through the spiders and other crepusculae. The circular stone stair emerged through a now uncovered hole in the stone roof, so that the top steps were shapeless and treacherous beneath deep, lumpy silt which had drifted in from the atmosphere.

And then there was a revelation indeed. As Grigg emerged and looked out over the low battlements, he saw on the instant that another boat had entered the small harbour, almost a ship; in fact, without doubt, *the* ship. She was painted green, and her single blue sail had already been struck. Grigg perceived that now he could hardly depart from the island without explanations.

He descended the tower, not having studied the other features of the prospect as carefully as he otherwise would have done. As he stumbled back through the débris and thick, dry vegetation, he grazed and sliced himself even more than on the outward scramble. He felt very undignified as he re-entered the citadel, especially as he was hotter than ever.

Standing in the courtyard were three women. They all appeared to be aged between thirty and forty, and they all wore identical greeny-brown dresses, plainly intended for service.

"Good afternoon," said one of the women. "Do you wish to stay with us?" She had a foreign accent, but it struck Grigg at once as not being Greek.

"Can one stay?" It was a foolish rejoinder, but instinctual.

"We do not run an hotel, but we sometimes have guests. It is as you wish."

"I am staying in the town. I couldn't find out anything about the island, so I borrowed a boat to see for myself."

"How did you do that?" asked one of the other women, in what seemed to Grigg to be the same foreign accent. She had dark hair, where the other two were fair, and a darker voice than the first speaker.

"Do what?"

"Borrow a boat. They would never lend you a boat to come here."

"No," said Grigg, certain that he was blushing under the singularly direct gaze of his interrogator's black eyes. "It was difficult." After pausing for a second, he took a small plunge. "Why should that be?"

"The Greeks are stupid," said the first woman. "Violent and vengeful, of course, too; quite incapable of government; but, above all, stupid. They can't even grow a tree. They can only cut them down." She placed her hand on the bole of the beautiful flowering tree which grew in the courtyard. It was a rather fine movement, Grigg thought, much more like the Greeks of myth than any of the Greeks he could remember actually to have seen.

"They certainly seem to have a particular feeling about this island."

No further explanation was forthcoming. There was merely another slight pause. Then the first woman spoke.

"Do *you* have any particular feeling about this island?"

"I think it is the most beautiful place I have ever visited," replied Grigg, hardly knowing whether or not he exaggerated.

"Then stay with us."

"I have to take back the boat. As I said, I have only borrowed it."

The third woman spoke for the first time. "I shouldn't take back the boat." She spoke with the same accent as the others, and her tone was one of pleasant warning.

"What do you mean?" asked Grigg.

"You'll be torn to pieces if you do."

"Oh, surely not," said Grigg, laughing uneasily.

"Didn't you steal the boat?" The woman was smiling quite amicably. "Or at least borrow it without asking?"

"As a matter of fact, yes."

"And haven't you borrowed it so as to come here?"

"Yes."

"They'll tear you to pieces." She spoke as if it were the most foregone of conclusions; but, seeing that Grigg still doubted, she added in friendly seriousness, "Believe it. It's true. If you leave us, you can't go back. You'll have to go somewhere else. A long way off."

Inevitably, Grigg was impressed. "But tell me," he said, "why shouldn't I—or anyone else—come here?"

The woman with the black eyes looked hard at Grigg. "They believe we're sorcerers—sorcer*esses,*" she corrected herself, tripping over the language.

Grigg was familiar with such talk among southern peasants. "And are you?" he asked lightly.

"Yes," said the dark woman. "We are."

"Yes," confirmed the first woman. "We are all sorceresses." There was about the statement neither facetiousness nor challenge.

"I see," said Grigg gravely; and looked away from them out to the open ocean, empty as before.

"People who come here usually know that already," said the first woman; again in simple explanation.

Grigg turned back to them and stared for a moment. They really were, he realized, most striking to see, all three of them: with beautifully shaped, muscular, brown limbs; strong necks and markedly sculptural features; and a casual grandeur of posture, which was perhaps the most impressive thing of all. And their practical, almost primitive, garments suited them wonderfully. The two fair women wore yellow shoes, but the dark woman was bare-footed, with strong, open toes. Grigg was struck by a thought.

"Yesterday I saw your ship," he said. "In a way, it was why I came. Do you sail her yourself?"

"Yes," said the first woman. "We have sometimes to buy things, and they will sell us nothing here. We built the boat on a beach in Albania, where no one lives. We took wood from the forests behind, which belong to no one."

"I believe that now they belong to the People's Republic," Grigg said, smiling.

"That is the same thing," said the woman.

"I suspect that you are right about my little boat," said Grigg. "They tell you to act more regularly on impulse, but I often act on impulse, and almost always find that it was a mistake, sometimes a surprisingly bad one."

"Coming here was not necessarily a mistake," said the first woman. "It depends."

"I wasn't thinking about that part of it," said Grigg, convicted of rudeness. "I like it here. I was thinking of what will happen when I go back—whenever I go back."

"One of us will guide you to somewhere where you'll be safe. Now, if you wish."

"Thank you," said Grigg. "But I only borrowed the boat and must really return it."

"Take it back during the night," said the third woman, with unexpected practicality.

And thus it was that Grigg decided to stay; at least until it was dark.

There was work to be done: first, the unloading of the ship. Grigg naturally offered to help, but the women seemed very cool about it.

"The tasks are disposed for the three of us," said the woman who had spoken first, "and you would find it very hot."

Grigg could not deny this last statement, as he was already perspiring freely, though standing still. None the less, he could hardly leave it at that.

"As you are permitting me to intrude upon you," he said, "please permit me to help."

"You are not an intruder," said the woman, "but you are a stranger, and the tasks are for me and my sisters."

She made Grigg feel so completely unqualified that he could think of nothing to say. "The house is open to you," continued the woman. "Go wherever you like. The heat is not good unless you are accustomed to it." The three women then went out through the harbour gateway and down the long flight of marble steps to the ship. Grigg looked after them as they descended, but none of them looked back.

Grigg entered through one of the doors and began to prowl about. There were many rooms, some big, some small, but all well proportioned. All were painted in different colours, all perfectly clean, all open to the world, and all empty. The whole place was beautifully tended, but it was hard to see for what, at least by accepted standards.

Grigg ascended to the floor above. The marble staircase led to a landing from which was reached a larger and higher room than any of the others. It had doubtless been the main hall of the citadel. Three tall windows opened on to small decorative balconies overlooking the courtyard. On a part of the floor against the wall opposite these windows were rectangular cushions packed together like mah-jong pieces, to make an area of softness. There were smaller windows high in the wall above them. There was nothing else in the room but a big circular bowl of flowers. It stood on the floor towards one corner, and had been hewn from pink marble. Grigg thought that the combined effect of the cushions, the flowers, and the proportions of the room was one of extreme luxury. The idea came to him, not for the first time, that most of the things which people buy in the belief that they are luxuries are really poor substitutes for luxury.

The other rooms on that floor of the citadel were as the rooms below, spotless, sunny, but empty. On the second floor there were several rooms furnished as the hall; with in one place a mass of deep cushions, in another a mass of flowers, and nothing else. Sometimes the flowers were in big iron bowls mounted on tripods; sometimes in reservoirs forming a part (but the dominant part) of a statuary group. On the first and second floors, the rooms led into one another, and most of them had windows in both the longer, opposing walls; one window, or set of windows, overlooking the larger island from which Grigg had come, the other overlooking the open sea. It was true that there were doors, in coloured wood; but all, without exception, stood open. There was nothing so very unusual about the building, agreeable though it was, and nothing in the least mysterious in themselves about its appurtenances, but before Grigg had completed his tour and emerged on to the flat roof, he had begun to feel quite depressed by the recollection of how he and his neighbours dwelt, almost immersed beneath mass-produced superfluities, impotent even as distractions.

On the roof was a single stone figure of a recumbent man, more than life-size. It reposed at one end of the roof with its back to the harbour, and it was from the other end of the roof that Grigg first saw it, so that he had a longish walk across the bare expanse before he came up to it, like a visitor to Mussolini in the great days.

The figure was, inevitably, of the kind vaguely to be termed classical; but Grigg doubted whether, in any proper sense, it was classical at all. It was not so much that it was in perfect order, as if it had been carved that same year, and glossy of surface, both of which things are rare with ancient sculpture, but rather the sentiment with which the figure was imbued, and which it projected as an aura, the compulsive implication of the artist's work, if indeed there had ever been an artist.

It was a male of advanced years, or alternatively, perhaps, ageless, who reclined with his head on his right hand which rose from the elbow on the ground, a position which Grigg had always found to be especially uncomfortable. The hair straggled unkempt over the low cranium. The big eyes

protruded above the snub nose, and from the thick lips the tongue protruded slightly also. There was a lumpy chin, unconcealed by a beard. The
rest of the body was hirsute, long-armed, and muscular; hands, feet, and
phallus being enormous. The man appeared to be lying on the bare and
wrinkled earth; or possibly, it struck Grigg, on rocks. The folds in the
stone ground of the statue (it seemed to be some other stone than the
usual marble) were very similar to the folds in the rock which he had
noticed as he walked up from the harbour. There was something compressed and drawn together about the man's entire attitude, almost like a
foetus in the womb, or an immensely strong spring, compressed against
the moment of use. Grigg thought that the man did not so much stare at
him, though staring he certainly was, as right through him and beyond
him, probably far beyond. As Grigg gazed back, a small spurt of dirty
water bubbled from the man's open mouth. It dribbled from his tongue
and discoloured the forearm supporting his head. There must have been a
pump to supply the fountain, and Grigg was not surprised, considering
the obvious mechanical problems, that it did not work very well.

Grigg advanced to the balustrade surrounding the citadel roof and
looked over to the harbour. The women were still at work unloading the
ship. One of them, the smaller of the two with fair hair, who had been the
last to speak when Grigg appeared, was carrying up the wide steps a large
green cask, mounted on her right shoulder.

Grigg felt very uncertain what to do. He could hardly just stand about
while the women were working so industriously, but he felt that the rejection of his services had been singularly final, and he also felt that if he
succeeded in insisting, then he would almost certainly make a fool of
himself in the great heat and with a routine of which he was ignorant. He
had nothing even to read, nor had he seen anything to read on the entire
island. He decided, pusillanimously, to stay where he was, until things
below perhaps quieted down.

He sank upon the stones of the roof at a place where the balustrade
gave a little shade. He had in mind to stretch out for a siesta, but the
stones were so hard and so level that he found himself propping his head
on his hand, like the stone man he had just been looking at. He gazed out
to sea between the columns of the balustrade, but the attitude soon
proved every bit as uncomfortable as he had always thought, and he
began instead to sprawl upon his back, pushed as close against the balustrade as he could manage, in the need for as much shade as possible. He
reflected that again he was imitating the stone man, so drawn in on himself.

It was, in any case, quite useless, and, like most useless things, useless
almost immediately. Not only was the sun unbearable, but the stored heat

of the stone was even more unbearable and worse even than its hardness, though stone is harder in the Hellenes than anywhere else. After only a few minutes, Grigg felt as stiff and parched as an old tobacco leaf; so much so that he had difficulty in rising to his feet, and was glad that his middle-aged muddling, the dropsy of a welfare society, was not under observation.

He descended to the floor below and sank himself on the cushioned area in one of the luxurious rooms; he neither knew nor cared which. Through the open windows had flown in some very tiny, curiously coloured birds. Grigg could not quite name the colour: some kind of bright blue, aquamarine perhaps. The birds fluttered immoderately, like moths; and, from their throats or wings or both, came a faint, high, silvery, unceasing chant, as of honey heard dripping from the very summit of Hymettus. Grigg normally liked a bird in the room no more than other men like it; but all he did about the birds now was fall dead asleep.

At some time during his sleep, he had a nightmare. He dreamed that lizards, not small blue ones, but quite large black ones, possibly eighteen inches long, were biting off his own flesh. Already they had devoured most of the flesh on his feet and legs, so that he could see the bare, red bones extending upwards almost to the knees. It was difficult to look, however. There was something in common between his attitude, lying uncomfortably on his back, and the attitude he had been forced into on the roof. He did not seem to be tied down in any way, or even drugged, but he was much too stiff to move very much, none the less. Gnawing away even now were eight or ten lizards, with long angular legs, big clawed feet, and oversized necks, heads, and eyes; and there were many other similar lizards, standing silently in the background, a terrifying number, in fact. Perhaps they are waiting their turn, Grigg thought; and then remembered that it was something which animals are seldom observed to do. One curious thing was that the gnawing did not exactly hurt: it was quite perceptible, but Grigg felt it as a nervous *frisson* charging his whole body, half painful but half pleasurable, like a mild current of electricity from a machine on the pier. Grigg could not decide whether or not he was wearing clothes. When he looked, he could see his bare legs (very bare in fact); while, at the same time, he *felt* as if he were fully dressed. But, then again, the lizards had already pecked at other patches of his body. He trembled to think what it would be like when they reached his head.

But before they did, Grigg was awake, or, rather, awakened.

The scene seemed hardly less strange, because there were several things to be taken in at once.

In the first place, the whole room was filled with a dim and dusky red light, which Grigg soon realized was probably just the last of the sunset, suggesting that he had slept a long time.

In the second place, the room seemed to be what he could only regard as moving about. There was a steady pitching, up, down, up; and with it was incorporated a sick-making diagonal tilt. It was by no means a single lurch, but a persistent, though far from regular, heaving and plunging.

"An earthquake," cried Grigg very loudly to the twilight; now much more fully awake.

He tried to leap up, but then realized a third thing: in some way he was being restrained.

He awoke completely. There was a weight on his chest, and bonds round his arms. He perceived that it was a human being who was imprisoning him, holding him down.

It was one of the three women. She lifted her head, though without releasing him, and he perceived that it was the woman he had last seen carrying the green cask on her shoulder up the steps.

"It will end," she said. "Lie still and it will be over."

"It *is* an earthquake?" enquired Grigg in a whisper.

"Yes," she said. "An earthquake." Her tonelessness was probably deliberate and intended to reassure. She tightened her hold of him, and as she moved her head, he felt her hair against his face in the near darkness.

"What's your name?" asked Grigg in the same whisper.

"My name is Tal."

"You are beautiful."

"You are strong."

Grigg had not, before she spoke, felt at all strong.

"I could hardly hold you." She spoke as if she had saved him from some great peril.

"I was dreaming. I still am dreaming."

"Then I am part of the dream."

"The whole island is a dream but it is a very lovely island."

"It is an island of love."

Suddenly he realized that she was naked.

The last of the sunset, setting fire to his body, kindled it into a blaze. The two of them rolled over onto the warm floor.

"It is my first earthquake," he said. "I always thought earthquakes were bad."

And in the few flushed minutes before it was absolutely and finally dark, in that region where darkness comes quickly, he had possessed her, with uttermost rapture, a rapture not previously imaginable.

*   *   *

He heard her voice through the darkness speaking, he divined, from the doorway. She sounded as cool as the night was still warm.

"There is a meal."

"I am hungry for it."

The earthquake had ended. It was as if they two had ended it.

"Can you find your way down without a light?"

"I'm sure I can." After all, she had given him the eyes of a cat, of a muscular, blonde cat.

"We eat in the courtyard."

"I could devour an ox," commented Grigg happily, and abandoning all restraint.

"We eat fruit," she said, and he could hear her leaving him through the darkness.

"Tal!" he cried after her, but softly. He wanted to kiss her, to ravish her again; but she did not return.

There she was, however, eating nectarines with the others, as soon as he had groped his way down. There were grapes, nuts, and oranges, not in dishes but strewn with the nectarines about the stones of the court. Grigg thought it was just as if all the fruit had been scattered from a cornucopia. There were also a whole chest of figs and heavy lumps of small dates in a big brown canvas bag. The three women had brought out cushions and were eating in what is supposed to have been the Roman style. There were cushions for Grigg, too, and soon he was peeling an orange. The sky was now full of stars.

"I am Lek," said the other fair woman.

"I am Vin," said the dark woman. She was still bare-footed, Grigg noticed.

As Tal said nothing, Grigg wondered how much was known.

"I am Grigg."

"Be welcome, Grigg," said Lek, the woman who had spoken to him first, that afternoon in this same courtyard; "be assured of all our loves."

"Thank you," replied Grigg. "I am happy."

Vin threw him a nut; or rather, if he had not been able to see her warm smile in the now clear starlight, he might have supposed that she had thrown a nut at him, so hard did it hit. What was more, he noticed that there were no nutcrackers and no substitute for them. The women split the nuts open by biting them, which was entirely beyond him to do. It was quite a serious matter, because he really could not subsist entirely on fruit. He had, after all, eaten nothing since breakfast. However, he looked with surreptitious meaning at Tal, and felt compensated but less than reas-

sured. Moreover, the night, instead of growing cooler, seemed to be growing steadily warmer.

"Don't earthquakes usually do damage?" he asked.

"Elsewhere they do," replied Lek, splintering a nut. "Not here."

"Our earthquakes are not like other people's earthquakes," said Vin.
She did not say it banteringly, but rather as if to discourage further questions. She, too, was carefully picking scraps of nut from splinters of shell.

"I see," said Grigg. "Or rather, I don't see at all."

"We do not claim to be like other people in any way," explained Lek.
"As I told you, we are sorceresses."

"I remember," said Grigg. "What exactly does that mean?"

"It is not to be described," said Lek.

"I feared as much," said Grigg, glancing again at Tal, who so far had
not spoken at all.

"You misunderstand," said Lek. "I mean that the description would be
without meaning. The thing can only be felt, experienced. It is not a
matter of conjuring, of turning lead into gold, or wine into blood. We can
do all those things as well, but they are bad and to be avoided, or left
behind."

"I think I have heard something of the kind," said Grigg. "I am sorry
to be inquisitive. All the same, it might have been nice if you could have
prevented that earthquake."

"There was no reason to prevent it."

"Sorry," said Grigg, tired of the mystification. "It is none of my business, anyway."

"That depends," said Lek.

"Upon whether you decide to stay or go," said Vin. As she spoke, she
took off her plain, greeny-brown dress. She did it casually, as a woman
might remove a scarf when she finds it too hot. Vin was wearing no other
garment, and now lay naked on the cushions, her back against the low
wall, behind which stretched the sea.

"On this island," continued Lek, "we live as all people once lived. But
long ago they thought better of it and started looking for something else.
They have been looking, instead of living, ever since."

"What have they been looking for?"

"They call it achievement. They call it knowledge. They call it mastery.
They even call it happiness. You called it happiness just now, when Vin
threw a nut at you, but we are prepared to treat that as a slip of the
tongue by a newcomer. And do you know who started it all?"

"I would rather you told me."

"The Greeks started it. It was their stupidity. Have you not seen how
stupid the Greeks are?"

"As a matter of fact, I have. It is not at all what one is led to expect. I have been continuously surprised by it."

"Nothing to be surprised at. It is the same quality that made the Greeks separate man from nature in the first place, or rather from life."

"You mean the ancient Greeks?" asked Grigg, staring at her.

"The same Greeks. All Greeks are the same. All stupid. All lopsided. All poisoned with masculinity."

"Yes," said Grigg, smiling. "As a matter of fact, I have noticed something like that. It is not a country for women." His eyes drifted to Vin's naked body, gleaming in the starlight.

"Once it was. We ruled once, but they drove us out," said Lek, more sadly than fiercely. "We fought, and later they wrote silly plays about the fight, but they defeated us, though not by the superior strength on which they pride themselves so much."

"How, then?"

"By changing our world into a place where it was impossible for us to live. It was impossible for them to live in such a world also, but that they were too stupid to know. They defeated us in the same way that they have defeated everything else that is living."

"Tell me," said Grigg. "What makes you think that _I_ am any different? After all, I am a man, even though not a Greek. Why on earth should I be any kind of an exception?"

"There is no earth here," said Lek. "Haven't you noticed?"

"Nothing but rock," cried Grigg. "But there are more flowers than anywhere? And these wonderful nectarines?"

"They live on rock," said Tal, speaking for the first time.

"You are different," said Lek, "simply because you have both set out and arrived. Few try and fewer succeed."

"What happens to them?"

"They have set-backs of various kinds."

"I didn't find it in the least difficult," said Grigg.

"Those meant to succeed at a thing never do find the thing difficult."

"Meant? Meant by whom?"

"By the life of which they are a part, whether they know it or not."

"It is very mystical," said Grigg. "Where is this life to be found?"

"Here," said Lek, simply. "And it is not mystical at all. That is a word invented by those who have lost life, or destroyed it. A word like _tragedy_. The stupid Greeks even called the plays they wrote about their fight with the women, _tragedies_."

"If I stay," began Grigg, and then stopped. "If I stay," he began again, "how do I make payment? I do not necessarily mean in money. All the same, how?"

"Here there are no bargains and no debts. You do not pay at all. You submit to the two gods. Their rule is light, but people are so unaccustomed to it that they sometimes find it includes surprises."

"I have seen one of the gods. Where is the other?"

"The other god is female and therefore hidden."

Grigg noticed that a considerable tremor, very visible in the case of Vin, passed through all three of their bodies.

"I still do not understand," he said, "why there is no one else. We are not all that far away. And the voyage is really quite easy. I should have thought that people would be coming all the time."

"It might be better," said Lek, "to rejoice that you are the one chosen. But if you wish to go, go now, and one of us will guide you."

Grigg didn't go. It wasn't Lek's riddling talk that prevented him, but much simpler things: Tal; the charm and strangeness of the empty rooms; not least the conviction that the women were right when they said he could not return to his starting-point, and uncertainty as to where else he could practically make for. He told them that he would stay for the night. A plan would be easier to evolve in the sunshine.

"You don't mind if I grow a beard?" he said. "I've brought nothing with me."

They were very nice about his having brought nothing with him.

"Enchanted islands are hard to understand," he said. "I've always thought that. It worried me even as a child. The trouble is that you can never be sure where the enchantment begins and where it ends."

"You learn by experience," said Tal.

"Do you—do we—really live entirely on fruit?"

"No," said Lek. "There is wine."

Vin rose and walked out through the gateway that led down to the harbour. She moved like a nymph, and her silhouette against the night sky through the arch was that of a girl-athlete on a vase.

Wine was not the sustenance that Grigg, fond though he was of it, felt he most needed at the moment, but he said nothing. They were all silent while waiting for Vin to return. The tideless waves flapped against the surrounding rock. The stars flickered.

Vin returned with a little porcelain bowl, not spilling a drop of the contents as she stepped bare-footed over the uneven stones. The bowl was set among them, small cups appeared, and they all drank. There was little wine left when all the cups had been filled. The wine was red. Grigg thought it was also extremely sweet and heavy, almost treacly in texture; he was glad that he did not have to drink more of it. They followed the wine by drinking water from a pitcher.

"Where do you find water?" asked Grigg.

"From springs in the rock," answered Lek.

"More than one spring?"

"There is a spring of health, a spring of wisdom, a spring of beauty, a spring of logic, and a spring of longevity."

"And the water we are drinking?"

"It is from the spring of salutation. Alas, we do not drink from it as often as we should like."

Here Tal departed and came back with the green cask which Grigg had earlier seen her carrying. It contained a different wine, and, to Grigg, a more accustomed.

Tal had also brought a lantern. They settled to ancient games with coloured stones, and lines drawn with charcoal on the rocky floor. These games again were new to Grigg: not only their rules and skills, but, more, the spirit in which they were played. The object appeared to be not so much individual triumph as an intensification of fellow-feeling; of love, to use Lek's word of welcome to him. Most surprising of all to Grigg was the discovery that he no longer felt underfed, although he had eaten neither meat nor grain. He felt agog (it was the only word) with life, air, warmth, and starlight. Time itself had become barbless and placid.

"Sleep where you will," said Lek. "There are many rooms." Vin picked up her dress and they all entered the citadel.

"Good night," they said.

He tried to catch Tal's eye, but failed.

They were gone.

Grigg did not feel like sleep. He decided to walk down to the harbour.

The lizards were still sprawling and squirming on the steps, which Grigg thought odd behavior for such creatures, and unpleasantly reminiscent of his dream. The scent of the massed flowers was heavier than ever. He went slowly down through the stars and the blossoms, and climbed aboard his boat, now lying alongside the much bigger sailing-ship; looked at the engine, which appeared to be untouched (though he could think of no real reason why it should be otherwise); and sat on the stern seat thinking.

He decided that though the way of life on the island seemed to him in almost every way perfect, he was far from sure that he himself was so innately the designated participant in it as to justify his apparently privileged journey and landfall. He was far from pleased by this realization. On the contrary, he felt that he had been corrupted by the very different life to which he had been so long accustomed, and much though he normally disliked it. He doubted whether by now he was capable of redemption from that commonplace existence, even by enchantment. The three women had virtually agreed that enchantment has its limitations. Grigg felt very much like starting the outboard forthwith, and making off to face the difficult music.

"Be brave."

Grigg looked up. It was Vin who had spoken. She had resumed her dress and was leaning over the gunwale of the ship above him.

"But what does courage consist in? Which is the brave thing to do?"

"Come up here," said Vin, "and we'll try to find out."

Grigg climbed the narrow harbour steps, walked round the end of the little basin, and stepped over the side of the curved ship. Vin had now turned and stood with her back against the opposite side, watching him. Grigg was quite astonished by how beautiful she looked, though he could hardly see her face through the darkness. It mattered little: Vin, standing there alone, was superb. She seemed to him the living epitome of the elegant ship.

"We don't really exist, you know," said Vin. "So, in the first place, you need not be scared of us. We're only ghosts. Nothing to be frightened of."

He sat on a coil of rope in front of her, but a little to the side, the harbour-mouth side.

"Do you chuck about ropes like this?"

"Of course. We're strong."

"Do you eat absolutely nothing but fruit?"

"And drink the wine I brought you to drink."

"I thought it was no ordinary wine."

"It makes you no ordinary person."

"I don't feel very different."

"People don't feel very different even after they have died. The Greek Church says that forty days pass before people feel any different."

"Is that true?"

"Quite true. Not even the Greeks are wrong all the time. And the dead still feel the same even *after* forty days unless the proper masses are said. You can't go to Heaven without the masses, you know."

"Or, presumably, to Hell?"

"As you say, Grigg."

Grigg was struck by a thought.

"Is that in some way why you're here now?"

Vin laughed, gurgling like her own thick, sweet, red wine. "No, Grigg. We're not dead. Feel."

She held out her left hand. Grigg took it. It was curiously firm and soft at the same time, strong but delicate. Grigg found himself most reluctant to relinquish it.

"You're alive," said Grigg.

Vin said nothing.

"Tell me," said Grigg, "what there is in the wine?"

"Rock," said Vin softly.

Grigg was absurdly reminded of those claims in wine-merchants' catalogues that in this or that brand can be tasted the very soil in which it was grown.

"Don't laugh," said Vin, quite sharply. "The rock doesn't like it."

Grigg had no idea what she meant, but he stopped laughing at once. The mystery made her words all the more impressive, as sometimes when an adult admonishes a child.

"Where did you all come from?" asked Grigg. "To judge by what you say, you can't be Greek. And you don't sound Greek. You speak English beautifully, which means you can't be English. What are you?"

"Lek comes from one place. Tal from another. I from a third. Where I come from the people wear no shoes."

"Lek spoke of you as sisters."

"We are sisters. We work and fight side by side, which makes us sisters."

"Are there no more of you?"

"Men have broken through from time to time, like you. The rock is surrounded, you know. But none of the men have stayed. They have killed themselves or sailed away."

"Have none of them sailed back? After all, it's not far."

"Not one. They have always had something to make it impossible. Like your stolen boat."

"I suppose that's inevitable. One couldn't think of finding a place like this and still being able to go back." He thought about it, then added, "Or forward either, I daresay."

"Grigg," said Vin, "burn your boat. I will make fire for you."

The shock of her words made him rise to his feet, charged with the instinct of flight.

On the instant her arms were round him, holding him very tightly. "Burn it, burn it," she was crying passionately. "Will you never understand? You might have done it hours ago."

Without thinking of what he was doing, he found that his arms were round her too, and they were kissing.

"Watch me make fire," she shouted. In the instant they had become lovers, true lovers, sentiment as well as passion, tender as well as proud.

She darted across the ship, leapt the gunwale, and ran round the little quay, all the while dragging Grigg by the hand. She seemed to part the thin painter with a single pull and drew the boat out of the basin. Despite the absence of tide or wind, the boat drifted straight out into the darkness of the open sea.

"Day and night, the sea runs away from the rock," cried Vin.

They stood together, their arms tightly round one another's waists, watching the boat disappear.

Grigg could not sense that she did anything more, but suddenly, far out, there was a beautiful rosy glow, like the sunset. It was contained and oval, and in the middle of it could be seen the transfigured outline of the boat, gleaming whitely, like the Holy Grail, too bright to stare at for more than a moment. Outside the fiery oval, the whole air was turning a faint, deep pink.

"My God," cried Grigg, "the petrol in the outboard. It will explode."

"On to the ship," said Vin, and hauled him back round the basin and aboard.

They hid, clinging together, in a small hold made simply by thick planks stretched at gunwale-level across the bow. The flush in the night sky was intensifying all the time. Then there was a loud concussion; the sky turned almost scarlet; and, not more than a few minutes later, he possessed Vin as if she had been hardly more than a little girl.

Hand in hand, they ascended the wide steps to the citadel. At the gateway, they looked back. The burning boat had still not sunk, because it could just be seen, a faint horizontal cinder, drifting into the blackness. The pink in the air was once more faint, and apparently turning to silver.

"The moon," said Vin. "The moon is drawing near and shining through the water."

"The flowers go to meet the moon even more eagerly than the sun. You can hear them. Listen, Vin."

They stood in silence.

"Sleep with me, Vin."

"We sleep apart."

It was as Tal had said, "We eat fruit." And it proved to be equally true.

He stole through the empty rooms, seeing no one. Now very tired, he lowered himself on to a pile of cushions, but not the pile on which he had lain with Tal, and not in the same room.

None the less, he could not easily sleep. It came to him with a nervous shock, as happens after long absorption, to recall that, only that same morning, the island, the rock, as the women always named it, had been no more than an obsessive premonition, he no other than an ordinary mortal, eternally going through the motions. He felt now that in the very moment he had first sighted the rock, he had begun to change. And there was almost certainly no going back; not just in symbol or allegory, but in hard, practical terms, as the world deems them.

Grigg lay listening to the lapping, trickling waves; smelling the night flowers. Was it never cooler or colder than this? Never?

Grigg would not have believed it possible, as he reflected on his third morning, that he could live so happily without occupation. There were a few jobs to be done, but so far the women had done all of them, and Grigg had felt no real compunction, as the jobs had seemed to be as complete a part of their lives as breathing—and as automatic and second-ary. There had been almost nothing else: no reading, no struggling with the environment, no planning. Grigg had always truly believed that he, like others, would be lost without tasks; that pleasures pall; and that ease exhausts. Now he was amazed not only by the change in his philosophy, but by the speed with which it had come about. Obviously, one had to say, it was far, far too soon to be sure; but Grigg felt that obviousness of that kind was, as far as he was concerned, already a thing of the past. Indeed, nothing, probably nothing at all, was obvious any more. Perhaps it was that Tal and Vin had purged him of the obvious within little more than his first twelve hours on the island.

Not that anything of that kind had so far happened again. Vin had withdrawn into an attitude of loving casualness, as Tal had done: the attitude which characterized all three of the women, and which Grigg found especially charming, so that he had not even made any serious attempt to intensify things with either of them.

Later that day, the three women had been singing. Now there was a pause, while they all lay listening to the waves and flowers singing for them.

"I am content," said Grigg. "But what do I do all day?"

Vin replied, "The Greek Church says that work was the fruit of sin. Here the fruit is more wholesome."

And, indeed, for a moment Grigg almost felt that he knew what the Garden of Eden had really been like: not the boring, moral attenuation of it; but the physical splendour, with flowers perfumed like these, with tiny, aquamarine birds, singing like honey, with indifference as to whether one was clothed or naked, with beauty to make it indifferent.

"The Greek Church," said Lek, "had once a prophet. 'Take no thought for the morrow,' he said; and spoke of lilies."

"But not of lilies only," said Grigg. "Far from it, alas."

"You must not expect a Greek prophet to be always wise. The Greeks used to decorate their houses with flowers, and sing songs. Now they buy tinsel from shops and listen to radios. The Greek radios are the noisiest in the world. It is not surprising that Greek prophets often make mistakes."

"You can't prophesy," said Tal, "when there's such a noise that no one can hear you."

"But the radio is new," objected Grigg.

Lek would have none of it. "The radio has been with us since the dawn of time," she said.

"I believe that men thought of it when they took over the world," said Tal.

"I prefer listening to you," said Grigg. "Sing me the song the sirens sang."

So they did.

On one occasion, two rather unpleasant things happened on the same day.

The first was that Grigg, roaming about the citadel, as he was so often told he was perfectly free to do, came upon a shut door. It was in the basement, or cellar, where he had previously hesitated to go: a sequence of low rooms, as it proved, sunk into the rock, which, quite unmodified, formed the irregular floor. The rooms were ill-lighted by small windows high in the walls. Grigg had tried the door, which was deep in the furthest rocky wall, and opened it, before he realized that it was the first door he had had to open at all; the others, as far as he could remember, having stood wide before him, at least when originally met with. He thought of Alfred de Musset's proverb: A door is either open or shut.

Inside, it was totally black; as thick, Grigg found himself thinking, as that wine. He hesitated to take even one step inside, but craned in, listening, and drawing the door close behind him. A long way below, as it seemed, was a noise: Grigg wondered if it could come from the bottom of a deep pit. At first he thought it sounded like the ebb and flow of the waves, and supposed there might be a rift in the rock; but then, in a curious way, it sounded more like a gigantic process of ingestion, as if, perhaps, a press were reducing a miscellany of organic matter to, as people say, pulp. The sound rose and fell, though something less than rhythmically, but never quite ceased; and every now and then a smell rose from the pit, if pit there was, a smell akin to the noise, in that it might have been of long-rotted tideless seaweed or, alternatively, of vaguer and terrestrial decomposition. The smell, though unpleasant, came only in strong whiffs, and Grigg wondered why it was apparently uncontinuous. Could something below be opening and shutting, appearing and withdrawing? Noise, smell, and darkness were plainly related to the formations of the rock, but Grigg found the place disturbing, as a child often finds a room he has entered without clear authority.

None the less, it was fascinating, and Grigg could not quite go, either: still like the transfixed child. He felt less than ever inclined to proceed further, but remained half-in, half-out, trying to peer through the blackness, but dreading at the same time. And, in the end, something terrible happened, or something which Grigg found terrible: it was as if the pit spoke. There was a sudden growling roar; a noise entirely different from what had gone before; and Grigg was sure that there were clear words. He could not understand them, and they did not sound like Greek, but words he knew they were, and addressed to him. The personal note was unmistakable. It was as if the pit and the darkness, the noise and the smell, had been watching him, and were now warning him off, and leaving no possibility of mistake.

Grigg reeled back and slammed the door. Stumbling over the rocky floor, he hastened into the sunlight. Even before he had reached the courtyard, he had begun to realize that he had merely been the victim of an aural hallucination—an hallucination of a quite common type, indeed; almost the sort of thing staged for tourists visiting Mediterranean grottoes. When he found himself alone in the courtyard, he realized that he had nearly made a serious fool of himself. Even though the first terror had by then ebbed, there was no knowing what idiotic thing he might have said if there had been anyone to listen.

He climbed over the courtyard wall and stretched out on the rock finally to recover his wits.

That same evening, he heard the women shouting and laughing, out beyond the gateway to the harbour. He went to look. The sky was almost emerald green and they moved in magnificent silhouette against it. The three of them stood above the water's edge and below the harbour causeway, on the side of the island away from the basin. Grigg found the beauty of their movement incomparable. He stood watching them for some time, as if they presented a merely formal spectacle, of maenads on a vase, or ballet dancers, before he clearly realized that they were not merely throwing stones, but very much aiming at a target. He walked down the causeway, and stood behind them, looking over their heads.

Floating in the emerald sea beneath the emerald sky was a body; though it was unlikely to be afloat much longer, as the women knew how to throw, and every stone hit true and hard. Grigg could see the body quite well: it had belonged to a fat, elderly, clean-shaven man with a big, bald head, and was dressed in a dark, conventional suit, of which the open jacket spread out in the water, like a pair of fins. All round the body the sea was red, like the death of a whale. Grigg shuddered as he thought of the whale.

The skilled throwing went on for another minute or two, a marvel of ancient beauty, and then, suddenly, the body collapsed and sank. Grigg could hear the water pouring in, as into a pierced gourd. The women, apparently still unaware of him, stood in lovely silent attitudes and watched it go. When there was nothing left but the fading patch of carmine, they turned, saw Grigg, and advanced laughing and gesticulating, their hair dishevelled and their faces flushed with excitement.

"Who was he?" asked Grigg.

"A tourist. They fall out of boats."

"They fall off pier-heads."

"They fall from Heaven."

Grigg felt as once he had done when he had found himself encompassed by English and American enthusiasts for the bull-fight. But now, at least, the central object had been dead to start with. Or so he could but suppose.

But this was not the only time when Grigg saw blood in the sea.

After he had been, as he thought, about three weeks on the island, or perhaps as much as a month, there was a great storm. There had been little forewarning, or little that Grigg had been able to sense; and the women had said nothing. The first lightning leapt at him in his room, taking him completely by surprise as he lay there musing in the warm darkness, some time after midnight. It was curious pink lightning, condensing, as it seemed, the entire firmament into a single second; and the thunder which followed might well have torn apart the total citadel . . . except that, to Grigg's astonishment, there was no thunder, nothing of the kind beyond a faint rumble, more as if the Olympians had been overheard conversing than as if there had been an electrical discharge. On the instant, there followed another flash and brief rumble of distant talk; and then another. Grigg now listened for rain, of which there had been none that he was aware of since his arrival; but though, according to the laws of nature, it must have been raining somewhere, all there seemed to be here was a rising wind. Lightning was flickering from cherry-blossom almost to scarlet; but Grigg hardly noticed it as the wind rose and rose, like a cataract of water charging through the widening burst in a dam and sweeping down a valley, presenting to Grigg a similar picture of instant danger and catastrophe. He caught up the garment the women had woven for him and hastened round the big dark room shutting windows, like a suburban housewife. Those in one of the walls were too high for him to reach, but at least there was as yet no question of water pouring in.

"There have always been storms like this."

It was Lek's voice. Grigg could just perceive her shape standing by the door. "There is nothing to be afraid of. The citadel is built to remain standing." A flash of rosy lightning filled the room, so that, for a second, Grigg saw her with unnatural clarity, as if she had been an angel. "Come and look."

Lek clasped his hand and led him out. They ascended the pitch-black, stone stair. "Do not falter," said Lek. "Trust me." Grigg, feeling no doubt at all, went up the hard, dark steps without even stubbing a toe. They came out on the roof.

The sky was washed all over with the curious pink of the lightning. Grigg had never seen anything like it before, and had never known so strange a wind, roaring, but warm, and even scented. Faintly massed against the rosy dimness at the other end of the flat roof was the recumbent shape of the male god. Lek stood looking at the god, herself a lovely, living statue. Grigg was filled with awe and revelation.

"Tal is earth," he said, somehow speaking above the roar of the wind.

As far as he could see, Lek moved not an eyelid.

"Vin is fire."

He thought she faintly smiled.

"And you are air."

A smile it was. There could be no doubt about it. And her eyes were far-distant vastnesses. The wind hummed and sang. Grigg kissed Lek, lightly as a leaf.

"Come nearer to the god," said Lek, drawing him onward through the hurricane. "It is for him. Everything is for him."

And for the prostrate Grigg, as the warm wind blew and blew, the heavens opened.

This time, just as much as he had finally forgotten to ask questions, so, at the end, he made no foolish demands.

On another night, conceivably a week later, Grigg was awakened by what must have been an unusual sound. He sat up and listened. There was nothing at all loud to be heard, but there was an unmistakable clinking and clanking in the island night, systematic, purposive, human. It occurred to Grigg immediately that there was an intruder—one intruder at least.

He put on his garment and descended, without disturbing the women, presumably on the floor below.

He stood in the courtyard avoiding the gaze of the stars in order the better to judge where the noise was coming from.

He padded across the courtyard stones to the gateway leading to the tower he had climbed when first he came.

On the top of the tower, visible above the roofs of the intervening ruins, he could just make out a figure; blacker than the night, and palpably at some manner of work.

Grigg hesitated for a considerable number of moments. Should he try to investigate on his own, or should he first rouse the women? He probably decided in favour of the former because he still felt short of experience and knowledge that were not mediated by what the women themselves had called sorcery. He half-welcomed a moment to investigate on his own.

He started to scramble, as quietly as was possible, through the rough foundations and tough thickets. Possibly he could not be quiet *enough* under such adverse conditions, because when at length he reached the tower, the black figure was gone, and a small black motor-boat was chugging across the black sea. The top of the tower had been screened from his view by the old fortress walls for much of the time he had been scrambling through the miniature Turkish jungle. The boat was the first he had seen so near the island. He watched it until, lightless, void of all detail, it merged into the black night.

He had little doubt that it meant trouble, and he made a considerable search, even climbing the spidery tower, only when half-way up reflecting that someone might still be there, someone who had remained when the boat had left. His heart missed a beat, compelling him to pause in the tight, dusty darkness, but he continued upwards. There was no one, nothing but the stars drawn nearer; and there was no sign of intrusion, change, or recent damage; either about the tower or about the entire extremity of the island: nothing, at least, that Grigg could find or see as he plunged about, slashing and abrading himself, in the darkness beneath the uninvolved stars. He could not even make out how the interloper could possibly have managed to moor a boat and mount the sharp rock.

Grigg sought and thought so conscientiously that the first light of dawn was upon him as he clambered back to the citadel. Ineffable, he thought, was the only word for such beauty: faint grey, faint blue, faint pink, faint green; and the entire atmosphere translucent right through to the centre of the empyrean, and on to the next centre, as if, while it lasted, distance was abrogated, and the solitary individual could casually touch the impersonal core of the universe.

Back in the courtyard, he stood with his hands on the familiar wall, gazing across the tranquilly colourless, early-morning sea.

Re-ascending the citadel staircase, he tiptoed into the big hall where the women slept. The three of them lay there, touching; in dark red robes (Grigg could think of no other noun); their faces pale and their lips full, with sleep; their relaxed bodies as undefined as the good, the true, and the beautiful. Grigg stood away from the wall, motionlessly gazing, filled with the apprehension of tragedy. He stood for a long time, then dragged at his numb limbs, and went on up. There was a scorpion-like creature on his coloured cushions, which, as it refused to be driven out, he had to kill before settling down to his resumed slumbers.

And the next morning, there, once more, was the redness in the sea; and this time, the sea was blood-red, not in a large, repulsive, but all too explicable patch, but red as far as Grigg, gazing appalled from his high window, could see; as if all the way across to the larger, mainland island. It was fearful, nightmarish, infernal. Macbeth's dream had materialized: the green *was* one red.

Moreover, there was a second sound that was new to the island.

Grigg went down, his feet heavy.

On the floor below, the women were lamenting. In their greeny-brown dresses, they clung together, shadowy and large-eyed, wailing and babbling in some tongue of which Grigg knew nothing, doubtless their own. Even in their mortification and misery, they were as beautiful as in their previous joy.

"What has happened?"

The women stopped wailing when they saw him, and Lek spoke.

"The rock is dead."

Not at all understanding, Grigg could not but blurt out, "There was a man here last night. One man at least. I saw him."

"You *saw* him," said Vin. "And you did not kill him?"

"Or let *us* kill him," said Tal.

There was a difficult pause. Grigg gazed into their tear-stained faces.

"I saw him on top of the tower. I could not get to him in time across the ruins in the darkness. When I reached the tower, he was gone. I saw and heard his boat quite a long way off."

"Why did you not tell us?" asked Lek. "Why did you not trust us?"

To such a question conventional answers abound, but Grigg could not bring one of them to his lips. Guilt in him was reinforced by fear. He felt that he might be made to suffer, and he felt that he deserved the suffering.

"What does it mean," he asked, "when you say the rock is dead?"

A tremor passed through them and Vin began once more to weep.

"The rock was a living rock," said Lek softly. "The rock gave us wine and water. The rock was the other god, the female god, so, while the rock was alive, you could not be told. Now they have killed the rock with a machine, so that it does not matter what is said." As Lek spoke, Tal burst into tears and moans.

"Is there nothing I can do?"

"There is nothing that anyone in the world can do."

"This was the last living rock, and now the last living rock is dead. There is nothing but to mourn, to forgive, and to go."

"I do not expect to be forgiven," said Grigg. "I deserve to die." The words came out quite naturally; which was something he would never before have thought possible.

Lek stepped forward, took his hands, and kissed him. Then Vin and Tal did the same, leaving their tears on his mouth.

"Let me at least mourn with you."

Lek smiled sadly, and indeed he found that the power to mourn, the power to mourn anything, was not in him.

They walked in line down the causeway, among the flowers, the birds, and the lizards; with Grigg bringing up the rear. The green and grey of the sea had absorbed nearly all the red, though there was still a faint, shimmering glow beneath the surface, melting away as Grigg watched. They took nothing.

The women spread the big, blue sail, and expertly steered the ship out of the basin into the hot morning. Grigg stood at the stern, looking back along the spreading plume of her wake.

Then Lek was standing beside him.

"How long can you swim?"

Grigg looked into her eyes.

"Possibly for half an hour," he said. "At least, in smooth, warm water."

So when they neared a spit of land, he went overside in the summer clothes he had worn when he had originally cast off in his borrowed motor-boat. It was his initiation into the last of the four elements. He went without again touching any of the women, and, in the event, he was immersed for not much more than ten minutes before fetching up, dripping and bearded, on a pebbly strand. Even so, it was enough for the ship to have sailed almost to the horizon, so skilfully was she navigated.

ᗧhe ᗧerries

Ramsey Campbell

WHEN BERRY REACHED Parkgate promenade he heard the waves. He couldn't recall having heard them during his stroll down the winding road from Neston village, between banks whispering with grass, past the netted lights of windows. Beneath clouds diluted by moonlight, the movement of the waves looked indefinably strange. They sounded faint, not quite like water.

The promenade was scarcely two cars wide. Thin lanterns stood on concrete stalks above the sea wall, which was overlooked by an assortment of early Victorian buildings: antique shops, cafés that in the afternoons must be full of ladies taking tea and cakes, a nursing home, a private school that looked as though it had been built for something else. In the faltering moonlight all of them looked black and white. Some were Tudor-striped.

As he strolled—the June night was mild, he might as well enjoy himself as best he could now he was here—he passed the Marie Celeste Hotel. That must have appealed to his uncle. He was still grinning wryly when he reached his uncle's address.

Just then the moon emerged from the clouds, and he saw what was wrong with the waves. There was no water beyond the sea wall, only an expanse of swaying grass that stretched as far as he could see. The sight of the grass, overlooked by the promenade buildings as though it was still the River Dee, made him feel vaguely but intensely expectant, as though about to glimpse something on the pale parched waves.

Perhaps his uncle felt this too, for he was sitting at the black bow window on the first floor of the white house, gazing out beyond the sea wall. His eyes looked colourless as moonlight. It took three rings of the bell to move him.

Berry shouldn't feel resentful. After all, he was probably his uncle's only living relative. Nevertheless there were decisions to be made in London, at the publishers: books to be bought or rejected—several were likely

to be auctioned. He'd come a long way hurriedly, by several trains; his
uncle's call had sounded urgent enough for that, as urgent as the pips that
had cut him off. Berry only wished he knew why he was here.

When at last his uncle opened the door, he looked unexpectedly old.
Perhaps living ashore had aged him. He had always been small, but now
he looked dwindled, though still tanned and leathery. In his spotless black
blazer with its shining silvery buttons, and his tiny gleaming shoes, he
resembled a doll of himself.

"Here we are again." Though he sounded gruff, his handshake was
firm, and felt grateful for company. When he'd toiled upstairs, using the
banisters as a series of walking-sticks, he growled, "Sit you down."

There was no sense of the sea in the flat, not even maritime prints to
enliven the timidly patterned wallpaper. Apart from a couple of large old
trunks, the flat seemed to have nothing to do with his uncle. It felt like a
waiting-room.

"Get that down you, James." His uncle's heartiness seemed faded; even
the rum was a brand you could buy in the supermarkets, not one of the
prizes he'd used to bring back from voyages. He sat gazing beyond the
promenade, sipping the rum as though it was as good as any other.

"How are you, Uncle? It's good to see you." They hadn't seen each
other for ten years, and Berry felt inhibited; besides, his uncle detested
effusiveness. When he'd finished his rum he said, "You sounded urgent on
the phone."

"Aye." The years had made him even more taciturn. He seemed to
resent being reminded of his call.

"I wouldn't have expected you to live so far from everything," Berry
said, trying a different approach.

"It went away." Apparently he was talking about the sea, for he continued: "There used to be thirteen hotels and a pier. All the best people
came here to bathe. They said the streets were as elegant as Bath. The
private school you passed, that was the old Assembly Rooms."

Though he was gazing across the sea wall, he didn't sound nostalgic.
He sat absolutely still, as though relishing the stability of the room. He'd
used to pace restlessly when talking, impatient to return to the sea.

"Then the Dee silted up," he was saying. "It doesn't reach here now,
except at spring tides and in storms. That's when the rats and voles flee
onto the promenade—hordes of them, they say. I haven't seen it, and I
don't mean to."

"You're thinking of moving?"

"Aye." Frowning at his clenched fists, he muttered, "Will you take me
back with you tomorrow and let me stay until I find somewhere? I'll have
my boxes sent on."

He mustn't want to make the journey alone in case he was taken ill. Still, Berry couldn't help sounding a little impatient. "I don't live near the sea, you know."

"I know that." Reluctantly he added, "I wish I lived further away."

Perhaps now that he'd had to leave the sea, his first love, he wanted to forget about it quickly. Berry could tell he'd been embarrassed to ask for help—a captain needing help from a nephew who was seasick on hovercraft! But he was a little old man now, and his tan was only a patina; all at once Berry saw how frail he was. "All right, Uncle," he said gently. "It won't be any trouble."

His uncle was nodding, not looking at him, but Berry could see he was moved. Perhaps now was the time to broach the idea Berry had had on the train. "On my way here," he said carefully, "I was remembering some of the tales you used to tell."

"You remember them, do you?" The old man didn't sound as though he wanted to. He drained a mouthful of rum in order to refill his glass. Had the salt smell that was wafting across the grass reminded him too vividly?

Berry had meant to suggest the idea of a book of his uncle's yarns, for quite a few had haunted him: the pigmies who could carry ten times their own weight, the flocks of birds that buried in guano any ships that ventured into their territory, the light whose source was neither sun nor moon but that outlined an island on the horizon, which receded if ships made for it. Would it be a children's book, or a book that tried to trace the sources? Perhaps this wasn't the time to discuss it, for the smell that was drifting through the window was stagnant, very old.

"There was one story I never told you."

Berry's head jerked up; he had been nodding off. Even his uncle had never begun stories as abruptly—as reluctantly—as this.

"Some of the men used to say it didn't matter if you saw it so long as you protected yourself." Was the old man talking to himself, to take his mind off the desiccated river, the stagnant smell? "One night we all saw it. One minute the sea was empty, the next that thing was there, close enough to swim to. Some of the men would almost have done that, to get it over with." He gulped a mouthful of rum and stared sharply out across the pale dry waves. "Only they could see the faces watching. None of us forgot that, ever. As soon as we got ashore all of us bought ourselves protection. Even I did," he said bitterly, "when I'd used to say civilised men kept pictures on walls."

Having struggled out of his blazer, which he'd unbuttoned carefully and tediously, he displayed his left forearm. Blinking sleepily, Berry made out a tattoo, a graceful sailing ship surrounded by a burst of light. Its masts resembled almost recognisable symbols.

"The younger fellows thought that was all we needed. We all wanted to believe that would keep us safe. I wonder how they feel now they're older." The old man turned quickly towards the window; he seemed angry that he'd been distracted. Something had changed his attitude drastically, for he had hated tattoos. It occurred to Berry, too late to prevent him from dozing, that his uncle had called him because he was afraid to be alone.

Berry's sleep was dark and profound. Half-submerged images floated by, so changed as to be unrecognisable. Sounds reached him rather as noise from the surface might try to reach the depths of the sea. It was impossible to tell how many times his uncle had cried out before the calls woke him.

"James . . ." The voice was receding, but at first Berry failed to notice this; he was too aware of the smell that filled the room. Something that smelled drowned in stagnant water was near him, so near that he could hear its creaking. At once he was awake, and so afraid that he thought he was about to be sick.

"James . . ." Both the creaking and the voice were fading. Eventually he managed to persuade himself that despite the stench, he was alone in the room. Forcing his eyes open, he stumbled to the window. Though it was hard to focus his eyes and see what was out there, his heart was already jolting.

The promenade was deserted; the buildings gleamed like bone. Above the sea wall the lanterns glowed thinly. The wide dry river was flooded with grass, which swayed in the moonlight, rustling and glinting. Over the silted river, leaving a wake of grass that looked whiter than the rest, a ship was receding.

It seemed to be the colour and the texture of the moon. Its sails looked stained patchily by mould. It was full of holes, all of which were mis-shapen by glistening vegetation. Were its decks crowded with figures? If so, he was grateful that he couldn't see their faces, for their movements made him think of drowned things lolling underwater, dragged back and forth by currents.

Sweat streamed into his eyes. When he'd blinked them clear, the moon was darkening. Now the ship looked more like a mound from which a few trees sprouted, and perhaps the crowd was only swaying bushes. Clouds closed over the moon, but he thought he could see a pale mass sailing away, overtopped by lurid sketches that might be masts. Was that his uncle's voice, its desperation overwhelmed by despair? When moonlight flooded the landscape a few moments later, there was nothing but the waves of grass, from which a whiter swathe was fading.

He came to himself when he began shivering. An unseasonably chill wind was clearing away the stench of stagnant water. He gazed in dismay at his uncle's blazer, draped neatly over the empty chair.

There wasn't much that he could tell the police. He had been visiting his uncle, whom he hadn't seen for years. They had both had a good deal to drink, and his uncle, who had seemed prematurely aged, had begun talking incoherently and incomprehensibly. He'd woken to find that his uncle had wandered away, leaving his blazer, though it had been a cold night.

Did they believe him? They were slow and thorough, these policemen; their thoughts were as invisible as he meant his to be. Surely his guilt must be apparent, the shame of hiding the truth about his uncle, of virtually blackening his character. In one sense, though, that seemed hardly to matter: he was sure they wouldn't find his uncle alive. Eventually, since Berry could prove that he was needed in London, they let him go.

He trudged along the sweltering promenade. Children were scrambling up and down the sea wall, old people on sticks were being promenaded by relatives. In the hazy sunshine, most of the buildings were still black and white. Everywhere signs said FRESH SHRIMPS. In a shop that offered "Gifts and Bygones," ships were stiff in bottles. Waves of yellowing grass advanced, but never very far.

He ought to leave, and be grateful that he lived inland. If what he'd seen last night had been real, the threat was far larger than he was. There was nothing he could do.

But suppose he had only heard his uncle's voice on the silted river, and had hallucinated the rest? He'd been overtired, and confused by his uncle's ramblings; how soon had he wakened fully? He wanted to believe that the old man had wandered out beyond the promenade and had collapsed, or even that he was alive out there, still wandering.

There was only one way to find out. He would be in sight of the crowded promenade. Holding his briefcase above his head as though he was submerging, he clambered down the sea wall.

The grass was tougher than it looked. Large patches had to be struggled through. After five hundred yards he was sweating, yet he seemed to be no closer to the far bank, nor to anything else. Ahead through the haze he could just distinguish the colours of fields in their frames of trees and hedges. Factory chimneys resembled grey pencils. All this appeared to be receding.

He struggled onward. Grass snagged him, birds flew up on shrill wings, complaining. He could see no evidence of the wake he'd seen last night; nothing but the interminable grass, the screeching birds, the haze. Behind him the thick heat had blurred the promenade, the crowds were pale shadows. Their sounds had been swallowed by the hissing of grass.

He'd been tempted several times to turn back, and was on the point of doing so, when he saw a gleam in the dense grass ahead. It was near the place where he'd last glimpsed the ship, if he had done so. The gleaming object looked like a small shoe.

He had to persuade himself to go forward. He remembered the swaying figures on the decks, whose faces he'd dreaded to see. Nevertheless he advanced furiously, tearing a path through the grass with his briefcase. He was almost there before he saw that the object wasn't a shoe. It was a bottle.

When inertia carried him forward, he realised that the bottle wasn't empty. For an unpleasant moment he thought it contained the skeleton of a small animal. Peering through the grime that coated the glass, he made out a whitish model ship with tattered sails. Tiny overgrown holes gaped in it. Though its decks were empty, he had seen it before.

He stood up too quickly, and almost fell. The heat seemed to flood his skull. The ground underfoot felt unstable; a buzzing of insects attacked him; there was a hint of a stagnant smell. He was ready to run, dizzy as he was, to prevent himself from thinking.

Then he remembered his uncle's despairing cry: "James, James . . ." Even then, if he had been able to run, he might have done nothing—but his dizziness both hindered him and gave him time to feel ashamed. If there was a chance of helping his uncle, however impossible it seemed— He snatched up the bottle and threw it into his briefcase. Then, trying to forget about it, he stumbled back towards the crowds.

His uncle was calling him. He woke to the sound of a shriek. Faces were sailing past him, close enough to touch if he could have reached through the glass. It was only a train on the opposite line, rushing away from London. Nevertheless he couldn't sleep after that. He finished reading the typescript he'd brought with him, though he knew by now he didn't want to buy the book.

The state of his desk was worse than he'd feared. His secretary had answered most of his letters, but several books had piled up, demanding to be read. He was stuffing two of them into his briefcase, to be read on the bus and, if he wasn't too tired, at home, when he found he was holding the grimy bottle. At once he locked it in a drawer. Though he wasn't prepared to throw it away until he understood its purpose, he was equally reluctant to take it home.

That night he could neither sleep nor read. He tried strolling in Holland Park, but while that tired him further, it failed to calm him. The moonlit clouds that were streaming headlong across the sky made everything beneath them look unstable. Though he knew that the lit houses beyond the swaying trees were absolutely still, he kept feeling that the houses were rocking slyly, at anchor.

He lay trying to relax. Beyond the windows of his flat, Kensington High Street seemed louder than ever. Nervous speculation kept him awake. He felt he'd been meant to find the bottle, but for what purpose? Surely it couldn't harm him; after all, he had only once been to sea. How could he help his uncle? His idea of a book of stories was nagging him; perhaps he could write it himself, as a kind of monument to his uncle— except that the stories seemed to be drifting away into the dark, beyond his reach, just like the old man. When eventually he dozed, he thought he heard the old man calling.

In the morning his desk looked even worse; the pile of books had almost doubled. He managed to sort out a few that could be trusted to readers for reports. Of course, a drain must have overflowed outside the publishers; that was why only a patch of pavement had been wet this morning—he knew it hadn't rained. He consulted his diary for distractions.

Sales conference 11 A.M.: he succeeded in being coherent, and even in suggesting ideas, but his thoughts were elsewhere. The sky resembled sluggish smoke, as though the oppressive day was smouldering. His mind felt packed in grey stuffing. The sound of cars outside seemed unnaturally rhythmic, almost like waves.

Back at his desk he sat trying to think. Lack of sleep had isolated him in a no-man's-land of consciousness, close to hallucination. He felt cut off from whatever he was supposed to be doing. Though his hand kept reaching out impulsively, he left the drawer locked. There was no point in brooding over the model ship until he'd decided what to do.

Beyond the window his uncle cried out. No, someone was shouting to guide a lorry; the word wasn't "James" at all. But he still didn't know how to help his uncle, assuming that he could, assuming that it wasn't too late. Would removing the ship from the bottle achieve something? In any case, could one remove the ship at all? Perhaps he could consult an expert in such matters. "I know exactly whom you want," his secretary said, and arranged for them to meet tomorrow.

Dave Peeples lunch 12:30: ordinarily he would have enjoyed the game, especially since Peeples liked to discuss books in pubs, where he tended to drink himself into an agreeable state. Today's prize was attractive: a bestselling series that Peeples wanted to take to a new publisher. But today he found Peeples irritating—not only his satyr's expressions and postures, which were belied by his paunch, but also the faint smirk with which he constantly approved of himself. Still, if Berry managed to acquire the books, the strain would have been worthwhile.

They ate in the pub just around the corner from the publishers. Before long Berry grew frustrated; he was too enervated by lack of sleep to risk drinking much. Nor could he eat much, for the food tasted unpleasantly salty. Peeples seemed to notice nothing, and ate most of Berry's helping before he leaned back, patting his paunch.

"Well now," he said when Berry raised the subject of the books. "What about another drink?" Berry was glad to stand up, to feel the floor stable underfoot, for the drinkers at the edge of his vision had seemed to be swaying extravagantly.

"I'm not happy with the way my mob are promoting the books," Peeples admitted. "They seem to be letting them just lie there." Berry's response might have been more forceful if he hadn't been distracted by the chair that someone was rocking back and forth with a steady rhythmic creaking.

When Berry had finished making offers Peeples said, "That doesn't sound bad. Still, I ought to tell you that several other people are interested." Berry wondered angrily whether he was simply touring publishers in search of free meals. The pub felt damp, the dimness appeared to be glistening. No doubt it was very humid.

Though the street was crowded, he was glad to emerge. "I'll be in touch," Peeples promised grudgingly, but at that moment Berry didn't care, for on the opposite pavement the old man's voice was crying, "James!" It was only a newspaper-seller naming his wares, which didn't sound much like James. Surely a drain must have overflowed where the wet patch had been, for there was a stagnant smell.

Editors meeting 3 P.M.: he scarcely had time to gulp a mug of coffee beforehand, almost scalding his throat. Why did they have to schedule two meetings in one day? When there were silences in which people expected him to speak, he managed to say things that sounded positive and convincing. Nevertheless he heard little except for the waves of traffic, advancing and withdrawing, and the desperate cries in the street. What was that crossing the intersection, a long pale shape bearing objects like poles? It had gone before he could jerk his head round, and his colleagues were staring only at him.

It didn't matter. If any of these glimpses weren't hallucinations, surely they couldn't harm him. Otherwise, why hadn't he been harmed that night in Parkgate? It was rather a question of what he could do to the glimpses. "Yes, that's right," he said to a silence. "Of course it is."

Once he'd slept he would be better able to cope with everything. Tomorrow he would consult the expert. After the meeting he slumped at the desk, trying to find the energy to gather books together and head for home.

His secretary woke him. "Okay," he mumbled, "you go on." He'd follow her in a moment, when he was more awake. It occurred to him that if he hadn't dozed off in Parkgate, his uncle might have been safe. That was another reason to try to do something. He'd get up in a few moments. It wasn't dark yet.

When he woke again, it was.

He had to struggle to raise his head. His elbows had shoved piles of books to the edge of the desk. Outside, the street was quiet except for the whisper of an occasional car. Sodium lamps craned their necks towards his window. Beyond the frosted glass of his office cubicle, the maze of the open-plan office looked even more crowded with darkness than the space around his desk. When he switched on his desk-lamp, it showed him a blurred reflection of himself trapped in a small pool of brightness. Hurriedly he switched on the cubicle's main light.

Though he was by no means awake, he didn't intend to wait. He wanted to be out of the building, away from the locked drawer. Insomnia had left him feeling vulnerable, on edge. He swept a handful of books into the briefcase—God, they were becoming a bad joke—and emerged from his cubicle.

He felt uncomfortably isolated. The long angular room was lifeless; none of the desks seemed to retain any sense of the person who sat there. The desertion must be swallowing his sounds, which seemed not only dwarfed but robbed of resonance, as though surrounded by an emptiness that was very large.

His perceptions must be playing tricks. Underfoot the floor felt less stable than it ought to. At the edge of his vision the shadows of desks and cabinets appeared to be swaying, and he couldn't convince himself that the lights were still. He mustn't let any of this distract him. Time enough to think when he was home.

It took him far too long to cross the office, for he kept teetering against desks. Perhaps he should have taken time to waken fully, after all. When eventually he reached the lifts, he couldn't bring himself to use one; at least the stairs were open, though they were very dark. He groped, swaying, for the light-switch. Before he'd found it, he recoiled. The wall he had touched felt as though it were streaming with water.

A stagnant stench welled up out of the dark. When he grabbed the banister for support, that felt wet too. He mustn't panic: a door or window was open somewhere in the building, that was all he could hear creaking; its draught was making things feel cold—not wet—and was swinging the lights back and forth. Yes, he could feel the draught blustering at him, and smell what must be a drain.

He forced himself to step onto the stairs. Even the darkness was preferable to groping for the light-switch, when he no longer knew what he might touch. Nevertheless by the time he reached the half-landing he was wishing for light. His vertigo seemed to have worsened, for he was reeling from side to side of the staircase. Was the creaking closer? He mustn't pause, plenty of time to feel ill once he was outside in a taxi; he ought to be able to hold off panic so long as he didn't glimpse the ship again—

He halted so abruptly that he almost fell. Without warning he'd remembered his uncle's monologue. Berry had been as dopey then as he was now, but one point was all at once terribly clear. Your first glimpse of the ship meant only that you would see it again. The second time, it came for you.

He hadn't seen it again. Surely he still had a chance. There were two exits from the building; the creaking and the growing stench would tell him which exit to avoid. He was stumbling downstairs because that was the alternative to falling. His mind was a grey void that hardly even registered the wetness of the banisters. The foyer was in sight now at the foot of the stairs, its linoleum gleaming; less than a flight of stairs now, less than a minute's stumbling—

But it was no linoleum. The floorboards were bare, when there ought not even to be boards, only concrete. Shadows swayed on them, cast by objects that, though out of sight for the moment, seemed to have bloated limbs. Water sloshed from side to side of the boards, which were the planks of a deck.

He almost let himself fall, in despair. Then he began to drag himself frantically up the stairs, which perhaps were swaying, after all. Through the windows he thought he saw the cityscape rising and falling. There seemed to be no refuge upstairs, for the stagnant stench was everywhere—but refuge was not what he was seeking.

He reeled across the office, which he'd darkened when leaving, into his cubicle. Perhaps papers were falling from desks only because he had staggered against them. His key felt ready to snap in half before the drawer opened.

He snatched out the bottle, in which something rattled insectlike, and stumbled to the window. Yes, he had been meant to find the bottle—but by whom, or by what? Wrenching open the lock of the window, he flung the bottle into the night.

He heard it smash a moment later. Whatever was inside it must certainly have smashed too. At once everything felt stable, so abruptly that he grew dizzier. He felt as though he'd just stepped onto land after a stormy voyage.

There was silence except for the murmur of the city, which sounded quite normal—or perhaps there was another sound, faint and receding fast. It might have been a gust of wind, but he thought it resembled a chorus of cries of relief so profound it was appalling. Was one of them his uncle's voice?

Berry slumped against the window, which felt like ice against his forehead. There was no reason to flee now, nor did he think he would be capable of moving for some time. Perhaps they would find him here in the morning. It hardly mattered, if he could get some sleep.

All at once he tried to hold himself absolutely still, in order to listen. Surely he needn't be nervous any longer, just because the ship in the bottle had been deserted, surely that didn't mean—But his legs were trembling, and infected the rest of his body until he couldn't even strain his ears. By then, however, he could hear far better than he would have liked.

Perhaps he had destroyed the ship, and set free its captives; but if it had had a captain, what else might Berry have set loose? The smell had grown worse than stagnant—and up the stairs, and now across the dark office, irregular but purposeful footsteps were sloshing.

Early next morning several people reported glimpses of a light, supposedly moving out from the Thames into the open sea. Some claimed the light had been accompanied by sounds like singing. One old man tried to insist that the light had contained the outline of a ship. The reports seemed little different from tales of objects in the skies, and were quickly dismissed, for London had a more spectacular mystery to solve: how a publisher's editor could be found in a first-floor office, not merely dead but drowned.

The Night
Sea-Maid Went Down

Brian Lumley

J. H. Grier (Director)
Grier & Anderson,
Seagasso,
Sunderland,
Co. Durham.

"Queen of the Wolds Inn,"
Cliffside,
Bridlington,
Yorks.
Nov. 29th

Dear Johnny;

By now I suppose you'll have read my "official" report, sent off to you from this address on the fourteenth of the month, three days after the old *Sea-Maid* went down. How I managed that report I'll never know—but anyway, I've been laid up ever since, so if you've been worried about me or wondering why I haven't let on about my whereabouts till now, well, it's not really been my fault. I just haven't been up to doing much writing since the disaster. Haven't been up to much of anything for that matter. But, as you'll have seen from my report, I've made up my mind to quit, and I suppose it's only right I give you what I can of an explanation for my decision. After all, you've been paying me good money to gang-boss your rigs these last four years, and no complaints there. In fact I've no complaints period—nothing *Seagasso* could sort out at any rate—but I'm damned if I'll sink sea-wells again. In fact I'm finished for good with *all* prospecting—sea, land . . . it makes no difference. Why!—when I think of what *might* have happened at any time in the last four years——

And now it *has* happened!

But there I go stalling again. I'll admit right now that I've torn up three versions of this letter, pondering the results of them reaching you; but now, having thought it all out, frankly I don't give a damn what you do with what I'm going to tell you. You can send an army of head-shrinkers after me if you like. One thing I'm sure of though . . . whatever I say you won't suspend the North Sea operations—"The country's economy," and all that.

At least my story will give old Anderson a laugh; the hard, unimaginative, stoic old bastard; and no doubt about it the story I have to tell is fantastic enough. I suppose it could be argued that I was "in my cups" that night (and it's true enough, I'd had a few) but I can hold my drink, as you well know. Still, the facts—*as I know them*—drunk or sober, remain simply fantastic.

Now, you'll remember that right from the start there was something funny about the "site" off Hunterby Head. The divers had trouble; the geologists, too, with their instruments; and it was the very devil of a job to float *Sea-Maid* down from Sunderland and get her anchored there; but nevertheless the preliminaries were all completed by late in September. Which, where I'm concerned, was where the trouble started.

We hadn't drilled more than six-hundred feet into the sea-bed when we brought up that first star-shaped thing. Now, Johnny, you know something?—I wouldn't have given two damns for the thing—except I'd seen one before. Old Chalky Grey (who used to be with the "Lescoil" rig *Ocean-Jem* out of Liverpool) had sent me one only a few weeks before his platform and all the crew, including Chalky himself, went down twelve miles out from Withner-sea. Somehow, when I saw what came up in the big core—that same star-shape—well, I couldn't help but think of Chalky and see some sort of nasty parallel. The one he'd sent me came up in a core, too, you see? And *Ocean-Jem* wasn't the only rig lost last year in so-called "freak storms"!

But anyway, regards those star-shaped stones, something more: I wasn't the only one to escape with my life on the night *Sea-Maid* went down. No, that's not strictly true, I was the only one to live through *that night*—but there was a certain member of the team who saw what was coming and got out before it happened—and it was mainly because of the star-shaped things that he went!

Joe Borszowski was the man—superstitious as hell, pannicky, spooked at the sight of a mist on the sea—and when he saw the star-thing . . . !

It happened like this:

We'd drilled that first difficult bore through some very hard stuff down to a depth of some six hundred feet when a core-sample produced the first of the stars. Now, Chalky had reckoned the one he sent me to be a fossilized star-fish of sorts, from some time when the North Sea was warm, a very ancient thing; and I must admit that with its five-pointed shape and being the size of a small star-fish I believed him to be correct. Anyway, when I showed the *Sea-Maid* star to old Borszowski he nearly went crackers. He swore we were in for trouble and demanded we all stop drilling and head for land right away. He insisted that our location was "accursed" and generally carried on like a mad thing without attempting to offer anything like a real explanation.

Well, of course I couldn't just leave it at that. If one of the lads was round the twist, as it were (meaning Borszowski) he could well affect the whole operation, jeopardize the whole thing, especially if his madness caught him at an important time. My immediate reaction was to want him off the rig; but the radio had been giving us a bit of bother so that I couldn't call in Wes Atlee, the chopper pilot. Yes, I'd seriously considered having the Pole lifted off by chopper. Riggers can be damned superstitious, as you well know, and I didn't want Joe "infecting" the others. As it turned out, that sort of action wasn't necessary, for in no time at all old Borszowski was round apologising for his outburst and trying to show he was sorry about all the fuss he'd made. Something told me, though, that he'd been quite serious about his fears—whatever they were. And so, to put the Pole's mind at rest (if I possibly could) I decided to have the rig's geologist, Carson, take the star to bits and have a closer look at it and let me know what the thing actually was.

Of course, he'd tell me it was simply a fossilized star-fish—I'd report the fact to Borszowski—things would be back to normal. So naturally when Carson told me that the thing *wasn't* a fossil, that he didn't know exactly *what* it was, well, I kept that bit of information to myself and told Carson to do the same. I was sure that whatever the trouble had been with Borszowski it wouldn't be helped any by telling him that the star-thing was not a perfectly ordinary, completely explicable object.

The drilling brought up two or three more of the stars down to about a thousand feet but nothing after that, so for a period I forgot all about them. As it happened I should have listened a bit more willingly to old Joe—and I would have, too, if I'd followed my intuition. You see, I'd been spooked myself right from the start. The mists were too heavy, the sea too quiet—things were altogether too queer all the way down the line. Of course, I didn't experience any of the early troubles the divers and geologists had known—I didn't join the rig till she was in position, ready to chew—but I was certainly in on it from then on. It had really started with the sea-phones, even before those stars came along.

Now you know I'm not knocking your 'phones, Johnny, they've been a damn good thing ever since *Seagasso* developed them, giving readings right down to the inch almost, so's we could tell just exactly when the drill was going through into gas or oil. And they didn't let us down this time either—we just failed to recognize or heed their warning, that's all.

In fact there were lots of warnings, but, as I've said, it started out with the sea-phones. We'd put a 'phone down inside each leg of the rig, right onto the sea-bed where they sat listening to the drill as it cut its way through the rocks, picking up the echoes as the bit worked its way down and the sounds of the cutting rebounded from the strata below. And of course, everything they heard we picked up on the surface—duplicated electronically and fed out to us through our computer. Which was why we believed initially that either the computer was on the blink or one of the 'phones was dicky. You see, even when we weren't drilling—when we were changing bits, joining up lengths or lining the bore—we were still getting readings from the computer!

Oh, the trouble was there all right, whatever it was, but it was showing up so regularly that we were fooled into believing the fault to be mechanical. On the seismograph it showed as a regular blip in an otherwise perfectly normal line; a blip that came up bang on time once every five seconds or so —blip . . . blip . . . blip—very odd! But, seeing that in every other respect the information coming out of the computer was spot on, no one worried over much about those inexplicable deviations. And, as you'll see, it wasn't till the very end I found a reason for them. Oh, yes, those blips were there right to the finish—but in between there came other difficulties; one of them being the trouble with the fish.

Now, if that sounds a bit funny, well, it was a funny business. The lads had rigged up a small platform, slung twenty feet or so below the main platform and about the same height above the water, and in their off-duty hours when they weren't resting or knocking back in a pint in the mess, you could usually see one or two of them down there fishing. First time we found anything odd in the habits of the fish around the rig was one morning when Nick Adams hooked a beauty. All of three feet long, the fish was, wriggling and yellow in the cold November sunlight. Nick just about had the fish docked when the hook came out of its mouth so that it fell among some support-girders down near where leg number four was being washed by a slight swell. It just lay there, flopping about a bit, writhing around in the girders. Nick scrambled down after it with a rope round his waist while his brother Dave hung onto the other end. And what do you think?—when he got down to it, damned if the fish didn't go for him! It actually made to *bite* him, flopping after him on the girders and snapping its jaws until he had to yell for Dave to haul him up. Later he told us about it—how the damned thing hadn't even tried to get back into the sea, seeming more interested in setting its teeth in him than preserving its own life! Now, you'd expect that sort of reaction from a great eel, Johnny, wouldn't you?—but hardly from a cod—not from a North-Sea cod!

From then on Spelmann, the diver, couldn't go down—not *wouldn't* mind you, *couldn't*—the fish simply would not let him! They'd chew on his suit, his air-hose—he got so frightened of them he became literally useless to us. I can't see as I blame him though, especially when I think of what later happened to Davies.

But of course, before Davies' accident, there was that further trouble with Borszowski. It was in the sixth week, when we were expecting to break through at any time, that Joe failed to come back off shore-leave. Instead he sent me a long, rambling letter—a supposedly "explanatory" letter—and to be truthful, when I read it I figured we were better off without him.

The man had quite obviously been cracking up for a long time. He went on about monsters (yes, *monsters!*), sleeping in great caverns underground and especially under the seas, waiting for a chance to take over the surface world. He said that those stone, star-shaped things were seals or barriers that kept these beings ("gods," he called them) imprisoned; that these gods could control the weather to a degree; that they were even capable of influencing the actions of lesser creatures—such as fish, or, occasionally, men—and that he believed one of them must be lying there, locked in the ground beneath the sea, pretty close to where we were drilling. He was afraid we were "going to set it loose"! The only thing that had stopped him pressing the matter earlier (when he'd carried on so about that first star-thing), was that then, as now, he believed we'd all think he was mad! Finally, though, and particularly since the trouble with the fish, he had *had* to warn me. As he put it: "If anything *should* happen, I would never be able to forgive myself if I had not at least tried."

Well, as I've said, Borszowski's letter was rambling and disjointed—but he'd written it in a rather convincing manner, hardly what you'd expect from a real madman. He quoted references from the Holy Bible (particularly Exodus 20:4) and emphasized again his belief that the star-shaped things were nothing more or less than prehistoric pentacles (pentagrams?), laid down by some great race of alien scientists many millions of years ago. He reminded me of the heavy, unusual mists we'd had and of the queer way the cod had gone for Nick Adams. He even brought up again the question of the dicky sea-phones and computer—making, in toto, an altogether disturbing assessment of *Sea-Maid*'s late history as applicable to his own odd fancies.

I did some checking on Joe's background that same afternoon, discovering that he'd travelled far in his earlier years and had also been a bit of a scholar in his time. Too, it had been noticed on occasion—whenever the mists were heavier than usual—that he crossed himself with a certain sign over his left breast. A number of the lads had seen him do it and they all told the same tale of that sign; it was pointed with one point straight up, two down and wide, two more still lower and closer together; yes, his sign was a five-pointed star!

In fact, Borszowski's letter so disturbed me I was still thinking about it that evening after we'd shut down for the day. That was why I was out on the main platform having a quiet pipeful—I can concentrate, you know, with a bit of baccy. Dusk was only a few minutes away when the *accident* happened.

Davies, the steel-rigger, was up tightening a few loosened nuts near the top of the rig. Don't ask me where the mist came from, I wouldn't know, but suddenly it was there; swimming up from the sea, a thick, grey blanket that cut visibility down to no more than a few feet. I'd just shouted up to Davies that he better pack it in for the night when I heard his yell and saw his lantern come blazing down out of the greyness. The light disappeared through an open hatch and a second later Davies followed it. He went straight through the hatchway, missing the sides by inches, and then there came the splashes as first the lantern, then the man, hit the sea. In two shakes of a dog's tail Davies was splashing about down there in the mist and yelling fit to ruin his lungs—proving to me and the others who'd rushed out from the mess at my call that his fall had done him little harm. We lowered a raft immediately, getting two of the men down to the water in less than a minute, and no one gave it a second thought that Davies wouldn't be picked up. He was, after all, an excellent swimmer. In fact the lads on the raft thought the whole episode was a big laugh—that is, until Davies started to scream.

I mean, there are screams and there are *screams*, Johnny! Davies wasn't drowning—he wasn't making noises like a drowning man! He wasn't picked up, either.

No less quickly than it had settled, the mist lifted, so that by the time the raft touched water visibility was normal for a November evening—but there was no sign of the rigger. There was something, though, for the whole surface of the sea was silver with fish; big and little, of almost every indigenous species you could imagine; and the way they were acting, apparently trying to throw themselves aboard the raft, I had the lads haul themselves and the raft back up to the platform as soon as it became evident that Davies was gone for good. Johnny!—I swear I'll never eat fish again.

That night I didn't sleep very well at all. Now you know I'm not being callous. I mean, aboard an ocean-going rig after a hard day's work, no matter what has happened during the day, a man usually manages to sleep. Yet that night I just couldn't drop off. I kept going over in my mind all the . . . well, the *things*. The occurrences, the happenings on the old *Sea-Maid*; the trouble with the instruments; Borszowski's letter; and finally, of course, the queer way we lost Davies—until I thought my head must burst with the burden of wild notions and imaginings going around and around inside it.

Next afternoon the chopper came in (with Wes Atlee complaining about having had to make two runs in two days), and delivered all the booze and goodies for the party the next day or whenever. As you know, we always have a blast when we strike it rich—and this time we figured we were going to. We'd been out of booze a few days by that time (bad weather had stopped Wes from bringing in anything heavier than mail) and so I was running pretty high and dry. Well, you know me, Johnny. I got in the back of the mess with all those bottles and cracked a few. I could see the gear turning from the window, and, over the edge of the platform, the sea all grey and eerie looking, and somehow the idea of getting a load of drink inside me seemed a good one.

I'd been in there topping-up for over an hour when Jeffries, my 2IC, got through to me on the 'phone. He was in the instrument-cabin and said he reckoned the drill would go through to pay-dirt within a few minutes. He sounded worried, though, sort of shaky, and when I asked him why this was he didn't rightly seem able to answer—mumbled something about the seismograph mapping those strange blips again; as regular as ever but somehow stronger, closer . . .

About that time I first noticed the mist swirling up from the sea, a real pea-souper, billowing in to smother the rig and turn the men on the platform to grey ghosts. It muffled the sound of the gear, too, altering the metallic clank and rattle of pulleys and chains to distant, dull *noises* such as I might have expected to hear from the rig if I'd been in a suit deep down under the sea.

It was warm enough in the back room of the mess there, yet unaccountably I found myself shivering as I looked out over the rig and listened to the ghostly sounds of the shrouded men and machinery.

That was when the wind came up. First the mist, then the wind—but I'd never before seen a mist that a good strong wind couldn't blow away! Oh, I've seen freak storms before, Johnny, but believe me this was *the* freak storm! She came up out of nowhere—not breaking the blanket of grey but driving it round and round like a great mad ghost—blasting the already choppy sea against the old *Sea-Maid*'s supporting legs, flinging up spray to the platform's guard-rails and generally (from what I could see from the window) creating havoc. I'd no sooner recovered from my initial amazement when the 'phone rang again. I picked up the receiver to hear Jimmy Jeffries' somewhat distorted yell of triumph coming over the wires:

"We're *through*, Pongo!" he yelled. "We're through and there's juice on the way up the bore right now!" Then his voice took the shakes again, turning in tone from wild excitement to terror in a second, as the whole rig *wobbled* on her four great legs. "Holy Heaven!—what . . . ?" the words crackled into my ear. "*What was that*, Pongo? The rig . . . wait. . . ." I heard the clatter as the 'phone at the other end banged down, but a moment later Jimmy was back. "It's not the rig—the legs are steady as rocks—*it's the whole sea-bed!* Pongo, what's going on. Holy Heaven——!"

This time the 'phone went completely dead as the rig moved again, jerking up and down three or four times and shaking everything loose inside the mess store-room. I still held on to the instrument, though, and just for a second or two it came back to life. Jimmy was screaming incoherently into the other end. I remember then that I yelled for him to get into a life-jacket, that there was something terribly wrong and we were in for big trouble, but I'll never know if he heard me. The rig rocked again, throwing me down on the floor-boards among the debris of bottles, crates, cans and packets; and there, skidding wildly about the tilting floor, I collided with a life-jacket. God only knows what the thing was doing there in the store-room; they were normally kept in the equipment shed and only taken out following storm-warnings (which, it goes without saying, we hadn't had) but somehow I managed to struggle into it and make my way into the mess proper before the next upheaval.

By that time, over the roar of the wind and waves outside (the broken crests of the waves were actually slapping against the outer walls of the mess by then) I could hear a whipping of free-running pulleys and a high-pitched screaming of revving, uncontrolled gears—and there was another sort of screaming. . . .

In a blind panic I was crashing my way through the tumble of tables and chairs in the mess towards the door leading out onto the platform when the greatest shock so far tilted the floor to what must have been thirty degrees and saved me my efforts. In a moment—as I flew against the door, bursting it open and floundering out into the storm—I knew for sure that *Sea-Maid* was going down. Before, it had only been a possibility; a mad, improbable possibility; but now—now I knew for sure. Half stunned from my collision with the door I was thrown roughly against the platform rails, to cling there for dear life in the howling, tearing wind and chill, rushing mist and spray.

And that was when I saw it.

I saw it—and in my utter disbelief—in one crazy moment of understanding——I relaxed my hold on the rails and slid under them into the throat of that banshee, demon storm that howled and tore at the trembling girders of the old *Sea-Maid*.

Even as I fell, a colossal wave smashed into the rig, breaking two of the legs as though they were nothing stronger than match-sticks, and the next instant I was in the sea, picked up and swept away on the great crest of that same wave. Even in the dizzy, sickening rush as the great wave hurled me aloft, I tried to spot *Sea-Maid* in the maelstrom of wind, mist and ocean. It was futile, and I gave it up in order to put all effort to my own battle for survival.

I don't remember much after that—at least, not until I was picked up, and even that's not too clear. I do remember, though, while fighting the icy water, a dreadful fear of being eaten alive by fish; but so far as I know there were none about. I remember, too, being hauled aboard the life-boat from the mainland in a sea that was flat as a pancake and calm as a mill-pond.

The next really lucid moment came when I woke up to find myself between clean sheets in a Bridlington hospital.

But there, I've held off from telling the important part—and for the same reason Joe Borszowski held off: I don't want to be thought a madman. Well, I'm not mad, Johnny, but I don't suppose for a single moment that you'll take my story seriously—nor, for that matter, will *Seagasso* suspend any of its North-Sea commitments—but at least I'll have the satisfaction of knowing I tried to warn you.

Now I ask you to remember what Borszowski said about great, alien beings lying asleep and imprisoned beneath the bed of the sea; "gods" capable of controlling the actions of lesser creatures, capable of bending the very weather to their wills—and then explain the sight I saw before I found myself floundering in that mad ocean as the old *Sea-Maid* went down.

It was simply a gusher, Johnny, a gusher—but one such as I'd never seen before in my whole life and hope never to have to see again. For instead of reaching to the heavens in one solid black column—it *pulsed* upwards, pumping up in short, strong jets at a rate of about one spurt in every five seconds—and it wasn't oil, Johnny—oh God!—it wasn't oil! Booze or none I swear I wasn't drunk; not so drunk as to make me *colour-blind*, at any rate!

Like I said, old Borszowski was right, he *must* have been right. There *was* one of those great god-creatures down there, *and our drill had chopped right into the thing!*

Whatever it was it had blood pretty much like ours—good and thick and red—and a great heart strong enough to pump that blood up the bore-hole right to the surface!

Think of it, that monstrous heart beating down there in the rocks beneath the sea! *How could we have guessed that right from the beginning our instruments had been working at maximum efficiency—that those odd, regular blips recorded on the seismograph had been nothing more than the beating of a great submarine heart?*

All of which explains, I hope, my resignation.

Bernard "Pongo" Jordan,
Bridlington,
Yorks.

Down by the Sea near the Great Big Rock

Joe R. Lansdale

OWN BY THE SEA near the great big rock, they made their camp and toasted marshmallows over a small, fine fire. The night was pleasantly chill and the sea spray cold. Laughing, talking, eating the gooey marshmallows, they had one swell time; just them, the sand, the sea and the sky, and the great big rock.

The night before they had driven down to the beach, to the camping area; and on their way, perhaps a mile from their destination, they had seen a meteor shower, or something of that nature. Bright lights in the heavens, glowing momentarily, seeming to burn red blisters across the ebony sky.

Then it was dark again, no meteoric light, just the natural glow of the heavens—the stars, the dime-size moon.

They drove on and found an area of beach on which to camp, a stretch dominated by pale sands and big waves, and the great big rock.

Toni and Murray watched the children eat their marshmallows and play their games, jumping and falling over the great big rock, rolling in the cool sand. About midnight, when the kids were crashed out, they walked along the beach like fresh-found lovers, arm in arm, shoulder to shoulder, listening to the sea, watching the sky, speaking words of tenderness.

"I love you so much," Murray told Toni, and she repeated the words and added, "and our family too."

They walked in silence now, the feelings between them words enough. Sometimes Murray worried that they did not talk as all the marriage manuals suggested, that so much of what he had to say on the world and his work fell on the ears of others, and that she had so little to truly say to him. Then he would think: What the hell? I know how I feel. Different messages, unseen, unheard, pass between us all the time, and they communicate in a fashion words cannot.

He said some catch phrase, some pet thing between them, and Toni laughed and pulled him down on the sand. Out there beneath that shiny-dime moon, they stripped and loved on the beach like young sweethearts, experiencing their first night together after long expectation.

It was nearly two a.m. when they returned to the camper, checked the children and found them sleeping comfortably as kittens full of milk.

They went back outside for awhile, sat on the rock and smoked and said hardly a word. Perhaps a coo or a purr passed between them, but little more.

Finally they climbed inside the camper, zipped themselves into their sleeping bags and nuzzled together on the camper floor.

Outside the wind picked up, the sea waved in and out, and a slight rain began to fall.

Not long after, Murray awoke and looked at his wife in the crook of his arm. She lay there with her face a grimace, her mouth opening and closing like a guppie, making an "uhhh, uhh," sound.

A nightmare perhaps. He stroked the hair from her face, ran his fingers lightly down her cheek and touched the hollow of her throat and thought: What a nice place to carve out some fine, white meat . . .

What in the hell is wrong with me? Murray thought, and he rolled away from her, out of the bag. He dressed, went outside and sat on the rock. With shaking hands on his knees, buttocks resting on the warmth of the stone, he brooded. Finally he dismissed the possibility that such a thought had actually crossed his mind, smoked a cigarette and went back to bed.

He did not know that an hour later Toni awoke and bent over him and looked at his face as if it were something to squash. But finally she shook it off and slept.

The children tossed and turned. Little Roy squeezed his hands open, closed, open, closed. His eyelids fluttered rapidly.

Robyn dreamed of striking matches.

Morning came and Murray found that all he could say was, "I had the oddest dream."

Toni looked at him, said, "Me too," and that was all.

Placing lawn chairs on the beach, they put their feet on the rock and watched the kids splash and play in the waves; watched as Roy mocked the sound of the *Jaws* music and made fins with his hands and chased

Robyn through the water as she scuttled backwards and screamed with false fear.

Finally they called the children from the water, ate a light lunch and, leaving the kids to their own devices, went in for a swim.

The ocean stroked them like a mink-gloved hand. Tossed them, caught them, massaged them gently. They washed together, laughing, kissing—

Then tore their lips from one another as up on the beach they heard a scream.

Roy had his fingers gripped about Robyn's throat, held her bent back over the rock and was putting a knee in her chest. There seemed no play about it. Robyn was turning blue.

Toni and Murray waded for shore, and the ocean no longer felt kind. It grappled with them, held them, tripped them with wet, foamy fingers. It seemed an eternity before they reached the shore, yelling at Roy.

Roy didn't stop. Robyn flopped like a dying fish.

Murray grabbed the boy by the hair and pulled him back, and for a moment, as the child turned, he looked at his father with odd eyes that did not seem his, but looked instead as cold and firm as the great big rock.

Murray slapped him, slapped him so hard Roy spun and went down, stayed there on hands and knees, panting.

Murray went to Robyn, who was already in Toni's arms, and on the child's throat were blue-black bands like thin, ugly snakes.

"Baby, baby, are you okay?" Toni asked over and over. Murray wheeled, strode back to the boy, and Toni was now yelling at him, crying, "Murray, Murray, easy now. They were just playing and it got out of hand."

Roy was on his feet, and Murray, gritting his teeth, so angry he could not believe it, slapped the child down.

"MURRAY," Toni yelled, and she let go of the sobbing Robyn and went to stay his arm, for he was already raising it for another strike. "That's no way to teach him not to hit, not to fight."

Murray turned to her, almost snarling, but then his face relaxed and he lowered his hand. Turning to the boy, feeling very criminal, Murray reached down to lift Roy by the shoulder. But Roy pulled away, darted for the camper.

"Roy," he yelled, and started after him. Toni grabbed his arm.

"Let him be," she said. "He got carried away and he knows it. Let him mope it over. He'll be all right." Then softly: "I've never known you to get that mad."

"I've never been so mad before," he said honestly.

They walked back to Robyn, who was smiling now. They all sat on the rock, and about fifteen minutes later Robyn got up to see about Roy. "I'm going to tell him it's okay," she said. "He didn't mean it." She went inside the camper.

"She's sweet," Toni said.

"Yeah," Murray said, looking at the back of Toni's neck as she watched Robyn move away. He was thinking that he was supposed to cook lunch today, make hamburgers, slice onions; big onions cut thin with a freshly sharpened knife. He decided to go get it.

"I'll start lunch," he said flatly, and stalked away.

As he went, Toni noticed how soft the back of his skull looked, so much like an over-ripe melon.

She followed him inside the camper.

Next morning, after the authorities had carried off the bodies, taken the four of them out of the blood-stained, fire-gutted camper, one detective said to another:

"Why does it happen? Why would someone kill a nice family like this? And in such horrible ways . . . set fire to it afterwards?"

The other detective sat on the huge rock and looked at his partner, said tonelessly, "Kicks maybe."

That night, when the moon was high and bright, gleaming down like a big spotlight, the big rock, satiated, slowly spread its flippers out, scuttled across the sand, into the waves, and began to swim toward the open sea. The fish that swam near it began to fight.

Message Found in a Bottle II

or

An Invitation from Your Captain

Nancy Holder

THIS IS HOW it will be when you drown:
   You start out, of course, in water. The particulars really don't matter, but for the sake of argument, let's say you're swimming. Of course, your boat might sink, or your plane may go down, and then there are ponds and lakes and rivers. And bath tubs. Or hot tubs. Dreadful things can happen in Jacuzzis. Have happened.

But imagine that it's a dazzling, warm day at the beach. You've arrived not half an hour before with friends, and you decide to take a dip while the others lie in the sun, play cards, and roast the weenies.

You shuffle through the velvet sand, watching the water roll ever closer to your toes. The rippled flow is frosted with bubbles that remind you of champagne; beneath the crystal-clear curtain, seashells glisten in the sun. You look up and down the deserted coastline at patches of grass and lavender boulders, planted by Nature in a thoughtful breakwater pattern, and you're grateful no one else bothers with the five-mile trek on the unpaved road that leads to this secret spot.

A breeze ruffles your hair, tickles the hair on your arms. The water laps at the ends of your toes; you jump playfully back, daring it to touch you. While it recedes into the ocean, you write your initials in the wet sand with your big toe, blot them out, jump back as the water rolls back in. It catches you this time, and licks your foot like a puppy; to your delight it is cool and refreshing, not cold at all. And quite clear: you can see your toenails as you wade deeper, up to your ankles, your shins, just below your knees.

You call to your friends—they're missing out! But they're hungry, and busy preparing lunch, and they tell you to go ahead and enjoy yourself. You, after all, are the one who loves the water most.

Knowing you're amusing them, you move faster, going deeper and making little noises because now the water's a tiny bit chillier. You prance up to your thighs and then you raise up on your toes as the swell gooses you. Then one, two, three big steps farther out, you dive into the rolling wave as it curls chest-high.

Cowabunga! It wakes you up! It's salty and clean, and washes the sweat and sand off your chest and arms. The sun dances on the droplets that cling to your hair and eyelashes as you pop up, shaking your head and wiping your eyes. You turn and wave, let out a whoop; your friends wave back. At this distance, you can hear the radio, see the smoke rising from the fire ring; and in the otherwise deserted parking lot your car sits, waiting to be refilled with damp bodies, sand, and the leftover firewood.

You swim a little farther out, waiting for the moment when the bottom dips and you lose contact. Whoops! You duck under for a second, bob back up, tread water while you get your bearings. The water is a deep, azure blue, like a picture in a resort brochure or a travelogue about the South Pacific. You cannot believe the perfection of this moment as, buoyed by the salt, you dip your head back so the water can slick your hair. You squint into the golden, gauzy sun. You wave again to your friends with a rush of shy tenderness, because they seem so happy to see you enjoying yourself.

Adventurous now, you flop onto your stomach and swim away from shore. You watch the waves; one swells beneath you, carrying you toward the beach as you ride it backwards. It was just a small one, so you cut the trip short by standing up. Eagerly, you swim back out. Jump headfirst into the next one and swim through before it crests.

The sky is a reflection of the water—or is it the other way around? There's not a single cloud up there, just the warm, gentle ball, a Goldilocks orb, not too hot, just right.

And then a wavelet smacks you. Your mouth is open and you swallow some sandy saltwater. Your throat and eyes sting a bit. A piece of seaweed brushes against you, lazes away. You wonder if there are any fish in the water. One of your friends brought a fishing pole, and has high hopes for later.

You give yourself a thrill by searching for jelly fish. But how could there be any, in this paradise? As if to confirm your opinion, a thirty-second scan of the area yields nothing.

You swim farther out. You watch the waves, travel over and up, waiting for just the one to ride in, anticipating the rough-and-tumble exit you'll make as you hit the shore. Your stomach rumbles and you imagine the tastes of potato chips and potato salad and remember you'll need to reapply your sunscreen after you dry off.

You turn around to see your friends again.

And they're farther away than you thought they'd be.

A lot farther.

For a moment you're puzzled, and then slightly panicked, as you understand you've been caught in an undertow. The current has dragged you out to sea. Yes, and why didn't you notice before that you're cold? In fact, you're shivering. You have another uncertain moment, but then you recall that now you must swim parallel to shore. Eventually you'll make your way out of the current—which is, by the way, growing still colder. It's practically frigid, and your muscles are cramping. Gooseflesh coats you like a wetsuit.

Swim parallel. You say it to yourself three or four times as you swim. Hand over hand, steady, legs kicking easily. You move right along; after all, everyone says you're part fish. You have it aced, you think; you're in no danger.

The undertow grabs hold of your ankles and drags you. You feel it this time, feel the process; have a frightening half-formed vision of someone actually wrapping their hands—

—their bony fingers—

around your ankles and swimming off with you, depositing you in deeper waters. You forget you must not fight directly against the force. Legs kicking, arms flailing like windmills, you lose the rhythm of your breathing and stop, gasping. Your lungs hurt.

The waves are surging around you; they're big enough to surf on. The water has deepened to a dark blue-gray like the skin of a humpback whale. You think you see things moving below the surface. Before you can be sure, a succession of waves crashes right over you, and you go under, gagging. You try repeatedly to catch one and bodysurf in. Each time, you fail. They roar and crash, pummeling you. You stop, because all you're doing is exhausting yourself.

You go back to treading water. The water is thick and cold. The sun, once so benevolent, beats down on your head and makes you squint hard at the coastline. Perhaps due to the harshness of the shadows it makes, the lavender boulders jut like hard, sharp rocks into the breakers, and you wonder, for the first time since you found this beach, if you could seriously hurt yourself riding the surf back to shore.

Something knocks into you, moves away. You don't bother with it now, because you see your friends on shore: tiny dots. Your heart clutches. The something bobs against you again, and you look around. In a different direction, you see five huge Portuguese man-of-war, stinging tentacles streaming behind them. They drift in front of you, another obstacle between you and the beach.

You wave at your friends. "Hey!" you call, but your voice is raw from the salt and it comes out scratchy and thin. Yet it must have done the trick: they're looking around, looking for you, so you relax a little. They're going to come for you and help you back. They'll razz you, but you won't mind, because you were pretty stupid to let this happen. You, after all, are an expert swimmer. But it'll feel so good to be back on land nothing can bother you. You'll let them tease you all they want.

All you need to do is wait. To conserve your strength, you flip over on your back and lay your head in the water, spread-eagle yourself. Your buddies are probably already on their way.

But how? They don't have a boat, or a raft, or even a life ring. And none of them can swim as well as you. Well, then, they'll get in the car and drive for help.

Except that you drove, and the keys are in your waterproof wallet, safety-pinned to the cutoffs you're wearing.

They'll flag someone down, someone else in a car.

But no one ever comes down that unpaved road. It's your secret spot. You read about it when you first moved to the area, in a book of local legends. Some ghostly nonsense you've forgotten now, evidently scary enough to keep everyone else away.

The undertow gives you another yank. You gasp, flip upright, and tread water again. You're pulled past the breakers, into an ice-cube sea that rolls and dips but has no waves. Then even those highs and lows flatten out, and you're floating on the liquid equivalent of a desert. The beating sun above, the cold depths below; the dark waters, where you can no longer see the lower half of your body. The ocean has swallowed it up and it's pulling the rest of you down, sucking at your tired back and arms like quicksand.

You scan the horizon for your friends.

They're gone.

The coastline itself is gone. You see nothing but endless, heartless gray. You turn in all directions, but there is nothing to see but more jelly fish and the painful reflections of the sun. No sailboats miraculously passing by, no other swimmers, no land. A line behind you where both the sea and sky bleach to gray and become the same horizon, where you might simply float away into oblivion.

You shout again for help. You realize you should have tried to shout louder when you were closer.

The shore, the world, is still gone.

You tread faster, comprehend that you're doing the wrong thing, and rest back into the water so you'll float again, while you consider your options.

But what you don't understand is that you have no options.

And then something bobs against you again, against your calf, then your hip, then your side, and you think *oh my god, it's a shark.* Your heart skips a couplet, you hold your breath, and touch the thing.

Not a shark. You exhale. Only a dark green flask you mistake at first for a 7-up bottle. But there are antique brown lines running through it, and dazzling red and blue stones circling the neck like a coronet. No, the brown is actually golden, and the bottle's corked; and there's something yellow and gooey half-covering the cork.

You pick it up. It's quite heavy, for something that's floating. As are you.

There's a piece of paper inside. A message in a bottle.

And because your hands are shaking, and you're already getting tired and trying to keep floating; because you're becoming giddy because you can't believe this is actually happening—that you've drifted out to sea and no one's come yet—*no one's come yet!*—because it makes for something to focus on, a diversion from the fact that you've just realized you can't swim or float or tread water too much longer—

—because you have nothing else to do but be so afraid you want to vomit, you pry off the coating, which is wax, pull out the cork, and tip the bottle upside down.

A piece of thick, yellowed paper slides into your hand. Decorated with an anchor—or is it a skull and crossbones?—the elaborately scrolled letterhead reads:

The Captain, H.M.S. Pandora.

Beneath it are engraved the following words:

The Captain respectfully requests your presence at the Captain's Table for dinner this evening.

And something rings a bell. Something in the local legends concerning messages in bottles.

And death warrants.

Because no one can swim for very long, and you certainly can't hold your breath forever.

And when the drowning itself begins? Your actual last few minutes?

You have some final throes, of course. You do not go gentle into that deep ocean. You tire, and so you struggle harder, which tires you more. You tell yourself to float, but you can no longer manage it. You're hyperventilating. You're crying. You wet yourself, and the warm stream reminds you how cold you are.

You sink, fight back to the surface, sink, surface, and so on, until you find yourself mindlessly reaching for a gasping, terrified gulp of air. It hurts when you inhale, feels better when you exhale. This seems to go on for an eternity, but ten, perhaps fifteen minutes elapse at most.

Your body is heavy and numb, and clumsy. You can no longer see because you're blind with fear. You can think of nothing but the next breath.

And you can no longer make your way to the surface. Down, down, you go, and then you struggle against your fate again, but to no purpose. Your eyes bulging, you stare up into the dazzling glare of the sun as it strikes the surface above you; and it looks unbelievably far away, that surface, that sunshine. Conversely, you can see nothing past your feet as they helplessly dangle.

Unbearable pressure pushes against your lungs, so you let the air out a bit at a time—a puff at a time, a slow leak, until your body aches. It feels thin and flaccid, like an empty balloon. Your throat tightens and aches. Your muscles tense and strain.

The surface above you dances and glitters.

Your lungs are almost drained, and you are hovering in the water, and that damn bottle knocks into your head once, twice, and you shut your eyes tight and hope it does the job. But it drifts a few feet away, suspended and unmoving as if it's waiting—and it is waiting. For your RSVP.

And you oblige. Because you are completely out of air, and now there is only one thing left for you to do.

Inhale.

And just as you do, and your eyes begin to roll back in your head, the shadow of a ship's hull casts a large, gray net over you and you think Thank God, thank God, you're saved.

But you're wrong. More wrong than you can imagine.

And that is what it will be like. And, more or less, how it will happen. And it *will* happen. Sooner. Or later.

So nice you can join us.

A Sailor's Pay

Jack Cady

ONLY THE SEA remains the same. The city of Portland grasps its way toward the surrounding hills of Maine where once stood the cold green of conifers. The port hums with off-loading of goods from container ships where once floated only trawlers and lobster boats. I return to a place where darkness is old, if not ancient. I carry an old clasp knife, one blade broken, but with a small marlinespike that is still intact.

The past compels me to deal with shades. Curious matters are reported in the press. I am the last man alive who understands them.

And, the coast of Maine is no wrong place to look for specters. Ships have passed the Portland Head for three hundred and fifty years. This harbor has recorded a thousand wrecks, and it has not recorded wrecks that happened in darkness when the sea swallowed hulls in one enormous gulp. At Portland Head the sea builds during northeast storms. Waves vacuum the bottom.

Expiation is being played out here in hideous resurrection. A Coastguardsman named Tommy pilots a steel-hulled forty-footer, twin diesels screaming wide at twenty-two hundred RPM. An engineman named Case dies horribly. A seaman named Alley fails a task, and an engineman named Wert turns coward; while a madman howls.

The newspaper reports that fishermen report ghosts. It does so tongue in cheek, inferring that the fishermen are drunk. I'll allow they may be drunk, but that doesn't mean their vision is unclear.

My name is Victor Alley. Immediately after WWII I was stationed here, doing harbor patrols from the Coast Guard base in South Portland. I was a very young man, and this is a young man's story.

When you are young, and when the world asks you to go into action, mistakes happen. Unseasoned men ride the great urgency of action and emotion, responding to feelings of duty and feelings of guilt. They do not have words or balance in emergencies. Sometimes people die in order for young men to learn how to handle themselves. Two days after my nine-teenth birthday our story went like this:

Winter darkness shrouded the inshore islands, and enclosed the harbor and channel and buoy yard at the Coast Guard base in South Portland. I shot pool in the barracks and hoped my girlfriend would phone. We had already made our evening harbor patrol. The boats were secured. When the call came over the PA to proceed with our boat I did not even rack my cue. Just laid it on the table and ran. Our Cap got fussy when those boats didn't move quick.

As I grabbed foul-weather gear, Wert still searched for his. Then he followed, trotting, not running. His rating called him a third-class engine-man, but nobody ever saw him get his hands dirty. He was football-player big, with a moon face.

Case, our first-class engineman, had the engines cracking and stuttering as I made it to the boat basin. Beneath the floodlights the forty-footer seemed more like a tiny ship than a big boat. It was painted white as snow on mountains, and it carried a high bow, a real wave buster. It sported low rails and plenty of working room aft. When we jumped aboard, and I cast off, our bosun mate, Tommy, sapped it hard.

Those engines could scream like animals. The stern grabbed deep, dig-ging in with the twin roar of diesels as the boat moved out. Those engines were still cold. Tommy knew better. He cleared the end of the pier and cut through shallow water, crosscutting flooded tideflats to the channel. Spray rose luminescent in the darkness. I climbed up beside Tom. He was hitting it just way too hard.

"You'll drag the bottom out," I yelled. I could feel fingers of rock reaching toward the hull. Tommy looked kind of crazy. Tall and skinny with thick black hair like a Portuguese. Just crazy. He muttered a name. He stood at the helm totally concentrated, and motioned me away.

I stepped aft. The engine ran at least two-thirds. Tom pushed it that way until we made the channel, and then he ran the engines full. They screamed in overspeed, the bow high and rock-steady in the hard hand of the water. Case tapped my shoulder, and we both moved forward to be away from the scream of engines. We did not know that Wert tagged along behind us.

"The Portland cops called. We're after a boat," Case told me. "Guy who stole it killed his old lady with a knife. He's got their kid in the boat with him. They think."

"Who thinks?"

"The cops didn't find a kid's body. The kid and all of her clothes are missing."

Tommy did not let up. He held it wide open in the middle of the channel, heading seaward. Distant lights of Portland and South Portland started looking fuzzy, the way they do just before winter fog arrives.

Wert interrupted us. The All-American Boy. His voice practically bubbled with excitement. "This beats towing in broken-down fishing boats. A murderer."

"Get back to those engines," Case told him. "Don't take your eyes off that oil pressure for a second."

"If we're going to have a murderer, we'd ought to have a gun." Wert acted conversational.

"You want a gun, join the Army," I told him.

Wert just asked for it, leaving those engines at those RPMs, and then refusing to hurry when Case gave an order.

"You done it this time," Case told Wert. He literally turned Wert around and gave him a shove aft. Then he turned back to me. "He lies better than I tell the truth. Waste of ink to put him on report." Case was tense, and that was unusual. He was mostly easygoing, a guy without enemies. Wert even liked him. He was the kindest man I ever knew. I'd learned a lot from him. Case had broad shoulders, broad face, a nice smile, and not much of a beer belly.

"I gotta talk to him." Case motioned at Tommy.

"The engines?"

"Sure," Case said, "and some other stuff."

I figured the engines were either okay, or wrecked by now. "What are we doing?" I asked Case.

"We're hurrying to put the cork in the bottle. There's a cutter checking the channel. We're blocking the seaward side. The killer can't escape through the harbor mouth. At least that's part of it."

"What's the other part?"

Case looked like he wondered if I would understand. "Tommy's acting weird," Case said. "He sorta gets his beanie unscrewed in emergencies. This ain't just about some nut and a stole boat."

I almost understood. I knew the story. During the war Tommy served on a cutter escorting convoys. On a dark night a freighter was torpedoed. There were survivors in the water. Tommy had the deck on the fantail because the gunnery officer was forward.

It was an awful story. Tommy spotted the survivors, and sonar picked up the German sub at the same time. The sub hovered a hundred feet down, directly below the freighter's surviving crew. The captain of the cutter made a command decision. He depth-charged the sub. Men struggling in the water turned to bloody pulp. A few survivors on the outskirts of the explosions did not die. The captain made the decision, but Tommy gave the order to drop the charges. It was one of those things that nobody talks about, and everybody seems to know.

"Tell him not to get too weird." I didn't know what else to say.

"C'mon," Case said. "Let's talk that poor fella out of wrecking those engines."

I followed Case, and he climbed up beside Tommy, who leaned way out around the spray shield. The engines screamed, and the bow rode so high at this speed that he could not see a thing. Case put one hand on Tommy's shoulder, grinned at Tom like Tom had just told a pretty good joke, and then Case eased the controls. Speed came off, the bow dropped, and the boat skidded a little sideways. We'd come far enough that we could see the lighthouse at Portland Head.

"Take a strain," Case said. "Guy with a wild hair crossways can't figure anything out."

"The police boat is out checking the islands," Tommy said. "If he gets in behind the islands, we've lost him." He did not even hear Case.

"Get it figured," Case said. "What you're doing ain't working." He paused as he figured the next move. He looked toward the misty lights that told of fog. "At best we've got an hour. Go up to the Head along the edge of the channel, then double back along the other side. He won't be riding the middle of the channel."

"I want a piece of that clown." Tommy's voice sounded in control, but it still sounded a little crazy.

It came to me, watching him, that Tommy had been quiet for too long. Been holding everything in. I figure he didn't care about the murderer. He just wanted to hit something that needed hitting.

"Cruise it slow," Case said. "Use the searchlight, because he'll be running without lights."

It's a big harbor, nearly as big as Boston. You could hide two hundred lobster boats in this harbor, and the odds on finding even a dozen of them would be pretty long.

"Because the guy's crazy," Case said. "He's runnin', but I doubt he's going to hide. If he hides, we won't find him."

We cruised the starboard side of the channel as far as Portland Head, then turned around and cruised the other side coming back. Fog gathered. An occasional horn or whistle sounded. Fog settled from above until it finally pressed against the water. It was thick above, thinner at the waterline.

A thousand-to-one shot, but there seemed nothing else to do except search the islands. Dull, freezing work. As the ice fog gathered the searchlight became useless. The fog did not lift after nearly five hours. It looked like it was going to be another one of those cold and futile nights.

Wert's teeth chattered. "It's cold."

"It's November."

"Take us home, Tommy."

"Go sit on an engine."

We traded off watching-standing in the bow. Tommy kept the engines barely turning. He searched along the beaches of the dark islands. Didn't use the searchlight. We just stood in the bow and listened, hoping to hear the sound of a lobster boat's engine. It was about 0330 when the cutter in the channel radioed, reporting a target on its radar. A small boat moved along the South Portland side of the channel.

"Got him," Tommy said. "Let's get him good." Tommy had sort of settled down, but now he started to get all ruffled again.

We were all tired, cold, and we had taken some spray five hours back. Nobody was wet, but nobody was exactly dry. Tommy shoved the RPMs ahead, then lowered them a little as he realized he was being stupid. That boat was forty feet of steel hull. Not something to shove through fog at high speed.

The cutter talked us across the harbor and through the fog. We moved too quick, taking radar readings from the cutter. I don't trust radar, and I sure don't trust a set I'm not looking at. I always trusted Tommy.

As we overhauled the cutter we could see its searchlights swallowed by fog. Just beyond the lights, right on the edge of the lights, the lobster boat looked like a little ghost. It was weaving in and out past the rocks.

It's a cliff along there. High-walled and granite and straight up. The lobster boat made its way toward a notch not big enough to be a tiny cove. It was just a place where the rock broke away and guys moored sometimes. We ran past the cutter, taking off speed, and coasted alongside the lobster boat. We were maybe twenty feet away.

The guy was hard to see in the dark and fog lying beneath that rock face. This close in, our searchlight helped. I ran it over the boat and the numbers checked. This was the man.

The guy stood behind the wheel. He turned when our light hit him. He shook his fist and yelled, maybe daring us to come in. The lobster boat edged nearer the rock. I did not believe the guy was insane. He ran the boat too well, discounting the fact that he was where you shouldn't run a boat.

Then he turned his face full to mine, and I believed it. He was like an abandoned beast, like a dog that's been run over and is not yet numb in its dying. The guy's eyes didn't seem like eyes; just sockets; deep, empty, vacant.

Tommy moved in closer, maybe six or eight feet away. The old lobster boat kept chugging. We were so close I could see blistered paint in the glow of our running lights. The madman started howling.

"Can't head him off," Tommy said. "He'll beach that thing. There's nothing but rock in there."

"Beach him," Wert said. "That kid ain't on that boat."

"Get back to those engines."

"If he'd swiped the kid in that kind of hurry, you think he'd have time to pack her clothes?"

"Move it aft," Case told Wert. "Get back to those engines." He paused, like he was thinking about what Wert had said. I couldn't figure if Wert was right or not. He sort of seemed right. "When we figure what we're going to do," Case told Wert, "I'll come and let you know."

Wert laid aft.

"We'll use three of us," Case said. He laid it out. Tommy was to bring the boat close alongside. Three of us would jump. I was to go forward and get the kid, who had to be in the wheelhouse. Wert would kill the engine on the lobster boat. Then Wert was supposed to help Case with the madman.

"And Tommy," Case said, "you hold steady. Because man, if he puts that thing on the rocks we're going to need you."

"He's got a knife."

"Yep," Case said, "and I got myself one hell of a big crescent wrench." He turned aft, yelling at Wert, who stood beside the engines looking determined. Wert rubbed a fist into the open palm of his other hand.

When Tommy closed I jumped. The lobster boat ran in the shadow of the rock face. It loomed over me, darker than the rest of the dark. As I hit I felt the lobster boat shudder and rub the rock someplace deep. I lost my balance. We were so close in that I actually shoved back to my feet by pushing on the rock face; while somewhere behind me Tommy yelled, "Left rudder. Left rudder."

I came from the bow, around the starboard side of the dinky wheelhouse. The madman stepped from the wheel to meet me. I was scared. Couldn't think of what to do, but my legs just ran me into him. Hit him like I was a fullback. He stumbled aft against Case, who was on his knees. I think maybe Case sprained or broke an ankle. That lobster boat was just trash, the decks full of junk and gear. Tommy was still yelling, "Left rudder, left rudder." I heard the forty's engines dig in as Tommy cut to port to give us running room. As the forty's stern slid past I looked up and across, into the pale moon face of Wert. He stood motionless. The guy looked frozen with fear, wide eyes staring. He hadn't jumped.

You never know—even after years you can never decide—if what you do is right. Everything happens so fast. If I didn't detest Wert so much, I would have listened to him. Maybe saved Case.

What happened is that I did what I'd been told. I grabbed the helm and threw it hard to port. The boat edged away from the rock. It handled sluggish, already sinking from the lick it took on the rocks. Forward of the wheel a red light burned in the little cabin. I was supposed to get the kid, and so I went down there. Old coats, old blankets, slickers, and boots. A gush of water through the ruptured hull. No kid. I must have wasted half a minute. I turned back to the deck just as a searchlight from the cutter swept us, and just as the forty's engines started howling.

It all happened in slow motion, or that's the way it seems. The madman stood above Case, and the madman howled almost like the engines. He had both hands raised high together, holding one of those long, thin stakes that lobstermen use to pin fish in their traps. The forty roared someplace real close. I heard a bow wave, but you never hear a bow wave —not like that—unless it's pointed right at you. Case yelled something, tried to throw something at the madman, but you can't throw much when you're on your knees. I dived over Case, trying to tackle the madman. There was a shock, the lobster boat driven sideways, a crash of timbers; and a fish smell came off the deck as I rolled. Something, a lobster trap maybe, clipped me alongside the head. Then I was in water that is death-dealing cold, struggling to stay up.

The boat crew from the cutter took us aboard, dried us out, and gave us clothes. At first I didn't remember much. I sat for a long time on the messdeck shivering and drinking coffee. Didn't see Tommy. Figured they were working on him. Didn't see Case. Saw Wert. He sat at a table facing me, sullen, wearing his own clothes. He'd got his feet wet, and he put them on a bench, rubbing his legs and rolling up the wet part of his dungarees so they came to his calf.

"There wasn't no kid. I told you. They beached what was left of that boat and there wasn't hide nor hair."

"What happened?" I couldn't remember anything. Then I started to remember a little.

"Tom lost his head and rammed you. Dumped you all in the water, then jumped in to pull you out. The forty's back there now, high and dry and cut wide open."

It was coming back now. "Case?"

Wert just plain looked sick. "Guy stabbed him. Tommy rammed you because he was trying to keep the guy from stabbing Case."

"The madman?"

"Jumped back and got himself killed when the bow of the forty pinched him."

And that's when the memory came clear of Wert's white face rising like a pale moon above the rail, the vacant look, the struggle and noise at my back and the roar of engines.

"Where were you?" I was getting cold again.

He had his story down pat. Like a first-grader reciting about Mary and the lamb. "We were about to jump, and the engines went rough. Case said to check it out because we couldn't afford to lose power. I checked, but before I could jump Tommy kicked it ahead." He turned his back to me, swinging away, and propped his leg up to inspect his toes.

They pulled me off of him, somebody did. Then their chief bosun sent me to wait it out on the fantail. Probably because I had shoes on and Wert didn't.

I went to the fantail figuring that things couldn't get any worse, and they got a million times worse right away.

Bodies are always stored on the fantail. I sat beside Case after I found which one he was. Kind of patted the old blanket he was wrapped in. I couldn't figure out why the best man I knew had to be dead. Wasn't thinking very straight.

Then I did start thinking straight, thinking about what I'd seen when I checked to see which one he was. Case was pretty tore up, but mostly just mangled. There was only one wound above the waist, and that was way above the heart, nearly in the left shoulder. That madman had not stabbed Case to death.

I'd always trusted Tommy. Tommy was my friend. He had taught me a lot. But, Tommy was the one who killed Case while trying to save him.

You never know if what you do is right, and that's especially true when you are young. You operate on the basis of what you know.

One thing I knew was that the local coroner was a lazy old drunk. Twice, while on Shore Patrol, we'd taken bodies to that coroner. He dumped them in a stainless steel tub, cut away the clothes, and said something like "This pore old buster drank hisself to death." I knew that coroner would do no autopsy.

If he saw a wound over the heart he would blame the madman. He'd not say a word about Tommy.

I pulled out my clasp knife. It carried a marlinespike, about the same diameter as a stake that runs through lobster traps. Even today I can't believe my courage and ignorance. I stabbed Case, stabbed a dead man, right where the heart would be. It was just a little blue hole that did not bleed, but, what with arterial damage and salt water, none of the other wounds were bleeding.

I remember vaguely wondering how much jail time you could get for stabbing a dead man.

* * *

Years pass, but memory is relentless. Such an act wears on a man's soul. Sometimes the memory lies faded and dull among brighter memories of youth. At the same time, the memory never leaves. Maybe I did Tommy a favor, maybe not. The police filed no civil charges, and the court-martial found him innocent. The court concluded that, although unable to save Case, he may well have saved me. The court did not like the destruction of an expensive boat.

Tommy came to a bad end. He started boozing when on liberty. We saw his tall frame and black hair bent over too many glasses of beer in too many sailor dives. He went AWOL for a month, was reclaimed from a drunk tank.

In those days the Coast Guard was a small and personal outfit. Our cap tried to save Tommy by transferring him to a weather cutter. The Cap figured, since the cutter stayed on station for a month at a time, Tommy would have to stay sober in thirty-day stretches. Tommy slipped overboard one night as the cutter passed the Portland Lightship. The investigating board called it an accident.

And Wert came to an even more macabre end. On a night of no wind he wandered among buoys in the buoy yard. The buoys stood silent, the giant whistles, the lighted bells, the racks of nuns. Some were barnacled, waiting to be sand-blasted and red-leaded. For no reason, and against known laws of physics, a lighted bell rolled on flat ground. It weighed maybe a ton, and it crushed Wert against the pavement of the storage area. There was not a breath of wind, but men on cutters swore they heard the bell toll, and clank, and toll.

When my hitch was up I did not reenlist, but fled from salt water. The next few years were dreary; odd jobs and bad jobs through the Middle West. I attended college at night, got married, finally graduated from college, got divorced. Nothing seemed to go exactly right. It came to me— in, of all places, the bus station in Peoria—that this awful incident of youth kept me from my true calling, the sea. I traded my bus ticket to Chicago for a ticket to Seattle. From Seattle I went to Ketchikan, fished salmon, then finally found a permanent berth on a tug hauling barges from Seattle to Anchorage. After many years I rose to master of my own vessel.

A lot of down-east sailors, mostly fishermen, drift into Alaska. On a snowy January afternoon in Sitka, forty years after the event, I heard stories from a couple of Maine men who vowed never again to enter Portland Harbor. There was enough in their drunken talk to convince me it was time to come to terms with the past. I booked a flight to Portland.

Through the years certain questions haunted that incident of youth. I thought about them on the plane. What happened to the child? What did Tommy see as he kicked the forty-footer ahead? What, for that matter, did I see? I am old now, and am well acquainted with the way the mind manufactures illusions. What did Wert see? What caused a puritanical lobsterman to suddenly sink into the depths of insanity?—for the lobstermen of Maine are usually stern and steady fellows.

After checking into a Portland hotel I went to the newspaper office. The report from so many years ago seemed sketchy, but it did contain the names of men and the name of the child. The child, it was reported, had been taken away by her grandmother before the ugly murder.

It was unlikely the grandmother still lived, but I searched the phone book. The grandmother was not listed, but the child's name was. Of course, she would now be a middle-aged woman. I phoned, made clumsy explanations, and she agreed to meet me for lunch.

To an aging man, the woman who met me in the hotel lobby seemed to shine with both dignity and beauty. The coast of Maine is hard on men, but often even harder on women. This slim lady's face was weathered, crow's-feet around bright gray eyes, and her hands showed that she was not afraid of work. Long, dark hair displayed streaks of gray, and her conservative gray dress fell well below the knee.

"It's a jigsaw puzzle," she told me once we were seated for lunch. "You must remember that I was little more than a baby."

"I wonder what is happening in the harbor," I said. "The newspaper just reports ghost stories." Beyond the windows, banks of piled snow lined streets that are asphalt now, but in my day were brick. Sun glistened on patches of ice, and the thermometer stood at zero.

"I know exactly," she told me. "I own a ship chandlery. The story comes together in bits and pieces. Men talk even when they want to keep quiet."

Men heard more than they saw. In winter darkness of early mornings, when ice fog covered the channel, fishermen reported the low sound of diesels. There would be a nearly hysterical cry of "Left rudder. Left rudder." When that happened men became terrified, and minded their own craft. A radar screen may be completely blank, but no sailor trusts the things, and no sailor fails to react when his vision is muffled by fog.

The sound of engines would then rise to a roar, as men blindly threw their helms over to get away. Then would come a great rip and tearing of metal and wood; and then silence. Into the silence a voice would speak: "A sailor's pay. A sailor's pay."

Men reported the voice as unworldly, or as worldly as the voice of the sea. They then heard the diminishing struggle of men overboard.

"I'll tell what my grandmother told," the woman said. She smiled as if distracted. "The people of Maine have a reputation for being taciturn, but among themselves they chatter like jays." She hesitated, and then made a whispered confession. "I never married. Old-fashioned, maybe, and partly superstitious. My father was insane, my mother no better."

"If this is too difficult for you . . ."

"I never really knew them," she reminded me, "but my grandmother was my best friend."

Beyond the windows bright colors of automobiles contrasted with piled snow and sun-glazed streets. Tall buildings rose to cast dark shadows beside the busy docks.

"Maine used to resemble Alaska," the woman said. "In Alaska people still know each other."

She was right about that. There is still, in Alaska, the feeling that "we are all in this together." When Alaskans meet in improbable places, say Indiana or Australia, they either know each other, or find that they have mutual friends. It's a big state with a small population.

"This was an incident of war," she told me. "Or, maybe it was an incident of youth. The sailor named Tommy came to visit my grandmother on two occasions. He knew my father. During the war they both sailed from this port. My father served aboard a freighter. Tommy sought forgiveness for my father's death."

Old memories stirred. At last there seemed to be some sense to all of this.

Her father, it developed, was one of the survivors from the torpedoing when Tommy followed that fateful order to drop depth charges. Her father was concussed, suffering what must have been awful brain damage. Her mother, who had a reputation for being fey, met his changed condition by sinking into a virulent brand of New England religion. She played the role of saint to his role of hapless sinner before an avenging God. It proved the wrong approach.

"I don't forgive my father," she said. "I don't even excuse him. There is no excuse for murder."

She was correct, of course. No one worth a dime resorts to murder, no matter how crazy he gets. Still, most murders come from situations and passions.

"Tommy believed himself doomed," the woman told me. "In a manner of speaking he saved my father's life during that depth-charging, because he was coxswain in the boat that picked up the few survivors. He felt that fate pushed him into a world where he was forced to kill my father. The depth charges failed, and it was terrible for him to think that he was forced to kill a man after failing to kill him the first time." She smiled, but the smile was small and tight. "Don't be fooled. If the roles were reversed, my father might have done the same thing, and reacted in the same way."

The woman prepared to leave, returning to her everyday work and everyday life. "Try to think about the minds of the men," she said. "And think about the sea, because the incident is only that, an incident."

I saw that she did not know more than she told, but that she *thought* more than she would say.

"Darkness tries to kill light," she murmured. "That is the business of darkness." As I helped her into her coat she added: "Remember that all of you were very young. My father was twenty-five, and Tommy could have been little more."

I thought of the immemorial voice of the sea as I sought to rent a boat. The sea speaks with the sounds of thunder, or it is susurrous, or it hisses, or it murmurs. It is nearly as ancient as the earth. The sea has swallowed men who have spoken a thousand different languages: it has taken into its restless maw Persians, Phoenicians, Romans, Spaniards and Englishmen.

And I thought of Maine and of Portland Harbor while checking the engine of a rented workboat, that, like myself, neared the end of a working life. A thousand vessels have died in these harsh waters, while on land people erected crosses facing the sea. Many of the graves of Maine are invested only by memories.

And I thought of youth, and of the great passions and inarticulateness of youth. I did not wonder why Tommy felt the need to strike out. It is clear that he was quiet because he was too young to mobilize words and alter his confusion. Little wonder he felt doomed.

And, as ice fog began to settle over the harbor around midnight, I thought of Wert. If the sea would not forgive Wert, if, in fact, the unforgiving sea had reached ashore for Wert by using a barnacled buoy, I could still understand. He had been a kid confronted by madness, and he had no experience with madness.

Finally, as I got underway, I thought of Case. He still stood in memory as the finest man I've known. I wondered if the memory were true.

The old boat ran smoothly enough. The gasoline engine puttered as I traced the starboard shoreline. Fog lay heavy above me, and tendrils of fog began to reach toward the surface of the restless and flowing water. The tide was running. Along the coast of Maine it will rise or drop seventeen feet during winter. I searched my memories, of Case smiling, teaching a young sailor how to bend lines, and of Case coaxing the roughness from an engine, as if the engine were a living thing.

Fog clustered on the rails and deck of the workboat. It froze in whitely glowing frost. Fog glazed the silent nuns which marked the channel. Small pieces of driftwood bobbed away from my low wake as I eased from the channel and toward the cliffs. After forty years it seemed a man would forget his local knowledge of rocks and current. Yet, I had total recall of the shoreline. I arrived at the scene of my worst memories.

When the small anchor held I cut the engine. Low sounds of moving water served as background for the muffled clank of a bell. In the far distance a ship's horn hooted, and from the shore a police siren wailed faint through the frozen night. Fog covered the water so absolutely that no light from the city penetrated this dark corner. No living man could discover me here. No living man would want to.

Faint and close astern a gasoline engine puttered. It was unmistakably a lobster boat headed toward this anchorage where sheer cliff gave way to broken rock.

Fear is an old friend. I have known fear in a thousand storms. I have heard fear, and felt it, when my vessel's radio picked up the terrified voices of doomed men; men giving last loran positions as their ship took its final dive. Fear always stands near those who go to sea. At first you learn to bear it, then, finding its true nature and depth, you befriend it.

Somewhere in that fog a ghostly forty-footer was even now being directed across the channel by radar from a ghostly cutter, a ship by now mothballed or sold for scrap. Somewhere close astern a spectral lobsterman puttered across the restless face of moving waters.

The sound of Tommy's diesels rose in the fog, as the sound of the lobsterman closed. The sounds converged, and it was then the lobster boat coasted past. It hugged the cliff.

Red light in the cabin, and red from the port running light, made a diabolic mask of the lobsterman's face. The mask blazed as true madness, not insubstantial apparition. Both man and boat seemed solid as the deck beneath my feet. If anything, it was madness that was spectral.

But, then, I have also known madness at sea. I, too, have wielded a knife, if only against a corpse.

The madman cut his engine to a low mutter, then turned to face me as the lobster boat slid past. Torment distorted that face, and it was torment I had never seen. I have seen men die, and seen them live when they wished to die. I have seen victims of hideous burns, and men flayed to pieces when lines or cables parted. Yet, this torment went deeper than physical pain. Forty years were as one hour to this man who had just killed his wife. His face twisted with guilt, and I looked at a man doomed to the perpetual retelling of his story. The face rose from the depths of certain, puritan hell.

The man laughed, his voice casting strokes of anguish through muffling fog. He motioned toward me, beckoning me to follow him. His boat began to rock. With the engine running low there was not enough power to keep the boat's head pointed toward the sea.

The bow of the forty-footer appeared, sliding whitely through mist. It was as insubstantial as the lobster boat was substantial. The forty-footer wavered, more ghostly than the surrounding fog. Were it not for the solid sound of engines, the forty would be vague as a cloud. I watched the drama unfold; watched ghostly forms of men huddling in quick conversation as the forty swept past, made a turn toward the channel, and eased back toward the lobsterman.

The forty made its turn, then pointed toward the cliffs, closing alongside the lobster boat. I could see Tommy clearly. His black hair glowed above a face only slightly less visible than darkness. For moments his face seemed only surreal as he concentrated on laying the forty alongside. Case and Wert—and a vague shape like an echo of me—stood at the rail. Two figures jumped, and to his credit, Wert tried. His shoulders moved forward, but his feet did not follow. He fumbled, fell against the low rail, regained his feet.

I watched us make mistakes, as young men in action almost always make mistakes. The few minutes of action aboard that lobster boat stretched toward timelessness. A slow-motion movie.

Case fell and rolled. My own vague form hesitated, finding its feet, as the madman stepped from the wheelhouse. The madman carried no weapon, and he raised his arms. As the form ran into him, I could see he only tried to shield his face. The madman fell against the wheelhouse, then rose slowly back to his feet. My form disappeared into the wheelhouse where it would port the helm, then search for a child who was not there. Case slowly stood, his left hand holding a wrench, and his right hand clasped to his left shoulder. His wound came from falling against a spike or a tool.

The madman howled and slowly retreated to the bow. He screamed, "Stay back, stay back, stay back." Then he screamed, "Tommy, Tommy, Tommy."

Case followed him as the forty made a tight sweep away and turned back toward us. Case should have waited for help. That madman was no threat. As the madman pulled a stake from a lobster trap, Case stumbled. He was on his knees, trying to throw the wrench, when my shade appeared from the wheelhouse. The two men were so close that my dive at the madman actually carried me over Case's back; and I, watching my own ghost, saw that the madman tried to stab no one but himself. The sound of the forty's engines rose.

How much did Tommy see? He saw it all. How much did Wert see? Practically none. Wert stood in the stern beside the engines.

And so it was that madness covered Tommy's face, and that in this time of torment two madmen sacrificed themselves on the altars of their guilt.

Tommy, who had killed with depth charges, now drove toward the rocks in a last and frantic display that may—or may not—have had the least thing to do with saving Case; a man who did not need saving. The madman stood facing the huge blade that was the forty's bow, and he screamed in exaltation or expiation, waving his arms toward him as if to attract the bow against his chest.

When the forty hit rock it stumbled, then drove its bow onto the beach, the tearing of steel striking showers of sparks as it crumpled against rocks. Wert tumbled against the engine house as water flooded the stern. Tommy cut the engines, ran aft where the lobster boat lay rolled on its side in shallow water. The bow was sheared away, and beneath the hull extended legs in sea boots; legs of the lobsterman, twisted and torn. Case lay against a crumpled rail with blood draining in arterial spurts, while my faint form lay halfway in shallow water, my head resting on a rock like a young boy nestled against a pillow. Tommy did not dive in, he fell in as he hurried first toward Case, then toward me.

I do not know whether it was my voice—although I think it was—or the voice of the sea that called forth: "A sailor's pay. A sailor's pay."

They gathered about me, the spirits of those four men, as I drew up the anchor and began working the boat back toward moorings in the city. The pale moon face of Wert lived faintly in the mist. It silently protested, explained, attempted to find language that would in some way speak inexpressible thoughts.

Case stood beside me at the helm—the wan form of Case, the kind face of Case—a man who had made his own young mistakes. He did not bare his chest, did not display his wounds. If anything he seemed proud that I had raised a knife to help a friend.

These were my comrades. In many ways they were closer to me than the living crew of my Alaskan vessel.

Tommy and the lobsterman seemed no more than tendrils of fog that intermixed, that somehow bonded together for the present, and perhaps for eternity. It came to me that all of us, or parts of us, are doomed to strut our roles on that obscure stage during all nights when ice fog lies across the harbor. The lobsterman will endure his earned portion of hell, and we, the crew of that forty-footer, will inflict our errors on him.

I now understand that Tommy's silence was the silence of madness. When he could not speak he took action, perhaps even trying to do the right thing; but I know now that no one could protect him from the knowledge that he had killed Case. I also know that Tommy protected me, for he had to have figured out my share of our mistakes. From that weather cutter to which our cap transferred him, he slipped overboard in search of silence. He knew that, sooner or later in his drunkenness, the story would get abroad.

Tommy was heroic in his way. Darkness reached for him twice, the first time with depth charges, the second time with the grounding of the forty. He fought against darkness in the only way he could. He sought the eternal silence of death.

Darkness tries to kill light. I pulled the old clasp knife from my pocket. Wert seemed only confused, while Case smiled. The interleaving forms of the lobsterman and Tommy appeared to express only sadness. It was not the knife that was wanted here, only my understanding. Perhaps the knife should have been thrown overboard.

But, it still rests in my pocket, to be carried until death, and perhaps carried to the grave. This knife is all I have of youth, because I know now that the part of me that remains on that cold coast is the ghost of my youth, forever tied to the rising scream of diesels.

The men disappeared into mist as I groped the final approach to moorage. There is little left to say. I will return to Alaska, and will make three more trips from Anchorage, maybe four. Then I will retire and find a small apartment near the docks. Although I will never finish my business with my comrades and the sea, I think perhaps they have finished their business with me. We, who were never really at war, have somehow still discovered peace. I think that between all of us, all has been forgiven.

Deep Sleep

Matthew J. Costello

H E LOOKED ACROSS the expanse of the first-class dining room, through the maze of bustling waiters sleekly presenting the passengers with their chosen dessert. A chocolate mousse perhaps, or fraise a la creme? Great dark wedges of Black Forest cake sailed across the room while the chamber quartet played too much Strauss.

Andre Farrand—such was the name on his passport—was traveling alone. But he felt them looking at him. One, two—yes—three pairs of eyes, ignoring their meal, their dessert course, their husbands. The room was filled with wealthy robber barons and overstuffed captains of industry.

The women looked at him. He felt their eyes devouring him hungrily.

"Monsieur, some café for monsieur?" The waiter was at his elbow. This was the first meal at which Farrand had made an appearance, nibbling some of the greens, tasting the escalloppe de veau before declaring the lemon sauce much too tart.

It was not uncommon for travelers to have distressed stomachs at sea.

Though—to be sure—that was not the reason Farrand didn't eat.

He caught the eye of one woman looking at him. Her eyes attempted to speak, urging him to confirm that they would dance again that evening, that they'd again take a walk on the first-class promenade. That—in the chill air of the North Atlantic—he'd pull her close, muttering words to make her forget her husband, then closer. . . .

"Still not feeling better, Monsieur Farrand?"

He looked up. A woman in a white dress heavy with brocade gave him a motherly purse of the lips. Perhaps the bejeweled dowager was so solicitous of his appetite since hers was never in disrepair.

He smiled. Monsieur Andre Farrand, a world-famous dealer in antiquarian furniture, favored the woman with a charming grin. "No, Madame Welch. I'm feeling much better. *Much* . . . but I'd best not test myself. A nibble here, a nibble there—it will more than satisfy me."

The dowager smiled, so pleased that he was well.

He felt the attentive gazes around the room, perhaps not quite in control, perhaps in danger of embarrassing him, of creating a scene. That would not do, not on this ship, not here. There was no place to hide . . . no place to go.

Monsieur Farrand pushed his chair back. He looked around at the table, smiling at the noisy Americans and a pair of British bankers with their wives—repulsive, cowlike creatures with no appeal, with rolls of skin that jiggled on their arms.

"But I think I'd like to take some air. And see if it's gotten any colder outside."

He nodded to the table. One of the American men stuck out his lip. "Perhaps I'll—"

The man was offering to join him, but Farrand pretended not to hear. He turned away and walked to the front of the grand dining hall, the hungry eyes still watching him, looking for a signal, something to give them hope. He forced his face to remain impassive.

Farrand pushed open one of the doors, pressing against the center section of the cut beveled glass. It led to the main hall and the giant staircase of first class. He walked out.

Just outside, he saw the purser talking to the captain. Captain Smith had excused himself early from dinner and now was engaged in what looked like a most serious conversation.

The captain saw him pass by. He turned, and nodded—a diplomat. "Good evening, Monsieur."

"Captain," he said, nodding to the man.

Farrand turned to go up the staircase. He looked up. At the landing where the staircase split in two there was a carved wooden panel and a clock—a frieze representing "Honor and Glory crowning Time."

He smiled at that, enjoying the irony, the private joke. Time is the ruler. Yes, it's the despot in people's lives. Unless . . . unless it can be defeated—and made the servant.

He walked up the stairs and stopped on the landing. He looked at the clock. It was 8 p.m. He touched the clock, and the two wooden figures holding the crown. And then he continued up the grand stairway.

Farrand went to his stateroom. It looked untouched, except for one open bag containing some clothes. He had given instructions, fortified with a ten pound note, that his room was to be left undisturbed. He didn't wish his bed to be made or his washroom to be cleaned. Nothing was to be done.

There was little need. He barely used it.

He stood in the darkness, feeling the rolling of the ship, the swells of the icy North Atlantic. He felt his hunger, and he stood there, savoring the warmth, the meaning it gave to him.

And when he was sure that supper had ended, he opened the cabin door and left his suite.

He made his way to another corridor, and the staterooms farther toward the bow.

She'd be waiting. They'd all be waiting, he knew, while their husbands played cards and smoked cigars and drank brandy.

He came to the door and knocked. If, perchance, the husband was there, Farrand would claim it was a mistake. It was so *easy* to get confused on this giant ship.

But the woman opened the door. She had the top of her dress open, wantonly, invitingly, so eager. She grabbed his hand.

"No," he whispered, gently shutting the door behind him. She was beautiful, with dark eyes and jet black hair. Her body pressed against him, lean, hungry. She was young, and so very unhappy with her life.

He grabbed her hand with his hands and pushed her away, fixing her with his gaze.

He heard sounds from the corridor. Some people were moving this way.

The woman looked hurt. Her lower lip—full, beet red—quivered in shock, in pain. He let go of her and brought his hand to her cheek. She brushed against it.

"Not here," he said. "You must wait. Meet me on the promenade deck. In an hour. Meet me there. . . ."

She licked her lips, the fever was on her. It was always this way, and he enjoyed her pain, her turmoil. To want something so badly, to crave it above all other things, something that would take everything away from you . . . your whole world.

It was wonderful.

He released her. He listened at the door. The corridor sounded empty.

He'd picked her because of her great need, the way she would kick and moan when he kissed her, when he touched her. I must not get carried away, he thought. Not on the ship. There was no way to explain such things. He turned and grabbed the door handle.

"You'll be there?" she said. Her voice had a wheedling quality, a small child, unsure, afraid.

He opened the door an inch. He looked at her again, his face not smiling.

"Don't ever doubt my word. *Ever.*"

He left the stateroom. He smelled the cigar smoke, lingering here, the hint of perfume. I can't wait too long, he thought.

My senses become aroused, inflamed.

Even *I* can't wait too long. . . .

He pulled his coat close. The churning water, white, frothing, spitting at the hull of the ship, was alive with phosphorescent specks. He wrapped his coat tight.

A couple walked by, their shoes clicking noisily on the wood of the deck. He turned to look at them, close together, perhaps newlyweds. They moved on, oblivious to him.

And then he was alone. He wondered if anyone doubted his name . . . Monsieur Farrand, from Paris. His accent was nearly *parfait*. Still, he wondered if he'd made any slips. There was a Frenchman, a writer, sitting two tables over, and a Marseilles businessman and his family sat all the way on the other side of the room.

But so far he had avoided meeting them, having them probe his background, asking questions, difficult questions.

It was cold, frigid. It felt as if the wet cold seeped right through his overcoat, through his suit, his shirt, and held his skin tight. It reminded him of what he faced every morning.

There is a price for conquering time. . . .

He turned his gaze away from the wake of the great ship, up to the stars. The sky was white with stars, the Milky Way was a gossamer belt around the night sky. Even in the mountains, in his homeland, there were never nights like this, so *clear,* so *bright.* He turned to search for Perseus, the Pleiades, other familiar constellations, his companions, friends in the night.

But the giant smokestacks of the ship blocked out the southeast sky, four great black columns outlined by the twinkling stars.

He heard a door creak open, yards away, leading from the first-class lounge to the open deck. He took a deep breath. The icy air stung his nostrils. He saw her outline, and he heard her steps on the wood.

He waited, arms open, ready to pull her close, to hold her tight, surrounding her warmth, possessing it.

"He—he came back, my husband," she said. Her words made small eddies of fog in front of her face. "I had to say I needed to walk. He wanted to come—"

He took her, grabbing her shoulders.

"But you told him no? You said that you needed to be alone. . . ."

There was just the glow of a few lights, the pale light of the stars, the billowing clouds of her breathing. He dug his hands into her shoulders, hard, locking her to him. He watched her face become delirious with joy. Her hands fiddled with the neck of her dress, unhooking it, exposing the creamy flesh to the icy air.

She was cold, shivering.

Slowly, savoring the moment, he pulled her close, hugging her tight against him. He saw the twin black dots on her neck.

"My sweet," he whispered. "My precious . . ."

"Andre . . ." she said, using a name that meant nothing to him. A convenience. It was best to be careful.

He opened his mouth. Her eyes were locked on his mouth. He pulled back, ready to hurry now, to quicken the moment when he'd open her skin again, and taste the warmth, let it drip onto his lips, sucking at it, not wasting a drop.

While she moaned and mewled.

He brought a hand behind her neck and pulled her to him. He bit down.

She gasped and kicked against him, quivering from pleasure.

And when he was done, she fell to the deck.

He waited, giving her a few minutes. And then he helped her up. She was dazed, shivering, weak, even confused.

He helped her button up her dress.

"You must go," he said. "Hurry back to your room. I'll see you tomorrow—"

There was a voice. It didn't come from the deck.

The woman started backing away. The voice yelled out something, and Farrand looked up. It was coming from the giant mast pole, a lookout, saying words.

The woman staggered backward, maybe too dazed, too confused to find her way back to her stateroom and her husband.

But again the words, and a bell ringing, so loud, raucous, disturbing the quiet. The bell ringing over and over. He understood the words this time.

"Iceberg! Right ahead . . ."

He looked up, and he saw the slab of white so close, as if it had suddenly appeared in the water. The ship was moving right toward it, as if it was making landfall.

We're going to hit it, Farrand knew. He had that thought, and there was an alarm attached. We're going to hit that iceberg.

And then—slowly—the blood still fresh on his lips—he started to think what that meant. . . .

* * *

He moved to the bow. People were coming on deck, a few summoned by the bell, others by the frantic shouting.

The iceberg was ahead, but already the ship was turning, cutting sharply to the left. But this ship, this *Titanic,* was moving too fast, and the berg looked so large, a great rectangular block with jagged white peaks jutting into the sky.

A crewman appeared beside him.

"We're goin' to hit 'er," he said.

Farrand recognized the accent. Cheapside, he thought. A thick, guttural accent used by sailors and fishmongers and the whores.

"But 'twill be aright." The crewman looked over at him. "We'll just graze the berg." The crewman laughed. "A bit of a bashing around, sir, I'say. That's all that will—"

Together, they watched the berg approach as if it were a white island, and S. S. *Titanic* was set to dock.

The accent. It brought memories. . . .

Farrand had to leave Carfax Abbey. They would have found him after one of his servants began to kill, crazily. When the man began to slaughter the whores—he had to do something.

The white island was close. . . .

"There we are, sir—" the crewman said. The bow was gliding past the berg.

And that's when Farrand heard the groan. The boat staggered as if it had beached, and then moved on, sluggishly, filling the night with the sound of metal tearing.

The man knew the ship was taking a gash on its side. He could *feel* it. But—we missed it, he thought. Didn't we? This isn't so bad.

It was over in a matter of seconds, the ship slowed, still veering away from the berg, the ghost island now left behind.

The deck was suddenly filled with people. From the other side of the promenade, someone tossed an icy snowball. It landed at Farrand's feet. He reached down and touched the ice, musing about where it had come from, how long it had been since it had fallen, and how many miles it had traveled to reach his fingertips. It felt so cold. . . .

People were talking excitedly.

The ship moved.

But—and here he hoped that he wasn't letting his senses, his finely tuned senses, run away with him—he thought he detected a difference, a subtle change in the motion of the ship.

He moved past the elegantly dressed first-class passengers, some pointing back at the berg, pulling their white silk scarfs tight around their neck, talking animatedly about the disaster narrowly averted.

He moved back into the ship.

The ship was—he had no doubt now—moving differently.

No . . . doubt.

He went down the stairs. The captain's office was located in a wing off the grand staircase. He hurried down an abandoned corridor, moving quietly on the red carpet. Everyone was outside, gathered together, chattering about this great event.

But he expected that the captain would be down here.

He saw the door. It was shut.

Farrand moved against it, breathing deeply. He pressed an ear close to the wood and listened.

He heard the fluttering rustle of paper, of big sheets being flipped, and then a voice. The captain, he wondered? Yes, it was Captain Smith.

"But how much could be damaged, Mr. Andrews?"

More rustling of paper.

Another voice, one he didn't know.

"There are tears, gashes here, and here, and here. Perhaps at least three more. There are three more bulkheads gone, all flooding."

"But the others? Surely, they are fine. And that leaves—"

"Ten. Yes, those compartments were spared any damage."

"Then—"

The papers rustled again, and Farrand could picture the blueprints, the giant schematic drawings of the ship. He imagined them with the water flooding in—

"*Titanic* can float with one, two, even three compartments completely flooded. But the berg tore a gash right along this line. With those six watertight compartments gone, she will sink."

There was silence. Farrand held his breath. His mind was racing now, calculating—what does this mean? What does this mean to me?

"How long?" Captain Smith asked.

"Two hours . . . maybe a bit longer. But only a bit."

He backed away. He turned, numb, his mind a jumble of ideas, of dangers met and surpassed, of moments when his victory was nearly snatched from him. This was all too incredible, too improbable.

He turned back to the staircase . . . back to the wooden frieze, the clock now ticking so noisily.

Two hours, maybe less. He stared at the wood carving, at honor and glory bowing before time.

Farrand pulled his lips back, and he snarled at the carving. He snarled, exposing his fangs, not caring who saw, not giving a goddamn who watched him rage at the stupid joke.

And then he drifted outside again. . . .

*   *   *

There were not enough lifeboats. Women and children first, those were the instructions. But some men were jumping right in. They'd be damned if they'd go down with the ship. Even some crewmen jumped in, leaving women and children crying, begging to get into the lifeboat.

Out in the dark sea, he could spot a few lifeboats already bobbing around the great ship, a funeral watch.

He saw John Jacob Astor back away from one boat. The American raised his hand to his wife as the lifeboat was lowered. Then the millionaire turned and looked over at Farrand. They had spoken briefly that day.

Other men looked around at the boats being loaded, looking for a chance to jump on.

But Astor looked over resignedly. He smiled.

Perhaps he respects me because I'm not getting into the boats, Farrand thought.

Farrand looked down at the water.

I would—if it was a possibility, if that was something that I could do—oh, yes, I wouldn't hesitate.

He shook his head. The ship was tilted now, the angle growing more severe by the minute. Signal rockets were being launched from the stern. There were muttered stories of a ship on the other side, a mystery ship sitting in the distance that wasn't answering the distress signal.

Some people had jumped into the water, the panic claiming them. And they screamed, crying out as the incredibly cold water squeezed their chests and made it impossible to breathe.

The boat's angle increased.

There was only one thing to do. He knew that. He had considered every other possibility, including getting into a lifeboat and chancing that it would be found before the sun came up, that he could somehow hide and—

Another lurch, more fireworks. The band was playing a hymn, treacle, the bleating sounding so pompous, so stupid while the hungry sea ate the ship and all who clung to it.

He turned away. He walked off the deck, and hurried inside, past gamblers playing a final hand of poker, and passengers drinking until the room wobbled, trying to blot out the last terrible moments.

He hurried. The ship groaned continuously now as if every rivet, every metal plate was under stress.

He reached a door that was marked "For Crewmen Only."

It was a door he had used before. It was supposed to be locked, but Farrand had arranged it so that with a jiggle of the handle, the bolt slipped open. Then he hurried down the metal staircase. He heard people yelling, perhaps second-class passengers searching for life vests or a way to the boats reserved for first class.

And on down deeper, to the nightmare corridors of steerage, past crying children, the angry sounds of crewmen trying to keep order, to make the poor passengers line up while they fought their way up the stairs, past Farrand.

Farrand stepped aside to let the first wave go, and then he pressed tight against the green wall of the stairwell and inched his way down.

One man punched him, screaming:

"Where ya goin', you fool? Go *up*, go—"

But Farrand kept sliding past them until he was finally able to move below the damp and smelly corridors populated by the lowliest passengers on the ship.

Just below was the cargo area. His heart beat madly.

What if it's already underwater? What if I can't get to it.

But the boat's tilt was making this part of the ship rise out of the water.

He lost his footing, and slid forward at one point, banging his head against a metal stair. But then he quickly scurried up.

The lights were still on, but surely the power, the electricity that fed them would be gone soon.

The boat moved, sliding down quickly now, the weight in the front pulling it down. He heard crashes and—even here, so far below the decks —he heard the screaming, the band playing, the noise of things collapsing, and—

He reached one cargo room. Great crates blocked his way and he had to clamber over them, digging his long, manicured nails into the wood, climbing over the jumbled hill to the next cargo compartment.

To the metal vault.

It looked like a silvery metal crate. An oddity to be sure, but no one questioned what valuable items Monsieur Farrand might be transporting.

It stood alone. No other heavy cargo had fallen to block the opening.

Again the ship moved, and the bow had to be fully in the ocean's grasp now.

Time . . . I have just moments, he knew.

He went to the metal vault. He felt the front, searching for the small moving pieces, imperceptible, unnoticeable, the panels of metal that were a secret lock, a combination.

He pushed at the shiny metal, but nothing happened.

I made a mistake, he thought. I'm rushing.

He took a breath. Another movement, and a stack of boxes fell into his arm, and he felt his skin tear. It would heal—quickly—but still there was pain, and now his arm did not move as swiftly, or as well. He shoved the boxes away and returned to the metal vault.

Again, he pushed at the moving pieces, the puzzle he'd devised from a Chinese box he'd purchased in his travels.

There was a click. And the vault opened.

And he saw—strapped to the other side, fastened with great metal clamps—the coffin.

He stepped into the vault. The lights sputtered outside, the naked bulbs protesting the loss of power.

Darkness is coming, he thought. For how long . . . for—

He pulled the metal vault shut. He felt his way to the coffin lid, feeling the letters, the name.

His hand ran across the metal plaque. Vlad Tepes.

And underneath . . . *Count Dracula.*

He opened the coffin. It smelled of his body, of centuries of sleep, and perfume, and blood drying on his lips, and now—of something new—a salty smell, oil, and soon—

He lay down.

The cracking sound, like an explosion, traveled even inside here, inside the watertight vault.

He shut his eyes.

Darkness, he thought. Darkness . . . for how long?

He felt movement, banging, even as he forced his consciousness to that near-death state. Movement, sliding down, *Titanic* breaking in two . . . groaning, the twisted metal crying out.

Until there was nothingness.

And nothing except waiting.

He slept for decades.

And then there was a sound.

He was sure of it. A sound here, and it wasn't just a natural movement, some shifting of the sea floor. It was a man-made sound. Dracula was sure of it.

Twice before he had made himself come to a state of awareness. There had been some earthquake, a tremendous movement of the sea floor. As he came to awareness, he listened to the rumbling, wondering whether something might make his vault pop open, exposing his coffin, his body, to the hungry creatures in the sea.

It had been years, maybe a decade or two after the accident.

Of course, that was his great fear. He was trapped here. What if he emerged? To do what? To crawl on the ocean floor, to make his way to a shore maybe a thousand miles away while sharks and hungry fish chewed at his withered flesh. They'd tear at him until he was nothing, his immortality squandered like grains of sand thrown into the sea.

He knew that, as dark as the ocean floor was, it offered him no escape from his tomb.

And of the lifeboats? What if he had still been in one when the sun rose? He would have been trapped in the open boat, seared on the small wooden ship like an animal cooked live in a skillet.

The sound again, a whirring, a noise—came closer. He opened his eyes in the darkness, looking at the total blackness inside his coffin.

Another time, there had been a noise overhead—certainly decades ago as much as he could figure time. There had been a sound of a motor overhead.

But it went away, and he waited.

Thinking, all the time thinking, that there was no way out. To be immortal and trapped at the bottom of the sea . . .

It was a terrible irony.

The sound grew in volume. A whirring noise, an engine of some kind. And he thought:

What could it be? It's not on the surface. It's not a ship. It's something down here, something outside the *Titanic,* looking at the ship.

That makes sense. He had no idea how many years had passed. But surely the day would come when people would be able to come down here, to see and—

The whirring seemed almost loud. It paused, just outside.

Perhaps—perhaps looking at his steel vault.

Then—a terrible moment—it moved on, growing fainter, moving to other parts of the ship, prowling over the *Titanic's* carcass which was probably broken into pieces, its innards exposed for this *thing* outside.

Then it went away completely.

But Dracula didn't close his eyes. He stayed awake, for just a bit. To savor the thought, the *realization.*

They'll be back. And someday when they return, they'll be able to bring things to the surface. They will see the silvery metal vault, and think it such an *odd* thing. They will wonder about it and, as people do, they will become even more curious until they must *have* it, must bring it to the surface.

It may not be for a very long time.

But I can wait. I'm used to waiting. I have all time to wait.

And only then did he shut his eyes and give himself over to the void, the blankness, the emptiness of his deep sleep.

Scape-Goats

Clive Barker

I T WASN'T A REAL ISLAND the tide had carried us on to, it was a lifeless mound of stones. Calling a hunch backed shit pile like this an island is flattery. Islands are oases in the sea: green and abundant. This is a forsaken place: no seals in the water around it, no birds in the air above it. I can think of no use for a place like this, except that you could say of it: I saw the heart of nothing, and survived.

"It's not on any of the charts," said Ray, poring over the map of the Inner Hebrides, his nail at the spot where he'd calculated that we should be. It was, as he'd said, an empty space on the map, just pale blue sea without the merest speck to sign the existence of this rock. It wasn't just the seals and the birds that ignored it then, the chart makers had too. There were one or two arrows in the vicinity of Ray's finger, marking the currents that should have been taking us north: tiny red darts on a paper ocean. The rest, like the world outside, was deserted.

Jonathan was jubilant of course, once he discovered that the place wasn't even to be found on the map; he seemed to feel instantly exonerated. The blame for our being here wasn't his any longer, it was the map makers': he wasn't going to be held responsible for our being beached if the mound wasn't even marked on the charts. The apologetic expression he'd worn since our unscheduled arrival was replaced with a look of self-satisfaction.

"You can't avoid a place that doesn't exist, can you?" he crowed. "I mean, can you?"

"You could have used the eyes God gave you," Ray flung back at him; but Jonathan wasn't about to be cowed by reasonable criticism.

"It was so sudden, Raymond," he said. "I mean, in this mist I didn't have a chance. It was on top of us before I knew it."

It had been sudden, no two ways about that. I'd been in the galley preparing breakfast, which had become my responsibility since neither Angela nor Jonathan showed any enthusiasm for the task, when the hull of the *Emmanuelle* grated on shingle, then ploughed her way, juddering, up on to the stony beach. There was a moment's silence: then the shouting began. I climbed up out of the galley to find Jonathan standing on deck, grinning sheepishly and waving his arms around to semaphore his innocence.

"Before you ask," he said, "I don't know how it happened. One minute we were just coasting along—"

"Oh Jesus Christ all-fucking Mighty," Ray was clambering out of the cabin, hauling a pair of jeans on as he did so, and looking much the worse for a night in a bunk with Angela. I'd had the questionable honor of listening to her orgasms all night; she was certainly demanding. Jonathan began his defense speech again from the beginning: "Before you ask—" but Ray silenced him with a few choice insults. I retreated into the confines of the galley while the argument raged on deck. It gave me no small satisfaction to hear Jonathan slanged; I even hoped Ray would lose his cool enough to bloody that perfect hook nose.

The galley was a slop bucket. The breakfast I'd been preparing was all over the floor and I left it there, the yolks of the eggs, the gammon, and the French toast all congealing in pools of split fat. It was Jonathan's fault; let him clear it up. I poured myself a glass of grapefruit juice, waited until the recriminations died down, and went back up.

It was barely two hours after dawn, and the mist that had shrouded this island from Jonathan's view still covered the sun. If today was anything like the week that we'd had so far, by noon the deck would be too hot to step on barefoot, but now, with the mist still thick, I felt cold wearing just the bottom of my bikini. It didn't matter much, sailing amongst the islands, what you wore. There was no one to see you. I'd got the best all over tan I'd ever had. But this morning the chill drove me back below to find a sweater. There was no wind: the cold was coming up out of the sea. It's still night down there, I thought, just a few yards off the beach; limitless night.

I pulled on a sweater, and went back on deck. The maps were out, and Ray was bending over them. His bare back was peeling from an excess of sun, and I could see the bald patch he tried to hide in his dirty yellow curls. Jonathan was staring at the beach and stroking his nose.

"Christ, what a place," I said.

He glanced at me, trying a smile. He had this illusion, poor Jonathan, that his face could charm a tortoise out of its shell, and to be fair to him there were a few women who melted if he so much as looked at them. I wasn't one of them, and it irritated him. I'd always thought his Jewish good looks too bland to be beautiful. My indifference was a red rag to him.

A voice, sleepy and pouting, drifted up from below deck. Our Lady of the Bunk was awake at last: time to make her late entrance, coyly wrapping a towel around her nakedness as she emerged. Her face was puffed up with too much red wine, and her hair needed a comb through it. Still she turned on the radiance, eyes wide, Shirley Temple with cleavage.

"What's happening, Ray? Where are we?"

Ray didn't look up from his computations, which earned him a frown.

"We've got a bloody awful navigator, that's all," he said.

"I don't even know what happened," Jonathan protested, clearly hoping for a show of sympathy from Angela. None was forthcoming.

"But where are we?" she asked again.

"Good morning, Angela," I said; I too was ignored.

"Is it an island?" she said.

"Of course it's an island: I just don't know which one yet," Ray replied.

"Perhaps it's Barra," she suggested.

Ray pulled a face. "We're nowhere near Barra," he said. "If you'll just let me retrace our steps—"

Retrace our steps, in the sea? Just Ray's Jesus fixation, I thought, looking back at the beach. It was impossible to guess how big the place was; the mist erased the landscape after a hundred yards. Perhaps somewhere in that grey wall there was human habitation.

Ray, having located the blank spot on the map where we were supposedly stranded, climbed down on to the beach and took a critical look at the bow. More to be out of Angela's way than anything else I climbed down to join him. The round stones of the beach were cold and slippery on the bare soles of my feet. Ray smoothed his palm down the side of the *Emmanuelle,* almost a caress, then crouched to look at the damage to the bow.

"I don't think we're holed," he said, "but I can't be sure."

"We'll float off come high tide," said Jonathan, posing on the bow, hands on hips, "no sweat," he winked at me, "no sweat at all."

"Will we shit float off!" Ray snapped. "Take a look for yourself."

"Then we'll get some help to haul us off." Jonathan's confidence was unscathed.

"And you can damn well fetch someone, you asshole."

"Sure, why not? Give it an hour or so for the fog to shift and I'll take a walk, find some help."

He sauntered away.

"I'll put on some coffee," Angela volunteered.

Knowing her, that'd take an hour to brew. There was time for a stroll. I started along the beach.

"Don't go too far, love," Ray called.

"No."

Love, he said. Easy word; he meant nothing by it.

The sun was warmer now, and as I walked I stripped off the sweater. My bare breasts were already brown as two nuts, and, I thought, about as big. Still, you can't have everything. At least I'd got two neurons in my head to rub together, which was more than could be said for Angela; she had tits like melons and a brain that'd shame a mule.

The sun still wasn't getting through the mist properly. It was filtering down on the island fitfully, and its light flattened everything out, draining the place of color or weight, reducing the sea and the rocks and the rubbish on the beach to one bleached-out grey, the color of over boiled meat.

After only a hundred yards something about the place began to depress me, so I turned back. On my right tiny, lisping waves crept up to the shore and collapsed with a weary slopping sound on the stones. No majestic rollers here: just the rhythmical slop, slop, slop of an exhausted tide.

I hated the place already.

Back at the boat, Ray was trying the radio, but for some reason all he could get was a blanket of white noise on every frequency. He cursed it awhile, then gave up. After half an hour, breakfast was served, though we had to make do with sardines, tinned mushrooms, and the remains of the French toast. Angela served this feast with her usual aplomb, looking as though she was performing a second miracle with loaves and fishes. It was all but impossible to enjoy the food anyway; the air seemed to drain all the taste away.

"Funny isn't it—" began Jonathan.

"Hilarious," said Ray.

"—there's no fog horns. Mist, but no horns. Not even the sound of a motor; weird."

He was right. Total silence wrapped us up, a damp and smothering hush. Except for the apologetic slop of the waves and the sound of our voices, we might as well have been deaf.

I sat at the stern and looked into the empty sea. It was still grey, but the sun was beginning to strike other colors in it now: a somber green, and, deeper, a hint of blue-purple. Below the boat I could see strands of kelp and Maiden's Hair, toys to the tide, swaying. It looked inviting: and anything was better than the sour atmosphere on the *Emmanuelle*.

"I'm going for a swim," I said.

"I wouldn't, love," Ray replied.

"Why not?"

"The current that threw us up here must be pretty strong, you don't want to get caught in it."

"But the tide's still coming in: I'd only be swept back to the beach."

"You don't know what cross currents there are out there. Whirlpools even: they're quite common. Suck you down in a flash."

I looked out to sea again. It looked harmless enough, but then I'd read that these were treacherous waters, and thought better of it.

Angela had started a little sulking session because nobody had finished her immaculately prepared breakfast. Ray was playing up to it. He loved babying her, letting her play damn stupid games. It made me sick.

I went below to do the washing up, tossing the slops out of the porthole into the sea. They didn't sink immediately. They floated in an oily patch, half-eaten mushrooms and slivers of sardines bobbing around on the surface, as though someone had thrown up on the sea. Food for crabs, if any self-respecting crab condescended to live here.

Jonathan joined me in the galley, obviously still feeling a little foolish, despite the bravado. He stood in the doorway, trying to catch my eye, while I pumped up some cold water into the bowl and half heartedly rinsed the greasy plastic plates. All he wanted was to be told I didn't think this was his fault, and yes, of course he was a kosher Adonis. I said nothing.

"Do you mind if I lend a hand?" he said.

"There's not really room for two," I told him, trying not to sound too dismissive. He flinched nevertheless: this whole episode had punctured his self-esteem more badly than I'd realized, despite his strutting around.

"Look," I said gently, "why don't you go back on deck: take in the sun before it gets too hot?"

"I feel like a shit," he said.

"It was an accident."

"An utter shit."

"Like you said, we'll float off with the tide."

He moved out of the doorway and down into the galley; his proximity made me feel almost claustrophobic. His body was too large for the space: too tanned, too assertive.

"I said there wasn't any room, Jonathan."

He put his hand on the back of my neck, and instead of shrugging it off I let it stay there, gently massaging the muscles. I wanted to tell him to leave me alone, but the lassitude of the place seemed to have got into my system. His other hand was palm down on my belly, moving up to my breast. I was indifferent to these ministrations: if he wanted this he could have it.

Above deck Angela was gasping in the middle of a giggling fit, almost choking on her hysteria. I could see her in my mind's eye, throwing back her head, shaking her hair loose. Jonathan had unbuttoned his shorts, and had let them drop. The gift of his foreskin to God had been neatly made; his erection was so hygienic in its enthusiasm it seemed incapable of the least harm. I let his mouth stick to mine, let his tongue explore my gums, insistent as a dentist's finger. He slid my bikini down far enough to get access, fumbled to position himself, then pressed in.

Behind him, the stair creaked, and I looked over his shoulder in time to glimpse Ray, bending at the hatch and staring down at Jonathan's buttocks and at the tangle of our arms. Did he see, I wondered, that I felt nothing; did he understand that I did this dispassionately, and could only have felt a twinge of desire if I substituted his head, his back, his cock for Jonathan's? Soundlessly, he withdrew from the stairway; a moment passed, in which Jonathan said he loved me, then I heard Angela's laughter begin again as Ray described what he'd just witnessed. Let the bitch think whatever she pleased: I didn't care.

Jonathan was still working at me with deliberate but uninspired strokes, a frown on his face like that of a schoolboy trying to solve some impossible equation. Discharge came without warning, signalled only by a tightening of his hold on my shoulders, and a deepening of his frown. His thrusts slowed and stopped; his eyes found mine for a flustered moment. I wanted to kiss him, but he'd lost all interest. He withdrew still hard, wincing. "I'm always sensitive when I've come," he murmured, hauling his shorts up. "Was it good for you?"

I nodded. It was laughable; the whole thing was laughable. Stuck in the middle of nowhere with this little boy of twenty-six, and Angela, and a man who didn't care if I lived or died. But then perhaps neither did I. I thought, for no reason, of the slops on the sea, bobbing around, waiting for the next wave to catch them.

Jonathan had already retreated up the stairs. I boiled up some coffee, standing staring out of the porthole and feeling his come dry to a corrugated pearliness on the inside of my thigh.

Ray and Angela had gone by the time I'd brewed the coffee, off for a walk on the island apparently, looking for help.

Jonathan was sitting in my place at the stern, gazing out at the mist. More to break the silence than anything I said:

"I think it's lifted a bit."

"Has it?"

I put a mug of black coffee beside him.

"Thanks."

"Where are the others?"

"Exploring."

He looked round at me, confusion in his eyes. "I still feel like a shit."

I noticed the bottle of gin on the deck beside him.

"Bit early for drinking, isn't it?"

"Want some?"

"It's not even eleven."

"Who cares?"

He pointed out to sea. "Follow my finger," he said.

I leaned over his shoulder and did as he asked.

"No, you're not looking at the right place. Follow my finger—see it?"

"Nothing."

"At the edge of the mist. It appears and disappears. There! Again!"

I did see something in the water, twenty or thirty yards from the *Emmanuelle*'s stern. Brown-colored, wrinkled, turning over.

"It's a seal," I said.

"I don't think so."

"The sun's warming up the sea. They're probably coming in to bask in the shallows."

"It doesn't look like a seal. It rolls in a funny way—"

"Maybe a piece of flotsam—"

"Could be."

He swigged deeply from the bottle.

"Leave some for tonight."

"Yes, mother."

We sat in silence for a few minutes. Just the waves on the beach. Slop. Slop. Slop.

Once in a while the seal, or whatever it was, broke surface, rolled, and disappeared again.

Another hour, I thought, and the tide will begin to turn. Float us off this little afterthought of creation.

"Hey!" Angela's voice, from a distance. "Hey, you guys!"

You guys, she called us.

Jonathan stood up, hand up to his face against the glare of sunlit rock. It was much brighter now: and getting hotter all the time.

"She's waving to us," he said, disinterested.

"Let her wave."

"You guys!" she screeched, her arms waving. Jonathan cupped his hands around his mouth and bawled a reply:

"What do you want?"

"Come and see," she replied.

"She wants us to come and see."

"I heard."

"Come on," he said, "nothing to lose."

I didn't want to move, but he hauled me up by the arm. It wasn't worth arguing. His breath was inflammable.

It was difficult making our way up the beach. The stones were not wet with sea water, but covered in a slick film of grey-green algae, like sweat on a skull.

Jonathan was having even more difficulty getting across the beach than I was. Twice he lost his balance and fell heavily on his backside, cursing. The seat of his shorts was soon a filthy olive color, and there was a tear where his buttocks showed.

I was no ballerina, but I managed to make it, step by slow step, trying to avoid the large rocks so that if I slipped I wouldn't have far to fall.

Every few yards we'd have to negotiate a line of stinking seaweed. I was able to jump them with reasonable elegance but Jonathan, pissed and uncertain of his balance, ploughed through them, his naked feet completely buried in the stuff. It wasn't just kelp: there was the usual detritus washed up on any beach: the broken bottles, the rusting Coke cans, the scum-stained cork, globs of tar, fragments of crabs, pale yellow durex. And crawling over these stinking piles of dross were inch-long, fat-eyed blue flies. Hundreds of them, clambering over the shit, and over each other, buzzing to be alive, and alive to be buzzing.

It was the first life we'd seen.

I was doing my best not to fall flat on my face as I stepped across one of these lines of seaweed, when a little avalanche of pebbles began off to my left. Three, four, five stones were skipping over each other towards the sea, and setting another dozen stones moving as they jumped.

There was no visible cause for the effect.

Jonathan didn't even bother to look up; he was having too much trouble staying vertical.

The avalanche stopped: run out of energy. Then another: this time between us and the sea. Skipping stones: bigger this time than the last, and gaining more height as they leapt.

The sequence was longer than before: it knocked stone into stone until a few pebbles actually reached the sea at the end of the dance.

Plop.

Dead noise.

Plop. Plop.

Ray appeared from behind one of the big boulders at the height of the beach, beaming like a loon.

"There's life on Mars," he yelled and ducked back the way he'd come.

A few more perilous moments and we reached him, the sweat sticking our hair to our foreheads like caps.

Jonathan looked a little sick.

"What's the big deal?" he demanded.

"Look what we've found," said Ray, and led the way beyond the boulders.

The first shock.

Once we got to the height of the beach we were looking down on to the other side of the island. There was more of the same drab beach, and then sea. No inhabitants, no boats, no sign of human existence. The whole place couldn't have been more than half a mile across: barely the back of a whale.

But there was some life here; that was the second shock.

In the sheltering ring of the large, bald, boulders which crowned the island was a fenced-in compound. The posts were rotting in the salt air, but a tangle of rusted barbed-wire had been wound around and between them to form a primitive pen. Inside the pen there was a patch of coarse grass, and on this pitiful lawn stood three sheep. And Angela.

She was standing in the penal colony, stroking one of the inmates and cooing in its blank face.

"Sheep," she said, triumphantly.

Jonathan was there before me with his snapped remark: "So what?"

"Well it's strange, isn't it?" said Ray. "Three sheep in the middle of a little place like this?"

"They don't look well to me," said Angela.

She was right. The animals were the worse for their exposure to the elements; their eyes were gummy with matter, and their fleeces hung off their hides in knotted clumps, exposing panting flanks. One of them had collapsed against the barbed-wire, and seemed unable to right itself again, either too depleted or too sick.

"It's cruel," said Angela.

I had to agree: it seemed positively sadistic, locking up these creatures without more than a few blades of grass to chew on, and a battered tin bath of stagnant water, to quench their thirst.

"Odd, isn't it?" said Ray.

"I've cut my foot." Jonathan was squatting on the top of one of the flatter boulders, peering at the underside of his right foot.

"There's glass on the beach," I said, exchanging a vacant stare with one of the sheep.

"They're so deadpan," said Ray. "Nature's straight men."

Curiously, they didn't look so unhappy with their condition, their stares were philosophical. Their eyes said: I'm just a sheep, I don't expect you to like me, care for me, preserve me, except for your stomach's sake. There were no angry baas, no stamping of a frustrated hoof.

Just three grey sheep, waiting to die.

Ray had lost interest in the business. He was wandering back down the beach, kicking a can ahead of him. It rattled and skipped, reminding me of the stones.

"We should let them free," said Angela.

I ignored her; what was freedom in a place like this? She persisted, "Don't you think we should?"

"No."

"They'll die."

"Somebody put them here for a reason."

"But they'll *die.*"

"They'll die on the beach if we let them out. There's no food for them."

"We'll feed them."

"French toast and gin," suggested Jonathan, picking a sliver of glass from his sole.

"We can't just leave them."

"It's not our business," I said. It was all getting boring. Three sheep. Who cared if they lived or—

I'd thought that about myself an hour earlier. We had something in common, the sheep and I.

My head was aching.

"They'll die," whined Angela, for the third time.

"You're a stupid bitch," Jonathan told her. The remark was made without malice: he said it calmly, as a statement of plain fact.

I couldn't help grinning.

"What?" She looked as though she'd been bitten.

"Stupid bitch," he said again. "B-I-T-C-H."

Angela flushed with anger and embarrassment, and turned on him. "You got us stuck here," she said, lip curling.

The inevitable accusation. Tears in her eyes. Stung by his words.

"I did it deliberately," he said, spitting on his fingers and rubbing saliva into the cut. "I wanted to see if we could leave you here."

"You're drunk."

"And you're stupid. But I'll be sober in the morning."

The old lines still made their mark.

Outstripped, Angela started down the beach after Ray, trying to hold back her tears until she was out of sight. I almost felt some sympathy for her. She was, when it came down to verbal fisticuffs, easy meat.

"You're a bastard when you want to be," I told Jonathan; he just looked at me, glassy-eyed.

"Better be friends. Then I won't be a bastard to you."

"You don't scare me."

"I know."

The mutton was staring at me again. I stared back.

"Fucking sheep," he said.

"They can't help it."

"If they had any decency, they'd slit their ugly fucking throats."

"I'm going back to the boat."

"Ugly fuckers."

"Coming?"

He took hold of my hand: fast, tight, and held it in his hand like he'd never let go. Eyes on me suddenly.

"Don't go."

"It's too hot up here."

"Stay. The stone's nice and warm. Lie down. They won't interrupt us this time."

"You knew?" I said.

"You mean Ray? Of course I knew. I thought we put on quite a little performance."

He drew me close, hand over hand up my arm, like he was hauling in a rope. The smell of him brought back the galley, his frown, his muttered profession ("Love you"), the quiet retreat.

Déja vu.

Still, what was there to do on a day like this but go round in the same dreary circle, like the sheep in the pen? Round and round. Breathe, sex, eat, shit.

The gin had gone to his groin. He tried his best but he hadn't got a hope. It was like trying to thread spaghetti.

Exasperated, he rolled off me.

"Fuck. Fuck. Fuck."

Senseless word, once it was repeated, it had lost all its meaning, like everything else. Signifying nothing.

"It doesn't matter," I said.

"Fuck off."

"It really doesn't."

He didn't look at me, just stared down at his cock. If he'd had a knife in his hand at that moment, I think he'd have cut it off and laid it on the warm rock, a shrine to sterility.

I left him studying himself, and walked back to the *Emmanuelle*. Something odd struck me as I went, something I hadn't noticed before. The blue flies, instead of jumping ahead of me as I approached, just let themselves be trodden on. Positively lethargic; or suicidal. They sat on the hot stones and popped under my soles, their gaudy little lives going out like so many lights.

The mist was disappearing at last, and as the air warmed up, the island unveiled its next disgusting trick: the smell. The fragrance was as wholesome as a roomful of rotting peaches, thick and sickly. It came in through the pores as well as the nostrils, like a syrup. And under the sweetness, something else, rather less pleasant than peaches, fresh or rotten. A smell like an open drain clogged with old meat: like the gutters of a slaughter house, caked with suet and black blood. It was the seaweed, I assumed, although I'd never smelt anything to match the stench on any other beach.

I was halfway back to the *Emmanuelle*, holding my nose as I stepped over the bands of rotting weed, when I heard the noise of a little murder behind me. Jonathan's whoops of satanic glee almost drowned the pathetic voice of the sheep as it was killed, but I knew instinctively what the drunken bastard had done.

I turned back, my heel pivotting on the slime. It was almost certainly too late to save one of the beasts, but maybe I could prevent him massacring the other two. I couldn't see the pen; it was hidden behind the boulders, but I could hear Jonathan's triumphant yells, and the thud, thud of his strokes. I knew what I'd see before it came into sight.

The grey-green lawn had turned red. Jonathan was in the pen with the sheep. The two survivors were charging back and forth in a rhythmical trot of panic, baaing in terror, while Jonathan stood over the third sheep, erect now. The victim had partially collapsed, its sticklike front legs buckled beneath it, its back legs rigid with approaching death. Its bulk shuddered with nervous spasms, and its eyes showed more white than brown. The top of its skull had been almost entirely dashed to pieces, and the grey hash of its brain exposed, punctured by shards of its own bone, and pulped by the large round stone that Jonathan was still wielding. Even as I watched he brought the weapon down once more onto the sheep's brain pan. Globs of tissue flew off in every direction, speckling me with hot matter and blood. Jonathan looked like some nightmare lunatic (which for that moment, I suppose, he was). His naked body, so recently white, was stained as a butcher's apron after a hard day's hammering at the abattoir. His face was more sheep's gore than Jonathan—

The animal itself was dead. Its pathetic complaints had ceased completely. It keeled over, rather comically, like a cartoon character, one of its ears snagging the wire. Jonathan watched it fall: his face a grin under the blood. Oh that grin: it served so many purposes. Wasn't that the same smile he charmed women with? The same grin that spoke lechery and love? Now, at last, it was put to its true purpose: the gawping smile of the satisfied savage, standing over his prey with a stone in one hand and his manhood in the other.

Then, slowly, the smile decayed, as his senses returned.

"Jesus," he said, and from his abdomen a wave of revulsion climbed up his body. I could see it quite clearly; the way his gut rolled as a throb of nausea threw his head forward, pitching half-digested gin and toast over the grass.

I didn't move. I didn't want to comfort him, calm him, console him— he was simply beyond my help.

I turned away.

"Frankie," he said through a throat of bile.

I couldn't bring myself to look at him. There was nothing to be done for the sheep, it was dead and gone; all I wanted to do was run away from the little ring of stones, and put the sight out of my head.

"Frankie."

I began to walk, as fast as I was able over such tricky terrain, back down towards the beach and the relative sanity of the *Emmanuelle*.

The smell was stronger now: coming up out of the ground towards my face in filthy waves.

Horrible island. Vile, stinking, insane island.

All I thought was hate as I stumbled across the weed and the filth. The *Emmanuelle* wasn't far off—

Then, a little pattering of pebbles like before. I stopped, balancing uneasily on the sleek dome of a stone, and looked to my left, where even now one of the pebbles was rolling to a halt. As it stopped another, larger pebble, fully six inches across, seemed to move spontaneously from its resting place, and roll down the beach, striking its neighbors and beginning another exodus towards the sea. I frowned: the frown made my head buzz.

Was there some sort of animal—a crab maybe—under the beach, moving the stones? Or was it the heat that in some way twitched them into life?

Again: a bigger stone—

I walked on, while behind the rattle and patter continued, one little sequence coming close upon another, to make an almost seamless percussion.

I began, without real focus or explanation, to be afraid.

Angela and Ray were sunning themselves on the deck of the *Emmanuelle*.

"Another couple of hours before we can start to get the bitch off her backside," he said, squinting as he looked up at me.

I thought he meant Angela at first, then realized he was talking about floating the boat out to sea again.

"May as well get some sun." He smiled wanly at me.

"Yeah."

Angela was either asleep or ignoring me. Whichever, it suited me fine.

I slumped down on the sun deck at Ray's feet and let the sun soak into me. The specks of blood had dried on my skin, like tiny scabs. I picked them off idly, and listened to the noise of the stones, and the slop of the sea.

Behind me, pages were being turned. I glanced round. Ray, never able to lie still for very long, was flicking through a library book on the Hebrides he'd brought from home.

I looked back at the sun. My mother always said it burned a hole in the back of your eye, to look straight into the sun, but it was hot and alive up there; I wanted to look into its face. There was a chill in me—I don't know where it had come from—a chill in my gut and in between my legs —that wouldn't go away. Maybe I would have to burn it away by looking at the sun.

Some way along the beach I glimpsed Jonathan, tiptoeing down towards the sea. From that distance the mixture of blood and white skin made him look like some piebald freak. He'd stripped off his shorts and he was crouching at the sea's edge to wash off the sheep.

Then, Ray's voice, very quietly: "Oh God," he said, in such an understated way that I knew the news couldn't be brilliant.

"What is it?"

"I've found out where we are."

"Good."

"No, not good."

"Why? What's wrong?" I sat upright, turning to him.

"It's here, in the book. There's a paragraph on this place."

Angela opened one eye. "Well?" she said.

"It's not just an island. It's a burial mound."

The chill in between my legs fed upon itself, and grew gross. The sun wasn't hot enough to warm me that deep, where I should be hottest.

I looked away from Ray along the beach again. Jonathan was still washing, splashing water up on to his chest. The shadows of the stones suddenly seemed very black and heavy, their edges pressed down on the upturned faces of—

Seeing me looking his way, Jonathan waved.

Can it be there are corpses under those stones? Buried face up to the sun, like holiday makers laid out on a Blackpool beach?

The world is monochrome. Sun and shadow. The white tops of stones and their black underbellies. Life on top, death underneath.

"Burial?" said Angela. "What sort of burial?"

"War dead," Ray answered.

Angela: "What, you mean Vikings or something?"

"World War I, World War II. Soldiers from torpedoed troopships, sailors washed up. Brought down here by the Gulf Stream; apparently the current funnels them through the straits and washes them up on the beaches of the islands around here."

"Washes them up?" said Angela.

"That's what it says."

"Not any longer though."

"I'm sure the occasional fisherman gets buried here still," Ray replied.

Jonathan had stood up, staring out to sea, the blood off his body. His hand shaded his eyes as he looked out over the blue-grey water, and I followed his gaze as I had followed his finger. A hundred yards out that seal, or whale, or whatever it was, had returned, lolling in the water. Sometimes, as it turned, it threw up a fin, like a swimmer's arm, beckoning.

"How many people were buried?" asked Angela, nonchalantly. She seemed completely unperturbed by the fact that we were sitting on a grave.

"Hundreds probably."

"Hundreds?"

"It just says 'many dead,' in the book."

"And do they put them in coffins?"

"How should I know?"

What else could it be, this Godforsaken mound—but a cemetery? I looked at the island with new eyes, as though I'd just recognized it for what it was. Now I had a reason to despise its humpy back, its sordid beach, the smell of peaches.

"I wonder if they buried them all over," mused Angela, "or just at the top of the hill, where we found the sheep? Probably just at the top; out of the way of the water."

Yes, they'd probably had too much of water: their poor green faces picked by fish, their uniforms rotted, their dog tags encrusted with algae. What deaths; and worse, what journeys after death, in squads of fellow corpses, along the Gulf Stream to this bleak landfall. I saw them, in my mind's eye, the bodies of the soldiers, subject to every whim of the tide, borne backwards and forwards in a slush of rollers until a casual limb snagged on a rock, and the sea lost possession of them. With each receding wave uncovered; sodden and jellied brine, spat out by the sea to stink awhile and be stripped by gulls.

I had a sudden, morbid desire to walk on the beach again, armed with this knowledge, kicking over the pebbles in the hope of turning up a bone or two.

As the thought formed, my body made the decision for me. I was standing: I was climbing off the *Emmanuelle*.

"Where are you off to?" said Angela.

"Jonathan," I murmured, and set foot on the mound.

The stench was clearer now: that was the accrued odor of the dead. Maybe drowned men got buried here still, as Ray had suggested, slotted under the pile of stones. The unwary yachtsman, the careless swimmer, their faces wiped off with water. At the feet the beach flies were less sluggish than they'd been: instead of waiting to be killed they jumped and buzzed ahead of my steps, with a new enthusiasm for life.

Jonathan was not to be seen. His shorts were still on the stones at the water's edge, but he'd disappeared. I looked out to sea: nothing: no bobbing head: no lolling, beckoning something.

I called his name.

My voice seemed to excite the flies, they rose in seething clouds. Jonathan didn't reply.

I began to walk along the margin of the sea, my feet sometimes caught by an idle wave, as often as not left untouched. I realized I hadn't told Angela and Ray about the dead sheep. Maybe that was a secret between us four. Jonathan, myself, and the two survivors in the pen.

Then I saw him: a few yards ahead—his chest white, wide, and clean, every speck of blood washed off. A secret it is then, I thought.

"Where have you been?" I called to him.

"Walking it off," he called back.

"What off?"

"Too much gin," he grinned.

I returned the smile, spontaneously; he'd said he loved me in the galley; that counted for something.

Behind him, a rattle of skipping stones. He was no more than ten yards from me now, shamelessly naked as he walked; his gait was sober.

The rattle of stones suddenly seemed rhythmical. It was no longer a random series of notes as one pebble struck another—it was a beat, a sequence of repeated sounds, a tick-tap pulse.

No accident: intention.

Not chance: purpose.

Not stone: thought. Behind stone, with stone, carrying stone—

Jonathan, now close, was bright. His skin was almost luminous with sun on it, thrown into relief by the darkness behind him.

Wait—

—What darkness?

The stone mounted the air like a bird, defying gravity. A blank black stone, disengaged from the earth. It was the size of a baby: a whistling baby, and it grew behind Jonathan's head as it shimmered down the air towards him.

The beach had been flexing its muscles, tossing small pebbles down to the sea, all the time strengthening its will to raise this boulder off the ground and fling it at Jonathan.

It swelled behind him, murderous in its intention, but my throat had no sound to make worthy of my fright.

Was he deaf? His grin broke open again; he thought the horror on my face was a jibe at his nakedness, I realized. He doesn't understand—

The stone sheered off the top of his head, from the middle of his nose upwards, leaving his mouth still wide, his tongue rooted in blood, and flinging the rest of his beauty towards me in a cloud of wet red dust. The upper part of his head was split on to the face of the stone, its expression intact as it swooped towards me. I half fell, and it screamed past me, veering off towards the sea. Once over the water the assassin seemed to lose its will somehow, and faltered in the air before plunging into the waves.

At my feet, blood. A trail that led to where Jonathan's body lay, the open edge of his head towards me, its machinery plain for the sky to see.

I was still not screaming, though for sanity's sake I had to unleash the terror suffocating me. Somebody must hear me, hold me, take me away, and explain to me, before the skipping pebbles found their rhythm again. Or worse, before the minds below the beach, unsatisfied with murder by proxy, rolled away their grave stones and rose to kiss me themselves.

But the scream would not come.

All I could hear was the patter of stones to my right and left. They intend to kill us all for invading their sacred ground. Stoned to death, like heretics.

Then, a voice.

"For Christ's sake—"

A man's voice; but not Ray's.

He seemed to have appeared from out of thin air: a short, broad man, standing at the sea's edge. In one hand a bucket and under his arm a bundle of coarsely cut hay. Food for the sheep, I thought, through a jumble of half-formed words. Food for sheep.

He stared at me, then down at Jonathan's body, his old eyes wild.

"What's gone on?" he said. The Gaelic accent was thick. "In the name of Christ what's gone on?"

I shook my head. It seemed loose on my neck, almost as though I might shake it off. Maybe I pointed to the sheep pen, maybe not. Whatever the reason he seemed to know what I was thinking, and began to climb the beach towards the crown of the island, dropping bucket and bundle as he went.

Half blind with confusion, I followed, but before I could reach the boulders he was out of their shadow again, his face suddenly shining with panic.

"Who did that?"

"Jonathan," I replied. I cast a hand towards the corpse, not daring to look back at him. The man cursed in Gaelic, and stumbled out of the shelter of the boulders.

"What have you done?" he yelled at me. "My Christ, what have you done? Killing their gifts."

"Just sheep," I said. In my head the instant of Jonathan's decapitation was playing over and over again, a loop of slaughter.

"They demand it, don't you see, or they rise—"

"Who rise?" I said, knowing. Seeing the stones shift.

"All of them. Put away without grief or mourning. But they've got the sea in them, in their heads—"

I knew what he was talking about: it was quite plain to me, suddenly. The dead were here: as we knew. Under the stones. But they had the rhythm of the sea in them, and they wouldn't lie down. So to placate them, these sheep were tethered in a pen, to be offered up to their wills.

Did the dead eat mutton? No; it wasn't food they wanted. It was the gesture of recognition—as simple as that.

"Drowned," he was saying, "all drowned."

Then, the familiar patter began again, the drumming of stones, which grew, without warning, into an ear-splitting thunder, as though the entire beach was shifting.

And under the cacophony three other sounds: splashing, screaming and wholesale destruction.

I turned to see a wave of stones rising into the air on the other side of the island—

Again the terrible screams, wrung from a body that was being buffeted and broken.

They were after the *Emmanuelle*. After Ray. I started to run in the direction of the boat, the beach rippling beneath my feet. Behind me, I could hear the boots of the sheep feeder on the stones. As we ran the noise of the assault became louder. Stones danced in the air like fat birds, blocking the sun, before plunging down to strike at some unseen target. Maybe the boat. Maybe flesh itself—

Angela's tormented screams had ceased.

I rounded the beachhead a few steps ahead of the sheep feeder, and the *Emmanuelle* came into sight. It, and its human contents, were beyond all hope of salvation. The vessel was being bombarded by endless ranks of stones, all sizes and shapes; its hull was smashed, its windows, mast, and deck shattered. Angela lay sprawled on the remains of the sun deck, quite obviously dead. The fury of the hail hadn't stopped however. The stones beat a tattoo on the remaining structure of the hull, and thrashed at the lifeless bulk of Angela's body, making it bob up and down as though a current were being passed through it.

Ray was nowhere to be seen.

I screamed then: and for a moment it seemed there was a lull in the thunder, a brief respite in the attack. Then it began again: wave after wave of pebbles and rocks rising off the beach and flinging themselves at their senseless targets. They would not be content, it seemed, until the *Emmanuelle* was reduced to flotsam and jetsam, and Angela's body was in small enough pieces to accommodate a shrimp's palate.

The sheep feeder took hold of my arm in a grip so fierce it stopped the blood flowing to my hand.

"Come on," he said. I heard his voice but did nothing. I was waiting for Ray's face to appear—or to hear his voice calling my name. But there was nothing: just the barrage of the stones. He was dead in the ruins of the boat somewhere—smashed to smithereens.

The sheep feeder was dragging me now, and I was following him back over the beach.

"The boat" he was saying, "we can get away in my boat—"

The idea of escape seemed ludicrous. The island had us on its back, we were its objects utterly.

But I followed, slipping and sliding over the sweaty rocks, ploughing through the tangle of seaweed, back the way we'd come.

On the other side of the island was his poor hope of life. A rowing boat, dragged up on the shingle: an inconsequential walnut shell of a boat.

Would we go to sea in that, like the three men in a sieve?

He dragged me, unresisting, towards our deliverance. With every step I became more certain that the beach would suddenly rise up and stone us to death. Maybe make a wall of itself, a tower even, when we were within a single step of safety. It could play any game it liked, any game at all. But then, maybe the dead didn't like games. Games are about gambles, and the dead had already lost. Maybe the dead act only with the arid certainty of mathematicians.

He half threw me into the boat, and began to push it out into the thick tide. No walls of stones rose to prevent our escape. No towers appeared, no slaughtering hail. Even the attack on the *Emmanuelle* had ceased.

Had they sated themselves on three victims? Or was it that the presence of the sheep feeder, an innocent, a servant of these willful dead, would protect me from their tantrums?

The rowing boat was off the shingle. We bobbed a little on the backs of a few limp waves until we were deep enough for the oars, and then we were pulling away from the shore and my savior was sitting opposite me, rowing for all he was worth, a dew of fresh sweat on his forehead, multiplying with every pull.

The beach receded; we were being set free. The sheep feeder seemed to relax a little. He gazed down at the swill of dirty water in the bottom of the boat and drew in half a dozen deep breaths; then he looked up at me, his wasted face drained of expression.

"One day, it had to happen—" he said, his voice low and heavy. "Somebody would spoil the way we lived. Break the rhythm."

It was almost soporific, the hauling of the oars, forward and back. I wanted to sleep, to wrap myself up in the tarpaulin I was sitting on, and forget. Behind us, the beach was a distant line. I couldn't see the *Emmanuelle*.

"Where are we going?" I said.

"Back to Tiree," he replied. "We'll see what's to be done there. Find some way to make amends; to help them sleep soundly again."

"Do they eat the sheep?"

"What good is food to the dead? No. No, they have no need of mutton. They take the beasts as a gesture of remembrance."

Remembrance.

I nodded.

"It's our way of mourning them—"

He stopped rowing, too heartsick to finish his explanation, and too exhausted to do anything but let the tide carry us home. A blank moment passed.

Then the scratching.

A mouse noise, no more, a scrabbling at the underside of the boat like a man's nails tickling the planks to be let in. Not one man: many. The sound of their entreaties multiplied, the soft dragging of rotted cuticles across the wood.

In the boat, we didn't move, we didn't speak, we didn't believe. Even as we heard the worst—we didn't believe the worst.

A splash off to starboard; I turned and he was coming towards me, rigid in the water, borne up by unseen puppeteers like a figure head. It was Ray; his body covered in killing bruises and cuts: stoned to death then brought, like a gleeful mascot, like proof of power, to spook us. It was almost as though he were walking on water, his feet just hidden by the swell, his arms hanging loosely by his side as he was hauled towards the boat. I looked at his face: lacerated and broken. One eye almost closed, the other smashed from its orbit.

Two yards from the boat, the puppeteers let him sink back into the sea, where he disappeared in a swirl of pink water.

"Your companion?" said the sheep feeder.

I nodded. He must have fallen into the sea from the stern of the *Emmanuelle*. Now he was like them, a drowned man. They'd already claimed him as their plaything. So they did like games after all; they hauled him from the beach like children come to fetch a playmate, eager that he should join the horse play.

The scratching had stopped. Ray's body had disappeared altogether. Not a murmur off the pristine sea, just the slop of the waves against the boards of the boat.

I pulled at the oars—

"Row!" I screamed at the sheep feeder. "Row, or they'll kill us."

He seemed resigned to whatever they had in mind to punish us with. He shook his head and spat onto the water. Beneath his floating phlegm something moved in the deep, pale forms rolled and somersaulted, too far down to be clearly seen. Even as I watched they came floating up towards us, their sea-corrupted faces better defined with every fathom they rose, their arms outstretched to embrace us.

A shoal of corpses. The dead in dozens, crab-cleaned and fish-picked, their remaining flesh scarcely sitting on their bones.

The boat rocked gently as their hands reached up to touch it.

The look of resignation on the sheep feeder's face didn't falter for a moment as the boat was shaken backwards and forwards; at first gently, then so violently we were beaten about like dolls. They meant to capsize us, and there was no help for it. A moment later, the boat tipped over.

The water was icy; far colder than I'd anticipated, and it took breath away. I'd always been a fairly strong swimmer. My strokes were confident as I began to swim from the boat, cleaving through the white water. The sheep feeder was less lucky. Like many men who live with the sea, he apparently couldn't swim. Without issuing a cry or a prayer, he sank like a stone.

What did I hope? That four was enough: that I could be left to thumb a current to safety? Whatever hopes of escape I had, they were short-lived.

I felt a soft, oh so very soft, brushing of my ankles and my feet, almost a caress. Something broke surface briefly close to my head. I glimpsed a grey back, as of a large fish. The touch on my ankle had become a grasp. A pulpy hand, mushed by so long in the water, had hold of me, and inexorably began to claim me for the sea. I gulped what I knew to be my last breath of air, and as I did so Ray's head bobbed no more than a yard from me. I saw his wounds in clinical detail—the water-cleansed cuts were ugly flaps of white tissue, with a gleam of bone at their core. The loose eye had been washed away by now, his hair, flattened to his skull, no longer disguised the bald patch at his crown.

The water closed over my head. My eyes were open, and I saw my hard earned breath flashing past my face in a display of silver bubbles. Ray was beside me, consoling, attentive. His arms floated over his head as though he were surrendering. The pressure of the water distorted his face, puffing his cheeks out, and spilling threads of severed nerves from his empty eye socket like the tentacles of a tiny squid.

I let it happen. I opened my mouth and felt it fill with cold water. Salt burned my sinuses, the cold stabbed behind my eyes. I felt the brine burning down my throat, a rush of eager water where water shouldn't go—flushing air from my tubes and cavities, 'til my system was overwhelmed.

Below me, two corpses, their hair swaying loosely in the current, hugged my legs. Their heads lolled and danced on rotted ropes of neck muscle, and though I pawed at their hands, and their flesh came off the bone in grey, lace-edged pieces, their loving grip didn't falter. They wanted me, oh how dearly they wanted me.

Ray was holding me too, wrapping me up, pressing his face to mine. There was no purpose in the gesture, I suppose. He didn't know or feel, or love or care. And I, losing my life with every second, succumbing to the sea absolutely, couldn't take pleasure in the intimacy that I'd longed for.

Too late for love; the sunlight was already a memory. Was it that the world was going out—darkening towards the edges as I died—or that we were now so deep the sun couldn't penetrate so far? Panic and terror had left me—my heart seemed not to beat at all—my breath didn't come and go in anguished bursts as it had. A kind of peace was on me.

Now the grip of my companions relaxed, and the gentle tide had its way with me. A rape of the body: a ravaging of skin and muscle, gut, eye, sinus, tongue, brain.

Time had no place here. The days may have passed into weeks, I couldn't know. The keels of boats glided over and maybe we looked up from our rock hovels on occasion and watched them pass. A ringed finger was trailed in the water, a splashless puddle clove the sky, a fishing line trailed a worm. Signs of life.

Maybe the same hour as I died, or maybe a year later, the current sniffs me out of my rock and has some mercy. I am twitched from amongst the sea anemones and given to the tide. Ray is with me. His time too has come. The sea change has occurred; there is no turning back for us.

Relentlessly the tide bears us—sometimes floating, bloated decks for gulls, sometimes half sunk and nibbled by fish—bears us towards the island. We know the surge of the shingle, and hear, without ears, the rattle of the stones.

The sea has long since washed the plate clean of its leavings. Angela, the *Emmanuelle,* and Jonathan, are gone. Only we drowned belong here, face up, under the stones, soothed by the rhythm of tiny waves and the absurd incomprehension of sheep.

ẞetween the ᶜWindows
of the Ṣea

Jack Dann

ITA STOOD at the end of the long, steel pier and stared into the black water below. Waves smashed in below her, the white froth turning to silver in the moonlight. Behind her, past the pier and the bottle-strewn, paper-littered beach, were modern balconied condos and hotels, one indistinguishable from another. A1A and the intersecting streets were quiet, except for the susurration of passing cars. Most of the chic little Soho-style shops were closed; and the college hangouts—the Elbo Room, The Button, Stagger Lee's, Durty Nelly's, and Nards—which had been packed with screaming, drinking students just a few days before, were almost empty. No one was on the beach drinking beer or making love to jangling rock-and-roll music turned up full blast. The large, "ghetto-box" radios had been all the rage, and there had been some talk about outlawing them. But spring break was over and the students were gone. Only their money and bottles and cans and used prophylactics remained behind. Fort Lauderdale was once again left to the locals and the wealthy retirees, to the tourists dressed in flowered shirts and floppy hats, and to the chairman-of-the-board executives and drug merchants who owned million-dollar homes on the intercoastals and whose children spent the long, languorous days cutting screaming wakes in the ocean with their "cigarette" speedboats.

It was cool out tonight, and Rita shivered as she contemplated suicide.

All she had to do was take another step. She could just let the water carry her away. She stared grimly downward at the angry, sudsy water below. No one could find her here. No one could rescue her, scream for her to stop, try to talk her out of it. She was completely alone. The pier was closed, and she'd locked all the doors behind her. The pier contained a restaurant and several overpriced sundry shops. Rita worked as the manager of the restaurant. In reality she was just another waitress, for The Pierpoint was just another diner with a fancy, pretentious name.

She tried to think of something profound to tell herself before she jumped off the pier, but she couldn't think of anything.

Before she could *really* decide if she wanted to do it right now, she jumped into the cold, dark water. It was an icy shock, and then her body became accustomed to it. She had a few seconds of blind panic, then realized that if she changed her mind and decided that she wanted to live after all, she could swim back to shore.

She swam slowly away from shore, and the undertow, flowing strong below her, helped her, pulling her toward that distant place where the starry sky met the dark ocean. The water now seemed warm as a womb.

Rita was calm. She waited for her life to pass before her as if in a dream, or an old movie—that's what was supposed to happen when you drowned. It was supposed to be a very pleasant experience, really—or so she'd been told. The water carried her along silently, and she bobbed and floated like a marker in her red-and-white, vertical-striped swimsuit. She looked up at the sky, counting the reddish-hued stars, and wondered when *it* was going to happen. But *it* could take hours, she told herself. By then she'd be too far out to swim back. . . .

So what? she asked herself. What else was there for her to do? Go back *there,* back to being a fat waitress in a crumby eat-out, back to her poster-walled little apartment off Commercial Boulevard, where there was nothing to do but watch television reruns or smoke another joint—or worse yet, back to the old hangouts, where bad, yet nostalgic memories were thick as smoke, back to being an over-the-hill '60s love child, a true flower-carrying protester who understood the metaphysical meaning of every one of Bob Dylan's songs . . . ?

Back to being achingly lonely?

I'd rather be dead, she thought.

And no one even *remembers* Bob Dylan anymore. . . .

A dark ocean swell swept over her and she choked, swallowing salty water. She lunged upward, gasping for air, churning the water with her arms, dog-paddling to keep her head as far above the surface as possible.

But the ocean was implacable. It had become cool again, even cold. It was dark and quiet. Rita looked toward the shore, toward the twinkling, hazy-distant city lights . . . looked over the glassy, undulating surface of the water. She had drifted too far out. She wouldn't be able to swim back.

It was too late!

She panicked, suddenly, desperately wanting to live. She just wanted to feel grass or cement under her feet, look in shop windows, be bored on a Saturday night, chain-smoke nonfilter cigarettes, go to a movie or watch television. Anything but death in an ocean where she could see no bottom where no one could hear her screams. She tried swimming back to shore, her fleshy arms banging into the water, her short legs kicking, splashing. In moments she was exhausted. She'd never been a good swimmer, certainly not a distance swimmer.

And the water kept carrying her away from the distant shore, as if it were quietly playing with her . . . as if it wanted her. Giving up, she floated—*that* she could do. She could float forever. Floating and waiting to drown, she cried and laughed at herself.

She'd *always* been a phony. Even now . . . especially now. She hadn't *really* expected to die when she jumped into the water. She was play-acting . . . acting out a private fantasy. She was just going to float for a while and then swim back to shore. She'd been a phony hippy, a phony radical, a phony feminist, a phony doper, a phony Protestant, and now a phony suicide.

But the ocean didn't care. It took her warmth and what strength she had. . . .

She started drowning at dawn, which was a rich, hot, ruddy sunrise bleeding into the water, turning blue, then green below. Rita fell asleep again, and inhaled water. She choked and, unable to scream, she kicked and twisted and tried to push herself to the surface, but she hadn't the strength. She felt electric, jolting pain, as if her head would burst. Then gradually the pain receded into darkness. She was falling into what looked like an endless black wall, a huge, curved well of darkness. No memory-movie of her life passed before her.

She passed through the wall into utter blackness.

Then she found herself falling slowly through greenish-gray depths, her arms outstretched as if she were flying. Her eyes were wide, and she could *see*. She tasted salt water, which filled her lungs. Her chest swelled and she exhaled a warm stream of water. She was breathing it. But she didn't need to "breathe" often; perhaps it was just to satisfy an old autonomic habit.

Rita could see the furrowed ocean bottom far below her, seventy or eighty feet down. For an instant, she experienced acrophobia, for the water was absolutely clear and still. She waved her arms and kicked her feet, testing. She hung midway, floating, slowly turning, free of the past, free of loneliness or emptiness.

Free. . . .

Rita wouldn't accept that she might be dead, or that these, her last thoughts, might be hallucinations, the last, synaptic coursings of a dying mind. She started swimming instead, feeling strong and lean and stream-lined and beautiful, sensitive to the private universe of water around her;

it was an ever-present pressure against her body, as if a beautiful man with cool skin and fresh breath were pushing against her, entering her. She cut easily through the water like a dolphin.

Sunlight shimmered through the water, turning it blue, which deepened to purple in the depths; but ahead the sea floor rose sharply like underwater crags, turning green, the living green and orange and yellow of a coral reef. Deeper, down the reef's side, the colors became muted, turning almost gray. There was life everywhere. Angelfish seemed to glow yellow and blue through black stripes. Four-eyed butterfly fish seemed to be swimming backward. Summer flounder, shark, and barracuda swam through cliff valleys and narrows; below were anemones and conchs and stars and sponges and long tendrils of seaweed, green against blue.

Rita swam over the reef, diving, as hundreds of tiny silvery fish sparkled all around her, slid past her arms and legs; and the world was color and light and life, every instant filled, as if loneliness and boredom were foreign sounds, words in a language she couldn't remember. She could hear the snapping of shells and a thrumming, a moaning. The ocean was life and sound and color. She could see clearly, as if she were wearing goggles or a face mask. She breathed water and light. She was free of constraint, an exultant ballerina who had conquered gravity.

She rested motionless, drifting downward to land gently upon a smooth, flat spot amid the coral. She stretched, unafraid, even as a huge shadowy manta soared slowly overhead.

She was happy. She had become much more than a client of the sea. She was home, finally . . . here by the large, rounded coral that looked like French modernist concretion sculpture, by the bony staghorn and rose and soft coral. A school of tiny blue damselfish flittered between mock-stone fronds and coral spikes. She reached out, as if awakening from a perfect dream, to grasp the tiny fish.

Suddenly she felt a sharp pain in her throat. She began to choke. She couldn't *breathe*. She tried to push herself away from the coral, struggled to reach the surface magnified above—an undulating mirror of light that seemed so near.

But the ocean burst into a kaleidoscope of coral color and then, just as quickly, dissolved into complete blackness. . . .

"Hey, are you all right?"

Rita opened her eyes, but everything seemed out of focus, as it used to when she had tried to swim underwater with her eyes open. Then her vision cleared. It was dark, and she was lying on the damp sand of the beach beside the steel pier. The moon was full and had a reddish halo. She shivered—the breeze skimming over the sea carried a northern chill.

"Miss, are you *all right?*"

Disoriented, she looked up at the man kneeling beside her. He was rather handsome, with a full mouth, a cleft chin, and a thin nose that was slightly too long for his squarish face. His thick shock of prematurely gray hair looked blond in the moonlight. Rita tried to sit up, but her body felt heavy and foreign. She leaned into the sand on her elbow and raised her head. Her long, bleached hair was still wet, as was her suit. "How long have I been here?" she asked.

"I don't really know," the man said. "I just came by. I thought something might be wrong."

Rita laughed weakly. "No . . . nothing's wrong."

"Is there anything I can do for you?" Rita shivered, and he took off his jacket and wrapped it around her shoulders. It was sky-blue imitation suede, and warm.

"Thanks," she said, feeling awkward sitting in the sand with this man kneeling beside her. But he *seemed* genuinely interested. Maybe he's just a good Samaritan, she told herself. He certainly wasn't dressed for the beach, not with those white bucks, white, high-waisted slacks that were now crusted with sand, and a starched white shirt that looked bluish in the moonlight. His tie was pulled loose below an open collar.

Rita thought he was beautiful, as cool and crisp as the water.

"Would you care to go and have a drink?" he asked cautiously. "Might warm you up."

"I'm not exactly dressed for it," she said, feeling self-conscious and fat in her sand-sticky swimsuit. She did feel better, though. She could even muse about her suicide attempt. It was as if it had happened to someone else; she felt distanced from it.

But she remembered jumping off the pier, floating out to sea, choking, drowning. She remembered the wall of darkness. She remembered swimming . . . and breathing under water. She could still taste the salty stuff.

"They're really not going to care how you're dressed," the man said. "Not on the strip, anyway. And you can wear my jacket." He seemed in earnest. "Come on, let me help you up."

Easier said than done, she said to herself. But she allowed him to help her to her feet. When she stumbled, he held her close for an instant. She felt dizzy . . . and hungry. It had been quite a while since she'd felt ravenously hungry.

He helped her along as they crossed the beach. Even after they were on the street, he kept his arm around her, his long fingers touching her flabby waist through the material of the jacket he had lent her. They crossed A1A, right on the corner of Las Olas, site of the famous Elbo Room Bar, tourist heaven. The streets were quiet. A few tourists were out. But the students who had been shouting and hanging out and showing off were gone. "Do you want to just stop in here?" he asked, looking into the Elbo Room's window.

"Are you kidding?" she asked, smiling at him—she had a beautiful smile. "It's a trap."

"I vaguely remember it from a long time ago," he said. "Do you know someplace better?"

"Yeah, a little bar down here a ways." They walked toward the inter-coastal; in fact a bridge was lifting to let a high-masted sailboat pass under. "You're just visiting, I take it," Rita said. She felt her strength returning.

"I had business in Jacksonville, and I thought that since I was in the neighborhood, so to speak, I'd come back down here for old time's sake. I used to come here for college break." He chuckled. "But that was a *long,* long time ago."

"You must have had some good times. . . ."

"That I did. But I think the real reason I came back was to try to feel the old sensation of being young again . . . you know, the sun all day, the lights and glitter and bars all night. Total freedom, no responsibility." Then, after a pause, he said, "And no money." They both laughed at that. "What about you . . . are you a native?"

"I came down here for spring break too . . . a *long,* long time ago." She smiled. "Only, I stayed."

"Maybe that's what I should have done."

Rita laughed and pointed out the cafe on the other side of the street. It was a gaily painted converted gas station. There were about a dozen outside tables, but only one was occupied, by a young couple sitting close together and sipping wine. They wore identical white shorts and tops. They *had* to be newlyweds. "I have no idea what you do or where you live," Rita said as they crossed the street, "but, believe me, you made the right decision not to stay here."

They sat down at one of the tables, and the waitress, who was about Rita's age, appeared to take their order.

"Hi, how you doin'?" Rita asked.

The waitress looked blankly at her for a second. "You know, you look *so* familiar."

"I'm Rita, from the Pier."

"Well, what can I get you?"

Rita felt herself burning with embarrassment. She'd wanted to impress her new friend, and not even a goddamn local could remember her. She wasn't friends with this waitress, certainly, but they'd seen each other around before. Her companion didn't seem to take any notice. He asked

Rita what she wanted—a glass of the house wine and a small chef's salad —and then ordered a Drambuie with a soda on the side for himself. After the waitress left, he finally asked her name.

"Rita . . . Rita Cobia," she replied.

"I'm Stephen Boden from Albany, New York." He grinned. "This whole thing's crazy, isn't it?"

"I guess it is." There was an embarrassing, awkward silence. Rita lowered her eyes and stared at her hands folded on the table.

She *had* tried to kill herself.

She *remembered* drowning.

"Rita . . . ?" Stephen asked. "What were you doing on the beach?"

The waitress came back with drinks and Rita's salad. What she *really* wanted was a hamburger, rare, with a great big Bermuda onion; but that would only bring attention to her weight. After all, fat people eat hamburgers on large, beautiful kemmelwick buns, and skinny people eat chef's salads with oil and vinegar. Heartburn city. . . . Rita took a forkful of meat and lettuce and chewed carefully. "I tried to kill myself last night," she said suddenly, as if she were testing Stephen. "I don't know how I got back on the beach." All that said flatly, matter-of-factly.

Stephen's eyes narrowed. He took another sip of his Drambuie, then followed it with a sip of soda.

"Sounds pretty nutty, huh," Rita said.

"Well . . . I guess it's a good thing I found you."

"It was all over but the chorus by then," and she told him the story, although she was certain that this guy was going to think her a nut case and get away as fast as he could. So what else was new. . . .

"Maybe you blacked out or something and dreamed it and then swam back to shore," Stephen said.

"I was out on the water for a long time," Rita said, musing. "I know that."

"Should I ask why you wanted to kill yourself?"

"If you wanted to relive the old memories, you should've been here last week when the kids were still on the streets," she said, ignoring his question. "But you did say you were down here on business."

"I did, but I guess I really didn't want to come back here until the party was over. I could have changed my schedule around. But the truth is that seeing all those kids would just remind me that I'm too *old* for spring break."

She giggled at that. "What do you do now?" she asked.

"Would you believe real estate?" Stephen seemed relaxed, yet animated; and as he talked to her, he leaned forward as if he were going to whisper, as if everything he had to tell Rita was privileged, secret. Rita found herself doing the same thing; they were blocking out all the noise and activity around them. This was more than just a pickup or a budding friendship. And right now, sitting with Stephen, she felt truly happy. She wouldn't ask for anything more.

"I would believe real estate," Rita said. She was full, and slightly high on the tangy wine.

"This whole place—Lauderdale, the beach, the bars, the sun—represented possibility to me," Stephen continued. "When I first came down here, I thought I could do *anything*: act, become a playwright, a novelist, a screenwriter, a director. I took film in college, which prepared me for absolutely nothing but making films . . . that's another story."

"Did you try to get into films?" Rita asked.

"Not hard enough. I was in advertising for a while, and used some of the stuff I learned in college."

"You didn't like it . . . advertising?"

"Actually, I liked it quite a bit," Stephen said, and he waved to the waitress to bring another round. "Maybe that was the problem. It kept reminding me that I *wasn't* doing film. Close, but no cigar. I'm making more money in real estate, anyway . . . and I'm *real* good at rationalizing. So, glutton for punishment that I am, I came back here to feel what it was like to have it all ahead of me."

"And what does it feel like?"

"I feel good because I'm here with you. But except for meeting you, which made the whole trip worth while, it's been a bust. I should have let well enough alone. I knew this place would look different . . . would be different when seen again through older eyes, but I thought I'd taste *something* of what it used to be like. Yet until now Florida had the same leaden 'feel' of everything else in my life." He laughed harshly. "I guess I've become dried-up and cynical. But what I'm feeling now is the real stuff." He seemed taken aback by that; he leaned backward, as if to think about it. After a long pause he said, "You know, *this* is what it felt like. Just sitting here with you makes me feel like I'm on . . . spring break." He laughed at that, and the harshness disappeared. "I'm starting to sound like a real jerk, aren't I?"

Rita felt her face become warm. "No . . . you're not."

They looked at each other. Rita felt awkward, and Stephen put his hand over hers. She felt her cheeks burn, but she couldn't stop herself from smiling, then giggling. "I'm sorry," she said. "I—"

"I feel the same way," Stephen said. The waitress came back with their drinks, and Stephen paid her. "Let's get out of here and walk around," he continued. "Unless you really want this drink. I feel full of energy; and if I don't walk some of it off, I'm going to be jumping around in my seat like this"—and he jumped up and down and made a silly face. Then he suddenly sat back in his chair. "I'm sorry. I can't believe that I'm trying to get you to take a walk after what you told me. You're probably ready to go home and sleep for forty hours."

"No," Rita said, standing up and leaning forward, reluctant to take her hand out of his. "Let's take a walk."

They walked back to A1A, crossed the street to the beach side, and cut through a well-lit parking lot and out onto the cool sand. A few tall palmettos cast long shadows on the beach. They passed a row of cabanas and a painted metal kiosk, where bathers could buy sundries—especially suntan oils—at outrageous prices. Then they walked in the wet sand along the ocean, sidestepping the angled paths of foamy water cutting into the beach.

Rita felt wonderful. Everything around her and Stephen seemed separate and perfect: the sea a darkness, a swelling; the sand seemed almost to glow in the wan moonlight. It was as if all her senses were heightened. She felt as if she were experiencing every smell and sight for the first time. The sea odors were sharp as horseradish and somehow poignant. The waves were a muffled roar, white noise swallowing the city sounds. The breezes were chilly, but the wine she had drunk kept her warm. The sky was a great vault reflected by the sea.

Every moment was magical . . . eternal.

Stephen took her hand. "What about you?"

"What do you mean?"

"You said you came here on college break and stayed."

"That's all there is to tell," Rita said. "I came from a small town in upstate New York, a blinker town."

"A what?"

"You blink, it's gone." He laughed and she continued. "I went to a small college, a religious school. Some friends were coming down here. They talked me into it and here I am."

Stephen didn't press her to speak. They kept walking, giving wide berth to several beached jellyfish in their path.

"My religious education and beliefs were almost the death of me," she said after some time passed. They both giggled and then broke into laughter like nervous high-school students on a first date.

"What do you mean?" Stephen asked.

"Well, this isn't exactly the kind of place a girl with traditional values chooses," Rita said. "I was rebelling, and I suppose it took everyone by surprise when I left the school. I was a good student, didn't get into trouble." There was a strain in her voice. "I'm your typical fat girl."

"You're *not* fat, nor typical, and here you are right in the middle of the sun and sex and drug belt," he said wryly.

"With my morals intact while I tried to off myself by jumping into the ocean." Again they laughed together, but there was a strain. The ocean seemed ominous. "I should have applied for a Guinness world record—I had to be the only sixties hippy, wearing tie-dyed jeans and beads, with my hair down to my ankles practically, who was also a virgin. I can tell you that religious fat girls make poor hippies. I used to sneak off to church. I'd put on my Sunday dress, put my hair up, slather on makeup to make me look middle class and proper, and go to Episcopalian services. I still do it . . . every Sunday."

"Look," Stephen said, stopping, pulling her to a halt too. "You're not skinny, but you're certainly not fat."

"Yes I am, but I've got a pretty face."

He put his arms around her. "When I saw you lying on the beach, I felt like I was eighteen and in love. And that's how I feel right now. . . ."

Rita blushed, not knowing what to say. Against all reason, her instincts were to trust this stranger. She nodded, brushing against his face, which was very close to hers.

They passed a large condo, and then more motels, priced high for the tourists. "I'm staying here," Stephen said, pointing at an old, two-story, white stucco motel. Rita knew of the place. It had a decent reputation, and the new owners had enough taste to do away with the flashing neon and 1950s pink plastic flamingos that had been its trademark for the previous twenty years.

"Why didn't you stay over at the Holiday?"

He grinned. "Over the years I've gotten tired of hassling with desk clerks to get a low floor. So I just go to motels where it's quiet and I can work and it doesn't take an act of bravery to get to my room."

"How do you fly, then?" Rita asked.

"Planes don't bother me . . . only elevators. You know what my shrink told me to do in elevators?" Before Rita could respond, he continued. "He said that every time I get into an elevator, I should force myself to have erotic fantasies. That way, I'd associate elevators with pleasure . . . that was the theory, anyway." He chuckled.

"Did it work?" Rita asked.

"Nah, I'd be too damn nervous and claustrophobic in the elevator to think about sex. In fact, I think it started working the other way around."

"What do you mean?"

"I started getting scared of *sex*." They both laughed, but there was a nervous tension working between them again. It was palpable, exciting. . . .

"Well, maybe we should give the elevator another chance," Rita said, surprised at herself.

They went to Stephen's room and turned on all the lights, as if they were both afraid of the dark; then they sat down on the large brown Naugahyde couch that faced sliding glass doors which opened onto a private patio. They looked out onto the beach but could see only reflections of the room in the glass. They joked and talked and became nervously silly.

When they ran out of small talk, Rita made the first move. She leaned against him, made herself vulnerable to him. There was a moment of shyness and awkwardness, as he began to caress and kiss her, exploring gently, as if searching for something precious that had been lost long ago. Passion was gradual, a soft falling, then a quickening. Rita felt as if she had two selves: one, who was burning . . . or choking, drowning; and another, who watched coolly, curiously, as if from a distance. Rita felt no shame, nor was she nervous; but Stephen got up and turned off all the lights, bringing the sand and sea outside the sliding doors into their private world.

Rita helped him remove her suit. But when he was ready to enter her, she pulled him away from the couch and led the way outside onto the damp sand.

"Someone might see us," he whispered, yet he didn't insist, for the beach was empty. They were hidden in shadow . . . hidden by the world. The sea was a dark, living thing before them, murmuring, speaking in a language just beyond sense. The moon was clear, a round white lantern turning the fine sand to opal.

Rita held Stephen close and looked up at the sky, as if studying the stars. She moaned softly, felt a bright flash of pain as he entered her. She could hear his labored breathing as if it were the surf pounding on top of her. His mouth locked on hers. Everything became liquid and slippery and clean. It was like washing . . . like swimming . . . like breathing water.

She awoke to his soft breathing beside her. She lay quietly and felt a strength, a muscular tightness throughout her body. She felt long and thin and beautiful. It was still dark; she couldn't have slept for more than an hour.

Stephen curled against her, murmured something in his sleep, and pressed his face into her breast. His tangled hair tickled her nut-brown shoulder. She giggled, feeling pleasure wash over her again. She caressed him, exploring. He felt as cool as the sea to the touch. He smelled as tangy and salty as the soapy whitecaps washing and smoothing over the sand.

She felt completely awake, alive, full of energy.

It was then she heard the sea. Amid its muted pounding and breaking and susurration, it seemed to speak to her . . . call to her. She could almost make out its words.

The sea wooed her with whisperings, and Rita found herself answering. Making love to Stephen had been a celebration, but now she wanted to go home.

Feeling the pull of the sea as if she were in its undertow, she kissed Stephen good-bye. She felt an instant of nostalgic regret, and then she stood up naked and ran toward the ocean. She took long strides, felt her scalp tingle as her long hair blew in the salty breeze, felt her body as her own, not as an ugly object worn like an oversized coat.

She jumped into the surf, which was refreshing and as cool as Stephen as he slept. She ran through the shallow water, lifting her legs high, splashing, and then swam. She was strength itself. She was a flowing. She cut through the sea like a fish sojourning from the deep.

The ocean was cool and patient and enveloping. It claimed her, as had Stephen. It breathed. It entered her. It pulled her down into its living stillness.

And once again, Rita took a deep breath . . . and became smooth and thin, formed by the sea.

Dip in the Pool

Roald Dahl

O N THE MORNING of the third day, the sea calmed. Even the most delicate passengers—those who had not been seen around the ship since sailing time—emerged from their cabins and crept on to the sun deck where the deck steward gave them chairs and tucked rugs around their legs and left them lying in rows, their faces upturned to the pale, almost heatless January sun.

It had been moderately rough the first two days, and this sudden calm and the sense of comfort that it brought created a more genial atmosphere over the whole ship. By the time evening came, the passengers, with twelve hours of good weather behind them, were beginning to feel confident, and at eight o'clock that night the main dining-room was filled with people eating and drinking with the assured, complacent air of seasoned sailors.

The meal was not half over when the passengers became aware, by the slight friction between their bodies and the seats of their chairs, that the big ship had actually started rolling again. It was very gentle at first, just a slow, lazy leaning to one side, then to the other, but it was enough to cause a subtle, immediate change of mood over the whole room. A few of the passengers glanced up from their food, hesitating, waiting, almost listening for the next roll, smiling nervously, little secret glimmers of apprehension in their eyes. Some were completely unruffled, some were openly smug, a number of the smug ones making jokes about food and weather in order to torture the few who were beginning to suffer. The movement of the ship then became rapidly more and more violent, and only five or six minutes after the first roll had been noticed, she was swinging heavily from side to side, the passengers bracing themselves in their chairs, leaning against the pull as in a car cornering.

At last the really bad roll came, and Mr. William Botibol, sitting at the purser's table, saw his plate of poached turbot with hollandaise sauce sliding suddenly away from under his fork. There was a flutter of excitement, everybody reaching for plates and wineglasses. Mrs. Renshaw, seated at the purser's right, gave a little scream and clutched that gentleman's arm.

"Going to be a dirty night," the purser said, looking at Mrs. Renshaw. "I think it's blowing up for a very dirty night." There was just the faintest suggestion of relish in the way he said it.

A steward came hurrying up and sprinkled water on the tablecloth between the plates. The excitement subsided. Most of the passengers continued with their meal. A small number, including Mrs. Renshaw, got carefully to their feet and threaded their ways with a kind of concealed haste between the tables and through the doorway.

"Well," the purser said, "there she goes." He glanced around with approval at the remainder of his flock who were sitting quiet, looking complacent, their faces reflecting openly that extraordinary pride that travellers seem to take in being recognized as "good sailors."

When the eating was finished and the coffee had been served, Mr. Botibol, who had been unusually grave and thoughtful since the rolling started, suddenly stood up and carried his cup of coffee around to Mrs. Renshaw's vacant place, next to the purser. He seated himself in her chair, then immediately leaned over and began to whisper urgently in the purser's ear. "Excuse me," he said, "but could you tell me something, please?"

The purser, small and fat and red, bent forward to listen. "What's the trouble, Mr. Botibol?"

"What I want to know is this." The man's face was anxious and the purser was watching it. "What I want to know is will the captain already have made his estimate on the day's run—you know, for the auction pool? I mean before it began to get rough like this?"

The purser, who had prepared himself to receive a personal confidence, smiled and leaned back in his seat to relax his full belly. "I should say so —yes," he answered. He didn't bother to whisper his reply, although automatically he lowered his voice, as one does when answering a whisperer.

"About how long ago do you think he did it?"

"Some time this afternoon. He usually does it in the afternoon."

"About what time?"

"Oh, I don't know. Around four o'clock I should guess."

"Now tell me another thing. How does the captain decide which number it shall be? Does he take a lot of trouble over that?"

The purser looked at the anxious frowning face of Mr. Botibol and he smiled, knowing quite well what the man was driving at. "Well, you see, the captain has a little conference with the navigating officer, and they study the weather and a lot of other things, and then they make their estimate."

Mr. Botibol nodded, pondering this answer for a moment. Then he said, "Do you think the captain knew there was bad weather coming today?"

"I couldn't tell you," the purser replied. He was looking into the small black eyes of the other man, seeing the two single little sparks of excitement dancing in their centres. "I really couldn't tell you, Mr. Botibol. I wouldn't know."

"If this gets any worse it might be worth buying some of the low numbers. What do you think?" The whispering was more urgent, more anxious now.

"Perhaps it will," the purser said. "I doubt whether the old man allowed for a really rough night. It was pretty calm this afternoon when he made his estimate."

The others at the table had become silent and were trying to hear, watching the purser with that intent, half-cocked, listening look that you can see also at the race track when they are trying to overhear a trainer talking about his chance: the slightly open lips, the upstretched eyebrows, the head forward and cocked a little to one side—that desperately straining, half-hypnotized, listening look that comes to all of them when they are hearing something straight from the horse's mouth.

"Now suppose *you* were allowed to buy a number, which one would *you* choose today?" Mr. Botibol whispered.

"I don't know what the range is yet," the purser patiently answered. "They don't announce the range till the auction starts after dinner. And I'm really not very good at it anyway. I'm only the purser, you know."

At that point Mr. Botibol stood up. "Excuse me, all," he said, and he walked carefully away over the swaying floor between the other tables, and twice he had to catch hold of the back of a chair to steady himself against the ship's roll.

"The sun deck, please," he said to the elevator man.

The wind caught him full in the face as he stepped out on to the open deck. He staggered and grabbed hold of the rail and held on tight with both hands, and he stood there looking out over the darkening sea where the great waves were welling up high and white horses were riding against the wind with plumes of spray behind them as they went.

"Pretty bad out there, wasn't it, sir?" the elevator man said on the way down.

Mr. Botibol was combing his hair back into place with a small red comb. "Do you think we've slackened speed at all on account of the weather?" he asked.

"Oh my word yes, sir. We slackened off considerable since this started. You got to slacken off speed in weather like this or you'll be throwing the passengers all over the ship."

Down in the smoking-room people were already gathering for the auction. They were grouping themselves politely around the various tables, the men a little stiff in their dinner jackets, a little pink and overshaved and stiff beside their cool white-armed women. Mr. Botibol took a chair close to the auctioneer's table. He crossed his legs, folded his arms, and settled himself in his seat with the rather desperate air of a man who has made a tremendous decision and refuses to be frightened.

The pool, he was telling himself, would probably be around seven thousand dollars. That was almost exactly what it had been the last two days with the numbers selling for between three and four hundred apiece. Being a British ship they did it in pounds, but he liked to do his thinking in his own currency. Seven thousand dollars was plenty of money. My goodness, yes! And what he would do he would get them to pay him in hundred-dollar bills and he would take it ashore in the inside pocket of his jacket. No problem there. And right away, yes right away, he would buy a Lincoln convertible. He would pick it up on the way from the ship and drive it home just for the pleasure of seeing Ethel's face when she came out the front door and looked at it. Wouldn't that be something, to see Ethel's face when he glided up to the door in a brand-new pale-green Lincoln convertible! Hello, Ethel, honey, he would say, speaking very casual. I just thought I'd get you a little present. I saw it in the window as I went by, so I thought of you and how you were always wanting one. You like it, honey? he would say. You like the colour? And then he would watch her face.

The auctioneer was standing up behind his table now. "Ladies and gentlemen!" he shouted. "The captain has estimated the day's run, ending midday tomorrow, at five hundred and fifteen miles. As usual we will take the ten numbers on either side of it to make up the range. That makes it five hundred and five to five hundred and twenty-five. And of course for those who think the true figure will be still farther away, there'll be 'low field' and 'high field' sold separately as well. Now, we'll draw the first numbers out of the hat . . . here we are . . . five hundred and twelve?"

The room became quiet. The people sat still in their chairs, all eyes watching the auctioneer. There was a certain tension in the air, and as the bids got higher, the tension grew. This wasn't a game or a joke; you could be sure of that by the way one man would look across at another who had raised his bid—smiling perhaps, but only the lips smiling, the eyes bright and absolutely cold.

Number five hundred and twelve was knocked down for one hundred and ten pounds. The next three or four numbers fetched roughly the same amount.

The ship was rolling heavily, and each time she went over, the wooden panelling on the walls creaked as if it were going to split. The passengers held on to the arms of their chairs, concentrating upon the auction.

"Low field!" the auctioneer called out. "The next number is low field."

Mr. Botibol sat up very straight and tense. He would wait, he had decided, until the others had finished bidding, then he would jump in and make the last bid. He had figured that there must be at least five hundred dollars in his account at the bank at home, probably nearer six. That was about two hundred pounds—over two hundred. This ticket wouldn't fetch more than that.

"As you all know," the auctioneer was saying, "low field covers every number *below* the smallest number in the range, in this case every number below five hundred and five. So, if you think this ship is going to cover less than five hundred and five miles in the twenty-four hours ending at noon tomorrow, you better get in and buy this number. So what am I bid?"

It went clear up to one hundred and thirty pounds. Others besides Mr. Botibol seemed to have noticed that the weather was rough. One hundred and forty . . . fifty . . . There it stopped. The auctioneer raised his hammer.

"Going at one hundred and fifty . . ."

"Sixty!" Mr. Botibol called, and every face in the room turned and looked at him.

"Seventy!"

"Eighty!" Mr. Botibol called.

"Ninety!"

"Two hundred!" Mr. Botibol called. He wasn't stopping now—not for anyone.

There was a pause.

"Any advance on two hundred pounds?"

Sit still, he told himself. Sit absolutely still and don't look up. It's unlucky to look up. Hold your breath. No one's going to bid you up so long as you hold your breath.

"Going for two hundred pounds . . ." The auctioneer had a pink bald head and there were little beads of sweat sparkling on top of it. "Going . . ." Mr. Botibol held his breath. "Going . . . Gone!" The man banged the hammer on the table. Mr. Botibol wrote out a cheque and handed it to the auctioneer's assistant, then he settled back in his chair to wait for the finish. He did not want to go to bed before he knew how much there was in the pool.

They added it up after the last number had been sold and it came to twenty-one hundred-odd pounds. That was around six thousand dollars. Ninety per cent to go to the winner, ten per cent to seamen's charities. Ninety per cent of six thousand was five thousand four hundred. Well —that was enough. He could buy the Lincoln convertible and there would be something left over, too. With this gratifying thought he went off, happy and excited, to his cabin.

When Mr. Botibol awoke the next morning he lay quite still for several minutes with his eyes shut, listening for the sound of the gale, waiting for the roll of the ship. There was no sound of any gale and the ship was not rolling. He jumped up and peered out of the porthole. The sea—Oh Jesus God—was smooth as glass, the great ship was moving through it fast, obviously making up for time lost during the night. Mr. Botibol turned away and sat slowly down on the edge of his bunk. A fine electricity of fear was beginning to prickle under the skin of his stomach. He hadn't a hope now. One of the higher numbers was certain to win it after this.

"Oh, my God," he said aloud. "What shall I do?"

What, for example, would Ethel say? It was simply not possible to tell her that he had spent almost all of their two years' savings on a ticket in the ship's pool. Nor was it possible to keep the matter secret. To do that he would have to tell her to stop drawing cheques. And what about the monthly instalments on the television set and the *Encyclopaedia Britannica?* Already he could see the anger and contempt in the woman's eyes, the blue becoming grey and the eyes themselves narrowing as they always did when there was anger in them.

"Oh, my God. What *shall* I do?"

There was no point in pretending that he had the slightest chance now —not unless the goddam ship started to go backwards. They'd have to put her in reverse and go full speed astern and keep right on going if he was to have any chance of winning it now. Well, maybe he should ask the captain to do just that. Offer him ten per cent of the profits. Offer him more if he wanted it. Mr. Botibol started to giggle. Then very suddenly he stopped, his eyes and mouth both opening wide in a kind of shocked surprise. For it was at this moment that the idea came. It hit him hard and quick, and he jumped up from his bed, terribly excited, ran over to the porthole and looked out again. Well, he thought, why not? Why ever not? The sea was calm and he wouldn't have any trouble keeping afloat until they picked him up. He had a vague feeling that someone had done this thing before, but that didn't prevent him from doing it again. The ship would have to stop and lower a boat, and the boat would have to go back maybe half a mile to get him, and then it would have to return to the ship, the whole thing. An hour was about thirty miles. It would knock thirty miles off the day's run. That would do it. "Low field" would be sure to win it then. Just so long as he made certain someone saw him falling over; but that would be simple to arrange. And he'd better wear light clothes, something easy to swim in. Sports clothes, that was it. He would dress as though he were going up to play some deck tennis—just a shirt and a pair of shorts and tennis-shoes. And leave his watch behind. What was the time? Nine-fifteen. The sooner the better, then. Do it now and get it over with. Have to do it soon, because the time limit was midday.

Mr. Botibol was both frightened and excited when he stepped out on to the sun deck in his sports clothes. His small body was wide at the hips, tapering upward to extremely narrow sloping shoulders, so that it resembled, in shape at any rate, a bollard. His white skinny legs were covered with black hairs, and he came cautiously out on deck, treading softly in his tennis shoes. Nervously he looked around him. There was only one other person in sight, an elderly woman with very thick ankles and immense buttocks who was leaning over the rail staring at the sea. She was wearing a coat of Persian lamb and the collar was turned up so Mr. Botibol couldn't see her face.

He stood still, examining her carefully from a distance. Yes, he told himself, she would probably do. She would probably give the alarm just as quickly as anyone else. But wait one minute, take your time, William Botibol, take your time. Remember what you told yourself a few minutes ago in the cabin when you were changing? You remember that?

The thought of leaping off a ship into the ocean a thousand miles from the nearest land had made Mr. Botibol—a cautious man at the best of times—unusually advertent. He was by no means satisfied yet that this woman he saw before him was *absolutely certain* to give the alarm when he made his jump. In his opinion there were two possible reasons why she might fail him. Firstly, she might be deaf and blind. It was not very probable, but on the other hand it *might* be so, and why take a chance? All he had to do was check it by talking to her for a moment beforehand. Secondly—and this will demonstrate how suspicious the mind of a man can become when it is working through self-preservation and fear—secondly, it had occurred to him that the woman might herself be the owner of one of the high numbers in the pool and as such would have a sound financial reason for not wishing to stop the ship. Mr. Botibol recalled that people had killed their fellows for far less than six thousand dollars. It was happening every day in the newspapers. So why take a chance on that either? Check on it first. Be sure of your facts. Find out about it by a little polite conversation. Then, provided that the woman appeared also to be a pleasant, kindly human being, the thing was a cinch and he could leap overboard with a light heart.

Mr. Botibol advanced casually towards the woman and took up a position beside her, leaning on the rail. "Hullo," he said pleasantly.

She turned and smiled at him, a surprisingly lovely, almost a beautiful smile, although the face itself was very plain. "Hullo," she answered him.

Check, Mr. Botibol told himself, on the first question. She is neither blind nor deaf. "Tell me," he said, coming straight to the point, "what did you think of the auction last night?"

"Auction?" she asked, frowning. "Auction? What auction?"

"You know, that silly old thing they have in the lounge after dinner, selling numbers on the ship's daily run. I just wondered what you thought about it."

She shook her head, and again she smiled, a sweet and pleasant smile that had in it perhaps the trace of an apology. "I'm very lazy," she said. "I always go to bed early. I have my dinner in bed. It's so restful to have dinner in bed."

Mr. Botibol smiled back at her and began to edge away. "Got to go and get my exercise now," he said. "Never miss my exercise in the morning. It was nice seeing you. Very nice seeing you . . ." He retreated about ten paces, and the woman let him go without looking around.

Everything was now in order. The sea was calm, he was lightly dressed for swimming, there were almost certainly no man-eating sharks in this part of the Atlantic, and there was this pleasant kindly old woman to give the alarm. It was a question now only of whether the ship would be delayed long enough to swing the balance in his favour. Almost certainly it would. In any event, he could do a little to help in that direction himself. He could make a few difficulties about getting hauled up into the lifeboat. Swim around a bit, back away from them surreptitiously as they tried to come up close to fish him out. Every minute, every second gained would help him win. He began to move forward again to the rail, but now a new fear assailed him. Would he get caught in the propeller? He had heard about that happening to persons falling off the sides of big ships. But then, he wasn't going to fall, he was going to jump, and that was a very different thing. Provided he jumped out far enough he would be sure to clear the propeller.

Mr. Botibol advanced slowly to a position at the rail about twenty yards away from the woman. She wasn't looking at him now. So much the better. He didn't want her watching him as he jumped off. So long as no one was watching he would be able to say afterwards that he had slipped and fallen by accident. He peered over the side of the ship. It was a long, long drop. Come to think of it now, he might easily hurt himself badly if he hit the water flat. Wasn't there someone who once split his stomach open that way, doing a belly flop from the high dive? He must jump straight and land feet first. Go in like a knife. Yes, sir. The water seemed cold and deep and grey and it made him shiver to look at it. But it was now or never. Be a man, William Botibol, be a man. All right then . . . now . . . here goes. . . .

He climbed up on to the wide wooden top-rail, stood there poised, balancing for three terrifying seconds, then he leaped—he leaped up and out as far as he could go and at the same time he shouted *"Help!"*

"Help! Help!" he shouted as he fell. Then he hit the water and went under.

When the first shout for help sounded, the woman who was leaning on the rail started up and gave a little jump of surprise. She looked around quickly and saw sailing past her through the air this small man dressed in white shorts and tennis shoes, spreadeagled and shouting as he went. For a moment she looked as though she weren't quite sure what she ought to do: throw a lifebelt, run away and give the alarm, or simply turn and yell. She drew back a pace from the rail and swung half around facing up to the bridge, and for this brief moment she remained motionless, tense, undecided. Then almost at once she seemed to relax, and she leaned forward far over the rail, staring at the water where it was turbulent in the ship's wake. Soon a tiny round black head appeared in the foam, an arm was raised above it, once, twice, vigorously waving, and a small faraway voice was heard calling something that was difficult to understand. The woman leaned still farther over the rail, trying to keep the little bobbing black speck in sight, but soon, so very soon, it was such a long way away that she couldn't even be sure it was there at all.

After a while another woman came out on deck. This one was bony and angular, and she wore horn-rimmed spectacles. She spotted the first woman and walked over to her, treading the deck in the deliberate, military fashion of all spinsters.

"So *there* you are," she said.

The woman with the fat ankles turned and looked at her, but said nothing.

"I've been searching for you," the bony one continued. "Searching all over."

"It's very odd," the woman with the fat ankles said. "A man dived overboard just now, with his clothes on."

"Nonsense!"

"Oh yes. He said he wanted to get some exercise and he dived in and didn't even bother to take his clothes off."

"You better come down now," the bony woman said. Her mouth had suddenly become firm, her whole face sharp and alert, and she spoke less kindly than before. "And don't you ever go wandering about on deck alone like this again. You know quite well you're meant to wait for me."

"Yes, Maggie," the woman with the fat ankles answered, and again she smiled, a tender, trusting smile, and she took the hand of the other one and allowed herself to be led away across the deck.

"Such a nice man," she said. "He waved to me."

The Night Ocean

Robert H. Barlow

I WENT TO ELLSTON BEACH not only for the pleasures of sun and ocean, but to rest a weary mind. Since I knew no person in the little town, which thrives on summer vacationists and presents only blank windows during most of the year, there seemed no likelihood that I might be disturbed. This pleased me, for I did not wish to see anything but the expanse of pounding surf and the beach lying before my temporary home.

My long work of the summer was completed when I left the city, and the large mural design produced by it had been entered in the contest. It had taken me the bulk of the year to finish the painting, and when the last brush was cleaned I was no longer reluctant to yield to the claims of health and find rest and seclusion for a time. Indeed, when I had been a week on the beach I recalled only now and then the work whose success had so recently seemed all-important. There was no longer the old concern with a hundred complexities of colour and ornament; no longer the fear and mistrust of my ability to render a mental image actual, and turn by my own skill alone the dim-conceived idea into the careful draught of a design. And yet that which later befell me by the lonely shore may have grown solely from the mental constitution behind such concern and fear and mistrust. For I have always been a seeker, a dreamer, and a ponderer on seeking and dreaming; and who can say that such a nature does not open latent eyes sensitive to unsuspected worlds and orders of being?

Now that I am trying to tell what I saw I am conscious of a thousand maddening limitations. Things seen by the inward sight, like those flashing visions which come as we drift into the blankness of sleep, are more vivid and meaningful to us in that form than when we have sought to weld them with reality. Set a pen to a dream, and the colour drains from it. The ink with which we write seems diluted with something holding too much of reality, and we find that after all we cannot delineate the incredible memory. It is as if our inward selves, released from the bonds of daytime and objectivity, revelled in prisoned emotions which are hastily stifled when we translate them. In dreams and visions lie the greatest creations of man, for on them rests no yoke of line or hue. Forgotten scenes, and lands more obscure than the golden world of childhood, spring into the sleeping mind to reign until awakening puts them to rout. Amid these may be attained something of the glory and contentment for which we yearn; some image of sharp beauties suspected but not before revealed, which are to us as the Grail to holy spirits of the medieval world. To shape these things on the wheel of art, to seek to bring some faded trophy from that intangible realm of shadow and gossamer, requires equal skill and memory. For although dreams are in all of us, few hands may grasp their moth-wings without tearing them.

Such skill this narrative does not have. If I might, I would reveal to you the hinted events which I perceived dimly, like one who peers into an unlit realm and glimpses forms whose motion is concealed. In my mural design, which then lay with a multitude of others in the building for which they were planned, I had striven equally to catch a trace of this elusive shadow-world, and had perhaps succeeded better than I shall now succeed. My stay in Ellston was to await the judging of that design; and when days of unfamiliar leisure had given me perspective, I discovered that—in spite of those weaknesses which a creator always detects most clearly—I had indeed managed to retain in line and colour some fragments snatched from the endless world of imagining. The difficulties of the process, and the resulting strain on all my powers, had undermined my health and brought me to the beach during this period of waiting. Since I wished to be wholly alone, I rented (to the delight of the incredulous owner) a small house some distance from the village of Ellston—which, because of the waning season, was alive with a moribund bustle of tourists, uniformly uninteresting to me. The house, dark from the sea-wind though it had not been painted, was not even a satellite of the village; but swung below it on the coast like a pendulum beneath a still clock, quite alone upon a hill of weed-grown sand. Like a solitary warm animal it crouched facing the sea, and its inscrutable dirty windows stared upon a lonely realm of earth and sky and enormous sea. It will not do to use too much imagining in a narrative whose facts, could they be augmented and fitted into a mosaic, would be strange enough in themselves; but I thought the little house was lonely when I saw it, and that like myself, it was conscious of its meaningless nature before the great sea.

I took the place in late August, arriving a day before I was expected, and encountering a van and two workingmen unloading the furniture provided by the owner. I did not know then how long I would stay, and when the truck that brought the goods had left I settled my small luggage and locked the door (feeling very proprietary about having a house after months of a rented room) to go down the weedy hill and on the beach. Since it was quite square and had but one room, the house required little exploration. Two windows in each side provided a great quantity of light, and somehow a door had been squeezed in as an after-thought on the oceanward wall. The place had been built about ten years previously, but on account of its distance from Ellston village was difficult to rent even during the active summer season. There being no fireplace, it stood empty and alone from October until far into the spring. Though actually less than a mile below Ellston, it seemed more remote; since a bend in the coast caused one to see only grassy dunes in the direction of the village.

The first day, half-gone when I was installed, I spent in the enjoyment of sun and restless water—things whose quiet majesty made the designing of murals seem distant and tiresome. But this was the natural reaction to a long concern with one set of habits and activities. I was through with my work and my vacation was begun. This fact, while elusive for the moment, showed in everything which surrounded me that afternoon of my arrival, and in the utter change from old scenes. There was an effect of bright sun upon a shifting sea of waves whose mysteriously impelled curves were strewn with what appeared to be rhinestone. Perhaps a watercolour might have caught the solid masses of intolerable light which lay upon the beach where the sea mingled with the sand. Although the ocean bore her own hue, it was dominated wholly and incredibly by the enormous glare. There was no other person near me, and I enjoyed the spectacle without the annoyance of any alien object upon the stage. Each of my senses was touched in a different way, but sometimes it seemed that the roar of the sea was akin to that great brightness, or as if the waves were glaring instead of the sun, each of these being so vigorous and insistent that impressions coming from them were mingled. Curiously, I saw no one bathing near my little square house during that or succeeding afternoons, although the curving shore included a wide beach even more inviting than that at the village, where the surf was dotted with random figures. I supposed that this was because of the distance and because there had never been other houses below the town. Why this unbuilt stretch existed, I could not imagine; since many dwellings straggled along the northward coast, facing the sea with aimless eyes.

I swam until the afternoon had gone, and later, having rested, walked into the little town. Darkness hid the sea from me as I entered, and I found in the dingy lights of the streets tokens of a life which was not even conscious of the great, gloom-shrouded thing lying so close. There were painted women in tinsel adornments, and bored men who were no longer young—a throng of foolish marionettes perched on the lip of the ocean-chasm; unseeing, unwilling to see what lay above them and about, in the multitudinous grandeur of the stars and the leagues of the night ocean. I walked along that darkened sea as I went back to the bare little house, sending the beams of my flashlight out upon the naked and impenetrable void. In the absence of the moon, this light made a solid bar athwart the walls of the uneasy tide; and I felt an indescribable emotion born of the noise of the waters and the perception of my smallness as I cast that tiny beam upon a realm immense in itself, yet only the black border of the earthly deep. That nighted deep, upon which ships were moving alone in the darkness where I could not see them, gave off the murmur of a distant, angry rabble.

When I reached my high residence I knew that I had passed no one during the mile's walk from the village, and yet there somehow lingered an impression that I had been all the while accompanied by the spirit of the lonely sea. It was, I thought, personified in a shape which was not revealed to me, but which moved quietly about beyond my range of comprehension. It was like those actors who wait behind darkened scenery in readiness for the lines which will shortly call them before our eyes to move and speak in the sudden revelation of the footlights. At last I shook off this fancy and sought my key to enter the place, whose bare walls gave a sudden feeling of security.

My cottage was entirely free of the village, as if it had wandered down the coast and was unable to return; and there I heard nothing of the disturbing clamour when I returned each night after supper. I generally stayed but a short while upon the streets of Ellston, though sometimes I went into the place for the sake of the walk it provided. There were all the multitude of curio-shops and falsely regal theatre fronts that clutter vacation towns, but I never went into these; and the place seemed useful only for its restaurants. It was astonishing the number of useless things people found to do.

There was a succession of sun-filled days at first. I rose early, and beheld the grey sky agleam with promise of sunrise; a prophecy fulfilled as I stood witness. Those dawns were cold and their colours faint in comparison to that uniform radiance of day which gives to every hour the quality of white noon. That great light, so apparent the first day, made each succeeding day a yellow page in the book of time. I noticed that many of the beach people were displeased by the inordinate sun, whereas I sought it. After grey months of toil the lethargy induced by a physical existence in a region governed by the simple things—the wind and light and water— had a prompt effect upon me, and since I was anxious to continue this healing process, I spent all my time outdoors in the sunlight. This induced a state at once impassive and submissive, and gave me a feeling of security against the ravenous night. As darkness is akin to death, so is light to vitality. Through the heritage of a million years ago, when men were closer to the mother sea, and when the creatures of which we are born lay languid in the shallow, sun-pierced water; we still seek today the primal things when we are tired, steeping ourselves within their lulling security like those early half-mammals which had not yet ventured upon the oozy land.

The monotony of the waves gave repose, and I had no other occupation than witnessing a myriad ocean moods. There is a ceaseless change in the waters—colours and shades pass over them like the insubstantial expressions of a well-known face; and these are at once communicated to us by half-recognized senses. When the sea is restless, remembering old ships that have gone over her chasms, there comes up silently in our hearts the longing for a vanished horizon. But when she forgets, we forget also. Though we know her a lifetime, she must always hold an alien air, as if something too vast to have shape were lurking in the universe to which she is a door. The morning ocean, glimmering with a reflected mist of blue-white cloud and expanding diamond foam, has the eyes of one who ponders on strange things; and her intricately woven webs, through which dart a myriad of coloured fishes, hold the air of some great idle thing which will arise presently from the hoary immemorial chasms and stride upon the land.

I was content for many days, and glad that I had chosen the lonely house which sat like a small beast upon those rounded cliffs of sand. Among the pleasantly aimless amusements fostered by such a life, I took to following the edge of the tide (where the waves left a damp, irregular outline rimmed with evanescent foam) for long distances; and sometimes I found curious bits of shell in the chance litter of the sea. There was an astonishing lot of debris on that inward-curving coast which my bare little house overlooked, and I judged that currents whose courses diverge from the village beach must reach that spot. At any rate, my pockets—when I had any—generally held vast stores of trash; most of which I threw away an hour or two after picking it up, wondering why I had kept it. Once, however, I found a small bone whose nature I could not identify, save that it was certainly nothing out of a fish; and I kept this, along with a large metal bead whose minutely carven design was rather unusual. This latter depicted a fishy thing against a patterned background of seaweed instead of the usual floral or geometrical designs, and was still clearly traceable though worn with years of tossing in the surf. Since I had never seen anything like it, I judged that it represented some fashion, now forgotten, of a previous year at Ellston, where similar fads were common.

I had been there perhaps a week when the weather began a gradual change. Each stage of this progressive darkening was followed by another subtly intensified, so that in the end the entire atmosphere surrounding me had shifted from day to evening. This was more obvious to me in a series of mental impressions than in what I actually witnessed, for the small house was lonely under the grey skies, and there was sometimes a beating wind that came out of the ocean bearing moisture. The sun was displaced by long intervals of cloudiness—layers of grey mist beyond whose unknown depth the sun lay cut off. Though it might glare with the old intensity above that enormous veil, it could not penetrate. The beach was a prisoner in a hueless vault for hours at a time, as if something of the night were welling into other hours.

Although the wind was invigorating and the ocean whipped into little churning spirals of activity by the vagrant flapping, I found the water growing chill, so that I could not stay in it as long as I had done previously, and thus I fell into the habit of long walks, which—when I was unable to swim—provided the exercise that I was so careful to obtain. These walks covered a greater range of sea-edge than my previous wanderings, and since the beach extended in a stretch of miles beyond the tawdry village, I often found myself wholly isolated upon an endless area of sand as evening drew close. When this occurred, I would stride hastily along the whispering sea-border, following the outline so that I should not wander inland and lose my way. And sometimes, when these walks were late (as they grew increasingly to be) I would come upon the crouching house that looked like a harbinger of the village. Insecure upon the wind-gnawed cliffs, a dark blot upon the morbid hues of the ocean sunset, it was more lonely than by the full light of either orb; and seemed to my imagination like a mute, questioning face turned toward me expectant of some action. That the place was isolated I have said, and this at first pleased me; but in that brief evening hour when the sun left a gore-splattered decline and darkness lumbered on like an expanding shapeless blot, there was an alien presence about the place: a spirit, a mood, an impression that came from the surging wind, the gigantic sky, and that sea which drooled blackening waves upon a beach grown abruptly strange. At these times I felt an uneasiness which had no very definite cause, although my solitary nature had made me long accustomed to the ancient silence and the ancient voice of nature. These misgivings, to which I could have put no sure name, did not affect me long, yet I think now that all the while a gradual consciousness of the ocean's immense loneliness crept upon me, a loneliness that was made subtly horrible by intimations—which were never more than such—of some animation or sentience preventing me from being wholly alone.

The noisy, yellow streets of the town, with their curiously unreal activity, were very far away, and when I went there for my evening meal (mistrusting a diet entirely of my own ambiguous cooking) I took increasing and quite unreasonable care that I should return to the cottage before the late darkness, though I was often abroad until ten or so. You will say that such action is unreasonable; that if I had feared the darkness in some childish way, I would have entirely avoided it. You will ask me why I did not leave the place since its loneliness was depressing me. To all this I have no reply, save that whatever unrest I felt, whatever of remote disturbance there was to me in brief aspects of the darkening sun or the eager salt-brittle wind or in the robe of the dark sea that lay crumpled like an enormous garment so close to me, was something which had an origin half in my own heart, which showed itself only at fleeting moments, and which had no very long effect upon me. In the recurrent days of diamond light, with sportive waves flinging blue peaks at the basking shore, the memory of dark moods seemed rather incredible, yet only an hour or two afterward I might again experience these moods once more, and descend to a dim region of despair.

Perhaps these inward emotions were only a reflection of the sea's own mood, for although half of what we see is coloured by the interpretation placed upon it by our minds, many of our feelings are shaped quite distinctly by external, physical things. The sea can bind us to her many moods, whispering to us by the subtle token of a shadow or a gleam upon the waves, and hinting in these ways of her mournfulness or rejoicing. Always she is remembering old things, and these memories, though we may not grasp them, are imparted to us, so that we share her gaiety or remorse. Since I was doing no work, seeing no person that I knew, I was perhaps susceptible to shades of her cryptic meaning which would have been overlooked by another. The ocean ruled my life during the whole of that late summer; demanding it as recompense for the healing she had brought me.

There were drownings at the beach that year; and while I heard of these only casually (such is our indifference to a death which does not concern us, and to which we are not witness), I knew that their details were unsavoury. The people who died—some of them swimmers of a skill beyond the average—were sometimes not found until many days had elapsed, and the hideous vengeance of the deep had scourged their rotten bodies. It was as if the sea had dragged them into a chasm-lair, and had mulled them about in the darkness until, satisfied that they were no longer of any use, she had floated them ashore in a ghastly state. No one seemed to know what had caused these deaths. Their frequency excited alarm among the timid, since the undertow at Ellston was not strong, and since there were known to be no sharks at hand. Whether the bodies showed marks of any attacks I did not learn, but the dread of a death which moves among the waves and comes on lone people from a lightless, motionless place is a dread which men know and do not like. They must quickly find a reason for such a death, even if there are no sharks. Since sharks formed only a suspected cause, and one never to my knowledge confirmed, the swimmers who continued during the rest of the season were on guard against treacherous tides rather than against any possible sea-animal. Autumn, indeed, was not a great distance off, and some people used this as an excuse for leaving the sea, where men were snared by death, and going to the security of inland fields, where one cannot even hear the ocean. So August ended, and I had been at the beach many days.

There had been a threat of storm since the fourth of the new month, and on the sixth, when I set out for a walk in the damp wind, there was a mass of formless cloud, colourless and oppressive, above the ruffled leaden sea. The motion of the wind, directed toward no especial goal but stirring uneasily, provided a sensation of coming animation—a hint of life in the elements which might be the long-expected storm. I had eaten my luncheon at Ellston, and though the heavens seemed the closing lid of a great casket, I ventured far down the beach and away from both the town and my no-longer-to-be-seen house. As the universal grey became spotted with a carrion purple—curiously brilliant despite its sombre hue—I found that I was several miles from any possible shelter. This, however, did not seem very important, for despite the dark skies with their added glow of unknown presage I was in a curious mood that flashed through a body grown suddenly alert and sensitive to the outline of shapes and meanings that were previously dim. Obscurely, a memory came to me; suggested by the likeness of the scene to one I had imagined when a story was read to me in childhood. That tale—of which I had not thought for many years—concerned a woman who was loved by the dark-bearded king of an underwater realm of blurred cliffs where fish-things lived; and who was taken from the golden-haired youth of her troth by a dark being crowned with a priest-like mitre and having the features of a withered ape. What had remained in the corner of my fancy was the image of cliffs beneath the water against the hueless, dusky no-sky of such a realm; and this, though I had forgotten most of the story, was recalled quite unexpectedly by the same pattern of cliff and sky which I then beheld. The sight was similar to what I had imagined in a year now lost save for random, incomplete impressions. Suggestions of this story may have lingered behind certain irritating unfinished memories, and in certain values hinted to my senses by scenes whose actual worth was bafflingly small. Frequently, in a momentary perception, we feel that a feathery landscape (for instance), a woman's dress along the curve of a road by afternoon, or the solidity of a century-defying tree against the pale morning sky (the conditions more than the object being significant) hold something precious, some golden virtue that we must grasp. And yet when such a scene or arrangement is viewed later, or from another point, we find that it has lost its value and meaning for us. Perhaps this is because the thing we see does not hold that elusive quality, but only suggests to the mind some very different thing which remains unremembered. The baffled mind, not wholly sensing the cause of its flashing appreciation, seizes on the object exciting it, and is surprised when there is nothing of worth therein. Thus it was when I beheld the purpling clouds. They held the stateliness and mystery of old monastery towers at twilight, but their aspect was also that of the cliffs in the old fairy-tale. Suddenly reminded of this lost image, I half expected to see, in the fine-spun dirty foam and among the waves which were now as if they had been poured of flawed black glass, the horrid figure of that ape-faced creature, wearing a mitre old with verdigris, advancing from its kingdom in some lost gulf to which those waves were sky.

I did not see any such creature from the realm of imagining, but as the chill wind veered, slitting the heavens like a rustling knife, there lay in the gloom of merging cloud and water only a grey object, like a piece of driftwood, tossing obscurely on the foam. This was a considerable distance out, and since it vanished shortly, may not have been wood, but a porpoise coming to the troubled surface.

I soon found that I had stayed too long contemplating the rising storm and linking my early fancies with its grandeur, for an icy rain began spotting down, bringing a more uniform gloom upon a scene already too dark for the hour. Hurrying along the grey sand, I felt the impact of cold drops upon my back, and before many moments my clothing was soaked throughout. At first I had run, put to flight by the colourless drops whose pattern hung in long linking strands from an unseen sky; but after I saw that refuge was too far to reach in anything like a dry state, I slackened my pace, and returned home as if I had walked under clear skies. There was not much reason to hurry, although I did not idle as upon previous occasions. The constraining wet garments were cold upon me, and with the gathering darkness, and the wind that rose endlessly from the ocean, I could not repress a shiver. Yet there was, beside the discomfort of the precipitous rain, an exhilaration latent in the purplish ravelled masses of cloud and the stimulated reactions of the body. In a mood half of exultant pleasure from resisting the rain (which streamed from me now, and filled my shoes and pockets) and half of strange appreciation of those morbid, dominant skies which hovered with dark wings above the shifting eternal sea, I tramped along the grey corridor of Ellston Beach. More rapidly than I had expected the crouching house showed in the oblique, flapping rain, and all the weeds of the sand cliff writhed in accompaniment to the frantic wind, as if they would uproot themselves to join the far-travelling element. Sea and sky had altered not at all, and the scene was that which had accompanied me, save that there was now painted upon it the hunching roof that seemed to bend from the assailing rain. I hurried up the insecure steps, and let myself into a dry room, where, unconsciously surprised that I was free of the nagging wind, I stood for a moment with water rilling from every inch of me.

There are two windows in the front of that house, one on each side, and these face nearly straight upon the ocean; which I now saw half obscured by the combined veils of the rain and the imminent night. From these windows I looked as I dressed myself in a motley array of dry garments seized from convenient hangers and from a chair too laden to sit upon. I was prisoned on all sides by an unnaturally increased dusk which had filtered down at some undefined hour under cover of the fostering storm. How long I had been on the reaches of wet grey sand, or what the real time was, I could not tell, though a moment's search produced my watch—fortunately left behind and thus avoiding the uniform wetness of my clothing. I half guessed the hour from the dimly seen hands, which were only slightly less indecipherable than the surrounding figures. In another moment my sight penetrated the gloom (greater in the house than beyond the bleared window) and saw that it was 6:45.

There had been no one upon the beach as I came in, and naturally I expected to see no further swimmers that night. Yet when I looked again from the window there appeared surely to be figures blotting the grime of the wet evening. I counted three moving about in some incomprehensible manner, and close to the house another—which may not have been a person but a wave-ejected log, for the surf was now pounding fiercely. I was startled to no little degree, and wondered for what purpose those hardy persons stayed out in such a storm. And then I thought that perhaps like myself they had been caught unintentionally in the rain and had surrendered to the watery gusts. In another moment, prompted by a certain civilized hospitality which overcame my love of solitude, I stepped to the door and emerged momentarily (at the cost of another wetting, for the rain promptly descended upon me in exultant fury) on the small porch, gesticulating toward the people. But whether they did not see me, or did not understand, they made no returning signal. Dim in the evening, they stood as if half-surprised, or as if they awaited some other action from me. There was in their attitude something of that cryptic blankness, signifying anything or nothing, which the house wore about itself as seen in the morbid sunset. Abruptly there came to me a feeling that a sinister quality lurked about those unmoving figures who chose to stay in the rainy night upon a beach deserted by all people, and I closed the door with a surge of annoyance which sought all too vainly to disguise a deeper emotion of fear; a consuming fright that welled up from the shadows of my consciousness. A moment later, when I had stepped to the window, there seemed to be nothing outside but the portentous night. Vaguely puzzled, and even more vaguely frightened—like one who has seen no alarming thing, but is apprehensive of what may be found in the dark street he is soon compelled to cross—I decided that I had very possibly seen no one; and that the murky air had deceived me.

The aura of isolation about the place increased that night, though just out of sight on the northward beach a hundred houses rose in the rainy darkness, their light bleared and yellow above streets of polished glass, like goblin-eyes reflected in an oily forest pool. Yet because I could not see them, or even reach them in bad weather—since I had no car nor any way to leave the crouching house except by walking in the figure-haunted darkness—I realized quite suddenly that I was, to all intents, alone with the dreary sea that rose and subsided unseen, unkenned, in the mist. And the voice of the sea had become a hoarse groan, like that of something wounded which shifts about before trying to rise.

Fighting away the prevalent gloom with a soiled lamp—for the darkness crept in at my windows and sat peering obscurely at me from the corners like a patient animal—I prepared my food, since I had no intentions of going to the village. The hour seemed incredibly advanced, though it was not yet nine o'clock when I went to bed. Darkness had come early and furtively, and throughout the remainder of my stay lingered evasively over each scene and action which I beheld. Something had settled out of the night—something forever undefined, but stirring a latent sense within me, so that I was like a beast expecting the momentary rustle of an enemy.

There were hours of wind, and sheets of the downpour flapped endlessly on the meagre walls barring it from me. Lulls came in which I heard the mumbling sea, and I could guess that large formless waves jostled one another in the pallid whine of the winds, and flung on the beach a spray bitter with salt. Yet in the very monotony of the restless elements I found a lethargic note, a sound that beguiled me, after a time, into slumber grey and colourless as the night. The sea continued its mad monologue, and the wind her nagging; but these were shut out by the walls of unconsciousness, and for a time the night ocean was banished from a sleeping mind.

Morning brought an enfeebled sun—a sun like that which men will see when the earth is old, if there are any men left; a sun more weary than the shrouded, moribund sky. Faint echo of its old image, Phoebus strove to pierce the ragged, ambiguous clouds as I awoke, at moments sending a wash of pale gold rippling across the northwestern interior of my house, at others waning till it was only a luminous ball, like some incredible plaything forgotten on the celestial lawn. After a while the falling rain— which must have continued throughout the previous night—succeeded in washing away those vestiges of purple cloud which had been like the ocean cliffs in an old fairy-tale. Cheated alike of the setting and rising sun, that day merged with the day before, as if the intervening storm had not ushered a long darkness into the world, but had swollen and subsided into one long afternoon. Gaining heart, the furtive sun exerted all his force in dispelling the old mist, streaked now like a dirty window, and cast it from his realm. The shallow blue day advanced as those grimy wisps retreated, and the loneliness which had encircled me welled back into a watchful place of retreat, whence it went no farther, but crouched and waited.

The ancient brightness was now once more upon the sun, and the old glitter on the waves, whose playful blue shapes had flocked upon that coast ere man was born, and would rejoice unseen when he was forgotten in the sepulchre of time. Influenced by these thin assurances, like one who believes the smile of friendship on an enemy's features, I opened my door, and as it swung outward, a black spot upon the inward burst of light, I saw the beach washed clean of any track, as if no foot before mine had disturbed the smooth sand. With the quick lift of spirit that follows a period of uneasy depression, I felt—in a purely yielding fashion and without volition—that my own memory was washed clean of all the mistrust and suspicion and disease-like fear of a lifetime, just as the filth of the water's edge succumbs to a particularly high tide and is carried out of sight. There was a scent of soaked, brackish grass, like the mouldy pages of a book, commingled with a sweet odour born of the hot sunlight upon inland meadows, and these were borne into me like an exhilarating drink, seeping and tingling through my veins as if they would convey to me something of their own impalpable nature, and float me dizzily in the aimless breeze. And conspiring with these things, the sun continued to shower upon me, like the rain of yesterday, an incessant array of bright spears; as if it also wished to hide that suspected background presence which moved beyond my sight and was betrayed only by a careless rustle on the borders of my consciousness, or by the aspect of blank figures staring out of an ocean void. That sun, a fierce ball solitary in the whirl-pool of infinity, was like a horde of golden moths against my upturned face. A bubbling white grail of fire divine and incomprehensible, it with-held from me a thousand promised mirages where it granted one. For the sun did actually seem to indicate realms, secure and fanciful, where if I but knew the path I might wander in this curious exultation. Such things come of our own natures, for life has never yielded for one moment her secrets, and it is only in our interpretation of their hinted images that we may find ecstasy or dullness, according to a deliberately induced mood. Yet ever and again we must succumb to her deceptions, believing for the moment that we may this time find the withheld joy. And in this way the fresh sweetness of the wind, on a morning following the haunted darkness (whole evil intimations had given me a greater uneasiness than any menace to my body), whispered to me of ancient mysteries only half-linked with earth, and of pleasures that were the sharper because I felt that I might experience only a part of them. The sun and wind and that scent that rose upon them told me of festivals of gods whose senses are a millionfold more poignant than man's and whose joys are a millionfold more subtle and prolonged. These things, they hinted, could be mine if I gave myself wholly into their bright deceptive power; and the sun, a crouching god with naked celestial flesh, an unknown, too-mighty furnace upon which no eye might look, seemed almost sacred in the glow of my newly sharpened emotions. The ethereal thunderous light it gave was something before which all things must worship astonished. The slinking leopard in his green-chasmed forest must have paused briefly to consider its leaf-scattered rays, and all things nurtured by it must have cherished its bright message on such a day. For when it is absent in the far reaches of eternity, earth will be lost and black against an illimitable void. That morning, in which I shared the fire of life, and whose brief moment of pleasure is secure against the ravenous years, was astir with the beckoning of strange things whose elusive names can never be written.

As I made my way toward the village, wondering how it might look after a long-needed scrubbing by the industrious rain, I saw, tangled in a glimmer of sunlit moisture that was poured over it like a yellow vintage, a small object like a hand, some twenty feet ahead of me, and touched by the repetitious foam. The shock and disgust born in my startled mind when I saw that it was indeed a piece of rotten flesh overcame my new contentment, and engendered a shocked suspicion that it might actually be a hand. Certainly, no fish, or part of one, could assume that look, and I thought I saw mushy fingers wed in decay. I turned the thing over with my foot, not wishing to touch so foul an object, and it adhered stickily to the leather of the shoe, as if clutching with the grasp of corruption. The thing, whose shape was nearly lost, held too much resemblance to what I feared it might be, and I pushed it into the willing grasp of a seething wave, which took it from sight with an alacrity not often shown by those ravelled edges of the sea.

Perhaps I should have reported my find, yet its nature was too ambiguous to make action natural. Since it had been partly *eaten* by some ocean-dwelling monstrousness, I did not think it identifiable enough to form evidence of an unknown but possible tragedy. The numerous drownings, of course, came into my mind—as well as other things lacking in wholesomeness, some of which remained only as possibilities. Whatever the storm-dislodged fragment may have been, and whether it were fish or some animal akin to man, I have never spoken of it until now. And after all, there was no proof that it had not merely been distorted by rottenness into that shape.

I approached the town, sickened by the presence of such an object amid the apparent beauty of the clean beach, though it was horribly typical of the indifference of death in a nature which mingles rottenness with beauty, and perhaps loves the former more. In Ellston I heard of no recent drowning or other mishap of the sea, and found no reference to such in the columns of the local paper—the only one I read during my stay.

It is difficult to describe the mental state in which succeeding days found me. Always susceptible to morbid emotions whose dark anguish might be induced by things outside myself, or might spring from the abysses of my own spirit, I was ridden by a feeling which was not fear or despair, or anything akin to these, but was rather a perception of the brief hideousness and underlying filth of life—a feeling partly a reflection of my internal nature and partly a result of broodings induced by that gnawed rotten object which may have been a hand. In those days my mind was a place of shadowed cliffs and dark moving figures, like the ancient unsuspected realm which the fairy-tale recalled to me. I felt, in brief agonies of disillusionment, the gigantic blackness of this overwhelming universe, in which my days and the days of my race were as nothing to the shattered stars; a universe in which each action is vain and even the emotion of grief a wasted thing. The hours I had previously spent in something of regained health, contentment, and physical well-being were given now (as if those days of the previous week were something definitely ended) to an indolence like that of a man who no longer cares to live. I was engulfed by a piteous lethargic fear of some ineluctable doom which would be, I felt, the completed hate of the peering stars and of the black enormous waves that hoped to clasp my bones within them—the vengeance of all the indifferent, horrendous majesty of the night ocean.

Something of the darkness and restlessness of the sea had penetrated my heart, so that I lived in an unreasoning, unperceiving torment; a torment none the less acute because of the subtlety of its origin and the strange, unmotivated quality of its vampiric existence. Before my eyes lay the phantasmagoria of the purpling clouds, the strange silver bauble, the recurrent stagnant foam, the loneliness of that bleak-eyed house, and the mockery of the puppet town. I no longer went to the village, for it seemed only a travesty of life. Like my own soul, it stood upon a dark enveloping sea—a sea grown slowly hateful to me. And among these images, corrupt and festering, dwelt that of an object whose human contours left ever smaller the doubt of what it once had been.

These scribbled words can never tell of the hideous loneliness (something I did not even wish assuaged, so deeply was it embedded in my heart) which had insinuated itself within me, mumbling of terrible and unknown things stealthily circling nearer. It was not a madness: rather was it a too clear and naked perception of the darkness beyond this frail existence, lit by a momentary sun no more secure than ourselves; a realization of futility that few can experience and ever again touch the life about them; a knowledge that turn as I might, battle as I might with all the remaining power of my spirit, I could neither win an inch of ground from the inimical universe, nor hold for even a moment the life entrusted to me. Fearing death as I did life, burdened with a nameless dread, yet unwilling to leave the scene evoking it, I awaited whatever consummating horror was shifting itself in the immense region beyond the walls of consciousness.

Thus autumn found me, and what I had gained from the sea was lost back into it. Autumn on the beaches—a drear time betokened by no scarlet leaf nor any other accustomed sign. A frightening sea which changes not, though man changes. There was only a chilling of the waters, in which I no longer cared to enter—a further darkening of the pall-like sky, as if eternities of snow were waiting to descend upon the ghastly waves. Once that descent began, it would never cease, but would continue beneath the white and the yellow and the crimson sun, and beneath that ultimate small ruby which shall yield only to the futilities of night. The once friendly waters babbled meaningfully at me, and eyed me with a strange regard, yet whether the darkness of the scene were a reflection of my own broodings or whether the gloom within me were caused by what lay without, I could not have told. Upon the beach and me alike had fallen a shadow, like that of a bird which flies silently overhead—a bird whose watching eyes we do not suspect till the image on the ground repeats the image in the sky, and we look suddenly upward to find that something has been circling above us hitherto unseen.

The day was in late September, and the town had closed the resorts where mad frivolity ruled empty, fear-haunted lives, and where raddled puppets performed their summer antics. The puppets were cast aside, smeared with the painted smiles and frowns they had last assumed, and there were not a hundred people left in the town. Again the gaudy, stucco-fronted buildings lining the shore were permitted to crumble undisturbed in the wind. As the month advanced to the day of which I speak, there grew in me the light of a grey infernal dawn, wherein I felt some dark thaumaturgy would be completed. Since I feared such a thaumaturgy less than a continuance of my horrible suspicions—less than the too-elusive hints of something monstrous lurking behind the great stage—it was with more speculation than actual fear that I waited unendingly for the day of horror which seemed to be nearing. The day, I repeat, was late in September, though whether the 22nd or 23rd I am uncertain. Such details have fled before the recollection of those uncompleted happenings—episodes with which no orderly existence should be plagued, because of the damnable suggestions (and only suggestions) they contain. I knew the time with an intuitive distress of spirit—a recognition too deep for me to explain. Throughout those daylight hours I was expectant of the night; impatient, perhaps, so that the sunlight passed like a half-glimpsed reflection in rippled water—a day of whose events I recall nothing.

It was long since that portentous storm had cast a shadow over the beach, and I had determined, after hesitations caused by nothing tangible, to leave Ellston, since the year was chilling and there was no return to my earlier contentment. When a telegram came for me (lying two days in the Western Union office before I was located, so little was my name known) saying that my design had been accepted—winning above all others in the contest—I set a date for leaving. This news, which earlier in the year would have affected me strongly, I now received with a curious apathy. It seemed as unrelated to the unreality about me, as little pertinent to me, as if it were directed to another person whom I did not know, and whose message had come to me through some accident. None the less, it was that which forced me to complete my plans and leave the cottage by the shore.

There were only four nights of my stay remaining when there occurred the last of those events whose meaning lies more in the darkly sinister impression surrounding them than in anything obviously threatening. Night had settled over Ellston and the coast, and a pile of soiled dishes attested both to my recent meal and to my lack of industry. Darkness came as I sat with a cigarette before the seaward window, and it was a liquid which gradually filled the sky, washing in a floating moon, monstrously elevated. The flat sea bordering upon the gleaming sand, the utter absence of tree or figure or life of any sort, and the regard of that high moon made the vastness of my surroundings abruptly clear. There were only a few stars pricking through, as if to accentuate by their smallness the majesty of the lunar orb and of the restless shifting tide.

I had stayed indoors, fearing somehow to go out before the sea on such a night of shapeless portent, but I heard it mumbling secrets of an incredible lore. Borne to me on a wind out of nowhere was the breath of some strange palpitant life—the embodiment of all I had felt and of all I had suspected—stirring now in the chasms of the sky or beneath the mute waves. In what place this mystery turned from an ancient, horrible slumber I could not tell, but like one who stands by a figure lost in sleep, knowing that it will awake in a moment, I crouched by the window, holding a nearly burnt-out cigarette, and faced the rising moon.

Gradually there passed into that never-stirring landscape a brilliance intensified by the overhead glimmerings, and I seemed more and more under some compulsion to watch whatever might follow. The shadows were draining from the beach, and I felt that with them were all which might have been a harbour for my thoughts when the hinted thing should come. Where any of them did remain they were ebon and blank: still lumps of darkness sprawling beneath the cruel brilliant rays. The endless tableau of the lunar orb—dead now, whatever her past was, and cold as the unhuman sepulchres she bears amid the ruin of dusty centuries older than men—and the sea—astir, perhaps, with some unkenned life, some forbidden sentience—confronted me with a horrible vividness. I arose and shut the window; partly because of an inward prompting, but mostly, I think, as an excuse for transferring momentarily the stream of thought. No sound came to me now as I stood before the closed panes. Minutes or eternities were alike. I was waiting, like my own fearing heart and the motionless scene beyond, for the token of some ineffable life. I had set the lamp upon a box in the western corner of the room, but the moon was brighter, and her bluish rays invaded places where the lamplight was faint. The ancient glow of the round silent orb lay upon the beach as it had lain for aeons, and I waited in a torment of expectancy made doubly acute by the delay in fulfillment and the uncertainty of what strange completion was to come.

Outside the crouching hut a white illumination suggested vague spectral forms whose unreal, phantasmal motions seemed to taunt my blindness, just as unheard voices mocked my eager listening. For countless moments I was still, as if Time and the tolling of her great bell were hushed into nothingness. And yet there was nothing which I might fear: the moon-chiselled shadows were unnatural in no contour, and veiled nothing from my eyes. The night was silent—I knew that despite my closed window—and all the stars were fixed mournfully in a listening heaven of dark grandeur. No motion from me then, or word now, could reveal my plight, or tell of the fear-racked brain imprisoned in flesh which dared not break the silence, for all the torture it brought. As if expectant of death, and assured that nothing could serve to banish the soul-peril I confronted I crouched with a forgotten cigarette in my hand. A silent world gleamed beyond the cheap, dirty windows, and in one corner of the room a pair of dirty oars, placed there before my arrival, shared the vigil of my spirit. The lamp burned endlessly, yielding a sick light hued like a corpse's flesh. Glancing at it now and again for the desperate distraction it gave, I saw that many bubbles unaccountably rose and vanished in the kerosene-filled base. Curiously enough, there was no heat from the wick. And suddenly I became aware that the night as a whole was neither warm nor cold, but strangely neutral—as if all physical forces were suspended, and all the laws of a calm existence disrupted.

Then, with an unheard splash which sent from the silver water to the shore a line of ripples echoed in fear by my heart, a swimming thing emerged beyond the breakers. The figure may have been that of a dog, a human being, or something more strange. It could not have known that I watched—perhaps it did not care—but like a distorted fish it swam across the mirrored stars and dived beneath the surface. After a moment it came up again, and this time, since it was closer, I saw that it was carrying something across its shoulder. I knew, then, that it could be no animal, and that it was a man or something like a man, which came toward the land from a dark ocean. But it swam with a horrible ease.

As I watched, dread-filled and passive, with the fixed stare of one who awaits death in another yet knows he cannot avert it, the swimmer approached the shore—though too far down the southward beach for me to discern its outlines or features. Obscurely loping, with sparks of moonlit foam scattered by its quick gait, it emerged and was lost among the inland dunes.

Now I was possessed by a sudden recurrence of fear, which had died away in the previous moments. There was a tingling coldness all over me —though the room, whose window I dared not open now, was stuffy. I thought it would be very horrible if something were to enter a window which was not closed.

Now that I could no longer see the figure, I felt that it lingered somewhere in the close shadows, or peered hideously at me from whatever window I did not watch. And so I turned my gaze, eagerly and frantically, to each successive pane; dreading that I might indeed behold an intrusive regarding face, yet unable to keep myself from the terrifying inspection. But though I watched for hours, there was no longer anything upon the beach.

So the night passed, and with it began the ebbing of that strangeness— a strangeness which had surged up like an evil brew within a pot, had mounted to the very rim in a breathless moment, had paused uncertainly there, and had subsided, taking with it whatever unknown message it had borne. Like the stars that promise the revelation of terrible and glorious memories, goad us into worship by this deception, and then impart nothing, I had come frighteningly near to the capture of an old secret which ventured close to man's haunts and lurked cautiously just beyond the edge of the known. Yet in the end I had nothing. I was given only a glimpse of the furtive thing; a glimpse made obscure by the veils of ignorance. I cannot even conceive what might have shown itself had I been too close to that swimmer who went shoreward instead of into the ocean. I do not know what might have come if the brew had passed the rim of the pot and poured outward in a swift cascade of revelation. The night ocean withheld whatever it had nurtured. I shall know nothing more.

Even yet I do not know why the ocean holds such a fascination for me. But then, perhaps none of us can solve those things—they exist in defiance of all explanation. There are men, and wise men, who do not like the sea and its lapping surf on yellow shores; and they think us strange who love the mystery of the ancient and unending deep. Yet for me there is a haunting and inscrutable glamour in all the ocean's moods. It is in the melancholy silver foam beneath the moon's waxen corpse; it hovers over the silent and eternal waves that beat on naked shores; it is there when all is lifeless save for unknown shapes that glide through sombre depths. And when I behold the awesome billows surging in endless strength, there comes upon me an ecstasy akin to fear; so that I must abase myself before this mightiness, that I may not hate the clotted waters and their overwhelming beauty.

Vast and lonely is the ocean, and even as all things came from it, so shall they return thereto. In the shrouded depths of time none shall reign upon the earth, nor shall any motion be, save in the eternal waters. And these shall beat on dark shores in thunderous foam, though none shall remain in that dying world to watch the cold light of the enfeebled moon playing on the swirling tides and coarse-grained sand. On the deep's margin shall rest only a stagnant foam, gathering about the shells and bones of perished shapes that dwelt within the waters. Silent, flabby things will toss and roll along empty shores, their sluggish life extinct. Then all shall be dark, for at last even the white moon on the distant waves shall wink out. Nothing shall be left, neither above nor below the sombre waters. And until that last millennium, and beyond the perishing of all other things, the sea will thunder and toss throughout the dismal night.

Spawn of the Sea

Donald Wandrei

OM GORDON HAD never paid any undue attention to the bottle until the moment he stumbled and knocked it from its shelf to shatter upon the floor, but from that instant his interest became prodigious.

Tom had been making a comfortable income from his gift shop for several years. He made a specialty of odd things—Oriental jewelry, antique terra-cotta figurines, illuminated parchment leaves, African sculptures, old Java batiks, and a thousand other things that were both unusual and artistic.

Every summer, during the slack season, he went abroad for a month or so and wandered from place to place purchasing as he went whatever odds and ends appealed to him. The bottle was one of the acquisitions of his most recent trip. It came to his attention when he was idling on the shore of Fezd-El-Tuah one morning and saw an Arab urchin playing with it. Tom wanted the bottle because it was obviously the craftsmanship of a bygone century. It looked something like a decanter, something like a Greek amphora, and was perfectly blown, with a long, slender neck and a gracefully rounded base. At one time it must have been buried, for stains and iridescent colors made even more opaque its original coloring of brown. It was stoppered and sealed with wax that had partly weathered away but still seemed almost as hard as stone.

Tom bargained with the shrewd gamin and finally obtained the bottle for the equivalent of fifteen cents. His Arabic was as poor as the lad's French, so that the two had difficulty in understanding each other. All that Tom discovered about the history of the curious bottle was that the urchin had recently found it half buried in the sand.

The bottle made its way back to America with the rest of Tom's purchases, and in due time was placed upon a shelf. No one priced it during the months it stood there, but Tom didn't mind, since he had bought it primarily to add a touch of atmosphere to his shop. And on the shelf it remained, half forgotten, until the accident that destroyed it.

Tom had little opportunity to regret his loss. His annoyance vanished when he saw the yellowed paper lying among bits of broken glass. Despite its apparent age, the paper was still strong and covered with quaint, fine script, though the writing on the outer leaf had faded for the most part to illegibility.

He took the tightly rolled manuscript home with him that night with as considerable interest as he had ever had in any of his purchases; and the dawn of another day was breaking before he had fully deciphered it and transcribed it into modern English. Most of the first page was hopelessly dimmed; he could make nothing of the superscription; and even the date was ambiguous. He deciphered a "17" but whether the year intended was "17—" or "—17" it was impossible to decide. Tantalized by the unreadable introduction, he eventually proceeded with the body of a manuscript that was in many ways even more tantalizing; and the hours flew by with never a thought from him as he pored over the script. To be sure, he grasped an occasional word on the outer leaf whose writing had been largely effaced by the action of sunlight, but nothing like a continuous narrative became possible until he turned to the second page, which began in the middle of a sentence.

"—day out the storm broke. We passengers were all ordered below deck while the crew raced above hauling in sail and trying to save the ship.

"May God's grace protect the seven seas from another such gale. Out of a sooty sky the rain lashed in torrents, the wind screamed through the rigging, and the vastest waves that ever were boiled up around us. The ship lurched and tipped as though any minute it would turn over or sink, and not one of us but was bruised from head to foot after an hour of wild pitching to and fro. The women, poor things, were all the more terrified, for it was dangerous to risk lighting the lamps; so we huddled in the dark and could hardly hear the shouting of the crew above the terrible uproar, what with the waves pounding, and thunder crashing, and the wind howling in a kind of fury. But besides these, we heard ominous cracks, and heavy objects smash across the decks; yet we knew not what went on up there.

"There was little food to be found, and that little of course went to the women and children. The rest of us did what we could to tie them and ourselves to anything solid, or brace ourselves against sudden lurches. We got no sleep, neither did we talk, such was the fear upon us.

"Many hours passed with the ship staggering and thus being battered; yet I knew not at what time God's wrath descended. There was a long, sickening slide of the ship, a groaning and bursting of timbers, and then a sudden deafening crash. We heard running feet, and next the panic caught us, poor devils, for the hatches were unbattened and a voice roared down that the ship was sinking.

"All was noise and confusion, the air a sound and frenzy, every one bawling and struggling and fighting to get out, only a few of us remembering that we were gentlemen, such was the terror. Up on deck we found the wildest disorder, two of the masts down, the other sail blown to tatters, and one of the boats squarely smashed. The crew were desperately trying to launch the seaworthy boats, but another was wrecked before it got clear. By the glare of lightning we saw the awful scene. The captain, God have mercy on his soul, stood by his post. He ordered the passengers off first. Gun in either hand, he shot down the cowards who tried to save themselves by leaving the women behind.

"I hastened toward the boat nearest me. That is the last I remembered save of hearing a sharp crack and receiving from behind a blow on my head. Pain numbed my limbs as total blackness blotted out the scene.

"For a very long time I must have lost my senses. I awakened with a throbbing headache and a thirst. I opened my eyes to the glare of sun. The sea was like a sapphire, smooth and motionless and bright as far as I could see, and no land anywhere.

"When I attempted to rise, my head throbbed so fiercely that I fell back. I felt it and discovered a swelling, with dried blood already caked into a scab, by which I judged that I must have lain unconscious for at least two days. I was weak, the pangs of hunger assailed me, and an intolerable thirst parched my mouth. With difficulty I finally dragged myself to a clogged scupper that retained some warm, dirty rain-water and drank it in gulps.

"Feeling considerably refreshed, I rested until my headache had subsided, then cautiously arose. I was still weak, but I needed to know the best—or the worst—about my predicament.

"The deck was swept clean of every movable object and the framework itself wrecked in places. Besides listing, the ship hung low. I surmised that it had sprung a leak or shipped a quantity of water. Not another soul appeared to be aboard.

"I made my way to a hatch and descended into gloom. The matches in my pocket were useless from having been soaked in the storm. I am no sailor, and knew little about the nature of ships, but I was acquainted with the general plan of this one and sloshed through a couple of inches of water to the galley. Long fumbling around in darkness was finally rewarded by the discovery of dry matches, one of which I promptly used to light a lamp. I satisfied my hunger with the first leftovers that came to hand—stale bread, a piece of salt cod, and some raw potatoes, washed down with a draft of English whisky that refreshed me greatly.

"I then set out to examine the ship. In the passengers' quarters I found three corpses, which I heaved overboard after brief prayers for the repose of their souls. I found two more bodies in the crew's quarters. And I discovered one living man.

"He must have been among those shot by the captain for disobeying the command to let the women and children escape first, and had crawled below later; for I came upon him hanging from a berth. At any rate, a ball had pierced his thigh and gone clean through. He suffered much from loss of blood, had a fever, and was delirious when I discovered him. But if gangrene did not set in, he had a fair chance to recover. I did what I could for him, glad of any companionship, even though it might not be of the best, and devoutly prayed that he would live. Whether the other passengers and the crew had taken to the boats or been claimed by the sea, I do not know. There was no one else aboard, and I can scarcely believe that anything human could have survived so terrific a storm.

"I next went over the remainder of the ship. The hold had filled with an amount of water that I considered dangerous, and I wondered how much longer the ship would last. I could not determine if it had sprung a leak and was still settling toward its grave, or if it had shipped an extraordinary amount of water in the gale. The hold was an evil-smelling place where the cargo had shifted and some boxes broken open, the others likewise being or becoming waterlogged. I do not know what the cargo was, but from as much as I could see of the shattered boxes, it appeared to consist equally of a greenish powder which I judged to be some chemical, a whitish salt that I also could not identify, a gummy, malodorous substance, and boxes simply marked 'seeds,' none of these latter being broken.

"My search then took me to the captain's quarters, which were a bitter disappointment. I hunted everywhere, but the ship's log was gone, including the sailing-chart. There were other maps and papers, but not a scrap that would indicate our position, even as it was at the height of the storm. Most of the instruments were hopelessly damaged and useless except to some one who might know how to repair them.

"In the galley I found a great many barrels of salt pork, salt cod, flour, potatoes, various condiments, five tubs of pickles, much liquor, and varying amounts of corn, nuts, rice, coconuts, venison, and so on, together with about two dozen live geese, chickens, and turkeys. Altogether there were ample provisions, upon which two men could subsist for many months, possibly a year even. The supply of fresh water was low, but I collected about two barrels more in different parts of the ship which retained rain-water from the recent blow.

"At intervals I ministered to the sick man. Toward evening he began to improve. A couple of days later, the fever left him and he thereafter grew rapidly better.

"I can not convey the loneliness of the next month, and it would be idle to make the attempt. Bill—his full name was William Gehrety—and I wore out our eyes peering vainly for sails that never came, and land that we could not find. We had no conception of where we were, since the ship might have been blown hundreds of miles off her course during the gale. According to the last reckoning he had heard, we were approximately nine hundred miles from the nearest known land. Nine hundred? It might as well have been nine thousand. Yet we continued to hope, even though we knew we were far off the trade route which, God knows, was travelled by no more than three or four ships a year, in this sea remote from the Americas, and farther still from England.

"We spent weary days building a crude boat, calked it with tar, rigged out a clumsy sail, and tested it. I doubt whether a craft was ever more unseaworthy. We hadn't the heart to go to certain death in it, for it wouldn't steer true, it pitched crazily, and we couldn't put into it a fraction of the water and provisions that we would need. We learned much by this experience, but we were also discouraged. Nevertheless, disheartened by the alternatives of eventual starvation on our prison, or certain death by sea, we set to work slowly erecting a more substantial boat.

"So the days went by, and the sun shone in deep blue skies, and the water lapped softly against the sides, and at night the stars came out brilliantly except when the moon rode high. Yet never a sail hove in sight, and though we probably drifted with currents, there was nothing to tell us how rapidly, and we saw no land. By ourselves, we could not repair and raise and rig a mast large enough to do us any good, for the season of calms had come, and since what canvas we had was too small for any benefit short of a stiff blow, we saved it for our boat.

"There was furthermore around the ship a bad smell that got on our nerves. It became stronger as the days passed until we determined to investigate its source. We traced it to the hold. We tried bailing the water out but the stench was so sickening that we were compelled to cease. The water in the hold was queer stuff, unusually warm, thick and slimy, and a pale green in color. The cargo had evidently gone bad, or the chemicals, if that's what they were, caused the smell. We decided that the odor would dissipate in time, but it was so bad below that we took to sleeping on deck and going down only for our meals.

"There were strange noises that also bothered us: not the usual creakings and strainings of an old ship, but something we couldn't quite place. We used to hear it, as though down in the hold, or far away, a stirring as of some one awakening and a simmer like water coming to a boil.

"The smell didn't vanish. It got worse, until even though it wasn't so bad in the daytime on deck, at night when we slept it seeped up and polluted the air. We tried closing the hatches but it did no good. Then it got into the food, and we not only had to smell the stench but taste it.

"I don't know when the combination of curious sounds and horrible odors became too much for our nerves. I think it was the forty-third day of our drifting, but it doesn't matter. All the preceding night, the stink had hung heavily like a smoke cloud, and the strange noise, almost like that of a heart, became a rhythmic pulse as the night wore on. I at first believed my nerves were beginning to give way, but since Bill had had the same impressions, I thought we couldn't both be wrong. Somehow, I felt uneasy. The monotony and solitude were bad enough. Now we had a rotten miasma and a singular noise to contend with besides.

"That morning we decided to make another investigation of the hold. Since we knew that the smell came from there, we suspected that the noises might have some connection with it. Perhaps a fermentation was going on. If worst came to worst, we might as well devote our time to carrying the bilge out or heaving the boxes and cargo overboard. I myself was rather sure that they were responsible for both the bad smell and the queer sounds.

"Going below was like walking into salt water, the odor was that strong, pushing and holding us back, a nauseating odor, filthy, abominable, and beast-like. I think I was faint when we reached the hold, for I can not otherwise quite account for what happened. Bill was carrying a lighted candle while I unbattened the hatch and looked in.

" 'Shut it! *Shut it!*' Bill screamed, and we hurled ourselves against the door, fastening it securely. Down in the hold we had seen a vast, shapeless mass of undulating greenish-white stuff, thick as skin, with a beating motion like a pulse. The revolting odor came from that mass, but what terrified us most was the way that pulpy substance leaped up at us when we opened the hatch! Leaped, like an unknown animal after prey, with a furious beating of the pulse, its surface writhing into tentacles that flung at us, and a hiss like an inarticulate cry.

"The candle went out when Bill jumped. Darkness dropped upon us like a shroud. We heard the thing undulating in the hold, and pounding against the hatch. Would the barrier hold? Or was the noise only that odd pulse beating? Or the hammering of our own hearts?

"Panic caught us. We dashed for the other hatchways and fought to get out. Once on deck, we felt a bit ashamed, with the morning sun shining hotly. We looked at each other, white and shaken, for all that. Then a wave of corruption eddied around us, and we knew it came from the thing in the hold.

"Tacitly, we avoided reference to the incident and made no further attempt to investigate. Who can say what we saw, or whether we really saw? Yet I was convinced that a sea-change had somehow come over the cargo, that a slow and abnormal and utterly loathsome transformation was taking place. How else account for it? The salt sea-water and the hot sun must have combined with the seeds and chemicals to germinate a hideous, perhaps unknown, form of life, down in the hold. Life? Not as I knew it, but something that was strangely and dreadfully alive.

"All that day we toiled, bringing food from the galley and stowing it on deck near the stump of the foremast. Every descent was a trip of unexpressed fear, for we could hear a distant heaving in the hold; but by nightfall we had carried everything that we would need above. Nothing could have persuaded us to leave the deck again. We battened the hatches and calked all places where the storm had smashed openings in the deck.

"It must have been long after sunset before our labors were ended. It is not strange, therefore, that when we retired, I quickly fell asleep, worn out from my exertions, despite the tension of peril that hung around, and the persistent throb which crept up from below, and the moldy reek that poisoned every breath I drew.

"I woke with a start, to hear a pulsing throb that made the whole ship quiver. But what brought me leaping to my feet in rage was the sight of Bill stealthily lowering himself over the side. The coward had filled our first crude boat with provisions and water. He was trying to steal away with our only means of escape, leaving me who had saved his life behind to face death and terror alone.

"I might have killed him, but I didn't. He was unprotected because he was lowering himself with both hands. I whipped out my pistol and had him covered before he could scramble back. He didn't risk dropping to the sea; for he knew that I could have and would have shot him before he could pull out of range. I made him haul back every scrap of food, and hoist the boat, after I had disarmed him. Then I tied him securely and went back to sleep. I knew he would be dangerous from now on, but I also knew he would be unnerved by that hellish pulse which sounded from the ship's hold and the commotion the shapeless thing made, and the stench that hung thicker than ever.

"Existence became a nightmare. I had long abandoned hope of rescue. The only recourse left was to finish the larger boat on which we were laboring, and trust that we made land. The stench on deck was horrible, and at night I heard that damnable pounding that became steadily more insistent. What if the thing broke out? I trembled at the thought of the consequences. And now I had to watch Bill every second. His aid was essential to finishing the boat, but the rat would kill me and flee the minute that he received the opportunity. Each long second I was under the greatest strain, listening to that maddening beat, watching the moves that Bill made, and always faint with the putrescence which assailed my nostrils. Yet I toiled as strenuously as Bill to finish our boat. And as if all this was not disaster enough, the food began to spoil, under the hot rays of the sun. The pork and cod became wormy. The venison dried out until it was tough as leather. Hardtack, pickles, potatoes, and nuts were about all we had left, except the flour that we occasionally made into soggy bread over a carefully guarded fire and munched without appetite.

"At night I trussed Bill up and obtained what fitful sleep I could. At morning I released him and kept a hawk-like watch over his movements while we sweated over the boat. He didn't say much. He was sullen, and by the wicked look in his eyes I knew he was still planning to escape.

"All through the night he would talk and mumble and try to keep me awake.

" 'You can't do this!' he would plead when the distant pounding became loud. 'What if that beast gets out? You'd run away and I'd get killed. It ain't fair. Damn you, take these ropes off—I won't try to escape,' on and on he would go until he fell asleep or I did.

"To make sure that he wouldn't try deserting again, I insisted on dismantling our first boat so that we could use the planks on our second one and progress faster. It took the heart out of him when he saw his way of escape disappear under his eyes, but I imagined he would work more willingly thereafter on the other boat. I realize now what a foolish action of mine that was, for I ought to have kept a means of escape in constant readiness. Bill suggested time after time that we draw lots to see who should win the first boat and take a chance on reaching land. I wouldn't listen to him. I felt in a way responsible for him, and I was determined that we would live or die together.

"Any one calamity would have been disheartening, and I had three battles to fight: the silent hostility of Bill, the eternal sea itself, and now this living creature that dwelt in the hold. Bill claimed that the thing was some sort of sea-monster that had been washed aboard during the storm and had kept on growing. I said and I still think that it was a fearful product of heat, seeds, and chemical action occurring in saline water, but no matter how rational our explanations were, they didn't help us keep a grip on ourselves. I remembered all too vividly that gluey, greenish mass quivering foully with a sub-human, less, and yet more, than animal life, and the hideously purposeful fashion in which it contracted and leaped at us.

"We raced against time trying to finish a seaworthy boat for our escape. It would have been an ardous task anywhere, even with adequate materials. Our nerves were ragged, our tools were inferior, and we had to employ any plank we could lay our hands on. It was a hopeless race from the beginning, and we knew it; but at any rate it kept us from brooding over our plight, and a kind of madness drove us on, to the heat of a tropical sun and the interminable sound of a heart beating with monotonous regularity.

"For three days we lived in a wretched hell. By the forty-sixth day, the far-away throb had swelled to a thud that was weirdly alive, louder than the faint lapping of waves or the blood that coursed in my temples. At night it fairly drove us wild. We listened to it with a sort of dreadful fascination, hardly conscious that for hours our movements had been rhythmically actuated by its tempo.

"I didn't sleep well, and I didn't sleep long after we turned in, that evening. I dozed a bit, only to wake from insane dreams to insane reality, and then doze again while that accursed heart beat steadily. I came to a sudden, terrified wakening when a heavy crash drowned out the sound. Bill screamed and I leaped over to him, freeing his bonds at a slash. Together we crouched in the darkness, listening.

"A sucky gurgling came from down in the hold, we heard a commotion as of oil bubbling, and the stench settled round us worse than ever. And closer yet, louder still, came the pounding that was shattering our nerves.

" 'My God! It's broken out!' whimpered Bill.

" 'Oh shut up!' I answered angrily. 'Crying won't help. The thing's loose. Our only chance is to kill it or get away, as fast as we can.'

" 'You can't kill a thing like that!' he mumbled.

"I knew he was right. There were plenty of balls for the guns, but most of the powder was ruined in the storm. Besides, what effect could the pellets have on a creature of such huge size and unfamiliar nature?

" 'Come on!' I ordered. 'We'll have to hurry.'

"But we halted in dismay before our boat. At least a week would be needed to complete it, and we felt certain that we would not have anywhere near a week's time.

"The way that that monster moved around below us made us shiver. It must have flowed along, for it made a sticky noise, and every once in a while we heard a sort of plop as if it had swallowed something, or maybe felt around with some tentacle like an octopus's that gave out a sucking smack when it jerked away. And ever the pulse drummed louder, hellishly regular, shattering our nerves with each thud.

" 'We'll have to dismantle the boat and make a raft,' I curtly told Bill.

"He started to complain.

" 'Then stay here and rot, unless the thing gets you first,' I cursed. 'We won't have much chance of coming out alive on a raft, but we won't have any chance if we remain here. And we'll have to work fast. It's only a question of hours before the thing breaks on deck.'

"As if to confirm my words, we heard a faint, tentative slithering underneath us.

" 'It's probably smelled us already,' I whispered. 'I think it's feeling around for a way to get at us. It may be able to slide through a crack, like water. Come on!'

"That was enough for Bill. Together we started our work all over again, tearing apart the half-finished dory.

"There was no moon, and the starlight was insufficient to see by. We set up a couple of tapers and labored as best we could in their feeble glow. Labored? It was a humid night. In ten minutes we were soaked with perspiration while we ripped the boards apart and began fastening them into a rude raft. And all the while, the thing throbbed in great beats underneath us, and made loathly noises that nauseated us. If it had been a definite kind of animal, we might have stood it better; but the beast was amorphous, or rather, protean; and the only sounds that it made were its movements and the pulse of its life, except once in long whiles when it emitted an inarticulate and dreadful unvocal cry. I could not help thinking of the beast as a disembodied stomach, expressing its hunger for food; and its audible desire was the more shocking for it implied neither the animal nor the organic, but the sub-vital, the sub-organic; as though the monster, God forgive me for the thought, belonged half-way between dead earth and living bodies.

"Desperate, anxious, fearing, and apprehensive, we worked in semi-darkness with reckless haste. The ship was ghostly on the dark waters, and the tapers shed a phantom glow; very close I heard the eery sounds of the thing below.

"I do not know how long we strove. An hour, perhaps two. The gray dawn was coming before our rough raft had been sufficiently completed to be launched.

" 'Two more planks and she'll be ready,' I told Bill. 'It'll only take me a minute or so to finish. We'll save time if you go over to the stores and bring the food back while I put the planks on. Better hurry!'

"Bill nodded and left. I had barely got one of the planks in place when he returned, staggering under a load of miscellaneous provisions.

" 'Good work!' I encouraged him. 'Now roll the keg of water here and we'll be set to leave.' I heard his steps move away while I prepared to finish my job.

"And I heard an ominous crack, a bursting smash that came without warning. I leaped to my feet and whirled around, suspecting treachery.

"Would God that it had been treachery—anything save the reality that stunned me into a momentary stupor!

"By the dim light of dawn, I saw the main hatch burst open; and out of it bubbled and flowed with torrential swiftness a mass of sickly green corruption, thick, horrible, noxious, suffocating by reason of its putrid stench, and sinisterly alive, and foully sentient with a purpose whose nature I could guess; a heap of crawling liquescence, formless yet held together and directed somehow by a rudimentary awareness; opaque, and yet with dark filaments like hairs or veins or vines weaving a webwork through it; moving swiftly and strangely, with a rhythmic advance and recession, a bloating expansion and contraction as the pulse that dominated the hellish mass rose and fell.

"Between it and me stood Bill, rigid with fright. Then he gave a strangled cry and bounded toward me.

"The scene that followed is burned for ever on the unfortunate altar of my thoughts. Even as Bill sprang, the pudgy heap vented a rustling hiss and surged outward with a turbulent rush, and flung after Bill a swath of greenish viscidity. He could not help himself, in midair as he was from his leap, and down he came in the green ichor.

"And he kept going down, oh God, he kept going down! He dissolved inch by inch in that gluey puddle, his furious thrashings could not budge him a step. Fire can not consume nor acid eat so rapidly as that thing consumed and ate and fed upon him and devoured him alive.

"When he first landed in it, he uttered a piercing shriek, shrill and terrible. I fired both my pistols at the monster, and saw the balls rip into the quivering jelly, but nothing indicated that they had had any effect. Then Bill screamed, a long series of uninterrupted screams, rising and falling, frenzied and tortured and insane, until his voice was raw and only a hoarse and hideous lowing came from his writhing mouth and convulsively cording throat.

"I prayed for blackest night, but the dawn grew lighter and the scene stood out with sickening clearness. I fumbled in haste to reload a pistol; then, with an arm that trembled, I took careful aim, and steadied myself, and fired true. The ball buried itself in Bill's heart.

"He sagged, and what was left of him fell. I hope that I was not wrong when I believed I saw the briefest shine of glad thanks in his eyes before they glazed and went blank.

"And the stuff welled interminably from the hatch, and the corpse dwindled while I watched. A rosy tint began to suffuse the webwork of the monstrous thing, a certain awful muscular distention and contraction shook it, its stench grew insufferable.

"A deep horror racked me with a shudder, then panic, ungovernable terror swept me and I dashed for the rail. I saw the glistening mass drive after me like a hurricane, and I knew that Bill's frightful fate would be mine before ever I could leap into the cleansing sea. And at that moment the sun's rim slid above the eastern horizon, and its golden rays slanted to the deck.

"The monster shrivelled as though tormented. A voiceless sibilance poured from it, it heaved and twisted and contracted madly down the hatch, leaving behind the back and part of the head of what ten minutes ago had been a man. Something in the monster's nature, or its long confinement in darkness, had made sunlight an agony which it could not endure.

"It is now mid-morning. I gave Bill a hasty sea-burial. I have written this narrative and am about to toss it overboard sealed in a bottle, so that if by chance it reach a passing ship, a watch may be kept out for me, and this derelict if it be sighted sunk from a distance or wholly avoided. For the monster still is living below, and its dreadful pulse dins through my thoughts, and its disgusting smell defiles the air with charnel odors. Cheated by sunlight it will emerge again at nightfall.

"I do not know what my fate will be. The raft may capsize when I launch it. If it does not, I may escape, or perish at sea. If it does, I may drown, or make my way back aboard. But here the coming of darkness means certain death—by the thing in the ship, or by my own hand, for sooner suicide than the consuming loathsomeness of the monster.

"May God's grace protect me. There is death whichever course I choose."